WILD
CARDS

As the nations struggled through four turbulent decades, from the end of World War II through the sleek New Wave '80s, the bizarre metahumans created by the wild card virus used their extraordinary abilities to shape the course of history. Now the district attorney is asking for Ace volunteers to step in when rival gangs wage a bitter war for control of the streets of Jokertown.

In this fifth mind-bending volume, here are some of the strange characters you'll meet as the battle rages between two ruthless criminal organizations.

BAGABOND
Bag lady and veterinarian of Jokertown, she surveys every niche of the city through the eyes of its animal inhabitants, who obey her every command, including the command to kill.

DEADHEAD
A ghoulish but highly useful individual, he steals people's memories by eating their brains.

CROYD
A speed freak with real electricity in his veins, he does some heavy stuff with burglar alarms, computers and telephones — as well as giving electroshock therapy to anybody he shakes hands with.

WATER LILY
She can use any water in her vicinity and control the force of its flow. If she chooses, she can quite literally drown her sorrows.

WILD CARDS

WILD CARDS

VOLUME FIVE

DOWN & DIRTY

a mosaic novel
edited by
George R. R. Martin
and written by:
John J. Miller
Roger Zelazny
Leanne C. Harper
Arthur Byron Cover
Melinda M. Snodgrass
Edward Bryant
Stephen Leigh
Pat Cadigan
Walter Jon Williams
George R. R. Martin

TITAN BOOKS
LONDON

WILD CARDS 5: DOWN & DIRTY
ISBN 1 85286 275 0

Published by Titan Books Ltd
58 St Giles High St
London WC2H 8LH

Published by arrangement with Bantam Books, a division of Bantam Doubleday Dell
Publishing Group Inc.

First Titan edition March 1990
1 2 3 4 5 6 7 8 9 10

Printed and bound in Great Britain by Cox and Wyman Ltd, Reading, Berkshire.

for Laura Mixon

we all miss you

Acknowledgment

The editor wishes to extend his thanks and appreciation to Melinda M. Snodgrass, his tireless, selfless, endlessly energetic right-hand man, who has put in long thankless hours as trademark attorney, mother confessor, negotiator, dinner coordinator, editor's assistant, babysitter, diplomat, and voice of reason amidst the slings and arrows, and without whose diligence, imagination, and sanity the Wild Card world would be a much duller place, if it existed at all. . . .

Note to Readers

In the real world there are always thousands of stories in progress, all of them happening at once. We try to make the world of the wild cards as real as we possibly can.

The previous volume in the Wild Cards series, *Aces Abroad*, chronicled the events of the World Health Organization global junket, which left New York on December 1, 1986, and returned on April 29, 1987.

The first part of the volume in hand tells what happened in Manhattan from the beginning of October through the end of April, before the tour made its departure and while it was wending its somewhat troubled way around the world.

The concluding portions of our present mosaic relate the events of May and June, after the travelers came home.

The Editor

October 1986 – April 1987

Only the Dead
Know Jokertown

by John J. Miller

I

Brennan moved through the autumnal night as if he were part of it, or it were part of him.

The fall had brought a coolness to the air that reminded Brennan, however palely, of the Catskills. He missed the mountains more than almost anything, but as long as Kien was free they were as unattainable as the ghosts of dead friends and lovers that had lately come to haunt his dreams. He loved the mountains as surely as he loved all the people he'd failed down through the years, but who could love the dirty sprawl of the city? Who could even *know* the city, could even know Jokertown? Not him, certainly, but Kien's presence bound him to Jokertown as solidly as chains of adamantine steel.

He crossed the street, entering the half block of urban debris that bordered the Crystal Palace. With the sixth sense of the hunter he could feel eyes follow him as he passed through the wreckage. He shifted the canvas bag that carried his broken-down bow to a more comfortable position, wondering, not for the first time, what sort of creatures chose to make the mounds of junk their home. Once or twice he heard twittering rustles that weren't the wind and glimpsed flashes of movement that weren't shifting moonshadow, but no one interfered as he swung up onto the rusted fire escape hanging down the Palace's rear wall. He climbed silently to the roof, went through the security system that would have given him pause if Chrysalis hadn't keyed him to it, and entered through the trapdoor that opened on the Palace's third floor, Chrysalis's private domain. The corridor was totally dark, but he

3

avoided, by memory the delicate stands cluttered with antique bric-a-brac and let himself into her bedroom.

Chrysalis was awake. Sitting naked on her plush wine-colored fainting couch, she was playing solitaire with a deck of antique playing cards.

Brennan watched her for a moment. Her skeleton, her ghostly musculature, her internal organs, and the network of blood vessels that laced through it all were delicately lit by rosy light from the Tiffany lamp hanging above the couch upon which she'd spread her cards. He watched the articulated skeleton of her hand flip through the deck and turn over the ace of spades.

She looked up at him and smiled.

Her smile, like Chrysalis herself, was an enigma. Difficult to read because her face was only lips and smudges of ghostly muscle on her cheeks and jaw, it could have meant any of the thousand things a smile could mean. Brennan chose to interpret it as a welcome.

"It's been some time." She looked at him critically. "Long enough for you to start a beard."

Brennan closed the door and set his bow case against the wall. "I've had business," he said, his voice soft and deep.

"Yes." Her smile continued until Brennan could no longer ignore the edge in it. "Some of which interfered with mine."

There was no doubt as to what she referred. Several weeks ago, on Wild Card Day, Brennan had broken up a meeting at the Palace at which Chrysalis was brokering a very valuable set of books that included Kien's personal diary. Brennan, hoping that volume had enough evidence in it to nail Kien's damnable hide to the wall, had eventually gotten it for himself, but it had proven to be worthless. All the writing in it had been destroyed.

"I'm sorry," he said. "I needed that diary."

"Yes," she repeated. Ghostly muscles bunched, indicating a frown. "And you've read it?"

Brennan hesitated a beat. "Yes."

"And you'll not be adverse to sharing the information in it?"

It was more of a demand than a request. It would do no good, Brennan thought, to tell her the truth. She probably would think he was trying to keep it all to himself.

"Possibly."

"In that case I suppose I coud forgive you," she said in a not-very-forgiving voice. She gathered her cards together slowly, careful of their age and value, and set them aside on a spider-legged table that stood next to the couch. She leaned back languorously, her nipples bobbing on invisible pads of flesh whose warmth and firm texture Brennan knew well.

"I've brought you something," Brennan said conciliatorily. "It's not information but something you might like almost as well."

He sat down on the edge of the couch, reached into the pocket of his denim jacket, and handed Chrysalis a small, clear envelope. When she reached out to take it, her warm, invisible thigh touched, then rested on, Brennan's own.

"It's a Penny Black," he said, as she held the glassine envelope up to the light. "The world's first postage stamp. Mint, in perfect condition. Rather rare in that state, rather valuable. The portrait is an engraving of Queen Victoria."

"Very nice." She smiled her enigmatic smile. "I won't ask you where you got it."

Brennan smiled in response, said nothing. He knew that she knew perfectly well where he'd gotten it. He'd asked Wraith for it when they were inspecting the stockbooks full of rare stamps she'd heisted from Kien's safe, the same safe from which she'd removed his diary during the early hours of Wild Card Day. Wraith had felt bad that Brennan hadn't gotten what he'd wanted from the worthless diary and had gladly given him the stamp when he'd asked for it.

"Well, I hope you like it." Brennan stood and stretched as Chrysalis set the envelope aside on her stack of cards. It had been a long day and he was tired. He went to the sidetable by Chrysalis's canopied four-poster bed and lifted the decanter of Irish whiskey that she kept there for him. He looked at it, frowned, and put it down. He rejoined Chrysalis on the couch.

She edged forward lithely and covered his body with hers. He drank in the musky, sexual scent of her perfume and watched the blood rush through the carotid artery in her neck. "Change your mind about the drink?" she asked softly.

"The decanter was empty."

Chrysalis drew back a little, stared into his questioning eyes.

"You only drink amaretto." It was a statement, not a question. She nodded.

Brennan sighed. "When I first came to you, I only wanted information. I didn't want anything personal between us. You started that. If it's to continue and become meaningful, I have to be the only one in your bed. It's the way I am. It's the only way I can give myself to anyone."

Chrysalis stared at him for several seconds before replying. "Whomever else I sleep with is no concern of yours," she finally drawled in the British accent that Brennan, with his ear for languages, knew was faked.

He nodded. "Then I'd better be going." He stood and turned.

"Wait." She stood too. They looked at each other for a long moment, and when she spoke, it was in a conciliatory voice. "At least have your drink. I'll go downstairs and fill the decanter. You can have your drink and we . . . we can talk."

Brennan was tired and had no other place in Jokertown he wanted to be. "All right," he said softly. Chrysalis wrapped herself in a silk kimono spattered with whisps of smoke shaped like galloping horses and left him with a smile that was more shy than enigmatic.

Brennan paced the room, watching his image shift across the myriad antique mirrors that decorated the walls of Chrysalis's bedchamber. He should get out, he told himself, and leave well enough alone, but Chrysalis was as fascinating out of bed as in it. His best intentions to the contrary, he knew that he needed her companionship and, he admitted to himself, her love.

It had been more than ten years since he'd allowed himself to love a woman, but as he'd been discovering since his arrival in Jokertown, the emotions that he allowed himself weren't the only ones he felt. He couldn't live on hate alone. He didn't know if he could love Chrysalis as he'd loved the French-Vietnamese wife whom he'd lost to Kien's assassins. He didn't even want to love a woman while he was on Kien's trail, but despite all his fixity of purpose, despite his Zen training, what he wanted and what actually happened were often two entirely different things.

He stood in the silence of Chrysalis's bedroom, studiously not thinking about his past. Long minutes passed and he suddenly realized that Chrysalis should have returned.

He frowned. It was almost inconceivable that something could happen to Chrysalis in the Crystal Palace, but the habitual caution that had saved Brennan's life more times than he cared to remember made him assemble his bow before going after her. He would feel foolish if he bumped into her in the dark, but he had felt foolish before. It was preferable to feeling dead, a sensation he was more intimately acquainted with than he liked.

Chrysalis wasn't in the corridors of the third floor, nor on the stairway leading down to the taproom, but he heard murmuring voices as he crept down the stairs.

He drew an arrow, placed it on the string of his bow, and peered around the edge of the stairwell where it opened up into the back of the taproom. He gritted his teeth. He had been right to be cautious.

Chrysalis was standing before the long, polished-wood bar that ran almost the entire length of the taproom. The whiskey decanter, still empty, was forgotten on the bar next to her. Her arms were crossed and her jaw was clenched. Her lips were compressed in a thin, angry line.

Two men bracketed her and a third sat facing her at a table in front of the bar. Brennan coud discern few details in the dimness of the night-light that burned above the bar, but the men all had hard, tough faces. The one facing her drummed his fingers on the tabletop next to a chrome-plated pistol.

"Come on," he said in a soft but dangerous-sounding voice. "We just want some information. That's all. We won't even say where we got it." He leaned back in his chair. "Soon there's going to be war, but we don't know who to hit."

"And you think I do?" Brennan recognized the edge anger put in Chrysalis's drawl, but he also recognized the fear under the anger.

The seated man smiled. "We know you do, babe. You know everything about this Jokertown shithole. All *we* know is that someone has put together these nickel-and-dime gangs into something called the Shadow Fists. They're moving into *our* territory, taking *our* customers, and cutting into *our* profits. It's got to stop."

"If I knew a name," Chrysalis said, coming down hard on the if, "it would cost you more than you can pay to learn it."

The man sitting at his table shook his head. "You don't understand," he said. "This is war, babe. And it's going to

cost you more than *you* can pay to keep your mouth shut."
He let his words sink in while he drummed his fingers on the
tabletop. "Sal," he said after a moment, nodding at the man
who stood to Chrysalis's right. "I wonder if her famous
invisible skin would scar?"

Sal considered the question. "Let's see," he finally said.

There was a loud snick and Brennan saw light glint off a
shiny blade. Sal waved it in Chrysalis's face, and she shrank
back against the bar. She opened her mouth to scream, but
the man standing on her left clamped his gloved hand over it.

Sal laughed and Brennan stood and loosed the arrow he'd
been holding. It struck Sal in the back and catapulted him
over the bar. No one had any idea what had happened,
except possibly Chrysalis. The man seated at the table snatched
his pistol and leaped to his feet. Brennan calmly shot him
through the throat. The thug holding Chrysalis let out a
startled stream of obscenities and fumbled under his jacket
for a pistol that he carried in a shoulder rig. Brennan shot
him through the right forearm. He dropped his gun and spun
away from Chrysalis, staring at the aluminum-shafted hunting
arrow skewering his arm and mumbling, "Jesus, oh, Jesus."
He stooped to pick up his pistol.

"Touch it," Brennan called from the darkness, "and I'll
put the next arrow through your right eye."

The thug wisely stood up and backed against the bar. He
clutched his bleeding arm and moaned.

Brennan stepped forward into the diffuse light cast by the
nightlamp burning over the bar. The man stared at the
razor-tipped arrow nocked to his bowstring.

"Who are they?" Brennan asked Chrysalis in a harsh,
clipped voice.

"Mafia," she replied, her voice cracking with tension and
fear.

Brennan nodded, never taking his eyes off the thug who
stared at the arrow that was pointed at his throat.

"Do you know who I am?"

The mafioso nodded violently. "Ya. You're that Yeoman
guy—the bow 'n' arrow killer. I read about you alla time in
the *Post*." The words tripped out of his mouth in a fear-filled
torrent.

"That's right," Brennan said. He spared the man who'd
been sitting at the table a quick glance and saw that he was

curled on the floor in a widening pool of blood, a foot of arrow sticking out from the nape of his neck. He didn't bother checking Sal. He'd had a clean heart shot on him.

"You're a lucky man," Brennan continued in his same dead voice. "Know why?"

The mafioso bobbed his head vigorously side to side, sighing in relief when Brennan relaxed the tension on the taut bowstring and set the bow aside.

"Someone has to deliver a message for me. Someone has to tell your boss that Chrysalis is off bounds. Someone has to tell him that I have an arrow with his name on it, an arrow I would not be slow in delivering if I heard that something had happened to Chrysalis. Do you think you could tell him that?"

"Sure. Sure I could."

"Good." Brennan reached into his back pocket and showed the thug a playing card, a black ace of spades. "This is so he knows you're telling the truth."

He grabbed the man's wounded arm by the elbow and yanked it straight. The thug groaned as Brennan stuck the card on the arrowtip.

"And this," Brennan said through gritted teeth, "is to make sure you don't loose it."

With a sudden, forceful jerk he impaled the man's other arm on the arrowpoint. The mafioso screamed at the sharp, unexpected pain. He sagged to his knees as Brennan bent the aluminum shaft of the arrow under and around both of his arms, pinning them together as tightly as handcuffs would.

Brennan yanked him to his feet. The man was sobbing in fear and pain and couldn't look Brennan in the eye.

"If I ever see you again," Brennan said, "you'll die."

The thug staggered away, sobbing and gibbering incomprehensible protestations. Brennan watched him until he tottered through the front door, then turned to Chrysalis.

She was looking at him with fear in her eyes, more than some of which, he was sure, was directed toward him.

"Are you all right?" he asked softly.

"Yes . . . yes, I think so. . . ."

"You'll have to answer a lot of questions," Brennan said, "unless we get rid of the bodies."

"Yes." She nodded sharply, suddenly decisive, suddenly in

control again. "I'll call Elmo. He'll handle it." She looked him straight in the eye. "I owe you."

Brennan sighed. "Does your entire life have to consist of rigidly tabulated credits and debits?"

She looked at little startled, but nodded. "Yes," she said firmly. "Yes, it does. It's the only way to keep track, to make sure . . ." Her voice trailed away, and she turned and went around the bar. She looked down at Sal's body, and when she spoke again, she voiced a totally different thought. "You know, Tachyon invited me to go on that world tour of his. I think I'll take him up on it. No telling what information I'll pick up rubbing elbows with all those politicians. And if there's going to be street warfare between the Mafia and Kien's Shadow Fists"—she looked into Brennan's eyes for the first time—"I would be safer elsewhere."

They looked at each other for a long moment, and then Brennan nodded.

"I'd better be going, then."

"Your whiskey?"

Brennan let out a long sigh. "No." He looked at the body at his feet. "Drink brings memories, and I don't need any tonight." He looked back at her. "I'm going to be . . . indisposed . . . for the next few weeks. I probably won't see you before you leave. Good-bye, Chrysalis."

She watched him go, a crystalline tear glistening on her invisible cheek, but he never looked back, he never saw.

II

The Twisted Dragon was located somewhere within the nebulous boundary of an interlocking Jokertown and Chinatown. One of Brennan's street sources had told him that the bar was the hangout of Danny Mao, a man who had a moderately high position in the Shadow Fist Society and was said to be in charge of recruitment.

Brennan watched the entrance for a while. The swirling snowflakes that missed the brim of his black cowboy hat caught on his thick, drooping mustache and in his long sideburns. A fair number of Werewolves—they were wearing Richard Nixon masks this month—were going into and out of the place. He'd also seen a few Egrets, though for the most part the Chinatown gang was too picky to hang out in a joint frequented by jokers.

He smiled, smoothing the tips of his mustache in a gesture that had already become habitual. Time to see if his plan was a stroke of genius, as he sometimes thought, or a quick way to a hard death, as he more frequently thought.

It was warm inside the Dragon, more, Brennan guessed, from the press of bodies than the bar's heating system, and it took a moment for him to spot Mao, who was, as Brennan's source had told him he'd be, sitting in a booth in the back of the room. Brennan threaded his way between crowded tables and the shuffling barmaids, staggering drunks, and swaggering punks who crossed his path as he headed toward the booth.

A girl, young and blond and looking vaguely stoned, sat next to Mao. Three men crowded the bench across the table from him. One was a Werewolf in a Nixon mask, one was a young Oriental, and the one in the middle was a thin, pale, nervous-looking man. Before Brennan could say anything a street punk stepped in Brennan's path, blocking his way.

He was a lean six four or five, so he towered over Brennan despite the cowboy boots that added an inch or two to Brennan's height. He wore stained leather pants and an oversize leather jacket that was draped with lengths of chain. His spiked hair added several inches to his apparent height, and the scarlet and black scars crawling on his face added apparent fierceness to his appearance, as did the bone—a human finger-bone, Brennan realized—that pierced his nose.

The scars that patterned his cheeks, forehead, and chin were the insignia of the Cannibal Headhunters, a once-feared street gang that had disintegrated when Brennan had killed its leader, an ace named Scar. Gang members not slain in the bloody power struggle after Scar's demise had for the most part gravitated to other criminal associations, such as the Shadow Fist Society.

"What do you want?" The Headhunter's voice was too reedy to sound menacing, but he tried.

"To see Danny Mao." Brennan spoke softly, his voice pitched in the slow drawl that he remembered so well from his childhood. The Headhunter bent lower to hear Brennan over the cacaphony of music, manic laughter, and half a hundred conversations that washed over them.

"'Bout what?"

"'Bout what's not your business, boy."

Brennan saw out of the corner of his eye that conversation in the booth had stopped and that everyone was watching them.

"I say it is." The Headhunter smiled a grin he fondly thought savage, showing filed front teeth. Brennan laughed aloud. The Headhunter frowned. "What's so funny, ass-hole?"

Brennan, still laughing, grabbed the bone in the Head-hunter's nose and yanked. The Headhunter screamed and reached for his torn nose and Brennan kicked him in the crotch. He fell with a choking moan, and Brennan dropped the bloody bone he'd ripped from his nose onto his curled-up body.

"You," Brennan told him, then slid into the booth next to the blond girl, who was staring at him in stoned astonishment. Two of the three men sitting across the table started to rise, but Danny Mao waved a negligent hand and they sat back down, muttering at each other and staring at Brennan.

Brennan took his hat off, set it on the table in front of him, and looked at Danny Mao, who returned his gaze with apparent interest.

"What's your name?" Mao asked.

"Cowboy," Brennan said softly.

Mao picked up the glass in front of him and took a short sip. He looked at Brennan as if he were some kind of odd bug and frowned. "You for real? I ain't never seen a Chinese cowboy before."

Brennan smiled. The epicanthic folds given his eyes by Dr. Tachyon's deft surgical skills had combined, as he had known they would, with his coarse, dark hair and tanned complexion to give him an Oriental appearance. This slight alteration of his features, his newly grown facial hair, and his western manner of speaking and dressing all added up to a simple but effective disguise. It wouldn't fool anyone who knew him, but he wasn't likely to run into anyone who did.

And the irony of his disguise, Brennan thought, was that every aspect of his new identity, except for the eyes given him by Tachyon, was true. His father had been fond of saying that the Brennans were Irish, Chinese, Spanish, several kinds of Indian, and all-American.

"My Asian ancestors helped build the railroads. I was born in New Mexico, but found it too limiting." That, too, was true.

"So you came to the big city looking for excitement?"

Brennan nodded. "Some time ago."

"And found enough so that you have to use an alias?"

He shrugged, said nothing.

Mao took another sip of his drink. "What do you want?"

"Word on the street," Brennan said, his intense excitement buried under his southwestern drawl, "is that your people are going to war with the Mafia. You've already hit them once—Don Picchietti was assassinated two weeks ago by an invisible ace who shoved an ice pick in his ear while he was eating dinner at his own restaurant. That was certainly a Shadow Fist job. The Mafia will undoubtedly retaliate, and the Shadow Fists will need more soldiers."

"Mao nodded. "Why should we hire you?"

"Why not? I can handle myself."

Mao glanced at his erstwhile bodybuard, who had managed to drag himself to a hunched position on his knees, his forehead resting on the floor. "Fair enough," he said thoughtfully. "But do you have the stomach for it I wonder?" He looked at the three men crowded together on the bench across the table, and Brennan, too, looked at them closely.

The Werewolf sat on the outside and the Oriental, probably an Immaculate Egret, was on the inside. The man they sandwiched, though, didn't look like a street tough.

He was small, thin, and palid. His hands looked soft and weak, his eyes were dark and bright. Many street toughs had a streak of madness in them, but even on first sight Brennan could see that this man was more than touched by insanity.

"These men," Danny Mao said, "are going on a mission. Care to join them?"

"What kind of mission?" Brennan asked.

"If you have to ask, maybe you're not the type of man we're looking for."

"Maybe," Brennan said, smiling, "I'm just cautious."

"Caution is an admirable trait," Mao said blandly, "but so is faith in and obedience to your superiors."

Brennan put his hat on. "All right. Where're we headed?"

The pale man in the middle laughed. It was not a pleasant sound. "The morgue," he said gleefully.

Brennan looked at Mao with a lifted eyebrow.

Mao nodded. "The morgue, as Deadhead says."

"Do you have a car?" the Werewolf asked Brennan. His voice was a mushy growl behind the Nixon mask.

Brennan shook his head.

"I'll have to steal one," the Werewolf said.

"Then we can go to the drive-up window!" the man called Deadhead enthused. The Asian sitting next to him looked vaguely disgusted but said nothing. "Let's go!" Deadhead pushed at the Werewolf, urging him out of the booth.

Brennan lingered to glance at Mao, who was watching him carefully.

"Whiskers," Mao said, nodding at the Werewolf, "is in charge. He'll tell you what you need to know. You're on probation, Cowboy. Be careful."

Brennan nodded and followed the unlikely trio onto the street. The Werewolf turned and looked at Brennan.

"I'm Whiskers," he said in his indistinct growl. "This is Deadhead, like Danny said, and this is Lazy Dragon."

Brennan nodded at the Oriental, realizing his initial assessment of the man had been wrong. He wasn't an Egret. He wasn't wearing Egret colors, and he didn't have the demeanor of a gang member. He was young, maybe in his early twenties, small, about five six or seven, and slender enough so that his baggy pants hung loosely on his lean hips. His face was oval, his nose slightly broad, his hair longish and indifferently combed. He didn't have the aggressive attitude of the street punk. There was a reserve about him, an air of almost melancholy thoughtfulness.

Whiskers left them waiting on the corner. Lazy Dragon was silent, but Deadhead kept up a constant stream of chatter, most of which was nonsensical. Lazy Dragon paid him no attention, and neither did Brennan after a while, but that seemed to make no difference to Deadhead. He burbled on and Brennan ignored him as best he could. Once Deadhead reached into the pocket of his dirty jacket and pulled out a bottle of pills of different sizes and colors, shook out a handful, and tossed them into his mouth. He chewed and swallowed noisily and beamed at Brennan.

"Take vitamins?"

Brennan wasn't sure if Deadhead was offering him some

or asking if he took vitamins himself. He nodded noncommittally and turned away.

Whiskers finally showed up with a car. It was a dark, late model Buick. Brennan hopped into the front seat, leaving the back for Deadhead and Lazy Dragon.

"Good suspension. Smooth drive," Whiskers commented as they pulled away from the curb. Brennan looked into the rear-view mirror and saw Lazy Dragon nod and reach into his pocket for a small clasp knife and a block of soft, white material that looked like soap. He opened the knife and began to whittle.

Deadhead kept up a stream of running chatter that no one listened to. Whiskers drove smoothly, cursing potholes, spot-lights, and other drivers in his muffled voice, continually glancing in the mirror to follow Lazy Dragon's progress as he carefully carved the small block of soap with delicate, skillful hands.

Brennan didn't know where the morgue was or what it looked like, but the dark, forbidding structure that they finally stopped before met all of his expectations.

"Here it is," Whiskers announced unnecessarily. They watched the building for a few moments. "Still looks busy." Occasional lights illuminated scattered rooms throughout the multistoried structure, and as they watched, people occasionally entered or left by the main entrance.

"Ready yet?" Whiskers growled, glancing into the mirror.

"Just about," Lazy Dragon said without looking up.

"Ready for what?" Brennan asked, and Whiskers turned to him.

"You gotta take Deadhead to the room they use for long-term body storage. It's in the basement. Deadhead will take it from there. Dragon will go first and scout. You're muscle in case anything goes wrong."

"And you?"

Whiskers may have grinned under his mask, but Brennan couldn't be sure. "Now that you're here, I just wait in the car."

Brennan didn't like it. This wasn't the way he liked to do things, but he was obviously being tested. Equally obviously, he had no choice. He made one more try for information.

"What are we looking for?"

"Deadhead knows," Whiskers said, and Brennan heard a

disquieting titter from the backseat. "And Dragon knows the general layout. You just deal with anyone who tries to interfere." He glanced back into the mirror. "Ready?"

Lazy Dragon looked up. "Ready," he said calmly. He folded his knife, put it away, and stared critically at what he had carved. Brennan, mystified and curious, turned around for a better look and saw that it was a small but credible mouse. Lazy Dragon studied it carefully, nodded as if satisfied, set it on his lap, settled back comfortably in his seat, and closed his eyes. For a moment nothing happened, then Dragon slumped as if asleep or unconscious, and the carving began to twitch.

The tail lashed, the ears perked up, and then, creakily at first but with increasing fluidity, the thing stretched. It stopped for a moment to preen its fur, then it leaped from Dragon's lap to the shoulder of the driver's seat. Brennan stared at it and it stared back. It was a goddamn living mouse. Brennan glanced back at Lazy Dragon, who seemed to be sleeping, then looked at Whiskers, who was watching impassively beneath his Nixon mask.

"Nice trick," Brennan drawled.

"It's okay," Whiskers said. "You carry him."

Lazy Dragon, who seemed to be vitalizing and possessing the little figurine he'd carved, climbed up on Brennan's shoulder, scurried down his chest, and popped into his vest pocket. He peeked out, holding the pocket-top with his little clawed paws. This was, Brennan thought, more than passing strange, but he had the feeling that things would get stranger before the night was over.

"Okay," he said. "Let's do it." Whatever *it* was.

They entered the morgue through an unlocked service entrance in a side alley and took the stairway to the basement. Lazy Dragon popped out of his pocket, ran down his vest and pant-leg, and scurried down the poorly lit corridor in which they found themselves. Deadhead started after him, but Brennan held him back.

"Let's wait until the mou—until Lazy Dragon gets back."

Deadhead's eyes were shiny and he was even more jittery than usual. His hands shook as he took out his pill bottle, and he dropped a dozen capsules on the floor as he gulped down a mouthful. The pills scattered on the concrete floor, making loud skittering noises. He grinned maniacally and the corner of his mouth kept twitching in a torturous grimace.

What the hell, Brennan thought, *am I doing in a morgue corridor with a madman and a living mouse carved out of soap?*

Lazy Dragon came scampering back before Brennan could think of a satisfactory answer to this disturbing question, his tiny feet moving as if he were being chased by the hungriest cat in the world. He stopped at Brennan's feet, dancing with excitement. Brennan sighed, bent over, and held out his hand. Lazy Dragon jumped up on his palm, and Brennan, still hunkered down, lifted the mouse close to his face.

Lazy Dragon sat up on his haunches, his beady eyes bright with intelligence. He drew his tiny right front paw over his throat repeatedly. Brennan sighed again. He hated charades.

"What is it?" he asked. "Danger? Someone in the corridor?" The mouse nodded excitedly and held up his paw.

"One man?" Again the mouse nodded. "Armed?" The mouse shrugged a very human-looking shrug, looked doubtful. "Okay." Brennan let the mouse down, then stood up. "Follow me." He turned to Deadhead. "You wait here."

Deadhead nodded a jittery nod, and Brennan went off down the corridor, Lazy Dragon scurrying at his heels. He had no confidence in Deadhead and wondered what part in the mission he could possibly play. *It's hard*, he thought to himself, *when your most dependable man is a mouse*.

Around the bend of the corridor a man was sitting in a metal folding chair, eating a sandwich and reading a paperback. He looked up as Brennan approached.

"Can I help you, buddy?" He was middle-aged, fat, and balding. The book he was reading was Ace Avenger #49, *Mission to Iran*.

"Got a delivery."

The man frowned. "I don't know nothing about that. I'm the night janitor. We usually get deliveries during the day."

Brennan nodded understandingly. "This is a special delivery," he said. When he was close enough, he reached behind his back and drew the stiletto he carried in a belt sheath under his vest, touching the tip of its blade lightly against the janitor's throat. The janitor's lips made a round *O* of astonishment and he dropped his book.

"Jesus, mister, what are you doing?" he asked in a strangled whisper, trying to move his throat as little as possible.

"Where's the long-term storage room?"

"Over there, over that way." The janitor made little
jerking motions with his eyeballs, afraid to move even a
muscle.

"Go get Deadhead."

"I don't know no one with that name," the fat man
pleaded, sweat beading his forehead.

"I wasn't talking to you. I was talking to the mouse."

"O Lord." The janitor started to mumble an incoherent
prayer, sure that Brennan was a crazed maniac who was going
to murder him.

Brennan waited patiently until Lazy Dragon returned
with Deadhead.

"Anyone else on this floor?" he asked, urging the janitor
up with a slight flick of his knife wrist. The janitor, catching
on quickly, stood immediately.

"No one. Not now."

"No guards?"

The janitor looked as if he wanted to shake his head, but
the proximity of the knife to his throat stopped him. "Don't
really need them. No one's broke into the morgue for, jeez,
months now."

"Okay." Brennan eased the knife away from the janitor's
throat and the man visibly relaxed. "Take us to the storeroom. Be quiet and no funny business." By way of emphasis
Brennan touched the tip of the janitor's nose with the tip of
his knife, and the janitor nodded carefully.

Brennan squatted and held out his palm, and Lazy Dragon
climbed onto it. He put the mouse in his vest pocket, holding
back a smile at the janitor's bug-eyed stare. He looked as
if he wanted to ask Brennan a question, then thought better
of it.

"It's this way," the janitor said, and Deadhead and Brennan, with Lazy Dragon peering from his pocket, followed
him.

The janitor let them into the room with his key. It was a
dark, cold, depressing room with floor-to-ceiling body lockers
in the walls. It was where the city kept all the corpses that no
one wanted or that no one could identify, before their pauper
burials.

Deadhead's jittery smile widened when they entered the room, and he hopped from foot to foot with ill-suppressed excitement.

"Help me find it!" he commanded. "Help me find it!"

"What?" Brennan asked, truly mystified.

"The body. Gruber's fat, cold body." He looked frantically at the lockers, capering in a macabre dance as he went along the wall.

Brennan frowned, herded the janitor in front of him, and started searching the opposite wall. Most of the name tags set into the little metal holders on the locker doors simply had anonymous ID numbers. A few had names.

"Say, this what you looking for?"

The docile janitor, who was preceeding Brennan, looked back helpfully. Brennan stepped to his side. The locker he was pointing at was third up from the floor, about waist high. The tag on it said *Leon Gruber, September 16*.

"Here it is," Brennan called softly, and Deadhead scuttled across the room. There had to be, Brennan thought, some sort of message on the corpse, something that only Deadhead could decipher. Perhaps this Gruber had smuggled something into the country in a body cavity... but surely, he thought, anything like that would've been found by the morgue technicians.

"The body's been here a long time," Brennan commented as Deadhead opened the locker door and pulled out the retractable table on which the corpse lay.

"Yes, it has, yes, indeed," Deadhead said, staring at the dingy sheet that covered the body. "They pulled strings. Pulled strings to keep it here until I... until I could get out."

"Get out?"

Deadhead pulled the sheet down, exposing Gruber's face and chest. He had been a fat young man, soft and pasty-looking. The expression of fear and horror pasted on his face was the worst that Brennan had even seen on a corpse. His chest was puckered with bullet holes, small caliber from the look of them.

"Yes," Deadhead said, but he never looked up from Gruber's dead, staring eyes. "I was in prison... hospital, really." From somewhere on his person he had produced a small, shiny hacksaw. His lips twitched in incessant, spasmodic jerks, and a line of spittle ran from the corner of his mouth to drip off his chin. "For corpse abuse."

"Are we taking the body with us?" Brennan asked through tightly clenched lips.

"No thanks," Deadhead said brightly. "I'll eat it here."

He began to saw Gruber's skull. The blade cut through the bone easily. Brennan and the janitor watched, horrified, as the top of the skull came off and Deadhead, with maniacal, somehow furtive glee, scooped chunks off Gruber's brain and stuffed them in his mouth. He chewed noisily.

Brennan felt Lazy Dragon dive into his vest pocket. The janitor vomited and Brennan fought off the rising tide of nausea that threatened to overwhelm him, holding on with grim, tight-lipped self-control.

III

Brennan gagged the janitor with his handkerchief and bound him at wrist and ankle with packing tape Lazy Dragon found in a corner of the storage room. He had to do all the work himself because Deadhead, mumbling incoherently, had sagged against the wall after wolfing down Gruber's brain. After Brennan took care of the janitor he guided the mumbling maniac out of the storeroom. Brennan wished that Lazy Dragon could tell him what the hell was going on.

"How'd it go?" Whiskers asked when Brennan threw open the Buick's rear passenger door and pushed Deadhead in. Brennan slammed the door and slid onto the front seat before answering.

"Fine, I think. Deadhead had a snack."

Whiskers nodded, started the car, and pulled away from the curb. Lazy Dragon climbed from Brennan's pocket, balanced precariously on the shoulder of the car seat, then leaped onto the lap of his human body, which, after a moment, awoke, yawned, and stretched. The mouse, undergoing a transformation somewhat analogous to that of Lot's overcurious wife, turned back into a block of soap.

"How'd it go?" Whiskers mumbled again, glancing up into the rearview mirror as he dove.

"Lazy Dragon dropped his mouse-sculpture in his jacket

pocket and nodded. "As planned. We found the body and Deadhead . . . dined. Cowboy did fine."

"Great. We'd better get Deadhead to the boss while he's still digesting."

"Now that we're all buddies," Brennan drawled, "maybe you can tell me what's going on."

Whiskers flipped off a driver who'd cut in front of them. "Well . . . I suppose it'd be all right. Deadhead there," he snickered, "is an ace, sort of. He can get people's memories by eating their brains."

Brennan made a face. "Jesus. So Gruber knew something that Mao wants to know."

Whiskers nodded and gunned the Buick, running a red light. "We think so. We hope so, anyway. You see, Danny Mao's boss is this guy named Fadeout who wants to find some ace who calls herself Wraith. Gruber was her fence before she bumped him off. Mao figures Gruber probably knew enough about her so we can use his memories to track her down."

Brennan pursed his lips, suppressing a smile. He knew more about this than these guys did. Fadeout was one of Kien's aces who had tried, and failed, to capture him and Wraith on Wild Card Day, and Wraith had told him that someone—not her—had killed her fence that very day.

"Why'd you wait so long to get to Gruber's corpse?" Brennan asked.

Whiskers shrugged. "Deadhead was in some kinda hospital. Cops caught him doing his thing with a body he'd found on the street back on Wild Card Day, and it took the lawyers a couple of months to spring him."

Brennan nodded, and to stay in his role as bewildered newcomer, he asked a question he already knew the answer to. "So why does Fadeout want to find this Wraith?"

Because she'd lifted Kien's private diary in the early morning hours of the wildest Wild Car Day ever, Brennan thought, but the Werewolf evidently didn't know that. He shrugged. "Hey, you think I'm Fadeout's confidant or something?"

Brennan nodded. He wasn't at least he tried not to be, introspective. His memories of the past were frequently painful, but Wraith—Jennifer Maloy—had often been on his mind since their meeting in September. It was more than the adventure they'd shared on Wild Card Day, more than the easy comradeship and grudging confidence between them, more than her tall, athletic-looking body. Brennan couldn't, wouldn't, admit why, but he knew that he'd try to get himself on the Shadow Fist task force that'd been given the job of hunting her. In that way he'd be in position to help her if the Fists got too close.

Not, he thought, that they'd be able to use Gruber's memories to track her down. Although Wraith had never told Brennan his name, she'd mentioned that she hadn't trusted her fence and had, in fact, never even told him her real name.

They drove on in silence. Whiskers finally pulled over and killed the engine in front of a three-story brownstone in the heart of Jokertown.

"Cowboy, you and Lazy Dragon help Deadhead. He can't do much on his own while he's digesting."

Brennan took his left arm, Lazy Dragon took his right, and they dragged him across the sidewalk and up the flight of stairs to the brownstone's entrance, where Whiskers was already talking with one of the Egrets who'd been standing in the foyer. They passed them on into the interior of the building, where another Egret guard spoke briefly into a house telephone and then told them to go upstairs. Getting Deadhead up two flights of stairs was like dragging a sack of half-set cement, but Whiskers didn't offer to help. Another Egret nodded to them on the third-floor landing. They went down a corridor with a threadbare carpet, and Whiskers rapped smartly on the door at the end of the hall. A masculine voice called out, "Come in," and Whiskers opened the door and preceded Brennan, Lazy Dragon, and Deadhead into the room.

It was a comfortably appointed room, rather luxurious compared to what Brennan had seen of the rest of the house. A man in his thirties, handsome, well-dressed, and fit-looking, was standing in front of a well-stocked liquor cart, having just fixed himself a drink.

"How did it go?"

"Fine, Fadeout, just fine."

Brennan didn't recognize him. He'd last seen him on Wild Card Day, but Fadeout had been invisible until Wraith had bashed him on the head with a garbage can lid and he'd fallen unconscious to the street. Brennan had had his hands full of Egrets at the time and had only spared the fallen ace the briefest of glances. It was evident that Fadeout also didn't recognize Brennan, who'd been masked at the time.

"Who's this?" the ace asked, nodding in Brennan's direction.

"New guy named Cowboy. He's all right."

"He'd better be." Fadeout stepped away from the cart, settled himself in a comfortable chair nearby. "Help youself," he said, gesturing at the liquor.

Whiskers stepped forward eagerly. Brennan and Lazy Dragon turned to dump the near-comatose Deadhead, who was now mumbling about excessive overhead and the price of cocaine, in a convenient chair, when a sudden, terrifyingly loud explosion boomed through the building, shaking it to its foundations. It seemed to come from the roof.

Fadeout's drink sloshed over his suit, Whiskers fell into the liquor cart, and Lazy Dragon and Brennan dropped Deadhead.

"Jesus Christ!" Fadeout swore, lurched to his feet, and staggered to the door as the ratcheting roar of automatic gunfire came from below.

Brennan followed Fadeout and found himself staring at three men armed with Uzis who'd come through a hole they'd blasted in the ceiling. Fadeout stood rooted in place by fear-induced paralysis. Brennan, acting instinctively, knocked the ace to the floor as a stream of slugs from their assailants' compact machine guns ripped into the wall above their heads. Brennan carried his Browning Hipower in a shoulder rig, and he knew that he couldn't draw it in time to return fire, he knew that he was going to be nailed to the floor by the next burst of slugs. Cursing the fate that had brought him to die among his enemies, he grabbed for his gun.

Something tossed from the room behind them fluttered in the hallway, a small sheet of paper that had been intricately folded. Before Brennan could draw his automatic, before their assailants could trigger another burst, there was a twisting shimmering in the air as the paper changed, transformed, *grew*, into a breathing, living, roaring tiger charging down the corridor, its eyes red and glaring, its mouth full of long, sharp teeth.

It caught a burst of slugs but didn't stop. It hurled itself at the three men at the end of the corridor, and Brennan heard bones splinter as it landed among them.

Brennan got to his knees, drew and aimed his Browning.

Lazy Dragon was holding one man down with his front paws, and with a single, quick motion bit cleanly through his throat. Blood sprayed over the hallway as a panicked gunman put a long burst through Dragon from point-blank range. The red dot from the sighting mechanism of Brennan's pistol shone on the gunman's forehead, and Brennan shot him as the tiger collapsed, falling with all its weight on the third assailant.

Fadeout had faded. Brennan half-stood and ran in crouching, crablike fashion down the corridor. He put a bullet through the head of the man who was trying frantically to pull himself out from under Lazy Dragon, then dropped to his knees before the gigantic cat. It was covered in blood, whether its own or from the slain men around it Brennan couldn't tell, but it was perforated by scores of wounds and was panting heavily. Brennan had seen enough mortally wounded creatures to know that Dragon was dying. He had no idea what he should do, or what this meant to Lazy Dragon's human form. He paused to pat the tiger sympathetically, then quickly moved on.

Bursts of automatic gunfire still rattled below as Brennan cautiously made his way down to the second-floor landing and carefully peered over the rail to the ground floor.

The foyer's double doors were open. Half a dozen Egrets, shot to pieces by automatic gunfire, lay on the stained marble floor. As Brennan watched, the few living members of the assault team backed grudgingly through the wreckage of the front door, swapping gunfire with the Egret guards and their reinforcements. Within moments the firefight had moved unto the stret outside, where gunfire echoed loudly in the night.

Brennan stood up.

"Goddamn wops."

He looked over his right shoulder. A pair of blue eyes, nerve tendrils and connective tissue dangling eerily from them, were floating five and a half feet above the floor. Fadeout blinked into existence, looking slightly rumpled and very, very angry.

"The Mafia?" Brennan asked.

"That's right, Cowboy. Rico Covello's men. I recognized what was left of their ugly faces from our dossiers." He paused, his anger replaced by sudden gratefulness. "I owe you one. They would've had me if you hadn't knocked me down."

Brennan shrugged. "If not for Lazy Dragon, we'd both be chopped meat. We'd better see if he's okay. His tiger got shot to shit."

"Right."

They went back upstairs. Brennan was relieved to see—then immediately angry at himself for the feeling—that Dragon was sitting calmly in one of Fadeout's comfortable chairs. He looked up as they entered the room.

"Everything is all right?" he asked.

"I wouldn't say that," Fadeout replied, still angry. "Those guinea bastards just waltzed in here and almost offed me." He looked angrily at Whiskers, who was standing uncertainly in the middle of the room. "What were you doing about it, you joker shitbag?"

Whiskers shrugged. "I-I thought someone should stay with Deadhead—"

"Take off that goddamned mask when you talk to me!" Fadeout ordered angrily. "I'm sick and tired of looking at Nixon's mug. No matter how ugly you are, it can't be worse."

Lazy Dragon watched Whiskers with calculated interest, and Brennan's hand crept closer to his holstered Browning. Werewolves had been known to fly into killing rages when unmasked, but Whiskers, as indicated by his earlier action—or lack of action—wasn't the fiercest of Werewolves. He took off his mask and stood in the center of the room uncomfortably shifting his weight from foot to foot.

Every bit of his face, except for his eyeballs, was covered with thick, coarse hair. Even his tongue, which was nervously licking his lips, was furred. No wonder, Brennan thought, his voice was so mushy.

Fadeout grunted, said something under his breath that Brennan didn't quite catch but had "joker bastard" in it, and turned away from the Werewolf.

"We've got to leave. The police will be here any minute. Dragon, you and Whiskers get that freak"—he nodded at Deadhead, who was still slumped muttering in his chair—"and bring him around back. Get the car and pick me up in front. Cowboy, come with me. I have to do a quick damage assessment."

Dragon stood. Brennan stopped in front of him and they

looked at each other for a long moment. There was something strange about Lazy Dragon, Brennan suddenly thought, something hidden, something utterly unfathomable that went beyond his unusual ace power. But the man had saved his life.

"Lucky you had a tiger on you."

Dragon smiled. "I like to have a backup handy. Something more deadly than a mouse."

Brennan nodded. "I'm in your debt," he said.

"I'll remember that." Dragon turned to help Whiskers with Deadhead.

Downstairs there were five dead Egrets, and half a dozen deceased mafiosi. The surviving Egrets were buzzing like angry bees.

Fadeout shook his head. "Damn. It's escalating. Little Mother isn't going to like this."

Brennan squelched the expression of sudden interest before it reached his face. He said nothing, because he was afraid his voice would betray him. Little Mother, Siu Ma, was the head of the Immaculate Egrets. If Fadeout was a lieutenant in Kien's organization, she was at least a colonel. In all his months of investigation he'd discovered only that she was an ethnic Chinese from Vietnam who'd come to the states in the late 1960s to become the wife of Nathan Chow, the leader of a penny-ante street gang called the Immaculate Egrets. Her arrival corresponded with a quick rise in the fortune of the Egrets, little of which was enjoyed by Chow. He had died under unspecified but mysterious circumstances in 1971, and Siu Ma took over the gang, which continued to grow and prosper. Kien, then still an ARVN general, used it to funnel heroin into the States. There was no doubt that Siu Ma was very high in Kien's organization, very high indeed.

"We have to split before the cops arrive," Fadeout said. He turned to an Ingram-toting Egret. "Leave this place. Take all the files, all valuables."

The Egret nodded, sketched an informal salute, and started shouting orders in rapid Chinese.

"Let's go," Fadeout repeated, carefully picking his way among the bodies.

"Where to?" Brennan asked as casually as he could.

"Little Mother's place in Chinatown. I've got to tell her what happened."

A sleek limo pulled up to the curb. Whiskers was driving, Deadhead lolled in the backseat with Lazy Dragon. Fadeout got in and Brennan followed him, excitement thrumming through his body like tautly stretched wire.

He carefully noted the route that Whiskers took, but he had no idea at all where they were when the limo finally stopped in a small, ramshackle garage in a dirty, garbage-choked alley. His unfamiliarity with the area irritated him and upset his fine-tuned sense of control. He hated the helpless feeling that had been plaguing him lately, but there was nothing to do but swallow it and go on.

Whiskers, his mask back in place, and Lazy Dragon dragged Deadhead from the limo on Fadeout's order. The significance of that wasn't lost on Brennan. He knew that he'd gone up a notch or two in Fadeout's estimation, which was exactly what he wanted. The closer he got to the core of Kien's organization, the easier it would be for him to bring it tumbling down like a house of cards.

The door they approached wasn't as flimsy as it appeared. It was also locked and guarded, but the sentinel let them in after peering through a peephole when Fadeout knocked.

"Siu Ma is asleep," the guard said. He was a large Chinese dressed in traditional baggy trousers, broad leather belt, and matching tunic top. The machine pistol holstered on his broad leather belt was a jarring anachronism with his antique style of dress, but, Brennan reflected, was a sensible compromise with what was apparently Siu Ma's strongly developed sense of tradition.

"She'll want to see us," Fadeout said grimly. "We'll be in the audience chamber."

The guard nodded, turned to a very modern intercom system, and spoke Chinese too quickly for Brennan to follow.

The audience chamber was as luxurious as the outside of the building was dilapidated. The decorating motif was dynastic China. There were rich rugs, beautiful lacquered screens, delicate porcelain, a couple of massive green bronze temple demons, and undoubtedly valuable knickknacks of ivory, jade, and other precious and semiprecious stones set about on tables of teak and ebony and other rare woods. Wraith, Brennan thought, would love this place.

Although it could have been overwhelming, the room's overall effect was actually quite pleasing. It was like a living museum exhibit that had been assembled with a discerning eye and in the utmost good taste.

Siu Ma was already waiting for them. She was seated on a gilt chair that dominated the chamber's rear wall, rubbing the sleep out of her eyes. She was short with a round, plump face, dark, long-lashed eyes, and black glossy hair. She looked to be in her early thirties. She stiffled a yawn with a pudgy hand and frowned at Fadeout.

"This had better be important," she said, glancing distastefully at Deadhead and his attendants, curiously at Brennan. Her English was excellent, with just a lingering trace of a French accent.

"It is," Fadeout assured her. He told her of the Mafia hit on his brownstone. As he spoke, a young girl bearing a tray came into the room and poured her a small cup of tea. Siu Ma sipped the tea as she listened to Fadeout's story, and her frown deepened.

"This is intolerable," she said when he'd finished. "We must teach those comic-book criminals a lesson they won't forget."

"I agree," Fadeout said. "However, our spies have told us that Covello has withdrawn to his estate in the Hamptons. It's one of the Mafia's most heavily fortified strongholds. It has two walls around it—an armored outer wall that encircles the entire estate and an inner electrified fence that protects the main building. Covello's entrenched there with a company of heavily armed Mafia thugs."

Siu Ma looked at Fadeout coldly, and Brennan could see ruthless strength in her near-black eyes.

"The Shadow Fists have weapons too," she said.

Fadeout bobbed his head. "I agree, but we don't want to expend our men in a futile attempt at revenge. And think of the unwanted attention such an assault would draw from the authorities."

There was an uncomfortable silence as Siu Ma sipped her tea and stared coldly at Fadeout. Brennan saw his chance.

"Excuse my interruption," he said in his soft drawl, "but one man can often go where many would be unwelcome."

Fadeout turned to him, frowned. "What do you mean?"

Brennan shrugged depreciatingly. "A one-man sortie might accomplish what a full-scale raid could never hope to do."

Brennan felt Siu Ma's eyes boring into him. "Who is this man?" she asked.

"His name's Cowboy," Fadeout said, distraction in his voice. "He's new."

Siu Ma finished her tea and set the cup down on the tray. "He sounds as if he has a head on his shoulders. Tell me," she said, speaking directly to Brennan for the first time, "are you volunteering to be this man?"

He bobbed his head in a respectful bow. "Yes, *Dama*."

She smiled, pleased as he'd hoped she'd be by the respectful form of address.

"It will be dangerous, very, very dangerous," Fadeout said cautiously.

Siu Ma turned her gaze to him. "Never," she said, "stop to count danger in a matter of revenge."

Brennan suppressed a smile. Siu Ma, it seemed, was a woman after his own heart.

IV

It was bone-chillingly cold at the West Thirtieth Street Heliport. The wind was an icy whip that cut through the stained jumpsuit that Brennan wore. The smell of immanent snow was in the air, though Brennan could barely discern it through the grease and oil odors of the heliport where, disguised as a mechanic, he waited patiently.

Brennan was good at waiting. He'd spent two days and nights doing just that in a hidden observation post across the road from Covello's Southampton estate. It was apparent that Covello, choosing discretion over valor, had decided to go to ground for the duration of the Mafia–Shadow Fist war. He was surrounded by a company of heavily armed Mafia goons and protected by walls that were safe to anything but a full-scale assault. The only vehicles allowed inside the grounds brought supplies to feed the don and underlings to consult with him, and even these were stopped and thoroughly checked at the front gate.

The only other way into the estate was the helipad on the mansion's roof. Brennan had watched Covello's helicopter come and go several times each day, on different occasions ferrying in and out expensive-looking women and dark-suited men. The men, when identified by snaps Brennan took of them with a telephoto lens, were mostly high-ranking members of the other Families. The women were apparently call girls.

His reconnaissance over, Brennan waited patiently at the heliport that was the Manhattan base of Covello's chopper. Since, he decided, he couldn't go through Covello's walls, he'd go over them. In Covello's own chopper.

Night had fallen before the chopper pilot showed up with a trio of shivering women dressed in fur coats. There was no one else near the chopper. As Brennan approached them, the pilot let down the ladder to the cabin. The first hooker was trying to climb aboard, but was finding it difficult to mount the metal stairs in her high-heeled boots.

It was too almost too easy. Brennan slugged the pilot, and he staggered backward, hit hard against the body of the chopper, and slid to the ground. The call girl who'd been clutching his arm teetered precariously, her arms windmilling vigorously, then Brennan steadied her with a hand on her rump.

"Hey!" she complained, either at the placement of Brennan's hand or his treatment of the pilot.

"Change in plan," Brennan told them. "Go on home."

They regarded him suspiciously. The one on the stairs spoke. "We haven't been paid yet."

Brennan smiled his best smile. "You haven't been killed yet, either." He reached for his wallet, emptied it of cash. "Cab fare," he said, handing the bills over.

The three glanced at each other, at Brennan, then back at each other. The one climbed down the stairs, and hunched over against the cold, walked away muttering. The others followed.

Brennan hauled the pilot into the chopper cabin. He was out cold, but his pulse was steady and strong. Brennan stared at him for a moment. The man, after all, was nothing to him, not even an enemy. He was just someone who happened to be in the way. Brennan took a ball of strong twine from his jumpsuit pocket, bound him, gagged him, and left him on the floor of the cabin. He stripped off his dirty jumpsuit, wadded it up, and flung it in a corner. He moved through the cabin into the cockpit and slid into the pilot's seat.

"I'm off," he said to the empty air, but those listening on

the chosen frequency heard him and started on their own way to Southampton.

Brennan hadn't piloted a chopper in more than ten years, and this was a commercial rather than a military model, but the old skills returned quickly to his hands. He asked for and received takeoff clearance, and scrupulously following the flight plan he'd found on a clipboard in the cabin, soon left behind the million twinkling jewels that was New York City.

Flying over Long Island in the cold, clear night gave him a fresh, clean feeling that he lost himself in. All too soon, however, Covello's brightly lit private helipad was below him. As he settled down as gently as a feather, a guard carrying an assault rifle waved at him. Brennan sighed. He shook the clean feeling of the night sky from his brain. It was time to get back to work.

The guard sauntered casually toward the chopper. Brennan waited until he was half a dozen steps away, then he leaned out the cockpit window and shot him in the head with his silenced Browning. No one saw him enter the mansion through the door in the roof, no one saw him flit from room to room, as quiet and purposeful as a haunting spirit.

He found Covello in a library that had rows and rows of unread books that had been bought by the mansion's interior decorator because of their matched bindings. The don, whom Brennan recognized from his photo in Fadeout's dossier, was shooting pool with his *consuláre* while a man who was obviously a bodyguard watched silently.

Covello missed an easy cushion shot, swore to himself, then looked up. He frowned at Brennan. "Who the hell are you?"

Brennan said nothing. He raised his gun and shot the astonished bodyguard. Covello started to scream in a curiously high-pitched, womanish voice, and the *consuláre* swung at Brennan with his poolstick. Brennan ducked out of the way and put three slugs in the *consuláre*'s chest, blowing him over the pool table. He shot the don in the back as he was running for the door.

Covello was still breathing as Brennan stood over him. There was a pleading look in his eyes and he tried to speak. Brennan wanted to finish him with a shot to the head, but couldn't. He had orders.

He pulled a small black nylon sack from his back pocket,

and a knife, much longer and heavier than the one he usually carried, from the belt sheath at the small of his back.

He was on the clock now. Covello's screams had certainly aroused the household, and he had little time before more goons would arrive. He bent down. The dying don closed his eyes in unutterable horror at the sight of the knife in Brennan's hands.

The man wasn't his enemy, but neither would his death be a great loss to society. Still, as he cut through Covello's throat, leaning hard on the blade to sever the spinal cord, Brennan couldn't help but feel that he deserved a cleaner death. That no one deserved a death like this.

He lifted Covello's head by his oiled hair and dropped it in the nylon bag. Moving quickly, he went back through the corridors that led to the roof and waiting chopper. He moved quickly and quietly, but he was seen.

A Mafia soldier let out a wild burst of gunfire and shouted to his companions. The burst didn't come close to hitting Brennan, but he knew now they were on his trail. He moved faster, running down corridors and up stairs. Once he blundered into a group of men. He had no idea who they were, and they looked surprised and not a little bewildered at the commotion. He emptied the Browning's clip at them as he charged, and they scattered without offering resistance as the sounds of pursuit drew closer and closer.

He spoke aloud to unseen listeners without breaking stride. "I've got the package and I'm coming home. I need backup." He reached into his vest pocket, dropped something to the carpet, and ran on.

A fluttering sheet of delicate paper, intricately folded into a small, complicated shape, fell from his hand. He didn't look back, but he heard the challenging roar of a big cat, terribly loud in the close confines of the corridor, reverberate and echo endlessly as it mixed with the sounds of gunfire and the screams of terrified men.

The route he flew to the small Suffolk County airport was on no authorized flight plan, and the flight itself was not as exhilarating with the stained and leaking black bag keeping him company on the copilot's seat.

Fadeout and Whiskers were waiting at the airport with a limo.

"How'd it go?"

"As planned." Brennan held out the bag and Whiskers took it.

Fadeout nodded. "Wrap it up in a blanket or something and put it in the trunk." He caught Brennan's look of disgust as Whiskers hustled off. He shrugged. "Yeah, it gets to me, too, sometimes. Deadhead is a useful tool, though. Think of all the inside info he'll pick up from Covello's brain."

"I thought Deadhead was working on another problem," Brennan said casually. "Some ace named Wraith?"

"Oh, that?" Fadeout waved a hand. "He solved it. Wraith apparently didn't like Gruber too much. Never even told him her real name. But she did let her birthday slip once. And Deadhead is a talented sketch artist—hard to think of him as having any real human qualities. We have deep connections in a lot of government agencies, the DMV, for example. Her birthday and Deadhead's sketch will be enough to nail that bitch to the wall."

A wave of fear washed through Brennan, sweeping away the fatigue that weighed heavily on his body and spirit. To hide it he rubbed his face and yawned hugely.

"Well," he said, desperately trying to sound casual, "it sounds pretty important. I'd like to be in on it."

Fadeout looked at him closely, but nodded. "Sure, Cowboy. You earned it. It won't come down for a day or two, but you look like you could sleep that long."

Brennan forced a grin. "I could at that."

They dropped Brennan at his Jokertown apartment, where he slept around the clock, then worried for another day before he got the call. It was Whiskers's mushy voice at the other end of the line.

"We got her name, Cowboy, and we got her address."

"Who's in on it?"

"You and me and two of my Werewolf pals. They're watching her place now."

Brennan nodded. He was glad that Lazy Dragon wouldn't be along. He had ample respect for the ace's power and adaptability.

"There's a problem, though." Whiskers hesitated. "She can turn into a ghost or something and walk right through walls and shit, so we can't even really threaten her."

Brennan smiled. Jennifer was extraordinarily difficult to deal with.

"Fadeout's got a plan though. We break into her place and see if we can find this book he's looking for. If not, we can try to deal with her. Buy it back or something. Then," Whiskers said, some satisfaction in his voice, "she can always catch a bullet in the back of her head sometime. She ain't always going to be a ghost."

"Good plan," Brennan made himself say. And it was. They knew her name. They knew where to find her. He had to do something or she wouldn't live out the month, even if they turned over the diary. His mind raced. "I'll meet you in an hour, at her place. Give me the address."

"Right, Cowboy. You know, it's too bad she can turn into a ghost. She's real good-looking. We could have a real party with her."

"Yeah, a real party." Brennan hung up after Whiskers gave him directions to the apartment. He stared at nothing for a moment, marshaling all his Zen training to calm his mind, to soothe his racing pulse. He needed calmness, not a brain drenched in hate, anger, and fear. Part of him wondered at his strong reaction to Whiskers's news. Part of him knew the reason, but the biggest part told him to forget it for now, to bury it and examine it later. There was a way out of this mess . . . there had to be. . . .

He sunk his consciousness in the pool of being, seeking knowledge through perfect tranquility, and when he brought his mind back from zazen, he had his answer. It was Kien, and what he knew of the man, his fears, his strengths, his weaknesses.

Some of the details would be tricky, and painful, to work out. He picked up the phone, dialed a number. It rang, then he heard the sound of her voice on the other end of the line: "Hello?" he held the phone tightly, realizing that he had missed her voice, and despite the circumstances, he was glad to hear it again. "Hello?"

"Hello, Jennifer. We have to talk . . ."

Snow was falling in blinding sheets and the wind was roaring like lost souls through the gray city canyons. Somehow winter seemed colder here than in the mountains, Brennan thought, colder and dirtier and lonelier. The maskless Werewolves, dressed as maintenance men, were waiting in the lobby of Jennifer's apartment building. One was tall and thin with acne-scarred cheeks. His joker deformities were hidden by the baggy coveralls he wore. The other was short and thin, his deformity evident in his sharply twisted spine that rotated his torso abnormaly from his hips. Whiskers and Brennan, also wearing coveralls, stamped the snow from their boots.

"Cold as hell," Whiskers offered. "She's gone?" he asked in a low whisper.

The tall and thin one nodded. "She left no more'n ten minutes ago. Caught a cab."

"Okay, let's do it."

No one saw them go up to Jennifer's apartment. Her front door yielded easily to the Werewolves' burglary tools. Brennan told himself that he'd have to speak to her about that, if, he amended, they were both still around when this caper was finished.

"We'll toss the bedroom first," Whiskers said as they entered the apartment. He stopped and frowned at the bookshelf-lined walls. "Shit, finding a book in this will be like looking for a needle in a goddamned haystack."

He led the way into a small bedroom that contained a single bed, a nightstand with a lamp, an ancient wardrobe, and more bookshelves.

"We'll have to check all those damn books," Whiskers said. "One might be hollowed out or something."

"Jeez, Whiskers," the short and thin Werewolf said, "you've seen too many mov—"

He stopped, stared, as a tall, slim, good-looking blonde in a black string bikini stepped out of the wall. She wavered, solidified, and pointed a silenced pistol at them. She smiled. "Freeze," she said.

They froze, more in astonishment than fear.

Whiskers swallowed. "Hey, we, we just want to talk. We were sent by important people."

The woman nodded. "I know."

"You know?" Whiskers asked, bewildered.

"I told her."

Everyone turned to stare at Brennan. He had opened the drawer of the nightstand, and he, too, had a gun. It was a long-barreled, peculiar-looking pistol. He pointed it at Whiskers.

The joker's eyeballs bulged from his furry face.

"What the hell are you doing, Cowboy? What's going on?"

Brennan looked at him with no expression at all. He

flicked his wrist, squeezed the trigger twice. There were two small, nearly soundless explosions of air, and the Werewolves stared in astonishment at the darts implanted in their chests. The tall, thin one opened his mouth to say something, sighed, closed his eyes, and slipped to the floor. The other didn't even try to speak.

"Cowboy!"

Brennan shook his head. "My name isn't Cowboy. It isn't Yeoman either, but that will do."

Whiskers's face took on an almost comical look of terror. "Look, let me go. Please. I won't tell anyone. Honest. Trust me—" He sagged to his knees, his hands clasped imploringly, tears soaking his furry cheeks.

Brennan's air pistol spat another dart, and Whiskers slipped facedown on the carpet. Brennan turned to Jennifer.

"Hello, Wraith."

She dropped the gun on the bed. "Can't you . . . can't you let them go?"

Brennan shook his head. "You know I can't. They know who I am. It'd blow my cover. It'd also ruin our plan."

"They have to die?"

He approached within reach of her but made his arms stay at his side. "This is deadly business you're involve in." He gestured at the drugged Werewolves. "No one can walk away from this, except me, if you want to live." He stopped, looked troubled. "Even then, there's no guarantee . . ."

Jennifer sighed. "Their lives are on my head—"

"*They* made the decisions and led the lives that brought them here. They were prepared to rape, maim, and kill you. Still"—Brennan looked away from Jennifer, looked inward to himself—"still . . ."

His voice ran down to silence. Jennifer put her hand on his cheek, and he looked up, his dark eyes haunted by memories of death and destruction that despite his Zen training, despite his dogged concentration, were never far from the surface of his thoughts.

Jennifer smiled slightly. "I like your new eyes." Brennan smiled back and almost unwillingly covered her hand with his.

"I have to get going. It'll be dark soon and I have to take care of them"—he nodded at the unconscious Werewolves—"and . . . other details."

Jennifer nodded. "Will I see you again? Soon, I mean."

Brennan took his hand away, half-turned, shrugged. "Don't you have enough problems?"

"Hey, the crime lord of New York City has marked me for death. How much worse could it get?"

Brennan shook his head. "You couldn't even *begin* to guess. Look, you'd better disappear. I have to take care of things."

Jennifer looked at him silently.

"I'll call you."

"Promise?" she asked.

Brennan nodded. She gave the Werewolves a final troubled glance, then faded through the wall again. Brennan had no intention of keeping the promise. None. Not at all. But by the time he'd hoisted the first unconscious joker to his shoulders, his resolve was already fading.

V

Fadeout, Siu Ma, and Deadhead were in conference when Brennan was admitted to the audience chamber. Deadhead was babbling lists of names, addresses, telephone numbers, bank accounts, and government connections. Everything that Covello had kept in the storehouse of his brain was Deadhead's. Everything the don had known. . . .

A sudden insight struck Brennan. Only the dead, he thought, could know everything. They were finished and done with. Their lives were complete. Only the dead could know Jokertown, totally and completely, for they had no need of new knowledge. Like him, when he'd been in the mountains. His life had been peaceful, unchanging, and serene. And quite dead. Now he was living again. The sense of uncertainty and loss of control that had increasingly been plaguing him was the price he paid for living. It was a high price, but so far, he realized, he could afford it.

Fadeout and Siu Ma exchanged concerned glances when Brennan entered the chamber alone.

"What happened? Fadeout asked.

"Ambush. That crazy Yeoman bastard. Killed Whiskers and the other Werewolves. Pinned me to the wall by my damn hand." Brennan held out his right hand. It was wrapped in a bloody rag torn from his shirt. It had hurt like hell to drive the arrow through his palm. It'd been, Brennan reflected, penance of a sort for what he'd done since his arrival in the city.

"He let you live?" Siu Ma asked.

"He wanted me to deliver this. He said it was no good to him." He held up Kien's diary, which had been blanked when Jennifer had ghosted it from Kien's wall safe. He hated like hell to give it back and let Kien know that he was safe from the secrets he'd written therein, but he had to give Kien something concrete to get him off Jennifer's back.

Fadeout took the diary from him and, mystified, riffled through its blank pages. "Did . . . did Yeoman do this?"

Brennan shook his head. "He said it happened when Wraith stole it."

Fadeout smiled. "Well, that's great. That's really great."

Even Siu Ma looked pleased.

"There was one more thing." Brennan forced himself to speak like a dispassionate messenger when he really wanted to brand the words on Fadeout's forehead so Kien would be sure to understand the iron behind them.

Fadeout and Siu Ma looked at him expectantly.

"He also had a message. He said to tell Kien—yeah, the name was Kien—that he knows where Kien lives, just as Kien knows where Wraith lives. He said to tell Kien that their feud goes beyond life and death, that it is one of honor and retribution, but that he will be satisfied with Kien's life if anything happens to Wraith. He says he has an arrow with Kien's name on it waiting . . . just waiting."

He'd delivered a similar promise a few months ago in behalf of another. But perhaps justifiably she had refused to accept his protection and chose instead to go away. Jennifer, though, had simply nodded when he'd told her his plan, had accepted it as if she truly, totally trusted him.

"I see." Fadeout and Siu Ma exchanged worried glances. "Well, yes, I'll pass that on." Fadeout nodded decisively. "I will indeed." He pulled worriedly at his lower lip.

Siu Ma stood up. "You have proven yourself worthy," she said. "I hope that your association with the Shadow Fists will be long and prosperous."

Brennan looked at her. He permitted himself to smile. "I'm sure it will," he said. "I'm sure it will."

All the King's Horses

by George R.R. Martin

I

Tom found the latest issue of *Aces* in the outer office, while the loan officer kept him waiting.

The cover showed the Turtle flying over the Hudson against a spectacular autumn sunset. The first time he'd seen that photograph, in *Life*, Tom had been tempted to have it framed. But that had been a long time ago. Even the shell in the picture was gone now, jettisoned somewhere in space by the aliens who'd captured him last spring.

Underneath, letters black against the scarlet-tinged clouds, the blurb asked, "The Turtle—Dead or Alive?"

"Fuck," Tom said aloud, annoyed. The secretary gave him a disapproving look. He ignored her and thumbed through the magazine to find the story. How the hell could they possibly say he was dead? So he got napalmed and crashed into the Hudson in full view of half the city, so what? He'd come back, hadn't he? He'd taken an old shell and crossed the river, flown over Jokertown near dawn the day after Wild Card Day, thousands of people must have seen him. What more did he have to do?

He found the article. The writer made a big deal of the fact that no one had seen the Turtle for months. Perhaps he died after all, the magazine suggested, and the dawn sighting was only some kind of mass hallucination. Wish fulfillment, one expert suggested. A weather balloon, said a second. Or maybe Venus.

"*Venus!*" Tom said with some indignation. The old shell he'd used that morning was a goddamn VW Beetle covered with armor plate. How the hell could they say it was Venus? He flipped a page, and came face-to-face with a grainy photograph of a shell fragment pulled out of the river. The

39

metal was bent outward, twisted by some awful explosion, its edges jagged and sharp. *All the king's horses and all the king's men couldn't put the Turtle together again*, said the caption.

Tom hated it when they tried to be clever.

"Miss Trent will see you now," the secretary announced.

Miss Trent did nothing to improve his disposition. She was a slender young woman in oversize horn-rimmed glasses, her short brown hair frosted with streaks of blond. Quite pretty, and at least ten years younger than Tom. "Mr. Tudbury," she said, from behind a spotless steel-and-chrome desk, when he entered. "The loan committee has gone over your application. You have an excellent credit record."

"Yeah," Tom said. He sat down, for a moment allowing himself to hope. "Does that mean I get the money?"

Miss Trent smiled sadly. "I'm afraid not."

Somehow he'd expected that. He tried to act as though it didn't matter; banks never lent you money if they thought you needed it. "What about my credit rating?" he asked.

"You have an excellent record of timely payment on your loans, and we did take that into account. But the committee felt your total indebtedness was already too high, given your present income. We couldn't justify extending you any further unsecured credit at this time. I'm sorry. Perhaps another lending institution would feel differently."

"Another lending institution," Tom said wearily. Fat chance. This bank was the fourth one he'd tried. They all said the same thing. "Yeah. Sure." He was on his way out when he saw the framed diploma on her wall and turned back. "Rutgers," he said to her. "I dropped out of Rutgers. I had better things to do than finish college. More important things."

She regarded him silently, a puzzled expression on her pretty young face. For a moment Tom wanted to go back, to sit down and tell her everything. She had an understanding face, at least for a banker.

"Never mind," he said.

It was a long walk back to his car.

It was just shy of midnight when Joey found him, leaning against a rusted rail and watching the moonlit waters of the Kill Van Kull. The park was across the street from his house, and from the projects where he'd grown up. Even as a kid, he'd found solace there, in the black oily waters, the lights of Staten Island across the way, the big tankers passing in the night. Joey knew that; they'd been friends since grade school, different as night and day, but brothers in all but name.

Tom heard the footsteps behind him, glanced over his shoulder, saw it was only Joey, and turned back to the Kill. Joey came up and stood beside him, arms folded on the railing.

"You didn't get the loan," Joey said.

"No," Tom said. "Same old story."

"Fuck 'em."

"No," Tom said. "They're right. I owe too much."

"You okay, Tuds?" Joey asked. "How long you been out here?"

"A while," Tom said. "I had some thinking to do."

"I hate it when you think."

Tom smiled. "Yeah, I know." He turned away from the water. "I'm cashing in my chips, Joey."

"What the fuck is that supposed to mean?"

Tom ignored the question. "I was getting nostalgic about that last shell. It had infrared, zoom lenses, four big monitors and twenty little ones, tape deck, graphic equalizer, fridge, everything on fingertip remote, computerized, state-of-the-art. Four *years* I worked on that mother, weekends, nights, vacations, you name it. Every spare cent I had went into it. So what happens? I have the damn thing in service for five months, and Tachyon's asshole relatives just toss it into space."

"Big fucking deal," Joey said. "You still got the old shells out in the junkyard, use one of them."

Tom tried to be patient. "The shell the Takisians jettisoned was my fifth," he said. "After I lost it, I went back to number four. That was the one that got napalmed. You want to look at the pieces, go buy a copy of *Aces*—there's a swell picture in there. We cannibalized all the useful parts from two and three years ago. The only one that's still more-or-less intact is the first."

"So?" Joey said.

"*So?* It's got wires, Joey, not circuit boards, twenty-year-old wires. Obsolete cameras with limited tracking capabilities, blind spots, black-and-white sets, vacuum tubes, a fucking gas heater, the worst ventilation system you've ever seen.

How I got it over to Jokertown back in September I still don't know, but I was in shock from the crash or I never could have tried such a fucking moronic thing. So many of the tubes burned out that I was flying half-blind before I got back."

"We can fix all that stuff."

"Forget it," Tom said with more vehemence than he knew was in him. "Those shells of mine, they're like some kind of symbol for my whole fucking life. I'm standing here thinking about it, and it makes me sick. All the money I've put into them, all the hours, the work. If I'd put that kind of effort into my real life, I could be somebody. Look at me, Joey. I'm forty-three years old, I live alone, I own a house and an abandoned junkyard, both of them mortgaged up to the hilt. I work a forty-hour week selling VCRs and computers, and I've managed to buy a third of the business, only now the business isn't doing so great, ha ha, big joke on me. That woman in the bank today was ten years younger than me, and she probably makes three times my salary. Cute too, no wedding ring, the secretary said Miss Trent, maybe I would've liked to ask her out, but you know what? I looked into her eyes, and I could see her feeling sorry for me."

"Some dumb cunt looks down at you, that's no reason to get bent out of shape," Joey said.

"No," Tom said. "She's right. I'm better than I looked to her, but there's no way she could have known that. I've put the best part of myself into being the Turtle. The Astronomer and his goons almost *killed* me. Fuck it, Joey, they dropped *napalm* on my shell, and one of them made me so sick I blacked out. I could have died."

"You didn't."

"I was lucky," Tom said with fervor. "*Damn* lucky. I was strapped into that motherfucker, every one of my instruments dead, with the whole fucking thing, all umpteen tons of it, headed straight for the bottom of the river. Even if I'd been conscious, which I wasn't, there would have been no way to get to the hatch and open it manually before I drowned. That's assuming I could even find the hatch with all the fucking lights out and the shell filling up with water!"

"I thought you didn't remember this shit," Joey said.

"I don't," said Tom. He massaged his temples. "Not consciously. Sometimes I have these dreams . . . fuck it, never mind about that, the point is, I was a dead man. Only I got lucky, incredibly lucky, something blew the goddamned shell apart, blew me right out without killing me, and I managed to make it to the surface. Otherwise I'd be down in a steel tomb on the bottom of the Hudson, with eels slithering in and out of my eyes."

"So?" Joey said. "You're not, are you?"

"What about next time?" Tom demanded. "I been breaking my back trying to figure some way to finance a new shell. Sell my share of the business, I thought, or maybe sell the house and move into some apartment. And then I thought, well, great. I sell my fucking house, build a new shell, and then the goddamned Takisians show up again, or it turns out the Astronomer had a brother and he's pissed, or some other shit goes down, the details don't matter, but *something* happens, and I wind up dead. Or maybe I survive, only the new shell gets trashed just like the last two, and I'm right back where I started, except now I don't have a house either. What's the fucking point?"

Joey was looking into his eyes, Joey who had grown up with him, who knew Tom better than anybody. "Yeah, maybe," he said. "So why do I think there's something you're not saying?"

"I used to be a pretty smart kid," Tom insisted, turning away sharply, "but somehow I got pretty dumb as I grew up. This double life shit is a crock. One life is hard enough for most people to manage, what the hell made me think I could juggle two?" He shook his head. "The hell with it. It's over. I'm wising up, Joey. They think the Turtle is dead? Fine. Let him rest in peace."

"Your call, Tuds," Joey said. He put a rough hand on Tom's shoulder. "It's a damn shame, though. You're going to make my kid cry. The Turtle's his hero."

"Jetboy was my hero," Tom said. "He died too. That's part of growing up. Sooner or later, all your heroes die."

Concerto for
Siren and Serotonin

by Roger Zelazny

I

Sitting shade-clad in a booth at Vito's Italian, odd-hour and
quiet, lowering a mound of linguini and the level in a
straw-bound bottle—black hair stiff with spray or tonic—the
place's only patron had drawn attention from the staff in the
form of several wagers, in that this was his seventh entrée,
when a towering civilian with a hand like a club came in off
the street and stood near, watching, also, through bloodshot
eyes.

The man continued to stare at the diner, who finally
swung his mirror lenses toward him.

"You the one I'm looking for?" the newcomer asked.

"Maybe so," the diner replied, lowering his fork, "if it
involves money and certain special skills."

The big man smiled. Then he raised his right hand and
dropped it. It struck the edge of the table, removed the
corner, shredded the tablecloth, and jerked it forward. The linguini spilled backward into the dark-haired man's lap. The
man jerked away as this occurred and his glasses fell askew,
revealing a pair of glittering, faceted eyes.

"Prick!" he announced, his hands shooting forward, paralleling the other's clublike appendage.

"Son of a bitch!" the giant bellowed, jerking his hand
away. "You fuckin' burned me!"

"'Fuckin' shocked,'" the other corrected. "Lucky I didn't
fry you! What is this? Why you taking my table apart?"

"You're hirin' fuckin' aces, ain't you? I wanted you to see
my shit."

44

"I'm not hiring aces. I thought you were, the way you came on."

"Hell, no! Bug-eyed bastard!"

The other moved quickly to adjust his glasses.

"It's a real pain," he stated, "looking at two hundred sixteen views of an asshole."

"I'll give you something up the asshole!" said the giant, raising his hand again.

"You got it," said the other, an electrical storm erupting suddenly between his palms. The giant stepped back a pace. Then the storm passed and the man lowered his hands. "If it weren't for the linguini in my lap," he said then, "this would be funny. Sit down. We can wait together."

"Funny?"

"Think about it while I go clean up," he replied. Then, "Name's Croyd," he said.

"Croyd Crenson?"

"Yeah. And you're Bludgeon, aren't you?"

"Yeah. What do you mean 'funny'?"

"Like mistaken identity," Croyd answered. "Two guys thinking they're each somebody else, you know?"

Bludgeon's brow was furrowed for several seconds before his lips formed a tentative smile. Then he laughed, four coughlike barks. "Yeah, fuckin' funny!" he said then, and barked again.

Bludgeon slid into the booth, still chuckling, as Croyd slid out. Croyd headed back toward the men's room and Bludgeon ordered a pitcher of beer from the waiter who came by to clean up. A few moments later, a black-suited man entered the dining area from the kitchen and stood, thumbs hooked behind his belt, toothpick moving slowly within a faint frown. Then he advanced.

"You look a little familiar," he said, coming up beside the booth.

"I'm Bludgeon," the other replied, raising his hand.

"Chris Mazzucchelli. Yeah, I've heard of you. I hear you can bash your way through nearly anything with that mitt of yours."

Bludgeon grinned. "Fuckin' A," he said.

Mazzucchelli smiled around the toothpick and nodded. He slid into Croyd's seat.

"You know who I am?" he asked.

"Hell, yes," Bludgeon said, nodding. "You're the Man."

"That I am. I guess you heard there's some trouble coming down, and I need some special kind of soldiers."

"You need some fuckin' heads broke, I'm fuckin' good at it," Bludgeon told him.

"That's nicely put," Mazzucchelli said, reaching inside his jacket. He removed an envelope and tossed it onto the tabletop. "Retainer."

Bludgeon picked it up, tore it open, then counted the bills slowly, moving his lips. When he was finished, he said, "Fuckin' price is fuckin' right. Now what?"

"There's an address in there too. You go to it eight o'clock tonight and get some orders. Okay?"

Bludgeon put away the envelope and rose.

"Damn straight," he agreed, reaching out and picking up the pitcher of beer, raising it, draining it, and belching.

"Who's the other guy—the one back in the john?"

"Shit, he's one of us," Bludgeon replied. "Name's Croyd Crenson. Bad man to fuck with, but he's got a great sense of humor."

Mazzucchelli nodded. "Have a good day," he said.

Bludgeon belched again, nodded back, waved his club-hand, and departed.

Croyd hesitated only a moment on reentering the dining room and regarding Mazzucchelli in his seat. He advanced, raised two fingers in mock salute, and said, "I'm Croyd," as he drew near. "Are you the recruiter?"

Mazzucchelli looked him up and looked him down, eyes dwelling for a moment on the large wet spot at the front of his trousers.

"Something scare you?" he asked.

"Yea, I saw the kitchen," Croyd replied. "You looking for talent?"

"What kind of talent you got?"

Croyd reached for a small lamp on a nearby table. He unscrewed the bulb and held it before him. Shortly it began to glow. Then it brightened, flared, and went out.

"Oops," he observed. "Gave it a little too much juice."

"For a buck and a half," Mazzucchelli stated, "I can buy a flashlight."

"You got no imagination," Croyd said. "I can do some

heavy stuff with burglar alarms, computers, telephones—not to mention anybody I shake hands with. But if you're not interested, I won't starve."

He began to turn away.

"Sit down, sit down!" Mazzucchelli said. "I heard you had a sense of humor. Sure, I like that stuff, and I think maybe I can use you in a certain matter. I need some good people in a hurry."

"Something scare you?" Croyd asked, sliding into the seat recently vacated by Bludgeon.

Mazzucchelli scowled and Croyd grinned.

"Humor," he said. "What can I do for you?"

"Crenson," the other stated, "that's your last name. See, I do know you. I know a lot about you. I've been stringing you along. That's humor. I know you're pretty good, and you usually deliver what you promise. But we got some things to talk about before we talk about other things. You know what I mean?"

"No," Croyd answered. "But I'm willing to learn."

"You want anything while we're talking?"

"I'd like to try the linguini again," Croyd said, "and another bottle of Chianti."

Mazzucchelli raised his hand, snapped his fingers. A waiter rushed into the room.

Linguini, e una bottiglia," he said. "*Chianti.*"

The man hurried off. Croyd rubbed his hands together, to the accompaniment of a faint crackling sound.

"The one who just left...," Mazzucchelli said at length. "Bludgeon...."

"Yes?" Croyd said, after an appropriate wait.

"He'll make a good soldier," Mazzucchelli finished.

Croyd nodded. "I suppose so."

"But you, you have some skills besides what the virus gave you. I understand you are a pretty good second-story man. You knew old Bentley."

Croyd nodded again. "He was my teacher. I knew him back when he was a dog. You seem to know more about me than most people do."

Mazzucchelli removed his toothpick, sipped his beer. "That's my business," he said after a time, "knowing things. That's why I don't want to send you off to be a soldier."

The waiter returned with a plate of linguini, a glass, and a bottle, which he proceeded to uncork. He passed Croyd a setting from the next booth. Croyd immediately began to eat with a certain manic gusto that·Mazzucchelli found vaguely unsettling.

Croyd paused long enough to ask, "So what is it you've got in mind for me?"

"Something a little more subtle, if you're the right man for it."

"Subtle. I'm right for subtle," Croyd said.

Mazzucchelli raised a finger. "First," he said, "one of those things we talk about before we talk about other things."

Observing the speed with which Croyd's plate was growing empty, he snapped his fingers again and the waiter rushed in with another load of linguini.

"What thing?" Croyd asked, pushing aside the first plate as the second slid into place before him.

Mazzucchelli laid his hand on Croyd's left arm in an almost fatherly fashion and leaned forward. "I understand you got problems," he said.

"What do you mean?"

"I have heard that you are into speed," Mazzucchelli observed, "and that every now and then you become a raging maniac, killing people, destroying property and wreaking general havoc until you run out of steam or some ace who knows you takes pity and puts you down for the count."

Croyd laid his fork aside and quaffed a glass of wine.

"This is true," he said, "though it is not something I enjoy talking about."

Mazzucchelli shrugged. "Everybody has the right to a little fun every now and then," he stated. "I ask only for business reasons. I would not like to have you act this way if you were working for me on something sensitive."

"The behavior of which you've heard is not an indulgence," Croyd explained. "It becomes something of a necessity, though, after I've been awake a certain period of time."

"Uh—you anywhere near that point yet?"

"Nowhere near," Croyd replied. "There's nothing to worry about for a long while."

"If I was to hire you, I'd rather I didn't worry about it at all. Now, it's no good asking somebody not to be a user. But I want to know this: Have you got enough sense when you start on the speed that you can take yourself off of my work? Then go crash and burn someplace not connected with what you're doing for me?"

Croyd studied him for a moment, then nodded slowly. "I see what you mean," he said. "If that's what the job calls for, sure, I can do it. No problem."

"With that understanding, I want to hire you. It's a little more subtle than breaking heads, though. And it isn't any sort of simple burglary either."

"I've done lots of odd things," Croyd said, "and lots of subtle things. Some of them have even been legal."

They both smiled.

"For this one, it may well be that you see no violence," Mazzucchelli said. "Like I told you, my business is knowing things. I want you to get me some information. The best way to get it is so that nobody even knows it's been got. On the other hand, if the only way you can get it is to cause somebody considerable angst, that's okay. So long as you clean up real good afterwards."

"I get the picture. What do you want to know, and where do I find it?"

Mazzucchelli gave a short, barking laugh.

"There seems to be another company doing business in this town," he said then. "You know what I mean?"

"Yes," Croyd replied, "and there is not usually room on one block for two delicatessens."

"Exactly," Mazzucchelli answered.

"So you are taking on extra help to continue the competition by heavier means."

"That is a good summary. Now, like I said, there is certain information I need about the other company. I will pay you well to get it for me."

Croyd nodded. "I'm willing to give it a shot. What particular information are you after?"

Mazzucchelli leaned forward and lowered his voice, his lips barely moving. "The chairman of the board. I want to know who's running the show."

"The boss? You mean he didn't even send you a dead fish in somebody's pants? I thought it was customary to observe certain amenities in these matters?"

Mazzucchelli shrugged. "These guys got no etiquette. Could be a bunch of foreigners."

"Have you got any leads at all, or do I go it cold?"

"You will be pretty much a ground-breaker. I will give you a list of places they sometimes seem to operate through. I also have names of a couple people who might do some work for them."

"Why didn't you just pick one of them up and pop the question?"

"I think that, like you, they are independent contractors rather than family members."

"I see."

Then, "And that may not be all they have in common with you," Mazzucchelli added.

"Aces?" Croyd asked.

Mazzucchelli nodded.

"If I've got to mess with aces it's going to cost more than if they're just civilians."

"I'm good for it," Mazzucchelli said, withdrawing another envelope from his inner pocket. "Here is a retainer and the list. You may consider the retainer ten percent of the total price for the job."

Croyd opened the envelope, counted quickly. He smiled when he finished.

"Where do you take delivery?" he asked.

"The manager here can always get in touch with me."

"What's his name?"

"Theotocopolos. Theo'll do."

"Okay," Croyd said. "You just hired subtlety."

"When you go to sleep you turn into a different person, right?"

"Yeah."

"Well, if that happens before the job is done, that new guy's still got a contract with me."

"So long as he gets paid."

"We understand each other."

They shook hands, Croyd rose, left the booth, crossed the room. Moth-sized snowflakes swirled in as he departed. Mazzucchelli reached for a fresh toothpick. Outside, Croyd tossed a black pill into his mouth.

Wearing gray slacks, blue blazer, and bloodclot-colored tie, his hair marcelled, shades silver, nails manicured, Croyd sat alone at a small window table in Aces High, regarding the city's lights through wind-whipped snow beyond his baked salmon, sipping Château d'Yquem, hashing over plans for the next move in his investigation and flirting with Jane Dow, who had passed his way twice so far and was even now approaching again—a thing he took to be more than coincidence and a good omen, having lusted after her in a variety of hearts (some of them multiples) on a number of occasions— and hoping he might fit the occasion to the feelings, he raised his hand as she drew near and touched her arm.

A tiny spark crackled, she halted, said, "Yike!" and reached to rub the place where the shock had occurred.

"Sorry—" Croyd began.

"Must be static electricity," she said.

"Must be," he agreed. "All I wanted to say was that you do know me, even though you wouldn't recognize me in this incarnation. I'm Croyd Crenson. We've met in passing, here and there, and I always wanted just to sit and talk a spell, but somehow our paths never crossed long enough at the right time."

"That's an interesting line," she said, running a finger across her damp brow, "naming the one ace nobody's certain about. I bet a lot of groupies get picked up that way."

"True," Croyd replied, smiling, as he opened his arms wide. "But I can prove it if you'll wait about half a minute."

"Why? What are you doing?"

"Filling the air with neg-ions for you," he said, "for that delightfully stimulating before-the-storm feeling. Just a hint at the great time I could show—"

"Cut it out!" She began backing away. "It sometimes triggers—"

Croyd's hands were wet, his face was wet, his hair collapsed and leaked onto his forehead.

"I'm sorry," she said.

"What the hell," he said, "let's make it a thunderstorm," and lightning danced among his fingertips. He began laughing.

Other diners glanced in their direction.

"Stop," she said. "Please."

"Sit down for a minute and I will."

"Okay."

She took the seat opposite him. He dried his face and hands on his napkin.

"I'm sorry," he said. "My fault. I should be careful with storm effects around someone they call Water Lily."

She smiled.

"Your glasses are all wet," she said, suddenly reaching forward and plucking them from his face. "I'll clean—"

"Two hundred sixteen views of moist loveliness," he stated as she stared. "The virus has, as usual, overendowed me in several respects."

"You really see that many of me?"

He nodded. "These joker aspects sometimes crop up in my changes. Hope I haven't turned you off."

"They're rather—magnificent," she said.

"You're very kind. Now give back the glasses."

"A moment."

She wiped the lenses on the corner of the tablecloth, then passed them to him.

"Thanks." He donned them again. "Buy you a drink? Dinner? A water spaniel?"

"I'm on duty," she said. "Thanks. Sorry. Maybe another time."

"Well, I'm working now myself. But if you're serious, I'll give you a couple of phone numbers and an address. I may not be at any of them. But I get messages."

"Give them to me," she said, and he scribbled quickly in a notepad, tore out the page, and passed it to her. "What kind of work?" she asked.

"Subtle investigation," he said. "It involves a gang war."

"Really? I've heard people say you're kind of honest, as well as kind of crazy."

"They're half-right," he said. "So give me a call or stop by. I'll rent scuba gear and show you a good time."

She smiled and began to rise. "Maybe I will."

He withdrew an envelope from his pocket, opened it, pushed aside a wad of bills, and removed a slip of paper with some writing on it.

"Uh, before you go—does the name James Spector mean anything to you?"

She froze and grew pale. Croyd found himself wet once again.

"What did I say?" he asked.

"You're not kidding? You really don't know?"

"Nope. Not kidding."

"You know the aces jingle."

"Parts of it."

"'Golden Boy ain't got no joy,'" she recited. "'If it's Demise, don't look in his eyes...'—that's him: James Spector is Demise's real name."

"I never knew that," he said. Then, "I never heard any verses about me."

"I don't remember any either."

"Come on. I always wondered."

"'Sleeper waking, meals taking,'" she said slowly. "'Sleeper speeding, people bleeding.'"

"Oh."

"If I call you and you're that far along..."

"If I'm that far along, I don't return calls."

"I'll get you a couple of dry napkins," she offered. "Sorry about the storms."

"Don't be. Did anyone ever tell you you're lovely when you exude moisture?"

She stared at him. Then, "I'll get you a dry fish too," she said.

Croyd raised his hand to blow her a kiss and gave himself a shock.

Breakdown

by Leanne C. Harper

The pair of bodyguards left Giovanni's first. Behind their dark glasses they immediately began scanning the street, looking for trouble. At a wave from the man on the right, another bodyguard preceded Don Tomasso, head of the Anselmi Family, onto the street. The don had to be assisted in walking. He was an old man, bent and in obvious pain, but his old-fashioned black suit had been hand-tailored and pressed into sharp creases. He surveyed the street as well, swiveling his shaking head from between his hunched shoulders like an aging turtle. The red and green neon of the restaurant's sign alternately revealed and hid his weathered face.

Don Tomasso's black Mercedes limousine was double-parked directly in front of Giovanni's entrance. Surrounded by his men, the don approached his car with his head held as high as possible in defiance to any unseen observers. A dark BMW pulled up behind Tomasso's Mercedes. He nodded in recognition at the driver before ducking his head and climbing into the limousine. One of the bodyguards followed him. The others moved back to the BMW. Both cars were in motion before the doors of the BMW were shut.

Lit by a dull orange streetlight, two children played on the sidewalk in front of a brownstone half a block down the street from the restaurant. The boy had just tossed the baseball to the younger girl when the Mercedes exploded, followed instantly by the BMW's destruction. The fireballs bloomed and met as pieces of the cars and bricks from the nearby buildings crashed back to earth.

Rosemary Muldoon continued to watch the flames on the oversize video screen in front of her. She said nothing until the tape ran down into static. She sat immobile in the carved black walnut chair at the head of the long table, but her hands clutched the chair's arms until her knuckles were white.

Chris Mazzucchelli got up from the chair beside her to pull the tape from the VCR. Rosemary glanced around her father's "library" where strategy meetings for his Family, the Gambiones, had always taken place. She had left almost everything in the penthouse the same, only bringing in some high-tech equipment such as the video and her computer to help her run the empire she had inherited. Right now, the room felt very empty, as if even her father had abandoned her.

When Chris came back to the conference table, he laid the tape down and stroked her dark brown hair. As his hand cupped her face, Rosemary roused herself.

"Only two of us left now. Don Calvino and I. Three dons dead in a matter of weeks, and we don't even know who's destroying us. All we know is who they are using." Rosemary shook her head. "The Five Families have never faced a threat like this. We're not prepared to fight on this scale. We've lost most of the drugs in Jokertown. Harlem has stopped paying our portion of the numbers. We're getting hit from the top and the bottom. They took *over* our biggest drug factory in Brooklyn."

"We've got to get prepared. You're the only active don left. I talked to Tomasso's capos; they're all with us just like the others. I only wish I could point them in the right direction. Right now, I'm just trying to keep business going so we have the money to survive and fight back. Calvino tried his hand at negotiating. So far, it doesn't seem to have worked. We had both of the remaining dons covered at all times. That's how we got this tape." Chris picked it up and tossed it into the air. "Remotely controlled explosives, P.E., we assume. They were probably within sight of the cars to make sure they got Don Tomasso."

"So they knew about the kids." Rosemary glanced up at him.

"Probably." Chris shrugged. "So far they haven't been particularly careful about civilian casualties. They're terrorists."

"They're bastards." Chris nodded and Rosemary knew he was already working out the details of backtracking the explosives. One of the things she had learned in the last few months of working with him was that he was superb at taking her objectives and desires and accomplishing them through his position as her front man to the Families. She had known she would never be accepted as the head of the Gambiones by the capos. They required a masculine figurehead. So Chris ran things in public, and she, Maria Gambione, pulled the strings. Except that it had not worked out quite like that. Chris could almost read her mind. He had the practical experience she lacked. They made a great team. Without him she would never have pulled it off.

"The Shadow Fist is causing us trouble, but I didn't think that it had the organization to accomplish all of this. On the other hand, we know they are working with the Immaculate Egrets and the Werewolves from Jokertown. Together, they're giving us a lot of trouble. But a bunch of gangs..."

"With the right leader..." Rosemary spread her hands.

"With the right leader anything's possible. But we would have heard something about him. How could they keep him under that sort of deep cover?" Chris shrugged. "I'll check it out, but I won't hold my breath. I had another idea. Think about Tomasso's murder. Those cars would have been under twenty-four hour guard by teams of his most trusted men. How the hell did they plant those bombs?"

Chris pulled a chair out and sat down backward.

"How?" Rosemary had learned not to get too impatient with Chris's occasional use of Socratic method. As in law school, it taught her much.

"Aces, again. Just like Don Picchietti. Who else could pop in and out without being seen? Nobody really knows how many there are or who they are or what they can do. What if some of them decided that wearing funky costumes and being altruistic was silly? Jokers, too. Look at the Werewolves. Get back at the nats. That's a pretty fierce army we're talking here. Look at where the action is going on most of the time. Jokertown. Maybe it's because we control it and they're trying to get us, or maybe it's because the jokers have decided that they want their own piece of the action." Chris had leaned forward to emphasize his point. "If these guys aren't all aces, they've got some working for them. And I think that's the way to go. If we don't get our own aces, we're going to get slaughtered. We can't compete."

"I like that. I could use the district attorney's office to get volunteers. A little steering of their efforts and a number of our troubles could get solved. We'll get higher-quality aces that way too. Pity a lot of the big names are still on that

WHO tour." Rosemary nodded, more enthusiastic about this plan than she had been about anything in some time. "Good. Can you pull in anyone?"

"To be honest, I already have. We've got a detective named Croyd doing some checking for us and a heavy name of Bludgeon who'll come in handy in a fight. 'Course they won't be as 'high quality' coming from the criminal element like me." Chris straightened and looked down his nose at her, trying to hide his grin.

"They'll do. The criminal element isn't all bad." Rosemary reached up and pulled him down to her to kiss him.

Bagabond walked down the crowded East Village street trying not to be impatient with C.C. Ryder's window-shopping. It seemed as though every ten feet the spike-haired redhead saw something she just had to have—as long as she didn't actually have to go in and talk to anyone about it. Bagabond was about to suggest going back to the songwriter's loft when she heard a bayou-accented voice behind her.

"Hey, y'all, *qué pasa?*" The teenage hyperactive body encased in a tiger-striped leotard with gold-lamé sneakers belonged to Jack's niece Cordelia. She bounced out of the restaurant she had been about to enter and grabbed both Bagabond and C.C. Ryder by the elbows to guide them into the Riviera with her before either could muster a protest. C.C. quickly shrugged her off when they were inside, but neither woman put up a struggle when Cordelia immediately got them a table. Bagabond had learned it was useless to resist unless one wanted an excessively hurt teenager on her hands.

"So, y'all seen Rosemary's television appeal to aces yet?" Cordelia opened and shut her menu with the same move-ment. "Gonna join up, Bagabond?"

"Haven't been asked." Bagabond chose to take her time with the menu. "What about you?"

Glancing up over the top of her oversize menu, Bagabond was surprised to catch the expression of revulsion on Cordelia's face. For possibly the first time she had stopped Cordelia cold in her tracks.

"I, uh, don't do that anymore." Cordelia opened her menu again and stared at it fixedly. "I could hurt somebody, y'know. I'm *never* going to do that again. It's not right."

"I'm not sure it's a good idea. Ace vigilantes are not what we need in this city." C.C. looked from Cordelia to Bagabond before excusing herself.

"So, you seen Jack lately?" Cordelia followed C.C.'s progress to the rear of the restaurant intently before turning to Bagabond with wide, innocent eyes.

"Yeah. He asked if I'd seen you. Ever think of calling your uncle once in a while?" Bagabond's irritation was evident in her rough voice.

"I've been so busy, what with working for Global Fun and Games an' all—"

"And you haven't wanted to talk to him anyway, right?"

"I don't know what to say..." Crodelia blushed. "I mean, it's like I don' know him anymore. You don' understand. I was raised in the Church. I was taught that bein' a homo—what Jack is, is one of the worst sins."

"It's not catching and he's your uncle. He's risked his life for you and you won't even give him a call. I'm glad you're so strong on right and wrong." Bagabond looked disgusted and unconsciously flicked her wrist at the girl. "Michael's good for him. I've never seen Jack so happy."

"Yeah, well, Michael's a son of a bitch! I saw him in a club in the Village last week. He was with someone and it wasn't Uncle Jack." Cordelia was furious.

"Everything okay here?" C.C. seated herself and looked at each woman in turn.

"Hey, no prob." Cordelia waved the waitress over. "You goin' to do my benefit or what?"

"You keep asking and I keep saying no." C.C. shook her head in affectionate exasperation. "I just want to write my songs, do some recording at home. I don't need a live audience and I certainly don't *want* one."

"C.C., de audience needs *you*. It's a benefit for wild card victims as well as AIDS. You of all people should have sympathy for the cause."

Bagabond watched C.C.'s face tighten at the mention of the wild card virus. It had taken years of drugs, therapy, and God knew what else to bring her back to humanity. C.C.'s very real nightmare was that she would again become a living subway car formed from nothing save hate. Or something much worse. C.C. had spoken of a little of this to Bagabond.

C.C. Ryder controlled her emotions rigidly, never allowing

them to exceed a certain low level. If she continued taking
the downs and antidepressants prescribed for her, she couldn't
write. Not being able to create her songs was even worse
than the prospect of changing back. So she avoided any
situation that might be more than she could handle. Not even
Tachyon could tell her what might set off the series of internal
changes that could result in another transformation. Bagabond
did not understand how C.C. could live in that state of
constant fear and still create the songs, but she did understand why she wanted to stay away from most humans. She
approved.

"No." C.C.'s voice had become as tense as her muscles,
although it was equally clear that she was controlling the
effect the discussion was having on her.

"It could be your big comeback—"

"Cordelia, you can't have a comeback if you were never
there in the first place." C.C. forced a smile. "I'm sure there
are many more likely candidates out there."

"Your songs have been recorded by the best: Peter
Gabriel—" Cordelia barely paused in her diatribe at the
arrival of their burgers. "Simple Minds, U2... It's time for
you to show them all what you can do."

Bored by the argument and reasured that C.C. was
holding her own, Bagabond reached out across the city,
flashing through the tangle of feral intelligences. Darkness,
bright light; hunger, fulfillment; the tense anticipation of the
hunter, the cold, shivering fear of the stalked; death, birth;
pain. So much pain in living each minute—why did these
human fools insist on creating even more for themselves by
their little games? Playing at living. She touched a squirrel
with a broken back. It had been struck by a passing car near
Washington Park, and she stopped its heart and brain
simultaneously. In Central Park the gray son of the black and
the calico dashed into a copse of oaks and sheltered by the
underbrush, spun and raked the nose of the Doberman that
had chased it. Bagabond felt the cat's triumph for an instant
before it recognized her touch and hissed in anger. Feeling
no need to force the contact, she moved on. She allowed
herself another instant to ascertain that the black and the
calico's most recent litter of kittens was well in the warm
service tunnels beneath Forty-second Street.

As her eyes rolled back down, Bagabond realized that Cordelia's conversation with C.C. had stopped.

"Suzanne, are you okay?" C.C. ran her gaze across Bagabond's face then nodded slowly.

"She's fine, Cordelia." C.C. brought the young woman's attention back to herself, giving Bagabond time to return. Sometimes it had become difficult to come back to the slow, jabbering world of the humans. Someday, she thought, looking at C.C. Ryder, she would not come back. C.C. was the only person she had ever met who understood that. One day she would ask what C.C. had felt as the Other. C.C. mentioned it rarely, but when she did, Bagabond had seen a haunted need still there behind her eyes.

"Um, okay. Anyway, GF & G, you know, would love to back you on your reintroduction. The Funhouse is an intimate venue. Perfect for you and your music." Cordelia leaned toward C.C., hand extended. "And you know Xavier Desmond's one of your biggest fans."

"Christ, girl, you're turning into a freaking *agent*." C.C. leaned back in the fifties plastic-covered chair. "And I've already got one agent. That's bad enough."

"Well, hey, I've got to get home. It's late. Good to see you guys." Cordelia dropped a few bills onto the table and got up. She swung the armadillo shoulder bag off her chair. Catching Bagabond's eyes on the dead animal, she elbowed it behind her and backed toward the door, still working on C.C. "You've got a few weeks to make your final decision. The show's not until late May. Bono said he was looking forward to meeting you. So'd Little Steven."

"Good *night*, Cordelia." C.C. Ryder had clearly reached the end of her patience. "I'm too old for this, Suzanne."

Wriggling underneath the padded shoulders of the business suit Rosemary had bought her, Bagabond stepped out of the elevator onto Rosemary's floor. The receptionist recognized her instantly.

"Good morning, Ms. Melotti. Let me buzz Ms. Muldoon."

"Thank you, Donnis." Bagabond sat down uncomfortably in one of the chairs scattered around the waiting area.

"I'm afraid you just missed Mr. Goldberg. He left a few minutes ago for his court appearances today." The older woman behind the word processor smiled at Bagabond indulgently while she punched Rosemary's intercom number and announced her.

"For once everything's running on time. Go right on in."

Bagabond nodded and got back up onto her high heels. With her back to the receptionist, she blinked at the pain in her feet. She hated these days when she played dress-up to talk to Rosemary. At Rosemary's closed door she knocked twice and walked in to see the assistant DA with a phone resting on one shoulder. As usual, Bagabond sat on Rosemary's big oak desk. She listened to the conversation.

"Wonderful, Lieutenant. I'm so glad that tip on the designer drug factory panned out." Rosemary rolled her eyes at Bagabond as she signed papers and balanced the receiver.

"So it wasn't a Mafia operation after all. Any clues as to the ownership? If we could just find out who's behind this senseless crime war with the Mafia, we could go a long way toward stopping it." Rosemary nodded to her unseen caller and almost dropped the phone. "True, but as long as they're wiping each other out, they're hurting innocent people.

"Well, you can rest assured that I'll be forwarding any other aces who volunteer over to you immediately. You're right—uncoordinated activity is dangerous for all concerned. I'm just glad to help. Right. I'll be in touch. 'Bye." Rosemary hung up the phone.

"We took out a drug plant last night." Rosemary leaned her chin on her hand and smiled up at Bagabond. "I'm pleased."

Bagabond nodded, looking across the office toward the dark wooden door.

"And I'm curious." Rosemary got up and checked to make sure that the door was securely closed. "Why haven't *you* volunteered?"

Bagabond noticed for the hundredth time that Rosemary had no trouble walking in her spike heels. She looked up to see Rosemary staring at her, a muscle jumping along her jaw.

"You never asked." Bagabond was uncomfortable. She hated it. Guilt was for humans. Or pets.

"I didn't think I had to. *I* thought we were friends."

They glared at each other like two cats in a territorial battle. Rosemary broke the impasse.

"And of course we are." The DA sat down and leaned back

in her chair. "I *should* have asked. I'm asking now. I need your help."

Rosemary's smile reminded Bagabond of a tiger's yawn. Teeth, lots of teeth. Bagabond felt cold.

"What can I do? I talk to pigeons." Bagabond examined Rosemary's face for duplicity.

"Well, pigeons see things. Sometimes I'm sure they see interesting things. I'd just like to hear about those things."

"Which one of you? The DA or the Mafia don?"

Rosemary's eyes flashed up to the door and back to Bagabond. After an instant of hesitation she smiled at the woman sitting on her desk.

"You'd be amazed to discover how much their interests are intertwined."

"Yes. I would." Bagabond shook her head. "No, I don't think I can help."

"Come on, Suzanne. People are getting hurt out there. We can stop that." Rosemary reached toward her window.

"People killing other people." Bagabond nodded. "Good. The fewer of them, the better I'll like it."

"Being a hard case today, I see." Rosemary relaxed back into her chair. "I've heard this one."

"I mean it." Bagabond looked down at her old friend.

"I know. But I do need you. I need your connections. I need your information. And it's not just humans getting hurt." Rosemary stretched her hands out on top of the papers on her desk. They both watched the fingers shake until they were clenched into fists. "Don Picchietti and Don Covello are already dead. They just took out Don Tomasso. He was my godfather. *Please*, Bagabond. Help me." Rosemary looked up at Bagabond, pleading her case with both her voice and her face.

"Picchietti was hit with an ice pick in his ear. Nobody around him saw anything." Rosemary smiled at her with a twisted and unamused grin. "And for once they weren't lying."

"You don't know what you're doing. But my help won't hurt anything either." Bagabond tasted bitterness at her surrender and felt anger at herself, but she could not abandon her friend.

"Thank you." Rosemary relaxed and picked up her pen, flipping it through her fingers. "Talk to Jack lately?"

"Almost never." Bagabond slid a part of her consciousness to the rat whom she had set to watch Jack as he worked his way through the subway tunnels. She smelled him first. Then, turning the rat's head toward Jack Robicheaux, she saw him in the rat's dim, black-and-white vision.

"Maybe you could pass on that I'd like to see him?" Rosemary had obviously tired of sparring with Bagabond.

"I can tell him." Bagabond nodded. "No promises. Who's the lieutenant I report to?"

"Don't be ridiculous, Suzanne. You'll give anything you come up with directly to me." When Rosemary met her eyes, Bagabond found no friendship at all.

Hands clenched atop a stack of case briefs, Rosemary stared out the window of her office. She was afraid for Chris. Until they found out who was behind the war on the Families, he was in extreme danger as the public chief of the Gambiones. And they still had few clues, although every day there was another Mafia loss. They'd hit all the numbers runners, dealers, small-timers, and extortionists they could find to try to get a lead to the top. It hadn't worked. The cells of lower-level criminals had no information about the cells above them. It was brilliant organization on someone's part, and it was destroying her people. She shook her head unconsciously, one part of her preoccupied with the Families while the other was trying to keep on top of her office's caseload. More and more she had come to depend on her assistants for aid in prosecuting the cases she would have dealt with personally a few months ago. She wondered if anyone had noticed and made a mental note to be more careful. But it was so hard to balance everything, so much more difficult than she had ever imagined.

"There's someone here to see you, Ms. Muldoon." Donnis's quiet voice broke into her thoughts so abruptly that she jumped.

"Who is it, Donnis? I've got a desk full of cases."

"Well, Ms. Muldoon, she says her name is Jane Dow."

The name was familiar although Rosemary failed to place it for a moment. Then she had it: Water Lily. What did the girl want?

"I'll see her."

Entering, the auburn-haired girl, no, young woman, Rosemary corrected herself, carefully closed the door after herself. "Thank you for seeing me, Ms. Muldoon."

"Please have a seat, Ms. Dow. What can I do for you?"

Water Lily looked down at her twisting hands, and Rosemary saw droplets of liquid forming on her forehead. Rosemary wondered if sweating was the extent of her "ace" power. Just what she needed.

"Well, I thought maybe I could do something for you. I heard that you were looking for aces and—I know I'm not much of one, but I thought I could work for you. Help out." For the first time Water Lily met Rosemary's eyes and shrugged. "If you have anything that I could do."

"Possibly." Rosemary sighed. She couldn't imagine what, but she was not about to turn down any help at this point. "Tell me what, precisely, is the extent of your power?"

"Well, I control water. I'm really good at floods." Water Lily turned pink and the water on her face shone. She seemed very young. Rosemary heard dripping but chose to ignore it.

"All water, everywhere? I mean, do you have a range? Do you generate it, or can you use the water around you?" Rosemary stopped and smiled apologetically. "Sorry about the third degree. I'm just trying to see where you'll fit in."

"It has to be fairly close, but I can use any water in my vicinity and control the force of its flow. And I can change the electrolyte balance in someone and knock them out." Water Lily was looking fractionally less embarrassed now that she was being taken seriously. Rosemary no longer heard the dripping. "I was thinking that I would be good with crowd control, sweeping people off their feet without really hurting them with a small flood, or causing distractions if you needed it."

"What about other forms of water, high-pressure steam, for example?"

"I don't know. I've never tried it." Water Lily appeared to be interested in the idea.

"Okay, that sounds as if it could be quite helpful. Welcome aboard, Water Lily. Or do you prefer Jane?" Rosemary thought about the raids she was trying to organize on some of the Shadow Fist drug operations. A few burst pipes could do an amazing amount of damage. She smiled broadly at the younger woman without seeing her.

"Jane, please. You can reach me at Aces High. I brought a card. Just let me know what I can do." Jane looked pleased by her acceptance.

Rosemary stole half an hour to familiarize herself with the cases stacked in front of her before she called in Paul Goldberg. His experience had made him an obvious choice to be her immediate aide, and Rosemary had taken advantage of it.

Paul came in and sat down uninvited. He held a fat sheaf of reports that he dropped on her desk with a thud.

"The latest info on our caseload. We won the case against Malerucci." Rosemary glanced up from the paperwork at the mention of the name. "I know you didn't think much of the case we had, but I decided to go ahead with it. It worked out. Maybe you're not aware of this, but we've been taking some heat about the number of Mafia cases we're prosecuting, or rather *not* prosecuting. The cops have come to me several times complaining about doing all the work and getting no support from this office."

"The cops are always complaining. You know that, Paul. They don't understand that we have this Constitution thing we have to pay attention to when we haul someone into court. Good work on the Malerucci case, but you took a chance there. The jury could have gone either way based on that evidence."

"Especially after somebody got to the Police Evidence Lab and destroyed most of the coke." Paul crossed his legs on Rosemary's desk and leaned back in the chair. "We haven't been able to trace that leak yet."

"In the future, please stick to my instructions on which cases to go after. I'd appreciate it, speaking strictly as your boss." Rosemary smiled at him and leaned back in her own chair.

"Boss, I've noticed a trend in the cases you okay, and I'm not the only one. Why aren't we going after the Mafia? With this war going on, we could put a lot of nasty people away. Their resources are stretched too thin to protect all of their people." He reached out and tapped the stack of papers with a rigid forefinger. "It's all right here. I've even got a possible tax evasion on Chris Mazzucchelli. What do you say? Let me at 'im."

"No." Rosemary put on her best inscrutable madonna look. "I want to wait until the war has shaken out some more.

The Mafia appears to be self-destructing anyway. We can just save ourselves the trouble."

"You know that if we put some of these people behind bars we might just be saving their lives." Paul was watching her closely. His scrutiny made Rosemary uncomfortable.

"I make the decisions here." The tone in her voice was meant to shut Paul up and it worked, but she still didn't like the stare she got after she said it.

After working out strategy for the twenty most urgent cases they had, Rosemary had relaxed and so had Paul. In many ways it reminded her of working with Chris. She came up with the plan and he carried it out. Only with Paul, everything was on the right side of the law. It was after six and she was leading Paul and his stack of cases to her door when he turned around to speak to her once more.

"You ever go to Holy Innocents?" Paul asked about her Catholic elementary school in offhand tones.

"Me, are you kidding? That's for rich Italian kids. I went to good old P.S. one ninety-two in Brooklyn." Rosemary studied his face.

"I didn't think so. Friend of mind went there. He said the craziest thing the other night. Thought you looked just like Rosa Maria Gambione grown up. What a crock, huh? She died back in the early seventies. See you in the morning." Paul nodded his farewell and Rosemary wondered if she had seen a warning in his eyes—or an indictment.

Bagabond moved quickly through the subway maintenance tunnels, accompanied by the black and one of his kittens. The kitten, a mottled ginger, was even bigger than he was. She had watched Jack return to his old home in the nineteenth-century abandoned station through the eyes of a succession of rats. Bagabond waited to catch him when he was still under-ground. It always felt more natural talking to him here. When she met him above, he was different. They both were. She pulled the ragged blue coat farther up above her knees and hurried to cut him off before he could go. The black paced her while his daughter loped ahead to spot trouble.

Bagabond reached the door and opened it onto Jack reach-ing for the knob. The compact, pale man smiled in surprise.

"'Allo dere." He set down the box he had been cradling and knelt to let the black sniff the back of his hand. The other cat kept her distance, standing in front of Bagabond to protect her.

"I haven't seen you for a long time. I've been a little worried." Jack stood up to face the woman in tattered clothing. "Come on in and sit down."

"You've been busy." Bagabond had swung her snarled hair back down across her face and hunched within the pile of ill-fitting dresses and pants she wore. She knew that with her rough voice and trembling manner she now looked at least sixty years old.

"So have you." Jack looked at her hesitantly making her way down the carpeted stairs. He grinned broadly. "You could win a Tony for that, you know. I met this Broadway producer, he's looking for an actress."

"Friend of Michael's?" Bagabond straightened as she sat on the edge of the Victorian horsehair sofa. The ginger sat tensely at her feet. The black leaned against Jack's leg and looked up at him.

"Yes, a friend of Michael's. Why won't you come over and spend some time with us? Get to know Michael. You'd like him."

"Why don't you get to know Paul?" Bagabond drew her feet up under her and looked at Jack sitting on the equally antique chair opposite her.

"I don't think a yuppie would see much in a blue-collar transit worker."

"*I* don't think Michael would approve of my style sense." Bagabond spread out her layers of mismatched clothing along the couch.

"So there we are, hmm? I don't like it and neither do you, but we've become trapped in our undercover lives as normal people." Jack looked sad. "Have you seen Cordelia?"

"Yeah." Bagabond shrugged. Another shrug, another avoidance of responsibility. She straightened her shoulders. "I tried. I don't know."

"When you see her again, tell her. . . tell her I understand. I grew up there too, after all." Jack ran the palms of his hands down his sharply creased black denim jeans. "So, you tracked me down. What can I do for you?"

Jack reached down to scratch behind the black's ears, and they both listened to the loud purring for a few moments.

"Rosemary wants to see you." Bagabond had pulled her

knees up and drawn her armor back around her. She refused to meet Jack's eyes.

"No."

"Jack, she's just trying to keep everything cool. She could use some help."

"For Christ sake, Bagabond, she's on the side of the bad guys. She's the head of the frigging Mafia." Jack got up and began pacing on the Oriental carpets. The black got up to join him, then looked at Bagabond and lay back down. Bagabond got a flash of warning from the cat. She didn't know if it was for her or for Jack. "What the hell does she need me for anyway?"

"Well, you could help with surveillance. You could keep your ears open for anything strange going on."

"Oh, right. Am I supposed to be her lead into the gay community? No, maybe she thinks the reptiles are against her too. Or maybe she just wants me to bite off a strategic foot or two." Jack turned to face Bagabond. "No fucking *way*."

"Jack, she just needs someone on her side—"

"Someone on her side! She's got the whole Mafia. I find it a little hard to believe that one were-alligator would make all that much difference." Jack walked over to the sofa and looked down on Bagabond. She refused to look up to meet his eyes. "Suzanne, you stay out of this. She doesn't care about you anymore. She'll use you too. Get you killed. And not even blink."

The black stood up and moved between Jack and Bagabond. The ginger began growling deep in her throat, the hair on her back standing up. Jack retreated a few steps.

Bagabond slid off the sofa onto her feet and stared back into Jack's green eyes.

"She's my friend. I guess she's my only friend."

She stalked to the stairs. The cats followed her. The ginger never took her eyes off Jack as she backed across the narrow room. The black walked a few steps, then stopped and looked back at Jack before leaping up the stairway to catch up with the others.

"Well, whoever they are, you're keeping them busy." Chris helped himself to a bite of Rosemary's grilled tuna.

"You said you weren't hungry." Rosemary swatted away his fork.

"I lied. It's definitely not the Yakuza. They're taking hits too. Lost one of their top men here in the city. It seems our friends are not above going after anybody if they can't have their Mafia for breakfast. Your program of authorized trouble is taking its toll. They may not be out, but they're definitely down. You having any trouble with that?"

"No. Now that the capos are all following our instructions I know everything that's happening anywhere among the Families. It makes it easy."

"I hate to say this, but you may need to arrange a hit on us. Nothing too severe, just something to ease off any suspicions." Chris glanced around the bright kitchen. It was the only cheery space in the otherwise dark and gloomy penthouse. "Got any cookies?"

"Afraid not. Do you know something I don't?" Rosemary examined Chris's face.

"No, I just believe in prevention. I don't want anyone to see a pattern in what your aces are doing."

"I'll be fine. Who'd connect me, assistant DA, with the Gambione Family? I'm more concerned with you." Rosemary pushed away her plate. She was not about to mention Paul's suspicions to Chris. She already knew what he would say. "What kind of security are you carrying?"

"Beretta, of course." Chris swung open his black leather jacket.

"That's not what I mean."

"All right, okay. You got no sense of humor sometimes, ya know. I've got some guys I know I can trust. They're with me twenty-four hours a day. One's outside right now. Three more are downstairs. I'm covered, babe. These guys owe me; their souls are mine."

"Tell me what's happening with our regular operations." Rosemary was annoyed at his possessiveness of his cadre of her men but decided it was only her native paranoia.

"Don't worry about it. I've got it all taken care of. Each of the other Families has a representative who reports to me directly. Any problems I take care of them. You need to come up with a way to find out who we're up against and how to take them out." Chris smiled happily at the ceiling. "You know, I think those boys still don't like my rattail."

"I'm still working on it. Have you investigated the Vietnamese? The Shadow Fist gang in Jokertown is involved in this somehow. That much has become clear." Rosemary decided not to press the issue of her normal briefing. Chris was right; she had more important things to think about.

"Well, I'm trying to get somebody to infiltrate them. You got any idea how hard it is to find an Oriental in the Mafia?" Chris sighed elaborately. "I'm trying to borrow somebody from the Yakuza."

"Good idea. Listen, Chris, I need some time by myself tonight, okay?" Rosemary hesitated. "To make plans."

"I can find something to keep myself busy." Chris smirked in a way that worried Rosemary.

"Stay out of trouble. I don't know what I'd do if I lost you."

"Me either." Chris got up and kised the top of Rosemary's head. "I may not be around for a few days. Don't worry about me. I'm just taking care of business."

When Chris had gone, Rosemary went to the library. She kept trying to keep her two lives straight, but it was getting more and more difficult. She had promised herself that she would get the Mafia out of drugs and prostitution. But now that the war was going on there was no way that she could do that. They needed the money desperately. Protecting her people was causing her trouble at the office. Paul Goldberg had openly asked her if her informants couldn't get more dirt on the Mafia. And that comment about Maria Gambione. Christ. There had to be something she could do about him. Kill him, before he passed on his suspicions? But he was Suzanne's boyfriend. What could she do?

She had thought it would be easy to run things from behind Chris. Instead it seemed that he was more and more in control of what was happening in the streets. Nothing was going the way she had planned. Rosemary rested her forehead on the table between her outstretched arms.

She knew that she was not doing her job in the DA's office. But it was only a matter of time until this damned war was over and she could get back to doing what she was supposed to be doing. Then she could get rid of the drugs, prostitution, and corruption. Just as soon as they had won the war.

She woke up from the nightmare with a small cry, quickly stifled by the heavy atmosphere of the library. She had been in a religious painting she had seen as a child, the Crucifixion. But it was her broken body on the center cross, with Chris hanging on her right and her father on her left. Rosemary put her arms around herself to stop the trembling.

Bagabond woke instantly, the warning of danger as insistent as a cat's claws set in her skin. She separated the thought-streams entering her own mind and found the sending carrying the cry for help. There was still a shock when she recognized Jack Robicheaux down the alley. The strength and clarity of the sending told her that the creature observing the scene in the alley was the black. So that's where he had been for the last few days. When he vanished, she had not followed him mentally except to make sure he was alive and well.

Silently she told him to return home. He snarled at the suggestion. He and Jack had been close since they had first met. The black's curiosity about the man/big-lizard had created a bond. The black focused on the tableau at the end of the streetlight-spotted alley. Jack was trapped by a much larger man who taunted him. Despite herself, Bagabond allowed the black to transmit more and draw her into the situation.

"Hey, fucking faggot! Guess taking off down this alley wasn't so smart, huh?" The hulk looming over Jack was ugly, with close-set eyes and a sloping forehead. Bagabond suddenly recognized him. Bludgeon. She'd seen him once before in the Tombs with Rosemary. He was just as mean and just as stupid as he looked. Jack was in trouble, but Jack could handle himself.

"All I wanted to do was play wit'cha a little. An' I know you faggots jus' love rough trade."

"You don't want to mess with me, man." Jack was plastered against the fence cutting off the alley. "I'm a lot more trouble than I look."

"Oh, I wanna mess wit' chou, pretty-boy. I'm gonna start wit' your face and work down, pervert. Ain't nobody gonna want you when I get through." Bludgeon reached out for Jack, but the smaller man ducked under the paw.

"Please, I don't want to hurt you. Just leave me alone." Jack's voice shook. Bagabond wondered why he was so afraid. "You won't like what you see."

"You think you know that gook chop-sockey stuff, huh?" Bludgeon laughed, and even Bagabond winced at the sound like gears stripping. "It's okay. I'm part of the Family now. I got me an insurance plan."

The black was more insistent as he sensed Bagabond's reluctance to help his other human friend. It transferred to pain in Bagabond's own mind. She sent Jack's refusal to help her and Rosemary back out to the black, but the cat would not turn away. Tiring of watching the two men spar, Bagabond called the black to return and showed him Jack's transformation to alligator. If he didn't want her help, fine. She wouldn't force it on him. He thought he didn't need her around, okay.

The black's wild anger at her stand surged back at her and she cut off contact. It wasn't her problem anymore. She lifted her hands to probe gently at the pain in her temples. The black had overridden her defenses because she had not expected his response. Christ, what was wrong with everyone? Why did everybody hate *her* now?

Curled upon a pile of rags in a steam tunnel yards below the surface, Bagabond had slept for hours. Despite her best efforts, the headache clung on. She couldn't reach the black either, although she knew he wasn't dead. She searched through her layers of clothing until she found the strapless wristwatch she used when she needed to keep track of time. Less than an hour until she was supposed to meet Paul. She'd be late. It would take half an hour to get to C.C.'s, where she had taken to keeping dresses and suits that had to be hung up. Stupid game. With a little luck C.C. would be working in the studio and never know she had been there.

The only luck she'd had all week actually happened. The red light was on over the door to C.C.'s studio, so Bagabond got in and out without distraction. Still, the always-late Paul was standing in the bar waiting at West Fourth Street where they were meeting for dinner before a movie. Dinner was pleasant, but Bagabond knew that Paul was not entirely there even as he regaled her with tales of the latest escapades and defenses he had encountered during the last week.

"So then this guy starts claiming that his what-do-you-call-it, his ancient Persian contact, told him that this other poor guy was really an ancient Greek and a personal enemy. And he starts "channeling" right there in the courtroom. Lots of grunts, rolling around on the floor, speaking in tongues—who knows if it's Persian. The judge breaks *two* gavels screaming for order while the schmuck's defense attorney is alternately calling for a doctor for his client and trying to build a defense based on this fit. He did get a continuance. Which means I have to go back in there with those idiots next week. Oy vay, as my sainted mother used to say." Paul Goldberg grinned over the cheesecake at her. "So, how was your week?"

"The animals are all okay. No major problems."

"What a city to be a veterinarian in. Between poodles and rottweilers, I don't know how you manage."

"That's why I try to stick to cats, with the occasional exotic rat or raccoon." Bagabond smiled across the table, wondering why she had ever come up with this story. Paul's mood changed abruptly.

"Listen, I need to talk to you. Can we skip the movie tonight?" Paul stared into his coffee cup as if the swirls of cream would reveal his future.

"Sounds serious."

"It is. At least I think it is. You're the sensible sort. You'll tell me if you think I'm crazy."

"Just don't start speaking in Persian."

"Right." He picked up the check. "This one's mine. Don't argue."

They took a cab over to Paul's huge two-level apartment on the upper East Side. He said almost nothing, just examined her hands with their short, blunt nails and joked about her lack of claws. Once up in the apartment he made coffee and put on Paul Simon. When he finally sat down, it was in a chair he pulled to face her rather than on the couch beside her.

"There are some things happening down at the office. Weird stuff. I need a second opinion. You're probably not the best person to ask, for a number of reasons, but you're a friend and that's what I need right now." He rolled the coffee cup between his palms.

"I'm here." Bagabond knew she wasn't going to like what he was about to say.

"I think somebody's gone bad. I've got people out on the street, snitches, we all do. Rumors are springing up about the DA's office. Rumors about Mafia connections."

"What sort of Mafia connections?" Bagabond got up and walked around the white-on-white living room.

"Nothing specific. But I do know that the last three raids

on Mafia operations have netted us nothing, just a few minor soldiers, virtually no drugs or guns. We're being given enough to keep us happy, but not enough to do actual damage." Paul looked up at Bagabond. "We're being used. The raids on the Mafia's enemies are always well-informed and almost always effective in hurting the opposition. And I think I know why."

"What are you going to do about it?" Bagabond sipped her coffee and pondered her options. If she killed him here, she had been seen and would be a suspect. Rosemary might or might not protect her.

"I can't trust anyone in the DA's office. And I'm not so sure about the mayor's office either." Paul put down his cup and paced across his living room in front of the fireplace. "I want to go to the press. The *Times*."

"Are you absolutely certain about your information?" Bagabond stared past Paul into the flames. Rosemary had left herself open to this. She had not been careful enough.

"Absolutely. I can corroborate everything I've said." Paul turned his back to her and warmed his hands over the fire. Bagabond stared into the back of his head. "But I'm hoping that the situation can be salvaged. If the person in question comes to their senses—maybe all this can be avoided. There are some other strange things going on here too. Some of this information that I have appears to have come directly from the Mafia. That I don't understand."

Bagabond remembered Chris Mazzucchelli. She had never trusted the man regardless of Rosemary's attachment to him. Was he betraying Rosemary?

"You have to do what your conscience tells you. But if these people are really mafiosi, isn't that a little dangerous?" Bagabond remembered Rosemary's telling her how everything was going to be different now that she was in charge. Rosemary had made her decision.

"True. That's one of the reasons I'm telling you. I've told some other people, given them the evidence. I didn't want to endanger you with it." Paul seemed relieved that she had not openly recognized Rosemary from the description. Bagabond wondered if this conversation had been a trap of some sort. Had she failed or won?

Paul put his arms around her and pulled her close. Bagabond did not resist, but she did not encourage him. She awkwardly embraced him in return.

"You could stay over tonight." Paul kissed her forehead.

"No. Paul, I'm just not ready to get involved that way. I'm old-fashioned, I guess." Bagabond pushed him away. "I need time."

"We've been seeing each other for months. I still don't know where you live. What is it about me that you don't trust?" Paul stood in front of her with his hands dangling at his sides.

"It's not you. It's me." Bagabond avoided his eyes. "Give me time. Or don't. It's your choice."

"*My* choice?" Paul shook his head in resignation. "This woud be easier if you weren't so damned intriguing. Next Friday, dinner and, I promise, a movie next time. Meet me here?"

"Okay. Good luck. At work." Bagabond didn't know whether she meant it for Paul or for Rosemary.

Bagabond watched the muzzle-flashes and heard the sound of pistols, rifles, and shotguns going off and destroying the night as she circled the building. With a small army of rats, cats, and a few wild dogs, she was patrolling the perimeter, as Rosemary had put it in their meeting two days ago. Whenever anyone tried to break and run, she and the animals drove them back to the waiting police.

She almost tripped over a body, face blown off by a shotgun blast. As she retreated, she ran into a black cop. He caught her gently and steadied her.

"Ma'am, it'd be better if you found someplace else to sleep tonight." His big hands turned her away from the battle toward the quiet surrounding streets. Those hands reminded her of Bludgeon's reaching for Jack. She twisted free, leaving a dirty leather coat in his hands, and limped swiftly away.

When she found herself hidden in the darkness again, she made contact with her animals. The ginger remained with her at all times, but the others ranged around the building. With the eyes of a rat crouched on a pile of garbage, she followed the slow progress of a young Oriental man who was attempting to flee the fight. A trail of blood followed him, dripping down the right leg of his pants. She smelled it and so did the escaped rottweiler that suddenly filled the mouth of the alley. The Vietnamese gasped and began to back slowly down the alley. Holding the dog back, Bagabond pulled the rottweiler onto her haunches, and the dog howled a summons to the sky.

There was water everywhere. Rosemary had said that a new ace named Water Lily would be there that night. Bagabond had grown tired of splashing through puddles. The bottom six inches of her coats and skirts were soaked through and so were her boots. Where was all the water coming from? She hoped there weren't any fires in Jokertown tonight.

Even though it revealed her presence, Bagabond had set up a fireline of feral cats to prevent any jokers from coning closer than a couple of blocks away from the fighting. The Jokertown warehouse at the center of the ring of protection was, according to Rosemary, one of the major Shadow Fist weapons storage areas. Bagabond's concentration was flagging. Rosemary had given little thought to how long her pet ace could continue to scan through animals' minds and control hundreds of them in coordinated action.

The ginger cat snarled and woke Bagabond from her reverie. She straightened up from the wall she had leaned against to conserve her strength. Holding an Uzi in firing position, another Vietnamese was making his way down the dark street, moving from shadow to shadow without a sound. Bagabond fixed on him, then called the rats. Within seconds a hundred rats attacked the man, driving him back. They leaped up his pants and ran up his flailing arms, biting his face and neck. Their sheer numbers tripped him as they covered the ground beneath his feet. He screamed. The Uzi began firing and did not stop, its pulsing fire echoing between the walls in an eerie rhythm to the man's screams. Both climbed the scale until the Uzi ran out of ammunition and the man's throat was too raw to make another sound. It was a silence broken only by the scrabbling rats. Bagabond sent them scurrying away to a new position. The sight of the man in his pool of blood disturbed her. He should not have struggled.

Lasers arced through the sky above the building, surgically cutting it apart. When the beams hit Water Lily's puddles, clouds of steam rose. The intermittently lit scene reminded Bagabond of a Ken Russell staging of hell.

Using the kitten Bagabond had left with her, Rosemary called her. Bagabond turned and left the body. He had done nothing to her. He would not feed her or the animals. What right did she have to kill him?

When Bagabond arrived, Rosemary had stepped back into a deep, shadowed doorway to wait for her. The bag lady slipped along the wall, remembering the Vietnamese maneuvering in the same way minutes before. No one saw her.

"What do you see?" Rosemary had no time for preliminaries.

"We got everyone. Nobody escaped through my eyes."

"Good, *good*. The bastards won't forget this one soon." Rosemary was pleased, but her thoughts were elsewhere. "You see, I knew you could do a lot for me."

Rosemary stepped out into the street as a policeman stepped up to greet her.

"Great job! Those aces of yours really made the difference, much as I hate to admit it. That black guy—the Hammer?—something else. Gave me a chill just being around him and that cloak of his." The captain thrust out his hand in congratulations.

"Glad we could help, Captain. But the Harlem Hammer is still out of the country. Sure it wasn't one of your undercover people?" Rosemary smiled and shook his hand. "By the way, could you have one of your officers help this lady out of the area?" Rosemary nodded toward Bagabond, who waited next to the doorway. "She got herself a little lost."

Before the cop could catch her, Bagabond moved down the sidewalk and ducked into an alley. She took a moment to scatter her gathered animals before following the ginger into a manhole she had left open earlier. In the wet night below the streets she considered what she had accomplished. To what end? So that Rosemary's Mafia could carry on? At least a score of rats, a cat, and one of the dogs had been lost tonight. *Not again, Rosemary. Your games aren't worth it to me*. Catching the gleam of the ginger's eyes, she followed her home through the tunnels.

When Rosemary got to the Gambione penthouse, Chris was already there. He was sitting in the chair at the head of the conference table in her father's library. He said nothing while she took a seat next to him.

"We've got trouble." Chris reached out and took her hand. "Paul Goldberg knows who you are."

"How?" Rosemary simultaneously felt fear and a strange, small relief that the masquerade was over.

"That we don't know, but it doesn't matter much now, does it? We've been watching your office on general principles and found this stuff in his apartment." Chris shoved an envelope across the table at her. When she opened it, she discovered pictures of herself and her father, records, everything they needed to pin her to a wall.

"We've got to get rid of him." Chris drummed his fingers on the oak tabletop. "But I wanted to get your okay first. He is one of your employees after all."

"Of course, immediately." Rosemary kept staring at the photographs and moving them around. "Did he give it to anyone? Who else knows?"

"I think we got him in time." Chris picked one of the pictures and looked at it almost idly. "I'd suggest you check with your great, good friend Suzanne, however. They've been seen together."

"Jesus, she and Paul have been dating. I don't know what she'll do if he's hit. She's not very stable sometimes."

"So you want us to wait on the hit? Come on, you know it's either him or you." Chris tipped the heavy chair back on its rear legs.

"No, take him out. Take him now. If he hasn't had time to tell anybody, I'll still be safe." Rosemary turned her head from side to side as if seeking an escape route.

"It's the only good choice. I'll take care of it. Unless . . ." Chris set the chair down with a small crash that was quickly dampened by the heavy rug.

"No. You do it." Rosemary looked up at him gratefully. "Thank you."

Smiling broadly, he leaned over and kissed her. "No problem. That's what I'm here for."

Walking around the corner of Paul's high rise, Bagabond simultaneously tugged her skirt down and tried to avoid the puddles left by the afternoon rain. The doorman held open the heavy glass door for her with a badly hidden smirk that told her he had seen her adjustments. She considered making his life a little more miserable by perching a pigeon directly above him, but he was not worth it. She had more important things on her mind. It would depend, she had decided, but she might stay with Paul tonight. She still felt a little queasy about the decision.

She waved at Marty, who nodded and checked her off on his guest register. As always, the echoes of her heels tapping across the marble made her self-conscious. The elevator took forever. She had determined that everyone who had seen her come in knew what she was thinking about Paul by the time it showed up. This was ridiculous. She was an adult for Christ's sake. One deep breath and she was in the car headed for Paul's thirty-second-floor apartment.

Mercifully there was no one in the hall when she got out of the elevator. Up here the carpet felt three inches thick, and she made no noise at all as she stepped up to Paul's front door and rang the bell. When several minutes had passed, she rang again and began paying attention to any sound from inside. She heard nothing. She mentally scanned for any creatures inside, a mouse or a rat, but Paul's building was much too classy for that. Failing to locate an animal inside, she pulled a pigeon across the windows. A couple of lights were on, but she didn't see Paul.

Great. What a night to stand her up. Good timing, Paul. Bagabond started back for the elevator with a certain lurking sense of relief that she kept shoving to the back of her mind. Riding down, she realized that she must have been expected or the security guard would not have let her up. For the first time she felt concern about Paul.

Marty, the guard, had seen Paul come in several hours earlier. They had chatted about the fact he had actually won a case for once and had left early to relax before Bagabond came over. Marty blushed as he mentioned that Mr. Goldberg had told him to look out for her. Paul had said they would be celebrating together. There was no record of Paul's going back out, and none of the doormen had seen him leave. Marty called another guard to take over his station and got the skeleton key for Paul's apartment.

As soon as the door opened, Bagabond knew that something was wrong. Following her sense of dread, she led Marty straight to the bathroom. Paul was naked in the black marble Jacuzzi. Blood swirled around him in the bubbling water. He had been shot in the eye at close range. She stared at him while Marty frantically dialed the police.

The police took her down to the station and questioned

her for hours. At first they were determined to get her to confess to the crime. When the initial coroner's report finally came in, they gave up and began asking her about her knowledge of Paul's activities. Who might have wanted him dead? She thought about Rosemary, over and over, but denied knowing anything.

Could Rosemary have had him killed? Rosemary knew that she cared about Paul. Rosemary had encouraged them. Was she capable of murdering someone she had worked with and respected? Bagabond did not allow herself to answer the questions.

It was almost six in the morning when C.C. finally got permission to take Bagabond home. Bagabond said nothing on the taxi ride back to C.C.'s loft. She reached out for the cats and mentally pulled them close to her, shivering. C.C. scooped her morning paper up off the sidewalk in front of her building and tucked it under her arm as she guided Bagabond into the lift. In the loft Bagabond stared blindly at the opposite wall while C.C. made tea.

Bagabond realized that C.C. was repeatedly calling her name. It had brought her back to herself. She preferred spreading her consciousness across the city. It spread her pain as well. Only the urgency in C.C.'s voice made her focus on the paper in front of her.

Rosemary Gambione Muldoon's picture took up a quarter of the front page.

Rosemary was icily calm. The warning had come from an obit writer who just happened to owe a lot of money in Vegas. She had bought his marker some time ago. Today had been the payoff. He had heard the excitement in the newsroom and checked it out. Seeing her picture on the front-page mock-up had been enough. He placed the call to his Family contact. Chris had pounded on her door at two A.M. and together they had thrown clothes into a suitcase.

Chris had brought four of his best men to guard her twenty-four hours a day. The six of them sat in the black limousine that took them to one of the Gambione safehouses. Rosemary said nothing. What was there to say? Part of her life had been destroyed. Only the Family was left. As she had begun, she was going to finish.

Rosemary sat alone in the house. Her bodyguards patrolled the exterior and kept watch on the windows and doors. Chris had left her to organize a safer retreat from which she could lead the Gambiones. She felt free and more alive than she had since she had taken over the task of living two lives. Her head swam with plans for keeping the Families alive and viable. Now that she could concentrate on the problems at hand, everything would be different. Paul had done her a favor. Pity he had had to die for it, but one couldn't show weakness, after all. She wondered when Chris would come back. She had so much to discuss with him.

All the King's Horses

II

The water made a sullen gurgling sound somewhere in the close, hot blackness. The world twisted and turned, sinking. He was too weak and dizzy to move. He felt icy fingers on his legs, creeping up higher and higher, and then sudden shock as the water reached his crotch, jolting him awake. He tore away his seat harness with numb fingers, but too late. The cold caressed his chest, he lurched up and the floor tumbled and he lost his footing, and then the water was over his head and he couldn't breathe and everything was black, utterly black, as black as the grave, and he had to get out, he had to get *out* . . .

Tom woke gasping for breath, a scream clawing at the inside of his throat.

In his first groggy waking moment he heard the faint tinkle of broken glass falling from the window frame to shatter on the bedroom floor. He closed his eyes, tried to steady himself. His heart was trip-hammering away in his chest, his undershirt plastered to his skin. Only a dream, he told himself, but he could still feel himself falling, blind and helpless, locked in a coffin of burning steel as the river closed in around him. Only a dream, he repeated. He'd lucked out, something had exploded the shell and he'd gotten out, it was over, he was alive and safe. He took a deep breath and counted to ten, and by the time he hit seven he'd stopped trembling. He opened his eyes.

His bed was a mattress on the floor of an empty room. He sat up, the bedclothes tangled around him. Feathers from a torn pillow floated in the shafts of sunlight that came through the broken window, drifting lazily toward the floor. The alarm clock he'd bought last week had been flung halfway across the room and had bounced off a wall. A series of random numbers blinked red on its digital LED display for an instant before it went dark entirely. The walls were pale green, utterly bare, and spiderwebbed with a growing network of cracks. A chunk of plaster dropped from the ceiling. Tom winced, untangled himself from the sheets, and stood up.

One of these nights his fucking subconscious was going to bring down the whole house on top of him. He wondered what his neighbors would make of that. He'd already reduced most of his bedroom furniture to kindling, and the plasterboard walls weren't holding up real well either. Then again, neither was be.

In the bathroom Tom dropped his sweat-soaked underwear into the hamper and stared at himself in the mirror over the sink. He thought he looked ten years older than he was. A couple of months of recurring nightmares will do that to you, he supposed.

He climbed into the shower, closed the curtain. A half-melted bar of Safeguard sat in a film of water in the soap dish. Tom concentrated. The soap rose straight up and floated into his hand. It felt slimy. Frowning, he gave the cold faucet a good hard twist with his mind, and he winced as the stream of icy water hit him. Very quickly he grabbed for the hot faucet—with his *hand*—turned it, and shuddered with relief as the water warmed.

It was getting better, Tom reflected as he lathered up. Twenty-odd years as the Turtle had atrophied his telekinetic abilities almost to nothing, except when he was locked inside his shell, but Dr. Tachyon had helped him understand that the block was psychological, not physical. He'd been working on it ever since, and it had gotten to the point where bars of soap and cold-water faucets were candy.

Tom stuck his head under the showerhead and smiled as the warm water cascaded down around him, washing away the last residue of nightmare. Too bad his subconscious didn't realize his limits; he'd feel a fuck of a lot safer going to sleep, and maybe his bedroom wouldn't be such a mess when he woke up. But when the nightmare came, he was the Turtle. Weak, dizzy, falling, and about to drown, but still the Great and Powerful Turtle, who could juggle locomotives and crush tanks with his mind.

The late great Turtle. All the king's horses and all the king's men, Tom thought.

He turned off the spray, shivered in the sudden chill, and climbed out of the tub to towel off.

In the kitchen he fixed himself a cup of coffee and a bowl of bran cereal. He'd always thought bran cereal tasted like wet cardboard, and these new extrahealthy bran cereals tasted like wood shavings, but his doctor said he had to get more fiber and less fat in his diet. He was also supposed to cut down on his coffee, but that was a hopeless case—he was an addict by now.

He turned on the small TV next to the microwave and watched CNN as he sat at the kitchen table. The city was launching a full-fledged investigation of corruption in the Manhattan district attorney's office, which seemed like the least they could do now that one of their assistant DAs had been exposed as a Mafia don. Indictments were promised. Rosa Maria Gambione, alias Rosemary Muldoon, was still being sought for questioning, but she'd vanished, gone underground somewhere. Tom didn't figure she'd be turning up anytime soon.

He'd felt guilty about ignoring Muldoon's appeal for ace volunteers when the gang war had begun raging in the streets of Jokertown. It wasn't like the Turtle to ignore a plea for help, and if he'd had a working shell or the money to build one, his resolve might have softened enough to bring the Turtle back from the dead. But he hadn't so he didn't and now he was glad of it. Pulse and Water Lily and Mister Magnet and the other aces who had responded had put their lives and reputations on the line, and now they had hack politicians going on the evening news demanding that all of them be investigated for ties to organized crime.

It was times like this that made Tom glad that the Turtle was dead.

On the tube, they moved to the international desk for an update on the aces tour. Peregrine's pregnancy was already old news, and there had been no new violence like the incident in Syria, thank god. Tom watched footage of the *Stacked Deck* landing in Japan with a certain dull resentment. He'd always wanted to travel, to see distant exotic lands, visit all the fabulous cities he'd read of as a child, but he'd never had the money. Once the store had sent him to a trade show in Chicago, but a weekend in the Conrad Hilton

with three thousand electronics salesmen hadn't fulfilled any
of his childhood dreams.

They should have asked the Turtle to be on the tour. Of
course transporting the shell might have been a problem, and
he couldn't get a passport without giving them his real name,
which he wasn't prepared to do, but those problems could
have been handled if anyone had cared enough to bother.
Maybe they really did think he was dead, though Dr. Tachyon
at least ought to have known better.

So here he was, still in Bayonne wth a mouth full of
high-fiber bran, while the likes of Mistral and Fatman and
Peregrine were sitting under a pagoda somewhere, eating
whatever the hell the Japanese ate for breakfast. It pissed
him off. He had nothing against Peri or Mistral, but none of
them had paid the dues he had. Jesus Christ, they'd even
invited that scumbag Jack Braun. But not him, oh no, that
would have been too much fucking trouble; they would have
had to make special arrangements, and besides, they had so
many seats allocated for aces and so many for jokers and
nobody knew quite where the Turtle fit.

Tom drank a mouthful of coffee, got up from the table,
and shut off the TV. Fuck it all, he thought. Now that he'd
decided that the Turtle was going to stay dead, maybe it was
time that he buried the remains. He had a notion or two
about that. If he handled it right, maybe by this time next
year *he* could afford to take a trip around the world too.

Concerto for
Siren and Serotonin

II

Checking to see that no one was watching, Croyd dropped a pair of Black Beauties with his espresso. He cursed softly as a part of the sigh that followed. This was not working out as he had anticipated. All of the leads he had tried during the past days had pretty much fizzled, and he was further along into the speed than he cared to be. Ordinarily this would not bother him, but for the first time he had made two separate promises concerning drugs and his actions. One being business and one being personal, he reflected, they kind of caught him coming and going. He would definitely have to keep an eye, or at least a few facets, on himself so as not to mess up on this job, and he didn't want to turn Water Lily off on their first date. Usually, though, he could feel the paranoia coming on, and he decided to let that be his indicator as to his degree of irrationality this time around.

He had run all over town, trying to trace two leads who seemed to have vanished. He had checked out every possible front on his list, satisfying himself that they had only been randomly chosen rendezvous points. Next was James Spector. While he hadn't recognized the name, he did know Demise. He had met him, briefly, on a number of occasions. The man had always impressed him as one of the sleazier aces. "If it's Demise, don't look in his eyes," he hummed as he signaled to a waiter.

"Yes, sir?"

"More espresso, and bring me a bigger cup for it, will you?"

"Yes, sir."

"For that matter, bring me a whole pot."

"All right."

He hummed a little more loudly and began tapping his foot. "Demise eyes. The eyes of Demise," he intoned. He jumped when the waiter placed a cup before him.

"Don't sneak up on me like that!"

"Sorry. Didn't mean to startle you."

The man began to fill the cup.

"Don't stand behind me while you're pouring. Stand off to the side where I can see you."

"Sure."

The waiter moved off to Croyd's right. He left the carafe on the table when he departed.

As he drank cup after cup of coffee, Croyd began thinking thoughts he had not thought in a long while, concerning sleep, mortality, transfiguration. After a time he called for another carafe. It was definitely a two-carafe problem.

The evening's snowfall had ceased, but the inch or so that lay upon the sidewalks sparkled under the streetlamps, and a wind so cold it burned whipped glittering eddies along Tenth Street. Walking carefully, the tall, thin man in the heavy black overcoat glanced back once as he turned the corner, breath pluming. Ever since he'd left the package store he'd had a feeling that he was being watched. And there was a figure, a hundred yards or so back, moving along the opposite side of the street at about the same pace as himself. James Spector felt that it might be worth waiting for the man and killing him just to avoid any possible hassle farther along the way. After all, there were two fifths of Jack Daniel's and a six-pack of Schlitz in his bag, and if someone were to accost him abruptly on these icy walks— He winced at the thought of the bottles breaking, of having to retrace his path to the store.

On the other hand, waiting for the man and killing him right here, while holding the package, could also result in his slipping—even if it was only when he leaned forward to go through the man's pockets. It would be better to find a place to set things down first. He looked about.

There were some steps leading up to a doorway, farther along. He headed for them and set his parcel down on the third one, against its iron railing. He brushed off his collar and turned it up, fished a package of cigarettes from his pocket, shook one out, and lit it within cupped hands. He leaned against the rail then and waited, watching the corner.

Shortly a man in gray slacks and a blue blazer came into sight, necktie whipping in the wind, dark hair disheveled. He paused and stared, then nodded and advanced. As he came nearer, Spector realized that the man was wearing mirrorshades. He felt a sudden jab of panic, seeing that the other possessed an adequate first line of defense against him. It wasn't likely to be an accident either, in the middle of the night. Therefore, this was more than some strong-arm hood on his tail. He took a long drag on his cigarette, then mounted several steps backward, slowly, gaining sufficient height for a good kick at the other's head, to knock the damned things off.

"Yo, Demise!" the man called. "I need to talk to you!"

Demise stared, trying to place him. But there was nothing familiar about the man, not even his voice.

The man came up and stood before him, smiling. "I just need a minute or two of your time," he said. "It's important. I'm in a big hurry and I'm trying for a certain measure of subtlety. It isn't easy."

"Do I know you?" Demise asked him.

"We've met. In other lives, so to speak. My lives, that is. Also, I believe you might once have done some accounting for my brother-in-law's company, over in Jersey. Croyd's the name."

"What do you want?"

"I need the name of the head of the new mob that's trying to take over operations from the kindly old Mafia, which has run this town for half a century or so."

"You're kidding," Demise said, taking a final drag on his cigarette, dropping it and moving his toe to grind it.

"No," said Croyd. "I definitely require this information so I can rest in peace. I understand you've done some work other than bookkeeping for these guys. So tell me who runs the show and I'll be moving along."

"I can't do that," Demise answered.

"As I said, I'm aiming for subtlety. So I'd rather not work this the hard way—"

Demise kicked him in the face. Croyd's glasses flew over his shoulder, and Demise found himself staring into 216 glittering eye-facets. He was unable to lock gazes with the points of light.

"You're an ace," he said, " or a joker."

"I'm the Sleeper," Croyd told him as he reached out and took hold of Demise's right arm, then broke it across the railing. "You should have let me be subtle. It doesn't hurt as much."

Demise shrugged even as he winced. "Go ahead and break the other one too." But I can't tell you what I don't know."

Croyd stared at the arm hanging at Demise's side. Demise reached across and caught hold of it, twisted it into place, held it.

"You heal real fast, don't you?" Croyd said. "In minutes, even. I remember now."

"That's right."

"Can you grow a new arm if I tear one off?"

"I don't know, and I'd rather not find out. Look, I've heard you're a psycho and I believe it. I'd tell you if I knew. I don't enjoy regenerating. But all I did was a lousy contract hit. I've got no idea who's on top."

Croyd reached out with both hands, catching hold of Demise's wrists.

"Breaking you up may not do much good," he observed, "but there's still room for subtlety. Ever have any electroshock therapy? Try this."

When Demise stopped jerking, Croyd released his wrists. When he could speak again, Demise said, "I still can't tell you. I don't know."

"So let's lose a few more neurons," Croyd suggested.

"Cool it a minute," Demise said. "I never learned the names of any of the big guys. Never meant dick to me. Still don't. All I know is this guy named Eye—a joker. He just has one big eye and he wears a monocle in it. He met me once, in Times Square, gave me a hit and paid me. That's all that matters. You know how it is. You freelance yourself."

Croyd sighed. "Eye? Seems I've heard of him someplace or other. Where can I get hold of the guy?"

"I understand he hangs around Club Dead Nicholas. Plays cards there awhile on Friday nights. Kept meaning to go by and kill the fucker, but I never got around to it. Cost me a foot."

"'Club Dead Nicholas'?" Croyd said. "I don't believe I know that one."

"Used to be Nicholas King's Mortuary, near Jokertown. Serves food and booze, has music and a dance floor, gambling in a back room. Just opened recently. Kind of Halloween motif. Too morbid for my taste."

"Okay," Croyd said. "I hope you're not bullshitting me, Demise."

"That's all I got."

Croyd nodded slowly. "It'll do." He released the other and backed away. "Maybe then I can rest," he said. "Subtle. Real subtle." He picked up Demise's package and put it in his arms. "Here. Don't forget your stuff. Better watch your step too. It's getting slippery." He continued to back away, muttering to himself, up the street, to the corner. Then he turned again and was gone.

Sinking to a seated position on the stoop, Demise cracked open a fifth and took a long swallow.

Jesus Was an Ace

by Arthur Byron Cover

*In these times of trouble and dark travail; in this fertile
land where the handiwork of Satan is on the verge of
bearing fruit: you don't need to pussyfoot with Marx; or
stick your nose in Freud; you don't need the help of
liberals like Tachyon; you don't need to open yourself up
to anyone but Jesus—because he was the first and the
greatest ace of them all!*

—REVEREND LEO BARNETT

I

There are a few blocks or so between Jokertown and the
Lower East Side that nats and virus victims alike call the
Edge. No one knows which group originated the term, but
it applies equally to either side. A joker might think of the
place as the edge of New York, a nat as the edge of
Jokertown.

People come to the Edge for the same reasons why some
people watch a slasher movie, or see a good speed metal rock
concert, or get wasted on the designer drug in fashion at the
moment. They come to the Edge drawn by the illusion of
danger, a safe, fleeting illusion that gives them something to
talk about at parties attended by people too timid to go to the
Edge themselves.

The young preacher thought about that as he watched the
television news team wandering the street below through the
bathroom window of the cheap hotel room he had rented for
the night, though he had intended to use it for only a few
hours. The team consisted of a male reporter in a coat and
tie, a Minicam operator, and a sound man; the reporter was
stopping pedestrians, nats and jokers alike, jabbing his microphone into their faces and trying to get them to say some-

thing. For a long, torturous moment the young preacher was afraid his tryst with Belinda May was the story the news team was searching for, but he comforted himself with the notion that the news team no doubt prowled this vicinity routinely. After all, where else did they have a better chance of finding a strong visual lead-in for the eleven o'clock news? The young preacher didn't like to think sinful thoughts, but under the circumstances he relished the hope the news team would be distracted by a spectacular auto accident a few blocks away, with lots of visual flair in the form of fire and crumpled hoods—but with no fatalities, of course.

The young preacher let the flimsy white curtain drop. He finished his business and while washing his hands with quick, efficient motions, stared at his cadaverous reflection in the mirror over the rust-stained sink. Was he really that unhealthy, or was his pale, yellowish complexion only the result of the unshielded glare of the two naked light bulbs above the mirror? The young preacher was a blond, blue-eyed man just turned thirty-five, with handsome features dominated by high cheekbones and a dimpled, square chin. Right now he was stripped down to a white T-shirt, light-blue boxer shorts, and socks. He perspired profusely. It was definitely hot in here, but he hoped to make it a lot hotter real soon now.

Even so, he couldn't help but feel out of place in this tacky little hotel room, with this particular woman who just happened to be one of the key staff members of his new Jokertown mission. Not that he was inexperienced. He had done it many times before, with many kinds of women, in rooms like this one. The women had done it because he was famous, or had felt good listening to his sermons, or wanted to feel closer to God. Occasionally, when he himself was having a little difficulty feeling close to God, they'd done it for money, the payments having been arranged by a trustworthy member of his most intimate circle. A few women had foolishly believed they were in love with him, a delusion he generally shattered without much trouble, but only after satiating their carnal desires.

But nothing in the young preacher's experience had quite prepared him for a woman such as Belinda May, who apparently was here for the sheer joy of it. He wondered if Belinda May's attitude was typical of unmarried big-city Christian women. *Where in the world is Jesus going to come from*, he thought, *when the time arrives for him to return again?*

He opened the door to the bedroom and, before he had taken a single step outside, received the shock of his life. Belinda May sat cross-legged on the bed, smoking a cigarette, as pretty as you please but as naked as a jaybird. He'd expected to see her naked, of course, but not right away. And even then, he'd thought she'd be discreetly under the sheets.

"About time you showed up," she said. She stubbed out her cigarette and stepped into his arms before he could take a breath. Now he knew how a frying pan felt on a hot stove. She clung to him as if she wanted to pull herself into his body. He was unbelievably aroused by the sensation of her breasts pressed against his chest, and by the way she had mounted his thigh, rubbing against it as if she were trying to sit on the bone. Her tongue was like an eel exploring his mouth. One hand was under his T-shirt, the other down his shorts, caressing his buttocks.

"Hmmm, you taste good," Belinda May whispered in his ear after what seemed like an eternity in a place that was an eerie combination of the stratospheres of heaven and the lower levels of hell. No doubt about it, Belinda May was more sexually aggressive than the kind of woman he was used to. "Come on, let's go to bed," she whispered, taking him by the hands and pulling him along. She climbed on the bed, got on her knees, and directing him to stand beside the bed, gently placed his right hand smack onto her pussy.

Though the young preacher experienced a deep and abiding satisfaction every time his foreplay brought her to orgasm, he felt strangely disjointed from the entire affair, as if he was watching the scene through a one-way mirror in the wall. Very self-consciously he wondered anew what he was doing in this dive, with its paint peeling off its badly plastered walls, those tacky lamps, the bed with creaky springs, and that television set staring at him with an unsleeping eye. He regretted going along with Belinda May's request that they pick a room here, at the Edge, to engage in their encounter. It disturbed him to think that in some part of his soul he so closely resembled the people who routinely came to the Edge in search of a safe chance to take. The young preacher wanted to believe God had already filled the important voids in his heart.

However, Belinda May's accessible beauty disturbed him on a deeper level than did his instrusive self-doubts. Gently he pushed her down, and with a strange thrill, not unlike the one he had experienced as a youth the first time he'd knelt alone before an altar, he noted how her blond hair was spread out over the pillow like the wings of an angel. She squirmed beguilingly as he kissed her ear and moved down to lick her neck. He moved down further to kiss her breasts and felt a renewed surge of heat in his scalp as she signaled the measure of her passion by running her hands through his hair and groaning softly. Then he was down at her stomach, running his tongue around the edges of her belly button—an outie—with what he hoped was a delicate, masterful touch. He was gratified beyond his capacity to understand when she at last spread her legs wide apart, an invitation he accepted almost instantly, burying his face and licking her with pagan ferocity. Never had he known a woman to taste so good. Never had he desired so fervently to serve another, instead of being served. Never had he worshiped so humbly, so eagerly at the altar of love. Never had he so gladly debased himself, or so wantonly. . . .

"Leo?" said Belinda May, moving back on her elbows. "Is something the matter?"

The young preacher rose onto his elbows and looked down between his legs, where his male member hung as limp as a man on a noose. *O Lord, why have you forsaken me?* He thought forlornly, reining in a childish urge to panic. He smiled sheepishly, looked past the altar with its still wide-open invitation, past her sweat-drenched body and those glistening breasts, to her sweetly smiling face. "I don't know. I guess I'm just not with it tonight."

Belinda May pouted and stretched as innocenty and as naturally as if she'd been alone. "Too bad. Is there anything I can do to help?"

For the next few seconds the young preacher weighed several factors in his mind, most of them having to do with the proper balance between frankness and delicate diplomacy. In the end he decided she would respond well to frankness, but he wasn't sure how much he could get away with. He smiled wolfishly. "Think you'd like to something to eat?"

His life passed before his eyes as she swung her left leg over his head, climbed off the bed, and exclaimed, "What a great idea! There's a sushi bar across the street! You can buy me dinner!" Her buttocks bounced enticingly as she disappeared into the bathroom, closing the door behind her. She turned on the water faucet and then, apparently before commencing her business, opened the door and stuck out her head just long enough to say, "Then we can come back here and try again."

The young preacher was speechless. He rolled over and stared at the ceiling, the random pattern of the intersecting cracks there enigmatically symbolic of his entire existence at this juncture. He sighed heavily. At least the possibility that the roving news team outside would discover his tryst was no longer the worst thing that could happen to him.

Now, the worst thing would be if they discovered he hadn't been able to get it up.

In that case, the damage done to his political ambitions would be incalculable. The American people were willing to forgive any number of sins in a presidential candidate, but at the very least they expected their sinners to be good at it.

"You really have a good pair of hands, you know that?" called out Belinda May from the bathroom.

Terrific, thought Leo Barnett, clinging to the precipice of despair with progressively weaker force. *Bye-bye, White House; hello, Heaven.*

II

Tonight he felt the city inside him, and he was inside it. He felt its steel and mortar and brick and stone and marble and glass, felt his organs touching the various buildings and places of Jokertown as their atoms phased in (and out) on their way (and back again) across the planes of reality. His molecules grazed the clouds swirling toward the city like an incoming black cotton tide; they mingled with air pregnant with moisture and the promise of more moisture to come, they trembled with the vibrations of distant thunder. Tonight he felt inexorably linked with Jokertown's past and future; the coming rainstorm would differ in no way from the last one, and would be exactly the same as the next. Just as the steel and the mortar were constant, the brick and stone forever, and the marble and glass immortal. So long as the city remained so, however tenuously, would he.

His name was Quasiman. Once he had had another name, but all he could remember about his previrus self was that he had been an explosives expert. Currently he was a caretaker of the Church of Our Lady of Perpetual Misery, and of him Father Squid relished saying, time and time again, "The bomb squad's loss has been the God squad's gain."

Usually it was all Quasiman could do to remember those bare facts, because the atoms of his brain, like those in the rest of his body, constantly, randomly, phased in and out of reality, soaring to extradimensional realms and snapping back again. This had the dual effect of making him more than a genius, and less than an idiot. Most days Quasiman considered it a victory to keep himself in one piece.

Tonight maintaining even that modest goal was going to prove more difficult than usual. Blood and thunder were in the air. Tonight Quasiman was going to the Edge.

As he reached the door at the top of the stairs leading to the roof of the cheapjack apartment building where he lived, portions of his brain glanced off the immediate future. Already he felt cool night air, saw distant flashes of lightning, felt rooftop gravel crunch beneath the soles of his tennis shoes, and saw an old bag lady, a joker, sleeping beside a warm-air duct, her belongings beside her in a cart she had pulled up the fire escape.

The intersection between present and future became stronger and more vivid the instant he actually touched the doorknob, and becoming stronger still once he turned it. Quasiman was used to this sort of minor precognition by now. For him the different levels of time constantly clashed together like discordant cymbals. Long ago he had accepted the only conclusion possible from living in such a mindworld: Reality was just the fragments of a dream shattered before the dawn of being.

Future and present merged seamlessly as he steped through the doorway. The lightning flashes and the gravel underfoot and the sleeping old woman were there, as he had known they would be. What he hadn't envisioned was the creaking of the door's rusty hinges, screeching like a buzz saw cutting through nails over the steady hum of the automobile traffic below, startling the old woman from her uneasy sleep. She had brown scaly skin, and the face of a furless rat. Her lips drew back and exposed sharp white fangs. "Who the fuck are you?" she demanded with false bravado.

He ignored her. A hunchbacked man with an unbending left hip, he shuffled to the building's ledge with the efficient grace of a dancer permanently engrossed in a sick, satirical joke.

Without the slightest hesitation he stepped off the ledge.

The old woman, mistakenly believing he was committing suicide, screamed. Quasiman didn't care.

He was too busy doing what he always did after stepping off a bulding: he willed himself to where he wished to be.

Time and space folded about him. In the following instant his rapidly fading intellect fought hard to hold on to his own self-image. For an enduring nanosecond he almost became lost in the fluidity of the cosmos. But he maintained, and when that moment ended, he was in an alley in the Edge.

He was one second closer to the thunder, one step closer to the blood, one event closer to the final blackout.

III

Tonight was the night of Vito's big break. The Man never would have instructed him to come along on this little excursion to the Edge if he hadn't already indicated his ability to handle responsibility. Of course that also meant Vito was a mite expendable, but that was okay, it came with the territory. You had to take risks if you wanted to move up in the Calvino Family.

And lately there had been a lot of openings in the Family hierarchy. Vito, an ambitious youngster, hoped to survive long enough to rise a few notches, just high enough to get somebody else to take the more obvious risks.

Unfortunately a truce of some sort seemed likely, if there was any truth to the scuttlebutt he had picked up from a few of the boys while he was busy waxing the Man's limo. Evidently the Man planned to hash over some important business with one of the high mucky-muck jokers pulling the strings on all the hits that had decimated the Five Families recently.

Some joker named Wyrm, yeah, that's his name, thought

Vito tensely as he walked down a sidewalk in the middle of
the Edge, weaving through a flood of tourists and jokers and
maybe even a few aces. He checked out the street scene for
potential trouble. It wasn't his job—that was to walk into the
lobby of the cheap dive just ahead and pick up the key to the
room where the Man and the joker had agreed to meet—but
he couldn't help hoping he'd notice something significant in
the security area anyway, so the Man and the boys would
maybe consider him a little less expendable.

Stepping into the lobby, however, Vito felt like a blind
bear walking into a campsite full of hunters. Trying to keep
his posture straight and his jaw tightly set, the way he'd seen
the boys do while rousting some welsher, he strode up to the
registry counter and slammed his palm on it with what he
hoped was an authoritative air. "I'm here for one of your, ah,
most important customers," he said with an unfortunate crack
in his voice.

The clerk, a seedy old man with white hair and a black
eyepatch, probably some joker passing for nat, barely looked
up from the girly magazine he was reading. The back of the
cover heralded some joker fetish article, and in the blurry
photo some beefy dude straddled a creature with gorgeous,
lusty eyes, but who otherwise resembled a giant scoop of
vanilla ice cream with skinny arms and legs and tiny hands
and feet. The clerk nonchalantly turned a page.

Vito cleared his throat.

The clerk cleared his. After a long pause he finally looked
up and said, "We've got a lot of important customers, young
man. Which one do you represent?"

"The one you owe so many favors to."

The words were barely out of Vito's mouth when the old
man jumped up and picked up a key from the rack and
dashed to the counter and held it out for Vito, saying,
"Everything's been taken care of, sir. Hope you find the
facilities to your liking."

"It's not my opinion that counts," Vito said, plucking the
key from the clerk's hand. "Watch it or else those pages will
stick together," he added, turning toward the exit. Briefly he
wondered if he should check out the room, but then he
remembered that his instructions had been very succinct and
to the point. *Go to the lobby and bring back the key.* Vito had

already learned from watching a few fellas learn the hard way, that the boys often didn't appreciate initiative.

So he went outside into the cool air and put his head down as if walking into a strong wind, although it was barely blowing and his posture allowed his greasy black hair to fall into his eyes. His confidence that things would go his way tonight, based on how things had gone so far, was almost immediately negated by the presence everywhere of men he recognized—on both sides of the street, standing around, sitting at the tables of junk food venues or in parked cars. Usually the only time that many family members and grunts were together in the same area was during a funeral. Now though, rather than being conspicuous in their clothing of mourning, they were trying to blend into their surroundings. Vito didn't recognize a few of the people accompanying the boys, but something about their cool confidence exuded an air of restrained cruelty that made even the roughest, toughest boys appear a little uneasy.

His mind racing with a hundred questions, Vito walked with a quickened pace to the streetcorner where Ralphy was waiting for him. Ralphy was one of the Man's most trusted assistants. Rumor had it he had been a hit man of such talent that he once shot a mayoral candidate from two hundred yards and disappeared into a crowd right in front of the television cameras. Vito didn't doubt it was possible. For him, Ralphy was more of a force than a human being. So when Vito halted a few respectful yards away from Ralphy, he looked up into those cold brown eyes above those pockmarked cheeks and saw a man who would snuff him out as casually as he would step on a bug. Vito held out the key. "Here it is!" he proclaimed, perhaps a trifle too loudly.

"Good," said Ralphy in his gravelly voice, pointedly not taking the key. "You check out the room?"

"No. I wasn't told to."

"Right. Check it out now."

"What's going on?" Vito blurted out. "I heard this was supposed to be a peace conference."

"You ain't heard nothing. We're just taking precautions, and you've been volunteered."

"What am I looking for?"

"You'll know if you find it. Now get."

Vito got. He didn't know if he should be elated or worried

that he was being trusted with this part of the operation. His musings were interrupted as he accidentally bumped into a hunchbacked joker with a stiff hip shuffling from an alleyway. "Hey—watch it!" he barked, pushing the joker away.

The joker stopped and drooled, nodding fearfully at Vito. Something flickered on in his dull eyes, lasting for only a second, as the joker clenched and unclenched his fist. During that second the joker straightened and Vito got the distinct impression he could crush granite in that massive fist.

Then the joker deflated, another stream of spittle drooled from his mouth, and he shuffled backward into the alley until he bumped into a garbage can. The joker ignored Vito and rummaged about in the garbage. He found a dried, half-eaten chicken and took a big chomp of it with his white, straight teeth, masticating it furiously.

Disgusted, Vito turned away and hastened back to the hotel. Only as he pushed his way through the rotating doors that led into the lobby did Vito note that the joker's clothing—a lumberjack shirt and blue jeans—had been very clean and tidy. He couldn't remember having seen before a street person, reduced to scrounging in garbage cans for food, with fresh patches on his jeans at the knees.

Vito put the picture of the man from his mind with a shrug. He walked past the counter where the clerk still had his nose buried in the magazine, and thinking he might be trapped in the elevator with an unsavory sort who could reduce his probability of surviving the peace conference to zero, he instead took the six flights of stairs to the third floor. The hallway was depressingly dark, the dim fluorescents casting as much haze as actual light, light that barely reflected off the grimy tan walls, infusing them with an unpleasant glare.

He found the room. He looked up and down the hall. No one was there. He could hear the muffled sounds of a few TV sets coming through the doors, as well as what seemed to be the sounds of the plumbing working in the room across the hall. All this was pretty normal hotel activity in Vito's opinion, but he nevertheless felt prickly and uneasy inside, the way he always felt when he beleieved he was being watched by unseen eyes. He inserted the key with trembling fingers and opened the door.

And found himself staring into the face of one ugly

motherfucker. The dude had virtually no jaw, two nostril pits instead of a nose, and a forked tongue that flicked in and out of his mouth. The way the joker grinned and looked at Vito with those predatory yellow eyes was definitely evil. Vito was used to a more banal, businesslike version. This joker savored the knowledge that he had already frightened Vito to the core.

The joker sneered. "I sssee the Calvinos are sending boysss to do their work now. Tell your boss it'sss all right for him to come in. I am quite alone."

IV

"Maybe you should try taking off your socks next time," said Belinda May mischievously as the young preacher pulled the door closed. He winced at the playful sting of her words as he twisted the knob to make sure the room was locked. Belinda May giggled and put her arm around him. "Lighten up, Reverend. You take yourself too seriously." She gave him a squeeze that started his heart pounding, and he attempted a smile. "Just remember what Norman Mailer said," she whispered seductively into his ear. "'Sometimes desire just isn't enough.' It doesn't make you any less of a man."

"I don't read Mailer," he replied as they walked toward the elevator.

"His books too dirty for you?"

"That's what I've heard."

"It's only life that he writes about. Life is what's happening to us now."

"The Bible tells me everything I need to know about life."

"Bullshit."

Shocked by her casual profanity, he opened his mouth to reply—

—but she continued before he could get a word in: "It's a little late to protest your innocence, Leo."

The young preacher supressed his anger. Normally he only became angry before his congregations, and he wasn't used to being talked back to. Furthermore he wasn't used to being in the company of a female who implied his understanding of the moral dilemmas of love, life, and the pursuit of happiness wasn't beyond questioning. But in this case he was forced to admit, though not aloud to Belinda May, he was in the wrong, because he had indeed read the works of Norman Mailer—in particular *The Executioner's Song*, the exhaustive case-study of the tormented young ace who had been executed for turning nine innocent people into pillars of salt. The young preacher still had a copy of the paperback edition, hidden away in a cabinet drawer in his study in his southwestern Virginia home, where it was unlikely to be seen by anybody else. Many other books of dubious moral content were hidden away in the same drawer, and in many others, concealed from the curiosity of his closest associates the way other evangelical preachers might conceal the contents of their liquor cabinets.

So what else could he do except let Belinda May get the better of him? He was satisfied with the prospect of getting the better part of her body later. Besides, he wasn't all that interested in her mind anyway.

She gave him another squeeze as they stood and waited for the elevator to arrive. The thrill was twice as great as before, because this time she squeeed a buttock. "You have such a cute ass for a possible presidential candidate," she said. "Most of the current crop looks like a bunch of hound dogs."

His eyes darted back and forth suspiciously.

"Don't worry," she said, giving him a pinch. "There's nobody here."

Then the elevator doors opened and they found themselves staring at four men with impassive faces and eyes of steel. The young preacher felt his knees quake, and Belinda May's squeeze this time conveyed her fear and need for protection, a signal direct and primal.

The two men in the middle were the focus of the young preacher's attention. One was short and corpulent, red-faced and thick-lipped, with a long patch of white hair combed over the top of his head in a failed attempt to conceal the bald dome glistening beneath the fluorescents. His big eyes looked as if they would pop out of his head if someone slapped him on the back too hard. His fingers were thick and meaty. Despite a well-tailored black suit, with a red carnation in the lapel, and a neat white shirt and a gray vest, his taste in clothing was questionable at best, thanks to a red tie whose shade practically sent it into the Day-Glo category. The man serenely puffed at a big Havana cigar. The tobacco at the end had been darkened by his spittle, making it resemble nothing so much as a dried turd.

The man blew cigar smoke into the young preacher's face.

The act was deliberately inconsiderate, and the young preacher might have responded had it not been for the cold brown eyes of the tall, pockmarked man beside the fat one. This man had thin, pale lips that looked like scars. His brown hair was pressed so flat against his skull the young preacher imagined he slept with a stocking over his head. He wore a beige trench coat with a decided bulge in the right pocket.

Two beefy men flanked them. They wore the brims of their hats tilted down so that most of their faces were concealed in shadow. One had his arms crossed, while the other, the young preacher belatedly noted, was waving the couple aside.

The couple obeyed. The four men left the elevator and walked down the hall without a backward glance. The young preacher couldn't help pausing to stare at them, even as Belinda May dashed inside. "Come on, Leo!" she whispered, holding open the closing doors with her body.

The young preacher hastened inside. "Who was that?"

"Not now!" Only when the elevator had begun its downward descent did Belinda May add, "That was the head of the Calvino Family. I saw him on the news once!"

"Who's the Calvino Family?"

"The mob."

"Oh, I see. We don't have the mob where I come from."

"The mob's wherever it wants to be. There are five Families in the city, though right now there're only three heads. Or maybe two. There've been a lot of gang murders lately."

"If that guy's such a bigwig, what's he doing here?"

"You can bet it was business. Calvino *número uno* will probably incinerate his shoes when he gets out of here." The elevator doors opened at the lobby. Completely oblivious to the fact that several people, including a beefy joker with a rhino face, were standing at the entrance. Belinda May put her hands around the young preacher's elbow and said, "Did you bring a box of prophylactics, by any chance?"

He felt his face blaze red. But if any of these people recognized him, he got no indication of it. At least he did not hear his name being spoken or the click of a camera. As they made their way through the rotating doors, he realized that his relief at having gotten out without being recognized could be illusionary. If he was being staked out by a muckraker, the young preacher would never know until he saw the proof on the evening news or read it on the front pages of the supermarket rags. "Belinda—why did you say that—?" he demanded.

"What? Do you mean about the prophylactics?" she asked innocently, reaching for a cigarette and lighter from her pocketbook. "It seems like a reasonable question. I think it's very important for sexually active people to practice safe sex, don't you?"

"Yes, but in front of all those people!"

She stopped at the edge of the sidewalk, turned away from him, cupped her hand over the cigarette in her mouth, and lit it. When she turned back to him, puffing smoke, she said, "What do they care? Besides," she added with a mischievous smile, "I should think you'd approve my inherent optimism."

The young preacher covered his face. He clenched his other hand into a fist. He felt as if the eyes of every individual on the street were upon him, even though the most casual appraisal of the situation demonstrated he was simply being paranoid. "Where do you want to eat?" he asked.

Belinda May playfully jabbed his ribs. "Brace up. Reverend! I was only kidding. You worry too much. Keep on worrying and we'll be in that room for weeks. I'm not sure I've got that much credit on my plastic."

"Oh, don't worry about that. I'll see that the church reimburses you somehow. Now, where do you want to eat?"

"That place looks good" she said, pointing across the street. "Rudy's Kosher Sushi."

"It's a deal." He took her by the elbow and walked her to the corner of the intersection. He looked both ways as the light at the crosswalk turned green, not just to make sure all the automobiles were stopping—something no big-city denizen took for granted—but to see if anyone was around whose presence he should be concerned with. The television crew was accosting a young woman at the end of the next block, but that was it. He felt reasonably certain they would be safely seated at a restaurant table in the back if the crew came this way again.

Before they had stepped off the curb, someone coming from his blind side bumped into him. On a usual night the young preacher would have turned the other cheek, but normally he wasn't so frustrated. He yelled, "Hey! Watch where you're going!" and then realized with a shock of horror that his harsh words had been spoken to a joker:

An obviously retarded joker with a hunchback and dim eyes. The man had curly red hair and wore a freshly pressed lumberjack shirt and denim jeans. "Sorry," said the joker, sticking the tip of his forefinger in his nostril, and then, as if thinking better of it, merely wiping his wrist across his nose.

The young preacher for some reason suspected the gesture as an affectation and became certain of it when the joker bowed stiffly and said, "I was just a tad preoccupied—lost in my own world, I suppose. You do forgive me—don't you?"

Then the joker stepped away from the curb as if he had completely changed his mind about which direction he was headed in. A trickle of drool dropped down his chin almost as an afterthought.

Wide-eyed and confused, the young preacher took a few steps after the man. Belinda May detained him, demanding, "Leo, where do you think you're going?"

"Uh, after him, of course."

"Why?"

The young preacher thought about it during a particularly uncomfortable moment. "I thought I would tell him about the mission. See if he couldn't use a little help. He looked like he could."

"Nice sentiments, but you can't. You're incognito, remember?"

"I am. All right." He couldn't see the hunchback anymore anyway. The pitiful creature had already disappeared into the crowd.

"Come on, let's feed our faces," she said, again taking him by the elbow. They weaved through a slew of automobiles gridlocked at the intersection.

The young preacher was still looking back, searching for a glimpse of the hunchback, when they came to an abrupt stop. He turned to see a microphone poised before his face. The television news team blocked their path.

"Reverend Leo Barnett," said the reporter, a clean-cut man with curly black hair, wearing glasses and a three-piece blue suit, "what in the world are you, with your well-known stance on jokers' rights, doing here in the Edge?"

The young preacher felt his life passing before his eyes. He managed a weak smile. "Ah, my date and I are simply having a bite to eat."

"Do you have an announcement for the society pages?" the reporter asked slyly.

The corners of the young preacher's mouth turned. "I make it a policy never to answer questions of a personal nature. This young lady is my companion for the evening. She works at the new mission my church has opened in Jokertown, and she suggested we sample some of the fine cuisine the Edge has to offer."

"Some commentators think it strange, peculiar even, that a man who has opposed jokers' rights so stridently at his pulpit would be so concerned with the day-to-day plight of jokers. Just why did you open the Mission?"

The young preacher decided he didn't like the reporter's attitude. "I had a promise to keep, that's why I did it," he said curtly, trying to imply the interview was over. That was precisely the opposite of his true intention.

"And what was that promise? Who did you make it to? Your congregation?"

The reporter had taken the bait. Now the young preacher's major difficulty was in keeping a straight face. The information on his mind hadn't been made public before, and his instincts guessed these were the right circumstances to do so. "Well, if you insist."

"There's been a great deal of speculation on the matter, sir, and I think the people have a right to know."

"Well, I met a young man once. He had been infected by the wild card virus and had gotten himself in a great deal of trouble as a result. He asked to see me, and I came. We prayed together and he told me he knew I couldn't do anything for him, but he wanted me to promise to help as many jokers as I could, so maybe they wouldn't get into the same type of trouble as he did. I was very moved and so I promised. A few hours later he was executed by electrocution. I watched as twenty thousand volts of current shot him in a hot flash and fried him like a piece of bacon, and I knew I would have to keep that promise no matter what anyone else thought."

"He was executed?" the reporter asked stupidly.

"Yes, he was a first-degree murderer. He had turned some people into pillars of salt."

"You made that promise to Gary Gilmore?" the reporter asked incredulously, his face ashen.

"Absolutely. Though maybe he wasn't a joker, maybe some people would call him an ace, or an individual with some of the powers you'd expect from an ace. I don't really know. I'm only finding some of these things out."

"I see. And has your opening of the Jokertown mission had any effect on your position toward jokers' rights?"

"Not at all. The common man still must be protected, but I have always emphasized that we must deal with the victims of the virus compassionately."

"I see." The reporter's face remained ashen, while the sound man and the Minicam operator smiled smugly. Evidently they realized, as the young preacher realized, that the reporter lacked the quick wit necessary to ask a logical follow-up question.

But since the young preacher was feeling fairly merciful—as well as confident that he had just achieved his sixty-second "bite" on the news—he felt like giving the reporter a break. A slight break. "My companion and I must get something to eat, but I think we have time for one more question."

"Yes, there is something else I'm sure our viewers would like to know. You've made no secret of your presidential ambitions."

"That is true, but I really have nothing further to add on the subject right now."

"Just answer this, sir. You've just turned thirty-five, the minimum age for that office, but some of your potential opponents have stated that a man of thirty-five can't possibly have the experience in life that's necessary for the job. How do you respond to that?"

"Jesus was only thirty-three when he changed the world for all time. Surely a man who's reached the grand old age of thirty-five can have some positive effect. Now if you'd excuse me . . ." Taking Belinda May by the arm, he brushed past the reporter and the crew and walked into the restaurant.

"I'm sorry, Leo, I didn't know . . ." she said.

"That's all right. I think I handled them well enough, and besides, I've been meaning to tell that story for some time."

"Did you really meet Gary Gilmore?"

"Yes. It's been a fairly well kept secret. There really hadn't been the need to publicize it before now, though it might do the mission some good in the public relations arena."

"Then maybe you have met Mailer? He said he hadn't been able to confirm all the identities of the people who saw Gilmore toward the end."

"Please, we have to have keep secrets from one another. Otherwise what would we discover about each other tomorrow?"

"Would you like a table for two?" asked the maître d', a tuxedoed, fish-faced man weaing a water helmet for breathing purposes. The words from the speaker grill on the helmet gurgled eerily.

"Yes, in the back, please," said the young preacher.

When they were alone at the booth, Belinda May lit yet another cigarette and said, "If those reporters find out about us, would it help if we assure them we're only going to use the missionary position?"

V

Quasiman did not fear death, and death certainly did not fear him. Quasiman lived with a little piece of death in his soul every day, a little bit of terror and beauty, of blood and thunder. Fragments of his forthcoming demise perpetually crashed together with fleeting images of his previral past inside his brain.

How distant were those fragments? Quasiman had the distinct sensation the future might be closer than he had hoped.

He shuffled up to a newsstand and stood before the rows of girlie magazines. He thought how there had been something tantalizingly familiar about the face of the man he had bumped into, something that eluded him as parts of his brain twisted into another dimension. Quasiman would have dropped everything until enough of his brain had reassembled in one plane for him to remember, but right now he figured it was more important to remember why he had come to the Edge tonight in the first place.

Suddenly his hand became very cold. He looked down at it. It had gone somewhere else, and his wrist tapered off into a stub as if the hand had become transparent. He knew it was still attached because otherwise he would be feeling intense pain, as he had when an extradimensional creature had eaten a stray toe. The extreme cold numbed his arm all the way to his shoulder, but there was nothing he could do about that, except suffer until the hand returned. Which would be soon enough. Probably.

Even so, he couldn't help thinking about how Christ had visited a synagogue and cured a man who had a withered hand.

Something in his heart like faith told him Father Squid had sent him to the Edge tonight on a mission. Whether or not the idea for the mission had originated in Father Squid's fevered mind was a moot point—many from all walks of life requested assistance from the Church of Our Lady of Perpetual Misery, and Father Squid was only too happy to provide it, if he saw that only good could result.

Quasiman shuffled up and down the street, casing out the scene. His suspicions were aroused by a few of the men sitting at some tables on the sidewalk. The rumpled clothing of a man at the newsstand, come to think of it, had indicated he probably wasn't the type who'd spend so much time looking at investors' magazines. Finally, an unusual number of alert, grim-faced men just sat in their cars, watching, waiting. Several little pieces of death manifested themselves in Quasiman's brain, death that pointed, thank God, at these grim-faced men.

For a moment Quasiman saw the streets running red with blood. But a closer inspection of the environment indicated the vision had just been an optical illusion, caused by reflecting red neon lights off water collecting in a few large, shallow potholes.

The revelation could not, however, explain the smell of blood and fear, permeating the air like a memory that hadn't happened yet.

As important parts of the muscle group in his right thigh phased into another plane of existence, where the air had a slightly acidic quality, Quasiman shuffled to a street corner.

There, pretending to be a beggar, he would wait for the blood
and the fear to become real.

The memory of thunder echoed in his ears.

VI

"War is a bad thing for business," said the Man philosophically.
He sat, legs crossed, in a chair in the corner of the room,
beside a table and the other chair. He absently rolled his
half-smoked cigar in his fingers.

"It'sss especially bad for the losssers," said Wyrm with a
grin, sitting in the other chair.

Vito stood at the door with his arms folded across his chest
and felt something inside turn to ice. He had assumed, as
presumably the Man and the boys had assumed, that this
joker was just another businessman whose interests lay outside the law, just as their own did. Vito couldn't help feeling,
however, this Wyrm character had a hidden agenda.

If the head of the Calvino clan was as disturbed as Vito,
though, he gave no indication of it. He conducted himself
forcefully, secure in his position as the person who pulled the
strings on the other four men in the room. Of these, Mike
and Frank were simple enforcers; Vito wasn't particularly
afraid of them, but he wouldn't want to be on their bad side
either. It was always prudent to be a little afraid to Ralphy,
even when he was in a good mood.

Even so, Vito couldn't help but notice that the Man was
deliberately acting defferentially to this joker who couldn't
keep his forked tongue in his mouth. Thus far in the course of
their conference, whenever Wyrm had raised his voice, the
Man had soothed his feelings. When Wyrm made demands,
the Man had said he would see what he and the boys could
do to strike a balance. And whenever Wyrm dared the Man
to step over a line, the Man politely declined. Vito had to
admit to nursing some concern for the future of the Five
Families, if they'd have to kowtow to the jokers to survive.

"Besidesss, a man diesss a little every day," said Wyrm
with a cryptic smile. "What difference doesss it make if he
diesss all at once?

The Man laughed. His smile was condescending. If Wyrm
noticed the implied insult, he gave no indication. "Once I

believed as you," said the Man. "I took delight in times of trouble and took great relish at seeing my enemies fall. But that was before I got married and began raising a family. I began to yearn for a more orderly way of resolving differences. That is why we are meeting now, so that we can resolve our differences like civilized human beings."

"I'm not particularly human."

The Man's face reddened. He nodded. "Forgive me. I did not mean to offend."

Vito glanced at Ralphy, leaning against the wall beside a desk. Ralphy's cheek was twitching, a sign he was getting suspicious. The fingers of his right hand twitched too. Ralphy and the Man exchanged glances, and then as the Man turned back to Wyrm, Ralphy looked meaningfully at Mike and Frank, who sat on the bed, carefully watching the proceedings. Mike and Frank nodded.

Vito wasn't exactly sure of the meaning of all those signals, but he definitely wasn't going to ask.

"There has been much killing, much bloodshed," said the Man. "And for what? I do not understand. This is a big town. It is a gateway to the rest of the country. Surely there is enough business for all."

Wyrm shrugged. "You don't undersssstand. My asssociates strive for sssomething more than just lining their pocketsss."

"That is what I am trying to say," replied the Man, "though please don't get me wrong. Greed is a great and noble thing. It makes the world go round. It makes for the bull market."

Wyrm shrugged. "Bull or bear, it isss all the same to the man who ownsss the building where the market standsss. My asssociates claim our fair share of every businesss operating in thisss market. What you get out of it isss your own affair, but you will have to bargain with usss first."

Ralphy stood straight up. Mike and Frank both reached toward the guns in the holsters beneath their jackets, but they were restrained by a signal the Man made with his forefinger. The silence filled the room like the scent of a crisp pizza in a microwave, and Wyrm ran his forked tongue over his face as if anticipating the tasty morsels to come.

Vito debated which way he should duck.

The Man stared at Wyrm for several moments. He thoughtfully rubbed his double chin. He put his cigar in his mouth, took a lighter from his pocket, and in a few seconds had filled the room with the pungent odor of burning Cuban tobacco. "Vito, I am hungry." He reached for his wallet, which Ralphy took and gave to Vito. "Take my credit cards," said the Man, "and go to that sushi bar across the street. Order a generous selection. For six! Who knows? By the time you return, our business might be concluded and we'll be comfortably watching a hockey game. Isn't that right, Mr. Wyrm?"

Wyrm hissed in agreement.

"It's amazing how the game becomes much more exciting every year," said the Man, settling back comfortably in his chair. "Tonight's Ranger game should be a good one, shouldn't it, Mr. Wyrm?"

This time Wyrm merely nodded.

Hustling down the hall toward the elevator, Vito realized how relieved he was to be out of Wyrm's company. he imagined the Man would feel the same way, and Vito admired the manner in which his boss hid his discomfort. Wyrm seemed not to notice.

Of course you could never really be sure what a joker noticed, and what he simply chose to ignore.

VII

"What is it you people want?" the Man asked Wyrm angrily after Vito had left. "We're both businessmen. What is it that we can *reasonably* do to help us live together?"

"Wyrm hissed. "Yesss, that isss the question. The organization I represssent, like the organization you represssent, isss very large. It already hasss consssiderable influence. Ssso naturally it wantsss more."

The Man puffed his cigar. "Your ambition has not escaped me," he said sarcastically.

Wyrm grinned. "I didn't think it would. I am merely emphasssizing that, like yourself, I can't make promisesss for othersss."

"Oh, but I can," said the Man, making a subtle gesture that restrained Ralphy from giving "the signal" to Mike and Frank. "And I gather you can too, otherwise you wouldn't have taken the trouble to have this meeting with us—alone. We're not naive, Mr. Wyrm. You must have some bargaining leeway, otherwise there'd be no point in you being so very, very alone."

"You are alone, aren't you?" said Ralphy, completely ignoring the irate glare the Man shot at him as he walked past Wyrm to the window and peeked out the curtain, looking to the streets below.

"Of courssse," Wyrm replied.

Suddenly they heard the sounds of two men arguing in the hall. The tone quickly became violent. They heard the sound of a fist striking a jaw. Someone grunted and *thumped* hard against a wall. The impact made the floor shake. One of the men snarled a curse and then went *thump!* against the other wall, twice as loud as before.

Ralphy turned from the window and said to Mike and Frank, "Check it out." The noise of the altercation in the hallway continued unabated.

Mike and Frank walked from the room. Ralphy followed them to the door to make certain it was locked. They heard Mike say something, then the hallway quieted down.

"You still haven't answered my question," the Man said.

"What quessstion isss that?" asked Wyrm, glancing up at Ralphy as the enforcer returned to his position at the window.

"What can we do to help us live together?"

"Oh, I think I can come up with a *reasssonable* ansssswer."

Then there was a knock at the door.

"What is it?" Ralphy called out.

"You better'd come here." It was Frank.

"Good," said the Man, responding to Wyrm's remark. "The Calvino interests want to be reasonable."

Wyrm hissed, his tongue darting in and out.

Ralphy opened the door and barked, "What, for Christ's sake?"

His answer was a gunshot. The bullet ripped a hole the size of a silver dollar in Ralphy's back and sprayed the room with bright red blood. Ralphy was dead before he hit the floor. He twitched, his eyes staring blankly at the ceiling.

Standing in the doorway were two toughs wearing Mackintosh coats. Their faces were concealed by plastic masks that, even in his state of surprise and shock, the Man found to be strangely, disturbingly familiar. Between them was Frank, a gun held to his head.

There was another shot, and an eruption of blood and

brains sprayed from Frank's temple and splattered the door.
Frank slumped to the floor.

"Mike?" said the Man softly. It had been many years since
he had personally witnessed violence. He hadn't refrained
because he was afraid, or gotten soft in his old age, but
because his lawyers had advised him to conduct his affairs in
this manner. So he was a little slow to react, a little slow to
realize he was one hundred percent alone.

By the time he stood up, with the intention of calling to
his men on the street, Wyrm had already grabbed him. The
Man struggled, but Wyrm was too strong. The Man was like a
rag doll in his grip.

The last thing the Man saw was Wyrm's open mouth,
coming closer to his face. The Man closed his eyes in panic
and kept them closed as Wyrm kissed him. The Man tried to
scream, then unconsciousness claimed him as Wyrm bit off
his lips and spat them across the floor.

VIII

"Where is our food?" the young preacher asked, half-impatiently,
half-rhetorically. He saw the waitress coming their way, carrying an array of trays on suspiciously wide arms.

She stopped at a foursome two booths down and served
two plates of steamed seafood in kelp boats, plus one of
chilled noodles with peanut-miso sauce and another of a
variety of meats and vegetables deep-fried tempura style. A
large bowl of rice and replenishment of refreshments were
quickly added for the entire table.

The air conditioner carried a fresh whiff of the tempura to
the young preacher, and his mouth watered in anticipation.
The worm of envy gnawed in his soul as he made a quick
inspection of the lucky ones whose food had already arrived.
They were a team of double-daters. Three, including an
Oriental man, seemed normal enough, but he found himself
unable to pry his eyes away from the scarlet-skinned victim of
the virus, a beautiful woman with soft pink compound eyes
like a butterfly's, and two large blood-red antennae protrud-
ing from her forehead. She wore a low-cut gown that revealed
her shape to be enticingly, even staggeringly normal. He

deduced that the scintillating silver cape hung up on a nearby coatrack belonged to her.

The dining area of the sushi bar itself was L-shaped, with the front door and the cash register in the middle corner. The young preacher and Belinda May sat in the row of booths at the discreet furthermost edge of the shorter corridor, which was hidden from the storefront window that ran along most of the longer corridor. The young preacher distracted himself from the beautiful ace by watching the fish-faced maître d' seat a couple who laughed and made jokes between themselves. At the register booth was a somber young man whose slick black hair made him resemble some juvie or punk from a gangster movie.

"Leo, you're staring at that woman," said Belinda May, a mischievous light appearing in her eyes.

"I was not. I was looking at that boy."

"Hmmm. I bet he's some kind of fledgling gangster. They're all over the streets tonight, for some reason. Did you notice?"

"No, I didn't."

"Anyway, you were looking at that ace earlier."

"Well, yes. Who is she?"

"Her name is Pesticide. She's becoming quite well-known, thanks to that society column she writes for the *Jokertown Cry*. Anyway, if you're going to stare at any woman tonight, it's going to be me."

The young preacher raised his cup of coffee as if to make a toast. "It's a deal."

Then the worm of envy finally knew defeat, as the waitress brought their meal. In a few moments all thoughts of small talk were erased as the young preacher reached out for a piece of hirame flounder, its tender white color, like glistening ivory, beckoning him like a white, cool light. The cold rice was scrumptious, the taste of the flounder delectable.

Belinda May's fingers flittered over the selection of sushi and tempura on her tray. Quickly she settled on a piece of dark red maguro. She bit the tuna in half and chewed with an expression of ecstasy he remembered all too well.

He picked up a fantailed shrimp and bit off all but the tip. The shrimp was nudging its way down his throat like a pebble in a narrow water pipe when a sudden chilly blast of air whipped through the sushi bar. He glanced up to see the patrons in the other booths, including Pesticide, looking toward the door. A gang of young toughs had entered, dressed in mackintosh coats to a man. It was evident they had some sinister purpose in mind.

The fish-faced joker gurgled something to them via his helmet speaker, probably urging them to vacate the premises at once. The short tough who appeared to be their leader responded threateningly with a hammer, directed at the joker's water helmet.

Their faces, Leo thought, the muscles in his gut tightening. He barely noticed the young juvie, if that's what he was, slipping out the door. *Something about their faces . . .*

The toughs' faces were all the same, immobile, strangely devoid of life. The young preacher realized with a start the toughs were wearing plastic masks. The familiar, grinning likeness—an exaggerated pug nose and a lick of blond hair falling across the broad forehead—was distorted with a tone that would have been satirical if the toughs hadn't exuded such dark menace.

With a bolt of horror he recognized the face as his own. The toughs were wearing Leo Barnett masks!

He barely felt the restraining touch of Belinda May on his arm as he stepped from the booth. "Don't go, don't draw any attention to yourself!" she hissed. "They're Werewolves! A joker streetgang! And they know who you are!"

Her words reminded him that many jokers had publicly spoken of their hatred of him for the political and the moral stands he had taken in the past. Their overreaction had only hardened his followers in the belief that something had to be done to end the problem of the wild card virus. This in turn had hardened victims in their belief that something had to be done to end political repression. The young preacher trembled. What would he do if the Werewolves recognized him?

Wild, fearful thoughts that made him ashamed flashed through his brain. A moment ago he had been a semi-anonymous patron of a sushi bar; now he was a lightning rod that anyone in danger could point to in order to distract the Werewolves.

"For God's sake, sit down!" hissed Belinda May, yanking him down beside her. He landed with a thump.

And a hollow chill tore through his being as he saw the nearest of the masked faces turn toward him. That thump had been just loud enough. He instinctively put his hand over his mouth, as if to hide a belch or an untimely remark. And for the next few moments he dared to hope his ploy had worked, for the tough seemed content to use his tentacle to scratch the folds of skin hanging below his mask.

The maître d', meanwhile, was held motionless by the threat of the hammer above his helmet. One tough withdrew a gun from beneath his mackintosh. There was a commotion at the far end of the sushi bar, as the other patrons reacted to the situation.

Another tough withdrew a machete from his coat and tossed it into the air. He tapped the forehead of his mask—a gesture evidently indicating his telekinetic power over the weapon, which spun out of sight down the far corridor like a giant version of those deadly ninja stars Leo had seen thrown in kung fu movies.

There was a loud *ssshhhick!*

People screamed. Drawing their knives, two other toughs moved out of sight. The machete returned to the hand of the thrower like a boomerang. The tentacled tough, meanwhile, nodded at two comrades, pointed at someone, then at someone else, and then at Leo. The trio walked up the corridor. The young preacher barely noted the screams from the other corridor.

Sweet Jesus, not me, don't let them be heading for me, he thought. Now very much afraid that even the slightest motion would make the Werewolves notice him, he refrained from wiping the beads of sweat on his brow. Regardless of what happened next, the spotlight of the nation would be thrown on him. He prayed to the Lord, asking for guidance.

But none came. He could only wait, and hope. The ensuing seconds seemed like eons, endless stretches of time punctuated by the sounds of gunfire from outside, or screeching tires, and of people screaming. The Edge had erupted into a war zone.

The toughs with the knives, now bloody, returned. Their leader shouted to the ones approaching the young preacher, "What are you assholes doing? Let's get out of here!"

The tentacled tough looked back just long enough to say, "In a minute, man. We've got some business to take care of."

An obese tough with lobster's claws instead of hands stopped by the booth where Pesticide sat, put one claw under her chin, and lifted her face to his. One of the men with her almost made a move but was detained by a look from the third tough, who signaled very clearly with his handgun.

"Pretty, pretty," said the clawed tough. "You wouldn't be so proud to show your face in public if it was anything like mine."

The tentacled tough turned toward the young preacher and motioned as if to say, "Be right with you."

The tough menacing Pesticide became distracted by staccato machine gun fire from outside, and Pesticide took advantage of the oppotunity to bat his claw from her face with a tiny hand and stand up defiantly. Compared to the man she saw facing, she seemed fragile, helpless, and small.

Meanwhile the young preacher's sense of outrage grew, overpowering both fear and common sense.

The sushi bar alarm began to clang deafeningly, with no sign of abating.

The leader of the toughs said, "That was a stupid thing to do, fishface!" and smashed his hammer down on the maître d's water helmet.

The joker immediately began coughing, unable to draw oxygen from the air. He cut his hands on the shards of his helmet as he brought them to his throat, as if warding off an invisible strangler.

While everyone was preoccupied with the maître d's death throes, a strange yellow light began to glow from within Pesticide. It became so bright that her clothing resembled gossamer thrown over a spotlight. Her entire skeleton became visible, sheathed by the outlines of her skin and the dim silhouettes of her inner organs.

A black force gathering inside her became evident.

She opened her mouth, as if to scream. Instead an intense light like that of a laser stabbed from her mouth and struck the lobster-handed tough.

The black force rushed up her throat.

And came out of her mouth.

And followed the path of the light.

It was a horde of scarlet insects, wing-backed and hideous, chirping like the incessant chorus of a nightmare. They covered the tough like a swarm of locusts before he could react. They began chewing immediately, chewing through his coat, through his mask, through the shells of his claws—burrowing inside him in a matter of seconds.

The tough screamed and fell backward onto the table of an empty booth. He rolled into the seat and beat what was left of his claws frantically on his body, futilely attempting to stop the horde of insects from continuing their grisly meal. Through it all Pesticide stood motionless, shining, staring at him with lifeless eyes that in the wake of her inner glow resembled ebony jewels.

She did not notice the tough with the gun point the barrel at her head. The shot that rang out was only dimly muffled by the clanging of the alarm. Presicide's brains splattered against the wall and onto the friend beside her. She fell, dead instantly, into his arms. The tough backed away, pointing his gun at her other two companions to hold them off.

The leader called out, "Come on! Let's get the fuck out of here!"

Belinda May shouted, "No, Leo, no!"

For the young preacher had already given in to his rage and charged the two remaining toughs in the corridor. He had no idea exactly what he planned to do. He only knew Pesticide's only crime had been defending herself, however strangely, against their aggression.

His ill-defined plans were quickly aborted when he was stopped by a tentacled tough—the Werewolf's arm was elongating from his sleeve! It wrapped around the young preacher's neck and lifted him from the floor like a doll caught in a hangman's noose. The young preacher kicked and waved his arms about; he attempted to scream in defiance, but the hold of the tentacle was too tight. All he could really do was choke. He had just enough air to breathe, no more. Still he continued to fight and kick.

Something hard struck him at the back of the head. It was the ceiling. He felt the world swirl around him as the tough partially retracted his tentacle.

The touch drew him close. He stared into the weird gray eyes behind the mask. "Look what I've got," the tough said. "How does it feel to be staring into your own face, preacher? It isn't pretty to live in fear, is it?"

The young preacher half-screamed, half-choked.

The tough laughed unpleasantly. "I have to thank you for providing us with something to play with after the evening's entertainment is over. Don't worry. She'll be returned to you unharmed. Only her pride will be a little damaged."

The young preacher turned into an animal at that moment, a trapped, frenzied animal. His weak fists beat furiously but vainly at the tentacle. He heard Belinda May scream but didn't catch exactly what was happening to her because he felt himself rising. His last coherent vision was that of the dead tough still being eaten by the insects, who were slowing down, now that their host had died. Even so, half the tough's torso had already been consumed, as well as most of his arms and thighs. Chirping insects listlessly poked through the joker's eyes and crawled out on what remained of the mask, to breathe their last.

The young preacher's last coherent thought was, *Oh, well. At least no one can fault me for fainting—not under these circumstances.*

Then his head struck a beam, and the lights went out.

IX

Mother of mercy, is this the end of Vito? thought the young hood as he ran from the sushi bar into the street. For a moment he hoped he had been imagining everything, that the Werewolves were just out on an insignificant robbing spree, and that he would return to the hotel room to find the Man incredibly incensed that he had left the sushi bar before even placing an order. Then the shooting started.

Vito hit the sidewalk and rolled beneath an automobile. He bruised his knee against the concrete and scraped his forehead against the metal, but except for being inconvenienced by the trickle of blood flowing into his left eye, he was way beyond caring about minor injuries. Judging from how things were going so far, he would be lucky to survive the night.

Across the street two of the boys were being attacked by more members of the Werewolves street gang. One of the boys managed to stab a Werewolf in the chest, but as the blood spurted high in the air, the Werewolf behind him cut his throat from ear to ear. It became difficult to tell who's blood was whose. The other boy pulled out his gun but only managed to get a single shot off—getting a Werewolf smack between the eyes of his plastic mask—before he was sliced to ribbons by a slew of attackers. Indeed the Werewolves, apparently unimpressed by the fact that their victims were decidedly dead, continued to cut them both up with such frenzy that Vito feared they might throw the ensuing pieces of meat to the rest of the gang.

Of course the rest of the Werewolves were a little too busy at the moment to notice. Chaos had erupted on the streets of the Edge. Nats and jokers alike ran in every direction, taking cover wherever they could find it, which was nowhere to be found. There were simply too many bullets flying about for anybody to be safe for long. Those Werewolves not engaged in personal combat with the members of the Calvino Family indiscriminately fired machine guns in every direction, sometimes cutting down their fellow gang members in their efforts to get everyone who even looked like they might be a Calvino. The members of the Calvino Family reacted pretty much in kind, except for those trying to get away in their cars.

Vito covered his head with his hands and watched as a Werewolf stood before an oncoming automobile and sprayed the front windshield with bullets. Vito couldn't tell if the driver bought it or if he merely ducked. In any case the guy in the passenger seat lost the majority of his brains. The car plowed into the attacking Werewolf and then carried along several pedestrians until it crushed them against a parked car. A few survived long enough to know their last few seconds would be spent waiting for the cars to erupt into flame. The plume of fire was spectacular. Pieces of flaming metal and scorched meat flew high in the air, and they landed on the ground in the sort of slow-motion ballet of violence Vito had thought only happened in the movies.

Vito scrambled to the rear of the car he was under, figuring he'd be safer if he was as far away as possible from all that hot debris. He saw a fight happening right next to him. He could only see the legs of the people involved, but he gathered a panic-stricken tourist was trying to wrestle a gun away from a Werewolf. The guy's girlfriend was trying to stop him. Vito was still trying to decide whom he should root for when the Werewolf succeeded in knocking the guy down. The guy landed on his butt, doubled over with the wind knocked out of him. His girl—a black chick in a tight green dress—knelt beside him and said something. Vito couldn't hear what because of all the noise going down, but whatever it was, it didn't do either any good, because two seconds later the pair was riddled with bullets and lying in a pool of blood.

Vito's stomach tightened into a slab as he watched the Werewolf walk away. Vito resolved to stay where he was until one side was wiped out or the cops arrived, whichever came first. He wasn't going to be like some fool showing off to his girlfriend, and he wasn't going to have any stories to brag about to whoever was left in the Calvino clan tomorrow. He was going to survive, and nothing more. That would be enough.

Across the street a couple of fool Werewolves threw Molotov cocktails. Vito imagined he was a bug, lying low in a pile of leaves, hoping if he imagined hard enough, then maybe on some level he would become one. Even then, he thought, being a bug might still be too big.

Vito turned around to see a familiar pair of legs kneeling beside the dead couple. The person was low enough so Vito could see his face. It was the hunchback, making the sign of the cross. Vito couldn't help wondering just how intelligent this nut-case really was.

Suddenly the hunchback turned his head, and Vito found himself staring directly into the nut-case's eyes.

He believed he saw many things happening there. The eyes quickly misted as if they were peering into some far-off place just around the corner. Fear manifested itself in the hunchback's eyes. His face lost all color, and he opened his mouth to say something.

But whatever he had on his mind, it was already too late to say it. In that brief second before Vito was engulfed in the flames of the Molotov cocktail that smashed under the car, he was curiously aware that the hunchback recoiled from something that hadn't happened yet.

X

The young preacher woke up on the floor of the sushi bar. The bar was packed with folks attempting to escape the chaos outside, which, from what he could hear, resembled one of the more horrendous visions from the *Book of Revelations*.

The place where the young preacher lay, however, was

nearly empty. It contained just a few corpses and a lot of dead insects.

Belinda May was nowhere to be found.

The young preacher rose, brushed off a few dead insects clinging to his jacket and trousers, and then sat down in the nearest booth to nurse his aching head. He touched the spot where the throbbing was the greatest. When he took his fingers away, they were flecked with dried blood.

From outside he heard the shrill sound of approaching sirens. The police were coming. He hoped they were bringing with them a full complement of paramedics. Of course there was still all that shooting and screaming going on outside too, so the scene from the good book wasn't over yet.

Suddenly the sushi bar was racked from the shock waves of a nearby explosion. The young preacher dived under the booth and struck his head against the pedestal. He didn't mind. After what he had already been through, a tad more excruciating pain wasn't going to make that much difference.

He crawled on the floor through a pile of dead bugs, under the limp legs of the dead Pesticide, and wondered where Belinda May was. He couldn't think straight, but he knew he couldn't let his mental fog prevent him from finding her. What would the people say? What would the Lord say, or the reporters? Worse, what would she say if he tried to have her again and discovered he didn't have the courage to brave fire and brimstone for the honor of parting her like the Red Sea?

He was vaguely aware of people trying to stop him as he got up and staggered into the street where the ruins of a car burned. There weren't nearly as many panic-stricken people running about as he had expected. Bodies, bloody or burned to a crisp, were strewn all over the sidewalks. The young preacher hoped the television crew was picking all this up.

Where's Belinda May? he wondered.

Then he saw the tentacled tough in the middle of the street. The tough held a limp Belinda May high, daring others to make her a target.

The tough approached some hoods with machine guns.

The hoods were beaten and battered, but they were still alive. And they were lifting their guns.

The tough lowered Belinda May. He was going to use her as a shield!

XI

Now that it was too late to make a difference, Quasiman remembered that Father Squid had sent him to the Edge to prevent Wyrm from making a hit on a Mafia don.

Of course neither Quasiman, Squid, or the individual who had provided the information about the hit had guessed that Wyrm would cover his tracks with a sea of blood. It was proving to be an effective, if brutal, idea. And although Quasiman knew no one would blame him for being unable to prevent the bloodshed of the evening, he hated himself for not having done anything to prevent all this suffering.

He had seen so many people die. A few details were lost as portions of his brain phased in and out of reality, but nothing could diminish the profound sense of desolation that assailed him. The worst death he had seen was that of the kid hiding beneath that car. He'd watched the flames engulf the kid before the event had actually happened. Maybe that was why it had been so unnerving.

But the night wasn't over yet. Quasiman had seen the blood, but the thunder was still to come.

Quasiman belatedly noticed the sounds of the approaching sirens as he decided he might as well split with the rest of the survivors. A few hoods and Werewolves still battled on the street, but Wyrm had doubtlessly made himself scarce long ago. Quasiman was still visualizing where he wanted to be when he saw the Werewolf, an unconscious woman in his tentacle above his head, walking down the middle of the street toward a couple of hoods. The hoods lifted their weapons.

Quasiman didn't need precognitive senses to guess what might happen next. He knew he had to help the woman, somehow.

He was about to make a turn through space when he saw

the man with the familiar face rushing toward the Werewolf
and the woman. The blasting reverberating in Quasiman's
head wasn't exactly thunder.

XII

If the young preacher had given the matter a serious thought,
he would have gotten down on his knees and prayed. Instead
he ran as fast as he could toward the Werewolf and knocked
him down. The hood's tentacle snapped like a whip, flinging
Belinda May to safety. She landed on the hood of an automobile. At the same time the Werewolf and the young preacher
struck the ground, the two members of the Calvino clan
pulled the triggers of their machine guns.

Surprisingly the young preacher felt no anticipation for
the next life to come. Instead he felt a curious sense of regret,
along with a particular, only slightly contradictory sense of
relief. He drew his mind in upon itself and tightening it up
into a psychic ball, hurled it to a place where he had once
dared not look.

The gunshots were like thunderclaps magnified to an
infinite power, and he almost visualized the bullets speeding
through the barrels. If this was to be the last nanosecond of
his life, well then, he would live it gladly. It was still a long
time.

Enveloped by cold, he felt himself going down. Going
down, down, down into a hell colder than any polar nightmare. He felt his soul dissipating. Was this what death was
like? Would he soon envision himself lying on the street,
surrounded by the others who had died before him? Would
he then be inexorably pulled toward a beckoning white light,
where the Virgin Mary and Jesus Christ stood side by side
with his own mother, awaiting him with outstretched arms?
Would he know at last what Heaven was like?

Why then did he feel as if his mind were being ripped
apart in a thousand directions? A hundred flashes of intense
heat alternated with a hundred flashes of absolute zero. He
suddenly believed all his concepts of eternity were just
timepieces glimpsed in a dream, his concepts of infinity
motes in a sandbox. The young preacher couldn't escape the

notion that he had merged, somehow, with all conceivable times and places—a prelude to merging with the inconceivable times and places that lay just beyond the confines of reality.

Death was turning out to be a more complicated experience than he had ever imagined. He wondered if the bullets had already penetrated his body, if his skull was being shattered, and his heart and lungs perforated.

Thankfully there was no pain. Yet. Perhaps he would be spared that one unpleasant aspect of his death.

It was strange, though, to feel so whole and complete when he was actually coming apart.

It was strange still that the nothingness, at first incomprehensible and indescribable, suddenly became just an expanse of concrete, lined at varying intervals, just like a sidewalk.

It was strangest of all to think that instead of lying in the street beside the dead tentacled Werewolf, he found himself still alive. The sidewalk was drenched with blood, none of it, thankfully, his.

But what was that weight on top of him? How had it gotten there?

The weight slid to the sidewalk beside him. It was the hunchbacked joker he had spoken harshly to earlier. Only this time the hunchback lay face up, as haggard as a corpse, and was sinking half an inch into the concrete. The young preacher could only guess how, but he was certain the hunchback was paying the price for saving him.

Suddenly someone jammed a microphone in his face. He looked up to see the television reporter, flanked by his remote team, leaning down. The sound man had a bloody, makeshift bandage over his wirst, and the reporter a fresh wound across his forehead. The camera was on. The sound was on. And the reporter said, "Hey, Reverend Barnett, how are you feeling? Do you have any words for your—"

But before the young preacher could answer, a policeman yanked the reporter away. Another policeman grabbed the young preacher and tried to pull him away from the hunchback. The wail of sirens blasted the air with shrill vibrations, and a horde of rotating red and blue lights added an entirely new level of surreality to the scene.

"Get the fuck away from me!" the young preacher shouted, breaking away from the policeman.

He was vaguely aware of the newsman saying softly into his mike, "You heard it on Channel Four first, folks—a minister using an expletive in public. I'm sure a lot of Reverend Barnett's constituents are wondering what this world's coming to. . . ."

The young preacher felt a flash of anger at the impertinent bozo, but he decided to be patient and beg God to curse him later. Right now all he was concerned about was the ace, or joker, or whatever, who had saved him. He knelt beside the man, who was already sinking deeper into the sidewalk. A paramedic with a confused expression knelt beside the pair.

"Save him!" the young preacher implored. "You've got to save this man!"

"How?" asked the paramedic helplessly. "I don't know what the matter is—and besides, I can't even touch him!"

It was true. The paramedic's hands had penetrated into the hunchback's body. The paramedic yelped and jerked them out and stuck them beneath his armpits. He shivered as if he had been immersed in a deep freeze. The young preacher remembered feeling cold while he thought he was dying. A small, dark part of that cold still resided in his soul like an unwanted friend.

He realized nothing the paramedic or anyone could do would help the hunchback. The hunchback was gradually becoming just an outline of his former self. Even as he watched, the hunchback sank another half inch into the concrete. The poor man's glazed eyes stared at the sky, and his breathing was tortured, as if whatever kind of air he was gasping at was unsuitable for the job at hand.

"Who are you?" Leo asked. "How can we help you?"

The man blinked his eyes. It was hard to tell just how lucid he was. "My name is . . . Quasiman," he whispered. "I've never jaunted with so much weight before . . . so hard . . . so hard even now to hold myself together. . . ." He coughed.

The young preacher looked up to see Belinda May kneeling down beside him. "Are you all right?" he asked curtly but not without feeling.

"Yes," she replied. "What happened to you?"

"I'm not sure, but I think this man was responsible."

"My God—I remember him! Leo, you've got to help him."

"How? I can't even touch him."

That old mischievous light returned to Belinda May's eyes. "You're a preacher," she said in a tone greatly resembling the one she had used when she'd said she wanted to go to bed with him. "Heal the poor bastard!"

It had been many years since the young preacher had performed an act of faith healing. He had refrained from the activity, having been advised that it didn't look good on videotape, especially for a man planning a presidential bid.

Even so, he couldn't let this noble spirit be snuffed out. Not if it was somehow in his . . . in *God's* power. He looked up to the sky. The clouds, pregnant with rain, were occasionally illuminated by flashes of lightning; their thunder was only a soft rumble. He breathed deeply. He reached out to those clouds, to the earth beneath the concrete of this city, to the dark forces of creation. He gathered it all into his spirit, and into a single ball of energy.

Then he reached inside Quasiman. The spectrum of sensations in his fingers clearly originated someplace he would never know—at least during this lifetime.

He forced himself to be calm, to ignore the cold, to disassociate himself from the itching of his hands, and the overwhelming numbness of his fingertips. And when he believed he had succeeded, he said with all the passion he could muster, "Heal, you goddamn son-of-a-bitch! *Heal!*"

Finally it began to rain. The thunder erupted directly overhead as if a nuclear device were ripping the sky apart.

XIII

That night over fifty people died at the Edge. A hundred more were seriously injured. The carnage, however, wasn't the lead-in story on the news that night, nor was it the biggest headline on most of the front pages across the country. After all, the gang war had been going on for some time, and the fact that scores of innocent people had been caught in that grisly crossfire was unfortunate, but not really of much consequence so far as the day-to-day development of the news was concerned.

There's a big place between New York and Los Angeles. It's known as the American Heartland, and for the people who live there, the story of the hour was the one about the

Reverend Leo Barnett proclaiming his candidacy for president of the United States. He had laid his hands on the outline of some poor joker and had brought him back from an involuntary trip to parts unknown. He had done something no one had ever done before—using only the power of his faith, he had healed a joker. He had proved that the grandest power on earth was the love of the Lord and of Jesus Christ, and he had put some of that love in the body of a creature whose body had been polluted by that obscene alien virus. Even the liberal news media, which had captured that event for all the world to see on videotape, had to admit that the Reverend Leo Barnett had done an amazing thing. Maybe it didn't qualify him to be president, but it certainly set him apart from the pack as someone to watch.

It also helped that immediately after healing the joker and watching the paramedics carry him off on a stretcher, the Reverend Leo Barnett didn't consult with his advisers or wait to see how the incident played on the news or how it sat with the public, he simply walked up to the array of cameras and microphones and announced that God had said the time had come for him to declare his candidacy. He demonstrated, clearly and forcefully, that he could make a decision and act on it.

Reverend Leo Barnett's standing in the polls became very high, very respectable, almost immediately. Of course a few of the voters were a little concerned about what he was doing in the Edge in the first place, especially with regard to that hotel room he and the young mission worker had checked into, but it wasn't as if either one was married or anything. And there had been talk, which neither would confirm or deny, of an impending engagement announcement. Women in the Democratic party, as it turned out, were particularly impressed that the Reverend Leo Barnett might have found his true love and his political destiny on the same night. If true, then perhaps all that carnage hadn't been in vain.

If God doesn't judge America, he'll have to apologize to Sodom and Gomorrah.

—REVEREND LEO BARNETT,
presidential candidate

All the King's Horses

III

The junkyard sat hard by the oily green waters of New York Bay, way at the end of Hook Road. Tom got there early, undid the padlock, and swung open the gates in the high chain-link fence. He parked his Honda beside the sagging tin-roofed shack where Joey DiAngelis had once lived with his father, Dom, back in the days when the junkyard had been a going concern, and sat for a moment with his arms folded across the top of the steering wheel, remembering.

He'd spent endless Saturday afternoons inside that shack, back when it had still been habitable, reading old issues of *Jetboy* to Joey after they'd heisted their comic book collections back from a PTA bonfire.

Over there, back behind the shed, was where Joey used to work on his cars, long before he turned into Junkyard Joey DiAngelis, king of the demolition derby circuit.

And way in back where no one ever went, behind that mountain of rusted junkers, that was where he and Joey had welded armor plate over the frame of a VW Beetle to make the first shell. Later, much later, after Dom had died and Tom had bought the junkyard from Joey and shut it down, they'd dug the bunker under the junkyard, but they hadn't been that sophisticated at the start. A greasy tarp was about all the concealment they had.

Tom climbed out of the car and stood with his hands shoved deep into the pockets of his shapeless old brown suede jacket, breathing the salt air off the bay. It was a chilly day. Out across the water a garbage barge passed slowly, flocks of seagulls circling around it like feathered flies. You could see the vague outline of the Statue of Liberty, but Manhattan had vanished in the morning haze.

Vanished or not, it was out there, and on a clear night you could see the lights shining off the towers. A hell of a view. In

130

Hoboken and Jersey City run-down houses and cramped condos that offered views like this went for six figures. Constable Hook was zoned for industrial use, and Tom's land was surrounded by an import-export warehouse, a railroad siding, a sewage treatment plant, and an abandoned oil refinery, but Steve Bruder said that none of that mattered.

That big a chunk of land, right on the waterfront, it was just *prime* for development, Bruder had said when Tom told him he was thinking of selling the old junkyard. He should know; he'd already made himself a millionaire with real estate speculation in Hoboken and Weehawken, rehabilitating old tenements into expansive condos for yuppies from Manhattan. Bayonne was next, Steve said. In ten years all this rust-belt industry would be gone, replaced by new housing developments, but they could be first and make the biggest killing.

Tom had known Steve Bruder since childhood and cordially loathed him most of that time, but for once Bruder's words were music to his ears. When Bruder offered to buy the junkyard outright, the price made Tom's head spin, but he resisted the temptation. He'd thought this all out beforehand. "No," he said. "I'm not selling. I want to be a full partner in the development. I provide the land, you provide the money and know-how, we split the profits fifty-fifty."

Bruder had given him a shark's slow smile. "You're not as dumb as you look, Tudbury. Someone been coaching you, or is this all your own idea?"

"Maybe I've finally gotten smart," Tom said. "Now what is it, yes or no? Shit or get off the pot, asshole."

"It's not nice to call your partner an asshole, wimp," Bruder said, extending his hand. He had a very firm handshake, but Tom was careful not to wince.

Tom looked at his watch. Steve would be bringing the bankers by in about an hour. Just a formality, he said. The loan would be candy; the property screamed with potential. Once they had the line of credit, they could get the zoning changed. By spring they'd have the junk cleared out and the land subdivided into building lots.

Tom wasn't sure why he'd come so early . . . unless it was just to remember.

It was funny that so many of his important memories were

rooted in this junkyard . . . but somehow appropriate, considering the way his life had gone.

But all of that was about to change. Forever. Thomas Tudbury was about to become a rich man.

Tom walked slowly around the shack, kicked at a threadbare tire in his path, then lifted it with his mind. He held it five feet off the ground, gave it a brisk telekinetic shove that set it spinning, and counted. At eight the tire began to wobble; at eleven it fell. Not bad. Back in his teens, before he'd crawled into a shell, he could have held that tire up all day . . . but that was when the power had been Tom's, before he'd given it away to the Turtle. Like he'd given so much else.

"Sell the junkyard?" Joey had said when Tom told him the plan. "You're serious about this, aren't you? That's one hell of a bridge to burn. What if they find the bunker?"

"They'll find a fucking hole in the ground. Maybe they'll worry about it for five, ten minutes. Then they'll push some dirt into it and it'll be over."

"What about the shells?"

"There are no shells," Tom said. "Just some junk that used to be shells. All the king's horses and all the king's men, remember? I'll go out there one night and turn Turtle just long enough to drop them into the bay."

"Hell of a waste," Joey said. "Weren't you the one telling me how much money and sweat you put into those fucking things?" He took a long swig of beer and shook his head. Joey looked more like his father Dom every year. The same skinny arms, the same rock-hard beer-belly, the same salt-and-pepper hair. Tom remembered when it had been pure black, always falling down into his eyes. In those days before pull-tabs, Joey used to wear a church key around his neck on a leather thong, even when he'd donned a cheap frog mask and gone to Jokertown with the Turtle to help roust Dr. Tachyon from an alcoholic pout.

That was twenty-three years ago. Tachyon hadn't aged, but Joey had, and so had Tom. He'd grown old without growing up, but all that was changing now. The Turtle was dead, but Tom Tudbury's life had just begun.

He strolled away from the shoreline. Broken headlights stared at him like so many blind eyes from mountains of dead cars, and once he felt live eyes and turned to see a huge gray rat peering out of the damp, rotten interior of a legless Victorian sofa. In the depths of the junkyard he passed between two long rows of vintage refrigerators, all the doors carefully removed. On the far side was a flat, bare patch of earth where a square metal plate was set into the ground. It was heavy, Tom knew from past experience. He stared at the big ring set into the metal, concentrated, and on the third try managed to shift it enough to reveal the dark tunnel mouth below.

Tom sat on the edge of the hole and dropped down carefully into darkness. At the bottom he fumbled against the wall and found the flashlight he'd hung there, then walked down the cold, damp tunnel until he emerged in the bunker.

The old shells waited for him in silence.

He'd have to get rid of them soon, he knew. But not today. The bankers wouldn't go poking around back here. They just wanted to eyeball the property, see the view, maybe sign a few papers. There was plenty of time to dump this junk in the bay; it wasn't going anywhere.

Painted daisies and peace symbols covered shell two, the once-bright paint now faded and chipped. Just looking at it was enough to bring back memories of old songs, old causes, old certainties. The March on Washington, folk-rock blaring from his speakers, MAKE LOVE NOT WAR scrawled across his armor. Gene McCarthy had stood on that shell and spoken with his customary wry eloquence for a solid twenty minutes. Pretty girls in halter tops and jeans would fight for the chance to ride on top. Tom remembered one in particular, with cornflower-blue eyes beneath an Indian headband and straight blond hair that fell past her ass. She loved him, she'd whispered as she lay across the shell. She wanted him to open the hatch, let her in; she wanted to see his face and look into his eyes; she didn't care if he was a joker like they said, she loved him and she wanted him to ball her, right then, right there.

She'd given him a hard-on that felt like a crowbar in his jeans, but he hadn't opened the shell. Not then, not ever. She wanted the Turtle, but inside the armor was only Tom Tudbury. He wondered where she was now, what she looked like, what she remembered. By now she might have a daughter as old as she'd been the night she'd tried to crawl inside his shell.

Tom ran his hand over the cold metal and traced another peace symbol in the dust that lay thick on the armor. He'd really felt as though he was making a difference in those days. He was a part of a movement, stopping a war, protecting the weak. The day the Turtle had made Nixon's enemy list had been one of the proudest of his life.

All the king's horses and all the king's men . . .

Beyond the painted shell was another hulk, larger, plainer, more recent. That one had seen some hard service too. He paused by the dent where some lunatic had bounced a cannonball off him. His head was ringing for weeks afterward. Underneath, Tom knew, if you looked in the right place, you could find the imprint of a small human hand sunk four inches deep into the armor plate, a souvenir left him by a rogue ace the press called the Sculptress. She was a cute bit of business; metal and stone flowed like water under her hands. She was a media darling until she started using those hands to shape doorways into bank vaults. The Turtle delivered her to the cops, wondering how they were going to stop her from just walking out again, but she never tried it. Instead she'd accepted a pardon and gone to work for the Justice Department. Sometimes it was a very strange world.

There wasn't much left of either shells two or three except for the frame and armor plate. The interiors had long since been gutted for parts. Cameras, electronics, heaters, fans, you name it; all that stuff cost money, of which Tom had never had an overabundance. So you borrowed from the old shells to build the new, where you could. It didn't help much, it still cost a fortune. By his rough figuring, he'd had about fifty grand tied up in the shell the goddamned Takisians had so casually spit out the airlock, most of it borrowed. He was still making payments.

In the darkest corner of the bunker he found the oldest shell of all. Even the layers of badly welded armor plate couldn't quite obliterate the familiar lines of the VW Beetle they'd started with back in the winter of 1963. Inside, he knew, it was dark and stuffy, with barely enough room to turn around, and none of the amenities of the later shells. Shining the flashlight over the exterior, he sighed at his naivete. Black-and-white TV sets, a Volkswagen body, twenty-year-old electrical wire, vacuum tubes. It was more or less intact, if only because it was so hopelessly obsolete. The very idea that he'd crossed the bay in it just a few months prior made him want to shudder.

Still . . . it was the first shell, with the strongest memories of all. He looked at it for a long time, remembering how it had been. Building it, testing it, flying it. He remembered the first time he'd crossed over to New York. He'd been scared shitless. Then he'd found the fire, teked that woman to safety—even now, all these years later, he could see the dress she'd been wearing vividly in his mind's eye, the flames licking up the fabric as he'd floated her down to the street.

"I tried," he said aloud. His voice echoed strangely in the dimness of the bunker. "I did some good." He heard scrabbling noises behind him. Rats probably. It had gotten so bad that he was talking to rats. Who was he trying to convince?

He looked at the shells, three of them in a crooked row, so much scrap metal, destined for the bottom of the bay. It made him sad. He remembered what Joey had said, about what a waste it was, and that gave him the beginnings of an idea. Tom pulled a pad out of his back pocket and jotted a quick note to himself, smiling. He'd been playing shell games for twenty years, and he never did find the pea beneath any of them. Well, maybe he could turn the old shells into a whole *can* of peas.

Steve Bruder arrived forty-five minutes later, wearing leather driving gloves and a Burberry coat, with two bankers in his long brown Lincoln Town Car. Tom let him do all the talking as they walked around the property. The bankers admired the view and politely deigned not to notice the junkyard rats.

They signed the papers that afternoon and celebrated with dinner at Hendrickson's.

Concerto for
Siren and Serotonin

III

The wind came and went like heavy surf, vibrating streetside windowpanes, driving icy pellets against the stone lions flanking the entranceway. These sounds were intensified as the door to the Jokertown Clinic was opened. A man entered and began stamping his feet and brushing snow from his dark blue blazer. He made no effort to close the door behind him.

Madeleine Johnson, sometimes known as the Chickenfoot Lady, doing a partial front desk deathwatch for her friend Cock Robin, with whom she had a good thing going, looked up from her crossword puzzle, stroked her wattles with her pencil, and squawked, "Close the damn door, mister!"

The man lowered the handkerchief with which he had been wiping his face and stared at her. She realized then that his eyes were faceted. His jaw muscles bunched and unbunched.

"Sorry," he said, and he drew the door closed. Then he turned his head slowly, seeming to study everything in the room, though with those eyes it was difficult to tell for certain. Finally, "I've got to talk to Dr. Tachyon," he said.

"The doctor is out of town," she stated, "and he's going to be away for some time. What is it that you want?"

"I want to be put to sleep," he said.

"This isn't a veterinary clinic," she told him, and regretted it a moment later when he moved forward, for he developed a distinct halo and began emitting sparks like a static electricity generator. She doubted this had much to do with virtue, for his teeth were bared and he clenched and unclenched his hands as if anticipating strenuous activity.

"This—is—an—emergency," he said. "My name is Croyd Crenson, and there is probably a file. Better find it. I get violent."

She squawked again, leaped and departed, leaving two pinfeathers to drift in the air before him. He put out a hand and leaned upon her desk, then mopped his brow again. His gaze fell upon a half-filled coffee cup beside her newspaper. He picked it up and chugged it.

Moments later there came a clattering sound from the hallway beyond the desk. A blond, blue-eyed young man halted at the threshold and stared at him. He had on a green and white polo shirt, a stethoscope and a beach-boy smile. From the waist down he was a palomino pony, his tail beautifully braided. Madeleine appeared behind him and fluttered.

"He's the one," she told the centaur. "He said, 'violent.'"

Still smiling, the quadrapedal youth entered the room and extended his hand. "I'm Dr. Finn," he said. "I've sent for your file, Mr. Crenson. Come on back to an examination room, and you can tell me what's bothering you while we wait for it."

Croyd took his hand and nodded.

"Any coffee back there?"

"I think so. We'll get you a cup."

Croyd paced the small room, swilling coffee, as Dr. Finn read over his case history, snorting on several occasions and at one point making a noise amazingly like a whinny.

"I didn't realize you were the Sleeper," he said finally, closing the file and looking at his patient. "Some of this material has made the textbooks." He tapped the folder with a well-manicured finger.

"So I've heard," Croyd replied.

"Obviously you have a problem you just can't wait for your next cycle to clear up," Dr. Finn observed. "What is it?"

Croyd managed a bleak smile. "It's the matter of getting on with the crapshoot, of actually going to sleep."

"What's the problem?"

"I don't know how much of this is in the file," Croyd told him, "but I've a terrible fear of going to sleep—"

"Yes, there is something about your paranoia. Perhaps some counseling—"

Croyd punched a hole in the wall.

"It's not paranoia," he said, "not if the danger is real. I could die during my next hibernation. I could wake up as the most disgusting joker you can imagine, with a normal sleep-cycle. Then I'd be stuck that way. It's only paranoia if the fear is groundless, isn't it?"

"Well," Dr. Finn said, "I suppose we could call it that if the fear is a really big thing, even if it is justified. I don't know. I'm not a psychiatrist. But I also saw in the file that you tend to take amphetamines to keep from falling asleep for as long as you can. You must know that that's going to add a big chemical boost to whatever paranoia is already present."

Croyd was running his finger around the inside of the hole he had punched in the wall, rubbing away loose pieces of plaster.

"But of course a part of this is semantics," Dr. Finn went on. "It doesn't matter what we call it. Basically you're afraid to go to sleep. This time, though, you feel that you should?"

Croyd began cracking his knuckles as he paced. Fascinated, Dr. Finn counted each cracking noise. When the seventh popping sound occurred, he began to wonder what Croyd would do when he was out of knuckles.

"Eight, nine, ten . . ." he subvocalized.

Croyd punched another hole in the wall.

"Uh, would you like some more coffee?" Dr. Finn asked him.

"Yes, about a gallon."

Dr. Finn was gone, as if a starting gate had opened.

Later, not telling Croyd it was decaf he was guzzling, Dr. Finn continued, "I'm afraid to give you any more drugs on top of all the amphetamines you've taken."

"I've made two promises," Croyd said, "that I'd try sleeping this time, that I wouldn't resist. But if you can't knock me out fast, I'll probably leave rather than put up with all this anxiety. If that happens, I know I'll be back on bennies and dexes fast. So hit me with a narcotic. I'm willing to take my chances."

Dr. Finn shook his mane. "I'd rather try something simpler and a lot safer first. What say we do a little brain wave entrainment and suggestion?"

"I'm not familiar with the procedure," Croyd said.

"It's not traumatic. The Russians have been experimenting with it for years. I'll just clip these little soft pads to your ears," he said, swabbing the lobes with something moist, "and we'll pulse a low amp current through your head—say, four hertz. You won't even feel it."

He adjusted a control on the box from which the leads emerged.

"Now what?" Croyd asked.

"Close your eyes and rest for just a minute. You may notice a kind of drifting feeling."

"Yeah."

"But there's heaviness, too, within it. Your arms are heavy and your legs are heavy."

"They're heavy," Croyd acknowledged.

"It will be hard to think of anything in particular. Your mind will just go on drifting."

"I'm drifting," Croyd agreed.

"And it should feel very good. Probably better than you've felt all day, finally getting a chance to rest. Breathe slowly and let go in all the tight places. You're almost there already. This is great."

Croyd said something, but it was muttered, indistinguishable.

"You are doing very well. You're quite good at this. Usually I count backward from ten. For you, though, we can start at eight, since you're almost asleep already. Eight. You are far away and it feels fine. Nine. You are already asleep, but now you are going into it even more deeply. Ten. You will sleep soundly, without fear or pain. Sleep."

Croyd began to snore.

There were no spare beds, but since Croyd had stiffened to mannequinlike rigidity before turning bright green, his respiration and heartbeat slowing to something between that of a hibernating bear and a dead one, Dr. Finn had had him placed, erect, at the rear of a broom closet, where he did not take up much space, and he drove a nail into the door and hung the chart on it, after having entered, "Patient extremely suggestible."

May 1987

All the King's Horses

IV

"I need a mask," he said.

The clerk towered above him, grotesquely tall and thin, with a manner as imperious as the pharaoh whose death mask he wore. "Of course." His eyes were gold, like the skin of his mask. "Perhaps you had something specific in mind, sir?"

"Something impressive," Tom said. You could buy a cheap plastic mask for under two bucks in any Jokertown candy store, good enough to hide your face, but in Jokertown a cheap mask was like a cheap suit. Tom wanted to be taken seriously today, and Holbrook's was the most exclusive mask shop in the city, according to *New York* magazine.

"If you'll permit me, sir?" the clerk said, producing a tape measure. Tom nodded and studied the display of elaborate tribal masks on the far wall as his head was measured. "I'll be just a minute," the man said as he vanished through a dark velvet curtain into a back room.

It was more than a minute. Tom was the only customer in the shop. It was a small place, dimly lit, richly appointed. Tom felt acutely uncomfortable. When the clerk returned, he was carrying a half dozen mask boxes under his arm. He set them on the counter and opened one for Tom's inspection.

A lion's head rested on a bed of black tissue paper. The face was done in some soft, pale leather, as buttery to the touch as the finest suede. A nimbus of long golden hair surrounded the features. "Surely nothing is as impressive as the king of beasts," the clerk told him. "The hair is authentic, every strand taken from a lion's mane. I couldn't help but notice your glasses, sir. If you'll provide us with your prescription, Holbrook's will be pleased to have custom eyepieces made to fit."

"It's very nice," Tom said, fingering the hair. "How much?"

The clerk looked at him coolly. "Twelve hundred dollars, sir. Without the prescription eyepieces."

Tom pulled back his hand abruptly. The golden eyes in the pharaoh's face regarded him with condescending courtesy and just a hint of amusement. Without a word Tom turned on his heel and walked out of Holbrook's.

He bought a rubber frogface for $6.97 in a Bowery storefront with a newspaper rack by the door and a soda fountain in the back. The mask was a little too big when he pulled it down over his head, and he had to wear his glasses balanced on the oversized green ears, but the design had a certain sentimental value. To hell with being impressive.

Jokertown made him very nervous. As many times as he had flown over its streets, walking those same streets was another proposition entirely. Thankfully the Funhouse was right on the Bowery. The cops avoided the darker alleys of Jokertown as much as any other sane person, even more so since the start of this gang war, but nats still frequented the joker cabarets along the Bowery, and where the tourists went the prowl cars went as well. Nat money was the lifeblood of the Jokertown economy, and that blood ran thin enough as it was.

Even at this hour the sidewalks were still busy, and no one took much notice of Tom in his ill-fitting frogface. By the second block he was almost comfortable. In the last twenty years he'd seen all the ugliness Jokertown had to offer on his TV monitors; this was just a different angle on things.

In the old days the sidewalk in front of the Funhouse would have been crowded by cabs dropping off fares and limousines waiting at the curb for the end of the second show. But the sidewalk was empty tonight, not even a doorman, and when Tom entered, he found the checkroom unattended as well. He pushed through the double doors; a hundred different frogs stared at him from the silvered depths of the famous Funhouse mirrors. The man up on stage had a head the size of a baseball, and huge pebbled bags of skin drooping all over his bare torso, swelling and emptying like bellows or bagpipes, filling the room with a strange sad music as air sighed from a dozen unlikely orifices. Tom stared at him with a sick fascination until the maître d' appeared at his side. "A table, sir?" He was squat and round as a penguin, features hidden by a Beethoven mask.

"I'd like to see Xavier Desmond," Tom said. His voice, partially muffled by the frog mask, sounded strange in his ears.

"Mr. Desmond only returned from abroad a few days ago," the maître d' said. "He was a delegate on Senator Hartmann's world tour," he added proudly. "I'm afraid he's quite busy."

"It's important," Tom said.

The maître d' nodded. "Whom shall I say is calling?"

Tom hesitated. "Tell him it's . . . an old friend."

When the maître d' had left them alone, Des got up and came around the desk. He moved slowly, thin lips pressed together tightly beneath a long pink trunk that grew from his face where a normal man would have a nose. Standing in the same room with him, you saw things you could not see in a face on a TV screen: how old he was, and how sick. His skin hung on him as loosely as his clothes, and his eyes were filmed with pain.

"How was the tour?" Tom asked him.

"Exhausting," Des said. "We saw all the misery of the world, all the suffering and hatred, and we tasted its violence firsthand. But I'm sure you know all that. It was in the papers." He lifted his trunk, and the fingers that fringed its end lightly touched Tom's mask. "Pardon, old friend, but I cannot seem to place your face."

"My face is hidden," Tom pointed out.

Des smiled wanly. "One of the first things a joker learns is how to see beneath a mask. I'm an old joker, and yours is a very bad mask."

"A long time ago you bought a mask just as cheap as this."

Des frowned. "You're mistaken, I'm afraid. I've never felt the need to hide my features."

"You bought it for Dr. Tachyon. A chicken mask."

Desmond's eyes met his, startled and curious, but still wary. "Who are you?"

"I think you know," Tom said.

The old joker was silent for a long moment. Then he nodded slowly and sagged into the nearest chair. "There was talk that you were dead. I'm glad you're not."

The simple statement, and the sincerity with which Desmond delivered it, made Tom feel awkward, ashamed. For a moment he thought he should leave without another word.

"Please, sit down," Des said.

Tom sat down, cleared his throat, tried to think how to begin. The silence stretched out awkwardly.

"I know," Desmond said. "It is as strange for me as it must be for you, to have you sitting here in my office. Pleasant, but strange. But something brought you here, something more than the desire for my company. Jokertown owes you a great deal. Tell me what I can do for you."

Tom told him. He left out the why of it, but he told him his decision, and what he hoped to do with the shells. As he spoke, he looked away from Des, his eyes wandering everywhere but on the old joker's face. But he got the words out.

Xavier Desmond listened politely. When Tom had finished, Des looked older somehow, and more weary. He nodded slowly but said nothing. The fingers of his trunk clenched and unclenched. "You're sure?" Des finally asked.

Tom nodded. "Are you all right?"

Des gave him a thin, tired smile. "No," he replied. "I am too old, and not in the best of health, and the world persists in disappointing me. In the final days of the tour I yearned for our homecoming, for Jokertown and the Funhouse. Well, now I am home, and what do I find? Business is as bad as ever, the mobs are fighting a war in the streets of Jokertown, our next president may be a religious charlatan who loves my people so much he wants to quarantine them, and our oldest hero has decided to walk away from the fight." Des ran his trunk fingers through thinning gray hair, then looked up at Tom, abashed. "Forgive me. That was unfair. You have risked much, and for twenty years you have been there for us. No one has the right to ask more. Certainly, if you want my help, you'll have it."

"Do you know who the owner is?" Tom asked.

"A joker," Desmond said. "Does that surprise you? The original owners were nats, but he bought them out, oh, some time ago. He's quite a wealthy man, but he prefers to keep a low profile. A rich joker is, well, something of a target. I would be glad to help set up a meeting."

"Yeah," Tom said. "Good."

After they had finished talking, Xavier Desmond walked him out. Tom promised to phone in a week for the details of the meeting. Out front, on the sidewalk, Des stood beside him as Tom tried to hail a taxi. One passed, slowed, then sped up again when the cabbie saw the two of them standing there.

"I used to hope you were a joker," Desmond said quietly.

Tom looked at him sharply. "How do you know I'm not?"

Des smiled, as if that question hardly deserved an answer. "I suppose I wanted to believe, like so many other jokers. Hidden in your shell, you could be anything. With all the prestige and fame the aces enjoy, why would you possibly hide your face and keep your name a secret if you were not one of us?"

"I had my reasons," Tom told him.

"Well, it doesn't matter. I suppose the lesson to be learned is that aces are aces, even you, and we jokers need to learn to take care of ourselves. Good luck to you, old friend." Des shook his hand and turned and walked away.

Another cab passed. Tom hailed it, but it shot right past.

"They think you're a joker," Des said from the door of the Funhouse. "It's the mask," he added, not unkindly. "Take it off, let them see your face, and you'll have no problem." The door closed softly behind him.

Tom looked up and down the street. There was no one in sight, no one to see his real face. Carefully, nervously, he reached up and pulled off the frog mask.

The next cab screeched to a stop right in front of him.

Blood Ties

by Melinda M. Snodgrass

I

"I QUIT! I QUIT! HE DOESN'T NEED A TUTOR, HE NEEDS A WARDEN! A GODDAMN ANIMAL TRAINER! A STINT IN THE PEN!"

The slam of the door shook papers from the stacks that stood on his desk like the bastions of a white cellulose fortress. Tachyon, a rental contract hanging limply from long fingers, stared bemusedly at the door. It cracked open.

A pair of eyes, swimming like blue moons behind thick lenses, peered cautiously around the door.

"Sorry," whispered Dita.

"Quite all right."

"How many does that make?" She eased one shapely buttock onto the corner of his desk. Tachyon's eyes slid to the expanse of white thigh revealed by the hitch of her miniskirt.

"Three."

"Maybe school?"

"Maybe not." Tach repressed a shudder as he contemplated the havoc his grandchild would wreak in the dog-eat-dog world of public school. With a sigh he folded the apartment lease and slipped it into a pocket. "I'll have to go home and check on him. Try to make some other arrangement."

"These letters?"

"Will have to wait."

"But—"

"Some have waited six months. What's another few days?"

"Rounds...?"

"I'll be back in time."

"Doctor Queen—"

"Is not going to be happy with me. A common enough event."

148

"You look tired."

"I am."

And so he was, he thought as he walked down the steps of the Blythe van Renssaeler Memorial Clinic without bestowing his usual pats on the heads of the stone lions that flanked the stairs. In the week since his return from the World Health Organization tour, there had been little time for rest. Worries snapped at him from all sides: his impotence, which left him (one should forgive the pun) with a growing sense of pressure and frustration; the candidacy of Leo Barnett; the crime wars that were threatening the peaceful (*peaceful*, ha!) life of Jokertown; James Spector wandering loose, and continuing to kill.

But all of this seemed oddly distant, so unimportant, mere bagatelles when compared with the arrival of a new presence in his life. An active eleven-year-old boy playing havoc with his routines. Making him realize just how very small a one-bedroom apartment could be. Making him realize how long it took to find something larger, and how much more it would cost.

And then there was the problem of Blaise's power. During his childhood Tachyon had frequently railed against the strictness of his Takisian psi lord upbringing. Now he wished he could apply some of that same severe punishment to his wayward heir, who *could not* be brought to realize the enormity of his sin when he casually exercised his psi powers on the mindblind humans that surrounded him.

But to be honest, it was not simply a matter of sparing the rod. On Takis a child learned to survive in the plot-ridden atmosphere of the women's quarters. Surrounded as they were by other mentats, children quickly became cautious about the unrestrained exercise of their power. No matter *how* powerful an individual might be, there was always an older cousin, uncle, or parent more experienced and more powerful.

Upon their emergence from the harem a child was assigned a companion/servant from the lower orders. The intent was to instill in the young psi lord or lady a sense of duty toward the simple folk they ruled. That was the theory—in actual fact it generally created a sort of indulgent contempt for the vast bulk of the Takisian population, and a rather offhanded atti-

tude that it really wasn't very interesting or sporting to
compel servants. But there were tragedies—servants forced
to destroy themselves upon a whim or a fit of fury on the part
of their masters and mistresses.

Tachyon rubbed a hand across his forehead and considered his options. To blather on about kindness and responsibility and duty. Or to become the most dangerous thing in
Blaise's life.

But I wanted his love, not his fear.

The boy reminded him of some feral woodland creature.
Coiled in the big armchair, Blaise warily eyed his grandsire
and tugged fretfully at the long points of the lacy Vandyke
collar that spilled over the shoulders of his white twill coat.
Red stockings and a red sash at the waist echoed the blood
red of his hair. Tach tossed his keys onto the coffee table and
sat on the arm of the sofa, keeping a careful distance from the
hostile child.

"Whatever he said, I didn't do it."

"You must have done something."

They spoke in French.

"No."

"Blaise, don't lie."

"I didn't like him."

Tach drifted to the piano and played a few bars of a
Scarlatti sonatina. "Teachers aren't required to be your friends.
They're meant to . . . teach."

"I know everything I need to know."

"Oh?" Tachyon drew out the word in one long, freezing
accent.

The childish chin stiffened, and Tach's shields repelled a
powerful mind assault. "That's *all* I need to know. At least for
ordinary people." He blushed under his grandfather's level
gaze. "I'm special!"

"Being an ignorant boor is unfortunately *not* terribly
unique on this world. You should find yourself with plenty of
company."

"I *hate* you! I want to go home." The final word ended on
a sob, and Blaise buried his face in the chair.

Tach crossed to him and gathered the sobbing boy into his
arms. "Oh, my darling, don't cry. You're homesick, that is

natural. But there is no one for you in France, and I want you
so very much."

"There's no place for me *here*. You're just fitting me in.
The way you make room for a new book on the shelves."

"Not true. You have given my life meaning." The remark
was too obscurely adult to reach the child, and Tachyon tried
again. "I think I've found a new apartment. We'll go there
this very afternoon, and you can tell me just how you want
your room."

"Really?"

"Truly." He scrubbed the child's face with his handkerchief. "But now, I must return to work so I will take you to
Baby, and she will tell you tales of your blood."

"*Très bien.*"

Tach felt a momentary flare of guilt, for this plan was
designed less for Blaise's pleasure than to assure his good
behavior. Locked within the walls of the sentient and intelligent Takisian ship, Blaise would be safe, and the world at
large would be safe from him.

"But only in English," Tachyon added sternly.

Blaise's face fell. "*Tant pis.*"

Back to the clinic for five hours of frenzied work. Most of
it unfortunately of the paper variety. With a start he remembered Blaise and hoped that *Baby* had been *very* entertain-
ing. Collecting the child, Tachyon hurried him to his karate
lesson. He then sat in the outer office reading the *Times*, a
wary ear cocked toward the dojo. But Blaise was behaving.

Wild Card/AIDS Benefit Concert to be Held at Funhouse.

How like Des, Tachyon reflected. Interesting that this
event was to take place in Jokertown. Probably no other
forum in New York would host it. They would want to place
plastic liners on the seats.

There were a number of emotional similarities between
the two scourges. As a biochemist, he saw a different correlation, herpes to wild card. But a herpes/wild card/AIDS benefit would offer far too many unfortunate opportunities for
sexual innuendo.

*Warning: The Surgeon General has determined that fucking
may be hazardous to your health.*

"Well, I ought to live to be two thousand," muttered
Tach, crossing his legs.

Blaise bounced out looking adorable in his little white gee. There had been an initial tussle with the manager of the karate school over that gee. The standard color was black, but despite forty years on Earth, Tach still held a stubborn bias against the color. Laborers wore black. Not aristocrats.

The boy thrust his clothes into Tach's arms.

"Aren't you going to change?"

"No." He climbed onto a chair to investigate a display of shurikiens, kusawagamas, and naginatas.

"Is the language barrier a problem?" he asked Tupuola as he wrote out a check.

"No. Even in just the past few days his English has improved remarkably."

"He's very bright."

"Yes, I am," said Blaise walking across the chairs to hug Tachyon around the neck. Tupuola frowned, twiddled a pen.

"I wish you would show *me* some of this English improvement."

"It's easier to speak French with you," Blaise said, lapsing into that tongue.

Tach ran a hand through his grandchild's straight red hair. "I think I shall have to develop selective deafness." He suddenly chuckled.

"What?" Blaise tugged at his shoulder.

"I was remembering an incident from my childhood. I wasn't much older than you. Fifteen or so. I had decided that physical workout was dull. Only the sparring really seemed to matter. So I had taken to ordering my bodyguards to do the workouts for me." Tupuola laughed, and Tach shook his head sadly. "I was an unbearable little prince."

"So what happened?"

"My father caught me."

"And?" asked Blaise eagerly.

"And he beat the crap out of me."

"I'll bet your bodyguards enjoyed it," chuckled Tupuola.

"Oh, they were far too well trained to ever show emotion, but I do seem to recall a few telltale lip twitches. It was very humiliating." He sighed.

"I would have stopped him," said Blaise, his eyes kindling.

"Ah, but I respected my father and knew he was right to chastise me. And it would have violated the tenets of psi to engage in a long, drawn out mind battle with my sire in front of servants. Also, I might have lost." He flicked a forefinger across the tip of the boy's nose. "Always a consideration when you're a Takisian."

"The tenets of psi. Sounds like a mystic book out of the sixties," mused Tupuola.

Tach rose. "Perhaps I'll write it." He turned to his grandchild. "And speaking of the sixties, there is someone I want you to meet."

"Someone fun?"

"Yes, and kind, and a good friend."

The corners of Blaise's mouth drooped. "Not someone I can play with."

"No, but he does have a daughter."

"Behold me! Mark, I am home!" Tach announced with a swirl of his plumed hat from the front door of the Cosmic Pumpkin ("Food for Body, Mind, & Spirit") Head Shop and Delicatessen.

Dr. Mark Meadows, aka Captain Trips, hung storklike over the counter, a freshly opened package of tofu balanced delicately on his fingertips.

"Oh, wow, Doc. Good to see ya."

"Mark, my grandson, Blaise." He pulled him from where the child had been hiding behind him and pushed him gently forward. "Blaise, *je vous présente, Monsieur Mark Meadows.*"

"*Enchanté, monsieur.*"

Mark flashed Blaise a peace sign, and Tach a sharp glance. "I can see you've got a lot to tell."

"Indeed, yes, and a favor to ask."

"Anything, man, name it."

Tachyon glanced significantly down at Blaise. "In a moment. First I want Blaise to makes Sprout's acquaintance."

"Uh . . . sure."

They climbed the steep stairs to Mark's apartment, left Blaise playing with Mark's lovely, but sadly retarded, ten-year-old daughter, and settled in the hippie's tiny, cluttered lab.

"So, like, tell all."

"Overall it was a nightmare. Death, starvation, disease— but at the end . . . Blaise, and suddenly it all becomes worthwhile." Tachyon halted his nervous pacings. "He's the focus of my life, and I want him to have everything, Mark."

"Kids don't need everything, man. They just need love."

Tach laid a hand fondly on the human's skinny shoulder. "How good you are, my dear, dear friend."

"But you haven't told me *anything*. How you found him, and what's the real poop on that shit that came down in Syria?"

"That's why I say it was a nightmare."

They talked, Tachyon touching on his fears for Peregrine, all of the events leading up to his discovery of Blaise. He omitted his final confrontation with Le Miroir, the French terrorist who had been controlling the quarter-Takisian child. He sensed that gentle, sensitive Mark might be shocked at Tachyon's cold-blooded execution of the man. It was something that, in retrospect, Tachyon wasn't very comfortable with himself. He reflected, a little sadly, that after an almost equal number of years on Takis and on Earth he was still more of Takis than of Earth.

He checked the watch set in his bootheel and exclaimed, "Burning Sky, look at the time."

"Hey, great boots."

"Yes, I found them in Germany."

"Hey, about Germany—"

"Another time, Mark, I must be going. Oh, what a fool I am! I came not only for the pleasure of seeing you, but to ask if I might occasionally borrow Durg? He's virtually immune to the effects of mind control, and I can't keep Blaise with me constantly, nor can I continue to lock him away in *Baby* everytime I have other responsibilities."

"Durg as a babysitter. It sorta boggles the mind."

"Yes, I know, and believe me it goes very much against the grain to have Zabb's monster guarding my heir, but Blaise is like a Swarm mother among planets if I leave him unattended with normal humans. You see, he has no self-discipline, and I'm damned if I can see how to instill it in him."

Trips dropped an arm over Tachyon's shoulders, and they walked to the door of the lab. "Time, give it time. And relax with it, man. Nobody's born a father."

"Or even a grandfather."

Mark looked down into the delicate, youthful face and chuckled. "I think he's going to have a hard time relating to you as Gramps. You're going to have to settle for—"

The sight in the living room knocked wind and words

from Mark's throat. Sprout was down to her teddy bear panties, daintily dancing while she sang a little song. Giggling, Blaise bounced on the sofa and manipulated her like a puppet.

"*K'ijdad*, isn't she funny? Her mind is so simple—"

Tachyon's power lashed out, and Sprout—suddenly freed from this terrifying outside control—burst into frightened and disoriented tears. Mark gathered her in a tight embrace.

"SIMPLE! I WILL SHOW YOU A SIMPLE MIND!" The boy jerked about the room like rusty automaton under the brutal imperative of his grandfather's mind. "IS THIS PLEASANT! DO YOU ENJOY—"

"NO, MAN, NO! STOP IT!" Tachyon rocked under the hard shaking. "It's okay," Trips added in a more moderate tone as the devil's mask that had slipped over Tachyon's normally pleasant features faded.

"I'm sorry, Mark," Tach whispered. "So very sorry."

"It's okay, man. Let's . . . let's just all calm down."

Tachyon dropped into telepathy. *Can you ever forgive me?*

Nothing to forgive, man.

Meadows dropped to one knee before the sobbing boy, took him gently by the shoulders. "You see, you're as scared as Sprout was. It's no fun to be in somebody else's power. And yeah, Sprout's mind is weak, but that's all the more reason for someone strong like you to be kind, and to look out for people like her. You understand?"

Blaise slowly nodded, but Tachyon didn't trust the shuttered expression in those purple/black eyes. And sure enough, as soon as they were out on the street in front of the Cosmic Pumpkin, the boy said, "What a wimp!"

"GET IN THAT TAXI."

"Ancestors!" Glass crunched under bootheels, and for a brief, breath-catching moment time rolled back, and the past clung like a gnawing animal at his throat.

Glass shattering and falling, mirrors breaking on all sides, silvered knives flying through the air . . . blood spattering against the cracked mirrors.

Tachyon shook himself free of the waking nightmare and stared at the carnage that filled the Funhouse. A janitor with enough arms to handle three brooms was busily sweeping up the broken glass that littered the floor. Des, grey-faced and frowning, was talking with a man in a business suit. Tachyon joined them.

"I'm not entirely certain your policy—"

"Of course not! Why should I think that twenty-four years of premiums paid on time, and no claims made, should entitle me to any coverage now," spat Des.

"I'll check, Mr. Desmond, and get back to you."

"What by the purity of the Ideal is going on here?"

"Do you want a drink?"

"Please." Tachyon pulled out his wallet, and Des stared down at the bills, a funny little smile twisting his lips, the fingers at the end of his incongruous trunk twitching slightly. The alien flushed and said defensively. "I pay for my drinks."

"Now."

"That was a long time ago, Des."

"True."

Tachyon kicked at a sliver of mirror. "Though God knows this brings it all back."

"Christmas Eve, 1963. Mal's been dead a long time."

And soon you will be too.

No, impossible to speak such words. But would Des ever speak? While Tachyon, of course, respected the old joker's desire for privacy as he prepared to die, it nonetheless hurt that he maintained his silence.

How am I to say farewell to you, old friend? And soon it will be too late.

The cognac exploded like a white-hot cloud on the back of his throat, banishing the lump that had settled there. Tachyon set aside the glass and said, "You never answered my question."

"What's to answer?"

"Des, I'm your friend. I've drunk in this bar for over twenty years. When I enter and find it busted all to hell, I want to know why."

"Why?"

"Maybe I can do something!" Tachyon tossed down the rest of his drink and frowned up into Des's faded eyes.

Des swept away the glass and refilled it. "For twenty years I've been paying protection to the Gambiones. Now this new gang is muscling in, and I'm having to pay off two of them. It's making it a little tough to meet overhead."

"New gang? What new gang?"

"They call themselves the Shadow Fists. Toughs out of Chinatown."

"When did this start?"

"Last week. I guess they waited until they knew I was back in town."

"Which means they made quite a study of Jokertown."

A shrug. "Why not? They're businessmen."

"They're hoodlums."

Another shrug. "That too."

"What are you going to do?"

"Keep paying both sides and hope they let me live in peace."

"However long that's going to be," Tachyon muttered, and drained the fresh cognac.

"What?"

"Oh, hell, Des, I'm not a blind man. I'm also a doctor. What is it? Cancer?"

"Yes."

"Why didn't you tell me?"

The old man sighed. "For a lot of complicated reasons. None of which I want to go into right now."

"Or ever?"

"That too is possible."

"I count you a friend."

"Do you, Tachy? Do you?"

"*Yes*. Can you doubt it? No! Don't answer that. I've already seen it; in your eyes and your heart."

"Why not my mind, Tachyon? Why not read it there?"

"Because I honor your privacy, and—" His face crumpled, and he sucked in a sharp breath. "Because I can't bear to face what I might read there," he concluded quietly. He tossed more bills on the bar and started for the door. "I'll see what I can do to make your hope a reality."

"What?"

"That you end your days in peace."

It had been the same story at Ernie's and Gobbler's Delicatessen and Spot's Laundry and so many others that he dreaded to even recall them all. Frowning, Tachyon tore the skin from an orange, the juice stinging briefly as it hit a hitherto unnoticed paper cut. Goons out of Chinatown. Goons from the Mob, and him with his big mouth promising to do something about it. *Like what?*

He finished peeling the orange and popped a segment into his mouth. A light breeze ruffled his curls and brought the sound of Blaise's delighted laughter. A rumbling call from Jack Braun sent the little boy scampering across the park, his red-stockinged legs a blur of motion. Braun leaned back the football cradled in his big hand and threw. He looked like a movie star; sun-bleached blond hair falling across his fore-head, tan sinewy legs thrusting out from a pair of safari shorts, a very attractive, brilliantly colored Hawaiian shirt.

Tach threw crusts of bread to some interested pigeons. *How ironic, Sunday in the park with Jack.* Hated enemy transformed into . . . well, perhaps not friend, but at least a tolerated presence. It didn't hurt that Jack's visit had been prompted by a desire to see Blaise, which raised him in Tach's estimation. To love Blaise was to find favor. And this outing had at least pulled Tachyon out of the brown study that had held him for days since his visit to the Funhouse.

The orange segment finally slipped down, and Tach's stomach rebelled. With a moan he rolled onto his back on the blanket and fought down nausea. The wages of worry. Over the past few days his stomach had closed down into a tight and painful ball. He began a litany of problems.

The fear that lay like a palpable shadow over Jokertown.

Leo Barnett offering to heal jokers with the power of his god, and if they failed to respond, then clearly it was an indication of the depth of their sin. What if he became president?

Peregrine. In a month her child was due. The ultrasound he'd run two days ago still indicated a normal, viable fetus, but Tach knew with soul-deep horror what the stress of the birth experience could do to a wild card babe. *Blood and Line, let this little one be normal.* If it wasn't, it would destroy her.

And he still hadn't been by the Jokertown precinct to work with a police artist on the preparation of a drawing of James Spector. . . .

A girl went jogging by, an Afghan hound loping at her heels. A sheen of sweat brought a golden glow to her skin, and several strands of long black hair lay plastered on her bare back. Tach watched the play of muscles in her legs and back, studied the ripe breasts bouncing beneath the halter top, and felt his mouth go dry and the urgent thrust of his penis against his zipper. It was a bitter and tantalizing glimpse of wholeness, for he knew after countless hopeless encounters that the power would fade when the moment came upon him.

Furious, he rolled onto his stomach and beat his fists on the ground—furious at his impotence, and at his flighty, undisciplined mind that could be distracted from concern over an ace killer by the sight of female flesh.

A toe nudged him in the ribs, and he shot to his feet.

"Hey, hey." Braun held up his hands placatingly. "Take it easy."

"Where's Blaise?" Tach stared anxiously about.

"I gave him some money for ice cream."

"You shouldn't have let him go alone. Something might happen. . . ."

"That kid can look out for himself." Braun dropped cross-legged onto the blanket, lit a cigarette. "Mind if I give you some advice."

"Yes."

"You're not on Takis now. He's not a prince of the blood royal."

Tachyon gave a bitter little laugh. "No, far from it. He's an abomination. On Takis he would be destroyed."

"Huh?"

The alien swept up the scattered orange peels and carried them to a garbage can. "The greatest penalties are reserved for those who mingle their seed outside their class. How could we rule if everyone possessed our powers?" he tossed back over his shoulder.

"Charming culture you come from. But it supports my point."

"Being what?"

"Stop driving him crazy. You're laying way too much pressure on him. You expect him to abide by rules of behavior that have no correlation on Earth, and you're also spoiling him rotten. Music lessons, karate lessons, dance lessons, tutoring in algebra and biology and chemistry—"

"Well, you're wrong there. His third tutor quit days ago, and I haven't been able to find a replacement. And *that* is why I have to expect so much of him. His power and his breeding make him special. At least to me."

"Tachyon, *listen* to me. You can't give a kid every toy and every gimcrack he desires, tell him he's special, special, special, and then expect him not to be an arrogant little bastard. Let him be a kid. Take his clothes."

"What's wrong with his clothes?" There was a threat in the husky voice.

"Get him out of the knee britches, and the lace, and the hats. Buy him some blue jeans, and a Dodgers cap. He's got to live in *this* world."

"*I* have not chosen to conform."

"Yeah, but you're a crank. It's a big flamboyant act with you. You're also an adult, and one incredibly arrogant son-of-a-bitch, and you could care less what people say about you. You don't want Blaise to abuse his power, but you've almost guaranteed that he'll have to. There's nothing crueler than kids, and he's going to be tormented until he lashes out. Then you'll be disappointed and disapproving, and he'll be resentful, and what a perfect vicious circle you've created."

"You should write a book. Clearly your vast experience has made you an authority on child rearing."

"Ah, hell, Tachyon. I like the kid. I even occasionally like you. Love him, Tachyon, and relax."

"I do love him."

"No, you love what he represents. You're obsessive about him because your im—" He bit off the words and flushed a deep red. "Ah, hell, I'm sorry. I didn't mean to bring that up."

"How do you even know?"

"Fantasy told me."

"Bitch."

"Hey, relax there too, and everything will probably work out. It's no big deal."

"Braun, you cannot conceive of what a *big deal* it is. Progeny, continuance—Oh, fuck! Are you also planning to offer psychiatric counseling at your new casino? Do what you do best, Jack—drift and make money. But leave me alone!"

"With pleasure!"

Seizing the picnic hamper and the blanket, Tachyon stormed away in search of Blaise.

"Where's Uncle Jack?"

"*Uncle* Jack had an appointment in Atlantic City."

"You two had a fight again. Why do you two fight so much?"

"Ancient history."

"Then you should forget it."

"Don't you start too." Tach waved down a cab.

"Where are we going?"

"To Mark's."

"Oh."

"Please wait for me," Tachyon instructed when they pulled up in front of the Cosmic Pumpkin.

"Hokay, but the meters she keeps running," the man replied in a thick and unplaceable accent.

"That's fine."

"I'll wait too," said Blaise in a small voice. And Tachyon felt a moment's shame, remembering his lack of control the last time they had visited the Pumpkin.

He stuck his head in the door. "Mark."

"Yo."

"Quick question. Have you been bothered with emissaries from various criminal organizations?" The handful of diners from CUNY stared at the Takisian wide-eyed.

"Huh?"

Tach expelled air in a sharp puff of irritation. "Have you been asked to pay protection?"

"Oh, is *that* what you meant. Oh, yeah, man, months ago, but I like . . . had one of my . . . *friends* show up, and they haven't been back."

"Would that everyone had friends like yours, Mark."

"Is that it?"

"That's it."

"Anything I can do to help?"

"I don't think so."

Tachyon slid into the cab and gave the hack the clinic's address.

"Ohhhh, Jokertowns. Yous that doctors?"

"Yes."

"I sees you on the televisions. Peri Green's Perches."

"That's Peregrine, and yes, that was me."

"Holy Jesus!"

The driver's exclamation jerked Tach's attention to the

road ahead. A jumble of police cars, their lights flashing, blocked Hester Street. With a wail an ambulance shot past.

"Shit, must be anothers, how you says, hits."

"Stop, stop at once."

Leaping from the cab, Tach darted under the police tape. A woman's keening filled the air, and a basso voice amplified by a bullhorn ordered knots of muttering people to move along. Tachyon spotted Detective Maseryk and pushed up to him.

"What?"

"How the hell . . . oh, hi, Doc." The detective stared curiously at the small boy who gazed with interest at the sprawled bodies in the shattered restaurant.

Tachyon rounded on Blaise. "Get back to the cab and wait there."

"Ahhh—"

"*Now!*"

"Looks like another little party," said Maseryk when Blaise had reluctantly drooped away. "But this time an uninvited guest got mixed up in it too." He jerked his head toward the sobbing woman, who was clutching at a small form in a bodybag being lifted into the ambulance.

Tachyon ran to the stretcher, unzipped the bag, and stared down at the child. He hadn't been very attractive to start with, a squat-bottomed heavy body sat upon broad flippers, and he looked a lot worse with half his head shot away. Spinning, the Takisian caught the woman in a tight embrace.

"MY BABY! MY BABY! DON'T LET THEM TAKE MY BABY!"

A rescue worker approached, hypodermic at the ready. Tachyon stilled the sobbing mother with a brief touch of his power and handed her to the man.

"Treat her kindly."

"Looks like Gambione boys," Maseryk called as he stared thoughtfully down at one sprawled body. Several strings of spaghetti hung from the corpse's mouth, leaving wet, red trails on his chin. "The Fists came cruising by and opened up. Car will be found, and be stolen, so that'll be another dead end. Too bad about the kid though. Talk about being in the wrong place at the wrong time."

The detective noticed Tachyon's continued silence and glanced down.

"I don't want dead ends, Maseryk, I want these men."

"We're working on it."

"Perhaps it is time I took a hand."

"No, for Christ's sake, the last thing we need are civilians getting in the way. Just stay out of this."

"Nobody kills *my* people in *my* town!"

"Huh? The mayor's going to be mighty surprised to hear he lost and you won the last election," he yelled after Tachyon's retreating back.

"Cognac," spat Tachyon to Sascha, the Crystal Palace's blind bartender. He threw his blue velvet hat, sewn with pearls and sequins, onto the bar and tossed back the drink. He extended the snifter. "Another."

A whiff of exotic frangipani perfume, and Chrysalis slid onto the stool next to him. The blue eyes floating within their hollows of bone stared impassively down at him.

"You're supposed to savor good brandy, not throw it down like a wino after a cheap drunk. Unless that's what you're after."

"You sound like a recruiter for AA."

Reaching out, Chrysalis wrapped one short red curl around her forefinger. "So what's the matter, Tachy?"

"This senseless gang war. Today an innocent caught in the crossfire. A joker child. I think he lives on this block. I remember seeing him on Wild Card Day last September."

"Oh." She continued playing with his short-cropped hair.

"Stop that! And is that all you have to say?"

"What should I say?"

"How about a little outrage?"

"I deal in information, not outrage."

"God, you can be a cold bitch."

"Circumstances have rather guaranteed that, Tachyon. I don't ask for pity, and I don't give any. I do what I have to do to survive with what I am. What I've become."

He reared back at the bitterness in her voice. For she was one of his bastard children—born of his failure and his pain.

"Chrysalis, we have to do something."

"Like what?"

"Prevent Jokertown from becoming a battlefield."

"It is already."

"Then make it too dangerous for them to fight here. Will you help me?"

"No. I take sides, and I've lost my neutrality."

"Willing to sell weapons to all sides, eh?"

"If that's what it takes."

"What is it you're after, Chrysalis?"

"Safety."

He slid off the stool. "There is none this side of the grave."

"Go be a fire-breather, Tachyon. And when you come up with something a little more concrete than an amorphous desire to protect Jokertown, let me know."

"Why? So you can sell me out to the highest bidder?"

And now it was her turn to rear back, the blood washing like a dark tide through the shadowy muscles of her face.

"Okay, let's come to order now," called Des, delicately tapping a spoon against the side of a brandy snifter.

The shifting throng gave a final shudder, like a beast falling into sleep, and silence filled the Funhouse. Mark Meadows, looking even more vacuous and absurd in the image-distorting mirrors of the Funhouse, was conspicuous for his very normalcy. The rest of the room looked like a gathering of carnival freaks. Ernie the Lizard had his rill raised, and it was flushed a deep scarlet under the emotion of the moment. Arachne, her eight legs catching at the thread of silk being extruded by her bulbous body, placidly wove a shawl. Shiner, with Doughboy huge and lumpish seated beside him, jiggled nervously in his chair. Walrus, in one of his loud Hawaiian shirts, fished a paper from his shoping cart and handed it back to Gobbler. Troll leaned his nine-foot length against the door as if ready to repel any outsiders.

"Doctor."

Des dropped into a chair like a discarded suit. As Tachyon stepped forward to face the crowd, he wondered how much longer until the old man was forced to enter the hospital for that final stay.

"Ladies and gentlemen, you've all heard about Alex Reichmann?" There were murmurers of assent, sympathy, and outrage. "I had the misfortune to stumble across that scene only moments after the Shadow Fists had made their hit and succeeded in killing not only their intended targets but one of our own. I've only been back a few weeks. I've heard the stories of intimidation and vandalism, but I thought I could stay neutral. In the words of another, and perhaps more famous, physician: "'I'm a doctor, not a policeman.'" That drew a couple of laughs.

"But the police are failing in their duty to us," Tachyon continued. "Not perhaps out of deliberate neglect, but because this war far exceeds their capacity to keep the peace. So I'd like to propose today that we form our own peacekeepers. A neighborhood watch on a grand scale, but with a twist. Many of you fall into that uncomfortable category of joker/aces." The alien nodded to Ernie and Troll, whose metahuman strength was well-known. "I propose that we also form response teams. Pairs of jokers and aces ready to respond to a call from any concerned citizen of Jokertown. Des has already offered the Funhouse as the central axis, the switchboard, if you will, for incoming calls. People who agree to be part of this effort will turn in times they would be available, and their work and home addresses. Whoever's on duty here will match a team to the problem spot and send them out."

"Just a point, Tachy," called Jube. "Those guys have *guns*."

"True, but they're also just nats."

"And some of my . . . er, the Captain's 'friends' are impervious to bullets," piped up Mark Meadows.

"As is Turtle and Jack and Hammer—"

"So you propose using aces as well?" asked Des, a slight frown between his eyes.

Tach looked at him in surprise. "Yes."

"May I point out that Rosemary Muldoon tried that back in March, and then it was revealed that she was a member of the Mafia herself. It's left rather a bad taste in people's mouths where aces are concerned."

Tachyon waved aside the objection. "Well, none of us are likely to be revealed as secret members of the Mafia. So what do you think? Are you willing to work with me on this?"

"Where does Chrysalis stand on this?" asked Gobbler. "And is it a comment that she's not here?"

"Well," began Tach, shifting uncomfortably.

"Yeah," called out Gills. "If Chrysalis isn't here, it's got to mean something. She may know something."

Tachyon stared in dismay at the sea of faces before him. They were closing down like night-blooming flowers retreating from the touch of the sun.

"Chrysalis and Des have always been two of the top figures in Jokertown. If she's not in on this, I don't trust it," cried Gobbler, his red wattle bouncing on his beak.

"What about *me*?" cried Tachyon.

"You're not one of us. Never can be," a voice called from the back of the room, and Tachyon couldn't pick out the speaker. A grinding weight seemed to have settled into the center of his chest at the woman's words.

"Look, we're not saying it's a bad idea," said the Oddity. "We're just saying that without Chrysalis it seems like we're missing a major part."

"If I get Chrysalis?" asked the Takisian a little desperately.

"Then we are with you."

Digger Downs was trotting down the stairs from Chrysalis's private third-floor apartments. Tachyon glared at him and nodded shortly. He noted that the journalist was carrying the current issue of *Time* with Gregg Hartmann's picture on the cover and the caption "Will He Run?" and a copy of *Who's Who in America*.

"Hey, Tachy. Des. What's the good word?"

"Beat it, Digger."

"Hey, you're not still sore—"

"Beat it."

"The public's got a right to know. My article on Peregrine's pregnancy did a valuable service. It pointed out the dangers of a wild card child."

"Your article was a sensational bit of garbage."

"You're just pissed because Peri got mad at you. You never are going to get a crack at her, Doc. I hear she and that boyfriend are thinking about getting—"

Tachyon mind-controlled him and marched him down the stairs and out the front door of the Crystal Palace.

"I'd consider that an assault," said Des.

"Let him prove it."

"You don't have a lot of sensitivity sometimes, Tachyon."

The alien turned, leaned against the banister, and frowned down at the joker. "Meaning what, Des?"

"You shouldn't involve aces in what should be a joker

project. Or don't you think we're capable of handling it ourselves?"

"Oh, burning sky! Why are you so touchy? There was no implicit slur in my inviting in aces. I would say the more firepower we have the better."

"Why are you doing this?"

"Because they're hurting my people, and no one hurts my people."

"And?"

"And Jokertown is my home."

"And?"

"And what!"

"You come from an aristocratic culture, Tachyon. Do you by chance view us as your own private fiefdom?"

"That's not fair, Des," he cried, but he knew that his hurt was tempered with a sudden flare of guilt. He climbed a few more stairs then paused and said, "All right, no aces."

Chrysalis was waiting for them, seated in a high-backed red velvet chair. Victorian antiques littered the room, and the walls were filled with mirrors. Tach suppressed a shudder and wondered how she could stand it. And again felt a stab of guilt. If Chrysalis wanted to look at herself, who was he to judge her? He who in many senses was her creator. He frowned at Des, wishing the old joker had not raised so many uncomfortable emotions.

"So without me you've got no goon squad," she drawled in her affected British accent.

"I should have known that you would have heard by now."

"That's my business, Tachy."

"Chrysalis, please, we need you."

"What are you going to give me for it?"

Des seated himself opposite her, hands clasped between his knees, leaned in intently. "Make a gift to yourself, Chrysalis."

"What?"

"For once in your life put aside profit and margin. You're a joker, Chrysalis, help your fellows. I've spent twenty-three years fighting for jokers, for this little piece of turf. Twenty-three years with JADL measuring my life by a few successes. Now I'm dying, and I'm watching it all erode away. Leo Barnett says we're sinners, and our deformities are God's judgment upon us. To the Fists and the Mafia we're just so many consumers. The ugliest, most hateful consumers they've got, but consumers nonetheless, and our town is their central marketplace. We're just things to them, Chrysalis. *Things* who stick their dope in our arms, and our cocks in their women. *Things* they can terrorize and *things* they can kill. Help us stop them. Help us force them to see us as men."

Chrysalis stared at him out of that impassive, transparent face. The skull without emotion.

"Chrysalis, you admire all things British. Then honor an old British custom of granting a dying man his last request. Help Tachyon. Help our people."

The Takisian held out his hand and twined his fingers through the fingers at the end of Des's trunk. Drew him close and embraced him. Said farewell.

Concerto for
Siren and Serotonin

IV

When Croyd awoke, he pushed aside mop handles, stepped into a bucket, and fell forward. The closet's door offered small resistance to the wild, forward thrust of his hands. As it sprang open and he sprawled, the light stabbing painfully into his eyes, he began to recall the circumstances preceding his repose: the centaur-doctor—Finn—and that funny sleep-machine, yes.... And another little death would mean another sleep-change.

Lying in the hallway, he counted his fingers. There were ten of them all right, but his skin was dead white. He shook off the bucket, climbed to his feet, and stumbled again. His left arm shot downward, touched the floor, and pushed against it. This impelled him to his feet and over backward. He executed an aerial somersault to his rear, landed on his feet, and toppled rearward again. His hands dropped toward the floor to catch himself, then he withdrew them without making contact and simply let himself fall. Years of experience had already given him a suspicion as to what new factor had entered his life-situation. His overcompensations were telling him something about his reflexes.

When he rose again, his movements were very slow, but they grew more and more normal as he explored. By the time he located a washroom all traces of excessive speed or slowness had vanished. When he studied himself in the mirror, he discovered that, in addition to having grown taller and thinner, it was now a pink-eyed countenance that he regarded, a shock of white hair above the high, glacial brow. He massaged his temples, licked his lips, and shrugged. He was familiar with albinism. It was not the first time he had come up short in the pigment department.

He sought his mirrorshades then recalled that Demise had kicked them off. No matter. He'd pick up another pair along with some sun block. Perhaps he'd better dye the hair too, he decided. Less conspicuous that way.

Whatever, his stomach was signaling its emptiness in a frantic fashion. No time for paperwork, for checking out properly—if, indeed, he'd been checked in properly. He was not at all certain that was the case. Best simply to avoid everyone if he didn't want to be delayed on the road to food. He could stop by and thank Finn another time.

Moving as Bentley had taught him long ago, all of his senses extended fully, he began his exit.

"Hi, Jube. One of each, as usual."

Jube studied the tall, cadaverous figure before him, meeting diminished images of his own tusked, blubbery countenance in the mirrorshades that masked the man's eyes.

"Croyd? That you, fella?"

"Yep. Just up and around. I crashed at Tachyon's clinic this time."

"That must be why I hadn't heard any Croyd Crenson disaster stories lately. You actually went gentle into your last good night?"

Croyd nodded, studying headlines. "You might put it that way," he said. "Unusual circumstances. Funny feeling. Hey! What's this?" He raised a newspaper and studied it. "'Bloodbath at Werewolf Clubhouse.' What's going on, a fucking gang war?"

"A fucking gang war," Jube acknowledged.

"Damn! I've got to get back on the stick fast."

"What stick?"

"Metaphorical stick," Croyd replied. "If this is Friday, it must be Dead Nicholas."

"You okay, boy?"

"No, but twenty or thirty thousand calories will be a step in the right direction."

"Ought to take the edge off," Jube agreed. "Hear who won the Miss Jokertown Beauty Pageant last week?"

"Who?" Croyd asked.

"Nobody."

*   *   *

Croyd entered Club Dead Nicholas to the notes of an organ playing "Wolverine Blues." The windows were draped in black, the tables were coffins, the waiters wore shrouds. The wall to the crematorium had been removed; it was now an open grill tended by demonic jokers. As Croyd moved into the lounge, he saw that the casket-tables were open beneath sheets of heavy glass; ghoulish figures—presumably of wax—were laid out within them in various states of unrest.

A lipless, noseless, earless joker as pale as himself approached Croyd immediately, laying a bony hand upon his arm.

"Pardon me, sir. May I see your membership card?" he asked.

Croyd handed him a fifty-dollar bill.

"Yes, of course," said the grim waiter. "I'll bring the card to your table. Along with a complimentary drink. I take it you will be dining here?"

"Yes. And I've heard you have some good card games."

"Back room. It's customary to get another player to introduce you."

"Sure. Actually, I'm waiting for someone who should be stopping by this evening to play. Fellow name of Eye. Is he here yet?"

"No. Mr. Eye was eaten. Partly, that is. By an alligator. Last September. In the sewers. Sorry."

"Ouch," Croyd said. "I didn't see him often. But when I did he usually had a little business for me."

The waiter studied him. "What did you say your name was?"

"Whiteout."

"I don't want to know your business," the man said. "But there is a fellow named Melt, who Eye used to hang around with. Maybe he can help you, maybe he can't. You want to wait and talk to him, I'll send him over when he comes in."

"All right. I'll eat while I'm waiting."

Sipping his comp beer, waiting for a pair of steaks, Croyd withdrew a deck of Bicycle playing cards from his side pocket, shuffled it, dealt one facedown and another faceup beside it. The ten of diamonds faced him on the clear tabletop, above the agonized grimace of the fanged lady, a wooden stake through her heart, a few drops of red beside the grimace. Croyd turned over the hole card, which proved a seven of clubs. He flipped it back over, glanced about him, turned it again. Now it was a jack of spades keeping the ten company. The flicker-frequency-switch was a trick he'd practiced for laughs the last time his reflexes had been hyped-up. It had come back almost immediately when he'd tried to recall it, leading him to speculate as to what other actions lay buried in his prefrontal gyrus. Wing-flapping reflexes? Throat contractions for ultrasonic wails? Coordination patterns for extra appendages?

He shrugged and dealt himself poker hands just good enough to beat those he gave the staked lady till his food came.

Along about his third dessert the pallid waiter approached, escorting a tall, bald individual whose flesh seemed to flow like wax down a candlestick. His features were constantly distorted as tumorlike lumps passed beneath his skin.

"You told me, sir, that you wanted to meet Melt," the waiter said.

Croyd rose and extended his hand.

"Call me Whiteout," he said. "Have a seat. Let me buy you a drink."

"If you're selling something, forget it," Melt told him.

Croyd shook his head as the waiter drifted away.

"I've heard they have good card games here, but I've got nobody to introduce me," Croyd stated.

Melt narrowed his eyes.

"Oh, you play cards."

Croyd smiled. "I sometimes get lucky."

"Really? And you knew Eye?"

"Well enough to play cards with him."

"That all?"

"You might check with Demise," Croyd said. "We're in a similar line of work. We're both ex-accountants who moved on to bigger things. My name says it all."

Melt glanced hastily about, then seated himself. "Let's keep that kind of noise down, okay? You looking for work now?"

"Not really, not now. I just want to play a little cards."

Melt licked his lips as a bulge ran down his left cheek, passed over his jawline, distended his neck.

"You got a lot of green to throw around?"

"Enough."

"Okay, I'll get you into the game," Melt said. "I'd like to take some of it away from you."

Croyd smiled, paid his check, and followed Melt into the back room, where the casket gaming table was closed and had a nonreflective surface. There were seven of them in the game to begin with, and three went broke before midnight. Croyd and Melt and Bug Pimp and Runner saw piles of cash grow and shrink before them till three in the A.M. Then Runner yawned, stretched, and turned out a small bottle of pills from an inside pocket.

"Anybody need something to keep awake?" he asked.

"I'll stick with coffee," Melt said.

"Gimme," said Bug Pimp.

"Never touch the stuff," said Croyd.

A half hour later Bug Pimp folded and made noises about checking on the line of joker femmes he hustled to straights wanting jittery jollies. By four o'clock the Runner was broke and had to walk. Croyd and Melt stared at each other.

"We're both ahead," said Melt.

"True."

"Should we take the money and run?"

Croyd smiled.

"I feel the same way," Melt said. "Deal."

As sunrise tickled the stained glass window and the dusty mechanical bats followed the hologram ghosts to their rest, Melt massaged his temples, rubbed his eyes, and said, "Will you take my marker?"

"Nope," Croyd replied.

"You shouldn't have let me play that last hand then."

"You didn't tell me you were that broke. I thought you could write a check."

"Well, shit. I ain't got it. What do you want to do?"

"Take something else, I guess."

"Like what?"

"A name."

"Whose name?" Melt asked, reaching inside his jacket and scratching his chest.

"The person who gives you your orders."

"What orders?"

"The ones you pass on to guys like Demise."

"You're kidding. It'd be my ass to name a name like that."

"It'll be your ass if you don't," Croyd said.

Melt's hand came out from behind his coat holding a .32 automatic, which he leveled at Croyd's chest. "I'm not scared of two-bit muscle. There's dumdum slugs in here. Know what they do?"

Suddenly Melt's hand was empty and blood began to ooze from around the nail of his trigger finger. Croyd slowly twisted the automatic out of shape before he tore out the clip and ejected a round.

"You're right, they're dumdums," he acknowleged. "Look at the little flat-nosed buggers, will you? By the way, my name's not Whiteout. I'm Croyd Crenson, the Sleeper, and nobody welshes on me. Maybe you've heard I'm a little bit nuts. You give me the name and you don't find out how true that is."

Melt licked his lips. The lumps beneath his glistening skin increased the tempo of their passage.

"I'm dead if they ever hear."

Croyd shrugged. "I won't tell them if you won't." He pushed a stack of bills toward Melt. "Here's your cut for getting me into the game. Give me the name, take it and walk, or I'll leave you in three of these boxes." Croyd kicked the coffin.

"Danny Mao," Melt whispered, "at the Twisted Dragon, over near Chinatown."

"He gives you a hit list, pays you?"

"Right."

"Who pulls his strings?"

"Beats the shit out of me. He's all I know."

"When's he at the Twisted Dragon?"

"I think he hangs out there a lot, because other people in the place seem to know him. I'd get a call, I'd go over. I'd check my coat. We'd have dinner, or a few drinks. Business didn't get mentioned. But when I'd leave, there'd be a piece of paper in my pocket with a name or two or three on it, and an envelope with money in it. Same as with Eye. That's how he worked it."

"The first time?"

"The first time we took a long walk and he explained the setup. After that, it was like I just said."

"That's it?"

"That's all."

"Okay, you're off the hook."

Melt picked up his stack of bills and stuffed it into his pocket. He opened his distorted mouth as if to say something, thought better of it, thought again, said, "Let's not leave together."

"Fine with me. G'bye."

Melt moved toward the side door, flanked by a pair of tombstones. Croyd picked up his winnings and began thinking about breakfast.

Croyd rode the elevator to Aces High, regretting the absence of a power of flight on such a perfect spring evening. Arriving, he stepped into the lounge, paused, and glanced about.

Six tables held twelve couples, and a dark-haired lady in a low-cut silver blouse sat alone at a two-person table near the bar, twirling a swizzle in some exotic drink. Three men and a woman were seated at the bar. Soft modern jazz sounds circulated through the cool air, accompaniment to blender and laughter, to the clicks and splashes of ice, liquid, and glass. Croyd moved forward.

"Is Hiram here?" he asked the bartender.

The man looked at him, then shook his head.

"Are you expecting him this evening?"

A shrug. "Hasn't been around much lately."

"What about Jane Dow?"

The man studied him. Then, "She's taken off too," he stated.

"So you really don't know if either of them'll be in?"

"Nope."

Croyd nodded. "I'm Croyd Crenson and I plan to eat here tonight. If Jane comes in, I'd like to know."

"Your best bet's to leave a note at the reservation desk before you're seated."

"Got something I can write on?" Croyd asked.

The bartender reached beneath the bar, brought up a pad and a pencil and passed them to him. Croyd scribbled a message.

As he set the pad down, his hand was covered by a more delicate one, of darker complexion, with bright red nails. His gaze moved along it to the shoulder, skipped to the silver décolletage, paused a beat, rose. It was the solitary lady with the exotic drink. On closer inspection there was something familiar . . .

"Croyd?" she said softly. "You get stood up too?"

As he met her dark-eyed gaze a name drifted up from the past.

"Veronica," he said.

"Right. You've a good memory for a psycho," she observed, smiling.

"Tonight's my night off. I'm real straight."

"You look mature and distinguished with the white sideburns."

"Damn, I missed some," he said. "And you're really missing a custom— Er, a date?"

"Uh-huh. Seems like we've both thought about getting together too."

"True. You have dinner yet?"

She gave her hair a toss and smiled. "No, and I was looking forward to something special."

He took her arm. "I'll get us a table," he said, "and I've already got a great special in mind."

Croyd crumpled the note and left it in the ashtray.

The trouble with women, Croyd reflected, was that no matter how good they might be in bed, eventually they wanted to use that piece of furniture for sleeping—a condition he was generally unable and unwilling to share. Consequently, when Veronica had finally succumbed to the sleep of exhaustion, Croyd had risen and begun pacing his Morningside Heights apartment, to which they had finally repaired sometime after midnight.

He poured the contents of a can of beef and vegetable soup into a pan and set it on the stove. He prepared a pot of coffee. While he waited for them to simmer and percolate, he phoned those of his other apartments with telephone answering machines and used a remote activator to play back their message tapes. Nothing new.

Finishing his soup, he checked whether Veronica was still asleep, then removed the key from its hiding place and opened the reinforced door to the small room without windows. He turned on its single light, locked himself in, and went to sit beside the glass statue reclining upon the day bed. He held Melanie's hand and began talking to her—slowly at first; but after a time the words came tumbling out. He told her of Dr. Finn and his sleep machine and talked about the

Mafia and Demise and Eye and Danny Mao—whom he hadn't been able to run down yet—and about how great things used to be. He talked until he grew hoarse, and then he went out and locked the door and hid the key again.

Later, a pallid dawn spreading like an infection in the east, he entered the bedroom on hearing sounds from within.

"Hey, lady, ready for a coffee fix?" he called. "And a little angular momentum? A steak—"

He paused on observing the drug paraphernalia Veronica had set out on the bedside table. She looked up, winked at him, and smiled.

"Coffee would be great, lover. I take it light. No sugar."

"All right," he replied. "I didn't realize you were a user."

She glanced down at her bare arms, nodded. "Doesn't show. Can't mainline or you spoil the merchandise."

"Then what—"

She assembled a hype and filled it. Then she stuck out her tongue, took hold of its tip with the fingers of her left hand, raised it, and administered the injection in the underside.

"Ouch," Croyd commented. "Where'd you learn that trick?"

"House of D. Can I fix you up here?"

Croyd shook his head. "Wrong time of month."

"Makes you sound raggedy."

"With me it's a special need. When the time comes, I'll drop some purple hearts or do some benz."

"Oh, *bombitas*. *Sí*," she said, nodding. "Speedballs, STP, high-octane shit. Crazy man's cooking. I've heard of your habits. Loco stuff."

Croyd shrugged. "I've tried it all."

"Not *yage*?"

"Yeah. It ain't that great."

"Desoxyn? Desbutol?"

"Uh-huh. They'll do."

"*Khat*?"

"Hell, yes. I've even done *huilca*. You ever try *pituri*? Now that's some good shit. Routine's a little messy, though. Learned it from an abo. How's about *kratom*? Comes out of Thailand—"

"You're kidding."

"No."

"Jeez, we'll never run out of conversation. Bet I can pick up a lot from you."

"I'll see that you do."

"Sure I can't set you up?"

"Right now coffee'll do fine."

The morning entered the room, spilling over their slow movements.

"Here's one called the Purple Monkey Proffers the Peach and Takes It Away Again," Croyd murmured. "Learned it—heard of it, that is—from the lady gave me the *kratom*."

"Good shit," Veronica whispered.

When Croyd entered the Twisted Dragon for the third time in as many days, he headed directly to the bar, seated himself beneath a red paper lantern, and ordered a Tsingtao.

A nasty-looking Caucasian with ornate scars all over his face occupied the stool two seats to his left, and Croyd glanced at him, looked away, and looked again. Light shone through the septum of the man's nose. There was a good-size hole there, and a patch of scabbed pinkish flesh occurred on the nose's tip. It was almost as if he had recently given up on wearing a nose ring under some duress.

Croyd smiled. "Stand too near a merry-go-round?"

"Huh?"

"Or is it just the *feng shui* in here?" Croyd continued.

"What the hell's *feng shui*?" the man said.

"Ask any of these guys," Croyd said, gesturing broadly. "Especially, though, ask Danny Mao. It's the way energy circulates in the world, and sometimes it gets you in a tricky bind. Lady from Thailand told me about it once. Like, killer *chi* will come blasting in that door, bounce off the mirror here, get split by that *ba-gua* fixture there and"—he chugged his beer, stepped down from his stool and advanced—"hit you right in the nose."

Croyd's movement was too fast for the man's eyes to follow, and he screamed when he felt that the finger had passed through his perforated septum.

"Stop it! My God! Cut it out!" he cried.

Croyd led him off his stool.

"Twice I've gotten the runaround in this joint," he said loudly. "I promised myself today that the first person I ran into here was going to talk to me."

"I'll talk to you! I'll talk! What do you want to know?"

"Where's Danny Mao?" Croyd asked.

"I don't know. I don't know any—aah!"

Croyd had crooked his finger, moved it in a figure eight, straightened it.

"Please," the man whined. "Let go. He's not here. He's—"

"I'm Danny Mao," came a well-modulated voice from a table partly masked by a dusty potted palm. Its owner rose and followed it around the tree, a middle-size Oriental man, expressionless save for a quirked eyebrow. "What's your business here, paleface?"

"Private," Croyd said, "unless you want to stand out on the street and shout."

"I don't give interviews to strangers," Danny said, moving toward him.

The man whose nose Croyd wore on his finger whimpered as Croyd turned, dragging him with him.

"I'll introduce myself in private," Croyd said.

"Don't bother."

The man's fist flashed forward. Croyd moved his free hand with equal rapidity and the punch struck his palm. Three more punches followed, and Croyd stopped all of them in a similar fashion. The kick he caught behind the heel, raising the foot high and fast. Danny Mao executed a backward flip, landed on his feet, caught his balance.

"Shit!" Croyd observed, moving his other hand rapidly. The stranger howled as something in his nose snapped and he was hurled forward, crashing into Danny Mao. Both men went down, and the weeping man's nose gushed red upon them. "Bad feng shui," Croyd added. "You've got to watch out for that stuff. Gets you every time."

"Danny," came a voice from behind a carved wooden screen beyond the foot of the bar, "I gotta talk to you."

Croyd thought he recognized the voice, and when the small, scaly joker with the fanged, orange face looked around the screen's corner, he saw it to be Linetap, who had erratic telepathic abilities and often worked as a lookout.

"Might be a good idea," Croyd told Danny Mao.

The man with the bleeding nose limped off to the rest room while Danny flowed gracefully to his feet, brushed off his trousers, and gave Croyd a quick burning glance before heading back toward Linetap.

After several minutes' conversation Danny Mao returned from behind the screen and stood before him.

"So you're the Sleeper," Danny said.

"Yep."

"St. John Latham, of the law firm Latham, Strauss."

"What?"

"The name you're after. I'm giving it to you: St. John Latham."

"Without further struggle? Free, gratis and for nothing?"

"No. You will pay. For this information I believe that soon you will sleep forever. Good day, Mr. Crenson."

Danny Mao turned and walked away. Croyd was about to do the same when the man with the nose job emerged from the rest room, holding a large wad of toilet tissue to his face.

"Hope you know you've made the Cannibal Headhunters' shit list," he snuffled.

Croyd nodded slowly. "Tell them to mind the killer *chi*," he said, "and keep your nose clean."

The Second Coming
of Buddy Holley

by Edward Bryant

Wednesday

The dead man slammed his fist through the pine door.

No knuckles broke, but his skin tore. Blood streaked the wooden shards of door panel. It hurt, but not enough. No, it didn't hurt much at all, other things considered. "Other things"—what a euphemistic code for people and relationships, lovers and kin. The dirty little politics of rejections and betrayals. Jesus god, *they* hurt.

Real mature, my frien', Jack Robicheaux thought. Going through the grieving process at Mach 10. Right past denial and directly to self-pity. Real grown-up for a guy into his forties. Fuck it.

He gingerly withdrew his hand from the shattered door. Naturally the long wooden splinters faced the wrong way. It was like trying to extract his flesh from some sort of toothy trap.

Jack turned and walked back into the shambles of his living room. It still looked like Captain Nemo's stateroom on the *Nautilus*—after the giant squid had wrestled with the submarine in the middle of the Atlantic's storm of a century.

He loved this room. "Love." Funny word to use anymore.

Kicking aside a shattered antique sextant, Jack crossed to the outside door—the one opening on a passage leading to the subway maintenance tunnels—and bolted it. As he did so, he caught a last whiff of Michael's sharp citrus after-shave. The image of Michael's retreating back, shoulders slightly hunched with denial, flickered in the space the door occupied, vanished, slipped out of existence with not even a whimper.

Jack stepped over the old-fashioned phone crafted as the effigy of Huey Long. Somehow it had miraculously ended on the floor upright with the earpiece still cradled in Huey's upraised right hand. Ol' Huey had communicated like a son-of-a-bitch. Why couldn't Jack?

He couldn't call Bagabond.

He wouldn't call Cordelia.

There was no one else he wanted to talk to. Besides, he thought he'd talked enough. He'd spoken to Tachyon. An apple a day hadn't worked. And he had talked to Michael. Who was left? A priest? Not a chance. Atelier Parish was too far behind. Too many years. Too much memory.

Jack stepped behind the carved mahogany bar with the brass fittings, smelled the dusty plush velvet hanging as he opened the cabinet. The brandy had cost close to sixty bucks. Expensive on a transit worker's salary, but what the hell, he'd always read in sea novels about brandy's being administered to survivors of wrack and storm, and besides, the cut-crystal decanter fit this Victorian room beautifully.

He poured himself a triple, drank it like a double, and filled the glass again. He didn't usually gulp like this, but—

"There is an interesting fact about Mr. Kaposi," Tachyon had said. His medical smock shone an immaculate white with almost the albedo of an arctic snowfield. His red hair seemed aflame under the examining-room lights. "Shortly before he discovered and named his sarcoma in 1872, Kaposi had changed his name from Kohn."

Jack stared at him, unable to form the words he wanted to say. What the fuck was Tachyon *talking* about?

"There was, of course, a pogrom in Czechoslovakia," Tachyon said, slender fingers gesturing expressively. "He reacted to the sort of ill-informed prejudice that has cursed both jokers, not to mention aces, of course, and AIDS patients alike. Exotic viruses might as well be the evil eye."

Jack looked down at his bare chest, gingerly touching the blue-black bruiselike markings above his ribs. "I don' need no double-barreled curse. One to a customer, no?"

"I'm sorry, Jack." Tachyon hesitated. "It's difficult to say when you were infected. The tumors are well-advanced, but the biopsy and the anomalous workup results suggest there's a synergy going on between the wild card virus and the HIV organism attacking your immunosuppressant system. I suspect some sort of galloping accelerated process."

Jack shook his head as though only half-hearing. "I had a negative test a year ago."

"It's as I feared then," said the doctor. "I can't forecast the progress."

"I can," said Jack.

Tachyon shrugged sympathetically. "I must ask," he said, "if you habitually use amyl nitrite."

"Poppers?" said Jack. He shook his head. "No way. I'm not much on drugs."

Tachyon marked something on Jack's chart. "Their use is frequently connected with Kaposi's."

Jack shook his head again.

"Then there is another matter," said the doctor.

Jack stared at him. It was like trying to look out from the center of a block of ice. He felt numb all over. He knew the psychic shock would go away soon. And then— "What?"

"I must ask you this. I need to know about contacts."

Jack took a deep breath. "There was one. *Is* one. Only one."

"I should talk to him."

"Are you kidding?" said Jack. "I will talk to Michael. An' den I'll have him come see you. But I'll talk to him first." His voice dropped off. "Yeah, I'll talk to him."

He proceeded to remind Tachyon of the confidentiality of the doctor-patient relationship. Tachyon seemed affronted. Jack didn't apologize. Then he left. That was in the morning.

—this was a special occasion. He felt as if he were drinking after his own funeral. "Cajuns do great wakes," he said aloud, pouring another brandy. Had the decanter been full? He couldn't remember. Now it was down close to half.

He glanced at the phone again. Why the hell did he want to talk to anyone? After all, no one wanted to talk to *him*. Now that he thought about it, for the last few months living with Michael had pretty much been like living alone. Now he might as well die alone. *Can the self-pity*. But it was so *easy*—

"So what's up?" Michael had said, closing the door after him before giving Jack a squeeze. No other greeting. No preamble. As light as Jack was dark, tall and slender-limbed, Michael had always seemed to bring something of the sunlit street-level spring down with him to Jack's subterranean dwelling. Not today. Jack couldn't read him at all.

"Huh?" Michael said. Jack turned his face away and disengaged himself from the other's arms. He stepped back. "Something wrong?" Jack scrutinized Michael's face. His lover's features were the very model of glowing health. Of innocence.

"You might want to sit down," said Jack.

"No." Michael stared at him. "Just say what whatever it is you want to say."

Jack's mouth was dry. "I went to the clinic today."

"So?"

"The tests—" He had to start over. "The tests were positive."

Michael looked at him blankly. "Tests?"

"AIDS." He said the hateful word. His stomach twisted.

"No," said Michael. He shook his head. "Naw. Not a chance."

"Yes," said Jack.

"But who—" Michael's eyes widened. "Jack, did you—"

"No." Jack stared back. "There's been no one. No one else, *mon cher.*"

Michael cocked his head. "There has to be. I mean, I wouldn't—"

"It isn't like immaculate conception, Michael. No miracle here. It *has* to be."

"No," said Michael. He shook his head vehemently. "It's impossible." His eyes flickered and he looked away. Then he turned on his heel, opened the door, and left.

"No," Jack had heard Michael say one more time.

—to feel the rusty blade twisting in his gut.

The brandy, it occurred to him, as like an emotional tetanus shot. Except it wasn't working. All it did was make him feel worse because it lessened his ability to control what he was feeling.

He felt suddenly as if he had inhaled all the oxygen there was to breathe in his home. He wanted to get out, to go up to the streets. So he carefully, with what he realized were exaggerated motions, put away the brandy decanter. Then

Jack left by the same door Michael had exited. He followed the ghost's footsteps to the tunnels and ladders that took him up to the streets.

He walked. Jack could have taken the track maintenance car down below but decided he didn't want to. The night was too chilly, but that was fine. He wanted something astringent to cleanse him, to flense the bruise marks, to clean out his flesh. He realized he was wishing there was now some overt pain.

He walked uptown, not truly comprehending where he was until he saw the sign for Young Man's Fancy. I shouldn't be here, of all places, he thought. He'd met Michael here. He shouldn't be in the West Village at all. And not at this bar. But by now it was too late. Here he was. Shit. He turned to leave.

"Hey, pretty boy, lookin' to get some tail? Or *you* the tail?"

The voice was all too familiar. Jack looked up and saw the memorably overmuscled face, not to mention the body, of Bludgeon emerge from the shadowed downstairs entrance to the closed laundry below the bar. Jack turned and started away.

There was the smack of size-eighteen Brogans on the sidewalk. Fingers like German sausages curled around his shoulder and spun Jack around. "The thing about them gorgeous eyes," said Bludgeon, "is that all I gotta do is dig my thumbs in there and they'll pop out like the green cherries onna wop cookies."

Jack shrugged the fingers away. He felt impatient and not terribly cautious. He just didn't give a damn. "Fuck off," he said.

"You *need* one of these too." Bludgeon put spurned fingers to his own cheek and touched the ragged, inflamed scar that ran all the way from the edge of his right eye to his bulbous chin.

Jack remembered the triumphant shriek of Bagabond's black cat. The feline was old but agile enough to have dodged Bludgeon's flailing fists after the claws had raked down the man's ugly features.

"Cat scratches get infected," Jack said, continuing to back toward the street. "You ought to see to those. I know a real good doctor."

"Chickenshit like you's gonna need an undertaker," Bludgeon threatened. "Mr. Maz'll be real pleased if I bring in your cock in a sammich bag. Them Gambiones love to make sausage, specially outta yellow dicks like you."

"I don't have time for this," said Jack.

"Gonna make time." Bludgeon's jaws split in the kind of smirk that can deform unborn babies. "You and me—I figure I can handle a little 'gator rassling."

The door of Young Man's Fancy swung open and a gaggle of about a dozen guys spilled out onto the street. Bludgeon stopped uncertainly in midstride.

"Witnesses," said Jack. "Down, boy."

"I'll take 'em all," said Bludgeon, surveying his prospective victims. He smacked the macelike mutation of his right hand into the palm of his left. It sounded like dropping a beef roast off a stepladder onto a tiled floor.

"A little gay bashing?" said the man apparently leading the others. He grimaced at Bludgeon. "You still hanging around, dork-breath?" His hand dipped inside his jacket and came out filled with blued steel. "Wanna see my Bernie Goetz impression?" He laughed. "It's a guaranteed killer."

Bludgeon looked around the semicircle of faces. "I gotta job to protect," he finally said to Jack. "You," he said to the man with the gun, "I'm gonna take out your guts with my thumb. Just wait. And you—" he said back to Jack, "you I'm gonna really hurt."

"But another time," said Jack.

"Fuckin' A." Bludgeon couldn't seem to find a better exit line. He lurched away from the growing crowd of onlookers and stomped down the street.

"Pretty rough trade," the man with the gun said to Jack. He put the pistol back under his coat. "I hope you know what you're doing."

"Thanks," said Jack. "I don't know the guy. He just stopped me for a light." He turned and headed the opposite direction, ignoring the murmurs.

"So you're welcome, man," said the man with the pistol. "Good luck, buddy."

Jack turned the corner and headed down a darker block. Christ it was cold. He hugged himself. He hadn't worn a coat. The chill was making him sluggish. Bad sign. He tentatively touched the back of his left hand with the fingers of his right. The skin felt rough, scaly, beginning to transform. No! He started to run. He didn't need this too. Not tonight.

Stress symptoms. He almost giggled.

He looked for a subway entrance. It didn't matter which. Red globe or green. BMT, IRT, or PATH. Uptown or downtown. Just as long as the stairs led down.

He searched for the telltale steam from a manhole cover. The sewers would do. That would be better. There'd be no people in the sewers. Those tunnels, warm and slimy, would lead toward the bay. Good hunting. Fine with Jack. He thought about his 'gator teeth ripping into albino gar. That was okay. Bagabond didn't give much of a shit about mutant fish. Food. Blood. Death. Exhaustion. Blankness.

Jack stumbled toward the deeper darkness, homing in on a warm grating.

I'm losing it, he thought.

He saw Michael's face. Bagabond's. Cordelia's.

Yeah, he'd lost it all right. Everything.

Jack plunged into the night.

Thursday

The volume of the bootleg mix of the new George Harrison album was sufficient to shiver the framed pictures on the office wall. But then the size of the office wasn't enough to provide much challenge to the cassette deck's amplifier. It wasn't a large office and didn't occupy the corner of the office tower, but it was a separate office regardless, with permanent walls, and it *did* have a window.

Cordelia Chaisson was happy with it.

Her desk was old and wooden and held, besides the computer, stacks of albums, tapes, and press kits. The pictures on the opposite wall were photos of Peregrine, David Bowie, Fantasy, Tim Curry, Lou Reed, and other entertainers, whether aces or not. In the midst of the photographs was a framed cross-stitch sampler reading DAMN, I'M GOOD. Tacked to the wall behind and to Cordelia's right was a large rectangle of poster board. It held a list of names, copiously emended with cross-outs, question marks, and shorthand notes such as "check film startup," "rel. fanatic," and "won't perform Brit. hol."

Her phone beeped to her. It was a few moments before Cordelia noticed. She thumbed down the volume control on the deck and picked up the receiver. Luz Alcala, one of her bosses, said, "My sweet lord, Cordelia, do you think you could perhaps use the headphones?"

"Sorry," said Cordelia. "I got carried away. It's a great album. I've already turned down the volume."

"Thank you," said Alcala. "Any word yet on who'll cut the promos for us?"

"I'm going down the list. Jagger, maybe." The young woman hesitated. "He hasn't said no."

"Have you called him in the last week?"

"Well . . . no."

Alcala's voice took on a mildly reproving tone. "Cordelia, I admire what you're accomplishing with the benefit. But GF and G has other projects to consider as well."

"I know," said Cordelia. "I'm sorry. I'm just trying to juggle a lot of things." She tried to sound more upbeat—and change the subject. "The clearances came through for China this morning. This means we'll be beaming to better than half the world."

"Not to mention Australia." Alcala chuckled.

"Including Australia."

"Call Jagger's agent," said Alcala. "Okay?"

"Okay." Cordelia hung up the phone. She picked up the small, intricately carved, stone lizard-shape from the desktop where it had nearly been covered over with a heap of glossies. It was actually an Australian crocodile, but she had been assured that it was her cousin and therefore appropriate as a fetish. She preferred to think of it as a 'gator. Cordelia replaced the figure, setting it in front of the small, framed black-and-white photo of a young aboriginal man. He scowled seriously out of the portrait. "Wyungare," she whispered. Her lips formed a kiss.

Then she swiveled her chair around to face the poster board on the wall. Taking a thick marker, she began crossing out names. What she ended up with was a list of U2, the Boss, Little Steven, the Coward Brothers, and Girls With Guns. Not bad, she thought. Not damn bad a-tall.

But—she chuckled with satisfaction—there was more. She reached up again with the marker—

*   *   *

The three of them had eaten an early lunch at the Acropolis on Tenth Street, just off Sixth Avenue. Cordelia had offered to take them to a plusher place. After all, she had an expense account now. The Acropolis was a mere café, indistinguishable from thousands of others in the city. "The Riviera's only a few blocks away," she'd said. "It's an okay place."

C.C. Ryder was having none of it. She wanted an anonymous meeting place. She asked that they meet well before the mealtime rush. She wanted Bagabond along.

She got what she wanted because Cordelia needed her.

So they ended up in the Naugahyde booth with C.C. and Bagabond on the side facing both Cordelia and the door. Cordelia looked up from the menu and smiled. "I can recommend the fruit cup."

C.C. didn't smile back. Her expression was serious. She took off her nearly shapeless leather porkpie cap and shook out her spiky red hair. Cordelia noticed that C.C.'s brilliant green eyes looked very much like Uncle Jack's. *I've got to call him*, she thought. She didn't want to, but she had to.

"See the raccoon rings?" said C.C., pointing to her own eyes. Today she didn't look much like one of rock's top lyricists and performers. The effect was deliberate. She wore jeans so old and worn, they looked acid-washed. Her floppy John Hiatt sweatshirt appeared to have endured almost as many washings.

"Nope," said Cordelia. C.C.'s skin looked smooth and white, almost albino in its lightness.

"Well, there ought to be." A bare smile ghosted across C.C.'s lips. "I've been losing sleep over this whole thing with the benefit."

Cordelia said nothing; kept looking the singer in the eye.

"I know this is Des's last hurrah," C.C. continued. "And I know the cause is a good one. A joint benefit for AIDS patients and the wild card victims is something whose time is long since due."

Cordelia nodded. This was looking good.

C.C. shrugged. "I guess I gotta come out of the anxiety closet sometime and perform in front of live folks." She smiled for real. "So the answer is yes."

"Super!" Cordelia leaned across the table and hugged C.C. fiercely. Startled, Bagabond half-rose from her seat, ready, it seemed to Cordelia, who saw the motion from the corner of her eye, to tear out her throat if she were actually attacking C.C. Cordelia did hear a low snarl, much like one of Bagabond's cats, as she disentangled herself from C.C. and settled back in her seat.

"That's wonderful!" said Cordelia. She stopped burbling when she saw C.C.'s face. She could read the expression. "I'm sorry." Cordelia sobered. "It's just that I've loved your music, loved *you* as a writer for so long, I've wanted to see you perform your songs more than just about anything."

"It's not going to be easy," said C.C. Bagabond looked at her concernedly. "What have we got, ten days?"

Cordelia nodded. "Barely."

"I'm gonna need every minute."

"You've got it. I'm going to give you someone as a liaison with me who will get you whatever you want, whenever you need it. Somebody I trust, and so do you."

"Who's that?" said Bagabond with evident suspicion. The muscles of her gaunt face tightened. Her brown eyes narrowed.

Cordelia took a deep breath. "Uncle Jack," she said.

The expression on Bagabond's face was not pleasant. "Why?" she said. C.C. glanced aside at her. "Why not me?"

"You can help C.C. as much as you want," said Cordelia hastily. "But I need Uncle Jack to be involved with all this. He's competent and he's levelheaded and he's trustworthy. I'm in over my head," she said candidly. "I need all the help I can scrounge."

"Jack know about this?" said Bagabond.

Cordelia hesitated. "Well, I been waitin' to tell 'im." She realized the Cajun was starting to creep through more as she got flustered. She took a mental grip on herself. "I been leavin' messages on his phone machine. He hasn't been answering."

Bagabond leaned back in her seat and closed her eyes. A minute went by. It seemed a long time. The Greek waiter came by to take their orders. C.C. told him to come back shortly.

When she opened her eyes again, Bagabond shook her head as though clearing it. "I don't know when the boy's going to answer your calls."

"What do you mean?" Cordelia felt a listing feeling as though her plans were papers sliding off a carefully leveled table.

"It's all broken up," said Bagabond. "Jack's a ways off—probably about New York Bay, I'd judge. He's getting his rocks off duking it out with the kind of critters you don't see in the Castle Clinton Aquarium. As much raw meat as he's getting"—she smiled humorlessly—"I couldn't say whether he's going to get home for dinner anytime soon."

"*Quelle damnation*," Cordelia muttered. "In any case," she said to C.C., "call me at the office tomorrow morning and I'll have something lined out. Either Uncle Jack or someone else."

"Make it someone else," said Bagabond.

Cordelia smiled placatingly. The waiter returned and she ordered the fruit cup.

—and marked C.C. down on the roster of benefit performers in bold, black letters.

"Doggonit," Cordelia said aloud to herself, "I'm good."

Then she hesitated and glanced back at the copy of the *Village Voice* lying on the desk. A small events notice in microscopic type was circled in red.

She scrawled one additional name on the board.

Friday

Merde.

No two ways about it. That's what he felt like as he dragged into his home in the early morning. There was nothing welcome about entering the shambles of his living room. Jack stumbled through the debris. Ahead of him he saw the shattered door to his bedroom. His hand still hurt. But now, so did his teeth. His head, his hands—it seemed to him that every bone in his body ached.

"*Enfer,*" he swore as he saw the blinking red light of his answering machine. He almost managed to ignore the single-eyed demon; then he bent and slapped the playback switch. Three of the messages were from his supervisor. Jack knew he'd better call back later in the morning, or he'd have no job to return to. He *liked* living down here, and he enjoyed the privilege of gainful employment down in the darkness.

The other eight messages were from Cordelia. They were not very informative, but neither did they sound like emergencies. Cordelia kept saying it was important for Jack to get back to her, but the tone didn't indicate mortal peril.

Jack rewound the message tape and turned off the machine, then went into the kitchen. He surveyed the refrigerator and didn't bother opening it. He knew what was inside. More, he simply wasn't hungry. He had some idea of what he had devoured over the past day and night and didn't want to think about it. Blind, albino gar. You wouldn't find that on the menu at any Cajun restaurant in New York.

He went into the bedroom and flopped down on the bed. There was no question of undressing. Jack only moved sufficiently to wind the antique quilt around himself. He was out.

The phone by the bed awoke him at eight A.M. precisely. He knew this because the red LED numerals on the clock burned themselves into his retinas when he finally opened his eyes and reached over to stop the shrilling that was scraping his inner ear into shreds.

"Mmmppk. Yeah?"

"Uncle Jack?"

"Yeah—uh, Cordie?" He came a good deal more awake.

"It's me, Uncle Jack. I'm sorry if I woke you. I've been tryin' to get you for better den a day."

He yawned and adjusted the receiver so the pillow would hold it snug. "'S okay, Cordie. I got to call the boss and tell him I'm down with something and been too sick to phone the last couple days."

Cordelia sounded alarmed. "You really sick?"

Jack yawned again. Remembered what he could have said. "Pink of health. Just went off on a bender, that's all."

"Bagabond said—"

"*Bagabond?*"

"Yes." Cordelia seemed to be picking her words carefully. "I asked her to look for you. She said you were out in the bay, uh, killing things."

"That about describes it," said Jack.

"Something wrong?"

He waited a few seconds before answering. Took a breath. "Stress, Cordie. That's all. I needed to unwind."

She didn't sound wholly convinced but finally said, "Whatever you say, Uncle Jack. Say, listen, do you mind if I come by tonight after work and bring along a friend?"

"Who?" Jack said guardedly.

"C.C."

Jack thought about her, remembered visiting her in Tachyon's clinic. He owned everything she'd ever recorded, albums and tapes both, shelved out in the next room. "I guess so," he said. "It'll give me an excuse to clean up the house."

"No need," said Cordelia.

He laughed. "Oh, yeah, dere is a need."

"Five-thirty okay?"

"Should be. By the way," he said, "what's this all about?"

She was candid. "I need your help, Uncle Jack." She filled him in on how things were proceeding with logistics for the benefit. "I'm snowed," she said. "I cannot do everything."

"I don' know much about putting on this kind of event."

"You know rock 'n' roll," she said. "Better, you can handle just about anything that happens."

Almost anything, he thought. Tachyon's face floated in front of him. Michael's. "Flatterer," he said.

"*Vérité*."

A few moments went by. "One thing I got to ask," said Jack. "We haven't been talkin' much . . ."

"I know," she said. "I know. For now I'm just not thinking much 'bout it."

"No resolution, then?"

"Not yet."

"Thanks for bein' honest."

More seconds went by. It seemed as though Cordelia wanted to say something, but finally all she said was, "Okay, thanks then, Uncle Jack. I'll be by with C.C. at half past five. 'Bye."

Jack listened to the silence until the circuit disconnected. Then he turned over and dialed his supervisor at the Transit Department. He wouldn't have to concentrate to sound convincingly sick.

When he opened the door to Cordelia and C.C. late in the afternoon, Jack realized that cleaning up his living room probably had been the easier part of the day. Cordelia's eyes seemed to squint as she looked at him, as though she were actually seeing two images and trying to choose the one she would perceive.

"Uncle Jack," she said. There was a stiff instant as she appeared to debate whether to give him a hug.

The woman standing beside her defused the moment. "Jack!" said C.C. "It's good to see you again." She stepped past Cordelia into the living room, giving Jack a firm hug and a warm kiss on the lips. "You know something?" she said. "Even though I didn't know what was going on for a long time, it really meant a lot, your coming to visit me in the clinic. Anything ever happens to you, you *know* I'll be there every visiting period, okay?" She grinned.

"Okay," he said.

"*Mon Dieu*," said Cordelia, looking around Jack's home. "What happened here?"

Jack's restoration efforts had not been totally successful. Some of the smashed antique furniture was stacked to one side of the room. He hadn't the heart to take it topside to a Dumpster. There was still the chance of careful repair and restoration.

"When I was coming in last night," he said. "I slipped."

"Shot while trying to escape," said Cordelia ironically. "Whatever happened, Uncle Jack, I'm really sorry. This was such a beautiful place."

"It still ain't shabby," said C.C., plopping down in a claw-footed love seat. She spread her arms as she sank into the overstuffed upholstery. "This is great." She smiled up at Jack. "Got some coffee?"

"Sure," he said. "It's all made."

"Bagabond was going to come along—" C.C. started to say.

"She had some errands uptown," said Cordelia.

"I think she'd want me to say hello," said C.C.

"Sure." Right, he thought. Cordelia offered to help with the coffee, but he shooed her back to the living room.

When everyone was settled with a steaming mug and a plate of scones with strawberry preserves, Jack said, "So?"

"So," said C.C., "your niece is very persuasive. But so's my own ego. I'm gonna come out of seclusion for the benefit, Jack. Back to public performance. Cold turkey. Nothing half-assed. A couple billion potential viewers. There I'll be, in front of God and everybody." She chuckled. "Nothing like hitting acute agoraphobia head on."

"Pretty gutsy," said Jack. "I'm glad you're doing it. New stuff?"

"Some old, some new," she said. "Some borrowed, some blues. It all depends on what the boss here"—C.C. gestured at Cordelia—"gives me for time."

"Twenty minutes," said Cordelia. "That's what everybody gets. The Boss, Girls With Guns, you."

"Equality's a great thing." C.C. looked back at Jack. "So you're gonna help me get ready for the big night?"

"Uh," said Jack.

"GF and G can persuade the Transit people to give you time off," said Cordelia quickly. "I talked to one of their guys in community relations. They think it'd be terrific to have one of their own involved in something like this."

"Uh huh," said Jack.

"With pay," Cordelia said. "And GF and G'll give you a fee too."

"I've got savings," Jack said quietly.

"Uncle Jack, I *need* you."

"I've heard that before." Gently, this time.

"So I say it to you again." It seemed to him Cordelia's voice, her expression, her eyes, were all one coordinated appeal.

"It would be good to work with you," said C.C. She winked one emerald eye. "Free backstage pass. Rub shoulders with the stars."

Jack looked from one woman to the other. "Okay," he finally said. "It's a deal."

"Great," said Cordelia. "I'll start feeding you the details. But there's one more thing I want to mention now."

"Why do I have the feeling," said Jack, "that I ought to be a 'gator at this very moment, lookin' up at the gaff?"

"You have plans for tomorrow night?" Cordelia said.

Jack spread his hands. "I thought I'd maybe refinish some chairs."

"You're coming with us to New Brunswick."

"New Jersey?"

Cordelia nodded. "We're going to the Holidome. We're going to see Buddy Holley."

Jack said, "*The* Buddy Holley? I thought he was dead."

"He's been on the lounge circuit for years. I saw a note about his appearance in the *Voice*."

"She wants him for the benefit," said C.C. again.

"A nostalgia act?" said Jack.

Cordelia was actually blushing. "I grew up with his music. I worship the man. I mean, nothing's set with the benefit and him. I just want us to go see him and find out if he's anything like he used to be."

"You may be in for a rude shock," said C.C. "Guitar of clay and all that."

"I'll risk it."

"'Not Fade Away''s one my favorite songs ever," said Jack. "Count me in."

"Tell him," C.C. said to Cordelia.

"Bagabond's going too," she said reluctantly.

"I don' know 'bout this," said Jack. He thought about his first encounter with Bludgeon, when the black cat had saved him from having to tangle with the psychopathic gay-basher. Had the cat been acting on his own, or at Bagabond's suggestion? He'd never asked the woman. Maybe he would tomorrow night.

"Uncle Jack?" said Cordelia.

He smiled at her. "Let's rock."

Saturday

"Oh, my god," C.C. said, sufficiently low that only Jack heard. "He's covering Prince, goddamned Prince!"

"And not very well," said Jack.

Cordelia had worried because of glacial traffic in the Holland Tunnel that the four of them would be late for Buddy Holley's first set. She also fretted that Jersey youth would make off with the Mercedes she'd borrowed from Luz Alcala.

"It's a Holiday Inn," said Jack as they pulled into the entrance.

"So?"

"The parking lot's illuminated," said Jack.

"There's an empty space close to the lobby," said Cordelia with relief.

"You want me to slip ten to the clerk to keep an eye on the car?"

"Would you?" said Cordelia seriously.

So they'd parked and secured the Mercedes and entered the New Brunswick Holidome.

The trip over from the city had been tense enough. Jack had ridden shotgun in front with Cordelia driving. Bagabond sat in back on the opposite side, as far from Jack as she could get. Both C.C. and Cordelia had done their best to keep a conversation going. Jack decided it was an inappropriate time to quiz Bagabond about whether his erstwhile rescuer, the black cat, had been acting autonomously or on his mistress's orders.

"Dis is gon' be great," said Cordelia. She had slotted a cassette of Buddy Holley and the Crickets' greatest hits into the Blaupunkt player. The speaker system was far, far better than adequate.

"Cordelia," said Bagabond, "I like Buddy a lot, but maybe so he doesn't hurt my ears?"

"Oh, sorry," said Cordelia. She turned the volume knob down to barely endurable.

Then Saturday-evening traffic slowed to a stop-and-go creep within the tunnel, the stench of auto exhaust rose up in visible clouds, and the four in the Mercedes listened to all of Cordelia's Buddy Holley tapes before they reached New Jersey.

Cordelia had become more nervous the later it got. "Maybe there'll be a warm-up group," she'd muttered.

There hadn't been, but it turned out not to matter. When the four walked through the door of the Holidome lounge, they saw there was no need to worry about seats. Perhaps half the booths and tables were vacant. Clearly Saturday-night bacchanalia in New Brunswick didn't center here. They took a table about ten feet from the low stage, Jack and Bagabond on opposite sides, buffered by C.C. and Cordelia.

And Buddy Holley covered Prince.

Jack recognized Holley from the album portraits. He knew the musician was forty-nine, close enough to Jack's own age. Holley looked older. His face carried too much flesh; his belly wasn't completely camouflaged by the silver-lamé jacket. He no longer wore the familiar old black horn-rims; his eyes were masked by stylish aviator shades that couldn't quite hide the dark bags. But he still played the Fender Telecaster like an angel.

The same couldn't be said for his sidemen. The rhythm

guitarist and the bass player both looked about seventeen. Their playing was not inspired. The muddy sound mix didn't help. The drummer flailed at his snares, the volume coming through at about the right level to completely mask Holley's vocal delivery.

In rapid order Buddy Holley segued from Prince into a bad Billy Idol and then a so-so Bon Jovi.

"I don't believe it," said C.C., drinking a healthy dollop of her Campari and tonic. "All he's doing is covering top-forty shit."

Cordelia watched silently, her expression of initial enthusiasm visibly fading.

Bagabond shook her head disapprovingly. "We shouldn't have come."

Maybe, Jack thought, *he's biding his time*. "Give him a little while."

As the desultory clapping faded after a game attempt at evoking Ted Nugent, a voice from the back of the lounge yelled, "Come *on*, Buddy—give us some oldies!" A ragged cheer went up. Most of the clapping came from Cordelia's table.

Buddy Holley took his Telecaster by the neck and leaned toward the audience. "Well," he said, the West Texas twang still pronounced, "I don't usually take requests, but since you've been such a terrific crowd . . ." He settled back and strummed out a rapid-fire sequence of opening chords that his backup group more-or-less followed.

"Oh, lord," said C.C. She took another drink as Buddy Holley tore into Tommy Roe's "Hurray for Hazel," then a quick verse of "Sheila," finally a lugubrious, almost-bluesy version of Bobby Vinton's "Red Roses for a Blue Lady." Holley continued in that vein. He played a lot of music made famous by Bobbys and Tommys in the fifties and sixties.

"I want to hear 'Cindy Lou' or 'That'll Be the Day' or 'It's So Easy' or 'T-town,'" said Cordelia, distractedly swirling her gin and tonic. "Not this shit."

I'll settle for "Not Fade Away," Jack thought. He watched Buddy Holley slog through the dismal pop retrospective and started getting real depressed. It was enough to make him maybe wish that Holley had died at the height of his initial popularity and not survived to fall into this ghastly self-mockery.

Inebriated conversation and drunken laughter escalated at

the surrounding tables. It appeared that most in the lounge had completely forgotten that Buddy Holley was performing onstage. When Holley came to the end of his set, he introduced the final number very simply. "This is something new," he said. The sparse crowd was having none of it; they had turned actively hostile.

"Fuck you!" somebody shouted. "Turn on the jukebox!"

Holley shrugged. Turned. Walked off the stage.

His backup guitarists quietly put their instruments down; the drummer got up and laid his sticks on an amp.

"Why doesn't he do his classics?" said Cordelia. "Hang on," she said to her companions. Then she got up and collared Buddy Holley as he headed toward the bar. They saw her talking earnestly to the man. She led him back to the table, dragged up a vacant chair, appeared to be making him sit through dint of sheer will. Holley looked bemused at the whole affair. Cordelia made introductions. The musician courteously acknowledged each name and shook hands in turn.

Jack found the man's grip warm and firm, not flabby at all. Cordelia said, "We're four of your greatest fans."

"Sort of sorry you're all here," said Holley. "I feel like I owe everyone an apology. This isn't a good show tonight." He shrugged. "'Course *most* nights in lounges are like that." Holley smiled self-deprecatingly.

"Why don't you play your own music?" said Bagabond without preamble.

"Your *old* music," said Cordelia. "The great stuff."

Holley looked around the table. "I've got my reasons," he said. "It ain't a matter of not wanting to. I just can't."

"Well," said Cordelia, smiling, "maybe I can help change your mind." She launched into her spiel about the benefit at the Funhouse, about how Holley could go on early in the following Saturday's performance, that maybe he could do a medley of the music that had propelled him to superstardom in the fifties and early sixties, that perhaps—just maybe—the concert and the telecast could rejuvenate his career. "Just like when the Boss found Gary U.S. Bonds playing in bars like this," she finished up.

Buddy Holley looked honestly astonished by Cordelia's outpouring of enthusiasm. He put his elbows on the table, closely studying the club soda and lime the waitress had brought him, finally looking up at her with a slight smile. "Listen," he said. "I thank you. I truly do. Hearing something like this makes my night—hell, the whole year." He looked away. "But I can't do it."

"But you *can*," said Cordelia.

He shook his head.

"Think about it."

"Won't do no good," he said. "It won't work." He patted her hand. "But thanks for the thought." And with that, he nodded to the rest of them, then got up and trudged through the smoke to the stage for his second set.

"Damn," said Cordelia.

Jack watched the musician's back as Holley hoisted himself up onto the stage. There was something familiar about how the man carried himself. It was the sense of defeat. Jack thought he'd last seen that slight slumping of shoulders and hanging of head when he'd looked in the mirror. *Just this morning*.

He wondered how many years and what disasters had beaten Buddy Holley down. *I wish*—At first the thought didn't complete itself. Then he said to himself, *I wish I could help*.

"You want to go or stay?" said C.C. to Cordelia.

"Go," said Cordelia. Almost too low to be heard, she continued, "But I think I'll be back."

"Like MacArthur?" said Bagabond.

"More like Sergeant Preston of the Mounties," said Cordelia.

Sunday

"So who are you calling a chickie?" said Cordelia, voice colder than the ocean off Jones Beach.

"What I be sayin'," said the Holiday Inn morning clerk, "is that we can't be givin' out guests' room numbers to just any chickie what comes along." He smiled at her. "Rules."

"You want to know how early I had to get up to catch a train out here?" Cordelia demanded. "Do you know how long I waited for a cab at the New Brunswick station?"

The clerk's easy smile started to fray at the lips. "Sorry."

"I'm not a goddamned groupie!" Cordelia slapped an

expensively embossed business card down on the counter.
"I'm trying to make Holley a star."

"Already was." The clerk picked up the card and examined
it. Below Cordelia's name it read 'Associate Producer.' The
escalated job title had been in lieu of a raise. "No shit? You
work with GF and G, the folks what do the Robert Townsend
show an' all that Spike Lee stuff?" He sounded halfway
impressed.

"No shit," said Cordelia. She tried smiling. "Honest."

"And you're gonna pull Buddy Holley out of this shithole?"

"Gonna try."

"O-kay," said the clerk, grinning. He glanced at the
registration spinner. "Room eighty-four twenty." He looked at
Cordelia significantly.

"So?"

With a tone of voice that suggested "Don't you know
nothin'?" the clerk said, "The main roads leadin' out of
Lubbock. The highway to Nashville."

"Oh," said Cordelia.

Buddy Holley had been asleep when Cordelia knocked on
the door of room 8420 at 9:25. That had been obvious when
he opened the door. His gray-streaked black hair was in
disarray. His glasses were slightly askew as he peered out into
the hallway.

"It's me, Cordelia Chaisson. Remember? From last night?"

"Um, right." Holley seemed to gather himself. "Can I
help you?"

"I'm here to take you to breakfast. I need to talk with you.
It's quite important."

Buddy Holley shook his head bemusedly. "Are you the
irresistible force? Or the immovable object?"

Cordelia shrugged.

"Give me ten," said Holley. "I'll meet you down in the
lobby."

"Promise?" said Cordelia.

Holley smiled slightly, nodded, and shut the door.

Buddy Holley came to the breakfast table in crisp denim
jeans, a flowered western shirt, and a brown corduroy jacket.
He looked somewhat the worse for wear, but comfortable.

He seated himself and said, "You gonna evangelize me again?"

"If I can. We can talk about dat after we get some coffee."

"Tea for me," he said. "Herbal. I brought my own. The tea selection in the kitchen is pretty shabby."

The waitress came and took their order.

"Around your neck," said Holley, pointing with his glance. "That a fetish? I saw it last night, but I was preoccupied."

Cordelia unhooked the clasp and passed the fetish over. The tiny silver alligator and the fossil tooth were bound to the delicate oval of sandstone with a tough strand of dried gut.

Holley turned the object over and over, examining it closely. "Doesn't look American southwest—Polynesian? Australia, maybe?"

"Pretty good," said Cordelia. "Aboriginal."

"What tribe? I know the Aranda pretty well, even the Wikmunkan and the Murngin, but this just ain't familiar."

"It was made by a young urban aborigine," said Cordelia. She hesitated a moment. It both excited and hurt her to think of Wyungare. And how, she wondered, was the central Australian revolution, such as it was, going? She'd been too busy with the benefit to watch much news. "He gave it to me as a going-away gift."

"Let me guess," said Holley. "The sandstone's from Uluru?" Cordelia nodded. Uluru, true name of what the Europeans called Ayers Rock. "And the reptile's your totem, of course." He held the object up to the light before passing it back over. "There's considerable power here. Not just a token."

She refastened the chain. "How do you know?"

He grinned crookedly at her. "Just don't laugh too loud, okay?"

Cordelia felt puzzled. "Okay."

"Ever since things went to hell—since they fell apart around 1972," he said hesitantly, "I been lookin' around." He contemplatively sipped his tea.

"For what?" Cordelia finally said.

"For whatever, for anything that meant something. I was just—searching."

Cordelia thought for a moment. "Spirituality?"

Holley nodded vehemently. "Absolutely. The limos were gone, the homes, the private jet and the high living, the—"

He stopped in midsentence. "All gone. There had to be something else besides hitting the bottle and the bottom."

"And you've found it?"

"I'm still huntin'." He met her gaze and smiled. "Lotta years and a lotta miles. You know something? I'm a lot more popular in Africa and the rest of the world than I am here. Back in '75 my agent gave me a last chance and booked me into this crazy pan-African tour. Things fell apart—well, *I* fell part. I really got screwed up after I backed out of a gig in Jo'burg. Somehow I stole a Land-Rover and ended up drinkin' two fifths of Jim Beam 'way out in the bush. You know how alcohol poisonin' works? Shoot, I was well on my way."

Cordelia stared at him, held entranced by the flat, West Texas twang. The man was a storyteller.

"Bushmen found me. Tribesmen from out of the Kalahari. First thing I knew was a !Kung shaman leanin' down over me and lettin' out the most ungodly screams you ever heard. Later I found out he was taking the sickness into himself and then gettin' shed of it into the air." Holley contemplatively touched the pad of his thumb to his incisors. "That was the beginning."

"And since?" said Cordelia.

"I keep lookin'. I search everywhere. When I played a string of bars in the Dakotas and the Midwest I learned about Rolling Thunder and the generations of Black Elk. The more I learned, the more I wanted to know." His voice took on a dreamy quality. "When I was with the Lakota, I cried for a vision. The shaman took me through the *inipi* ceremony and sent me up the hill to receive the *wakan*, the holy beings." Holley smiled ruefully. "The Thunder Beings came, but that was about all. I got wet and cold." He shrugged. "So it goes."

"You keep searching," said Cordelia.

"I do that," said Holley. "I learn. I been off booze since South Africa. No more drugs either. As for what I'm learnin', it ain't easy to work with a hardshell Baptist growin' up, but that's what I've tried to do."

It occurred to Cordelia that, for all he'd been saying, Buddy Holley still seemed very anchored in the physical universe. She didn't have the same sense of ethereal dissociation that she'd gotten from spiritually transformed rock stars such as Cat Stevens or Richie Furay. She nibbled a bite from her neglected English muffin. "Most of what I know about this, I learned from my aboriginal friend, but I've thought about it. Sometimes, in my job, I wonder whether rock stars, pop singers, entertainers in the public eye in America, are sort of the contemporary equivalent of shamans."

Holley nodded seriously. "Men and women of power. Absolutely."

"They have the magic."

Buddy Holley laughed. "Fortunately the ones who believe they do, usually have nothing. And the ones who truly possess the power, don't consciously know it."

Cordelia finished her muffin. "The performers at the benefit concert next Saturday all have the power." Holley looked wary. "I'm changing the subject," Cordelia said lightly.

"I don't think things have changed since last night. You want me to play all my old standards. I just can't do that."

"Is this—" Cordelia hunted for words. "Is this a crisis of confidence?"

"That's probably part of it."

"Same thing happened with C.C. Ryder," said Cordelia. "But she changed her mind. She's gonna appear."

"Good for her." Holley hesitated. "The truth is, I *can't* play the songs you want me to do."

"Why not?"

"I don't own them anymore. 'Long about the time things went to hell, a New York outfit called Shrike Music bought up my entire catalog. They're real sweethearts. Ever see their logo? A quarter-note stuck on a spike. They been keeping my songs on ice. I hate it, but I can't do spit to get them back." Holley spread his hands helplessly.

"We'll see," said Cordelia without hesitation. "GF and G's got some pull. Is that the only other catch?"

"You think you can do anything, don't you?" Holley smiled as he shook his head. This time it was a genuine smile. His teeth were even and white. "Okay, look. You spring some of my music loose and maybe we've got a deal. Just for old times' sake."

"I don't understand," said Cordelia.

"Well, let me tell you something," said Buddy Holley. Animation filled his features and his voice. "Back in high school in Lubbock? Back when Bob Montgomery and I were first putting together a band and doin' some crazy recordings, there was a girl. I thought she was just—well—" He took a

deep breath and smiled shyly. "You know the story line. She
never noticed me a-tall. Couple years later, she was still in
my head when I recorded 'Girl on My Mind' in Nashville.
That was about the time Decca wanted me to sound like
everyone else with a rock 'n' roll hit in 1956. I sort of got out
of the formula with 'Girl.'" He shook his head. "So anyway,
you remind me of her. She knew her own way too." He
leaned back in his seat and regarded her.

"That's a great story," said Cordelia. "It's just like—"

"Rock 'n' roll," Holley finished.

They both laughed. Things, thought Cordelia, were back
on track.

Monday

First thing Monday morning, Cordelia sat at her desk and
contemplated her sins while she waited on hold with the
rights and permissions department at Shrike Music. The
background tape for Shrike's hold circuit was classical, somber and dirgelike. Cordelia suspected it was a deliberate
psych-out tactic.

It occurred to her as she examined her nails that she had
not yet tried to contact Mick Jagger. Luz Alcala would not be
happy. At least she had gotten the Mercedes back to Luz
without a scratch or dent. Well, there were priorities. It
seemed very important to secure Buddy Holley for the
Funhouse benefit.

She riffled through the phone messages that had been
stacked on her desk. U2's manager wanted her to know that
The Edge had got his fingers caught in a car door over the
weekend. U2 just might be without the services of their
guitarist. Maybe, she thought, she could convince Bono to do
an acoustic set?

The tech people had left a note alerting her that ShowSat
III was acting up over the Indian Ocean. They were working
on it. They were somewhat confident that malfunctioning
relays could be cleared. *Somewhat?* she thought. Shit.
"Somewhat" had better translate into "absolutely." She knew
damn well she didn't have the clout to get GF&G to commis-
sion a shuttle repair flight with five days notice. With *any*
notice. Christ, what was she *thinking*? Cordelia gulped some

coffee and glared down at the phone. How long was Shrike going to hang her up?

Another note was from Tami, the half-Eskimo lead guitarist of Girls With Guns. The world's greatest all-women neopunker band was stranded in Billings. And could Cordelia wire just enough cash so that *all* the members of the band could get to New York by Saturday? Probably. Cordelia jotted a note. Talk to Luz.

There was a double beep on the phone and a voice said, "Miss Delveccio, rights and permissions."

Cordelia introduced herself, sounding as calm, self-assured, and in control as she could manage. She sounded good to *her*. "I want to talk about Buddy Holley's catalog," Cordelia said. "I understand Shrike holds the rights. Here at Global Fun and Games we're very much looking forward to having Mr. Holley perform a selection of his past hits at this weekend's global benefit for medical victims."

There was a brief silence. "What sort of medical victims?"

Cordelia didn't like the sound of her voice. South Bronx, probably. "Um, AIDS and the wild card virus. The live video feed will reach—"

Miss Delveccio interrupted her. "Oh, right, *that* benefit. I'm sorry, Ms. Chaisson, but it will be quite impossible to cooperate with Global on this project. I am sorry." She didn't sound sorry.

"But surely there—"

"Shrike owns Mr. Holley's music under an exclusive license. We just won't be able to release the permissions you need." The tone of her voice said, *and that's final*.

"Perhaps if I could speak with your department head—"

"I'm afraid Mr. Lazarus isn't in today."

"Well, maybe—"

"Thank you for thinking of us, Ms. Chaisson," said Miss Delveccio. "Have a nice day." And she hung up.

Cordelia stared at the phone for a minute or two. Damn it. She hoped Miss Delveccio would have an extremely difficult period. After another minute she switched on the desk terminal and pulled up the on-line *Variety*. She flipped through a few electronic pages at random and then turned on the modem and dialed up *Variety*'s index base. While there were quite a few key-word entries for Shrike Music, but not many for Buddy Holley, there was one story that flagged both. It was dated nearly three months before, while she had been in Australia. It seemed that Shrike Music had inked a megabucks deal with America's second-largest advertising firm. The advertising company was a client of a major evangelical organization that was looking to market its theme amusement parks and other commercial subsidiaries through what the article, quoting Leo Barnett, termed "the innocent, but energetic, nostalgia" of Buddy Holley's music.

Oh, Cordelia thought. Oh, no. No wonder Shrike wasn't eager to have Holley's songs associated with the benefit. This was going to be a problem.

Luz Alcala stuck her head through the office door and said, "Good morning, Cordelia, did you have a good weekend?"

Cordelia looked up. "Definitely. You get your keys okay? Thanks again for the car."

Luz nodded. "You all right? You look a bit distracted."

"It's just Monday morning."

Luz smiled sympathetically. "By the way, did you reach our lycanthropic friend?"

Cordelia shook her head. Thought fast. "Still can't find him."

"Let me give you a suggestion. After you try their management, call the presidents of the companies they record for. When you can't get satisfaction, go upstairs. It almost always works."

Aha! thought Cordelia. "Thanks," she said.

After Luz chatted a little more and then left, Cordelia dialed Shrike back and asked for the president's office. After two layers of secretaries, she finally reached one Anthony Michael Cardwell. Cardwell was more sympathetic than Miss Delveccio, but ultimately no more helpful. "True, Shrike Music has a responsibility to the community—and we participate in *many* projects toward that end—but ultimately we are responsible to our shareholders and our corporate owners," he said. "I believe you can appreciate the difficulty of our position."

Bullshit, Cordelia thought, furious. What she said was much the same thing. Definitely too blunt. The president of Shrike Music cut the conversation short.

After setting the phone down, Cordelia drummed her fingers on the desktop. Go upstairs, Luz had said. Cordelia touched the terminal keyboard and called up GF&G's re-

search list of entertainment industry data bases. As she
started to dig out the roots of Shrike's corporate family tree,
she wondered how Jack was doing.

Naturally Jack had believed Cordelia when she had told
him Sunday night that things looked good so far as obtaining
permission for Holley to play his own music. More, GF&G
would take care of Jack's leave of absence Monday morning.
That would free Jack so he could help move Holley into
Manhattan. Cordelia had arranged a room downtown at the
Hotel California, Manhattan's premiere hostelry for visiting
musicians. "The management," Cordelia had said, "doesn't
care what happens to a room so long as the damage gets paid
for. Platinum Amex cards are welcome."

By noon Monday, while Cordelia was playing silicon Nancy
Drew, Jack had moved Buddy Holley into his eighth-floor
room at the Hotel California. "You've got an open account,"
the desk clerk had said, so they ordered up sumptuous
lunches.

Jack watched as Holley unpacked a compact tape deck
and a box of cassettes. There was an eclectic selection of new
age music—lots of Windham Hill albums, along with starkly
packaged relaxation tapes of wind, storm, sea, rain—and a
varied lot of early rock, blues, and country. "Got some scarce
stuff here," said Holley, picking up a handful of what were
obviously home-dubbed tapes. "Tiny Bradshaw, Lonnie Johnson,
Bill Doggett, King Curtis. Got the better-known stuff too—
Roy Orbison, Buddy Knox, Doug Sahm." He chuckled. "A
real Texas collection, those last boys. Also have some George
Jones—got a soft spot in my heart for that boy too. Me and
my first band played behind him back in '55 on the Hank
Cochran show."

"What's that?" Jack pointed at what seemed to be the only
vinyl record in the box of tapes.

"I'm real proud of that." Holley held up the 45. " 'Jole
Blon.' Waylon Jennings's first record. I produced that for him
back when he was playin' with the Crickets."

Jack took the record and examined it gingerly, as though
looking at a holy relic. "I guess maybe I heard this on WSN."

"Yep," said Holley. "Just about everybody I respect from
that era learned about music first from listenin' to the Grand
Ole Opry."

Jack set down the 45 of "Jole Blon." A tremendous lassitude swept across him. He looked at the remains of lunch. Nausea rocked back and forth in his belly. He sat back on the hotel couch and tried to keep his voice steady. " 'Fore I came to New York, I listened to the Opry all the time. Once I was here, I found a station out of Virginia dat carried it."

"You come from the same place as your niece?" Holley said interestedly.

Jack nodded.

"Alligator your totem too?"

Jack said nothing, trying to control the new pain in his gut.

" 'Gator's a powerful guardian animal spirit," said Holley. "I wouldn't mess with one."

Jack doubled up and tried not to whimper.

Holley was at his side. "Somethin' wrong?" He ran his hands down Jack's chest and stomach. His fingers fluttered lightly over the man's belly. He whistled. "Oh, man, I think you've got some trouble here."

"I know," said Jack. He groaned. Any other year he'd be pretty sure he could avoid the flu-type stomach bugs. But Tachyon had briefed him about opportunistic infections. He'd had the instant image of viruses zeroing in on him from every pesthole in the world. "I think maybe it's just the flu."

Holley shook his head. "It's a heavy-duty power intrusion I'm pickin' up here."

"It's a bug."

"And the bug's gettin' through to you because your protection, your personal mantle is screwed."

"Couldn't have put it better myself," said Jack.

Holley took his hands away from Jack's abdomen. "Sorry, nothin' personal. I don't know if Cordelia told you, but I—well, I know something about this stuff." Jack looked back at him bewilderedly. "What you need," said Holley seriously, "is a traditional treatment. You need to have the intrusion sucked out. I think it's the only way."

Jack couldn't help himself. He started chuckling, then guffawing. He couldn't remember the last time he'd laughed like this. It hurt to laugh, but it helped as well. Buddy Holley looked on, apparently astonished. Finally Jack straightened a bit and said, "Sorry, I just don't think, uh, sucking an intrusion out of *my* body would be a real wise idea right now."

"Don't get me wrong," said Holley. "I'm talkin' about a psychic thing, pullin' out the cause of the discomfort usin' the power of the soul and the mind."

"I'm not." Jack started laughing again. But *Dieu*, he *did* feel better.

By two in the afternoon Cordelia had accessed both the New York Public Library Reference Base and the Public Records DB in Albany. She covered several notebook pages with scrawled numbers and notes. Her task was akin to one of the thousand-piece jigsaw puzzles she never had the patience to finish.

Shrike Music was a wholly owned subsidiary of Monopoly Holdings, a New York corporation. Cordelia had dialed Monopoly's central Manhattan number and tried for the president. Whom she eventually got was the executive vice president for corporate affairs. That man told her the Buddy Holley matter was not his to comment upon, but that she should send a detailed letter to Monopoly's president, one Connel McCray. But couldn't Cordelia speak to McCray directly? she inquired. The president was indisposed. It was hard to say when he'd be back in the office.

Cordelia ascertained from Public Records that Monopoly Holdings was a division of the Infundibulum Corporation, a consortium controlled by CariBank in Nassau. The call to Infundibulum netted her a frustrating twenty minutes holding for an equally unsatisfactory conversation with the CEO's executive assistant. The long distance call to Nassau got her a heavily accented Bahamian voice claiming complete confusion about this Holley chap.

After hanging up, Cordelia regarded the frustration the phone represented. "I think I go home now," she said to herself. A break was in order. She could come back to the office later and work all night.

Veronica and Cordelia shared a high-rise apartment downtown on Maiden Lane. There wasn't much of a view—the living room windows looked out on a narrow courtyard with eleventh-floor neighbors only thirty feet away. At first it had been like watching very dull big-screen TV. Cordelia quickly learned to ignore the rest of the building. It was pleasant just having her own small room. Veronica could use the rest of the apartment as she pleased.

Cordelia had made the maximum use of her room, engaging a Soho carpenter to build an inexpensive frame of two-by-fours to support her bed. Instant sleeping loft. She just had to remember not to roll off the top during the night. The six feet of space beneath the mattress allowed her a closet, book shelves, and space to store her albums. That left her most of the wallspace for prints and posters. One wall was dominated by a color poster of Ayers Rock at dawn. The opposite wall had the common WHEN YOU'RE UP TO YOUR ASS IN ALLIGATORS poster, but with the tired maxim's payoff amended in black marker to read YOU KNOW YOU'RE HOME.

Cordelia was slotting a Suzanne Vega tape into the deck when her roommate walked in. Veronica was wearing a slinky white gown, along with a platinum wig and violet contacts. "Masquerade?" Cordelia said.

"Just a date." Veronica rolled her eyes. "It's a guy from Malta with a crush on both Marilyn Monroe and Liz Taylor." She changed the subject. "Listen, any good tickets left for Saturday?"

"At twenty-five hundred dollars a pop, I can't really comp you," said Cordelia.

"No problem. These are for management. Miranda and Ichiko can afford them. They just would like a little consideration about table placement. Close to the stage okay?"

"I'll see what I can do." Cordelia jotted a note and put her book of Things to Do back in her handbag.

"So how's work?" said Veronica innocently.

Cordelia told her.

"Sounds like you could use a *real* detective."

"If I knew one, I'd ask. I'm desperate."

"Well," said Veronica. "It just so happens maybe I can help you out."

"You want to tell me what you're talking about?" It would be *so* good, thought Cordelia, to turn this over to someone else.

"Not yet," Veronica said. "Let me work on it. And you can make sure those seats are good ones."

"Help me get Buddy Holley in front of the cameras," said Cordelia, "and I'll let Miranda and Ichiko sit onstage behind the monitors. They can hold the microphones. Anything their hearts desire."

"It's a deal. Now then," continued Veronica, "before I go uptown, whose turn is it to buy cat food?"

The men sat and listened to music and drank. Buddy Holley drank soda. Jack drank dark beer. Room service was accommodating. They talked. Every once in a while Holley would get up to change the tapes. They went through Jimmie Rodgers and Carl Perkins, Hank Williams and Jerry Lee Lewis, Elvis Presley and Conway Twitty. Jack was surprised that the singer had some tapes of newer artists: Lyle Lovett and Dwight Yoakum and Steve Earle. "Like the monkey said," Holley said simply, "you gotta keep up with evolution."

They talked about the fifties—about Louisiana bayou country and the dry vastness of West Texas. "Tell you," said Holley, "it ain't sayin' much about Lubbock when about the only place to go on Saturday night is Amarillo. I went back there after the oil boom, and then again after the crash, and nothin' much had changed either time."

"No Buddy Holley Day?" said Jack.

"Figure I'll have to die before that happens."

They had a lot in common, Jack decided. Except there'd never be a Jack Robicheaux Day in Atelier Parish. Not even after he'd died. He fumbled through the box of cassettes and held up one that was unlabeled except for the word "new." "What's this?"

"Aw, that's nothin'," said Holley. "Nothin' you'd want to hear."

There was something about the way he'd protested, Jack thought. When Buddy Holley went into the bathroom, Jack set the mysterious cassette in the deck and punched "play." The music was simple and unadorned. There was no backup, no double-tracking, no layered sound. The singing was reflective in the first song, exuberant in the second. The lyrics were mature. The characteristic hiccup in the vocal line was there. This was Buddy Holley. Jack had never heard either of these songs before.

He heard the bathroom door open behind him. Buddy Holley said, "After the plane went down with my family, and Shrike bought all my music, people seemed to think I just

wasn't gonna write anymore. And for a few years, I guess I
didn't."

The third song began.

"All dis is new," said Jack reverently. "Is it not?"

Buddy Holley's voice was soft and powerful. "Just as fresh
as resurrection."

Tuesday

The Funhouse was no Carnegie Hall, and as with virtually
any other Manhattan club, daylight didn't become it. This
morning the mirrors were streaked and dusty. They'd be
polished to a high sheen by Saturday. As Jack looked across
toward the stage, what he mostly saw were chairs stacked on
tables. The few windows and skylights admitted bars of
spring sunlight that contained myriad dancing dust motes.
The place smelled stale. The other predominating odor was
that of machine lubricant.

Jack stood beside Buddy Holley. Holley stood beside
C.C. Ryder. On the other side of C.C. was Bagabond. It
was an unbreakable protocol. Bagabond had chosen to be
C.C.'s constant companion and protector. Jack realized he
had consciously picked a similar role with Buddy Holley.
He genuinely liked the singer, and it wasn't merely a matter
of nostalgia for the fifties and sixties. He felt he was becoming genuine friends with the Texan, though *too bad*, whispered
the nasty voice in his head, *you're not going to be buddies
for very long*. Jack had seen Dr. Tachyon earlier in the
morning. Tachyon had proposed hospitalizing him. "No
way," he'd said. Tachyon appealed to his reason. "Can you
really predict what my version of the virus is going to do?"
he'd asked. Tachyon admitted that he didn't truly know. But
there were precautions . . . Jack had shrugged ruefully and
left.

Xavier Desmond, his elephantine trunk seeming to wilt
down his chest, watched over the stage preparations. He
moved slowly, in the manner of a man knowing the real
proximity of death, yet he seemed proud beyond words. For
a night the eyes of most of the world would be on his beloved
Funhouse.

The limited space in the club was being further curtailed by the camera tracks laid in front of and to the side of the stage. The tech people had cleverly rigged a superthin Louma boom from the ceiling. "Don't let it brush the chandelier!" Des said as the remote operator put the mantislike camera mount through its paces.

Even with the shafts of sun glinting off the mirror balls, the club looked drab.

Buddy Holley scratched his head. "Shoot, I've seen worse stages."

C.C. laughed and said, "I've *played* them."

"Guess there won't be no chicken wire around the stage, huh?"

C.C. shrugged and affected a deep, deep Texas accent. "Joe Ely used to tell me about places so tough, you had to puke three times and show a knife before they'd let you in. And that was if you was singin'."

"Des runs a classier dive," said Jack. "I figure people laying out twenty-five hundred dollars a seat aren't gonna heave Corona bottles at the band."

"Be more real if they did." Holley glanced at C.C. "I gotta tell you, I'm pretty excited about hearing you sing."

"Same here," said C.C., "though I'm still edgy as a cat. You decided to go on for sure?"

Holley turned to Jack. "Anything from your niece?"

Jack shook his head. "I talked to her this morning. I guess things are going slow with Shrike, but she said no sweat. Just bureaucratic runaround."

C.C. poked Holley in the ribs. "Listen, man, I will if you will."

"A challenge?" Holley slowly grinned. "Think this'll be as much fun as racin' for pink slips? What the hell. Okay. I'll go on first like the Ghost of Charts Past, and if I have to, I'll cover—oh, Billy Idol."

"No!" Bagabond spoke up. "No, you won't."

Things weren't going terribly well for Cordelia. She had gotten into the office by seven. It was too bad about being so phased that she forgot about the sequence of time zones west. Little Steven's road manager wasn't terribly happy about being awakened in his hotel room at a little past four in the morning.

On the other hand, better news had come in about ten. X rays had determined that The Edge's fingers were mildly sprained rather than fractured. Even though U2's performance that night in Seattle was being scrubbed, the guitarist had a good shot at being operational by Saturday.

Then there was the matter of Shrike Music. Cordelia had a terrific flow chart with lines and arrows indicating the tangled skein owning the music publishing firm. She had lists of CEOs, presidents, vice presidents, and heads of promotion departments. And lawyers—lord, hordes of attorneys. But no one would talk to her. *How come?* she wondered. *Is it my breath?* She giggled. Fatigue, she thought. Early burn out. Way too soon. There would be time to collapse after Saturday night. She poured another cup of high-caf Columbian and started thinking seriously about Shrike and its masters, and why everyone was evading as if she were a Congressional investigator out bird-dogging payola charges.

The phone beeped. Good. Maybe it was one of a dozen executives connected with Shrike or its Byzantine ownership returning her calls.

"Hi," said her roommate. "You got the tickets for me?"

"Have you lined up Spenser, or maybe Sam Spade?"

"Even better," said Veronica. "Got somebody here I want you to talk to."

"Veronica—" she started to say. Why was everyone playing cloak-and-dagger?

"This is Croyd," said an unfamiliar male voice. "You met me. We had a little date, you, me, and Veronica."

"I remember," said Cordelia, "but—"

"I'm in investigations." Flatly.

"I guess I knew that, but I didn't think—"

"Just listen," said Croyd. "This is Veronica's idea, not mine. Maybe I can help. Maybe not. You want to know something about Shrike Music."

"Right. Buddy Holley and I need to find out who really owns his music, so I can get permission for him to sing it, and I can convince him to appear Saturday—"

"So isn't Shrike in the phone book?" said Croyd.

"They've been stonewalling me like they were the Mafia or something."

She heard a dry chuckle. "Maybe they are."

"Anything you can do," Cordelia said, "I'll be very—"

Croyd broke in again. "I'll see what I can find out. I'll get back to you." The connection clicked off.

Cordelia set the phone down and allowed herself a smile. She crossed her fingers. Both hands. Then she picked up from the desk the next note begging her attention. This one was simpler. Maybe she could find out in less than an hour exactly why Girls With Guns seemed to be hung up in Cleveland.

Wednesday

GF&G had decided that the Funhouse club band would back both C.C. Ryder and Buddy Holley. Actually it was C.C. who approved them; GF&G paid the checks.

"They're all sound musicians," said C.C. to Holley.

"Good enough for me." He watched and listened as the two guitarists, drummer, keyboard woman, and sax player tuned.

Jack observed too. Practice would be long and tedious. But if you were an observer, it was show business in action. It was diverting. Glamorous. It was heaven.

C.C. led Holley onto the stage. Bagabond sat down at a front table, though the action looked performed under duress. Jack knew that she really did want to follow C.C. on up there.

"Mind if I sit here?" he said to her, setting his hand on the back of the chair opposite. Bagabond's dark eyes fixed on him fiercely for just a split second; she shrugged slightly and Jack sat.

"Okay," C.C. was saying to the musicians on the stage. "Here's what I'm gonna want to start with. Or maybe end with. Damned if I know yet. All I really know is that it's new and it's part of my twenty minutes." She jacked in her ebony twelve-string and strummed a chord progression. "We got a whole three days to get in tune. So remember the advantage we have over dudes like the Boss or U2." Everybody grinned. "Okay, let's do it. This is called 'Baby, You Been Dealt a Winning Hand.' One, two, three, and—"

The moment C.C. started to play, she looked stricken. "Nervous," Jack thought, was too mild a word for it. There was no crowd. There was no audience save the musicians, the technicians working on sound and lights, and the few odd observers such as Jack and Bagabond. C.C.'s lead went hideously flat. She stopped, looked down at the stage while everyone in the club seemed to hold a collective breath. Then C.C. looked up, and to Jack it seemed the motion was executed with enormous effort. Her fingers caressed the strings of her guitar. "Sorry," she said. That was all. And then she played.

> Baby, the cards are out
> > Baby, there is no doubt
> That when the dealer calls
> > You been dealt a winning hand

The drummer picked up the backbeat. The bass player chugged in. The rhythm guitar softly filled the spaces. Jack saw Buddy Holley's fingers lightly stroking the strings of his Telecaster even though it wasn't jacked in.

> You played since you were just a kid
> > You played till you got old
> Baby, you never knew a thing
> > Cause all you ever did was fold

The woman on keyboards ran an eerie, wailing trill out of her Yamaha. Jack blinked. Holley smiled. It sounded like the rinky-tink Farfisas both remembered from the presynthesizer, good old days.

> Baby, don't ever fold
> > Not when you got
> > That winning hand

When it was done, there were a long few moments of absolute silence in the Funhouse. Then the tech people started to clap. So did C.C.'s backup musicians. They cheered. Bagabond get to her feet. Jack saw Xavier Desmond in the back of the room; it looked as if there were tears on his face.

Buddy Holley scratched his head and grinned. A little like Will Rogers, Jack thought. "You know somethin', darlin'? I think maybe all of us here were privileged this mornin' to see the high point of the concert."

C.C. looked pale, but she smiled and said, "Naw, it's pretty rough. It's only gonna get better."

Holley shook his head.

C.C. Ryder marched over to him and tilted her face up toward his. "Your turn in the barrel, boyo."

The man shook his head, but his fingers were caressing the guitar.

C.C. tapped the side of her head. "I showed you mine."

Holley made a little shrug. "What the heck. Gotta do it sometime, I reckon."

"No Billy Idol," Ragabond said.

Holley laughed. "No Billy Idol." He strummed contemplatively for a moment. Then he said, "This is new." He glanced over at Jack. "This one ain't even on the tape you heard." The strum deepened, picked up strength. "I call this one 'Rough Beast.'"

Then Buddy Holley played.

"It was incredible, Cordie. It's the old Buddy Holley with all the maturity laid in." Jack's voice was exuberant and uncritical. "Everything he played was new, and it was absolutely great."

"New, huh?" Cordelia tapped the earpiece with her right index finger. "As good as 'That'll Be the Day' and 'Oh, Boy'?"

"Is 'Maxwell's Silver Hammer' better than 'I Want to Hold Your Hand'?" The excitement crackled in Jack's voice. "It isn't even apples and oranges. The new stuff's as energetic as his early songs—it's just more"—Jack seemed to be searching for the precise word—"sophisticated."

Cordelia stared at the photographs across the office but wasn't seeing them. *Click. There might as well be a light bulb switching on above my head,* she thought. *I've gotta slow down. I'm starting to miss a lot.* "What I'm guessing," she said, "is that Shrike doesn't have any claim on the new stuff. What I can do is put him in the hammock in the middle of the show. Maybe cut him down to ten minutes."

"Twenty," said Jack firmly. "It has to be as much as everyone else."

"Maybe," said Cordelia. "Anyhow, he's in the center so the audience warms up before they have to decide whether they're gon' be disappointed when Buddy Holley don' sing 'Cindy Lou.'"

There was a silence on the line. Jack finally said, "I don't think he'll mind."

"Okay, then. Great. This is really gon' simplify matters. I can tell the wet-brains at Shrike to screw off." Cordelia felt the crushing weight start to lift from her head. "You sure he'll do the show with new material?"

Jack's words were a verbal shrug. "The ice do seem to be broken. He and C.C. are reinforcing each other. I think it's all gon' work out."

"Great. Thanks, Uncle Jack. Keep me current."

Cordelia's mood was cheerful after she hung up the phone. So Buddy Holley was in. And now she could call Croyd off the wild-goose chase. But when she phoned the apartment, no one answered. All she reached was the answering machine.

Maybe, she thought cheerfully, *it's all gon' be downhill from here*.

Thursday

Cordelia realized she was humming "Real Wild Child." The up-tempo rocker perfectly matched her hyper mood this afternoon. She wondered for a moment where she'd heard it as she identified the tune. She knew it was on none of her Buddy Holley albums. The song must just be in the air.

She tapped along with her fingers to the guitar runs in her head as she dialed her postlunch calls. Cordelia had phoned over to the Funhouse just about the time her take-out Vietnamese soup had arrived. Jack was sounding up.

"Practice is going great," he had said. "C.C. and Buddy are getting along fine. And Bagabond even nodded to me when I said good morning."

"How's the music?"

"They're both doing mostly new stuff—well, Buddy's is *all* new."

"Can he fill the whole twenty minutes?" Cordelia had said.

"Just like before—when I said he wouldn't have any

problem? He still won't. You really ought to give him an hour."

"I'm not sure how U2 or the Boss would like that," Cordelia said dryly.

"I bet they'd love it."

"We won't be finding out." Cordelia sniffed the fragrance of crab and asparagus wafting out of the styrofoam soup bucket. "I've got to go, Uncle Jack. My food's here."

"Okay." Jack's voice hesitated. "Cordie?"

"Mmmp?" She already had the first spoonful in her mouth.

"Thanks for asking me to do this. It's a terrific thing. I'm grateful. It's . . . keeping my mind off everything else going on in the world."

Cordelia swallowed the hot soup. "Just go on keeping C.C. and Buddy Holley happy. And Bagabond, too, if it's possible."

"I'll try."

About two o'clock Cordelia was dialing the contract firm that was trying to exorcise the demons from ShowSat III when, out of the corner of her eye, she caught an unfamiliar figure silhouetted in the office doorway. Setting down the phone, she saw a distinguished-looking middle-aged man dressed in a cream silk suit that she knew had to be worth two or three months of her salary. Tailored to the final angstrom unit. Knotted foulard precisely positioned. Head cocked, he regarded her with sharp eyes.

"You're too well-dressed to be Tom Wolfe," she said.

"Indeed I am not. Tom Wolfe, that is." He didn't smile. "Do you mind if I come in and chat with you?"

"Did we have an appointment?" Cordelia said puzzledly. She glanced down at her calendar. "I'm afraid I don't—"

"I was in the neighborhood," said the man. "We have an appointment. It's just I'm afraid you were not informed." He extended one hand. "Forgive the lack of formal introduction. I'm St. John Latham, at your service. I represent Latham, Strauss. I expect you've heard of us."

Cordelia caught a gleam of intensely manicured nails as she grasped his hand. His grip was dry and perfunctory. "The attorneys," she said. "Uh, yes, please, do sit down."

He took the guest chair. As a backdrop for Latham's suit,

the Breuer looked a mite shabby. "Let me get to the point, Ms. Chaisson—or may I call you Cordelia?"

"If you wish." Cordelia tried to gather her thoughts. For the senior partner of one of Manhattan's priciest and nastiest law firms to be sitting in her office just might not be a good omen.

"Now," said Latham, his fingers steepled, the index fingers just brushing his thin chin, "I am informed you have been causing considerable commotion with a number of Latham, Strauss's client corporations. As you doubtless discovered, we are retained by the CariBank Group, and thus have an interest in their respective subsidiary holdings."

"I'm not sure I see—"

"You have obviously been rather inventive with your computer and modem, Cordelia. You've not been terribly discreet with your calls to a variety of corporate officials."

It was suddenly coming very clear. "Oh," said Cordelia, "this is about Shrike Music and Buddy Holley, right?"

Latham's tone was even—and functioned at about the same temperature as a superconductor. "You seem to have an extreme interest in CariBank's corporate family."

Cordelia smiled and held up her hands. "Hey, no problem, Mr. Latham. It's not my hassle any longer. Holley's got a whole collection of new music that Shrike can't touch."

"Ms. Chaisson—Cordelia—Shrike Music Corporation is the least consequential of your enquiries. We at Latham, Strauss are concerned about your apparent need for information about the rest of CariBank's family. Such information could be . . . a bit troublesome—"

"No, really," said Cordelia decisively. "This is a nonproblem. Honest, Mr. Latham. No problem." She smiled at him. "Now, if you don't mind, I've got an incredible amount of work to catch—"

Latham stared at her. "You will desist, Ms. Chaisson. You will pay attention to your own business, or, I assure you, you shall be very, very sorry."

"But—"

"*Very* sorry indeed." Latham looked at her levelly until she finally blinked. "I hope you understand me." He turned on his heel and exited with a whisper of expensive tailoring.

It hit her. *Hang me with* corde à boyau, she thought. *I've*

*just been threatened by one of Manhattan's most powerful
and predatory attorneys. So sue me.*

Cordelia had plenty to do that helped take her mind away
from Latham's visit. She called the tech people in charge of
satellite transmissions and discovered the happy fact that
ShowSat III was operational again. A healthy chunk of the
other side of the world would have a shot at viewing the
Funhouse benefit after all. "I guess the gremlins are on
vacation," said the consulting engineer.

Then GF&G's switchboard relayed a collect call from
Tami in Pittsburg.

"What on earth are you doing *there*?" Cordelia demanded.
"I sent enough cash so all the Girls With Guns could fly into
Newark today."

"You're not gonna believe this," said Tami.

"Probably not."

"We bought a lot of feathers."

"Not coke?"

"Of course not!" Tami sounded scandalized. "We ran into
a girl who had an incredible selection. We need 'em for our
costumes Saturday night."

"Feathers don't cost six hundred bucks."

"These do. They're rare."

"'Dose feathers gon' to help you fly?" Cordelia said
dangerously.

"Well . . . no," said Tami.

"I'll wire some more money. Just give me an address."
Cordelia sighed. "So. You ladies enjoy riding the bus?"

Friday

Jack and Buddy Holley headed back to the latter's
dressing room after they'd both watched the Boss do his
run-through. Holley's final rehearsal session was sched-
uled for ten o'clock, later that night. Little Steven, U2,
and the Coward Brothers had gotten in their licks early in
the afternoon. The Edge had winced a lot, but he'd
played. Then came the Boss and the other guys from
across the river.

"Not too shabby," said Holley.

"The Boss?" said Jack. "Damn straight. So how did it feel,

him treating you as though you were one of the faces on Mount Rushmore come to life?"

"Shoot." Holley said nothing more.

"I thought it was pretty impressive when he asked if you'd play 'Cindy Lou.'"

Holley chuckled. "Funny thing about that tune. You know it almost wasn't gonna be 'Cindy Lou'?"

Jack looked at him quizzically.

They rounded the corner of the hallway behind the stage. The lighting was something less than adequate. "Watch out for the wire on the floor," said Holley. "Good old 'Cindy Lou.' Well, that was the original title all along, but about the time the Crickets and me were gonna record it, our drummer, Jerry Allison, asked if I'd change it."

"Change the music?" said Jack.

"Change the title. Seems as if Jerry was marryin' a gal named Peggy Sue, and he thought she'd be just tickled to death havin' a song named after her."

"But you didn't."

Holley laughed. "She jilted him, broke the engagement before anything permanent could be done about the song. So 'Cindy Lou' it's stayed."

"I like it better," said Jack.

They turned a final corner and came to the small room where Holley was keeping his guitar and the other things he'd brought over from the hotel. Holley went in first. When he flipped the light switch, nothing happened. "Blamed bulb must be out."

"Not quite," said a voice from inside.

Both Jack and Holley jumped. "Who's in dere?" said Jack. Holley started to back out of the doorway.

"Hold it," said the voice. "Everything's fine as long as you two're Buddy Holley and Jack Robicheaux."

"You got that right," said Holley.

"The name's Croyd."

Holley said, "I don't know any Croyd."

"I do," said Jack. "I mean, I know who you are."

The voice chuckled. "I'm in a bit of a hurry, and I'm trying to be subtle, so why don't the two of you come on in and shut the door."

The two men did so. Croyd snapped on a penlight and let the beam play briefly across their faces. "Okay, you're who

you say." He set the light down on the makeup table but
didn't turn it off. "I've got some information for your niece,"
he said to Jack, "but her office doesn't know where she is, and
I don't have time to wait around on her."

"Okay," said Jack. "Tell me. I'll get it to her. She's
jumping around like a frog in a tub of McIlheney's, what with
about ten thousand things to get done before tomorrow night."

"She asked me to look into Shrike Music," said Croyd.

"Oh, yeah?" Holley sounded interested.

"I thought it might be one of the Gambione fronts; you
know, a Mafia laundering operation."

"So?" said Jack. "Are Rosemary Muldoon's hands dirty
there too?"

"No," said Croyd. "'I don't think so. Whatever Shrike
is—and I think it's dirty as hell—I really don't think it's
connected with the Gambiones or the other Families. Tell
Cordelia Chaisson that."

"Anything else?" said Jack.

"Yeah. As far as I could follow the trail back, I got some
hints that the brain behind Shrike is Loophole. You know, the
lawyer, St. John Latham. If I'm right, you better tell your
niece to be real careful. With Loophole, I'm talking one
dangerous son-of-a-bitch."

"Okay," Jack said. "I'll tell her."

"If you find out more—" Holley said.

"I won't. I've got my own problems to deal with." Croyd's
chuckle was very dry.

"Oh," said Holley. "Well, thanks anyhow. At least I know
my songs aren't tied up in pasta."

"Listen," said Croyd, some animation coming into his
voice. "'Shake, Rattle and Roll' is one of the best rockers
ever recorded. Don't let anyone ever tell you different. I just
wanted to say that before I took off."

"Well," said Holley. "Thank you very much." He strode
forward in the darkness, toward the makeup table. "I'll shake
the hand of any man who tells me that."

"What can I say?" said Croyd. "I've liked your work for a
long time now. Glad you're back."

Jack had the impression of a pale albino face in the dark.
Pink eyes flashed as the penlight snapped off.

"Good luck with the concert." Then Croyd's indistinct
form was out the door and gone.

"Okay," said Jack, "let's see if we can round up a fresh light bulb." He winced. The pain was coming back, the pain and something else. In the darkness he touched his own face. The skin felt scaly. The virus was eroding his control. It was getting harder to remain— He didn't like filling in the blank. *Human* was the word he was looking for.

Saturday

The audio ocean combers of U2 crashed over them. The Edge's picking fingers had healed just fine for tonight. Bono swung into "With or Without You" with his exuberant never-sing-the-song-the-same-way-twice voice in great form.

C.C. abruptly stared at Buddy Holley with concern. She reached out to steady him. Jack moved in from the other side. "What's wrong, babe?" She touched his forehead with the back of her right hand. "You're burning up."

Bagabond looked concerned. "You need a doc?"

The four of them stepped back as a cameraman with a SteadiCam double-timed by, heading for the stage.

Holley straightened. "It's okay. I'm all right. Just a little flop-sweat."

"You sure?" said C.C. skeptically.

"I guess," said Holley, "maybe I was feeling some momentary melancholy." His three companions registered uniform incomprehension. "Waitin' to go on out there, it's getting to me in a strang way. I'm looking at all this and I'm thinking about Ritchie and the Bopper and how they both went down with Bobby Fuller in that Beechcraft back in '68 when Bobby was tryin' his comeback tour. Lord, I do miss 'em."

"You're alive," said Bagabond. "They're not."

Holley stared at her. Then he slowly smiled. "That's putting it straight." He looked past the curtains toward the full house. "Yep, I'm alive."

"You're gon' sit down for a bit," said Jack. "Rest just a while."

"Remind me," said Holley. "When do I go on?"

"The Coward Brothers are on next. Then Little Steven and me," said C.C. "I'll warm 'em up for you. You'll be up before Girls With Guns and the Boss."

"Comfortable in the hammock, huh? Heavy-hitter company." Holley shook his head. "You know how the world would change if somebody nuked this club tonight? Not a bit." He staggered. "Well, maybe just a little bitty bit."

"You're gonna sit down," said C.C. firmly.

Jack looked toward the stage. This was probably the only rock concert he'd been to that wasn't choked with smoke. But in the confined space of the Funhouse, the management, the Health Department, and some of the performers had begged for abstinence. The tech crew was using a fog machine to get the right lighting. With the lights in his face Jack could see nothing. But he knew who was out there.

Cordelia was sitting next to the small, roped-off space where the floor director was sequestered with her video monitors. Everything looked good. The satellite feeds were webbing the globe satisfactorily, though god only knew if any eyes out there were actually watching.

Every seat was taken. People had paid two grand just for standing room. Cordelia had checked around her chair before U2 had been announced. The table immediately behind her was occupied by New Jersey's junior U.S. senator, the senator's wife—Hoboken's head of cultural development—a hot, teen heartthrob actor, and the actor's ICM agent. The next table to the left held Senator Hartmann and his party. Tachyon was back there too. A beaming Xavier Desmond was right up front.

Off to her right, Miranda and Ichiko had seen her looking and had waved and smiled. Cordelia had smiled back. Luz Alcala and Polly Rettig, GF&G's top management, also sat at Cordelia's table. Now and then they said appropriately laudatory things to her. Obviously they were enjoying how the benefit concert was progressing. *Boffo*, thought Cordelia. *That's how* Variety *will describe this. Dey better damn better.*

U2 ended its set and the Irish quartet trooped offstage. The applause thundered on, and they came back for a quick encore. That had been budgeted into the schedule. It was assumed.

After the encore the screen dropped down from the Funhouse's ceiling, barely missing the Louma crane, and the slick, donated media spot for the New York AIDS Project blazed forth. This was the commercial. No one minded.

Cordelia wondered if she should go backstage and check that all was in order. No, she decided. She needed to be in place where she was—waiting for hideous crises. No use seeking them out.

The Coward Brothers came out to a storm of applause. T-Bone and Elvis burned the place up with "People's Limousine" and another sixteen minutes that flashed by like no time at all.

Between sets, when the broadcast had gone to a taped message, the lighting director turned the spots on the Funhouse's mirror balls and chandelier. The interior of the club exploded in a phantasmagoria of shattered light.

Little Steven and his band came on. The roadies had been fast and accurate. The musicians plugged into the house system and were off. Little Steven had a new scarf for each song in the set. The crowd loved it.

It was C.C. Ryder's time. She held the neck of her shining black twelve-string with both hands.

"Don't strangle it," said Holley. He wrapped his hands loosely around hers.

"Break a leg." Jack gave her a hug. Bagabond didn't seem to mind.

The latter hugged C.C. in turn for a few seconds and said, "You'll be great."

"If I'm not," said C.C., "I hope this time I'm an express."

Jack knew she was referring to her years-ago wild card transformation when trauma had catalyzed her into becoming a more than reasonable facsimile of a local subway car.

C.C. hit the stage running and never stopped. It was as though she was casting a net of power over the audience. There was a moment at first when she faltered. But then she seemed to gather strength. It was as though energy were flowing out into the people in their seats, then being amplified and broadcast back to the singer. The magic, Jack thought, of genuine empathy.

She started with one of her old standards, then quickly segued into her new ballads. Her twenty minutes flashed past for Jack. C.C. ended with the song she had publicly debuted at the first rehearsal.

*Baby, you never have to fold
  'Cause what you've got
    Is a winning hand*

...*Is a winning hand*, came the refrain. *Never forget*.
C.C. bowed her head. The applause had megatonnage.
When she came offstage, she waited until she was past the
curtains before collapsing. Jack and Bagabond both caught her.
"What's the matter?" said Bagabond. "Oh, C.C.—"
"Nothing," said C.C. She grinned up at them, her face
lined with exhaustion. "Absolutely nothing."
"Okay," Cordelia muttered as the Jokertown Clinic spot
unspooled above her. "Buddy Holley's next." In spite of what
Uncle Jack said, she wondered if she should cross her fingers.
Maybe toes too.
"Hold on a sec," said the floor director. She leaned toward
Cordelia. "Change in plans."
Shit, thought Cordelia. "What?"
"Seems to be a minor rebellion among the musicians. It's
still getting sorted out."
"Better be quick." Cordelia glanced at the LED counting
down on the director's console. "Like in about twenty-two
seconds."

"But *I'm* supposed to go on now," said Buddy Holley
stubbornly.
"The deal is," said Jack, "both the Boss and Girls With
Guns have decided they want to go now and let you be the
final act."
Bagabond glanced beyond them. "The Boss and that girl
Tami are arm wrestling. Looks like she's winning."
"But it's *my* gig," said Holley.
"Shut the fuck up," said the Girls With Guns' leader,
Tami, as she strutted up, rubbing her right shoulder. She
uttered the words with considerable affection. "Him and
I"—she gestured at the Boss, who was ruefully grinning—
"we both figure we learned most all we know from you. So
you're gonna be the climax. That's it, Bud." She leaned up on
tiptoes and kissed him on the lips. Holley looked startled.
The stage director was signaling frantically.
The glass eyes of the SteadiCams implacably zoomed in.
Girls With Guns upped the energy ante by tearing out

the heart of Tommy Boyce and Bobby Hart's bubblegum standard "I Wonder What She's Doing Tonight," stomping it into jam, smearing the residue on their sneering lips, and just generally raising hell. They ended up with "Proud Flesh," a razor-edged anthem of romance and nihilism.

"So," said Tami to the Boss as she led her sisters swaggering offstage, "top that."

The Boss did his best.

Oh, god, thought Cordelia as the echoes finally died. She watched the Boss raise his guitar in one hand and elevate a fist with the other. Let Buddy work out. Please. The Boss gave the audience another bow, then led his band backstage.

Cordelia blinked. She thought she'd seen St. John Latham at a table in the back of the club. *Latham, Strauss's cash is as good as anyone else's,* she thought. The problem was, Latham seemed to be staring directly at her.

She sighed as the penultimate PSA faded to black and the director cued in the Louma. The monitor showed a wide tracking shot sweeping back and up from the stage.

"And . . . go!" said the director into her mike.

Please, Cordelia again mentally implored.

"Hello, Lubbock!" Buddy Holley said to the immediate audience and their five hundred million electronic shadows. The crowd smiled.

Jack smiled too from his vantage at the edge of the stage. He crouched down to avoid getting in the way of the camera dollying past on its track. The pain was gnawing regularly at his gut, and he didn't know how long he'd be able to hold this position. He realized that what he wanted now more than anything else was simply to lie down. He wanted to rest. *Soon enough,* he thought morbidly. *I'll rest all I want. For good.*

Holley hit his first note, then brushed his fingers across the chord. The magic Buddy Holley touch. Now it might be a standard technique, but three decades before, it had signaled a revolution.

Rou-ou-ou-ou-ough beast

The characteristic hiccup was still there, though no one in the paying audience had ever heard this Buddy Holley tune before.

> *When the moon slides low*
> * And lo-ove rubs thin*
> *I'll be knockin'*
> * Askin' to be let in*

To Jack it seemed a little like vintage Dylan. Maybe a dash of Lou Reed. But most of it was just pure Holley.

> *Rou-ou-ou-ou-ough beast*—almost a wail.

Jack realized he could easily cry.

> *When my friends*
> * Like my center*
> *Cannot hold*
> * And every feeling I got*
> *   Has just been sold*

He *was* crying.

> *I'm the rough beast's prey*
> * In the rough beast's way*

Buddy Holley's Telecaster sobbed. Not in self-pity, but in honest grief.

> *Without friends*
> * Without love*
> *   Forever*

Jack loved the music, but the pain was horrendous. When he could no longer withstand it, he got up and quietly left. He missed the encore.

Cordelia was already looking ahead to the final extravagant encore when every performer would come onto the stage and all would stand there with hands and arms linked. She blinked and registered a double take as she realized Buddy Holley looked about ready to fall flat on his face as he stood there taking the applause from his final song. She was close enough that she could see the flush in his face. Holley staggered. *Oh, Jesus*, she thought, *he's sick. He's going to collapse.*

But he didn't. It was as though the flush in his skin metamorphosed into a ripple of heat that ran along his body from feet to head.

What the hell? thought Cordelia.

Then it was Buddy Holley's flesh itself that rippled. A transforming nimbus of energy seemed to glow around his body. He held the Fender Telecaster out in front of him and something astonishing happened. The steel strings became ductile, melting like taffy, flashing away from the frets, stretching out and out like lines of silver sparks. They whipped around camera mounts and lights, anchoring themselves like jungle snakes.

Illusion? Cordelia thought. Maybe it *was* telekinesis.

The guitar strings formed a kind of enormous cat's cradle.

Buddy Holley looked around at this, then at his hands. He slowly raised his head and gazed upward. Holley seemed to be seeing something nobody else could comprehend. He smiled and the smile transformed into a joyous grin.

And then he danced. Slow and deliberate at first, the pace grew more rapid as Holley began to whirl around the stage. The audience stared, gaping.

She had seen this dance before—or something like it. Cordelia recalled the memory. Wyungare. She had seen the young aboriginal man dance in this manner deep within the Dreamtime, far into the desert heartland of Australia. This was a shaman's dance.

Holley's grin widened. He leaped and gyrated. Screamin' Jay Hawkins and James Brown could have done no better. Then Holley leaped into the shimmering, almost invisible webwork of silver sparks.

He whirled and his right hand came off, severed at the wrist with a gush of crimson smoke.

Someone in the audience gasped.

Holley continued to dance. The other hand. The right arm, up to the elbow. His left leg at the knee. Scarlet smoke fanned out like the curving trails of fire from a catherine wheel.

Cordelia became aware the director was addressing her. "Should we go to a spot?" The director's voice was taut.

It was all coming clear to Cordelia. "No," she said. "No. Leave it. Broadcast everything."

Buddy Holley whirled within the cradle of sparking tracers. He disassembled himself as the audience murmured and cried out.

From the chair beside her at the table Cordelia heard Polly Rettig say, "God almighty, it's just like with Kid Dinosaur."

"No." Cordelia said aloud. "It's not. It's the death and resurrection show. It's just—a joke. It's entertainment."

"*Entertainment*?" said Rettig. "He's . . . killing himself."

"I don't think so," said Cordelia. "He's transforming, but he's not dying. This is a shaman's trick."

The last of Buddy Holley, a nearly limbless torso, wavered and tumbled to the stage. The body parts lay stacked in a haphazard heap. Curtains of bright smoke rose up. Sparks shot up in fountaining streamers.

The audience watched, uncertain how to react.

Cordelia felt calm and sure. She trusted Wyungare. She wondered if Holley's transmogrification was a direct result of the wild card virus. That would explain his apparent illness.

The pile of arms and legs stirred. The bones began to reconnect, joint to joint. The muscles and ligaments wound around them. The skin slithered onto the limbs, and the limbs rejoined the body.

Buddy Holley stood before them, whole again. He wasn't completely the physical original. This Buddy Holley was fitter, the spare tire around his waist and the bags under the eyes gone. His hair was a glossy black again, with no gray. His skin was smooth and unwrinkled.

The crowd began to clap. The cheering rose as the audience's collective tension released. Someone behind Cordelia said, "That's the absolute fucking performance of a lifetime."

The guitar had also reassembled. Holley picked up the Telecaster and held it loosely.

He got what he wanted, Cordelia thought. "He's become a shaman," she said aloud.

"Buddy Holley and the Shamans," said a voice behind her. "Bitchin' name. After this, it'd sell like Fawn Hall's underwear. Man, this Holley could become a presidential candidate."

Cordelia turned and saw it was the ICM man who had spoken. She gave him a frigid stare and turned back toward the stage. The new being that had been Buddy Holley smiled reassuringly. Then he brought his hand across the guitar strings. The chord throbbed as though resonating with every heart in the audience.

The sound, thought Cordelia. *It's a trigger for states of heightened consciousness. This is the power of rock and roll.*

Then Buddy Holley, the reborn man of power, stood before the awestruck audience and played the best version of "Not Fade Away" that had ever been performed.

It was, Cordelia suspected, a portent.

As Jack slipped away from the alley door of the Funhouse, he felt sick in heart and body. *I should have stayed for Buddy's encore*, he thought. But Buddy would do just fine.

There was the scraping on asphalt of something inhumanly large shifting its weight.

Jack stopped abruptly as a shadow deeper than the darkness in the rest of the alley fell across him.

"I figured a blue-ribbon fag party like this would draw all my little buddies," said Bludgeon. "But I didn't even hope the first fucker would be you." Without warning, his deformed right hand whistled out, catching Jack across the head and slamming him back into the brick side of a building.

Jack felt something give, bone or cartilage he couldn't tell. All he knew was that he was slipping away from what light there was. He wanted the darkness, but not yet, not this way. He tried to struggle. He was aware that Bludgeon was grasping him tightly and holding him upright. Bludgeon jerked loose Jack's belt and pulled down his pants.

"Got a little going-away thing for you, Jack. Something I figure you'll love. I bet your niece Cordelia'll eat it up when I get around to her too."

Jack tried to will himself back into full consciousness. Then he felt what Bludgeon was shoving between his buttocks. Into him. Spreading and tearing. Nothing had ever hurt this much. *Nothing!*

"I'll save the little girl for later," said Bludgeon.

Jesus, thought Jack through the agony. Cordelia. "Let her alone you rat-bastard *cochon!*"

"Sticks and stones," said Bludgeon, emitting a high-pitched giggle, "but only the Fatman can hurt me..." He thrust forward and Jack screamed.

Where was the *other*? Jack thought desperately, his brain seeming to heel over in a grinding haze of pain. *I need you. Now. I've got to transform. This once. Just to kill the son-of-a-bitch.*

And then he felt the change coming.

He also knew he was dying.

Good, he thought. Good to both. And a surprise for Bludgeon.

Jack felt the teeth springing up as his jaw elongated. *Pestilence or claw, you son-of-a-bitch, you're gon' die.* The fierce anger carried him a little further.

Bagabond! his thought shouted into the night. *Hear me! Save Cordelia.*

I'll save the little girl for later, Bludgeon's threat echoed. It all rippled into a void. And died.

The dead man plunged into darkness.

Blood Ties

II

The seven-to-midnight shift was just coming off. The midnight-to-five-A.M. shift was preparing to sally forth from the Crystal Palace onto the streets of Jokertown. Coughs, hacks, a few subdued laughs as they lined up at the long trestle tables to be served. Hiram Worchester, the immensely large and immensely elegant owner of Aces High, oversaw the feeding effort. It was his way of showing support, and a very welcome one to the always-tired Jokertown patrols.

Tachyon, seated on a table, with a booted foot propped on the chair, sniffed appreciatively. *Coq au vin.* He noticed Sascha pausing to speak with Hiram. The big ace jerked his head toward one of the secluded alcoves, and they moved away. Business of some sort, mused Tachyon. Everyone did business at the Crystal Palace.

The door to the Palace was flung open, and Mr. Gravemold surveyed the room. He brought with him an indescribable smell, and the chill of the grave seemed to wash from his tall, wiry person. Beneath his absurd porkpie hat a skull mask decorated with black and white feathers leered about the room. There were some muttered curses from the assembled jokers. It was going to be tough to choke down even Hiram's delicious food with Mr. Gravemold stinking up the place.

Tachyon, a scented handkerchief held to his nose, was about to slide to the floor and join the line when the brash voice of Digger Downs riveted him in place.

"Oh, no, you don't, Doc, interview time."

"Why me, Digger?"

"Because you owe me for that mind control last week. Not nice, Tachy, not nice."

"Digger, if you weren't so goddam irritating and unscrupulous—"

"Captain Ellis doesn't approve of this protection racket,"

the reporter bulled ahead. "She says somebody's going to get hurt, and it ain't gonna be the bad guys."

"I would submit to the good captain that the protection rackets have all been coming from one direction. And she's being unduly pessimistic. I think we can look out for ourselves. Ideal knows we've had enough practice," he added dryly, recalling all the years when the police were curiously uninterested whenever a joker was beaten or killed, but Johnny-on-the-spot whenever a tourist howled. Things were better now, but it was still an uneasy relationship between New York's jokers and New York's finest.

Digger licked the tip of his ballpoint pen, a silly, affected gesture. "I know my readers will want to know why these patrols consist only of jokers. With you heading up this effort why not pull in some of the big guns? The Hammer for example, or Mistral or J.J. Flash or Starshine."

"This is a joker neighborhood. We can take care of ourselves."

"Meaning there's hostility between jokers and aces?"

"Digger, don't be an ass. Is it *so* surprising that these people choose to handle this themselves? They are viewed as freaks, treated like retarded children, and ignored in favor of their more fortunate and flamboyant brethren. May I point out that your magazine is titled *Aces*, and no one is panting to found a concomitant magazine entitled *Jokers*? Look around you. This is an activity born out of love and pride. How could I say to these people you're not tough enough or smart enough or strong enough to defend yourselves? Let me call in the aces."

Which was of course precisely what he had been going to do until Des had opened his eyes. But Digger didn't need to know that. Still, Tach had the grace to blush as he shamelessly appropriated Des's lecture and passed it on to the journalist.

"Comment on Leo Barnett?"

"He is a hate-mongering lunatic."

"Can I quote you on that?"

"Go ahead."

"So who's going to be the white knight? Hartmann?"

"Maybe. I don't know."

"I thought you two were real tight."

"We're friends, but hardly intimates."

"Why do you think Hartmann's been such a friend to the

jokers? Personal interest? His wife a carrier, or maybe an illegitimate joker baby hidden away somewhere?"

"I think he is a friend to the wild cards because he is a good man," replied Tachyon a little frigidly.

"Hey, speaking of monstrous joker babies, what's the latest poop on Peregrine's pregnancy?"

Tachyon went rigid with fury, then carefully uncoiled his fists, and relaxed. "No, Digger, you're not going to get me again. I will never stop regretting that I let slip that the father of Peregrine's child was an ace."

"Have a drink on me, Tachy?" asked the journalist hopefully, eying the almost empty snifter.

"NO!"

"Just a little hint to reassure all those breathless fans who are worried about Peri?"

"Oh, go away, Digger, do. You plague me worse than horse flies." He waved a hand toward the jokers. "Interview them, and leave me in peace. I'm far less important in all of this than they are."

"Jesus, Tachy! Modesty, from you?"

The Takisian stared hard, and Digger lifted the glass from the table and dribbled the remaining brandy over his head.

"I'm not . . . in a very good mood . . . right now."

The journalist mopped at his wet neck. "No fuck! And that makes two, Tach. I'll be collecting on that next interview soon."

"I'll count the moments."

"Asshole."

Tachyon stared morosely at his empty glass, then scanned the room for a waiter. Durg at'Morakh bo-Isis Vayawand-sa had been stolidly eating his way through an enormous plate of food, but Tachyon noticed that his pale eyes kept drifting toward the staircase. Chrysalis appeared and the Morakh killer, light-footed despite his incredible bulk, moved swiftly to her side. He lifted her hand with courtly grace and bestowed a fervent kiss upon it. Chrysalis snatched it back and stared coldly down at him. Drawn despite himself, Tach drifted toward them, trying to overhear. Suddenly Chrysalis's hand shot out, and the sharp slap echoed about the crowded bar.

"Tachyon!" she gritted. He obediently followed her to her private table. Lifting her deck of antique cards, she shuffled quickly several times and laid out a solitaire hand. "Will you keep your pet freak away from me!"

"He's not mine, he's Mark's, and what's the problem?"

"He wants me."

"Good god!"

A tangle of conflicting emotions washed through him. Disgust and amazement that Durg could be attracted to the joker. Monster he might be, but he was still a Takisian. Shame for his reaction, and pity for Chrysalis beset by such a monstrous lover.

"Will you get him off my back?"

"I'll do what I can, but remember he was raised from childhood to hate and despise me; first by the Vayawand and then by my cousin Zabb. He tolerates me now solely for Mark's sake."

"*Please.*"

"All right, but be a bit more forbearing, I beg you. The Morakh may be a perversion, but they are Takisians, and as such used to getting what they want from groundlings. Never forget he's a killing machine."

"Thanks so much, Tachy, I feel so much better now."

"Sorry."

"Well, maybe the Mafia or the Fists will beat my head in before he does. And to think I let you talk me into this. You know this really is all your fault. Oh, stop looking so stricken. It was a joke."

"Not to me."

Dita came toddling down the hall, the heels of her improbably high heels clicking on the faded tile floor.

"Doctor, Mr. Marion quit!"

Tachyon looked up from the chart he was studying. "Who?"

"Mr. Marion, the tutor."

"Oh, shit." It was not a common expletive from him and Dita stared. "Dita, I'm far to busy to deal with this right now, and since it's a losing proposition anyway, would you please hire a new tutor for me."

"But I wouldn't know what to look for."

"A thorough grounding in mathematics, and the sciences. Some history and literature, and a knowledge or at least an appreciation for music would be nice."

The click and hiss of the pager, and the smooth voice of

the switchboard interrupted. "Dr. Tachyon to emergency. Dr. Tachyon to emergency."

"But . . ."

"Just use your judgment." Looping his stethoscope around his neck, Tach lifted the phone from the third-floor nurses' station. "What is it?"

"Wild card," came the terse response from Dr. Finn.

He wasted no more time but headed for the elevator.

The child was writhing on the examnation table. Finn's hooves were clattering nervously on the tile as he sought to restrain her. He was the first joker physician at the Blythe van Renssaeler Memorial Clinic, and there had been some initial resistance from the joker community fearful that he had gotten through medical school because of affirmative action and not through merit. After two weeks of working with the young man, Tach could assure them that their fears were unfounded.

The child's mother stared with panicked eyes at Tachyon. Superficially she was a nat; what her genetic code held was of course another matter. Manifestation, or new infection? Only testing would show.

"Initial exam indicates no transformation. We've managed to stabilize pressure and heart rate, and I've ordered up a trump, but . . ."

"Thank you, Doctor. Mrs. . . . ?"

"Wilson," supplied a nurse.

"Wilson." Tachyon took her arm, urged her away frm the convulsing child. "Your daughter has contracted the wild card, and its fairly evident that she's drawn a Black Queen." The woman gasped, whimpered, clapped a hand over her mouth. "We must very quickly make a decision. We can give her a dose of a countervirus which I have developed—"

"Give it to her!"

"But I must warn you that this treatment is successful only twenty percent of the time. The usual result is that there is no improvement. The virus runs its course. There is also a very slight chance of death in reaction to the trump."

"She's dyin' anyway. It don't matter if she does it faster." A nurse appeared at her elbow with the release.

Tachyon was already preparing the syringe. It took Finn and three nurses to hold the girl quiet. The plunger was depressed. Tach held her wrist, the flutter of pulse beneath his fingers. Fainter, fainter. The monitor went flat. The deadly keen was echoed in the mother's cry.

The aftermath was always so hateful. The inadequate words of comfort, obtaining consent for an autopsy, blood tests on both parents—in this case unfortunately incomplete for Beth Wilson was a welfare mother, and the man who'd sired little Sara had long since vanished from her life. She had spent the last thirty dollars of her welfare check on taxis shuttling from hospital to hospital, being turned away when the virus was discovered, until at last she reached the Jokertown clinic. Tach gave her money and sent her home with Riggs in the limousine.

Sprawled back in his chair, Tach pulled a flask from the desk drawer and slugged back a large swallow.

"Mind if I have one?" asked Finn.

He was on the floor with all four legs curled neatly beneath him. His golden hide twitched slightly over one haunch, and he cranked around to scratch the itch. Tach, canted back in his chair, studied the young man and decided that Finn looked like a Disney character. Small pointed face, tipped-up blue eyes, a riot of white curls that tumbled over his forehead and ran down his spine to form a mane. His tail spread behind him like a white cloak. When he was in surgery they braided it up and wrapped surgical tape around it. Tach had suggested that he bob it and gotten a horrified look in response. He then realized that that floor-length fall of hair was Finn's pride and joy.

Staring at those four teacup-size hooves, Tach wanted to ask if Finn had been born this way or metamorphosed after birth. If his had been an *in utero* transformation, Tachyon sure as hell bet he had been delivered by cesarean section. But it would be gauche to ask. Although Finn seemed incredibly well adjusted Tachyon would be the first to admit that he didn't know the man at all well.

The doctor turned the flask slowly between his fingers and frowned off into space.

"What's the matter?" asked Tach.

"I've never worked among jokers until now."

"Oh?"

"Yeah, my old man had enough clout and money to send me to the finest medical schools and get me into a residency program at Cedars in L.A."

"So why are you here?"

"I thought it was about time I got to know some jokers. To take a look at the joker experience."

"That's quite noble."

"No, it's guilt. I grew up in a Spanish colonial palace in Bel Air. If dad couldn't buy people to accept me, he'd intimidate them until they did."

"What did your father do?"

"'Does.' He's a movie producer. A very successful one."

"And you became a doctor."

"Well, I could hardly become an actor."

"True." Tachyon rose. "If you'd like a bit more joker experience, I'm on my way over to the Crystal Palace for the daily report. If you would care to accompany me?"

"Sure. Beats staying here waiting for another Black Queen to be rolled in. Wish you guys had done a little more lab work before field-testing xenovirus Takis-A."

"But Finn, by anyone's standards it was an astounding success."

"Yeah, tell that to Mrs. Wilson."

Even the lights had been turned off in an effort to make the skinny teenager who huddled in a chair next to Chrysalis comfortable. Video was an undersize sixteen-year-old who would never dance at her senior prom or go to the movies or, in short, live with any of the modern conveniences that make life comfortable. For the presence of any electrical equipment in her vicinity sent her into ventricular fibrillation, and without immediate aid she would die.

Until one noticed her eyes, Video seemed normal. Long brown hair, parted in the middle, fell straight to her shoulders. A narrow, worried face peered out from behind this curtain of hair. And the eyes. White and perfectly round, they seemed to billow and change like whitetops on waves, or clouds torn by a passing wind.

"Hi, Dr. Tachyon," she muttered around a mouthful of gum.

"Hi, Video, how are you today?"

"Pretty good."

"This is Dr. Finn."

"Hi."

"So what have you got for us today?"

"I got around pretty good so I got quite a bit."

"Excellent."

"Uh . . . Doctor?"

"Yes?"

"Ummm . . . you're a friend of Senator Hartmann's, right?"

"Yes."

"Is he gonna run?"

"For president, you mean?"

"Yeah."

"I don't know, Video."

"Well, I wish he would. One of my friends got beat up near that Barnett mission."

"Were Barnett's people behind it?"

"I don't know. He thinks so. The cops thought it was probably the Werewolves."

"In other words, no proof."

"Paul was sure," she said with a mulish expression.

"But that's not proof."

"Well, I don't think this guy ought to become president."

"I doubt he will, Video," said Tachyon, and wished he was as certain as he sounded.

"Senator Hartmann oughta run."

"I'll ask him next time I talk to him."

"I'd vote for him. If I were eighteen."

"I'll tell him. Now, the replay."

"Oh, okay."

The girl stared hard at the clear space before Chrysalis's table. Figures sprang to life.

. . . An Oriental man in gang colors stuck the tip of a switchblade up Gobbler's nose slit. A flick, and blood poured over the old man's beak. With a screech he collapsed onto the floor. A lean, ganglingly tall street punk dressed in stained leather pants and chains grinned, pulling the crawling scarlet and black scars on his face into hideous relief. Spiked hair made him seem seven feet tall as he gripped the joker by the tuft of feathers sprouting from his bald skull and pulled him up. The feathers came loose in his fist.

"Put 'em on a hat," yelled the Oriental gleefully.

Suddenly Elmo boiled in the door of the deli. Launched himself at the tall, scarred Occidental. They wrestled. The dwarf leaned forward, his powerful jaws closing on his opponent's bandaged nose. Elmo reared back, and the man screamed and clapped a hand over the raw, bleeding wound where his nose had been. Elmo spat the nose into his palm...

"Gross," said Finn.

... The Twisted Sisters shuddered and clung more tightly to one another's waist. Gray hair twisted like smoke about their gaunt bodies. It snaked out as soft and insubstantial as cobwebs, as insinuating as a sigh. It crept up nostrils and past lips. Thickened until it lay like cotton wadding in windpipes and lungs. The bully boys collapsed onto the floor of the deli like deflated balloons.

... A pair of men in polyester sports jackets and a wealth of gold chains thrust Spots's head into one of her own washing machines at the Spots Out Laundromat. They dragged her out gasping and dripping, soap clinging to her piebald hair and skin. Mister Gravemold slipped through the door, flexed his fingers, and laid a hand on one goon's shoulder. The man reared back, cried out, and collapsed. The other soon joined him....

"What's he using?" asked Tachyon with a glance to Chrysalis.

"Hypothermia."

"Oh." He waved to Video to proceed.

... The back door of the bakery spilling light into the alley. Screams from the kitchen. Shadow Fists pausing like alert hounds in the cluttered alley. Rushing in to join in a fight with their Mafia competitors. Terrified jokers backed against the walls, smoke rising from doughnuts boiling to ash in the hot oil.

In the distance a clear whistle floating over the bleat of horns, and the rumble of subways. The theme to *High Noon*...

Tachyon dropped his face into his hands. "I didn't know you were there."

"I can be pretty sneaky," said Video with pride.

Chrysalis shot the Takisian an ironic glance. "Very interesting. So our little doctor is riding with the posse. Go ahead, Video, I want to see this."

"Doug's bakery is a block from the clinic. I buy doughnuts there in the morning. When the call came, Troll and I were convenient."

"Right," she drawled.

... Tachyon, the .357 Magnum like a cannon in his small hand, entering from the alley. Troll roaring in from the front of the bakery. Troll doubled up a ham-size fist and beat heads like a man playing bongos. One of the Mafia thugs drew a .22 pistol. Fired point-blank into Troll's massive chest. The bullet ricocheted off the joker's thick greenish skin with a whine. The man went white. Troll lifted him by his shirt front.

"You shouldn't have done that, mister, because now I'm *really* mad."

Troll coolly broke both the man's arms, then his legs, and then propped him in a corner like a discarded sack. A sack that screamed.

Tachyon switching his gaze from man to man. Each one dropping in a snoring heap as soon as those strange lilac eyes were leveled upon him. One of the Fists succeeded in unlimbering a .45 automatic. Tachyon shot the gun from his hand. Raised the gun to his lips, and blew lightly across the barrel . . .

"Show off," said Chrysalis.

The alien shrugged. "I'm a good shot."

"I don't believe for a moment that you didn't know Video was there. That has got to have been a performance for the benefit of the applauding masses."

"Chrysalis, you wound me."

"Tachyon, you're an arrogant son-of-a-bitch, and don't try to tell me otherwise."

"I didn't know you were taking part in all this," said Finn.

"I organized it . . . helped organize it. I should share in the risks." The alien drained his drink and bowed to Video and Chrysalis. "Ladies, I thank you." He paused at the door. "By the way, Chrysalis. How do you think we're doing?"

"I think we've got them on the run. I just hope they don't decide to take a crack at us."

"Scared?"

"You bet your sweet little alien ass I am. I know more about this situation—who's behind it—than you do."

"And you're not going to tell me."

"You've got *that* right."

June 1987

All the King's Horses

V

ADMISSION ONLY $2.50 said the sign over the darkened ticket booth in front of the Famous Bowery Wild Card Dime Museum.

The booth was empty, the museum doors locked. Tom rang the bell by the ticket window. After a minute he rang it again. There were shuffling noises from within, and a door in the back of the booth opened. An eye appeared, a rheumy pale-blue eye on a long fleshy stalk that curled around the doorframe. It fixed on Tom, blinked twice.

A joker stepped into the booth. He had a dozen eyes on long prehensile stalks that sprouted from his forehead and moved constantly, like snakes. Otherwise he was unremarkable. "Cancha read?" he said in a thin, nasal voice. "We're closed." In one hand he had a small sign, which he slid in front of the ticket window. It said CLOSED.

The way the joker's eyes kept moving gave Tom a queasy feeling in the pit of his stomach. "Are you Dutton?"

One by one the eyes turned, stilled, until every last one of them was fixed on him, studying him. "Dutton expecting you?" the joker asked. Tom nodded. "All right, c'mon round the side." He turned and left the booth, but two or three of his eyes stared back at Tom, curious and unblinking, until the door shut.

The side entrance was a heavy metal fire door opening on an alley. Tom waited nervously while locks were unlocked and bolts lifted inside. You heard stories about Jokertown alleys, and this one seemed to him especially dark and gloomy. "This way," eye-stalks said when the door finally opened.

The museum was windowless, its interior hallways even gloomier than the alley. Tom looked around curiously as they passed down several long corridors, with dusty brass railings

247

and waxwork dioramas to either side of them. He had floated
over the Dime Museum thousands of time as the Turtle, but
he'd never set foot inside.

With the lights out, the figures in the shadows seemed
remarkably lifelike. Dr. Tachyon stood on a mound of white
sand, his spaceship painted on the backdrop behind him,
while nervous soldiers climbed from a Jeep. Jetboy clutched
his chest as steel-faced Dr. Tod pumped bullets into him. A
blond in a torn teddy struggled in the grasp of the Great
Ape as he scaled a model of the Empire State Building. A
dozen jokers, each more twisted than the last, writhed
suggestively in some dank basement, clothing strewn all
around them.

His guide vanished around a corner. Tom followed, and
found himself face-to-face with a roomful of monsters.

Drenched in shadow, the creatures looked so real that
they brought him up short. Spiders the size of minivans,
flying things that dripped acid, gigantic worms with rings of
serrated teeth, humanoid monstrosities whose skin quivered
like gelatin; they filled the room behind the curving glass,
surrounding him on three sides, crowding each other, slavering
to break out.

"Our newest diorama," a quiet voice said behind him.
"Earth versus the Swarm. Try the buttons."

Tom looked down. A half dozen large red buttons were set
into a panel by the railing. He pressed one. Inside the
diorama a spotlight picked out a wax simulacrum of Modular
Man suspended from the ceiling, as twin beams of scarlet
light flashed down from his shoulder-mounted guns. The
lasers struck one of the swarmlings; thin tendrils of smoke
rose, and a long hiss of pain issued from unseen speakers.

Tom pushed a second button. Modular Man vanished
back into the shadows, and the lights found the Howler in his
yellow fighting togs, outlined against a plume of smoke from a
burning tank. The simulacrum opened its mouth; the speakers shrieked. A swarmling quivered in agony.

"The children love it," the voice said. "This is a genera-
tion raised on special effects. I'm afraid they demand more
than simple waxworks. One must adapt to one's times."

A tall man in a dark suit of old-fashioned cut stood in a
doorway to one side of the diorama, the joker with the
eyestalks hunched over beside him. "I'm Charles Dutton," he

said, offering a gloved hand. A heavy black cape was thrown over his shoulders. He looked as though he'd just stepped from a hansom cab in Victorian London, except for the cowl drawn up over his head that kept his face in shadow. "We'll be more comfortable in the office," Dutton said. "If you'll step this way."

Tom was suddenly very uneasy. He found himself wondering, once again, what the hell he was doing here. It was one thing to float over Jokertown as the Turtle, secure in a steel shell, and quite another to venture into its streets in his own all-too-vulnerable flesh. But he'd come this far. There was no backing out now. He followed his host through a door marked EMPLOYEES ONLY and down a narrow flight of steps. They passed through a second door, through a cavernous basement workshop, into a small but comfortably furnished office.

"Can I get you a drink?" the cowled man asked. He went to a wet bar in the corner of the office and poured himself a brandy.

"No," Tom said. He was a cheap drunk, too easily affected by booze, and he needed all his wits about him today. Besides, drinking through the damned frog mask would be a bitch.

"Let me know if you change your mind." Cradling the snifter, Dutton crossed the room and seated himself behind an antique clawfoot desk. "Please, sit down. You look terribly uncomfortable standing there like that."

Tom wasn't listening. Something else had caught his eye.

There was a head on the desk.

Dutton noticed his interest and turned the head around. The face was remarkably handsome, but the oh-so-perfect features were frozen in a rictus of surprise. Instead of hair, the top of the skull was a plastic dome with a radar dish beneath. The plastic was cracked. Severed cables, blackened and half-melted, dangled from the jagged stump of its neck.

"That's Modular Man," Tom said, shocked. Numbly he eased himself down onto the edge of a ladderback chair.

"Only his head," Dutton said.

It had to be a wax replica, Tom told himself. He reached out and touched it. "It's not wax."

"Of course not," Dutton said. "This is authentic. We bought it from one of the busboys at Aces High. I don't mind telling you, it cost us quite a tidy sum. Our new diorama will dramatize the Astronomer's attack on Aces High. You'll recall that Modular Man was destroyed during that fracas. His head will give a certain verisimilitude to the display, don't you think?"

The whole notion made Tom ill. "You planning to put Kid Dinosaur's body on display too?" he said testily.

"The boy was cremated," Dutton replied in a matter-of-fact tone. "We have it on good authority that the mortuary substituted a John Doe, cleaned his bones with carpet beetles, and sold the skeleton to Michael Jackson."

Tom found himself at a loss for words.

"You're shocked," Dutton said. "You wouldn't be, if you were a joker beneath that mask. This is Jokertown." He reached up, pulled back the cowl that covered his face. A death's head grinned at Tom across the desk; dark eyes sunk deep beneath a heavy brow ridge, leathery yellow skin stretched taut across a noseless, lipless, hairless face, teeth bared in a rictus of a smile. "When you've lived here long enough, nothing shocks you," Dutton said. Mercifully he yanked up the cowl again to conceal the living skullface, but Tom could feel the weight of his eyes. "Now," he said. "Xavier Desmond gave me to understand that you have a proposition for me. A major new exhibit."

Tom had seen thousands of jokers in his long years as the Turtle, but always at a distance, on his TV screens, with layers of armor plate between them. Sitting alone in a gloomy basement with a cowled man whose face was a yellowed skull was a little different. "Yeah," he said uncertainly.

"We are always in the market for new exhibits, the more spectacular the better. Des is not normally given to hyperbole, so when he tells me you're offering us something truly unique, I'm interested. Exactly what is the nature of this exhibit?"

"The Turtle's shells," said Tom.

Dutton was silent for a moment. "Not a replica?"

"The real thing," Tom told him.

"The Turtle's shell was destroyed last Wild Card Day," Dutton said. "They dredged up pieces of it from the bottom of the Hudson."

"That was one shell. There were earlier models. I've got three of them, including the very first. Armor plate over a Volkswagen frame. It's got some burned-out tubes, but otherwise it's pretty much intact. You could clean it up, rig the TV screens for closed circuit, make a real ride out of it. Charge extra for people to crawl inside. The other two shells are just empty hulls, but they'd still make quite a draw. If you have a big enough hall, you could hang 'em from the ceiling, like the airplanes in the Smithsonian." Tom leaned forward. "If you want to make this place into a real museum instead of just a tacky freak show for nat tourists, you need real exhibits."

Dutton nodded. "Intriguing. I'll admit I'm tempted. But anyone could build a shell. We'd need some kind of authentication. If you don't mind my asking, how did they chance to come into your possession?"

Tom hesitated. Xavier Desmond said Dutton could be trusted, but it was not easy to set aside twenty-four years of caution. "They're mine," he said. "I'm the Turtle."

This time Dutton's silence was even longer. "There are those who say the Turtle is dead."

"They're wrong."

"I see. I don't suppose you'd care to give me proof."

Tom took a deep breath. His hands curled around the armrests of his chair. He stared across the desk, concentrated. Modular Man's head rose a foot into the air and turned slowly until its eyes were fixed on Dutton.

"Telekinesis is a relatively common power," Dutton said, unimpressed. "The Turtle is distinguished not by the mere fact of his teke, but by its strength. Lift the desk and you'll convince me."

Tom hesitated. He didn't want to queer the deal by admitting that he couldn't lift the desk, not when he was out of his shell. All of a sudden, without thinking, he heard himself say, "Buy the shells, and I'll fly them here. All three of them." The words slipped out glib and easy; it wasn't until they were there hanging in the air that Tom realized what he'd said.

Dutton paused thoughtfully. "We could videotape the arrival, run the loop as part of the exhibit. Yes, I'd think that would be all the authentication we'd need. How much are you asking?"

Tom felt a moment of blind panic. Modular Man's head thumped back onto Dutton's desk. "One hundred thousand dollars," he blurted. It was twice what he'd intended to ask.

"Too much. I'll offer you forty thousand."

"Fuck that," Tom said. "This is a one-of-a-kind exhibit."

"Three-of-a-kind, actually," Dutton pointed out. "I might be able to go to fifty thousand."

"The historical value alone is more than that. This is going to give this fucking place respectability. You'll have lines going around the block."

"Sixty-five thousand," Dutton said. "I'm afraid that's my final offer."

Tom stood up, relieved but somehow disappointed as well. "Okay. Thanks for your time. You don't happen to have a number for Michael Jackson, do you?" When Dutton didn't answer, he started for the door.

"Eighty thousand," Dutton said behind him. Tom turned. Dutton coughed apologetically. "That's it. Really. I couldn't do better if I wanted to. Not without liquidating some of my other investments, which I'm not prepared to do."

Tom paused in the doorway. He'd almost escaped. Now he was stuck again. He didn't see any way out that wouldn't make him look like a fool. "I'll need cash."

Dutton chuckled. "I don't imagine a check made out to the Great and Powerful Turtle would be very easy to negotiate. It will take me a few weeks to raise that much cash, but I imagine I can work it out." The cowled man unfolded from his chair and came around the desk. "Are we agreed, then?"

"Yeah," Tom said. "If you'll throw in the head."

"The head?" Dutton sounded surprised, and a little amused. "Sentimental, aren't we?" He picked up Modular Man's head and stared into the blind, unfocused eyes. "It's just a machine, you know. A broken machine."

"He was one of us," Tom said with a passion that surprised even him. "It doesn't feel right, leaving him here."

"Aces," Dutton sighed. "Well, I suppose we can do up a wax replica for the Aces High diorama. It's yours, as soon as we can take delivery on the shells."

"You get the shells when I get my money," Tom said.

"Fair enough," Dutton replied.

Jesus, Tom thought, *what the fuck have I gone and done?* Then he got a grip on himself. Eighty thousand dollars was one hell of a lot of money.

Enough money to make it worth turning turtle one last time.

Concerto for
Siren and Serotonin

V

After running a small favor for Veronica, reporting his progress to Theotocopolos, and phoning Latham, Strauss for an appointment, Croyd met Veronica for dinner. As he told her of the day's doings, she shook her head when he told her about St. John Latham.

"You're crazy," she told him. "If he's that well-connected, what do you want to fool around with him for, anyway?"

"Somebody wanted to know about something he was up to."

She frowned. "I find a guy I like, I don't want to lose him so quick."

"I won't get hurt."

She sighed, put a hand on his arm. "I mean it," she said.

"So do I. I can take care of myself."

"What does that mean? How dangerous is it?"

"I've got a job to finish, and I think I'm almost there. I'll probably wrap it up soon without any sweat, get the rest of my money, and maybe take a little vacation before I sleep again. Thought we might go someplace real nice together—say, the Caribbean."

"Aw, Croyd," she said, taking his hand, "you've been thinking of me."

"Of course I've been thinking of you. Now, I've got an appointment with Latham for Thursday. Maybe I can finish this thing by the weekend. Then we'll have some time for just the two of us."

"You be careful, then."

"Hell, I'm almost done. Haven't had any problems yet."

                              *   *   *

After stopping at one of his banks for additional funds, Croyd took a taxi to the building that held the law offices of Latham, Strauss. He had made the appointment by describing a fictitious case designed to sound expensive, and he arrived fifteen minutes ahead of time. On entering the waiting room he suppressed a sudden desire for medication. Hanging out with Veronica seemed to have him thinking about it ahead of schedule.

He identified himself to the receptionist, sat and read a magazine till she told him, "Mr. Latham will see you now, Mr. Smith."

Croyd nodded, rose, and entered the inner office.

Latham rose from his seat behind his desk, displaying an elegantly cut gray suit, and he offered his hand. He was somewhat shorter than Croyd, and his refined features remained expressionless.

"Mr. Smith," he acknowledged. "Won't you have a seat?"

Croyd remained standing. "No."

Latham raised an eyebrow, then seated himself. "As you would," he said. "Why don't you tell me about your case now?"

"Because there isn't one. What I really need is some information."

"Oh? That being?"

Instead of replying Croyd looked away, casting his gaze about the office. Then his hand moved forward, to pick up an orange and green stone paperweight from Latham's desk. He held it directly before him and squeezed. A cracking, grinding sound followed. When he opened his hand, a shower of gravel fell upon the desk.

Latham remained expressionless. "What sort of information are you seekng?"

"You have done work for the new mob," Croyd said, "the one trying to move in on the Mafia."

"Are you with the Justice Department?"

"No."

"DA's office?"

"I'm not a cop," Croyd responded, "and I'm not an attorney either. I'm just someone who needs an answer."

"What is the question?"

"Who is the head of this new family? That's all I want to know."

"Why?"

"Perhaps someone wishes to arrange a meeting with that person."

"Interesting," Latham said. "You wish to retain me to arrange such a meeting?"

"No, I only want to know who the person in charge is."

"Quid—pro—quo," Latham observed. "What are you offering for this?"

"I am prepared to save you," Croyd said, "some very large bills from orthopedic surgeons and physiotherapists. You lawyers know all about such matters, don't you?"

Latham smiled a totally artificial smile. "Kill me and you're a dead man, hurt me and you're a dead man, threaten me and you're a dead man. Your little trick with the stone means nothing. There are aces with fancier powers than that on call. Now, was that a threat you just made?"

Croyd smiled back. "I will die before too long, Mr. Latham, to be born again in a completely different form. I am not going to kill you. But supposing I were to cause you to talk, to stop the pain, and supposing that later your friends were to put out a contract on the man you see before you. It wouldn't matter. He would no longer exist. I am a series of biological ephemera."

"You are the Sleeper."

"Yes."

"I see. And if I give you this information, what do you think will happen to me?"

"Nothing. Who's to know?"

Latham sighed. "You place me in an extremely awkward position."

"That was my intention"—Croyd glanced at his watch—"and I'm on a tight schedule. I should have begun beating the shit out of you about a minute and a half ago, but I'm trying to be a nice guy about this. What should we do, counselor?"

"I will cooperate with you," Latham said, "because I don't think it will make an iota of difference in what is going on right now."

"Why not?"

"I can give you a name, but not an address. I do not know

from where they do business. We have always met in no-man's-land or spoken over the telephone. I cannot even give you a telephone number, however, for they have always gotten in touch with me. And I say that it will make no difference because I do not believe that the interests you represent are capable of doing them harm. This group is too well staffed with aces. Also, I am fully convinced that they are going to manage what we might refer to as a "corporate takeover" very soon. Should your employer wish to save lives and perhaps even settle for a bit of pocket money as something of a retirement bonus, I would be happy to try to arrange the terms for such an agreement."

"Naw," Croyd said, "I don't have any instructions for that kind of deal."

"I'd be surprised if you did." Latham glanced at his telephone. "But if you would like to relay the suggestion, be my guest."

Croyd did not move. "I'll pass the word along, with the name you're going to give me."

Latham nodded. "As you would. My offer to negotiate does not assure the acceptance of any particular terms, though, and I feel obliged to advise you that it may not be acceptable at all to the other side."

"I'll tell them that, too," Croyd said. "What's the name?"

"Also, to be completely scrupulous, I ought to tell you that if you force me to divulge the name, I have a duty to inform my client that this information has been given out, and to whom. I cannot take responsibility for any actions this might precipitate."

"The name of my client has not been stated either."

"As with so much else in life, we must be guided by certain suppositions."

"Stop beating around the bush and give me the name."

"Very well," Latham told him. "Siu Ma."

"Say again."

Latham repeated the name.

"Write it down."

He jotted the name on a pad, tore off the sheet, and handed it to Croyd.

"Oriental," Croyd mused. "I take it this guy is head of a tong or a triad or a yakuza—one of those Asian culture clubs?"

"Not a guy."

"A woman?"

The attorney nodded. "Can't give you a description either. She's probably short, though."

Croyd looked fast, but he could not decide whether the residue of a smile lay upon the other's lips.

"And I'll bet she's not in the Manhattan directory either," Croyd suggested.

"Safe bet. So I've given you what you came for. Take it home, for all the good it will do you." He rose then, turned away from his desk, moved to a window, and stared down into traffic. "Wouldn't it be great," he said after a time, "if there were a way for you wild card freaks to bring a class action suit against the Takisians?"

Croyd let himself out, not totally pleased with what he had let himself in for.

Croyd required a restaurant with a table within shooting distance of a pay phone. He found what he was looking for on his third try, was seated, placed his order, and hurried to make his first call. It was answered on the fourth ring.

"Vito's Italian."

"This is Croyd Crenson. I want to talk to Theo."

"Hold on a minute. Hey, Theo!" Then, "He's coming."

Half a minute. A minute.

"Yeah?"

"This Theo?"

"Yeah."

"Tell Chris Mazzucchelli that Croyd Crenson's got a name for him and needs to know where he wants to hear it."

"Right. Call me back in half an hour, forty-five minutes, okay?"

"Sure."

Croyd phoned Tavern-on-the-Green then and was able to make reservations for two at eight-fifteen. Then he phoned Veronica. It was answered on the sixth ring.

"Hello?" Her voice sounded weak, distant.

"Veronica, love, it's Croyd. Not to be carried away, but I think I'm just about done with this job and I want to celebrate. What say we cut out about seven-thirty and start doing it?"

"Oh, Croyd, I really feel shitty. I ache all over, I can't

keep anything down, and I'm so weak I can hardly hold the phone up. It's gotta be flu. All I'm good for is sleeping."

"I'm sorry. You need anything? Aspirins? Ice cream? Horse? Snow? *Bombitas*? You name it and I'll pick it up."

"Aw, that's sweet, lover. But no. I'll be okay, and I don't want to expose you to this thing. I just want to sleep. Okay?"

"All right."

Croyd headed back to his table. His food arrived moments later. When he finished it, he ordered again and rolled a pair of pills between his thumb and forefinger. Finally he took them with a swallow of iced tea. Then he ordered again and checked various of his personal phones for messages till his next order arrived. He went back and took care of it, then buzzed Theo again.

"So what'd he say?"

"I haven't been able to get hold of him, Croyd. I'm still trying. Get back to me in maybe an hour."

"I will," Croyd said, and he called Tavern-on-the-Green and canceled his reservation, then returned to his table to order a few desserts.

He phoned before the hour had run as there were a number of matters he was anxious to attend to. Fortunately Theo had made a connection in the meantime, and he gave him an apartment address on the upper East Side. "Be there nine o'clock tonight. Chris wants you to make a full report to the management."

"It's just a lousy name I could give him over the phone," Croyd said.

"I am only a message service, and that is the message."

Croyd hung up and paid his tab, the afternoon open before him.

As he stepped outside, a short, broad-shouldered man with an Oriental cast to his features emerged from a doorway perhaps ten feet to the left, hands within his blue satin jacket, gaze focused on the ground. As he turned toward Croyd, he raised his head and their eyes met for a moment. Croyd felt later that he had known in that instant what was to occur. Whatever the case, he knew for certain a moment later when the man's right hand emerged from his jacket, fingers wrapped in an unusual grip about the hilt of a long, slightly curved knife, its blade extending back along the man's forearm, edge outward. Then his left hand emerged as he moved forward, and it held a matching blade in an identical grip. Both weapons moved in unison as his pace accelerated.

Croyd's abnormal reflexes took over. As he moved forward to meet the attack, it seemed as if the other had suddenly dropped into slow motion. Turning to match the double-bladed pass, Croyd reached across a line of gleaming metal, caught a hand, and twisted it inward. The weapon's edge was rotated back toward the attacker's abdomen. Its point entered there, moved diagonally upward, and was followed by a rush of blood and innards. As the man doubled, Croyd beheld the white egret that decorated the jacket's back.

Then the window at his side shattered and the sound of a gunshot rang in his ears. Turning, drawing his collapsed assailant before him, he saw a dark, late-model car moving slowly along the curbside, almost parallel to him. There were two men in the vehicle, the driver and a passenger in the rear seat who was pointing a pistol in his direction through the opened window.

Croyd moved forward and stuffed the man he held into the car. He did not fit through the window easily, but Croyd pushed hard and he went in nevertheless, losing only a few pieces along the way. His final screams were mixed with the roar of the engine as the car jumped forward and raced off.

It had been, he realized, a kind of proof that Latham had told him the truth and nothing but, though not necessarily the whole truth; and by this he was pleased with his work, after a fashion. Now, though, he had to start looking over his shoulder and keep it up till he had his money. And this was aggravating.

He stepped over some of his attacker's odds and ends and felt in his pocket for one of his pillboxes. Aggravating.

As Croyd approached the apartment building that evening, he noted that the man in the car parked before it appeared to be speaking into a small walkie-talkie and staring at him. He'd grown very conscious of parked cars following the second attempt on his life, a little earlier. Massaging his knuckles, he turned suddenly and stepped toward the car.

"Croyd," the man said softly.

"That's right. We'd better be on the same side."

The man nodded and shifted a wad of chewing gum into his left cheek. "You can go on up," he said. "Third floor, apartment thirty-two. Don't have to ring. Guy by the door'll let you in."

"Chris Mazzucchelli's there?"

"No, but everyone else is. Chris couldn't make it, but it don't matter. You tell those people what they want to know. It's the same as telling him."

Croyd shook his head. "Chris hired me. Chris pays me. I talk to Chris."

"Wait a minute." The man pressed the button on his walkie-talkie and began speaking into it in Italian. He glanced at Croyd after a few moments, raised his index finger, and nodded.

"What's comin' down?" Croyd asked when the conversation was concluded. "You find him all of a sudden?"

"No," the guard answered, shifting his wad of gum. "But we can satisfy you everything's okay in just a minute."

"Okay," Croyd said. "Satisfy me."

They waited. Several minutes later a man in a dark suit emerged from the building. For a moment Croyd thought it was Chris, but on closer inspection he realized the man to be thinner and somewhat taller. The newcomer approached and nodded to the guard, who nodded at Croyd and said, "There he is."

"I'm Chris's brother," the man said, smiling faintly, "and that's as close as we can get at the moment. I can speak for him, and it's okay for you to tell the gentlemen upstairs what you've learned."

"Okay," Croyd said. "That's good. But I was thinking about collecting the rest of my money from him too."

"I don't know about that. Maybe you better ask Vince about it. Schiaparelli. He sometimes does payroll. Maybe you shouldn't, though."

Croyd turned toward the guard. "You've got the bitch-box. You call the guy and ask him. The other side's already hit on me today for what I got. If my money's not here, I'm walking."

"Wait a minute," Chris's brother said. "No reason to get upset. Hang on."

He pointed at the walkie-talkie with his thumb and the guard spoke into it, listened, waited, glanced at Croyd.

"They're getting Schiaparelli," the guard said. After a longer while he listened to a low squawking, spoke, listened

again, looked at Croyd again. "Yeah, he's got it," he told
Croyd.

"Good," Croyd said. "Have him bring it down."

"No, you go up and get it."

Croyd shook his head.

The man stared at him and licked his lips, as if loathe to
relay the message. "This does not make a very good impression, for it is as if you had no trust."

Croyd smiled. "It is also correct. Make the call."

This was done, and after a time a heavyset man with
graying hair emerged from the building and stared at Croyd.
Croyd stared back.

The man approached. "You are Mr. Crenson?"

"That is correct."

"And you want your money now?"

"That's the picture."

"Of course I have it here," the other told him, reaching
into his jacket. "Chris sent it along. It will grieve him that
you are so suspicious."

Croyd held out his hand. When the envelope was placed
in it, he opened it and counted. Then he nodded. "Let's go,"
he said, and he followed Schiaparelli and Chris's brother into
the building. The man with the walkie-talkie was shaking his
head.

Upstairs, Croyd was introduced to a group of old and
middle-aged men and their bodyguards. He declined a drink,
just wanting to give them the name and get out. But it
occurred to him that giving them the money's worth might
entail stretching the story out a bit to show that he'd earned
it. So he explained things, step by step, from Demise to
Loophole. Then he told them of the attempt to take him out
following that interview, before he finally got around to giving
them Siu Ma's name.

The expected question followed: Where could she be
found?

"This I do not know," Croyd replied. "Chris asked me for
a name, not for an address. You want to hire me to get that
for you, too, I suppose I could do it, though it would be
cheaper to use your own talent."

This drew some surly responses, and Croyd shrugged,
said goodnight, and walked out, stepping up his pace to the

blur level as the muscle near the door looked about, as if for orders.

It was not until a couple of blocks later that a pair of such street troops caught up and attempted to brace him for a refund. He tore out a sewer grating, stuffed their bodies down through the opening and replaced it, for his final bit of subtlety before closing the books on this one.

The Hue of a Mind

by Stephen Leigh

Wednesday, 9:15 A.M.

For seven days, since Misha had arrived in New York, she had met nightly with the joker Gimli and the abominations he had gathered around him.

For seven days she had lived in a festering sore called Jokertown, waiting.

For seven days there had been no visions. And that was most important.

Visions had always ruled Misha's life. She was Kahina, the Seeress: Allah's dreams had shown her Hartmann, the Satan who danced puppets from his clawed hands. The visions had shown her Gimli and Sara Morgenstern. Allah's visions had led her back to the desert mosque the day after she'd slit her brother's throat, there to be given by one of the faithful the thing that would give her revenge and bring Hartmann down: Allah's gift.

Today was the day of the new moon. Misha took that as an omen that there would be a vision. She had prayed to Allah for well over an hour this morning, the gift He had bestowed upon her cradled in her arms.

He had granted her nothing.

When she rose from the floor at last, she opened the lacquered clothes trunk sitting beside the rickety bed. Misha took off her *chador* and veils, changing into a long skirt and blouse again. She hated the light, brightly colored cloth and the sinful nakedness she felt. The bared arms and face made her feel vulnerable.

Misha covered Allah's gift with the folds of the *chador* she didn't dare wear here. She had just hidden it under the black cotton when she heard the scrape of a footstep behind her.

Mingled fear and anger made her gasp. She slammed down the lid of the clothes trunk and straightened.

"What are you doing in here?" She whirled around, not even realizing she was shouting in Arabic. "Get out of my room—"

She'd never felt safe in Jokertown, not once in the week she'd been here. Always before there had been her husband, Sayyid, her brother, the Nur. There had been servants and bodyguards.

Now Misha was in a country illegally, living alone in a city full of violence, and the only people she knew were jokers. Only two nights before, someone had been shot and killed in the street outside these ramshackle sleeping rooms near the East River. She told herself that it had only been a joker, that the death didn't matter.

Jokers were cursed. The abominations of Allah.

It was a joker standing at the door of her dingy room, staring at her. "Get out," she said in shaky, accented English. "I have a gun."

"It's my room," the joker said. "It's my room and I'm taking it back. You're just a nat. You shouldn't be here." The thin, scrawny shape took a step forward into the light from the room's one window. Misha recognized the joker immediately.

Gray-white rags of torn cloth were wrapped around his forehead, and the grimy bandages were clotted and brown with old blood. His hair was stiff with it. His hands were similarly covered, and thick red drops oozed through the soaked wrappings to fall on the floor. The clothing he wore over his emaciated body bunched here and there with hidden knots, and she knew that there were other seeping, unclosing wounds on the rest of his body.

She'd seen him every day, staring at her, watching. He would be in the hallways outside her door, on the street outside the tenement, walking behind her. He'd never spoken, but his rancor was obvious. "Stigmata," Gimli had told her when she'd confessed his fear of him the first day. "That's his name. Bleeds all the fucking time. Have some goddamn compassion. Stig's no trouble to anyone."

Yet Stigmata's sallow, drawn stare frightened her. He was always there, always scowling when she met his gaze. He was a joker, that was enough. One of Satan's children, devil-marked by the wild card. "Get out," Misha told him again.

"It's my room," he insisted like a petulant child. He shuffled his feet nervously.

"You are mistaken. I paid for it."

"It was mine first. I've always lived here, ever since—" His lips tightened. He drew his right hand into a fist; the sopping bandages rained scarlet as he brandished it before her. His voice was a thin screech. "Ever since this. Came here the night I got the wild card. Nine years ago, and they kick me out 'cause I don't pay the last couple months. I told 'em I was gonna pay, but they wouldn't wait. They'll take nat money instead."

"The room's mine," Misha repeated.

"You got my things. I left everything here."

"The owner took them, not me—they're locked in the basement."

Stigmata's face twisted. He spat out the words as if they burned his tongue, almost screaming them. "He's a nat. You're a nat. You're not wanted here. We hate you."

His accusations caused Misha's masked frustrations to boil over. A cold fury claimed her, and she drew herself up, pointing at the joker. "You're the outcasts," she shouted back at Stigmata, at Jokertown itself. She might have been back in Syria, lecturing the jokers begging at the gates of Damascus. "*God* hates you. Repent of your sins and maybe you'll be forgiven. But don't waste your poison on me."

In the midst of her tirade there was suddenly a whirling, familiar disorientation. "No," Misha cried against the on- slaught of the vision, and then, because she knew there was no escape from *hikma,* divine wisdom: "*In sha'Allah.*" Allah would come as He wished, when He wished.

The room and Stigmata wavered in her sight. Allah's hand touched her. Her eyes became His. A waking nightmare burst upon her, melting away the gritty reality of Jokertown, her filthy room, and Stigmata's threats.

She was in Badiyat Ash-sham again, the desert. She stood in her brother's mosque.

The Nur al-Allah stood in front of her, the emerald glow of his skin lost beneath impossibly thick streams of blood that trailed down the front of his *djellaba*. His trembling hand pointed at her accusingly; his chin lifted to show the gaping, puckered, bone-white edges of the wound across his throat. He tried to speak, and his voice, which had once been compelling and resonant, was now all gravel and dust, choked. She could understand nothing but the hatred in his eyes.

Misha gasped under that baleful, accusing gaze.

"It wasn't me!" she sobbed, falling to her knees before him in supplication. "Satan's hand moved mine. He used my hatred and my jealousy. Please..."

She tried to explain her innocence to her brother, but when she looked up, it was no longer Nur al-Allah standing before her but Hartmann.

And he laughed.

"I'm the beast who rips away the veils of the mind," he said. His hand lashed out, clawing for her as she recoiled belatedly. Like talons his nails dug into her eyesockets, slashed the soft skin of her face. Blinded, she screamed, her head arced back in torment, writhing but unable to get away from Hartmann as his fingers tore and gouged.

"We don't wear veils here. We don't wear masks. Let me show her the truth underneath. Let me show you the color of the joker below." He clenched harder, ripping and tearing. Ribbons of flesh peeled away as he clawed at her, and she felt hot blood pouring down her ruined features. She moaned, sobbing, her hands trying to beat him away as he raked again and again, shearing flesh from muscle and muscle from bone.

"Your face will be naked," Hartmann said. "And they will run in horror from you. Look, look at the colors inside your head—you're just a joker, a sinner like the rest. I can see your mind, I can taste it. You're the same as the rest. You're the same."

Through the streaming blood she looked up. Though the apparition was still Hartmann, he now had the face of a young man, and the whine of a thousand angry wasps seemed to surround him. Yet in the midst of her torment, Misha felt a comforting hand on her shoulder and turned to see Sara Morgenstern beside her. "I'm sorry," Sara told her. "It's my fault. Let me send him away."

And then Allah's vision withdrew, leaving her gasping on the floor. Trembling, sweating, she raised her hands to her face. Marveling, she touched the unbroken flesh there.

Stigmata stared at the woman sobbing on the splintery pine boards.

"You ain't no damn nat," he said, and his voice was touched with a gruding sympathy. "You're just one of us." He sighed. Slow droplets of blood welled, fell. "It's still my room and I want it," he added, but the bitter edge was gone from his voice. "I'll wait. I'll wait."

He walked softly to the door. "One of us," he said again, shaking his gory, swaddled head, and went out.

Friday 6:10 P.M.

"So all the rumors are true. You *are* back again."

The voice came from behind him, in the shadow of an overflowing trash container. Gimli whirled, scowling. His feet kicked up oil-filmed water pooled in the alleyway, the remnants of the afternoon's showers. "Who the fuck are you?" The dwarf's left hand was fisted at his side; his right stayed very close to the open flap of the windbreaker he wore despite the warm night, where the weight of a silenced .38 hung. "You've got about two seconds before you become gossip yourself."

"Well, and as temperamental as ever, aren't we?" It was a young man's voice, Gimli decided. Streetlight flowed over a figure beside the trash. "It's me, Gimli," the man said. "Croyd. Move that damn hand from the gun. I ain't no cop."

"Croyd?" Gimli squinted. He relaxed slightly, though his squat, muscular body stayed low. "Your ace sure screwed up this time. I've never seen you look like that."

The man chuckled without mirth. His face and arms were a shocking porcelain white, his pupils dull pink; the tousled dark brown hair only accentuated the pallor of the skin. "Shit, yeah. Gotta stay out of the sun, but then I've always been a night person. Dyed the hair and started wearing sunglasses, but I lost the shades. Still got the strength this time, though. It's a damn good thing too," he added reflectively.

Gimli waited. If this guy *was* Croyd, fine; if he wasn't, Gimli didn't intend to give him a chance to do anything. Being in New York again made him edgy. Polyakov wouldn't meet with them until Monday, when Hartmann was rumored to be making his bid; the fucking Arab woman was a joker-hater who spouted religious nonsense half the time and had "visions" the other; his old JJS people had lost their fire while he'd been in Europe and Russia; and with the Shadow Fist/Mafia wars and Barnett's rabble-rousing, no one felt safe.

Yet staying cooped up in the warehouse made him edgy.

He had told himself that taking a brief night walk would take some of the edge off.

Another fucking bad idea.

Gimli was seeing enemies in every shadow—that was the only way to stay alive and free. It was bad enough that Hartmann had the federal and state authorities digging up the old JJS network and hassling everyone. With the joker-nat underground skirmishes, it seemed like every fucking cop in New York was in Jokertown and Gimli was too recognizable to feel comfortable on the streets, no matter what precautions he took. He wasn't going to pretend that Hartmann wouldn't prefer Gimli was shot "resisting arrest" than jailed—he wasn't that damned stupid.

Better to be cautious. Better to be furtive. Better to make a mistake and leave someone else dead than to be noticed. "Look, Croyd, I'm just a little paranoid at the moment. I'm real uneasy about people I don't know seeing me..."

Croyd took a step closer. Crooked teeth snagged his lower lip—the albino's gums were a startling bright red. Gimli was reminded of a B-movie zombie. "You got any speed, Gimli? Your connections were always good."

"I've been away. Things change."

"No speed? Shit."

Gimli shook his head. That, at least, sounded like Croyd. The man frowned, shuffling from foot to foot.

"So it goes," he said. "I've got other sources, though they're drying up or dying on me. Listen, the talk on the streets is that the JJS is reforming. Let me give you some free advice. After Berlin, you should give up on Hartmann; he's a good guy, anyway, no matter what you think. Take out that s.o.b. Barnett instead. I might have considered it myself, if I'd woken up with the right power. Everyone in Jokertown'd thank you for it."

"I'll think about it."

The albino laughed again, the same dry cackle. "You don't believe it's me, do you?"

Gimli shrugged. His hand moved significantly back toward the windbreaker; he saw the man watching the movement carefully. "You're still alive, aren't you? That's something."

The albino who might or might not be Croyd sidled closer until Gimli could smell his breath. "Yeah," he said. "And maybe next time around I'll just pound you a lot closer to the pavement than you already are. Croyd remembers things, Miller."

Croyd coughed, sniffed, and wiped his nose on his sleeve. With a bloodshot, overdone leer, he moved off. Gimli watched him, wondering if he was making a mistake. If he wasn't Croyd . . .

He let him go. Gimli waited in the alley until he'd turned the corner back onto the street and then headed off again, taking a few extra turns just to see if he was being followed.

In time he came to the back door of a dilapidated warehouse near the East River.

Gimli could see Video on the roof. He waved to her and nodded to Shroud, who materialized from the shadows of the entrance. Gimli grimaced. He could hear the argument inside the frame building—twined voices snarling like a rumbling thunderstorm heard just over the horizon. "Fuck, not again," he muttered.

Shroud adjusted the strap of his machine pistol and shrugged. "We need some entertainment," he said. "It's almost as good as Berlin."

Gimli shoved open the door. Muffled words coalesced into intelligibility.

File was shouting at Misha, who stood with arms folded and a righteous expression on her face as Peanut tried to hold back the rasp-skinned joker. File waved a fist at Misha, shoving at Peanut. ". . . your self-centered, blind fanaticism! You and the Nur are just Barnetts in Arabian drag. You have the identical hatred in your pompous souls. Let me show you hatred, bitch! Let me show you what it feels like."

As the rusty hinges of the door screeched, Peanut glanced over, his arms still wrapped around File. Peanut was scraped from the effort of holding the joker, his forearms scored with long, bloody scratches. A nat's skin would have been scoured entirely off, but Peanut's chitinous flesh was more durable. "Gimli," he said pleadingly.

File spun in Peanut's grip, tearing a pained screech from Peanut. He pointed at Misha as he glanced at the dwarf. "Get *rid* of her!" he shouted. "I won't put up with this crap much longer." Twisting, he tore himself away from Peanut, who let him go this time.

"Just what the fuck's going on?" Gimli slammed the door

shut behind him and glared. "I could hear you people halfway down the alley."

"I won't tolerate any more insults." File stalked toward Misha threateningly, and Gimli planted himself between the two.

"She said Father Squid's going to hell when he dies," Peanut added, dabbing at his cuts with a handkerchief. "I told File she just don't understand, but—"

"I told the truth." Misha sounded bewildered, as if she failed to believe their lack of comprehension. Her head shook, her hands were spread wide as if to absolve herself of guilt. "God showed His displeasure with the priest when He made him a joker. Yes, this Father Squid might be sent to hell, but Allah is infinitely merciful."

"See?" Peanut smiled at File tentatively. "It's okay, huh?"

"Yeah, and I'm a joker and Gimli and you are jokers and we're *all* being punished too. Right? Well, that's bullshit and I'm not gonna listen to it. Screw you, cunt." File flipped a finger in Misha's direction and spun on the balls of his feet. The slamming of the door reverberated for several seconds after his exit.

Gimli looked over his shoulder at Misha. To him she was quite remarkably good-looking out of the frigging black funeral dress, but she never seemed at ease in Western clothing. Her mysticism and bluntness unsettled his people. File, Shroud, Marigold, and Video absolutely loathed her, while Peanut—oddly enough—seemed utterly infatuated even though she gave the half-witted joker nothing but scorn.

Gimli had already decided he hated her. He regretted the impulse that had led him to meet with her after the Berlin fiasco; he wished he'd never steered her toward Polyakov. If it weren't for the evidence she claimed to have against Hartmann and the fact that they were still waiting for the Russian's information, the Justice Department would have received an anonymous tip. He'd like to see what fucking Hartmann would have them do with her.

She was a damn ace. Aces only cared about themselves. Aces were worse than nats.

"You got remarkable tact, you know that?" he said.

"He asked. I only told him what Allah told me. How can truth be wrong?"

"You want to live very much longer in Jokertown, you'd

better learn when to keep your fucking mouth shut. And *that* is the truth."

"I'm not afraid to be a martyr for Allah," she answered haughtily, her accent blurring the hard consonants. "I would welcome it. I'm tired of this waiting; I would rather attack the beast Hartmann openly."

"Hartmann's done a lot for the jokers..." Peanut began, but Gimli cut him off.

"It'll be soon enough. I talked to Jube tonight, and the word is Hartmann's going to speak at the rally in Roosevelt Park on Monday. Everyone thinks he'll make his announcement then. Polyakov said he'd contact us as soon as Hartmann made things official. We'll move then."

"We must contact Sara Morgenstern. The visions—"

"—don't mean anything," Gimli interrupted. "We'll make plans when Polyakov's finally here."

"I will go to this park, then. I want to see Hartmann again. I want to hear him." Her face was dark and savage, almost comically fierce.

"You'll stay away, goddammit," Gimli said loudly. "With all the shit going down in this city, the place'll be crawling with security."

She stared at him, and her gaze was more intense then he had thought it could be. He blinked. "You are not my father or my brother," she told him as if speaking to a slow child. "You are not my husband, you are not the Nur. You can't order me as you do the others."

Gimli could feel a blind, useless rage coming. He forced it down. *Not much longer. Only a few more days.* He stared back at her, each reading the other's dislike.

"Hartmann might make a good president..." Peanut's voice was almost a whisper as he glanced from one to the other. They ignored him. The scratches on his arms oozed blood.

"I hate this place," Misha said. "I look forward to leaving." She shuddered, breaking eye contact with Gimli.

"Yeah, there's a lot of fucking people about here who feel the same way." Misha's eyes narrowed at that; Gimli smiled innocently.

"A few more days. Be patient," Gimli continued. *And after that, all bets are off. I'll let File and the rest do whatever they damn well please with you.*

"Until then, keep your goddamn opinions to yourself," he added.

Monday, 2:30 P.M.

Misha, who had once been known as Kahina, remembered the sermons. Her brother, Nur al-Allah, had been at his most eloquent describing the torment of the afterlife. His compelling, resonant voice hammered the faithful from the *minbar* while noontime heat swirled in the mosque of Badiyat Ashsham, and it had seemed that the pits of hell gaped open before them.

Nur al-Allah's hell had been full of capering, loathsome jokers, those sinners Allah had cursed with the affliction of the wild card virus. They were an earthly image of the eternal torment that awaited all sinners: the vile underworld was slathered with twisted bodies that were a mockery of the human form; slick with puss oozing from scabrous faces; full of the stench of hatred and revulsion and sin.

The Nur had not known, but Misha did: Hell was New York. Hell was Jokertown. Hell was Roosevelt Park on a June afternoon. And the Great Satan himself capered there, before all his adoring followers: Hartmann, the devil with strings lacing his fingertips, the phantom who haunted her waking dreams. The one who had with Misha's own hands destroyed her brother's voice.

She'd seen the papers, the headlines praising Hartmann and extolling his coolness in crisis, his compassion, his work to end the sufferings of jokers. She knew that the thousands in the park were there to see him, and she knew what they hoped he would say. She knew that most considered Hartmann to be the one voice of sanity against the pious, hate-filled ravings of Leo Barnett and the others like him.

Yet Allah's dreams had shown her the real Hartmann, and Allah had placed in her very hands the gift that would bring him down. For just a moment the reality of the gathering in the park shimmered and threatened to give way to the nightmare again, and Misha nearly cried out.

"You okay? You shivered."

Peanut touched her on the arm, and Misha felt herself draw away involuntarily from contact with his hornlike, inflexible fingers. She saw hurt in his eyes, nearly lost in the scaly shell of his face.

"You're not supposed to be here," she told him. "Gimli said—"

"It's all right, Misha," he whispered. The joker could barely move his lips; the voice was a poor ventriloquist's rasp. "I hate the way I look too. A lot of us do—like Stigmata, y'know. I understand."

Misha turned from the guilty pain that the sympathy in his ruined voice gave her. Her hands ached to pull the veils over her face and hide herself from Peanut. But the *chador* and veils were locked away in the trunk in her room. Her hair was unbound and loose around her shoulders.

"When you are in New York, you can't wear black, not on a summer day. They'll already suspect that you're there. If you must go out, at least take care that you blend in if you intend to stay free. Be glad you can at least go walking in daylight; Gimli won't dare show his face at all." Polyakov had told her that before she'd left Europe. It seemed small consolation.

Here in Roosevelt Park, despite what Gimli had said the night before, there was no chance she would be conspicuous. The place was packed and chaotic. Jokertown had spilled its vibrant, strange life onto the grass. It was '76 again, the masks of Jokertown placed gleefully aside. They walked unashamed of Allah's curse, flaunting the visible signs of their sins, mixing unchecked with the one they called nats. They stood shoulder to misshapen shoulder around the stage set at the north end of the park closest to Jokertown, cheering the speakers who preached solidarity and friendship. Misha listened, she watched, and she shivered again, as if the afternoon heat was a chimera, a dream-phantom like the rest.

"You really hate jokers, don't you?" Peanut whispered as they moved closer to the stage. The grass was torn and muddy under their feet, littered with newspapers and political tracts. It was another thing she detested about this hell; it was always crowded, always filthy. "Shroud, he told me what your brother preached. The Nur don't sound awful different from Barnett."

"We . . . the Qur'an teaches that God directly affects the world. He rewards the good and punishes the wicked. I don't find that horrible. Do you believe in God?"

"Sure. But God don't punish people by giving them no damn virus."

Kahina nodded, her dark eyes solemn. "Then yours is either an incredibly cruel God, who would inflict a life of pain and suffering on so many innocents; or a poor, weak one who cannot stop such a thing from happening. Either way, how can you worship such a deity?"

The sharp rebuttal confused Peanut—in the days since she'd been here, Misha had found the joker to be friendly but extraordinarily simple. He tried to shrug, his whole upper body lifting, and tears welled in his eyes. "It ain't our fault—" he began.

His pain touched Misha, stopping her even as she started to interrupt. Again she wished for the veil to hide her empathy. *Haven't you listened to what Tachyon and the others have hinted at between the lines?* she wanted to rage at him. *Don't you see what they don't dare say, that the virus amplifies your own foibles and weaknesses, that it only takes what it finds inside the infected person?* "I'm sorry," she breathed. "I'm very sorry, Peanut." She reached out and brushed her shoulder with her hand; she hoped he didn't notice how the fingers trembled, how fleeting the touch was. "Forget what I said. My brother was cruel and harsh; sometimes I'm too much like him."

Peanut sniffed. A smile dawned on his sharp-edged face. "S'okay, Misha," he said, and the instant forgiveness in his voice hurt more than the rest. He glanced at the stage, and the valleys deepened in his craggy skin. "Look, there's Hartmann. I don't know why you and Gimli got such a beef against him. He's the only one who helps . . ."

Peanut's observation trailed off; at that moment the packed masses around them shoved fists toward the sky and cheered.

And Satan strode onto the stage.

Misha recognized some of those around him: Dr. Tachyon, dressed in outrageous colors; Hiram Worchester, rotund and bloated; the one called Carnifex, staring at the crowd so that she wanted to hide herself. A woman stood beside the senator, but it wasn't Sara, who had also been in her dreams so often, with whom she'd talked in Damascus—Ellen, his wife, then.

Hartmann shook his head, grinning helplessly at the adulation that swept through the crowd. He raised his hands, and the cheering redoubled, a roaring crowd-voice echoing from the skyscrapers to the west. A chant began somewhere near the stage, rippling back until the entire park resonated. *"Hartmann! Hartmann!"* they shouted to the stage. *"Hartmann! Hartmann!"*

He smiled then, his head still shaking as if in disbelief, and then he stepped to the battery of microphones. His voice was deep and plain and full of caring for those before him. That voice reminded Misha of her brother's; when he spoke, the very sound was truth. "You people are wonderful," he said.

They howled then, a hurricane of sound that nearly deafened Misha. The jokers pressed around the stage, Misha and Peanut thrust forward helplessly in the tidal flow. The cheering and chanting went on for a long minute before Hartmann raised his hands again and a restless, anticipatory hush came over the crowd.

"I'm not going to stand up here and feed you the lines you've come to expect of politicians like me," he said at last. "I've been a long time away and what I've seen of the world has, frankly, made me feel very frightened. I'm especially frightened when I return and find that same bigotry, that same intolerance, that same inhumanity *here*. It's time to quit playing politics and taking a safe, polite course. These aren't safe, polite times; these are dangerous times."

He paused, taking a breath that shuddered in the sound system. "Almost exactly eleven years ago, I stood in the grass of Roosevelt Park and made a 'political mistake.' I've thought about that day many times in the past years, and I swear to God that I've yet to understand why I should feel sorry for it. What I saw before me on that day was senseless, raw violence. I saw hatred and prejudice boiling over, and I lost my temper. *I. Got. Mad.*"

Hartmann shouted the last words, and the jokers shouted back to him in affirmation. He waited until they had settled into silence again, and this time his voice was dark and sad. "There are other masks than those which Jokertown has made famous. There is a mask which hides a greater ugliness than anything the wild card might produce. Behind that mask is an infection that's all too human, and I have heard its voice in the tenements of Rio, in the *kraals* of South Africa, in the deserts of Syria, in Asia and Europe and America. Its voice is rich and confident and soothing, and it tells those who hate that they are *right* to hate. It preaches that anyone who is *different* is also *less*. Maybe they're black, maybe they're Jewish or Hindu, or maybe they're just *jokers*."

With the emphasis on the last word the crowd-beast howled again, a wall of anguish that made Misha shiver. His words echoed the visions uncomfortably. She could almost feel his fingernails clawing at her face. Misha looked to her right and saw that Peanut was craning forward with the rest, his mouth open in a cry of agreement.

"I can't let that happen," Hartmann continued, and now his voice was louder, faster, rising with the emotions of the audience. "I can't simply watch, not when I see that there's more I can do. I've seen too much. I've listened to that insidious hatred, and I can no longer abide its voice. I find myself becoming angry all over again. I want to rip the mask off and expose the true ugliness behind, the ugliness of hatred. The state of this nation and the world frightens me, and there's only one way that I can do something to ease that feeling." He paused again, and this time waited until the entire park seemed to be holding its collective breath. Misha shuddered. *Allah's dream. He speaks Allah's dream.*

"Effective today, I have resigned my seat in the Senate and my position as chairman of SCARE. I've done that to give full attention to a new task, one that will need *your* help as well. I am now announcing my intention to be the Democratic candidate for president in 1988."

His last words were lost, buried under the titanic clamor of screaming applause. Misha could no longer see Hartmann, lost in the rippling sea of arms and banners. She had not thought that anything could be so loud. The acclamation deafened her, made her clap hands to ears. The chant of *Hartmann! Hartmann!* began once more, joker fists pumping in time with the beat.

Hartmann! Hartmann!

Hell was noisy and chaotic, and her own hatred was lost in the joyous celebration. Beside her, Peanut chanted with the rest, and she looked at him with revulsion and despair.

He is so strong, Allah, stronger than the Nur. Show me that this is the right path. Tell me that my faith is to be rewarded.

But there was no answering dream. There was only the beast-voice of the jokers and Satan basking in their praise.

At least now it would begin. Tonight. Tonight they would meet and decide how to best destroy the devil.

Monday, 7:32 P.M.

Polyakov was the last one to arrive at the warehouse.

That pissed Gimli off. It was bad enough that he wasn't sure he could trust any of the old New York JJS organization. It was enough that he'd been dealing with Misha for nearly two weeks now, putting up with her contempt for jokers. It was enough that Hartmann's Justice Department aces were prowling all over Jokertown after him; that Barnett's rabble-rousing had made any joker fair game for the nat gangs; that the continuing battles between the underworld organizations had made the streets a gamble for all.

On top of everything else, he could feel a cold coming on.

Gimli sneezed and blew his nose into a large red handkerchief.

It was shit time in Jokertown.

Polyakov's arrival only made Gimli's temper more vile. The Russian stamped into the place without a knock, throwing the door back loudly. "The joker on the roof is standing against streetlight," he proclaimed loudly. "Any fool can see her. What if I'd been police? You would all be under arrest or dead. Amateurs!" *Dilettante!*

Gimli wiped his bulbous, tender nostrils and glanced at the handkerchief. "The joker on the roof's Video. She threw an image of you in the room to let us know you were on the way—she needs the light to project. Peanut and File would have taken you out at the door if I hadn't recognized you." Gimli stuffed the damp handkerchief back in his pocket and pounded on the wall twice with his fist. "Video," he shouted to the ceiling. "Give our guest a replay, huh?"

In the center of the warehouse the air shimmered and went dark. For a moment they were all looking at the alleyway outside the warehouse, where a portly man stood in shadow. The darkness coalesced, pulsed, and they were seeing a head-and-shoulders view of the man: Polyakov, grimacing as he looked toward Video. Then the image faded to Gimli's laughter.

"And you never fucking *saw* Shroud behind you, did you?" he said.

A slender figure materialized out of the shadow behind Polyakov. He poked a forefinger in Polyakov's back. "Bang," Shroud whispered. "You're dead. Just like a Russian joker." Alongside the door Peanut and File grinned.

Gimli had to admit that Polyakov took it gracefully enough for a nat. The burly man just nodded without looking at Shroud at all. "My apologies. You obviously know your people better than I."

"Yeah. Don't I." Gimli sniffed; his sinuses were dripping like an old faucet. He waved to Shroud. "Make sure nobody else gets in—there's no more invitations." The thin, dark joker nodded. "Dead meat time," Shroud said—another whisper. A grin came from the vaporous form, and then he dissolved into shadow.

"We have aces with us, then," Polyakov said.

Gimli laughed without amusement. "Get Video near an electrical device and her nervous system overloads. Put her in front of a damn television and her heart will go into arrhythmia. Too close and she'll die. And Shroud loses substance every day, like he's evaporating. Another year and he'll be dead or permanently immaterial. Aces, shit, Polyakov—they're jokers, just like the rest. You know, the ones you cull out in the Russian labs."

Polyakov merely grunted at the insult; Gimli felt disappointed. The man brushed his fingers through stubbly gray hair and nodded. "Russia had made her mistakes, as has America. There are many things I wish had never happened, but we're here to change what we can, are we not?" He fixed Gimli with an unblinking stare. "The Syrian ace has arrived?"

"I'm here." Misha came from the rear of the warehouse. Gimli saw her glance sharply at Peanut and File. Her attitude was sour and condescending. She walked as if she expected to be catered to. Gimli might find her Arabian darkness extremely attractive, but—except in late-night fantasies—he didn't delude himself that anything might come of it. He knew what he looked like: "a warty, noxious little toadstool feeding on the decaying log of ego"—Wilde's phrase.

Gimli was a joker; that was the bottom line for the bitch. Misha had made certain that Gimli knew he was tolerated only to gain revenge on Hartmann. She didn't see him as a person at all; he was just a tool, something to use because nothing else would do. The realization gigged him every time he looked at her. Just seeing the woman was enough to make him want to shout at her.

I'll make you a fucking tool of my own one day.

"I'm ready to begin. The visions"—she smiled, making Gimli scowl in response—"have been optimistic today."

Gimli scoffed. "Your goddamn dreams ain't gonna worry the senator, are they?"

Misha whirled around, eyes flaring. "You mock Allah's gift. Maybe your scorn is why He made you a squashed mockery of a man."

That was enough to shatter what little restraint he had. A quick, molten rage filled Gimli. "*You fucking bitch!*" he screeched. The dwarf's stance widened on muscular legs, his barrel chest expanded. A finger stabbed from the fist he cocked at her. "I won't take that shit, not from you, not from anyone!"

"*STOP THIS!*" The shout came from Polyakov as Gimli took a step toward Misha. The roar brought Gimli's head around; the movement made his stuffy head throb. "Amateurs!" Polyakov spat out. "This is the stupidity that Mólniya said destroyed you in Berlin, Tom Miller. I believe him now. This petty bickering must end. We have a common purpose; focus your anger on that."

"Pretty speeches don't mean shit," Gimli scoffed, but he stopped. The fist lowered, the fingers loosened. "We're a damn unlikely conspiracy, ain't we?—a joker, an ace, and a nat. Maybe this was a mistake, huh? I'm not so certain anymore that we share much of a common purpose." He glared at Misha.

Polyakov shrugged. "None of us want Hartmann to gain political power. We have our separate reasons, but on this we agree. I would not care to see an ace with unknown powers as president of the nation that opposes my own. I know the Kahina would like to exact revenge for her brother. You have a long-standing grudge of your own against the senator. And as little as you may care for this woman, she has brought hard evidence against Hartmann."

"So she claims. We ain't seen it yet, have we?"

Polyakov grunted. "Everything else is circumstantial: hearsay and speculations. So let us begin. I, for one, would like to see Misha's 'gift.'"

"Let's talk reality first. Then we can indulge in religious fantasies," Gimli argued. He could feel control of the meeting slipping from him; the Russian had presence, charisma. Already the others were watching Polyakov as if he were the head of the group. *Forget how lousy you're feeling. You've got to watch him or he'll take over.*

"Nevertheless," the Russian insisted.

Gimli cocked his head at Polyakov. Polyakov stared back at him blandly. Finally Gimli cleared his throat noisily and sniffed. "All right," he grumbled. "The stage is yours, Kahina."

When Gimli glanced at her, she gave a quick, triumphant smile. That decided Gimli. When this was over, the bill would come due for Misha's arrogance. He'd exact the payment himself if he had to.

Misha went to the rear of the warehouse again and came back with a rolled bundle of cloth. "When the aces attacked us in the mosque, Hartmann was wounded," she said. "His people examined him there, quickly, but they retreated immediately afterward. I"—she stopped, and a look of remembered pain darkened her face—"I had already fled. My brother and Sayyid, both horribly wounded, gathered their followers and went deep in the desert. The next day a vision told me to return to the mosque. There, I was given this: It is the jacket Hartmann was wearing when he was shot."

She unrolled her package on the cement floor.

The jacket wasn't all that impressive—a gray-checked sports coat, dusty and bedraggled. The cloth held a faint stench of mildew. At the right shoulder a frayed hole was surrounded by an irregular splotch of brown-red, spreading as it crept down the chest. Packed inside were a sheaf of papers in a manila envelope. Misha riffled through them.

"I went to four doctors in Damascus with the jacket," she continued. "I had them examine the bloodstains independently, and each gave me a report that said the blood had definitely come from someone infected with the wild card virus. The blood type matches Hartmann—'A' positive. I have verification from the man who gave it to me that this is Hartmann's jacket—he picked it up after the fighting, thinking to keep it as a relic of the Nur."

"A verification letter from a terrorist, and blood that could have come from fucking anyone." Gimli snorted. "Look, all of us here might believe it's Hartmann's blood, but alone it's nothing. The bastard's got his blood test on record. You think he can't produce another negative one with the people he knows?"

Polyakov nodded ponderously. "He can. He would."

"Then attack him physically," Misha said, wondering at these people. "If you don't want my gift, kill him. I will help."

The look on her face made Gimli laugh, and the laughter brought on a hacking, phlegm-filled cough. "Christ, all I need is a cold," he muttered, then: "Awfully fucking blood-thirsty, ain't we?"

Misha folded her arms beneath her breasts, defiant. "I'm not afraid. Are you?"

"No, goddammit. Just realistic. Look, your brother had him surrounded by guards with Uzis and he got away, didn't he? *I* had the fucker tied to a chair, all of us armed, and one by one most of us left, a decision we can't believe we made an hour later. Then Mackie Messer—who was a loaded gun with no safety anyway—goes fucking berserk and slices up every-one that's left, yet somehow doesn't hurt the good senator at all." Gimli spat. "He can make people *do* things—that's got to be his power. He's got aces all around him. We ain't gonna get to the man, not that way."

Polyakov nodded. "Unfortunately, I must agree. Misha, you don't know Mólniya, the ace who was with Gimli in Berlin," he said. "He could have killed Hartmann with a simple touch. I spoke to him at length. He did things there that were sloppy and senseless for a man of his loyalty and experience. His performance was utterly inconsistent with his past record. He was manipulated: part of the evidence I have is his deposition."

File elbowed Peanut. "'Seventy-six," he said to Gimli. "I remember. You talked to Hartmann when we were all ready to march. Suddenly, you were telling us to turn around and go back into the park."

The memory was as sour now as it had been eleven years ago. Gimli had brooded on it many times. In '76 the JJS had been on the verge of becoming a legitimate joker voice, yet somehow he'd lost it all. The JJS and Gimli's power had fallen apart in the aftermath of the rioting. Since Berlin, since his meeting with Misha, that brooding had taken a different turn.

Now he knew who was to blame for his failure.

"Damn right. The son-of-a-bitch. That's why I want him taken down. With Barnett or any of the other nat politicians we know what we're dealing with. They're all known quantities. Hartmann's not. And that's why he's more dangerous than any of the rest. You remember Aardvark, Peanut? Aardvark died in Berlin, along with a lot of others—his death and all the fucking rest are ultimately Hartmann's fault."

Peanut's entire body moved as he tried to shake his head. "That ain't right, Gimli. Really. Hartmann *does* work for the jokers. He got rid of the Acts, he talks nice to us, he comes to Jokertown . . ."

"Yeah. And I'd do the same damn thing if I wanted to lull everyone's suspicions. I tell you, we know where Barnett stands. We can deal with him anytime. I'm more afraid of Hartmann."

"Then do something about him," Misha interjected. "We have his jacket. We have your story and Polyakov's. Take it to your press and let them remove Hartmann."

"Because we still ain't got shit. He'll deny it. He'll produce another blood test. He'll point out that the 'evidence' was produced by a joker who kidnapped him in Berlin, a Russian who has connections with the KGB, and you—who says that her *dreams* tell her Hartmann's an ace and who's suffering under the lunatic delusion that she was *made* to attack her terrorist brother. A fucking classic example of guilt transference."

Gimli enjoyed the flush that climbed Misha's neck. *Yeah, that one hit home, didn't it, bitch?* "We've circumstantial evidence, sure," Gimli continued, "but if *we* bring it forward, he'll just laugh it off and so will the press. We have to link with someone else. Let them be the front."

"I take it you have someone in mind?" Polyakov commented. Gimli thought he heard a faint challenge in the man's voice. "Yeah, I do," he told Polyakov. "I say we take what we have to Chrysalis. From what I hear, she's awfully damn interested in Hartmann herself, and she doesn't have any grudges. No one knows more about anything in Jokertown than Chrysalis."

"Know one knows more about Hartmann than Sara Morgenstern." Misha waved away Gimli's suggestion. "Allah's dreams have shown me her face. She is the one who will destroy Hartmann, not Chrysalis."

"Right. She's Hartmann's lover. We think Hartmann's got mind powers—so who's he most likely to control?" The headache was slamming at Gimli's temples now, and his head felt packed full of mucus. "We have to go to Chrysalis."

"We don't know that Chrysalis would have any interest in helping us. Maybe Hartmann controls her as well. My visions—"

"Your visions are crap, lady, and I'm getting fucking tired of hearing about them."

"They are Allah's gift."

"They're a gift from the wild card, and every last joker knows what's in *that* package." Gimli heard the door to the warehouse open. His gaze spun away from Misha to see Polyakov standing there. "Where the hell are you going?"

Polyakov exhaled sharply. "I've heard enough. I won't be caught with fools. Go to Chrysalis or go to Morgenstern—I don't care which. I even wish you luck; it may work. But I won't be associated with it."

"You're walking?" Gimli said in disbelief.

"We have a common interest, as I've said. That seems to be all. You do as you like; you don't need me for that. I will pursue this my own way. If I uncover anything of interest, I will contact you."

"You try something on your own and you're more likely to get caught. You'll alert Hartmann that people are after him."

Polyakov shrugged. "If Hartmann is the threat you think he is, he already knows that." He nodded to Gimli, to Misha, to File and Peanut. He stepped outside and closed the door softly behind himself.

Gimli could feel the gazes of the others on him. He gestured obscenely at the door. "To hell with him," he said loudly. "We don't need him."

"Then I go to Sara," Misha insisted. "She will help."

You don't have a choice. Not now.

Gimli nodded reluctantly. "All right," he sighed. "Peanut will get you a plane ticket to Washington. And I'll see Chrysalis." He touched his hand to his forehead; it felt suspiciously warm. "In the meantime, I'm going to bed."

Tuesday, 10:50 P.M.

Gimli had told her that she must be careful that no one was watching Sara's apartment. Misha thought the dwarf paranoid, but she waited several moments before crossing the street, watching. There was never a way to be sure—Sayyid, her husband, who had been in charge of all aspects of the Nur sect's security, would have agreed.

"No amateur will ever see a professional unless he wants to be seen," she remembered his saying once. Thoughts of Sayyid brought back painful memories: his scornful voice, his overbearing manner, his monstrous body. She'd felt relief mingled with horror when he'd been struck down in front of her, his bones snapping like dry twigs, a low animal moaning coming from his crumpled body. . . .

Misha shuddered and crossed the street.

She pressed the intercom button at the front door, marveling again at the American obsession with ineffectual security— the door was beveled glass. It would hardly stop anyone desperate to enter. The voice that answered sounded tired and cautious. "Yes? Who's there?"

"This is Misha. Kahina. Please, I must talk with you. . . ."

There was a long silence. Misha thought that perhaps Sara wasn't going to answer when the intercom's speaker gave a dry click. "You may come up," the voice said. "Second floor. Straight ahead."

The door buzzer shrilled. For a moment Misha hesitated, not certain what to do, then pushed the door open. She entered the air-conditioned foyer and went up the stairs. The door was cracked open; in the space between the door and jamb, an eye stared at her as she approached. It withdrew, and Misha heard a chain rattling. The door opened wider, but only enough to let her pass. "Come in," Sara said.

Sara was thinner than Misha remembered, almost gaunt. Her face was sallow and drawn; there were pouchy dark bags under the eyes. Her hair looked as if it hadn't been washed in days, lying limp and lusterless around her shoulders. She locked the door behind Misha, then leaned back against it.

"You look different, Kahina," Sara said. "No *chador*, no veils, no bodyguards. But I remembered the voice, and your eyes."

"We've both been changed," Misha said softly, and saw pain flicker in Sara's dark-rimmed pupils.

"I guess we have. Life's a bitch, huh?" Sara pushed away from the door, knuckling at her eyes.

"You wrote about me, after. . . after the desert. I read it. You understood me. You have a kind soul, Sara."

"I don't write much lately." She went to the center of the living room. Only one lamp was on; Sara turned in dim shadow. "Listen, why don't you sit down? I'll get something to drink. What would you like?"

"Water."

Sara shrugged. She went into the kitchen, came out a few minutes later with two tumblers. She handed one to Misha; Misha could smell alcohol in the other. Sara sat on the couch across from Misha and took a long swallow. "I've never been more frightened than the day in the desert," she said. "I thought your brother—" She hesitated, glancing at Misha over the rim of the glass. "I thought he was utterly mad. I knew we were all going to die. And then . . ." She took a long sip.

"Then I cut his throat," Misha finished. The words hurt; they always did. Neither one of them looked at the other. Misha put her tumbler on the table beside the couch. The chiming of ice against glass seemed impossibly loud.

"That must have been a very hard decision."

"Harder than you could believe," Misha answered. "The Nur was—and still is—Allah's prophet. He is my brother. He is the person my husband followed. I love him for Allah, for my family, for my husband. You've never been a woman in my society; you don't know the culture. You can't see the centuries of conditioning. What I did was impossible. I would rather have cut off my hand than allow it to do that."

"Yet you did."

"I don't think so," Misha said softly. "I don't think you believe it, either."

Sara's face was in darkness, haloed by backlit hair. Misha could see only the gleam of her eyes, the shimmer of water on her lips as she raised her glass again. "Kahina's dreams again?" Sara mocked, but Misha could hear the words tremble.

"I came to you in Damascus because of Allah's visions."

"I remember."

"Then you remember that in that vision Allah told me you and the senator were lovers. You remember that I saw a knife, and Sayyid struggling to take it from me. You remember that I saw how Hartmann had taken your distrust and transformed it, and how he would take *my* feelings and use them against me."

"You said lots of things," Sara protested. She huddled back deeper in the couch, hugging her knees to her chest. "It was all symbols and odd images. It could have meant anything."

"The dwarf was in that vision, too," Misha insisted. "You must remember—I told you. The dwarf was Gimli, in Berlin. Hartmann did the same thing there."

Sara's breath was harsh. "Berlin—" she breathed. Then: "It's all coincidence. Gregg's a compassionate and warm man. I know that, better than you or anyone. I've seen him. I've been with him."

"*Is* it coincidence? We both know what he is. He is an ace, a hidden one."

"And I tell you that's impossible. There's a blood test. And even if it *were* true, how does that change things? He's still working for the rights and dignity of all people—unlike Barnett or your brother or terrorists like the JJS. You've given me nothing but innuendo against Gregg."

"Allah's dreams—"

"They're *not* Allah's dreams," Sara interrupted angrily. "It's just the damned wild card. Flashes of precognition. There are half a dozen aces with the same ability. You see glimpses of the possible futures, that's all: useless little previews that have nothing to do with any god."

Sara's voice had risen. Misha could see her hand trembling as she took another drink. "What did *you* think he'd done, Sara?" she asked. "Why did *you* once hate him?"

Misha had thought that Sara might deny it; she didn't. "I was wrong. I thought . . . I thought he might have killed my sister. There were coincidences, yes, but I was *wrong*, Misha."

"Yet I can see that you're frightened because you might have been right, because what I'm saying might be the truth. My dreams tell me—they tell me you've been wondering since Berlin. They tell me you're frightened because you remember one other thing I told you in Damascus: that what he did to me, he would also do to you. Don't you notice how your feelings for him change when he's with you, and doesn't that also make you wonder?"

"*Damn* you!" Sara shouted. She flung the tumbler aside.

It thudded against the wall as she rose to her feet. "You have no *right!*"

"I have proof." Misha spoke softly into Sara's rage. She looked calmly upward into the woman's glare.

"Dreams," Sara spat.

"More than dreams. At the mosque, during the fighting, the senator was shot. I have his jacket. I had the blood analyzed. The infection is there—your wild card virus."

Sara shook her head wildly. "No. That's what *you* want the tests to show."

"Or Hartmann had his own blood test falsified. That would be easy for him, wouldn't it?" Misha persisted. The wild agony in Sara tore at Misha, yet she persisted. Sara was the key—the visions all said that she was. "And it would mean that perhaps you were right about your sister. It would explain what happened with me. It would explain what happened in Berlin. It would explain everything, all the questions you've had."

"Then go to the press with this proof."

"I am. Right now."

Sara's head swayed back and forth in dogged refusal. "It's not enough."

"Maybe not by itself. We need all that you can tell us. You must know more—other strange incidents, other deaths..."

Sara was still shaking her head, but her shoulders slumped and the anger had drained away. She turned from Misha. "I can't trust you," she said. "Please. Just go away."

"Look at me, Sara. We're sisters in this. We've both been hurt, and I want justice for that, as you want justice for your sister. We cry and bleed and there's no healing for us until we *know.* Sara, I know how we can mix love and hate. We're related in that strange, awful way. We've both allowed love to blind us. I love my brother, but I also hate what he's done. You love Hartmann, and yet here's a darker Hartmann underneath. You can't move against him because to do so would prove that giving yourself was a mistake, because when he's *here* all you can think about is the Hartmann you love. You'd have to admit that you were wrong. You'd have to admit that you let yourself love someone who was using you. So you wait."

There was no answer. Misha sighed and nodded. She couldn't say any more, not when each word tore a visible

wound in Sara. She moved toward the door, touching Sara
gently on the back as she passed. Misha could feel Sara's
shoulders moving with silent tears. Misha's hand was on the
knob when Sara spoke behind her, her voice choked.

"You swear it's his jacket? You have it?"

Misha kept her hand on the knob, not daring to turn, not
allowing herself to feel hope. "Yes."

"Do you trust Tachyon?"

"The alien? I don't know him. Gimli doesn't seem to like
him. But I will trust him if you do."

"I have to be in New York later this week. Meet me in
front of the Jokertown Clinic Thursday evening at six-thirty.
Bring the jacket. We'll have Tachyon examine it, and then
we'll see. We'll see, that's all. Is it enough?"

Misha almost gasped with the relief. She wanted to laugh,
wanted to hug Sara and cry with her. But she only nodded.
"I'll be there. I promise you, Sara. I want the truth, that's
all."

"And if Tachyon says it proves nothing?"

"Then I'll learn to accept the guilt for what I did myself."
Misha started to turn the knob, stopped. "If I'm not there,
know that it's because he stopped me. You'll have to decide
what to do then."

"Which gives you a convenient out," Sara said derisively.
"All you have to do is not show."

"You don't believe that. Do you?"

Silence.

Misha turned the knob and went out.

Tuesday, 10:00 P.M.

Chrysalis swung open the door to her office. She paid very
little attention to the dwarf who sat in her chair, his bare feet
propped up on her desk. She shut the door—the sounds of
another busy night at the Crystal Palace dropped to a distant
tidal soughing. "Good evening, Gimli."

Gimli was feeling rotten. The lack of surprise in Chrysalis's startling eyes only made him feel worse. "I should learn
that you're never caught off guard."

She gave him a tight-lipped smile that floated over a
webbing of muscles and tendons. "I've known you were back
for weeks. That's old news. So how's your cold?"

Gimli sniffed, a long, wet inhalation. Another chill rattled down his spine like a tray of ice cubes. "Shitty. I feel like hell. I've had a fever I haven't been able to kick for two days now. And I've evidently got somebody in my organization who can't keep his or her mouth shut." He gave her a rueful grimace.

"You wouldn't get colds if you'd wear shoes. You brought me a package, too."

"Fuck," Gimli spat out. He swung his legs down and hopped from the chair with a grimace. The sudden movement made him dizzy, and he steadied himself against the desk with a hand. "I might as well have come in the front door. Why don't we just skip the conversation entirely and you just give me an answer?"

"I really don't know the question yet, for certain." Her laugh was short and dry. "There are some limits after all, and I've been concerned about more immediate things than politics recently. It's not safe out there for *any* joker, not just you. But I *can* make an educated guess," Chrysalis continued. "I'd say that your visit concerns Senator Hartmann."

Gimli snorted. "Shit, after the fuckup in Berlin that doesn't take much of a guess."

"You're the one who's impressed by what I know, not me. You're the one who has to hole up near the East River so the feds don't snatch him."

"I've got a *big* goddamn leak." He shook his head. Gimli lurched around the side of the desk and hauled himself into her chair again. He closed his eyes for a second. *When you get back, you can go to bed again. Maybe this time when you wake up it'll be gone.* "God, I do feel like crap."

"Nothing infectious, I hope."

"We've both already had the worst fucking infection we're ever like to get." Gimli glanced at Chrysalis with a sidelong, bloodshot stare. "And speaking of which, I suppose you already know that our Senator Hartmann's a goddamn ace?"

"Really?"

Gimli scoffed. "There are things I know too, lady. One of them is that Downs has been asking odd questions, and that you've been seeing a lot of each other. My guess is that you're thinking the same thing."

"And if I am? Even granting that you're correct—and I'm not—why should you care about it? Maybe an ace president would be good. A lot of people feel Hartmann's done more for the jokers than the JJS."

Gimli shot to his feet at that, his illness forgotten. Rage eroded deep canyons in his pudgy face. "The goddamn JJS was the only organization that told the fucking nats that they can't jerk us jokers around. We didn't stand there holding our hats in our trunks like old kiss-ass Des. The JJS made 'em pay attention, even if we had to do it by beating them in the face. I'm not going to listen to crap about Hartmann being better than the JJS."

"Then I suggest you leave."

"If I do, then you don't see the fucking package."

He could see Chrysalis considering that, and he smiled, the anger quickly forgotten. *Yeah, you're hungry for that. Old Chrysalis's just playing it cool. I knew she'd want to see it. And fuck Misha if she doesn't like it.*

"You've never been one to be free with things, Gimli. What's the payment for the package?"

"You go public with this. You spill it with the rest of what I've got for you, along with anything you and Downs have dug up. We take Hartmann out of the race."

"Why? Because he's an ace? Or because it's Gimli's personal little vendetta?"

Gimli gritted his teeth and then destroyed the image with a sneeze. "Because he's a power-hungry bastard. He's just like the rest of the money-grubbing, self-centered bureaucrats in government, only he's got his ace to help him. He's dangerous."

"You get rid of Hartmann, and the next president might be Leo Barnett."

"Shit." Gimli spat; Chrysalis looked at the globule on her rug in dismay. "He might get the nomination, but that's not the presidency. Barnett's just a nat; he can be removed if he has to be. With Barnett we at least know what to expect. Hartmann's a fucking unknown. You don't know what he's got or what he's going to do with it."

"Like maybe make a few things right."

"Like maybe make things worse. This ain't for me; this is for the jokers. Look at the damn facts you prize so much. What Hartmann touches gets destroyed. He uses people. Chews 'em up and spits out the carcass when the flavor's gone. He used me, he used the Nur's sister, he fucked with

the minds of the people around me in Berlin. He's a goddamn bottle of nitro. God knows what else he's done."

He paused, waiting for her to object, but she didn't.
Gimli pulled a wad of tissues from his pocket, blew his nose,
and grinned at her. "And you suspect the same thing," he
continued. "I fucking know it, 'cause you wouldn't have stood
there and listened to me for this long if you thought otherwise. You want my little package because it might prove it
true."

"Proof is a nebulous thing. Look at Gary Hart. No one
needed 'proof' with him, just a lack of denial."

"There *is* proof with the wild card. In the blood. And I've
got Hartmann's blood." Gimli brought out Misha's jacket. As
he spread the bloodstained cloth on Chrysalis's desk, he gave
her the story. When he'd finished, a faint flush had appeared
in Chrysalis's transparent skin, the lacework of blood vessels
spreading and widening in excitement. Gimli laughed even
though his head pounded from the fever.

"It's yours, free," he told her. A coughing fit took him,
deep hacking spasms, and he waited until they'd passed,
wiping his nose on his sleeve. "You know me, Chrysalis. I
might do a lot of things, but I don't lie. When I tell you that's
Hartmann's blood, it's the truth. But it ain't enough, not
without more. You just have to do something with it.
Interested?"

She took the cloth between her fingers, touching the
bloodstains tentatively. "Let me keep it," she said. "I want a
friend to run the tests—it might take a few days. If the stains
are from an ace, then yes, we might have a deal."

"I thought so," Gimli said. "Which means you have more
on Hartmann, don't you? Take good care of the jacket. I'll
check with you later. Right now, I'm going to go home and
fucking die."

Tuesday, 11:45 P.M.

Gimli was shaking with fever by the time he left Chrysalis.
He'd ridden over in the back of File's van but had told the
joker that he'd get back himself. *Fuck the risk,* he'd said. *I'm
tired of playing the fugitive. I'll be careful.*

He let himself out the back door of the Crystal Palace into
an alleyway that reeked of stale beer and rotting food. Quick

nausea slammed him in the gut; leaning with one hand against the Dumpster, he heaved violently, emptying his stomach with the first wave and then retching uselessly. Afterward he felt no better. His stomach was still knotted, his muscles felt as if he had been beaten, and the fever was getting worse. "Oh, fuck," he gasped. He spat dry-mouthed.

He wished he'd listened to File and let him wait. He pushed off the Dumpster and holding his stomach, began to walk toward the warehouse. *Six damn blocks. It ain't so far.*

He'd made it four when his stomach rebelled again. This time it was far worse. There was nothing in his stomach. Gimli tried to ignore it, shuffling forward.

"Christ!" he shouted, his face twisting with surprised agony. The pain drove him to his knees; he knelt behind a row of trash cans, desperately trying to breathe between the waves of helpless retching. His insides were on fire, his head pounded, sweat soaked his clothing. He pummeled the concrete with his fists until they were torn and bloodied, trying to block the inner torment with outside pain.

It got worse. Every muscle in his body seemed to go into spasm at that moment, and Gimli bellowed, a shrill inhuman screeching. He rolled on the gound, twitching, the muscles of his body in uncontrolled rebellion—legs flailing, hands clenched, spine arched in torment. His arm snapped under the pressure of wildly contracting biceps and triceps, the jagged end tearing through skin. The bone wriggled before his eyes like a live thing, tearing the wound wider. His intestines felt as if acid had been poured on them, but somehow the pain seemed to be receding, and that scared him worst of all.

He was going into shock.

The spasms ended abruptly, leaving him in a curled fetal position. Gimli couldn't move. He tried, willing himself to blink his eyes, bend a finger; he had no control of his body at all. For a moment Gimli thought that at least it was over. Someone would find him; someone would have heard his screams. The denizens of Jokertown knew what to do—they'd take him to Tachyon.

But it wasn't over. His broken arm was sitting in front of his open, staring eyes, and as he watched, the spear of bone from his arm was melting like a candle in an oven. He could *feel* his body sagging, shifting inside, liquefying. His skin bulged, spread like a huge balloon filled to bursting with scalding water. He tried to scream and could not even open his mouth. His eyes, too—the trash cans, the wall, his broken arm in front of him all dissolved in his sight, distorting as the world turned dim and then was gone. He could not draw a breath. He felt himself suffocating, unable to take in air.

At least Chrysalis has the fucking jacket. The thought had a finality that surprised him.

There was a sound like tearing paper, startling a curious rat that had crept closer to the strange mound. Gimli couldn't see it or hear it, but the feeling was there, like a white-hot poker rammed into his spine. A small rent appeared in the middle of his back. Slowly the fissure grew, his flesh tearing open in long, jagged strips.

In his soundless, anguished void, Gimli wondered if he hadn't already died, if this wasn't the eternal hell Misha had promised him waited for all jokers. He mind-screamed, cursing Misha, cursing Hartmann, cursing the wild card and the world.

And then, blessedly, he lost consciousness.

Wednesday, 12:45 A.M.

The waking dream hit her just as she pushed open the door to the warehouse. The graffiti-scrawled paint became fluid; the door sagged like a lead figurine thrown into a fire.

In the darkness beyond she could hear laughter—Hartmann's laughter, and the strings of a puppet danced in the air before her. As Misha recoiled, the strings tightened and rose, and she could see a hunchbacked figure lolling on the ends. The malevolence of that face staggered her—a pimply boy's face, but one so infused with evil that its very breath seemed a poison. She remembered that face from her visions. The smile was twisted and cruel, and the bright eyes held the promise of pain. The creature stared at her, twisting in the strings, silent and unmoving as Hartmann's laughter boomed.

And then it was gone. There was the door, and her hand ready to twist the key. "Allah," she breathed, and shook her head. The motion did nothing to dispel the lingering feeling of dread. The images of the dream stayed with her, and she could hear her heart pounding. The lock clicked open and she pushed the door wide. "Gimli?" she called "Hello?"

The warehouse was as dark as her dream, and empty.

Misha's pulse roared in her head and the dream-demon threatened to reappear; in the dim reaches of the warehouse, whirling splotches of light moved with her momentary dizziness.

The door to the office swung wide, the glare from behind the lamps inside nearly blinding her. A shadow loomed— Misha cried out.

"Sorry, Misha," Peanut's voice said. "I didn't mean to scare you."

His hand reached out as if he was going to pat her shoulder, and Misha drew back, leaving his hand extended awkwardly. She frowned as she regained her composure. "Where's Miller?" she asked sharply.

Peanut's hand dropped, his sad gaze regarding the stained concrete floor. Heavy, clumsy shoulders lifted. "Dunno. He should'da been here hours ago, but I ain't heard from him. File and Video and Shroud was here, said they'd be back later. They wouldn't stay with me."

"What's the matter, Peanut? You've been here alone before."

"Polyakov—he phoned. Said to tell Gimli that Mackie was here, in the States. Said that the paper trail was all official stuff: government. He told me to tell Gimli that he was afraid Hartmann knew it all—everything."

"Does Gimli know?"

"Not yet. I gotta tell him. You wait with me?"

"No." She said it too quickly, too harshly, but she didn't try to soften the word with an explanation. "I talked to Sara; I need the jacket—we're going to take it to Tachyon."

"You can't have the jacket. Gimli took it with him. You'll have to wait."

Misha only shrugged at that, surprising Peanut, who had expected her to fly into a rage. "I'm going to my place. I'll come back here later."

She turned to leave.

"I don't hate you," Peanut's childlike voice said behind her. "I don't hate you 'cause you got lucky with the wild card and I didn't. And I don't even hate you for what you and the Nur did to people like me. I think I got a lot more reason to hate than you, but I don't, 'cause I think maybe the damn virus has hurt you more than me, after all."

Misha had kept her back turned, stiffly, from his first words. "I don't hate you, Peanut," she answered. She was tired from the long day, from the flight, from the meeting with Sara and the inchoate feeling of dread that still enveloped her. There was no energy in her to argue or explain.

"The Nur hates jokers. Barnett hates jokers. Sometimes jokers hate jokers. And you and Gimli and the Russian want to hurt the one guy who looks like he might care. I don't understand." Peanut sighed. "So what if he's an ace? Maybe that explains why he works so hard for the jokers. I might keep it secret, too, if I could. I know how people treat you different and stare at you and try to pretend it doesn't matter when it does."

"Haven't you listened to us, Peanut?" Misha swung around, sighing. "Hartmann's a manipulator. He plays with his power. He uses it for his own ends. He hurts and kills people with it."

"I'm still not sure I believe that," Peanut insisted. "Even if I did, didn't what you and the Nur preached kill? Didn't you cause hundreds of jokers to die?"

His mild voice only made the truth of the accusation sting more. *Blood on my hands, too.* "Peanut—" she began, then stopped. She wanted to bring the veils over her eyes and hide her feelings behind black cloth. But she couldn't. She could only stand there, unable to look away from his sad, puckered face. "How can you not hate me?" she asked him.

He almost seemed to smile. "I did, once. Till I met you, anyways. Hey, your society fouled you up. Does that to everyone, huh? I see you fight against it, and I know you care, underneath. Gimli says you didn't like a lot of what the Nur said, either." Now he did smile, a tentative grin that heightened the ridges in his thick flesh. "Maybe I could come with you and protect you from Stigmata."

She could only smile in return.

"Well, ain't this touching?"

The voice, so utterly unexpected, caused them both to whirl —the words had a strong Germanic accent. A hunchbacked, anemic young man in black stepped through the wall of the warehouse as if it were a mist. Misha knew that cruel, lean face instantly, knew the sickness that lurked behind the eyes. The hammering of fear in her body was reminder enough, and he had the same feral casualness of the figure hanging in Hartmann's strings.

"Kahina," he said in a jittery, quick voice, and with the use of that honorific she knew it was over. The youth was breathing like a nervous thoroughbred, smiling lopsidedly. *Hartmann knows. He's found us.* "It's time."

She could only shake her head.

Peanut moved to put himself between the intruder and Misha. The boy-man's sardonic gaze flicked toward the joker. "Ain't Gimli told you about Mackie? Man, everyone's scared shitless of Mackie. You should have seen the Fraction bitch's eyes when I offed her. I've got an ace better than anything. . . ." There was an eager satisfaction in Mackie's rambling voice. He reached for Misha. Peanut tried to strike Mackie's hand aside, but suddenly the hand shivered and began to vibrate with a fierce thrumming.

Blood fountained impossibly. Peanut's severed forearm dropped to the floor.

Peanut stood for a moment, staring in disbelief as pulsing red jetted from the stump. Then he screamed. His legs buckled; he collapsed. Mackie raised his hand again, a deep buzz-saw whine coming from the blur.

"*No!*" Misha shouted. Mackie hesitated, looking at her. The pleasure she saw in the boy made her sick—it was a look she'd seen in her brother, it was a look she'd seen on Hartmann's face in Allah's dreams. "Don't," she pleaded. "Please. I'll go with you. Whatever you want."

Mackie's breath was harsh and loud; emotions crossed his pinched face like quick cloud-shadows. Peanut moaned beneath him. "He's a damn joker. I thought you wanted them all dead. I can do it for you. It'd be quick; it'd be good." His face had gone serious now, and the sickness was like a lust in him.

"Please." Mackie didn't answer. Misha stopped and ripped a strip of cloth from the hem of her dress. She knelt beside the stricken joker, who writhed on the floor. "I'm sorry, Peanut," she said. She wrapped the cloth around his arm above the stump, pulled it tight until the blood flow eased, and knotted it. "I didn't hate you. I just couldn't manage to say it."

Mackie's hand touched her arm, and Misha flinched. Though the horrible vibration was gone, his fingers gripped her until she cried out in pain. "Now," Mackie said. He glanced down at Peanut. His tone was almost conversational. "Next time you see Gimli, tell him Mackie said 'Auf Wiedersehen' "

And then he was grinning again as he pulled Misha up.

"Don't be frightened," he told her. "This is going to be fun. Lots of fun." His manic laughter cut into her like a thousand glass shards.

Thursday, 3:40 A.M.

In the alley behind the Crystal Palce a bulky figure in a black cloak approached a man wearing a clown's mask. The cloaked figure's hooded face was hidden behind what looked to be a fencing mask.

"Okay, Senator, we were the last ones out," the apparition said. "The rest of the customers are gone. The staff just left; the place is empty. Chrysalis is in her office with Downs."

The quiet voice sounded female, which meant that the Patti persona was in charge of Oddity tonight. Gregg's understanding was that the joker had once been three people, two men and a woman involved in a long-standing love relationship. The wild card had joined them into one being, though the fusion had been incomplete and fluid. Shapes humped and shifted under Oddity's cloak. Oddity's body was never at rest—Gregg had once seen it without the concealing fabric, and the sight had been disturbing. It (or perhaps "they," since Oddity always referred to itself in the plural) was constantly undergoing metamorphosis. Patti, John, Evan: never entirely any one of them, never stabilizing, always struggling against itself. Bones creaked, the flesh bulged and twisted, the features came and went.

The endless process was agonizing—Puppetman knew that best of all. Oddity gave him the emotional nourishment he craved simply by existing. Oddity's world was a wash of pain, and the trebled matrices of its mind were quick to shift into black, sullen depression.

The only constant of Oddity was the strength of its malleable form. In that, Oddity surpassed Carnifex and perhaps rivaled Mordecai Jones or Braun. Oddity also had a great loyalty to Senator Hartmann.

After all, Oddity knew that Gregg was compassionate. Gregg cared about the jokers. Gregg was the voice of reason against fanatics such as Leo Barnett. Why, he was one of the few who ever asked Oddity about itself, and he listened sympathetically to the long tale of the joker's like. Gregg might be a nat, but he came among the jokers and talked to them and shook their hands and then kept his political promises.

Oddity would have done anything Senator Hartmann asked it to do. The thought made Puppetman wriggle with delight inside Gregg. Tonight... tonight held the promise of being delicious.

Puppetman was tired of playing it safe, even if Gregg was not.

Gregg forced that hidden personality into the recesses of his mind. "Thanks, Patti," he said. Through Puppetman he could feel a tinge of pleasure at that—the individual psyches in Oddity liked to be recognized. "You know the rest?"

Oddity nodded. What might have been a breast pushed sluggishly at the left side of the cloak. "I'll watch the place. No one gets in or out but the two you told me about. Simple enough." The words were slurring as the shape of the mouth altered behind the fencing mask.

"Good. I appreciate this."

"No problem for you, Senator. All you ever have to do is ask."

Gregg smiled and forced himself to clap Oddity on the shoulder. There were sliding *things* underneath. He suppressed a shudder as he squeezed slightly. "Thanks again, then. I'll be out in twenty minutes or so."

The gratitude and loyalty radiating from Oddity made Puppetman laugh, inside. Gregg adjusted the clown's mask as Oddity leaned against the back doors. They groaned; a metal chain snapped inside. Gregg strode through the sagging doors and into the club.

"We're closed." Chrysalis was standing at the door to her office with a nasty-looking gun in her hand; behind her, Gregg could see Downs.

"You were expecting me," Gregg said softly. "You sent me a message." He took off the clown's mask. Even without a puppet's link to the woman, he could sense the mingled fear and defiance in her, a bitter metallic tang that roused Puppetman. Gregg chuckled, letting a little of his own nervousness into the sound.

Why so uncertain?

That should be obvious. Even with the information Video fed us we don't know everything. Gimli didn't trust Video

*enough; he didn't let her see everything. They have whatever
it was Kahina and Gimli had.*

And you have me.

Gregg had planned it well: Video had been a wonderful,
pliant puppet for years. Yet even with what she'd managed to
funnel to him, even with what he'd garnered from government intelligence agencies and other sources, he was still
grasping in twilight. A misstep here, and it might all be over.

Gregg had always been cautious, had always sought the
safe path. Recklessness was not something with which he was
comfortable, and this was reckless. But since Syria, since
Berlin, it seems he'd been forced to choose this path. "Sorry I
couldn't make it during your business hours," he continued,
his voice nearly apologetic. "I felt your meeting might be too
private for that."

*Good. Let them think they're negotiating from strength,
at least for a bit. You need to know what they know.*

Chrysalis lowered the gun; muscles expanded under her
transparent arm and across her chest—the dress she wore did
little to conceal her body. Red lips that seemed to float on
glassy flesh pursed. "Senator," she said with that breathy fake
accent that Gregg disliked, "I assume you know what Mr.
Downs and myself would like to discuss."

Gregg took a breath. He smiled. "You want to talk about
aces," he said. "Especially ones who are—so to speak—up
the sleeve and who intend to stay that way. You want to see
what I might be able to do for you. I think it's usually called
blackmail."

"Aah, that's such an ugly word." She stepped back into the
office. Her lips tightened, the horror-show skull eyes blinked.
"Please come in."

Chrysalis's office was luxurious. A polished oak desk,
plush leather chairs, an expensive rug over the center of the
hardwood floor, wooden bookcases on which gold-leaf spines
were lined neatly in sets. Downs was sitting nervously. He
smiled tentatively at Gregg as the senator entered.

"Hey, Senator. What's shakin'?"

Gregg didn't bother to answer. He stared hard at Downs.
The little man sniffed and sat back in the chair. Chrysalis
brushed past him in a wave of perfume and took her seat
behind the desk. She waved at one of the empty chairs.

"Have a seat, Senator. I don't believe our business will take that long."

"Exactly what are we talking about?"

"We're talking about the fact that I'm considering telling the public that you're an ace. I'm sure you'd be very unhappy with that."

Gregg had expected Chrysalis to threaten; she was no doubt used to getting results from that tactic, and he didn't doubt that she considered herself safe from physical violence here. Gregg watched Downs from the corners of his eyes. The reporter had shown himself to be the nervous type on the wild card tour, and he couldn't control his agitation now. Sweat beaded on his forehead; he rubbed his hands and squirmed in his seat. If Chrysalis was at ease with this, Downs was not. *Good.* Puppetman came alert. *We made a mistake not taking him. Let me have him now.*

No. Not yet. Wait.

"You are an ace, aren't you, Senator?" Chrysalis asked the question coolly, pretending nonchalance.

He knew they expected him to deny it. So he simply smiled. "Yes," he answered just as calmly.

"Your blood test were faked?"

"As they can be faked again. But I don't think I'll have to do that."

"You're rather overconfident in your ability, then."

Gregg, looking at Downs rather than Chrysalis, could see the uncertainty. He knew what the man was thinking: *A projecting telepath? A mental power like Tachyon's? What if we can't control him?*

Gregg smiled calmly to lend credence to that misconception. "Your friend Downs isn't so certain," he told Chrysalis. "Everyone in Jokertown knows about Gimli's empty skin being found last night in an alleyway, and he wonders about whether I had anything to do with that." It was a bluff—Gregg had been as surprised (and delighted) as anyone else at the news—but Gregg saw the color drain from Downs's face. "He wonders if I might not be able to coerce your cooperation through my ace."

"You can't. And whatever happened to Gimli had nothing to do with you, not directly," Chrysalis answered forcefully. "No matter what he thinks. My best guess is that you've a mind power, but with a rather limited range. So even if you can make us say yes now, you can't enforce it."

She knows! Puppetman's wail echoed in Gregg's head. *You've got to kill her. Please. It will taste good. We could make Oddity do it....*

She suspects, that's all, he answered.

What's the difference? Have them killed; we have puppets who would find pleasure in it. Have them killed and we don't have to worry.

Kill them now and we have more trails to cover up. Misha wouldn't talk; we still don't know what evidence Chrysalis was given. Gimli's taken himself out of the picture, but there's still the other man in Video's memory—the Russian.

And Sara. Puppetman's scorn was a barb.

Shut up. Sara we can control. Chrysalis will have plans made against her own death. We can't risk that.

The inner debate took only a moment. "I'm a politician. This isn't France, where the wild card is chic. I'm in a fight where Leo Barnett will use joker hatred as a tool. I've already seen Gary Hart's career wiped out by innuendo. I'm not going to let that happen to me. Still, people might look at whatever evidence you have and wonder. I might lose votes. People will say that blood tests can be faked, they'll look at Syria and Berlin with suspicion. I can't afford to lose ground to speculation."

"Which means we can come to an accommodation," Chrysalis smiled.

"Maybe not. I think you still have a problem."

"Senator, the press has its obligations..." Downs began, then fell silent with the withering gaze Hartmann gave him.

"*Aces* magazine is hardly the legitimate press. Let me put it this way—your problem is that you don't know what I'm capable of. I *will* tell you that Berlin and Syria weren't accidents. I'll tell you that even now Gimli's little cadre is being arrested. I'll tell you that there's no way you can escape me if I want to find you." He turned his head slightly toward the door. "Mackie!" he called.

The door opened. Grinning, Mackie entered, supporting a stumbling woman wrapped in a long cloak. Mackie jerked the cloak from the woman's shoulders, revealing her naked and streaked with blood. He shoved the woman from behind, and she sprawled on the carpet in front of the horrified Chrysalis.

"I'm a reasonable man," Gregg said as Chrysalis and Downs stared at the figure moaning on the floor. "All I ask is that you think about this. Remember that I *will* contest any evidence. Remember that I can and will produce that negative blood test. Think about the fact that I don't even want to hear the faintest whisper of a rumor. And realize that I leave the two of you alive because you're the best sources of information I know—you hear everything, or so you'd have me believe. Good. Use those sources. Because if I hear any rumors, if I see a piece in the papers or *Aces*, if I notice that people are asking strange questions, if I'm attacked or hurt or even feel vaguely threatened, I'll know where to come."

Downs was staring slack-jawed at Misha; Chrysalis had sunk back against her desk. She tried to meet Gregg's eyes and failed. "You see, I intend to use *you*, not the reverse," Gregg continued. "I hold the two of you responsible for silence and safety. You're both so damned good at what you do. So start learning who my enemies are and work at stopping them. I'm vindictive, and I'm dangerous. I'm everything Gimli and Misha were afraid I might be.

"And if anyone else ever learns that, I'll consider it *your* fault. You might damage my presidential campaign by being heroes, but that's all. You can't prove anything else. After all, I've never actually killed or hurt anyone *myself*. I'd still be on the streets, afterward. And I'd find you without any trouble at all. And then I'd do to you what I'd do to any enemy."

Puppetman was chuckling in his mind, anticipating. Gregg smiled at Chrysalis, at Downs. He hugged Mackie, who was watching him eagerly. "Enjoy yourself," Gregg told him. He gave Chrysalis a small nod that was chilling in its nonchalance and left the office. He shut the door behind him, leaning against it until he heard the whine of Mackie's ace.

He let Puppetman loose to ride with the youth's strange, brightly colored madness. He hardly had to nudge Mackie at all.

Inside, Mackie knelt and cradled Misha's head in his arms. Neither Chrysalis nor Downs moved. "Misha," he crooned. The woman opened her eyes, and the pain he saw behind them made him sigh. "Such a good little martyr," he told her. "She wouldn't talk no matter what I did, you know," he said to the others admiringly, his eyes skittering, bright. His hands roamed over her lacerated body. "She could be a saint. Such silence in suffering. So frigging noble." The smile he gave Misha was almost tender. "I took her like a boy first, before I cut her at all. Anything to say now, Misha?"

Her head rolled side to side, slowly.

Mackie was smiling fitfully, breathing hard and fast. "You couldn't really have hated the jokers," he said, looking down at her face. "You couldn't, or you would have talked." There was a strange sadness in the way he said it.

"*Shahid.*" The word was a whisper from swollen; blood-caked lips. Mackie leaned close to hear it.

"Arabic," he told them. "I don't understand Arabic." His hands were buzzing now, screaming. He ran his fingers around her breasts like a caress, and blood followed. Misha shrieked hoarsely; Downs gagged and threw up. Chrysalis remained stoic until Mackie slid his hand down Misha's stomach and let the coils of intestines spill wetly out over the carpet.

When he was done, he stood up and brushed away the gore covering the front of him. "The senator said you'd know how to take care of the mess," he told them. "He said you knew everything and everybody." Mackie chuckled, high and manic. He began to whistle: Brecht, the *Threepenny Opera*.

With a casual wave he strolled through the wall and away.

Thursday, 7:35 P.M.

Sara stood on the corner of South across from the Jokertown Clinic. A cool front had moved in from Canada; low, scudding clouds spat wet circles on the pavement.

Sara glanced again at her watch. Misha was over an hour late. "*I'll be there. I promise you, Sara. If I'm not there, know it's because he stopped me.*"

Sara cursed under her breath, wishing she knew what to think, what to feel.

"*You'll have to decide what to do then.*"

"Can I help you, Ms. Morgenstern?" Tachyon's deep voice made her start. The scarlet-haired alien peered down at her with a look of intense concern on his face that she might have found comical at another time; during the recent junket, he'd more than once indicated he found her attractive. She laughed, hating the hysteria she heard in the sound.

"No. No, Doctor, I'm all right. I was . . . I was waiting for someone. We were supposed to meet here. . . ."

Tachyon nodded solemnly, his startling eyes refusing to let her go. "You seemed nervous. I watched you from the clinic. I thought perhaps there was something I could do. Are you sure there's nothing I can help you with?"

"No." Her denial was too sharp, too loud. Sara was forced to smile to soften the effect. "Really. Thank you for asking. I was just about to leave, anyway. It doesn't look like she's going to show."

He nodded. He stared. At last he shrugged. "Aah," he said. "Well, it was good seeing you again. We don't need to be strangers now that the trip is over, Sara. Perhaps dinner one night?"

"Thank you, but . . ." Sara bit her lower lip in agitation, just wanting Tachyon to leave. She needed to think, needed to get away from here. "Maybe next time I'm in the city?"

"I'll hold you to that." Tachyon inclined his head like a Victorian lord, staring at her strangely, then turned. Sara watched Tachyon make his way across the street to the clinic. The sky was beginning to let down a steady drizzle. Street-lights were flickering in the early dusk. Sara looked again up and down the street. A joker with oddly twisted legs and a carapace scuttled from the sidewalk to the cover of a porch. Rain began to pool in the trash-clogged glutters.

We're sisters in this.

Sara stepped from the curb and hailed a cab parked down the street. The nat driver stared at her through the rear-view mirror. His gaze was rude and direct; Sara turned her face away. "Where you going?" he asked with a distinct Slavic accent.

"Head uptown," she said. "Just get me out of here."

What he did to me, he would also do to you. Don't you notice how your feelings for him change when he's with you, and doesn't that also make you wonder?

Aah, Andrea. I'm sorry, I'm so sorry.

Sara sat back and watched the rain smear the towers of Manhattan through the windows.

Blood Ties

III

A grid map of Manhattan from Eighty-seventh down to Fifty-seventh Street glowed on the computer. Tachyon punched in a marker. Brought up another thirty-block section. Studied the two red dots. Wished he had a really big screen that could give him a full view of all of Manhattan. Decided that despite the growing crises at the clinic he would have to spend several hours aboard *Baby*. Her wetware and hardware were far superior to anything on Earth, and she could give him a full-screen view of this mysterious and elusive wild card source.

Victoria Queen, the clinic's chief of surgery, entered without knocking.

"Tachyon, you can't go on like this. Spending time with the joker patrols, working with patients, doing research, and racing around with your grandson trying to be superdad."

He dug his thumbs into his gritty eyes, then rapped his knuckles against the CRT screen. "The answer is here somewhere. I just have to find it. Eighteen new cases of wild card in a four-day period. It's not rational, it shouldn't be happening. I had hoped it was something simple. A hitherto undisturbed cache of spores. But the dispersal of the cases makes that impossible. I put in a call to the National Weather Service, and they're up sending weather tapes covering the past two weeks. Perhaps that will be the key. Some climactic and seismic anomoly that has caused this outbreak."

"Pointless and hopeless, and a waste of your already limited time."

"GODDAMN IT!" He used the desk to lever himself out of his chair. "I've got the goddamn press breathing down my neck, demanding answers, demanding some reassurance for their readers. How long can I continue to make reassuring noises before this becomes a full-scale panic? And just think what Barnett will do with that!"

She gripped his wrists, pinning his hands to the desk. Leaned in until their noses were almost touching. "You *can't* be responsible for every damn thing that happens in the world! For gang wars in Jokertown, and right-wing cranks running for President! Or for wild card either."

"I am bred to be responsible. By blood and bone. By a thousand generations. This is *my* town, *my* people, MY GRANDSON, AND MY CLINIC, AND YES, MY VIRUS!"

"DON'T BE SO FUCKING PROUD OF IT!"

"I'M NOT!" Snatching his hands away, he stormed across the room.

"YOU'RE ARROGANT AND IRRATIONAL!"

"SO WHAT DO YOU SUGGEST? TO WHOM DO I ABDICATE THIS RESPONSIBILITY? WHOM DO I CON- DEMN TO BEAR THE GUILT AND THE HATE! MY PEOPLE, YES, AND AT BASE EVERYONE OF THEM HATES MY GUTS!" Laying his head against the wall, he burst into wild sobs.

The woman's face hardened. Filling a glass with water from the bathroom tap, she yanked him around by a shoulder and flung it full in his face.

"That's enough! Get hold of yourself!" She punctuated each word with a hard shake.

Coughing, he mopped his face, drew a shaky breath. "Thank you, I'm all right now."

"Go home, get some sleep, accept some goddamn help. Get Meadows in here to help with the research, and let Chrysalis run the goddamn patrols."

"And Blaise? What do I do with Blaise?" He scrubbed at his face. "He's the most important thing in my life, and I'm neglecting him."

"The problem with you, Tachyon," she said as she walked out of the office, "is that *everything* is the most important thing in your life."

A routine appendectomy. He shouldn't have taken the time, but Tommy was Old Mr. Cricket's nephew, and you don't ignore old friends. Tach stripped out of the bilious green scrubs, brushed out his cropped hair, and made a face. He then took a turn through each of the clinic's four floors.

The hospital had been dimmed for the evening. From various rooms he heard muted televisions, the low hum of conversation, and from one a sad, hopeless sobbing. For a moment he hesitated, then entered. Powerful mandibles and opaque oval eyes stared out framed by stringy gray hair. The emaciated body beneath the hospital gown revealed it to be a woman.

"Madam?" He lifted the chart. Mrs. Willma Banks. Age seventy-one. Cancer of the pancreas.

"Oh, Doctor, I'm so sorry. I didn't mean... I'm fine really. I don't mean to be a bother... that nurse was so sharp—"

"You're not a bother. And what nurse?"

"I don't mean to be a talebearer or unduly troublesome."

It was obvious that she was, but Tachyon listened politely. No matter how tiresome a patient might be, he insisted upon courtesy and service from his staff. If someone had violated this most basic rule, he wanted to know.

"And my children never come to see me. I ask you, what's the good of children if they abandon you when you most need them? I worked every day for thirty years so they could have the advantages. Now my son, Reggie—he's a stockbroker with a big Wall Street firm—he has a house in Connecticut, and a wife who can't stand to look at me. I've only been to their house *once* when *she* was away with my grandchildren."

There was nothing to say. He sat, her hand resting lightly in his, listening. Brought her a glass of cranberry juice from the nurses' station, and had a few rather sharp words with the floor staff. Moved on.

The coffee he'd been drinking all day was jumping in the back of his throat, sour with stomach acid. Well, if he was going to feel bilious he might as well get it over all at once. He pushed open the door to a private room and entered. He could ill afford the space, but no patient deserved to be placed with the horror that lay comatose behind his door. After forty years of viewing wild card victims he had thought he was inured to anything, but the man who lay twisted on the bed made a mockery of that assumption.

Caught partway between human and alligator, Jack's body was warped by the unnatural pressures of the wild interacting with the AIDS virus. The bones of the skull had elongated, producing the snout of an alligator. Unfortunately the lower jaw had not transformed. Small and vulnerable, it hung below the razor-sharp teeth of the upper jaw. Stubble darkened the chin. In the torso area, skin melded to scales. The line between the intersecting areas had split into angry red lines, and serum oozed from the cracks.

Tachyon shuddered and hoped that deep within his coma Jack was beyond pain. For this had to be agony. For years Jack had faithfully, patiently visited C.C. Ryder. Now, ironically, she had been cured and released into a new life while the faithful, patient Jack had taken her place.

"Oh, Jack, what lover grieves for you, or did he die before you entered this living death?" he whispered.

Lifting the chart, Tachyon read again his notes, which indicated that the AIDS virus did not advance when Jack was in his alligator form.

Memories lay like scattered leaves, black and sear. Tachyon walked among them, flushing with guilt for this was an intrusion. Deep within Jack's dying mind lay a spark of light, a fitful glitter. The human soul. Deeper yet the trigger that would throw Robicheaux completely into his alligator form. A touch from Tachyon, and the transformation would be permanent.

He was a physician. Sworn to the task of saving lives. Jack Robicheaux lay under sentence of death. The presence of the wild card twined into the code of his cells currently held the AIDS virus at bay. But it merely delayed the inevitable. Eventually Jack would die.

Unless.

Unless Tachyon changed him forever. What was not human could not die from a human disease.

But was life worth any price?

And did he have the right?

What should I do, Jack? Do I make this choice for you since you can't make it yourself?

Was it any different than unplugging a respirator?

Oh, yes.

Later, as he leaned back against the elevator wall as it whined slowly to the ground floor, he considered again Queen's advice that he bring in help. *But so much of this only I can do. And there's only one of me. And everyone wants a piece.* Shaking his head like a tired pony, he stepped out into the emergency room.

And was nearly run down by a nurse hurrying past with a

vial of the trump. *Thirty-two*, he thought, upping the count, and followed her through the screen. Finn was preparing the injection. Stepping to the gurney, Tachyon began a fast exam. The woman's blouse was open, revealing the rich *café au lait* of her skin. Monitors were taped to her chest; a nurse held a mask over mouth and nose. A noxious slime covered the patient's body, wetting her clothing, pouring from every pore. It was a measure of his physician's detachment that he didn't recognize her until he peeled back an eyelid. The nurse removed the mask to give him room to work, and...

Gagging, he pushed aside the smelling salts. Fought free of the restraining hands.

"Are you all right?"

"Doctor?"

"Drink this."

"Forget me!" Clinging like a drunk to a nurse's arm, he struggled to his feet. Catching Finn's wrist, he forced away the syringe. "WHAT THE HELL ARE YOU DOING?"

"It's... it's our only shot... it's wild card."

"IT CAN'T BE! I KNOW THIS WOMAN! SHE'S AN ACE!" The joker recoiled from the madness in Tachyon's face.

The Takisian resumed his examination. Finn pranced forward and gripped him hard. "You're wasting time! You're costing her the one chance she's got! It's wild card!"

"Impossible! The virus was designed to *resist* mutation. She's a stable ace. She's can't be reinfected."

"*Look* at her!"

Panting, Tach stared from the syringe to Roulette's oozing body and back again. "Give it to me!"

His fingers slipped on the foul-smelling mucous film, and the needle scraped across the vein. Roulette cried out.

"Wipe this away."

But as fast as they wiped, it bled still faster from her pores. Finally Tachyon jammed home the needle.

Ancestors. Let it work. Let this be one time when it works!

But recently it seemed his prayers had only been met with silence.

Roulette was beginning to resemble a thousand-year-old mummy as the moisture leached from her body. Suddenly her lids fluttered open; she stared blankly up into his face.

"Tachyon." A croaking whisper. "I was coming back. To

you." She sucked in air—a sound like a dying accordian. "Are
you still waiting?"

"Yes."

"Liar. I'm dying. You're off the hook."

"Roulette." His skin crawled to touch her, but he forced
himself to lay his cheek against hers. His tears mingled with
mucus.

"You destroyed my life. You and your disease. Finally it's
finishing the job. I'm . . . so . . . glad."

Long minutes later Finn tugged Tach away and drew up
the sheet. Pain shot through the alien as his knees cracked
onto the cold tile floor. Hands balled against his mouth, he
fought back sobs. Partly from grief. Partly from guilt, for he
hadn't been waiting.

Mostly from terror.

"I got really mad today, but I thought about it like you
said, and I didn't control them."

"Good." Tachyon stared into the refrigerator as if seeking
enlightenment from a carton of sour milk and a bowl full of
moldy peaches. "What was that?" The boy stiffened. "Oh,
Blaise, I'm so proud of you." The rigidity went out of the
small body under Tachyon's tight embrace. "And you're speaking English. I noticed that, too. I'm just so tired it takes me a
few beats to catch up."

Blaise reached up and laid his fist against Tachyon's mouth.
Tach kissed it. In a sudden, abrupt topic change the boy
asked. "Uncle Claude wasn't a very good person, was he?"

"No, but one can partially understand his reasons. It's
never easy to be a joker."

"What would you do if you were a joker?"

"Kill myself." Blaise gaped up at the indescribable expression on his *k'ijdad's* narrow face.

"That's silly. Anything is better than dead."

"I can't agree. You'll understand when you're older."

"Everybody tells me that." Pouting, Blaise left the kitchen
and flung himself on the sofa. "Jack, Durg, Mark, *Baby*. I
suppose it must be true if ships and humans and Takisians all
agree. But I didn't mean being a yucky joker like Snotman.
What if you were like Jube, or Chrysalis or Ernie?"

"I still couldn't live with it." Tach joined him on the sofa.
"My culture idealizes the perfect. Defective children are

destroyed at birth, and otherwise normal individuals are sterilized if it's determined that they lack sufficient genetic worth."

"So to be ordinary is as bad as being de...defective," he asked, stumbling over the unfamiliar word.

"Well, not quite, and too random a gene pattern can also endanger a person. I was almost sterilized because of my Sennari blood, but my outstanding mental abilities were deemed to outweigh the unpredictable Sennari, and my other...failings."

"Do you have a little boy on Takis?"

"No."

Tachyon briefly wondered if the sperm he had left banked on Takis still existed, or if Zabb's supporters had seen it destroyed. Or even worse, had Taj impregnated some female? It was ironic that in a culture as technologically advanced as the Takisian, there was a fundamental distrust of artificial insemination, and artificial wombs. The wombs made a certain degree of sense; in a telepathic culture it was best that the child be linked with its mother, but there was little justification for the sex act.

Except for the obvious ones.

Ten months! Ten months without sex.

He jerked his mind from that unpleasant thought and focused again on Blaise. There was so much to teach him about his Takisian culture, and yet should he really bother? The child could never be presented to the family. He was an abomination. Also there was much in Takisian culture that didn't bear close scrutiny. How to indicate to an eleven-year-old child that the blood feuds, the controlled breeding, the tension and almost unbearable expectations that were part and parcel of life among the psi lords, were not romantic or wonderful, but rather deadly in the extreme, and had driven his grandsire to this alien world?

"Tell me a story."

"What makes you think I know any stories?"

"You're more like a fairy tale than real. You have to know stories."

"All right. I'll tell you how H'ambizan tamed the first ship. Long ago—"

"No."

"No?" Blaise's expression suggested that his grandfather

was an idiot. "Ahhh, of course. Once upon a time." He cocked an inquiring eyebrow. Blaise nodded, satisfied, and snuggled in closer under Tachyon's arm. "And so long ago that even the oldest *Kibrzen* would lie if they told you they remembered, the people were forced to journey through the stars aboard ships of steel. What was worse, they weren't allowed to build these ships, for the Alaa—may their line wither—had signed a contract with Master Traders, and the people were forbidden to build space-going vessels. So the wealth of Takis bled into space, and into the pockets of the rapacious Network."

"What's the Network?"

"A vast trading empire with one hundred and thirty member races. One day H'ambizan, who was a notable astronomer, was drifting among the clouds in the birthplace of stars, and he came upon an amazing sight. Playing among the clouds of cosmic dust like porpoises in the waves, or butterflies through flowers, were vast incredible shapes. And H'ambizan fell to the deck, clasping his ringing skull, for his head was filled with a great singing. His assistants died of joy and shock for their minds could not absorb the thoughts of the creatures. But H'ambizan—being of the Ilkazam—was made of sterner stuff. He controlled his fear and pain and lanced out with a single thought. A single command. And so great was his power that the honor of ships fell silent and gathered like nursing whales about the tiny metal ship.

"And H'ambizan choose the leader of the honor, and suited against the vacuum, he stepped upon the rough surface of the ship. And curious, Za'Zam, father of ships, made a cavity to receive the man."

"And then H'ambizan mind-controlled the ship and made him carry him home!" cried Blaise.

"No. H'ambizan sang, and Za'Zam listened, and they both realized that after a thousand thousand years of loneliness they had found the separate halves of their souls. Za'Zam realized that guided by these strange small creatures the 'Ishb'kaukab would leave their nomadic pastoral lives and achieve greatness. And H'ambizan realized he had found a friend."

Tach leaned in and kissed the top of the boy's head. Blaise, chewed thoughtfully on his lower lip, glanced up.

"Why didn't H'ambizan realize that now he could fight the Network? Why did he realize something silly?"

"Because this is a story of longing and regret."

"Is this supposed to be subtle?"

"Yes."

"But did H'ambizan and Za'Zam fight the Network?"

"Yes."

"And did they win?"

"Sort of."

"Is this true?"

"Sort of."

"Isn't that like being a little bit pregnant?"

"What would you know about that?" Blaise lifted his nose and looked superior. "Someday when I'm not so tired, I'll tell you about the genetic manipulation and eon-long breeding program that took place before we had ships like *Baby*."

"So there weren't wild ships?"

"Oh, yes, there were, but they weren't as bright as this tale indicates."

"But—"

Tach laid a finger on the child's lips. "Later. Your stomach's been growling so loud I was afraid it would jump out and take a bite out of my arm."

"A new wild card power! Killer stomachs!"

Tach threw back his head and laughed. "Come, little *kukut*, I'll buy you dinner."

"At McDonald's."

"Oh, joy."

The tutor hasn't quit.

The thought was so breathtaking that it brought him up short.

"The tutor hasn't quit!" Tachyon repeated with dawning wonder.

He ran to the office door, flung it open. Dita slewed around to stare nervously at him.

"The tutor hasn't quit!" he shouted. "Dita, you're wonderful!" Blood washed into her cheeks as he kissed her and pulled her around the office in a lurching polka. He dropped her back into her chair and collapsed on the sofa, panting and fanning himself. The weeks of unremitting work and strain were taking their toll. "I must see this paragon for myself. I'll be back in one hour."

*   *   *

He could hear Blaise's voice piping like a young bird, or a silver flute, and the deeper rumbling tones of the man's voice. A cello or a bassoon. There was warmth in that voice, and comfort, and something tantalizingly familiar. Tachyon stepped out of the tiny foyer and into the living room. Blaise was seated at the dining room table, a stack of books before him. A heavyset older man with graying hair and a faintly melancholy expression kept the boy's place with a blunt forefinger. His accent was musical, rather like Tachyon's.

"Oh, Ideal . . . no!"

Victor Demyenov raised his dark eyes to meet Tachyon's lilac ones. His expression was both ironical and slightly malicious.

"*K'ijdad,* this is George Goncherenko." His grandsire's alarming rigidity seemed to penetrate, and the boy faltered and added, "Is something wrong?"

"No, child," said George/Victor. "He is merely surprised to see us getting along so well. You have terrified so many of my predecessors."

"But not you," said Blaise. Then he added to Tachyon, "He's not scared of anything."

You had better be afraid of me! Tachyon shot at the KGB agent telepathically.

No, we hold one another in the palms of our hands.

"Blaise, go to your room. This gentleman and I need to talk."

"No."

"DO AS YOU'RE TOLD!"

"Go, child." George/Victor coaxed him with a gentle hand. "It will all be all right." Blaise gripped the older man in a fierce hug, then ran from the room.

Tachyon flung himself across the room and poured a brandy with hands that shook with fear and shock.

"You! I thought you were out of my life! You told me you were retiring. It was finished. You lied—"

"Lied! Let's talk about lying! You withheld something I needed. Something which cost me everything!"

"I . . . I don't know what you're talking about."

"Oh, come now, Dancer, I trained you better than that. You deliberately withheld the information about Blaise. You have enough tradecraft to have known the value of that little piece of information."

Hamburg, 1956. A shabby but clean boarding house, and Victor doling out booze and women in limited doses while he trained and questioned the shattered Takisian. A few years, and they had kicked him loose to continue his descent into the gutter. He had given them all that he had, and it hadn't been enough. The secret had gnawed at him for years, but thirty years was a long time, and he had begun to think himself safe. And then had come the phone call during the final leg of the World Health Organization tour, and his KGB control was back in his life.

"My superiors learned of Blaise, his potential and power, but *I* who trained you and ran you was left ignorant. They did not assume it was stupidity, but rather duplicity. They drew the only conclusion." His raised eyebrows drew the answer from his former pupil:

"They assumed you had rolled over, become a double agent."

Victor grimaced a bit at the theatrical phrase. The brandy exploded in the back of his throat as Tachyon tossed it down. Some explanation, some justification seemed necessary.

"I wanted him safe from you."

"I would say I am the least of his problems."

"What do you mean? What do you mean by that?"

"Nothing. Never mind."

"Is that a comment on me?"

"Good god, no. I merely point out that we live in dangerous times."

"Victor, are they looking for you?" Tachyon asked, not certain if he referred to the Russian's KGB masters or to the CIA.

"No, they all think I'm dead. All that remains is a charred car and a pair of corpses burned past recognition."

"You killed them."

"Don't look so shocked, Dancer. You too are a killer. In fact we have more in common then you might think. Like that child."

"I want you out of my life!"

"I'm in your life for good. You better get used to it."

"I'll fire you!"

Demyenov's voice froze him before he had taken three steps. "Ask Blaise."

Tachyon remembered the hug. Never in the weeks since

he had smuggled Blaise out of France had the child given him so affectionate a gesture. The boy obviously loved the grizzled Russian. What would it do to Tach and the boy's relationship if he now abruptly removed this man? He sank onto the sofa and dropped his head into his hands.

"Oh, Victor, why?" He didn't really expect an answer, and he didn't get one.

"Oh, yes, since we're going to be friends you should know my true name. Friends don't lie to each other. My name is Georgi Vladamirovich Polyakov. But you can call me George. Victor is dead—you killed him."

Addicted to Love

by Pat Cadigan

The view of the city from Aces High was breathtaking, even inspirational. Beached on the shores of the afternoon, Jane stared blindly down at it from the kitchen window, frustration and unhappiness doing their usual waltz in her stomach. Behind her the kitchen staff worked away at winding down the afternoon luncheon service before preparing for the dinner custom, politely ignoring the fact that she'd left the salad they'd made for her untouched. Her appetite was poor these days. Lately she had even abandoned the pretense of wrapping the food up for later and tossing it out on the sly.

She knew there were whispers that she'd gone anorexic, not exactly the best advertisement for a place such as Aces High. It was like a bad joke on Hiram, after he'd increased her responsibilities at the restaurant from hostessing to pinch-hit supervising. Hiram was pretty weird himself these days, but he wasn't shedding any weight. He'd been on a round-the-world goodwill tour. Hiram Worchester, Goodwill Ambassador. It beat the hell out of Jane Dow, Mafia Dupe.

Memories of the time with Rosemary drove her deeper into depression. She missed her; rather, she missed the person she'd thought Rosemary had been and the work she'd thought she'd been doing for her. It had all sounded so fine and noble—trying to counteract the antiace, antijoker hysteria that had been building up, fueled by hysterical extremist politicians and evangelists. Rosemary had been a real hero to her, someone with a shining light around her; she'd needed a hero very badly after all the nastiness with the Masons and the terrible, grotesque murder of Kid Dinosaur. Her own brush with death had not left much of an impression on her, except for the contact with that horrible, evil little creature called the Astronomer. She had seldom thought of it after-

ward, and Rosemary had been the antidote to the Astronomer's poison.

Until March, when she began to find herself thinking that
it might have been better if Hiram had just let her plummet
to the street.

She seemed to have an unerring instinct for getting mixed
up with exactly the wrong people. Maybe that was her real
ace power, not the water-calling ability. She could hire
herself out as a bad-guys detector, she thought sourly, change
her name from Water Lily to Dowsing Rod. *Yes, I just love
these people, I'd follow them anywhere, do anything for
them—call the cops, they must be white slavers and kiddie
pornographers.*

Her mind gave her an image of Rosemary Muldoon,
smiling at her, praising her for her hard work, and she felt a
pang of disloyalty and guilt. There was no way she could
think of Rosemary as a truly bad person. A big part of her still
wanted to believe that Rosemary had been sincere about the
work, that whatever else she had been involved with as the
head of a Mafia family, Rosemary really had wanted to do
something for the victims of the wild card virus.

Yes, she thought fiercely, there was plenty of good in
Rosemary, she wasn't like all the others. Maybe something
awful had happened to her that had driven her to accept and
embrace the Mafia. She could understand that; God, could
she understand it.

Her mind shoved aside the memory and came to rest on
the man named Croyd. She still had the phone numbers he'd
given her. *Anytime you want some company, someone to talk
to . . . I bet I could listen to you for hours. Maybe even all
night, but that would be up to you, Bright Eyes.* No one had
ever showed quite so much panache flirting with her.
Mirrorshades Croyd, calling *her* Bright Eyes; she was un-
aware of smiling at the memory. There had been no link
exposed between him and Rosemary's organization, Either it
was buried too deeply or he'd been another idealist like
herself. Since she wanted to believe it was the latter, that
most likely meant it was the former—and she was still
tempted to take out those phone numbers and surprise him
by calling him. There was no way she could ever really bring
herself to do it, which could well have been why he'd given
her the numbers in the first place.

Her whole life was upside down and backward. Maybe that was what the wild card virus had really done to her, fixed it so she would live as the butt of every practical joke the world could play on her.

Abruptly Sal's voice seemed to be speaking to her in her head: *You're not being fair with yourself. You never believed the Masons were good, you weren't blind to what the Astronomer really was. And as for Rosemary, she was just a whole lot smarter than you, street smart—she took advantage of you and that should be her shame, not yours. If she even has the capacity to feel shame.*

Yeah, Salvatore Carbone would have said something very like that to her if he'd been alive. The fact that she could come up with it herself must have meant she wasn't completely hopeless, she thought. But the idea didn't improve her mood or bring her appetite back.

"Excuse me, Jane," said a voice behind her. It was Emile, who had started at Aces High not long before she had and was now the new maître d'. She wiped at her wet face hastily, glad that she had managed to gain more control over her tendency to pull enormous amounts of water out of the air when under stress, and turned around, trying to smile at him politely. "I think you'd better come down to the loading dock."

She blinked at him in confusion. "Pardon?"

"A situation has developed and we think you're the only one who could handle it."

"Mr. Worchester always—"

"Hiram isn't here and frankly we doubt he'd be much use if he were."

She stared up at Emile tensely. Emile was one of the most vocal (and unforgiving) critics of Hiram's behavior, a group that seemed to gain more members every day, all of them disgruntled employees and all of them, to her complete dismay, more in the right than she wanted to admit.

Ever since his return from the tour Hiram had been ...strange. He seemed to have little real interest and no enthusiasm for Aces High these days, acting as if the restaurant were some awful albatross around his neck, a burdensome annoyance that was keeping him from something of greater importance. And he was behaving abominably toward his staff; his almost courtly manners had disappeared, and he

ranged from distracted to abusively rude. Except for herself.
Hiram was still friendly toward her, though it seemed to be
an enormous and obvious effort to control himself and focus
his attention. He had always been attracted to her; she'd
known that since the night he had saved her life; and she felt
guilty for not feeling the same way toward him. Being obligated
to someone who cared for her when she couldn't return the
affection was one of the most uncomfortable situations she
could imagine. She had repaid him for the expensive clothes,
and she had made every effort to be the best employee he
could have asked for in exchange for the security of the job
(and the generous salary) he'd given her. Lately that meant
taking up for him, even against people who had known him
far longer than she had and supposedly had many more
reasons to be devoted to him. Some of these were the most
virulent, maybe because they had so many more better days
to remember at Aces High. If only she could get through to
Hiram, she thought, looking into Emile's cold green eyes. If
only she could make him understand how badly he was
eroding his own authority and credibility and respect, he
would be able to halt this terrible decline, turn it around, and
become Hiram Worchester, Grand Master Restauranteur,
again. Right now, it was as if he were dying.

"What kind of situation?" she asked carefully.

Emile shook his head in a small, tight way that was more
shudder than anything. "It's easier if you just come," he said.
"What we need right now is quick, decisive action from
someone who has the authority to take it. Please. Just come
down with me."

Taking a deep breath, she forced composure on herself
and went with Emile to the elevator.

The scene on the loading dock was like something out of a
Marx Brothers movie, only not quite so funny—like something out of a *remake* of a Marx Brothers movie, she thought,
watching the dock crew work furiously at reloading a truck
while two employees of the Brightwater Fish Market kept
unloading it (or perhaps *re*-unloading it, while a third Brightwater employee stood on a box nose to nose with Tomoyuki
Shigeta, the new sushi chef. Brightwater's man was a short,
stocky nat who appeared to have high blood pressure; Tomoyuki
was a slender seven-foot ace who, during the period of the
new moon, lived as a dolphin between the hours of eleven

P.M. and three A.M. Together they looked like a comedy team rehearsing an act, although Brightwater's man was doing all the yelling, with Tomoyuki occasionally putting in a couple of soft words that seemed to provoke the other man to higher volume.

"What's going on here?" Jane asked in her most business-like voice. No one heard her. She sighed, glanced at Emile, and then hollered, "Everybody, *shut up!*"

This time her voice cut through the air, and everyone *did* shut up, turning toward her almost as one.

"What's going on?" she asked again, looking up at Tomoyuki. He made a slight bow.

"Brightwater has delivered a shipment of bad fish. The entire load has gone over, and it went over quite some time ago." Tomoyuki's cultured, Boston Brahmin tones held no hostility or impatience. Jane thought he was the most profes-sional person she had ever met, and she wished she were more like him. "Some time before it was loaded onto this truck for delivery here. Unless Hiram has another source, we will be unable to offer the twilight sushi bar this evening."

Jane tried to sniff the air without being obvious about it. All she could smell was overwhelming *fish*, as though the greater part of the ocean had been caught and dumped in the immediate vicinity. She could not tell whether the odor was good or bad, only that it was offensively strong, and if the load stayed on the dock much longer, it *would* go bad if it weren't already.

"Look, lady, this is fish and fish stinks," said Brightwater's man, rubbing his upper lip directly under his nose, as though to emphasize the point. "Now, I been deliverin' loads of stinkin' fish to Hiram Worchester and a good many other people for a long, long time, and the stuff always smells like this. I don't like the way it smells, either, but that's just how it is." He glanced up at Tomoyuki in disgust. "Fish is *supposed* to smell bad. Nobody's gonna tell me different. And *nobody's* gonna tell me to take my load back unless it's Hiram Worchester himself."

Jane nodded very slightly. "Are you aware that Mr. Worchester has empowered me to act as his agent for all business transactions having to do with the Aces High menu?"

Brightwater's man—*Aaron* was the name on his shirt pocket—tilted his wide head and looked at her through half-closed eyes. "Just say it, okay? Don't try and jack me around with double-talk, just look me in the eye and spit it out."

"What I meant," Jane said, slightly embarrassed, "is that any decision I make is a Hiram Worchester decision. He will back it one hundred percent."

Aaron's gaze traveled from Jane to Emile to one of the dock crew and came to rest on Tomoyuki, who stared down at him impassively. "Oh, for chrissakes, what am I lookin at *you* for? *You'll* back her up a hundred percent."

Tomoyuki turned to Jane, raising his eyebrows in a silent question.

"Is the fish bad, Tom," she said quietly.

"Yes. Definitely."

"Is that what you would tell Mr. Worchester?"

"In a minute."

She nodded. "Then it goes back to Brightwater. *No arguments,*" she added as Aaron opened his mouth to protest. "If it isn't off this loading dock in fifteen minutes, I'll call the police."

Aaron's broad face twisted into an expression of hostile disbelief. "You'll call the cops? On what charge?"

This time Jane's sniff was as audible as she could make it. "Littering. Illegal dumping. Air pollution. Any of those would stick. Good day to you." She turned sharply and fled back into the building with her hand over her mouth and nose. The smell had suddenly become too nauseating to bear.

"Well done, Jane," Tom said as he and Emile caught up with her at the elevator. "Hiram himself couldn't have carried it off much better."

"Hiram couldn't carry it off, period," Emile muttered darkly.

"*Don't,* Emile" she said, and felt him staring at her in surprise.

"Don't what?"

The elevator doors slid open and they all got in.

"Don't badmouth Hiram. Mr. Worchester, I mean." She pushed the button for Aces High. "It's bad for morale."

"*Hiram's* bad for morale, in case you hadn't noticed. If he'd been on top of things, Brightwater wouldn't have even *thought* of trying to pass their rotted stuff off on us. It just

shows the word must be out on him, everyone must know
he's no good anymore—"

"*Please*, Emile." She put a hand on his slender arm,
looking into his face imploringly. "We all know something's
wrong, but every time you or one of the other employees says
something like that, it diminishes the chances of his being
able to put it right again. He can't recover from whatever is
wearing on him if we're all against him."

Emile actually looked mildly ashamed of himself. "God
knows if anyone wishes him well, I do, Jane. But the way he
is these days, he reminds me of a—well, a junkie," He
shuddered. "I *detest* junkies. And *all* addicts."

"What you say is very true, Jane," said Tom, from the
opposite corner of the elevator where he was standing with
his arms folded against his sleek body, "but none of it gets
us a twilight sushi bar for this evening, and Hiram never
saw fit to let me in on his backup plan for this kind of
eventuality. So unless you know what to do, or can find
Hiram and get him to tell you, Aces High is actually going
to renege on an offering. Which may well be its ruination.
A little bird told me Mr. Dining Out has reservations here
tonight, specifically to review the sushi bar for *New York
Gourmet*. I don't have to tell you what it would mean for
Aces High to get a bad review."

Jane rubbed her forehead tiredly. This must be what they
call black comedy, she thought. When everything just gets
worse and worse and you think you might start laughing and
never stop till they take you away.

Casually Tom moved to the other side of the elevator to
stand near Emile. Just as casually she turned away so they
could touch without her seeing. No one was supposed to
know they were lovers, but she wasn't sure why they were so
fanatical about keeping it secret. Something to do with AIDS
perhaps, she thought. The perception of all gays as AIDS
carriers had brought renewed persecution to homosexuals.
She could almost be glad that Sal hadn't lived to see that.

"I can find Hiram," she said after a bit. "I'm pretty sure I
know where he is. Emile, you keep order until I get back."
She handed Emile the spare key to Hiram's office. "You won't
need this, but just in case of something. When I come back,
we'll have a sushi bar. The selection might be a little more

limited than we'd like, but we can carry it off if we do it with enough . . . um . . . panache. Can we, Tom?"

"I *am* panache," Tomoyuki said, his face completely impassive while Emile suppressed a smile. The sight of the two of them made her feel suddenly and unbearably alone.

"Good," she said miserably. "I'll just get my purse and be on my way." The elevator stopped to let them off at the Aces High dining room. "With any luck you'll hear from me in about an hour."

"And without any luck?" said Emile, pressing, but, she could tell, not unkindly.

"Without any luck," she said thoughtfully, "do you think you could get sick, Tom?"

"I could have done that to begin with," he said, a little curtly.

"Yes, but then we would not have tried. Would we." She tried to look up at him as if they were eye to eye. "We'll continue to try until there's nothing to try for. Do you understand?"

Both men nodded.

"And one more thing," she said as they started to turn away. "From now on, refer to him as Mr. Worchester." Emile frowned slightly. "To everyone, even to me. It will help morale. Even ours."

Emile bit his lip tensely and then, to her relief, nodded. "Understood, Jane. Or should that be Ms. Dow?"

She let her gaze drop for a moment. "I'm not power mad, Emile. If you really understand, you know that. I'm trying to save him. Mr. Worchester. I owe him that." She looked up at him again. "We all do, in our own particular ways."

Tom was staring at her, and for the first time she saw a fondness in his smooth, cold face. Feeling awkward, she excused herself to retrieve her purse from Hiram's office and call a cab. There was a sense of victory within her as she rode down in the elevator again. The temperamental Tomoyuki *liked* her, no small achievement, and she had managed to get Emile on her side, at least for a while. He must like her, too, she thought, almost giddy. Perhaps it was a terrible weakness to want to be *liked* so much, but she certainly was getting a lot accomplished because of it. Or she would if she could just get Hiram to come through on the promises she'd made, or implied.

The cab was waiting in front of the entrance for her; she climbed in and gave the driver an address in Jokertown, ignoring the double-take he gave her. *I know, I don't look like much beyond a bite for the Big Bad Wolf,* she thought at him acidly as she settled back in the seat. *Wouldn't you be surprised to know that I've killed people—and that I could return you to the dust, too, if you gave me any trouble.*

She suppressed the thought, feeling ashamed. She'd lied when she'd said she wasn't power mad. Of course she was—it was hard not to be when you had an ace ability. It was the dark side of her talent, and she had to struggle against that all the time, or she might become like that awful Astronomer, or poor Fortunato. She wondered briefly where he was now and if he remembered the way she did.

They stopped at a red light and a ragged joker with enormous donkey ears threw himself halfway onto the hood to wash the windshield. Blocking out the sound of the cab driver's yelling at him, she tried to compose herself for the inevitable confrontation with Hiram. She wasn't supposed to have this address, and she wasn't supposed to know whose address it was. Hiram might just fire her and throw her out without letting her get a word in edgewise, while Ezili stood behind him laughing.

Jane dreaded facing Ezili—Ezili Rouge everyone called her. The scuttlebutt around Aces High was that she had been some kind of superprostitute in Haiti whom Hiram had "rescued" from the crushing poverty of the slums—i.e., she was virtually an ace in the sex department and any man (or woman) who had ever had the experience was spoiled for anyone else. And Hiram had supposedly had the experience. There were other rumors—she was the ex-toy of a super-drug kingpin, in hiding; she was a drug kingpin herself; she had blackmailed Hiram or somebody into bringing her to the States; and any number of other things.

Whatever the truth might have been, Jane didn't like her and the feeling was mutual. The one time Ezili had come to Aces High, it had been hate at first sight for both of them. She'd been completely taken aback by the overbearing *heat* that seemed to pour out of her, and she was completely intimidated by her strange eyes—what should have been whites were blood red instead. Ezili haughtily addressed her as *Ms. Dow,* mispronouncing it to rhyme with *cow* instead of *low*, with a sneering intonation that produced an instant rise in her. What made it worse was the fact that Hiram really did seem to be under her influence. Whenever he had looked at her or even mentioned her, Jane could read a bizarre mixture of desire, subservience, and helplessness in his face, although occasionally an expression of pure loathing surfaced, making Jane suspect that at heart Hiram really didn't like Ezili any more than she did.

"Hey, gorgeous!"

She looked up, startled, to see the joker pressing his face against the back window.

"Get on outta that cab, baby, and I'll take you to heaven! I got more than just the *ears* of a donkey!"

The light changed and the cab lurched forward, knocking the joker away. In spite of herself Jane found herself almost wanting to laugh. There was no comparison between the joker's crudeness and the genteel come-ons she politely turned away at Aces High, but for some reason something about it had touched her. Maybe just because it was so funny, or because the joker was a victim refusing to kneel to his affliction, or because he hadn't actually come out and said what else it was he had. Someone earthier than she *would* have laughed out loud. *I'm just a hothouse flower,* she thought, a bit ruefully. *A hothouse killer-flower.*

The cab turned a corner sharply and went down two blocks before pulling over in the middle of the third. "This's it," the driver said sullenly. "You mind hurrying?"

She looked at the meter and pushed several bills through the slot in front of her. "Keep the change." The door was stuck, but the driver showed no inclination to get out and help her. Disgusted, she kicked it open on the second try and got out. "Just for that, I won't bother telling you to have a nice day," she muttered as the cab roared away from the curb, and then she turned to look at the building in front of her.

It had been renovated at least twice, but nothing had helped; it was just plain ugly and shabby though obviously solid. It wasn't going to fall down unless the Great Ape kicked it down, except, she remembered, the Great Ape didn't exist anymore. Five stories, and the place she wanted was on the top floor. She'd grown up in an apartment on the top floor of a seven-story tenement building, the kind with no elevators, and she'd sprinted up and down all seven flights without stopping several times every day of her young life. Five floors wouldn't give her any problem, she thought.

Her sprinting gave out in the middle of the second flight, but she did manage to keep going without pause, albeit more slowly, catching her breath on each landing. The darkness was relieved by the frosted skylight directly over the squared-off spiral of the stairs, but the light was anemic and depressing.

There was only one apartment on the top floor. Hiram might as well have had his name on it, she thought as she paused at the head of the stairs, panting a little. Instead of the drab, grayish door that all the other apartments had, there was a custom hardwood job with an ornate brass knocker and an old-fashioned handle instead of a doorknob. The lock above it was completely modern and secure but made to look just as refined. *Hiram, Hiram,* she thought sadly, *does it pay to advertise in a place like this?*

What would he say when he opened the door and saw her? What would he think? It didn't matter. She had to make him see what was happening because then it would save him—save his *life*. It would be a bit different from the way he had saved hers, but Aces High was his life, and if she could save that for him, then she would have repaid him for her own life. The balance between them would be restored after all, whereas before she hadn't thought there'd be any way to do that.

No way but one, and she couldn't. The feeling wasn't there. She knew Hiram would have welcomed her regardless, that he would be considerate and tender and funny and loving and everything a woman could want in a lover. But ultimately it would be horribly unjust to him, and when it came to its inevitable end, it would be painful and scarring to both of them. Hiram deserved better. Such a good man deserved someone whose devotion would match his, someone who would enter fully into every part of his life and give him all the pleasures of attachment. He needed someone who could not live without him.

Instead of someone who would have died without him? her mind whispered nastily, and she felt another hard pang of guilt. *All right, all right, I'm a bitch and an ingrate,* she scolded herself silently. *Maybe it's some fatal flaw in me that*

I don't love him, as good as he is. Maybe if gratitude could make me fall in love with him, I'd be a better person.

And maybe he wouldn't be holed up in a Jokertown apartment with poison like Ezili Rouge, either.

God, Jane thought. She had to talk to Hiram. She couldn't believe he would really want to keep company with such a creature. She had to help him get away from her, find some way to bar her from Aces High. Whatever she had to do to help him, anything, anything at all, she would do it especially if saving Hiram meant she never had to see that woman again.

She forced herself to walk along the landing to the apartment and gave the brass knocker three sharp taps. To her dismay, it was Ezili who answered.

Ezili was dressed, if that was the word for it, in a whisper of transparent gold material over nothing. Jane looked steadily into Ezili's face, refusing to let her gaze fall below the woman's chin, and said in her driest, most controlled voice, "I've come for Hiram. I know that he's here, and it's imperative that I see him."

A slow hot smile spread across Ezili's face as if Jane had said the one thing in the world she could possibly have wanted to hear. Swaying a little, as though dancing to some inner music she moved back and gestured gracefully for Jane to enter.

The apartment was a surprise. The living room had been carefully decorated in a completely Haitian motif that also reflected Hiram's high tastes. Jane found herself unable to look at anything except the deep brown carpet, exactly like the one in Hiram's office. The place was so *Hiram,* but Hiram changed, Hiram the stranger who had come back from the tour. With Ezili, who was moving leisurely around her like some sort of predatory creature whose favorite dinner had walked obligingly into its claws.

"Hiram's in the bedroom," she said. "I guess if it's *imperative* that you see him, then you can see him there." Standing in front of Jane, she lifted her arms to run her hands along the back of her own neck, practically thrusting her large breasts into Jane's face. Jane maintained her steady, even gaze, refusing to look. Something shiny flashed on Ezili's right hand as she brought it around.

Blood. Jane's severe composure almost broke. *Blood?* What in God's name could Hiram have gotten himself into?

Ezili's reddened hand undulated through the air in a pointing gesture. "That way. Just walk in and you'll see him. In bed."

Jane marched past her to the shadowy doorway and stepped into the bedroom. She cleared her throat, started to speak, and then froze.

He was not in bed but kneeling on the floor next to it in an attitude of prayer. But he was definitely not praying.

At first she thought she had surprised him in the act of giving a piggyback ride to a small child, and it flashed through her mind that it was his child by Ezili, the pregnancy, birth, and growth drastically foreshortened by the wild card infection, which had also made the child a hideously deformed joker.

She took a step toward him, her eyes filling with tears of pity. "Oh, Hiram, I . . ."

The look on Hiram's face went from rage to agonized sorrow, and she saw what it really was on his back.

"H-H-Hiram . . ."

Her voice died away as a bizarrely alien expression of curiosity spread over Hiram's face. It was not the expression of a father interrupted while tending to his child, and no child would have been fastened to a father's neck by the mouth. The wizened creature on Hiram's back quivered in a way that reminded her of Ezili's movements. Even as she turned to bolt for the door, she knew it was too late.

She thought she must have weighed at least three hundred pounds when she hit the floor.

Later on, when she thought of it, when she could bring herself to think of it, she knew that it could have been at most half a minute before Hiram moved from the bed to where she was anchored to the floor on her stomach. It was completely silent in the apartment for what seemed to Jane like an excruciating stretch of time before Hiram finally rose and came to stand over her where she lay with water pouring off her, soaking her clothes and the carpet.

She tried to say something to him, but all the breath had been knocked out of her by the fall. In a minute, when she could talk, she would tell him he hadn't had to do that, that no matter what kind of trouble he was in, she wouldn't give him away to anyone, and she would try to help him in any way she could—

There was a quiet rustle as Hiram lay down on the carpet next to her, facing her with that same peculiar expression of curiosity. *He doesn't recognize me,* she thought with horrified amazement. The creature was still on his back, and she squeezed her eyes shut against the sight.

"In a few moments you won't find me so hard to look at," Hiram said. His voice sounded strange, as if someone were doing a creditable imitation of him.

"Hi-Hiram," she managed in a whisper. "I—I w-wouldn't—h-hurt—"

Small fingers touched her back, and she realized what was happening. She opened her eyes,

"No, Hiram," she begged, her voice getting stronger, "don't let it—don't let it—"

Hiram's curious look had vanished. In its place was an expression so griefstricken, she automatically tried to reach out to him, but the weight barely let her move her hand. He looked into her eyes and she had the impression he was struggling with something.

The thing was fully on her back now, nestling in; she could feel something moving along her neck.

Suddenly the weight was gone. Tears glittered in Hiram's eyes, and she thought she heard him whisper, *Run.*

And then something stabbed her neck.

She must have blacked out at the first contact; she felt as though she were swimming through the air, or being carried to and fro by air currents. *The weight's gone,* she thought, *Hiram's made me weightless and I'm floating through the room.* Then her vision cleared and she saw she was still lying on the floor. Hiram was reaching for her, intending to gather her to him in an embrace.

"Stop." It was her voice, but she had no control over it. Something else was speaking through her. The panic that rose in her at the realization transmuted into a mild pleasure that began to grow more intense.

Hiram hesitated for a moment and then continued to pull her close.

"*I said, stop!*" The command in her voice stopped Hiram

cold. From the last tiny part of her that was still herself, Jane watched as her hand lifted and paused; a small waterfall congealed out of the air and splashed down on the carpet. A wave of pleasure swept through her, overruling that little bit of her that was horrified. It was as though she had been split into two people, one very large one full of irresistible pleasure and energetic appetites, and one very, very small Jane Dow confined in a cage and buried too deeply to surface and regain control, but able to observe—and feel—everything the large one did. The large one, she realized, was the creature on her back.

She got to her feet and stretched, feeling her muscles. Hiram sat up and watched her with hurt, suspicious eyes.

"You promised," he said sulkily, as though he were a little boy deprived of a treat.

"I promised you pleasure beyond anything in your artificial, white world," the creature said with her voice. "You have that. Please do not disturb me when I am getting the feel of a new mount." The little tiny Jane gave a surge of outrage but was quickly subdued. Somewhere in her mind she felt the presence of humiliation and panic, but it was so far away, it might as well have been happening to someone else. The pure pleasure coursing through her body in ever-strengthening waves, *that* was the only thing really happening to her.

"Why not?" Hiram said, sounding almost whiny. "Haven't I been good to you? Don't I give you everything and everyone you ask for? I even gave you *her*. I wanted her all to myself, but I didn't hold out on you."

The creature used Jane's laugh. There was another surge of outrage that turned to pleasure even more quickly than before. "You're in love with this little white flower?"

Hiram dropped his gaze for a moment and muttered something she couldn't hear. It might have been *yes*. There was a part of her that was important to, but the rising pleasure displaced everything. Nothing could be important next to that.

"Ah, but you love me more. Don't you."

Hiram raised his head. "Yes," he said tonelessly.

Jane felt the creature move her hand to touch Hiram's head with the benevolence of superiority, noblesse oblige, and every movement sent new waves of pleasure through her.

She had not thought it possible that just simple movement could suffuse her with pure ecstasy. That was the only word for it: ecstasy. "And I love you, too, of course." The creature was feeling around in her mind for all her thoughts of Hiram. She had a faint, distant sense of wanting to shut him off, evict him, how dare he—but the pleasure. No. He could take what he wanted, take anything he wanted, take it all if it meant that she could go on feeling like this. "How could I not love such tastes and appetites, such a capacity to enjoy life?" The creature probed more deeply, and Jane thought she must be ringing like a bell, vibrating with heaven. "I'm quite—*attached* to you. I couldn't live without you."

She knelt down beside him and touched his face. Hiram looked as though he were about to cry. "Is it hard for you to hear those words from this mouth?" The creature poured its knowledge into her mind and she wanted to be sorrowful, but it seemed that even the chemical reactions in her brain cells detonated more pleasure within her. How could someone feel so much of this without dying, she wondered. Perhaps she was dying. If so, that was fine, she would die, too, if it felt this good. *Whatever,* she promised the creature, begging it to like her, love her. *Whatever. Always.* She was telling it something it already knew, and such a superior form of life could hardly be bothered with her supplications, but she made the offering anyway. It deserved no less.

"We must *always* do *whatever* is in our best interests," the creature told Hiram through her, and she felt herself wiggling inwardly like a delighted puppy because it had chosen to acknowledge her by using her words. "Hiram, my own. This is a mount with everything to discover. Everything." *Yes, everything, anything,* she gibbered. *Whatever. Always.* "This will be a new pleasure for me, the pleasure of discovery, of gratification finally taken." The creature using her face to smile was a sun shining within her. "Call Ezili to us."

Hiram went to the doorway. Jane pulled herself up onto the bed, enjoying each separate part of the movement and all of it together. How was it she had never realized what a good body she had, how much feeling it was capable of? Well, she would not waste any more time. The world was full of pleasure.

"Ah. As I thought."

She turned at the sound of Ezili's voice and laughed. "Ezili-je-rouge, my own. See this unexpected pleasure." Jane stood up, rejoicing in the sensation, and smoothed her hands over her hips.

Ezili walked over to her and looked her up and down. "Does it please you, then?"

She was looking into Ezili's face as though it were the most fascinating thing she had ever seen. How could she have ever thought Ezili's eyes were evil? The red in those eyes was pleasurable to see; seeing was another act of pleasure, and seeing Ezili was even more pleasure because she pleased *him* so much. She could only love Ezili helplessly because Ezili made her Master so happy, and her Master's happiness meant more ecstasy for herself. "It pleases me so much."

Jane's hand moved toward Ezili and then paused, shaking a little. Her vision swam and darkened, and for a moment she was thinking. *What am I doing, no, stop, STOP!*

And then the pleasure was back, bringing with it the anticipation of even greater pleasures, and her hand was moving on Ezili's breast. Ezili quickly pulled down the front of her dress.

Jane looked over at Hiram with a smile. "Here's something I bet you never thought you'd see." Moisture condensed out of the air and fell on herself and Ezili in a gentle mist, moving over them selectively. She bent her head to Ezili's breast. The wet flesh was soft and firm and very warm. Hiram made a small noise. It registered on her only as the vague noting that hearing, too, could turn the pleasure up higher and higher.

Absolute pleasure, she discovered, could make a person swoon. At least it did her. Sometimes it seemed she was nearly at the point of blacking out, and then she would find herself following a smooth curve of hip, or gazing down at Ezili's face. The pleasure pulsing through her would grow again until it overwhelmed her.

Once she found herself staring into Hiram's eyes while Ezili knelt before her, and she felt an almost psychic connection with him. He was hungry for her, for Ezili, for both of them, but even more for the thing on her back. He felt a bit bewildered and abandoned. He knew this pleasure, not just the pleasure of Ezili's body but of this contact, the ecstasy of

the kiss. The kiss. Ezili's mouth, skilled as it was, paled next
to the real kiss.

Absently she pushed Ezili away and gave herself over fully
to the creature, obeying its silent commands, reveling in
what it could do for her all by itself.

Eventually she found herself languid on the bed, drifting
in half-consciousness, still aglow with pleasure. She was
aware of the way the covers felt against her skin, of the
wetness between her thighs and the water still slowly caressing
her body, of the murmur of Hiram and Ezili's talking. It
should have been uncomfortable with her Master on her back
(*Ti Malice,* her mind told her, and she accepted the name),
but it felt perfectly natural there, as though it were something that always should have been there and had been
missing until now. She sighed with contentment. How had
she gone all her life without the comfort of the weight there,
the sweet pressure at her neck? She had been incomplete
before, pathetically unfinished. Now she was whole, more
than whole; perhaps even more than human.

Yes, much more than human. She had been waiting for
this all her life without knowing it, to be ridden by this
creature of beauty that could bring her spirit to new heights
of awareness. This was living a plane above human. All the
new thoughts it gave her . . . but most of all, the pleasure. She
had been made for pleasure, she thought happily; how fortunate that she had been able to find that out.

"Ezili," her voice said. Somewhere out of the range of her
vision she felt Ezili snap to attention.

"I have been waiting," Ezili said, sounding acquiescent
and yet petulant all at once.

"It is not done yet."

Ezili sighed. A moment later she felt the touch of Ezili's
hand.

"No, not that. Is your traveling cloak here? We wish
to . . . travel." Jane heard herself laugh softly.

"What about me?" Hiram said.

"You can help me dress." Jane's hand lifted in his direction. "Come, help me up."

The traveling cloak was a long, flowing cape with a cowl
and a large collar in layered ruffles. The ruffles hid the hump
the creature would have made under the more conventional

covering of a sweater or a jacket. The cloak itself was a bit ostentatious, but on the streets of wild card New York, it wouldn't cause much comment. The shrouded forms of jokers hiding some prominent feature or another had been commonplace for years.

Ezili pulled up the cowl so that it hid Jane's face completely. Jane gathered the cloak about herself, enjoying the small pleasure of the way it touched her.

"Somewhere interesting," she told Ezili. "Something in a man this time."

"And I just stay here and wait for you?" Hiram said. His tone was satisfyingly servile.

"You know I will come back for you later. Be here."

"Yes," said Hiram. "Always." He kept his gaze on the carpet. "I'll phone for the car."

Jane was delighted to see that Hiram was traveling by private limo these days, with a driver who left the soundproofed partition up at all times. It gave her the privacy she wanted, with Ezili or anyone else.

It was like being a queen, Jane thought; a queen or an empress. Now she could understand what it must have been like to be the Astronomer, the way he was. She had been calling him poison and resisting certain aspects of her own power—it was to laugh. What she had thought of as evil was just a matter of power. There wasn't really even such a thing as evil or good—only power and the pleasure that it brought. And anything could be sacrificed for that, anything at all, and everything if necessary. *Whatever. Always.*

They passed a newsstand and she had a glimpse of a magazine with a picture of Jumpin' Jack Flash on the cover. Something twanged within her. How nice it would have been to have him now. But there were plenty of good-looking men in the world, red-haired or not. And what did good-looking have to do with it anyway? There were whispers about jokers, about how sometimes the more grotesque the deformity, the more endowed and skilled they were for certain things. . . .

Hey, baby, I got more than just the ears *of a donkey!*

She gave Ezili an attention-getting pinch, once more generating a burst of pleasure just in the movement, and told her where she wanted to go. Then she sat back while Ezili told the driver, experiencing the ecstasy of just breathing in and out. In and oūt.

If the joker with the donkey ears recognized her, he gave no sign. He stood gawking with his squirt bottle in one hand and a filthy rag in the other as Jane beckoned through the open door to him. For a moment he looked as though he were going to climb in, but when he saw Ezili, he suddenly bolted. Surprise and anger surged through Jane, and that, too, was great pleasure to feel. From now on she would feel every emotion there was to feel, anything that pleased her Master. *Whatever. Always.*

Ezili shut the door and told the driver to go on. "Don't worry," she purred, to Jane or to Ti Malice, it didn't matter. Sound was exquisite. "We'll find another that isn't all talk."

The next joker they found was eyeless, but he had no problem climbing into the back of the limo. Jane studied him; his head was elongated, bullet-shaped, with just a blank expanse of skin running from the straight hairline to his nose. Seeing deformity was as delicious as seeing Ezili naked.

The joker sniffed suspiciously and turned his face to her. "How many of you are there?" he said in a ridiculously high voice. Jane reached down between his legs and he jumped. Ezili held him back against the seat.

"Hey, hey," the joker shrilled. "You don't have to pin me down, I know what you want." He began to undo his baggy trousers.

Her Master rode her awe as if it were a wave. "Is that . . . standard equipment?" she was allowed to ask.

The joker gave a high laugh. "It is on this model. God bless the wild card, hey, ladies?"

Her Master bent her head for her; even the anticipation of pleasure was a whole pleasure in itself. As was having Ezili watch.

The bar was dark, except for the hot, white spotlight on the small stage where a many-breasted hermaphroditic joker and a normal man did unusual things to each other in time to music. Jane watched through her new eyes, embracing the experience of curiosity and interest. Even more interesting was the way the other patrons cruised her and Ezili. They moved past their corner table, ostensibly on their way to the bar or to the rest room, slowing to make eye contact. It was exhilirating to find she could dismiss someone with a look. They all wanted her; some of them stared at Ezili, but they all looked at her, nestled in her cloak, hiding the spirit of power on her back. They knew, she thought. They all knew that she was the real presence and Ezili wasn't much more than her servant, if that. Servant to the thing on her back, yes, but it was on *her* back. No matter what happened later, it was on her back now, and even if it should leave, if she should never have it again, she had been the Queen of Pleasure for a little while and she could not imagine *not* feeling that way ever again.

There was a young man standing in front of the table expectantly. Her Master told Jane to appraise him—skinny, young, probably not more than seventeen or eighteen. No visible distinguishing characteristics other than his shaggy red hair. A little pretty boy. She leaned forward.

"You're blocking our view. Why don't you sit down?" She indicated the chair beside her.

The boy sat down, staring at her intently. Then, without a word, he slid off the chair and knelt in front of her. When she pulled up her dress, she knew it was the creature moving her arms, but she poured all her enthusiasm into it, going with him joyfully, accepting the pleasure of her fingers twisting in the boy's hair. *Red hair,* she thought dreamily; *I'll pretend it's him, Jumpin' Jack Flash.* . . .

There was a mild ripple in the pleasure running through her, as though something in her had been distracted. Without volition she looked over her shoulder at Ezili.

"It's starting to bore me," she heard herself say in a flat voice. "Perhaps it doesn't fight me enough, or perhaps it just doesn't have enough ideas of its own. Take the cape, Ezili."

Ezili's eyes seemed to glow in the darkness.

"Move carefully, my own."

Ezili whispered something in French and slipped under the side of the cloak, putting one arm around Jane.

Jane held tighter to the boy's head, feeling something like hurt surprise. It was leaving her? Now? Even as she thought it, she felt it withdraw from her neck. There was a moment of sharp pain, followed by a sudden blankness, as if a switch had been thrown to *off*. She was aware of the creature's moving from her back to Ezili's, and she wanted to turn and grab it back, but she couldn't move.

And the cloak was resettled around Ezili's shoulders and *she* was now the Queen of Pleasure.

Ezili rose from her chair as if she were levitating and looked down at Jane with scornful triumph.

"*Why?*" Jane pleaded. "I thought—I thought—"

Ezili stroked Jane's head roughly, as if she were a dog. "Old favorites are not forgotten. New pleasures bring great thrills, yes, but the old favorites such as this mount, it knows how to please me. And the richness of its appetites—you have far to go, little mount, before you can compare with this." Ezili cupped her hands around her breasts and held them out proudly.

Jane turned away, starting to tremble. Ezili bent down and put her mouth close to her ear. "Goes right to the pleasure place in your brain, did you know that?" she said in her own, hateful Ezili-voice. "Yeah. Maybe you can get hold of some drug does the same. Might get you through the hours without him. You can try that, might help. And maybe you be a lot nicer to me now, white meat. If you want the kiss again." She thrust her tongue into Jane's ear, and Jane gave a little screech, slapping at her. Ezili laughed and moved around the table, going toward the exit.

"Wait!" Jane shouted over the music. "Where are you going?"

Ezili paused, sneering at her. "Out for some real action."

"What about me?" she cried desperately.

Ezili laughed again; the cape swirled gracefully as she headed for the exit.

Jane sat frozen for a moment. *Drown her!* she thought, but her mind shied away from the necessary concentration. The pleasure that had been thrumming all through her like the vibrations from some smooth-running engine were gone, and in its place was a terrible hollowness as if, when the creature had pulled away from her, it had taken everything inside of her with it.

Then she looked down and saw the boy between her legs, grinning up at her, his mouth and chin shining wetly in the faint light.

"*Get away!*" she shrieked and beat at him madly, horrified at herself and him and at the way the creature had left her.

"Hey, *hey!*" the boy yelled, trying to fend off her flailing hands. "Handyman, *help!* Cunt gone crazy!"

Several arms grabbed her from behind, pinning her arms to her sides.

"Let me go!" She tried to twist away and the arms hugged her tighter, threatening to crush her rib cage. She tried to call water to dash it into her captor's face, but her ability seemed to have deserted her; there was only hollowness where it had once been. Panic jumped in her. "Help, police, somebody!"

"Shut your fucking mouth, cunt," said a deep male voice close to her ear, the same ear where Ezili had stuck her tongue. Jane squirmed in revulsion and the arms squeezed again painfully. She forced herself to go limp. After a moment the arms relaxed slightly, ready to tighten again if she started to struggle.

"Now what were you saying about the police? Maybe you seen a crime being committed?"

Jane looked around. They were all staring at her, all the people at the little tables spread through the room, but there was no emotion in most of the faces. On stage the hermaphrodite and the man had paused, sitting on a platform with legs entwined, squinting out at the room in annoyance. The hermaphrodite shielded his/her eyes from the spotlights with one hand, searching for the cause of the disturbance.

"Hey, do you fucking *mind?*" s/he yelled, his/her face turned in Jane's direction. "I'm trying to *concentrate* up here. You think this she-male shit's *easy* or something?"

"Go fuck yourself!" someone yelled hoarsely.

"That's the late show, sweetheart!"

"Okay, cunt, let's go," said the male voice in Jane's ear. "You ruined the show." The arms lifted her and dragged her across the back of the room to a different exit than the one Ezili had taken. The red-haired kid ran to open the door, and Jane was shoved out into a narrow, dirty alley. She hit the ground on hands and knees, crying out in rage and pain.

"Blow, cunt. And don't bring it around here again."

She scrambled up, ready to protest, and then jumped back, falling against some garbage cans. The man standing in the doorway was no taller than she was, but his torso was wide and misshapen, to accommodate the three pairs of arms.

Behind him the red-haired boy glowered at her and wiped his mouth showily. "She didn't pay, Handyman," he said.

The man glanced at the kid and then came at Jane, moving more quickly than she had thought he would have been able to. "Nobody stiffs one of my boys," he said, "especially not some skinny fucking cunt who yells for the cops. Give it up, dickhole, and you're free to go." Before she could run, he was on her, running all of his hands over her body in a rough search. "Come on, where do you keep your wad?" One hand clamped between her legs. Jane opened her mouth to scream, and another hand clamped over it while four hands continued to pat her down.

"Shut up. You keep it down there, in the safety deposit box? I'll give you one chance to get it yourself and then I go in after it."

Jane stared at him pleadingly; he pulled the hand at her mouth away.

"Well?"

"I don't have anything," she whispered. "They left me here with nothing."

The man picked her up and tossed her away. She landed heavily on her side in a spill of garbage.

"Tough stuff, cunt. But I'll let you off with a warning. This time. Don't bring it back here, I mean it."

Jane raised herself slowly to a sitting position, drawing her legs up protectively. The man started to turn away and then feigned a lunge at her. She gave a small yelp and he laughed at her, the red-haired boy joining in from where he stood at the doorway, hanging on the jamb by one arm as though this were some idle, late-summer afternoon and he was being entertained by the antics of his friends. In the light it was obvious that he was younger than she'd thought. Revulsion and pity for him began to well up in her and suddenly cut off as it met the great hollowness of Ti Malice's absence from her body and mind. She burst into tears and something in her gave. Suddenly she was covered with water.

"What the fuck is that?" the man shouted at her. "What the fuck are you?" He backed away from her. The sight of the six-armed joker flinching from her water-calling power gave her small, bitter amusement; she concentrated and this time found the power, pulling a couple of gallons of water out of the air to fling in his face. Then, while he was still sputtering and roaring with anger, she got up and ran.

She called the water out of her clothing as best she could, but the power was weak and she stayed moderately damp as she wandered aimlessly through Jokertown in the deepening twilight. Aimless? Not quite—lifeless, perhaps, lifeless and empty, but on the lookout for Hiram's car. Perhaps Ezili had gone back to Hiram, or Hiram had gone back to Aces High. If she called Hiram, he might send someone out for her—

The memory of what had happened with Hiram was like a fist in her stomach. She could see his face, the sorrow, the anger, the despair, that alien curiosity, and then Ezili, Ezili and *herself* . . .

She bent over, choking and gagging, unmindful of the stares from people passing by. Oh, God, how could she have, what had made her—with Ezili, *Ezili*—she must have been mad, crazed, *possessed*—

Someone bumped into her and she staggered against the side of a building, sobbing into her hands. Possessed, yes, but now it was gone, leaving her worse than alone. The hollowness inside of her seemed to swell, and she had an image of herself being sucked down a huge drain. To live without the fullness the creature brought her, to exist with no pleasure at all, was unbearable.

Trembling doubled her over again and she sobbed harder. More. She needed more, she needed to feel herself whole again, nestled in the glow of pleasure that only the creature could give her, and if she had to go to Ezili again, to Ezili and Hiram together, if she had to go to that bar and walk up onstage to the hermaphrodite and the man and the six-armed joker and the red-haired boy all at the same time, it would not have been too much to ask of herself, if the thing asked her to cut her own throat at the end of it—

"Hey. *Hey.* Easy, now."

Gentle hands were on her shoulders. She twisted around, desperate hope rising and then plummeting to despair as she looked into the grotesque clown face. "Go away," she said, pushing at the strange man feebly.

"There, now, I'm just trying to help you. Don't let the face put you off. I know it's silly. Just my bad luck to be in makeup when the virus showed, now I can't get it off. Not the

worst thing that could happen, I guess, just looking at you."
The man hauled her to her feet and stood her against the
wall, dabbing at her face with a handkerchief. The sadness in
his eyes made the clown white and the big red nose even
more absurd, but she didn't feel much like laughing.

"Go away," she moaned, "you can't help me, no one can
help me, only *him*. I have to find *him*." Weeping, she looked
down at her arms. Dry. She touched her face; it, too, was dry.
She couldn't even call her own tears anymore. Had that been
the last of it, back there in the alley?

"Water!" she cried. "I want the water!"

"Shh, shh, we'll get you some water," said the clown man,
trying to hold her still.

"Please! He's taken the water!" She collapsed against the
man, crying weakly, but still without tears.

Curled up on the bed in the fetal position, she heard the
clown man talking to one of the clinic nurses without really
listening to what he was saying. Every so often her body gave
an uncontrollable shudder, but she remained dry. *Dried up,*
she thought; *all dried up without him, without the kiss and
the pleasure and the fullness.*

". . . something about water," the clown man was saying.

"Hysterical," said the nurse. "Hysteria seems to be the
condition of the moment around here."

"Nah, it's more than that. I've got a bad feeling. She
oughta be watched."

The nurse sighed. "Maybe, but we just don't have the
people. The new cases are coming in almost faster than we
can log them, all jokers and worse. If we don't find the cause,
the whole city could get infected. You're running a pretty bad
risk yourself, Boze."

The clown man grunted. "What's a joker got to lose?"

"You'd know the answer to that if you saw the locked
ward."

"That's just a small locked ward you got here. Out there,
it's a big locked ward, and we're all locked into it. And when
I walk around it, I just see my brother again, turned inside
out. Screaming every time his heart beat. Hell, you don't
have the people to stay with her, I'll stay with her, watch her
for signs that she's been infected."

A fresh bout of shuddering racked Jane's body; she tried to quell it and listen to what they were saying.

"That's big of you, Boze, but just from the quick exam we gave her in the emergency room, I'd say she's suffering from drug withdrawal, not a new wild card infection."

The idea seemed to flood Jane's mind with a bright light. She sat up and turned to the nurse. "Drugs. I need a drug."

The nurse glanced at the clown man. "What'd I tell you, Boze? Just another junkie courting AIDS."

"*I am NOT a junkie, you bitch, I am an ACE and I demand to see Dr. Tachyon AT ONCE!*" The scream tore out of Jane's throat, leaving it raw; she imagined she could hear her words echoing all through the clinic, reaching all the way to Tachyon himself, wherever he was.

And apparently she had imagined it right; a few moments later Tachyon appeared in the doorway, alarm large on his drawn, tired face.

The nurse started to speak to him; he waved away her words and went to the bed, taking Jane's hand in his.

"Water Lily," he said, his voice full of compassion. "What has happened to you?"

This undid her completely and she clung to him, sobbing dryly. He held her, letting her get it all out, and then gently pushed her back down on the bed.

"Don't leave me like this!" she cried, grabbing at his hands.

"Shh, Jane, I won't leave you, not for a few minutes anyway."

She saw that he was not just weary but near complete exhaustion; then she brushed the fact aside. He was here to help her. He *had* to help her. It was all his fault to begin with, and if that meant he had to work exhausted once in a while, that was *his* tough stuff, which was nothing compared to what *she* was going through.

"I need a drug," she said shakily. "I was given something—it wasn't my fault, I didn't want to take it, it was forced on me. I don't want it anymore but I have to have it. I might die without it. I don't know—"

"What was it?" he asked quietly, pushing her down as she tried to rise.

"I don't *know!*" she snapped impatiently. "Just something, it goes right to the pleasure place, it makes—it does—I had to—but *you* must have a drug. Something you can make from your world. Something that will cure me, or replace it, like methadone—"

"You need *methadone*?" His expression was stricken.

"No, no, not methadone, something *like* methadone, but from your world, something that will make me stop *craving*—"

Tachyon wiped a hand over his face. "Please. You're babbling. Please try to calm down. If you're addicted to a drug I can send you to another clinic—"

"It's not a drug!" she screamed, and Tachyon put his hands over his ears. "I'm sorry, oh, I'm so sorry," she went on in a whisper, "but it's not a drug, not exactly, but it's *like* a drug—"

Tachyon pulled away from her, pressing his palms against his forehead. "Jane, please. I've lost count of the number of hours I've been up. I can't even put forth my mind to calm you. The nurse will give you a sedative and we'll transfer you to another hospital."

"No, please, don't send me away!" She grabbed at his arm and he twisted away from her.

"You can't stay here. We need the beds for the new cases."

"But—"

Tachyon pulled away from her firmly. "The nurse can give the name of a clinic not far from here. They can help you. Or just outside, I'm sure there's someone who can give you the name of a source, if that's what you're really after." He got up and walked wearily to the door, pausing to look back at her. "I had expected you to end up differently, Water Lily. You must be a great disappointment to Hiram Worchester." He was gone.

Speechless, Jane fell back against the pillow and stared at the ceiling. He was tired, so exhausted that he saw her as just another drug addict. *A great disappointment to Hiram Worchester.* At the thought of Hiram the craving burst upon her with an intensity that brought her up out of the bed and sent her charging for the doorway.

Just at the threshold she collided with the nurse. "Whoa, wait a minute," the nurse said, thrusting a piece of paper at her. "Dr. Tachyon told me to give you the name of this clinic—"

Jane snatched the paper from her and stared at it, trying to drown it in a gout of water that would turn it to mush, but the terrible need blocked her again. She looked up at the nurse.

"No drug?" she said belligerently.

The nurse's eyes were hard. "Not here, lady."

She could still call a little water, albeit in a rather conventional way. She spat on the paper and flung it in the nurse's face. Then she turned and ran down the hall to the exit.

On the fourth number she dialed, the answering machine message cut off and a low voice said, "It better be good."

Jane's voice suddenly deserted her. She hung on the pay phone in the telephone booth, her mouth opening and closing impotently.

"Okay, kid. We had Prince Albert in a can but we let him out last week. Now go call your mommy." She heard him start to hang up.

"Croyd!" she wailed.

She could actually sense him shifting gears at the sound of a female voice. "Go ahead, I'm listening."

"It's—it's me, Jane. Jane Dow," she added, trying to force herself to sound calm.

"Jane. *Well*." His pleasure-filled laugh grated on her painfully. "So you didn't throw away the numbers I gave you. You sound a little breathless. Everything okay?"

"No. Yes. I mean—" She slumped against the wall of the phone booth, gripping the receiver with both hands.

"Jane? You still there?"

"Yes. Of course." Slowly she straightened up and tried to compose herself into the Aces High hostess who flirted so easily with the man with the faceted eyes. The overwhelming emptiness inside of her made that woman a stranger to her now. "I'm still here and you're there. I think that means one of us is definitely in the wrong place." Her voice broke on the last word, and she jammed her knuckles into her mouth to smother the sound of her crying.

"If you're saying you'd like to rectify that situation, that's the best thing I've heard today." He paused. "Are you sure everything's okay?"

Something in the back of her mind was trying to tell her Croyd sounded as though he were on the thin edge himself, but she ignored it. If there was anyone who could get her a drug, it was Croyd. Whatever she had to do for him in return was not too much to ask.

"Everything *will* be okay when you give me your address," she said shakily. When he didn't answer, she added, "I *really* want. to see you. Please?"

"I never could resist a woman who said please. Tell me where you are and I'll tell you the best way to get to where I am. . . ."

The door opened a wide crack to reveal the mirrorshades, gleaming at her with an insectile coldness. Croyd licked his lips and opened the door wider. "Come into my parlor, Bright Eyes. If you'll pardon the expression. I'm afraid parlor is all there is." The voice was different; the man was taller and his skin was white all over, but the words were pure Croyd.

She stepped into a shabby one-room apartment lit only with a few small lamps scattered in odd spots. The furniture was negligible—a bureau that might have come from the same flea market as the lamps, an old wooden table and a couple of chairs, a broken-down sofa near the windows. It was not the most reassuring place she had ever come to, but, she reminded herself, she had not come for reassurance.

"This is not the place I usually choose to entertain in," Croyd was saying as he shut the door and ran down a line of four locks. He turned to her, raising a hand to his mirrorshades, and licked his lips again. "So. I'm afraid I don't have a lot to offer you in the way of refreshment, but I can make any kind of gin and tonic you like."

She laughed nervously, hugging herself. "How many kinds are there?"

"Well, there's gin and tonic, of course. Tonic and gin," he said, moving closer to her. She made a countermove farther into the room, hugging herself tighter. "Gin and not much tonic. Gin and no tonic at all. Gin and an ice cube. Which sounds great to me. You think it over." He licked his lips for the third time in as many minutes and went to the kitchenette.

Jane turned away, trying to get the shudder building inside of her under control. In the company of this man who wanted her, the void was eating away at her like acid. It would make no difference if Croyd's latest persona were the god of eros. Just being in the same room with him was an excruciating reminder that pleasure could only be *Ti Malice;*

anything else was a pale, crude substitution to force time to pass.

"Decided?"

She jumped as he touched her shoulder and moved away from him, rubbing the spot as if it were bruised. "No, I—nothing for me, I guess." She gave another nervous laugh and winced. He tilted his head curiously and she saw two Janes in the mirrorshades. The distortion made her look as if she were trying to disappear into herself.

"You sure?" Croyd upended the glass and took a couple of ice cubes into his mouth, crunching them noisily. There were only ice cubes in his glass, she saw. "Nothing at *all*?"

"Well, not *nothing*...." She made a face, giving a long sigh. "God, I'm no good at this."

"At what?" Croyd had another ice cube. "What is it you're not good at, Bright Eyes?" He came a little closer and she backed away. "And why is it so important to be good at it?"

Something caught her abruptly behind the knees, and she plumped down hard on the couch. Croyd moved in quickly beside her, rolling another ice cube around in his mouth. His left arm slid along the back of the sofa and she shrank away from him. His knee touched hers just as his hand went from the couch to her shoulder, moving very lightly. He reached over and set the glass on the windowsill behind the couch, disturbing the drawn shade; his hand, she saw, was trembling slightly. Jane looked from the glass to Croyd. His tongue flicked out and ran along his lips every few seconds now. It was more like a tic than an expression of desire.

"Talk to me, Jane," he said gently as she reached the corner of the couch. He put his other hand on her arm. She flinched at the contact; there was another sensation under the displeasure of a touch that was not Ti Malice's, a tremor, as if he were running a long distance and going as fast as he could instead of sitting here on the couch trying to take her in his arms. "Come on, talk to me. Tell me."

The words came to her unbidden. "'Sleeper speeding, people bleeding.'"

He froze. Jane looked into the mirrorshades, seeing only her twin reflections. Impulsively she reached for the glasses and he pulled back. "Don't." He twisted around, looking for the ice cubes, and Jane nodded at the windowsill. "Thanks. Speed dries you out."

"Where do you get it?" she asked.

"What, the speed? Why?" He crunched a couple of ice cubes. "You planning to stay up all night?"

"I was just wondering if whoever you got it from might... well, stock other things." She took a deep breath. "Other kinds of drugs."

He looked at her sharply for a moment and then suddenly lunged at her, grabbing her upper arm to pull her close.

"Stop, you're hurting me!" Jane flinched from the mirrorshades thrusting themselves into her face and tried to pry his fingers off her arm.

"Are you strung out? Is *that* why you came here?" He was almost laughing. She twisted away from him, started to get up, and stumbled, landing on the floor in a heap.

"Get up." He pulled her back onto the couch roughly. "Talk to me, and this time, tell me something I don't know. *Are* you strung out."

"It's not what you think," she said, not looking at him.

"It never is, Bright Eyes." He was licking his lips again. It was beginning to drive her crazy. "So, what kind of drug were you shopping for—horse? Lady? Blue dreamers? Reds? White crossroads? Black bombers, screaming yellow zonkers? What's your *pleasure*?" His voice was hard and ugly and she was aware, with no little amazement, that he was as disappointed in what he thought she was as Tachyon had been.

"God, what am I supposed to be, everyone's idea of Rebecca of Sunnybrook Farm, the Sweet Virgin Ace?" she shouted at him. "Am I supposed to stand up here on my pedestal, playing God's Good Girl, just so you can all pat me on the head and call me virtuous in between your own debaucheries? Dear little Water Lily, *lily white* Water Lily, *virgin-white* Water Lily! It doesn't work that way! You all had to drag me into this, you had to involve me in your stupid games, in your fucking gang wars, you all had to use me for your own purposes, and now everyone's so shocked because I've turned up with the same filth you wallow in splashed all over me. *What did you expect!*"

She realized she was kneeling over him on the couch, screaming into his face. A few flecks of saliva were spattered on the mirrorshades. He stared up at her openmouthed.

"I guess," he said, pausing to lick his lips, "speed isn't the only thing that can dry you out."

Jane doubled over with a sob as the aching emptiness

renewed its attack on her. She felt Croyd's hand lightly on her hair and shouted, "Don't touch me, *it hurts!*"

"I thought it was kind of strange that you weren't, ah, moist, but I wasn't sure. Everything seems a little strange at this point." He crunched the last of the ice cubes. "What is it? Plain old heroin, or something more exotic?"

She raised her head from the musty cushion. "You wouldn't believe me if I told you."

"Try me. Tell me what you're looking for."

With great effort she pulled herself all the way up and sat with her legs tucked under her. "I need something that goes directly to the pleasure center of the brain and stimulates it continuously."

"Don't we all," Croyd said grimly, tapping the last drop of water from his empty glass.

"Well?" she said after a moment.

"Well what?"

"Do you know of anyone who has such a drug and will sell it to me?"

He gave a short, humorless laugh. "Hell, no."

She stared at him, feeling the void consume her hope along with the rest of her, and then, absurdly, she sneezed.

"Gesundheit," he said automatically. "Listen, there's no such thing, not animal, vegetable, or mineral. Except maybe about five hours of good, dirty sex, and frankly I'm not up to more than an hour at a time. Terrible to have to admit that—"

She was off the couch, heading for the door.

"Hey, wait!"

She stopped and turned, looking at him questioningly.

"Where are you going?"

"The only place I *can* go."

"And where might that be?"

She shook her head. "You're wrong, Croyd. There is such a thing. It exists. I know it. And I hope you never do. It's the worst thing in the world."

He licked his lips again and wiped his mouth with the palm of his hand. "I doubt that, Bright Eyes."

"Good," she said. "I hope you always will. Stay where you are. I'll let myself out."

But she couldn't. She had to wait patiently while he undid

all four locks before she could rush away from the twin reflections of her own hopeless face.

Hiram opened the door to her this time, Hiram all alone in the empty apartment. She didn't have to ask to be let in.

"It left you," he said quietly.

"Yes." Her voice was a whisper as she stood with her head bowed.

"Are you..." his voice failed him for a moment. "Are you... all right?"

She looked up at him and his eyes reflected the emptiness she felt inside. "You know I'm not, Hiram. And neither are you."

"No. I suppose we're not." He paused. "Can I get you anything? A glass of water or something to eat or..." His words hung in the air between them, futile absurdities. He was offering a teardrop to a forest fire.

It was too painful to leave at that. Jane raised her head with as much dignity as she could muster. "A cup of hot tea would be nice, thank you." It would be no such thing, and she almost never drank hot tea anyway, but it would be something they could do besides just stand there and ache together.

He busied himself in the kitchenette while she sat at the small table, staring at nothing. If pleasure was real, then the absence of pleasure was a palpable thing as well; where there had been rapture in every movement there was now the pain of the void *he* had left. *My Master,* she thought with dull revulsion. *I called him My Master.*

"I couldn't let you go after you'd seen," Hiram said abruptly. He didn't turn around and she didn't look up. "I'm sure you understand that, now that you know."

She made a small murmur but said nothing else.

"And he'd seen you in my thoughts many times as well. So when you showed up..." Pause. "Why *did* you come here?"

The memory made her burst out laughing. Alarmed, Hiram turned around from the counter where the tea was brewing and stared at her. He looked so frightened that she tried to stem her laughter, but she had no control. She only laughed harder, shaking her head and waving him away as he made a move toward her.

"It's all right," she gasped after a while. "Really. It's

just—just so—" She was off again for nearly a minute while he stood watching her, misery emanating from him in waves she could almost feel.

"It's just so . . . *insignificant*," she said when she could finally speak again. "Brightwater delivered a load of rotten fish and I had to send it back. Nobody knew what to do about getting in a replacement shipment for the sushi bar, and Tomoyuki said that Mr. Dining Out was coming from *New York Gourmet* to review the twilight sushi bar—" She laughed again but weakly this time. "I guess we won't be offering the sushi bar tonight. I told Tom to get sick if I weren't back in an hour. That was—I don't know. What time is it?"

Hiram didn't answer.

"No, I guess it doesn't matter, does it?" she said, staring at him. "I got the address off the back of your desk blotter, but I wasn't going to use it unless I really had to, and I felt like I did. They're all turning against you, Hiram. Emile's walking around saying he thinks you're a junkie."

"I am," Hiram said bleakly. He checked the teapot and then set it on the table with two cups. "And so are you. And Ezili. And everyone else he's kissed."

"Is that what you call it?" she said as he poured the tea.

"Do you have a better word for it?"

"No."

"It's an instant, permanent addiction," Hiram went on, almost matter-of-factly. "He connects directly to the pleasure center of your brain. That's why everything feels so good. Eating. Moving. Making love. Just breathing. And when he leaves you—it's like death. There's no cure, no relief. Except the kiss. I'll do anything for it. And so will you."

"*No.*"

Hiram paused in the act of raising his teacup.

"We've got to pull ourselves together. There must be some kind of cure we could take, or even a drug that could act as a block or a replacement—"

"No, nothing." Hiram shook his head with finality.

"There *must* be. We could look for it together, you and I. I went to Tachyon's clinic—"

Hiram's cup clattered into the saucer. "You *what*? You went to *Tachyon*?" His face had actually gone gray; she thought he might drop dead of horror.

"Don't worry, I didn't tell him. And he didn't find out.

He's swamped with new wild card cases. He didn't bother reading my mind. But if you went back there with me and talked to him—"

"*No!*" he roared, and she jumped, spilling tea all over the table. Hiram immediately went for a dish towel and began wiping up the mess. "No," he said again, much more quietly. "If anyone finds out, they'll kill him. He can't survive without a human host. We'd lose him and we still wouldn't have a cure. We'd have to be like this for the rest of our lives. Could you stand that?"

"God, no," she whispered, putting her forehead in her hand.

"Then don't talk crazy." Hiram tossed the dish towel at the sink and took her hand. "It'll be all right. Really. It's not so bad a lot of the time. Not really. I mean, does he demand *that* much for the pleasure he gives? And he does leave you alone a lot, and it's not like he's evil, not really. If you were the only mount, could you deny him his life? If you knew he would die without you, could you let that happen?"

She pulled her hand away, shaking her head. "Hiram, you don't know what's happened to me."

"You don't know what's happened to *me!*" he cried. He knelt down to look into her face, and she was horrified to see tears in his eyes. "Whatever you've done is nothing compared to what I've done! Don't you think it's been horrible for me? The fear of detection, the powerlessness—I've considered suicide, don't think I haven't, but the awful part is, there might be an afterlife and he wouldn't be there and that really *would* be hell! What happened to *you*—! Know what happened to *me?* I let him take a friend! I swore I would not, and I did it anyway! *I let him take you!*"

She pulled away from him. "Oh, Jesus, Hiram, I wish I'd died that night when the Astronomer came to Aces High. I wish you had let me fall!"

"I wish I had, too!" he bellowed at her.

Hiram's statement seemed to echo in the silence that followed. It was over, she realized wonderingly. Aces High, her obligation to Hiram, her life as an ace if she'd ever really had one, everything. It had all been wiped out, leaving both of them with nothing.

"You're not wet," Hiram said, belatedly aware.

Before she could answer him, there was a knock at the door.

Hiram jerked his head at the bedroom and she went without protest, pulling herself into a huddle on the floor next to the bed. Whatever was coming next, she wasn't ready for it.

Exhaustion suddenly swept over her; she leaned her head against the side of the mattress and let herself fall into a strange half-sleep. She heard the voices in the other room, but they made no impression on her, even when Hiram's rose angrily. Some uncounted time later she sensed someone's approaching and she tried to push down into unconsciousness, away from the presence, fantasizing again that Hiram had made her weightless so she could drift off into the sky.

But strong hands pulled her up and flung her down on the bed. She struggled feebly, her eyelids fluttering with groggy alarm. Then she felt the feather touch of small fingers along her back, and she stretched her neck obligingly for the kiss.

The scene in the living room was troublesome, but she was far above it, riding in a state of transport with her Master. There was Hiram of course, and Ezili, and two men she didn't recognize and couldn't be bothered to care about, and Emile, of all people, bound and gagged and lying on the carpet. Her Master forced her attention to him and she acquiesced, all the while reveling in the renewed contact.

"Jane," Hiram said tensely. She turned to look at him through pleasure-glazed eyes. He seemed to be having some difficulty keeping his gaze on her, or perhaps on her Master. It didn't matter, though. Everything was all right again.

"*Jane.*"

"Heard you," she said, completely happy. "What is it?"

"Why did you give Emile the spare key to my office?"

Her Master commanded that she answer, and it was exquisite to obey. "I put him in charge while I was gone. It seemed to be the logical thing to do."

"When I gave you that key, I told you no one—*no one*—but you was to have it, for *any* reason."

"You gave me that key ages ago, before you left on the trip, and after you came back, I thought you'd forgotten all about it. It just didn't seem to make any difference because you didn't seem to care anymore." She smiled dreamily.

Hiram's fist was clenched but she wasn't worried. With Her Master there was nothing to worry about. She marveled at how the surrender could be so much more profound on the second time. On the third time she would probably lose herself to him completely and *that* would be absolute perfection. She could hardly wait.

"You don't understand what you've done, Water Lily," Hiram said miserably. "You've killed this man."

Something in her started at the use of her ace name, but she let it go. Her Master liked it. He liked the water that was trickling down her face and running from her hair, saturating her clothes and soaking the carpet around her feet.

"If she was responsible," her voice said at her Master's command, "then she can take care of it, yes, Hiram?"

"It will kill her," Hiram said. "Or drive her mad."

"She's already mad." Her Master had her laugh for him. "And she's not really so terribly interesting, except for her power." Her face turned to Emile. His eyes widened, and he made desperate little noises against the gag.

"Get him ready for her, Ezili," said her Master. "I am so curious as to what it will be like."

Ezili struggled to pull down Emile's trousers while he tried to wiggle away from her. One of the men Jane didn't know forced Emile over onto his back, crushing his bound hands against the floor, and knelt on his shoulders. Emile began to scream against the gag, but it came out as muffled bleats. His bound legs kicked upward, and the man pressed harder on his shoulders until he was still.

After a while Ezili got up, wiping her mouth delicately. "Show him a good time, little girl."

Jane moved to Emile and knelt beside him. Her Master had already explained wordlessly what was required of her. It wasn't too much to ask. He wanted to know how it would feel; her only mission in life was to show him. She pulled up her dress and casually ripped away her underpants.

The horror in Emile's eyes fed her sensation as she straddled his body and lowered herself onto him. He stiffened and she heard him grunt in pain. Water poured down on him in rhythmic splashes. More sensation. She gave herself over to it, letting her consciousness dissolve so that it, too, was like fluid. Somewhere lost in the pleasure was the little tiny Jane screaming against this atrocity, but little tiny Jane didn't count for much in the face of this magnificent pleasure-power. What had to be sacrificed for Ti Malice's enjoyment would be; if Emile could have known, he might have offered himself up willingly. It was more than an honor. It was a blessing; it was a state of grace. It was—

Her eyes met Emile's. Motionless and stiff beneath her, he was staring at Ti Malice. The waves of pleasure parted suddenly, and for a moment there was a small rift between her and her Master. She opened her mouth to scream, and then the waves crashed together again and she fell forward. Water poured over her and Emile in a small flood.

Ti Malice was talking to her as he rifled through her sensations and thoughts. He laughed at the memory of the clinic and Dr. Tachyon (*No, little mount, there is no drug that could go directly to the pleasure place, as you call it*) and took special note of the information about the contagious virus (*You would never expose me to that, little mount, you will give your life before you allow that to happen to me*). Even as her body moved and twisted and reveled, she worshiped the thing at her neck, promising everything to it, offering everything she had. *Whatever. Always.*

She felt him bring her up to full awareness to concentrate on Emile.

Whatever. Always. He had her bring tears to Emile's eyes, and together they watched as he struggled, trying to blink them away. Her Master found the calling of the water a wonderful sensation and wanted more. She did more, calling the water only from his body and not out of the air around him, because her Master liked it so much. He made another suggestion, and pleasure surged anew as Emile bucked beneath her, the involuntary action turning quickly to pain for him. If he only knew what his body was serving, she thought.

The power seemed easier to wield now than it ever had before. Because she was whole again, she thought, watching with Ti Malice's pleasure as the blood swelled from Emile's pores and he screamed against the gag. She had never realized how good it felt to do that, to call the moisture from a living being instead of the lifeless air. If she really let herself go with it, it was better than anything, even better than the sex Ti Malice enjoyed so much.

And at last the permission was given and she did let herself go with it, all the way to finality. *Whatever. Always.*

It was an explosion that went beyond pleasure, into something that was completely alien, a ripping away of whatever humanity had been left to her and Ti Malice, leaving the hard, bright, burning thing that had thrust itself upon them in an act of irrevocable conquest. For one single eternal instant they were purely the living wild card virus, not just living but *sentient*.

Then she was herself again, watching through a haze of dying sensation as Ti Malice himself trembled under this new awareness. This had almost been too much even for him. She cold not even raise a protest as he left her for Ezili again.

A little later she realized she had been blinded by the last of the fluids she had called out of Emile's body, and there were only his clothes and some substance that looked like a spill of powder on the floor where he had been.

She took a long fall into blackness, screaming all the way down.

Faces came out of the darkness at her; she made them fade away. At some point she was looking at Hiram's face, and try as she would, she couldn't make him vanish. He seemed to be trying to explain something to her, but none of it made any sense. *I quit*, she told him at last, and that finally made him go.

Clean her up, get her some clothes, and get her out of here. For now, said Ezili in her own voice. *She makes me . . . uncomfortable.* Laughter.

Then the craving hit her and the lack of Ti Malice was too much to bear. Her mind folded itself up into a tiny little box and flushed itself away.

She was walking through a bizarre, wasted wonderland and Sal was at her side. She was only mildly surprised that he was there with her; she thought it might have been because Ti Malice had left her with so little that she wasn't completely in existence anymore. But it was nice that of all the ghosts she could have run into, she had somehow met up with Sal. Meeting Emile would have been terribly unpleasant; perhaps he hadn't been dead long enough to have become a ghost yet.

She covered everything that had happened within the

first few minutes they were together, all the degradation, the lies, the broken promises.

Sal asked her what broken promises those were.

Why, that I was done leaning on anyone, Sal. Remember? I promised that after the Cloisters. And now look at me. I'm leaning so hard I'm tipped over. Then she realized he'd known and he'd just wanted her to say it, to admit it.

All right. I admit it. I admit it all. I said I'd never kill anyone again, no matter how bad they were, even if it meant they'd kill me first. And I killed Emile because he wanted to watch how he'd die. She didn't have to explain who *he* was; Sal knew that, too.

And I always promised I'd be . . . responsible with my body. Maybe it was easier to lock myself up than finally accept that we would never be together.

Sal thought that was kind of funny. After all, he wasn't just gay, he was gay and *dead*; been that way for quite some time, too.

Well, Sal, being dead, you wouldn't have any idea how easy it can be to remain faithful to someone's memory. It's real easy when you're too scared to face a living person. Live men are real intimidating, Sal.

Sal said he knew what she meant.

Yeah, I guess you would, wouldn't you. I guess it's kind of a funny coincidence, then, that the first time I'd be with a woman, and then the first man I ever really had would also be gay.

Sal said he didn't see what that had to do with anything.

Well, it's like a recurring theme.

Sal said he still couldn't see it.

Never mind. I'm just glad now that you didn't live to see what I've come to. That's something you missed by drowning in the bathtub, Sal, that and the big AIDS epidemic. I mean, if you really had to go and die, drowning was the better way. You wouldn't want to die of AIDS. Or of me.

Sal said he'd never been *that* paranoid.

Well, there's plenty to be paranoid about these days. I found out there's a contagious form of the wild card virus. No one knows how it's being transmitted. And most people die from it.

Sal said that certainly was a revolting development.

Yes, it certainly is. And you know what else, Sal?

Sal asked her what that was.

There's no way to tell if you've been exposed. Till it happens. Maybe I've been exposed. Maybe I'll get it and die. I just hope I can't give it to anyone else.

"Honey, you're not the only one."

Jane was about to answer when she realized she had heard Sal's voice for real. But it didn't sound very much like Sal. She turned to him in surprise and found it hadn't been Sal beside her after all but some stranger, a skinny man with a ratlike face, down to the mangy fur covering his cheeks, the pointed nose, and the whiskers.

"It's a mouse face, lady, not a rat face," the man said wearily. "You can tell by the teeth, if you know anything about rodents. I used to be an exterminator, okay? Gimme a hard time about it, why doncha. I tagged along with you to see what a little piece of chicken could want wandering around in Jokertown at this hour of the night. Frankly, lady, you got a lot more problems than I have, and I don't want none of them."

He was gone and she was standing in the middle of a sidewalk under a buzzing streetlamp.

"Sal?" she asked the air. There was no answer.

At first she'd been afraid she'd come back to the same bar, but then she saw it was different. No stage set up for a live sex show, for one thing, and the clientele was a lot livelier, more brightly dressed, some of them even in costumes and masks.

When she saw the eyeless man behind the bar, she panicked, and then she realized it couldn't be the same one she'd taken into the limousine. When had that been? At least a thousand years ago. Like a sleepwalker she moved to the bar and took one of the high stools. The eyeless bartender, working expertly, suddenly straightened up and turned his face in her direction.

"Trouble, Sascha?" A dwarf materialized at her side and clamped one thick hand on her arm.

The bartender backed away. "I don't want to be near her. Get her away from me."

"Come on, honey. You don't have to go home, but you can't stay here." The dwarf started to pull her off the stool.

"No, please," she said, trying to twist her arm out of his grasp. "I have to see someone." She knew where she was now and it was the only place she could have come to find what she needed; Chrysalis or someone around Chrysalis would know where she could get a drug that would fill in the void Ti Malice had eaten away in her. She turned to look at the bartender. "Please, I'm not going to hurt anyone—"

"Get her out," the bartender said urgently. "I can't stand the way she feels."

Jane looked around wildly and then spotted Chrysalis at a corner table. She gave a mighty tug and slipped out of the dwarf's grip.

"Hey!" he yelled.

Ignoring the stares of the other patrons, she darted between the tables to the corner where Chrysalis was sitting, watching with those strange, floating blue eyes.

"Gotcha!" The dwarf seized her around the waist, and she fell to her knees, crawling the last few feet to Chrysalis's chair, dragging the man with her.

Chrysalis lifted a finger. The dwarf's arms loosened but he didn't let go of her completely.

"I need information," Jane said in a low voice. "About a drug."

Chrysalis didn't answer. Whatever expression might have been on her peculiar face was impossible to read.

"I've been addicted to something against my will. I need—I need—" She dug in her pants pocket and miraculously there was money there, a small, flat fold of bills. Hurriedly she unfolded them and held them out. "I can pay, I can pay for—"

Chrysalis flicked briefly at the bills Jane was thrusting at her. Jane looked; there were three bills, two tens and a twenty. Forty dollars. Bad joke.

Chrysalis shook her head and waved a hand.

"Like I said, honey," the dwarf said, "you were just leaving."

She leaned against the side of the building with the bills crumpled in her hand. The void in her widened until she thought the craving had to split her open right there.

"Excuse me."

Kim Toy.

She blinked and then realized it wasn't Kim Toy after all. This woman was younger and taller and her features were different.

"I saw Chrysalis give you the bum's rush. Some nerve she's got, huh. The twerp took you by my table, and I couldn't help thinking I knew you from somewhere."

Jane turned away from her. "Leave me alone," she muttered, but the woman moved closer.

"Like, I think you used to work for Rosemary Muldoon. Didn't you?"

Jane stumbled away from the woman and then fell to her hands and knees, shaking all over. Underneath the ache she felt something else, a sickness that was more physical. As if she were coming down with the flu or something worse. The idea was so absurd she could almost have laughed.

"Hey, are you sick or something?" The woman bent down, putting concerned hands on her shoulders. "You strung out?" she asked in a low voice.

Jane could feel herself weeping without tears.

"Come on," said the woman, helping Jane to her feet. "Any friend of Rosemary Muldoon's is a friend of mine. I think I can help you out."

In spite of the hollowness eating away at her, Jane was overwhelmed by the luxurious apartment. The sunken living room was as large as a ballroom. The predominant color was a delicate, pearlized pink, even to the silk wallpaper and the enormous crystal chandelier.

The woman led her down the steps and sat her on an overstuffed sofa. "It's something, isn't it? Looks like a dump on the outside and heaven on the inside. Had to grease a lot of palms to keep the CONDEMNED sign out front. Just finished the place last week, and I've been dying to entertain. What are you drinking?"

"Water," Jane said weakly.

Across the room, at the ornate wet bar, the woman looked over her shoulder with a near smile. "Thought *you* could get your own."

Jane stiffened. "You—you know—?"

"Didn't I say I knew you? You think I'd really bring anyone here I wasn't sure of?" The woman brought her a cut-glass goblet of ice water and sat down next to her. "Of course, it isn't *all* mine. It really belongs to the people I work for. Best job I ever had, needless to say."

Jane sipped her water. Her hands began to shake

uncontrollably, and she handed the goblet to the woman before she could spill it. The physical illness was crawling over her again, like a cramp, except it was all over her body. She held very still until it subsided.

"Whatever you've got, I hope it isn't catching," the woman said, not unkindly. "What happened—you fall in with one of those sleaze-bags around Rosemary and get turned on to junk?"

Jane shook her head. "Not Rosemary."

"Oh? That's too bad. I mean, I was sort of hoping you were still in touch with Rosemary because I'd like to see her again." She leaned over to open a pink laquered box on the oversize coffee table. "Joint? It'll take the edge off. It really will. This is like nothing you've ever had before."

"No, it isn't," Jane said, looking away from the proffered joint.

"What *are* you on, anyway?"

"It's something that goes straight to the pleasure center of the brain. You don't want to know." Or perhaps she would, Jane thought suddenly. Her thoughts began to coil toward a plan. What if she could get this woman to go back to the apartment with her and offered her to Ti Malice? He loved new mounts, she knew that . . .

"Oh, that's easy," the woman said.

"What?" Jane looked at her, startled.

The woman tilted her head to one side, eyeing her curiously. "I've got an associate who's developed something that'll go straight for the pleasure center of the brain."

"Who is it?" Jane said, grabbing the woman's shoulder. "Can I meet him? Where can I find him? How—"

"Whoa, whoa now. Slow down." The woman plucked Jane's hand off herself and moved away slightly. "This is top secret stuff. Stupid of me to mention it, but you being a friend of Rosemary's and all, I kind of forgot myself. Come on. Mellow out and let's talk about Rosemary." She lit the joint with a crystal table lighter, took a deep drag, and offered it to Jane.

She accepted the joint and tried to do exactly as she'd seen the woman do. The smoke burned in her lungs, and she coughed it out.

"Keep practicing," the woman said, laughing a little. "It'll really take the edge off."

A few drags later she had gotten more than just the hang of it. So this was what they meant by getting a buzz on, she thought. It was a buzz you felt rather than heard, and it would have been pleasant, except that it couldn't get between herself and the gnawing void. She tried to give the joint back to the woman, but she told Jane to keep at it, she needed it more. Instead she put it out carefully in the cut-glass ashtray on the table.

"Don't like it?" the woman said in surprise.

"It's . . . okay," Jane said, and her voice seemed to stretch out and out and out like long, slow elastic. Her head felt ready to float off her shoulders like a helium balloon and rise up to the ceiling. She wondered if Hiram knew about this.

But the woman wanted to talk about Rosemary, and between trying to keep her head on her shoulders and fighting against the need for Ti Malice, it was hard to keep track of what she was saying. If the woman would just shut up, she might achieve some kind of equilibrium, something that would steady her long enough to break the water glass on the table and use one of the shards on her throat. That was the only answer now; the dope was helping her see that. She would never be free of the need for Ti Malice, and if she went back—*when* she went back—she could only look forward to worse things, more degradation, more killings, all done willingly, just to feel the bliss of his presence within her. All the things she had wished for Hiram, that he would find someone to make his life complete, she had inadvertently gotten for herself, except it was Ti Malice instead of the vague, unidentifiable man she had always dreamed of, who had sometimes resembled Sal and sometimes Jumpin' Jack Flash and sometimes even Croyd. Another bad joke in an ongoing series. It had to end.

The woman kept on talking and talking. Occasionally there were long periods of silence, and Jane came out of her fog to find that the woman was no longer on the couch with her. She would lie back against the cushion, glad of the silence, and then the woman would magically rematerialize next to her, going on and on and on about Rosemary Muldoon until she thought she might cut her throat just to get away from that voice.

But that was awfully ungrateful. The woman was just

trying to help her. She knew that. She should do something in return. Offer her something.

Rosemary's phone number swam to the surface of her mind and waited for her to pick it up. And after a while she did, and the woman disappeared for the longest time ever.

Someone was shaking her awake. The first thing that hit her was the *need,* and she doubled over, beating her fist on the couch cushion because it wasn't Ti Malice there but a slender Oriental man kneeling on the carpet next to her, smiling polite concern at her.

"This is the associate I was telling you about," the woman said, pulling her to a sitting position. "Roll up your sleeve."

"What? Why?" Jane looked around, but the room wouldn't come clear yet. Her head felt heavy and thick.

"Just my way of saying thanks."

"For what?" She felt her sleeve being pushed up and something cold and wet on the inside of her arm.

"For Rosemary's phone number."

"You called her?"

"Oh, no. You're going to do that for me." The woman tied a piece of rubber around Jane's upper arm and pulled it tight. "And in return, you get a trip to heaven."

The Oriental man held up a syringe and grinned as though he were a game show host showing off a prize.

"But—"

The woman was shoving a cordless receiver into her hand. "You'd like to see her again, wouldn't you?"

Jane let the phone drop to her lap and wiped her face tiredly. "I'm not so sure, really."

"Then maybe you'd better *get* sure." The woman's voice hardened. Jane looked up at her in surprise. "I mean, *I'm* sure. I have a lot to talk about with Rosemary. The sooner you contact her, the sooner you go to heaven. You want to go to heaven, don't you?"

"I don't know if I can—I don't know if she'll even take my call—"

The woman leaned down and spoke directly into her face. "I don't see where you've got a choice. You're strung out and you've got nowhere to go. I can't let you stay here indefinitely, you know. The company that owns this place might not want me to have a roommate. Of course, they'd feel differently if you did something for me."

Jane drew back a little. "Who do you work for?"

"Don't be so nosy. Just make the call. Get her to meet you here, if possible, anywhere else if necessary."

She was about to say no when the craving gnawed at her again, shutting off the word in her throat. "This drug," she said, looking at the syringe. "It's—good?"

"The best." The woman's face was expressionless. "You want me to dial?"

"No," she said, picking up the phone. "I'll do it."

The man put the point of the needle to the inside of her elbow and then held it there, waiting, still wearing his wide, game-show-host grin.

She could hardly keep her mind on Rosemary's voice; there was no way she could keep her own voice steady. At first she tried to sound friendly, but Rosemary got it out of her that she was in trouble. The man and the woman didn't seem to mind what she said, so she plunged on, begging Rosemary to come to her.

But maddeningly, Rosemary kept telling her she would send someone to pick her up, and she had to insist over and over that *that* wouldn't do at all, she didn't want anyone but Rosemary. Nobody else, especially no men. She would run away if she saw any men. This seemed to please the man and the woman a great deal.

And at last she got Rosemary's consent and read the address to her off a card the woman held in front of her. Rosemary hesitated, but she pleaded again, and Rosemary gave in. But not there, not at that address. Someplace out in the open. Sheridan Square. A glance told Jane that would be fine with her new friends, and she told Rosemary she would be there.

"Once a social worker, always a social worker," the woman said, hanging up the phone. She nodded at the man. "Give it to her."

"Wait," Jane said weakly. "How can I get there if—"

"Don't worry about a thing," said the woman. "You'll be there."

The needle went in and the lights went out.

The lights came up dimly and she saw she was leaning against the side of a building. It was the Ridiculous Theatre

Company, and she was waiting to get in to see a play. Late
performance, very late, but she didn't care. She loved the
Ridiculous Theatre Company best and she'd been to lots of
theatres, the small ones in Soho and the Village and the
Jokertown Playhouse, which had closed down shortly before
she'd gone to work for Rosemary...

Rosemary. There was something she had to remember
about Rosemary. Rosemary had betrayed her trust. But perhaps that was only fair, since she was such a great disappointment to Hiram—

It hit her so powerfully she thought it had to knock her
down, but her body didn't move. Warm maple syrup was
running through her veins. But underneath the warmth and
the languor the void remained, wide open, eating away at
her, and whatever this lassitude was only made it possible for
the wanting to crunch at her bones without a struggle. Her
stomach did a slow forward roll and her head began to pound.

A shadow by her feet chittered softly. She looked down. A
squirrel was staring up at her as if it were actually considering
her in some way. Squirrels were just rats with fancier tails,
she remembered uneasily, and tried to edge away from it, but
her body still wasn't moving. Another squirrel chittered
somewhere above her head, and something else ran past,
almost brushing her legs.

When was the theatre going to open so she could get away
from all this vermin? Sheridan Square had gotten really bad
since she'd last been there, to see the late Charles Ludlam in
a revival of *Bluebeard*. Charles Ludlam—she'd loved him,
too, and it had been so unfair that he'd had to die of
AIDS....

She sighed and a voice said, "Jane?"

Rosemary's voice. She perked up. Had she been going to
the theatre with Rosemary? Or was this just a happy coincidence? No matter, she'd be so happy to see her—

She tried to look around. It was so dark. Was there really
a performance *this* late? And the squirrels, chittering and
chittering to the point of madness—it would have been
exquisite with Ti Malice, but by herself it was only excruciating.

A thin flashlight beam cut through the darkness and she
winced.

"Jane?" Rosemary asked again. She was closer now. "Jane,
you look awful. What happened? Did someone—"

There was the sound of claws scratching on the side of the building. Jane turned in the direction of the sound and saw Rosemary standing a few yards away. The dim illumination from the streetlamps made her little more than a detailed silhouette. Funny, Jane thought suddenly, that the theatre had no outside security lights to discourage burglars or vandals. A darker shadow was flowing back and forth around Rosemary's ankles; it eventually resolved itself into a cat. Rosemary looked down at the cat and then up at Jane again.

"What kind of trouble are you in, Jane?" she asked, and her voice had a slight edge to it.

"The worst," said a man's voice. "Just like you, Miss Muldoon."

Jane shook her head, trying to clear it. Something was coming back to her, something about an Oriental woman who was not Kim Toy, and a man with a needle, and dialing the telephone . . .

A larger shadow swept up behind Rosemary, and suddenly she was standing with an arm around her throat and the barrel of a gun jammed up against the side of her face.

"It is appropriate we meet in the *shadows*," a man's voice said. Rosemary stood perfectly still, staring past Jane. Jane followed her gaze and saw the other man leaning casually at the opposite end of the building with his own pistol up and ready. Jane felt herself starting to nod out and forced herself to hold her head up. Her face felt itchy and uncomfortable and the craving for Ti Malice burst on her with a strength that made her want to double over. But her body could manage no more than a mild spasm. *They lied,* she thought miserably. *The woman and her friend lied. How can people lie so easily?*

There were more people, more men, melting out of the darkness to surround her and Rosemary. Even through the soupy fog that was her mind, Jane could sense the weapons and the malignant intent. The woman who had taken her home had been no friend of Rosemary's, or hers, either. But it was a little late for clever deductions.

"Aren't junkies funny, Ms. Muldoon?" said the man holding Rosemary. "That one sold you out for a mere dime of garden-variety heroin."

No, no, it isn't true! she wanted to scream, but her voice was stuck in the craving. Her eyes had adjusted to the darkness now, and she could see that Rosemary was staring at her with a stricken expression.

"Jane," she said, "if there's anything left of the person you used to be, you could turn this around—"

"N-not . . . junkie," Jane said heavily. Her eyes began to roll up.

"Hopheads don't make great aces," the man said with a laugh. "She's not about to—" There was the sound of wings and something whirred out of the night, fluttering and flapping directly onto his head.

"Hey!" he yelled, letting go of Rosemary, who pushed away from him. She tripped and went down on her hands and knees just as several other things raced past Jane, parted themselves fluidly around Rosemary, and launched themselves at the men.

"Bagabond—" Rosemary said breathlessly, and then there was an explosion of angry cries and wails, both human and not. The man who had been standing so insouciantly at the other end of the building was now batting at a pigeon flapping around his head while he tried to kick something loose from his pant leg. Rat, Jane realized dully. She had never seen a rat so bold.

Rosemary had gotten to her feet and was backing away from the embattled group of men. More shapes of various sizes were streaking out of the night to throw themselves onto the men, hissing, screeching, howling with unmistakable anger. Someone tore himself loose from the group and ran past Rosemary and Jane, screaming as he tried to shake the rat off his arm and pull the squirrel away from his neck. Something clattered at Jane's feet, and she looked down at it: a gun.

Her legs gave out and she slid down the building onto her knees. She picked the gun up and stared at it for a moment. Then Rosemary was shaking her.

"Come *on*," she said, pulling Jane to her feet and forcing her to run along the walk in front of the theatre, out to the sidewalk on the other side of Sheridan Square.

Several large stray dogs were waiting for them in a strange, loose formation. Jane blinked at them groggily, barely aware of Rosemary's arms around her. After a moment the dogs broke and ran back the way she and Rosemary had come. The shouts of the men turned to screams over the sounds of growling and baying.

Jane staggered along the street, still in Rosemary's grasp. "Goddamn you, *run*," Rosemary said close to her ear. On the edge of consciousness, she stumbled along until the awful noise began to fade behind them. The absence of Ti Malice was gaining on her again, countering the drug in her system, making each step more painful than the last as it brought her back into full awareness.

She gave Rosemary a mighty shove and broke away from her, staggering up against a lightpole. Catching herself, she looked around; the streets were deserted except for the two of them.

"Jane," Rosemary said tensely. "I'll take you somewhere you'll be safe. And then you can explain—"

"Stay away from me!" she shouted, raising her hand. Rosemary backed off quickly and she saw why; she still had the gun and she was pointing it at the other woman. Her first impulse was to toss it away and tell Rosemary she meant her no harm, she'd been tricked and she hadn't even realized she'd been holding a gun. But it didn't matter whether she meant Rosemary any harm or not—anyone around her would be in terrible danger for as long as she lived.

"*You* get out of here, Rosemary," she said shakily, keeping the gun on her. "*You* go someplace you'll be safe, and you thank God there still is such a place for you. Because there's no place like that for me anymore!"

Rosemary opened her mouth to say something, and Jane thrust her gun hand forward.

"Go on!"

Rosemary backed away a few steps, then turned and broke into a run.

Still hanging on the lamppost as if she were some kind of comical, innocent drunk, Jane studied the gun in her hand. She didn't know anything about guns except for what was generally known. But that would be enough.

You just put it in your mouth. Aim the barrel toward the top of your head and count to three and you'll be free. Nothing could be easier.

Her hand turned very slowly, as if there was still some reluctance somewhere in her.

Unless, of course, you want to walk around like this for

the next forty or so years. The craving flared in her and her hand moved quickly. *Barrel in the mouth. Just turn it around so the trigger faces the sky.* The metal tasted sour and made her lower teeth ache. She swallowed openmouthed and took a firmer grip on the gun.

Count to three and you'll be free. She remembered how it felt the first time Ti Malice had climbed onto her back, the way his small hands had touched her, eager, greedy, confident. She must have looked at Hiram the way Rosemary had been looking at her. (A spasm of shuddering swept over her, the strange, physical sickness she'd been feeling, but she managed to keep the gun in place.)

Count to three and you'll be free. She remembered the feel of Ezili's skin and the taste of her. Ezili would have enjoyed the sight of her standing on a deserted street with a gun in her mouth. (Now there was a prickly sensation crawling over her shoulders and down her arms, her torso, her legs, as though a small fire had broken out in her skin.)

Count to three and you'll be free. She remembered Croyd; she remembered walking with Sal only to have him turn into a man with a mouse's head. It was Sal she was a great disappointment to, not Hiram Worchester. Sal had believed in what she was. Hiram had never really known her. (Her flesh began to simmer.)

Count to three and you'll be free. She remembered that none of it would matter if someone would bring Ti Malice to her right now, right this very second, and set him on her shoulders. She would toss the gun away and welcome his blissful presence inside of her, and he would make all of it unimportant in the universe of pleasure that he could pour into the void widening in her even as she stood there, feeling the hardness of the pistol against the roof of her mouth. (She was broiling alive now.)

Count to three and you'll be free. A small movement caught her eye; on the curb a squirrel was staring up at her with bright, curious little eyes. She swallowed openmouthed again and counted without hurrying.

One. Two. Three.

Her fingers squeezed the trigger. Absurdly, Sal's voice spoke in her mind. *Hey, cara mia,* now *what the hell you doin'?*

In the total silence of the street the click was deafening.

Misfire.

She sank down to the pavement, and the warm dark tide of the fever covered her over.

She was in a soft realm of many colors. They came and went, conversing in human voices, sometimes speaking directly to her. She couldn't answer; this wasn't her realm, she was just waiting here. Besides, they said such funny things. Things like, *The coma is unmistakable, it doesn't happen that way to all of them, but when it does, we know what it is,* and *Why don't we just put her in a bathtub and be done with it. The way the water's pouring off her, her skin will rot before she has a chance to die,* and oddest of all, *Jane, why couldn't I have helped. I should not have let my fatigue cause me to fail you.* That was the brightest color, an extraordinary shade of red, sometimes with bright yellow accents.

A little later all the colors went away (*Unplug the machines and get them out of here, she's not going to wake up*), and there was only peace for a while. Then, somewhere far away, a phone rang. It's for you, someone said, and she imagined that meant her.

Jane. It's time.

She roused to a strange, soft awareness that reminded her of a lucid dream. The voice that had spoken sounded familiar. That you, Sal? I've been looking all over for you. Where are you?

Never mind that now. It's time.

Time for what, Sal?

Time for you to get up. There's something very important you have to do. Come on now, open your eyes and get out of bed.

She sat up, looking around. Tachyon's clinic; how had she ended up back here? she wondered.

Don't worry about that. You have to hurry.

All right, Sal.

She slipped out of bed and padded across the room to the door barefoot. Just at the doorway she turned to look back at the bed. There was a pale shape on the mattress, slowly fading away like trick photography.

Was that me, Sal?

It was you. It isn't you anymore. Go down the hall. Quickly now, there's no time to lose.

She seemed to float down the hall, her bare toes just a few inches above the cold floor. It was a great way to travel, she thought. Being dead had a lot to recommend it in the comfort department.

You're not dead.

She accepted that with equanimity. It didn't seem to be worth arguing about.

This door. On your right. Go into that room.

She wafted into the room and hovered next to one of the two beds, looking down at the occupant. Once she might have found his appearance frightening and pitiable. Now she looked down at him with complete and rational calm, taking in the sight of the enormous head on the pillow, cratered like the moon, except each crater was filled with an eye, most of them open. They watched her just as calmly, or so it seemed.

A small hole near one of the craters opened, and she heard a whistle of breath. "Who are you? Are you a doctor?"

Listen very carefully, because I have to leave now and you must remember this.

She felt a small pang of fear. *Leaving me again? Do you have to?*

Yes. But I am leaving you with a gift. It's a very important gift. It's a gift that Croyd gave you.

What is it?

You'll find out.

Something in the soft air around her changed, and she knew she was alone with the joker.

Acting without her volition, her hand pulled the sheet back, exposing the rest of the joker's body, which was cratered with more eyes, almost all over. They seemed to be forming as she watched. She would have to work fast so as not to hurt him.

She climbed onto the mattress next to him and smiled. One area, fortunately, had been spared so far, and it was there that she began, moving with gentleness.

"Lady, what the hell are you doing?"

She couldn't answer him, but it wasn't necessary. Certainly he could see very well what she was doing.

"Hammond. Hey, Hammond! Wake up! Tell me this isn't a dream!"

She ignored the sounds from the next bed, ignored everything except the task at hand, except *task* was entirely the wrong word for it. Loving someone was not a *task*. Loving someone could perform miracles.

She felt his hands moving carefully on her, felt him quiver with pain. The eyes. How they all must hurt when anything touches him, she thought, and wondered who had been so thoughtless as to cover him with a sheet. Perhaps they'd just been waiting for him to die; this was the terminal ward, after all.

"Don't worry," she told him. "I'll do it all."

"Do anything you like!" he said, and groaned with enjoyment as he felt her enfold him.

It was different when it was love, she thought happily. When it was love, there was no pain, no shame; of course. When it was love, you wanted to heal the other person of all hurts. And when it was love, that was really possible.

She smoothed her hands over his chest and laid her head down on it to listen to his heartbeat. His arms went around her, and she could feel the new strength in them as they rocked together. Next to this, Ti Malice was a sad, sorry imitation of a kiss.

And with that thought, she realized that the terrible void within her had vanished and she was free. She rose up and gave a shout of joy.

A roomful of voices answered her.

It was like a switch being thrown—suddenly she was awake, *really* awake, and she realized she was straddling a man in a hospital bed, a perfectly normal man with two, only two, green eyes, and sandy hair, who was looking up at her with a beatific smile on his young, plain face.

"Lady," he said, "*this* is what I call *medication!*"

She twisted around and saw that the room behind her was filled with jokers of every variety, and among them, forcibly restrained, were two nurses and a doctor.

They broke loose from their captors and rushed the bed, pulling her off and examining the man.

"I saw it, but I don't believe it!"

"Right before my very eyes—"

"I thought this one was already dead—"

"Who are you? What room are you in?"

She backed away from their questions, into the waiting arms of the jokers. A misshapen man whose features had been scrambled thrust his distorted face into hers and demanded, "Can I be next?"

"No, *me!*" shouted someone else, and then hands were grabbing at her, pulling her every which way, trying to throw her down on the floor.

"*SAL!*" she screamed.

The room was suddenly filled with fog, and then a wall of water crashed through the door, slapping them all down. Jane let it carry her across the room, onto the ex-joker's bed. She rolled into the headboard and slipped down to the floor. More fog poured into the room as she crawled around the confused, shouting, drenched mob splashing about in the ankle-deep water, and she fled through the open doorway.

By the time the alarms went off, she had already left the building.

The luncheonette was a far cry from Aces High, and the clientele didn't tip nearly as well, but they didn't expect a whole lot. Most of them hardly looked at her—a waitress with a short, punkish haircut and an ill-fitting, baggy white uniform wasn't especially noteworthy in that part of town. The owner was a big motherly woman named Giselle who called her Lamb and asked nothing more of her help than their being on time and trying to remember any good jokes they overheard from the customers. Giselle collected jokes, and the regulars were always happy to supply them.

Like the two-headed man who came in every Monday, Wednesday, and Thursday morning for a bacon-and-egg sandwich. He/they always had a new one to offer.

"Hey, have you heard the latest?" he/they said as she was setting the dish down in front of him/them. "There's good news and there's better news."

She smiled at each head politely. The two-headed man was one/two of the better tippers.

"The good news is, there's this woman that can turn you back into a nat by screwing you!"

Her smile froze, but he/they didn't seem to notice.

"You know what the *better* news is?"

She shook her head, unable to speak.

"She's really good-looking!" Both heads roared with laughter, accidently bonking into each other. She tried to laugh with them, but she couldn't manage even a mild ha-ha-ha.

The heads sobered and looked up at her, slightly disappointed in her lack of reaction. "Hey, we guess you gotta be a joker—"

"—to really appreciate it," finished the other head, and giggled a little more.

"It's—it's very good, really," she said in a too-cheery voice. "I'll have to remember to tell it to Giselle when she comes in. I don't think she's heard it yet."

"Well, don't forget—"

"—to tell her where—"

"—you heard it first!"

"I won't," she said, still smiling her frozen smile at each head. "I won't forget. I promise."

Takedown

by Leanne C. Harper

Rosemary stared out into the spring rain. Gray and dirty, outside it looked more like winter. Chris Mazzucchelli droned on in the background. Christ, how had she ever gotten involved with a jerk like him? Living underground with him had shown her the difference between dealing with Chris on an occasional basis and being together nearly twenty-four hours a day. He was no longer a romantic rebel in her eyes; he was a vicious punk. The problem was he was *her* vicious punk.

She returned her attention to the crisis at hand, but her eyes were immediately caught by the sight of Chris's rattail bouncing up and down on his back as he paced the dingy little Alphabet City hotel room they were using as a safe house.

"We lost eight capos to this double cross. Fiore, Baldacci, Schiaparelli, Hancock, and *my brother*. Dead. Vince Schiaparelli looked like he had been turned inside out. Fiore's skin turned into stone and he choked to death. Hancock and Baldacci weren't there anymore—just puddles with bones sticking out. My brother—" Here even he gagged and hesitated. "Three more, worse than dead. Matriona and Cheng walked away. They're fine, just *fine*. Since then we've been able to do nothing more than stay even, if that."

"And what did we get? Siu Ma. We already knew about her. We've tried to kidnap her twice, for Christ's sake. We know who's behind the Immaculate Egrets. But we still don't know who the ultimate leader is." Rosemary Gambione shook her head. "Even if Croyd knew something truly useful, they didn't get it out of him. Great. The Shadow Fists must have gotten to him. *We* hit a few more Shadow Fist operations, lose some more of our people, and we're just as far away as ever. Even worse, they've started using some kind of biological warfare against us. I wonder whose side this Croyd is really on."

"Well, O fearless leader, any ideas? I've done everything I can think of." Chris spun on her, anger and fear mixed evenly on his face. "And do me a favor, don't bring up your fucking father again. I've had about all I can take of that, too."

"Find your informer, this Croyd. Maybe he does have something more. Let's try to find out how the Shadow Fists got hold of this wild card virus they used. If they have it, we need it." Rosemary thought but did not voice her apprehension that if the Families were this far behind, they had already lost the war. She was the sole surviving don. The Shadow Fists had gotten all the others. This war had begun to feel like Vietnam, and they weren't on the right side.

"I'll do what I can. By this time he's probably in Outer fucking Mongolia." Chris looked unimpressed by her request.

"Chris. Get him." Rosemary used the drill sergeant tone deliberately. She suspected that he did not always follow her orders. She wondered at the speed with which the papers had gotten hold of her true background and whether the source could have been within the Family. Mazzucchelli looked back at her with swiftly concealed loathing.

"Anything you say. Dear." Chris stalked across the room before turning back at the door. "By the way, you might find it amusing that our boy Bludgeon apparently beat the shit out of Sewer Jack Robicheaux a few nights ago. He found out that Jack turned us down, I guess, and took it upon himself to teach the dirty little Cajun a lesson in manners. I gave him a little bonus for the job, in your name, of course."

Rosemary sat on the bed. It wasn't supposed to be this way. She was completely isolated from her people. Chris told her it was the only way to guarantee her security, but the situation was getting to her. She looked across the room to the door. She didn't feel like an all-powerful Mafia don. She felt like a prisoner.

Bagabond let herself into C.C. Ryder's loft expecting that C.C. would be in the studio. Instead, Cordelia was bothering C.C. again. She wondered what Cordelia wanted this time. Bagabond had had to dodge around even more people wearing the useless surgical masks. She had no sympathy for those panicked by this new outbreak of the wild card virus. Maybe it would do them some good. Paced by the ginger cat, Bagabond walked over to the couch and sat down on the floor beside C.C. The ginger put her head in Bagabond's lap. Both women nodded to her before continuing their discussion.

"There's something weird about that Shrike. I can feel it." Cordelia leaned forward to make her point. "And what they're doin' to Buddy just isn't right. He wrote those songs!"

"Cordelia, Shrike Music is a perfectly legitimate business. I know people who record for them. They're good business people. If Holley gave up the rights to his songs, that was his decision to make." C.C. shook her head wearily. "This business is full of trade-offs. That's the way it works. You know that by now. Buddy's got his new songs. They're good. Let it be."

"But I can tell by talking to Buddy that it wasn't his decision. He jus' won't tell me what happened." Cordelia got that look on her face that told Bagabond that she was not about to give up. Bagabond got up and went into the kitchen. Cordelia's obsession with saving the world reminded her uncomfortably of some of the younger nuns she'd met as a child. They had all wanted to be saints, real ones.

"The old-timers got ripped off. Look at Little Richard. It wasn't right; it wasn't fair. But it was legal. You can't do anything about that. Buddy has other preoccupations now. The concert went fine. Leave it."

"But you saw him a few weeks ago. Playing in a Holiday Inn in New Jersey! Somebody has to help him, and I'm going to do it." Cordelia's eyes shone with the fervor of the converted.

"Let Buddy get on with his life."

"Hey, it's not even my idea dis time. They want to see *me*." Cordelia waved her hands innocently in the air.

C.C. shook her head in resignation. "So what's this great plan of yours?"

Bagabond hacked off a chunk of cheddar cheese for herself and another for the cat. Nibbling at hers, she walked back into the living room.

"I have an appointment to meet a Shrike exec tomorrow. I put him off until well after the concert." Cordelia scooted down on the couch and put her arms around her knees. "And I need to know what to ask him."

"Me." C.C. sighed and reached down for a bite of Bagabond's cheese.

"Right. You. My expert on recording contracts." Cordelia bounced once in triumph and grinned over at C.C. "I want to see the original contracts, right?"

"I *guarantee* you that they are not going to let you see Holley's contract."

"I'll find a way." Cordelia grinned unself-consciously. "Woo, hey, I gotta go."

Cordelia was up and headed for the door. "I see you two later. Bye, y'all."

Chris Mazzucchelli burst into the room to face Rosemary's drawn Walther. He waved both hands in the air languidly, then dropped them and threw himself down on the bed.

"Put that silly thing away before you shoot yourself. Jesus Christ, woman."

"I haven't seen you for days. Where the hell have you been?" Rosemary lowered the pistol but did not holster it.

"I've been a good little boy. I've been out finding Croyd just like you wanted." Chris rolled over onto his elbows. "I've got an address all ready for you."

"Don't be ridiculous, Chris. I'm not leaving this room." Rosemary sat down on a chair across the narrow room from Chris. "It's too dangerous."

"Maybe if you exposed yourself to a little 'danger,' you'd get some idea what we're up against. You sure as hell don't know anything now." Chris sat all the way up on the bed. "Or is that more than your heart would take? Your *father* would never be caught dead hiding his face like this."

"All right." Rosemary knew she was being baited, but the question was whether Chris had the guts to kill her. "Where?"

"In Jokertown, in a hotel near the docks." Chris smiled openly in triumph. "Fitting, don't you think?"

Chris got up and walked over to her. He stroked her cheek. She tensed but did not pull away.

"C'mon, baby, we've got until tomorrow."

It took hours to get rid of him. When he finally left—to

make final preparations for her security, or so he said—she went to the bathroom and pried open the window. With one foot on the sink and the other on the water tank, she levered herself outside onto the fire escape.

Rosemary climbed the fire escape to the roof, silently cursing at the least rusty squeak it gave. On the roof she walked as quietly as possible to a small flock of pigeons cooing on the edge of the building. When they did not fly off at her approach, she scattered some crumbs from the sandwiches she had been eating for weeks.

"Bagabond, help me." She tried to catch the eyes of each pigeon, wondering how long it could carry her image in its tiny brain. There was no other chance. "Bagabond, I need you. Chris is going to kill me."

Bagabond was her last hope. Chris wouldn't dare just shoot her. It would be too obvious to the few mafiosi still loyal to her father and the Gambione name. He had had to find another way. This was it, she could feel it.

Bagabond pulled off her headphones. Something, like a fading echo within her mind, had broken her concentration on C.C.'s newest tapes. She tracked it back through the lines of consciousness that intersected in her mind, identified the medium as a bird's mind, then found the pigeon who carried the vision. Rosemary called to her again out of the pigeon's memory.

Rosemary had given her address. Bagabond knew the area. She sat stroking the ginger's back as she debated meeting Rosemary. She couldn't trust the woman anymore. In the message she had left among the pigeons, Rosemary promised to tell Bagabond who really killed Paul. The Mafia leader sounded sincere, but Bagabond had seen her in action before. She was a lawyer. She was trained to say whatever would best serve her purposes at that moment.

But even Rosemary's training could not hide the fear that was carried by every pigeon she had reached. Rosemary was terrified. Bagabond remembered the first time they had met. The social worker, frightened then but frightened of not being able to help, had done everything she could for the street people. Bagabond remembered Rosemary's teasing questions about her dates with Paul and going shopping together for just the right outfit to impress him. Rosemary had given her back part of her life.

But she had paid that debt. She'd already saved Rosemary's life once when Water Lily had betrayed her. Betrayal. What about Paul? Wasn't helping Rosemary betraying Paul? Bagabond still suspected that Rosemary was more involved in his death than she would admit.

Bagabond stood up and dumped the cat onto the floor. She picked up her old coats and wrapped them around her. If she decided that Rosemary was lying about Paul's death, she had meant too much to her for too long to abandon her now. She turned off the tape deck and amplifier. The green telltales that had illuminated the room dimly faded to black. Bagabond's eyes adjusted almost instantly as she walked unhesitatingly across the loft toward the door and the New York City night.

Down on the street she began gathering her forces. Bagabond contacted the pigeons, the cats and the dogs, and the rarer ones: the pair of peregrine falcons, the wolf who had escaped from his would-be owners, and the ocelot who spent her time prowling the parks for stray dogs. The wild ones listened to her call and were ready to follow her.

Rosemary was north near Jokertown. It would be a long walk to this hotel where she would be meeting someone who planned to harm her. Bagabond slipped into a subway entrance and began working her way through the tunnels toward Jokertown. She had gone almost a mile underground when Jack called.

Jack had been missing since the night of the concert. Cordelia had been concerned, but she had assumed that he was doing what he wanted and had not tried to find him. He and Bagabond continued to avoid each other, and she had not tracked him down either. The strength of his sending was incredible. Bagabond fell to one knee, then collapsed under the weight of it.

She caught snatches of images. It was enough to tell her he was in a hospital. But that was not the message. Jack was cycling through the human-alligator as fast as he could, using the alligator-persona to contact her and the human to communicate. It was Cordelia. She was in trouble. Filtered through Jack's perceptions, Bagabond understood that Cordelia had called for Jack but he was physically unable to help her.

Not only was he switching between alligator and human, he was alternating between consciousness and coma. Jack was expending all the energy he could muster to ask her for help.

Bagabond concentrated. Cordelia's fear resonated through everything Jack sent. Images cascaded through Bagabond's mind. A needle, the pain of an injection. A street empty of pedestrians or traffic. Anonymous buildings. They looked like apartments, but Bagabond did not recognize the neighborhood.

"Where, Jack? Where?" Somewhere else rough concrete cut into her hands and knees. It was to the north, it had to be. She could tell that much from what she had seen of the apartment houses crowded onto hills. With part of her fragmented mind she tried to match what she had seen with the views of the birds and the animals in the north end of Manhattan. Abruptly she lost Jack.

"Jack!" For long seconds he was gone entirely. He was dead to her and she feared that his efforts had been fatal. Then abruptly she was seeing the numbers over the building's front door through Cordelia's eyes. "The street, Cordelia, the street?"

She did not know if Cordelia had heard her or not, but corner street signs appeared. Washington Heights. She also felt the rough hands on her arms and the gun at her head. There was a haze across the images that she recognized. Cordelia had been drugged with something psychoactive and disorienting that would prevent Cordelia from concentrating enough to harm her attackers even if she would betray her principles.

Cordelia's face floated in her mind shaded by both her own memories and Jack's. Cordelia's young enthusiasms and energy, her devotion to life and helping others, pulled Bagabond north toward her. But Cordelia's face was overlaid by Rosemary's. The ginger screamed her empathy with the turmoil in Bagabond's brain.

She had promised to help Rosemary. Cordelia had the ability to help herself, if she would use it. But could she, drugged, and would using it destroy the girl, as Bagabond had been destroyed. Rosemary had killed Paul, or caused his death. Bagabond knew that as well as she knew anything. She had been blinding herself to it because of her overwhelming desire to keep Rosemary as her friend. Rosemary had chosen her path. Cordelia had not had time to choose hers.

The falcons wheeled in midflight and headed north, and the ocelot bounded after them.

Her bodyguards followed Rosemary down the filthy hallway of the flophouse where Croyd was hiding. If Croyd was there at all. Rosemary remembered the men she had seen in prison movies being escorted to their deaths. The two big mafiosi said nothing to her. She didn't even know their names. Chris had told her he would wait outside to keep watch. The walls were mildewed and stained, and the hallway smelled of cigarette smoke and urine. Abruptly the two men stopped. The dark-haired man on her right motioned her forward.

She couldn't tell if Bagabond was there, watching and waiting. Rosemary had come up with a plan to take care of two of her problems. She knew she could convince Bagabond that Paul's death had all been Chris's doing. Bagabond would kill Chris in revenge. With Chris out of the way maybe she could make some kind of deal with the Shadow Fists. Get out alive. Maybe.

Please, God, Bagabond, be here.

Bagabond found one of Jack's underground motorized carts. He had made her memorize the tunnel system underlying the entire island. She silently thanked him as she switched from one passage to another, risking a crash by pushing the cart as fast as it would go. The markings on the walls passed as she sped north. Above her and through the tunnels paralleling her route, her animals kept pace as best they could.

The hawks arrived first and circled the building. Through their eyes Bagabond could see the motions of the men inside. Cordelia was huddled in a corner but still alive. Bagabond tried to send that information to Jack, but she got no response. Ignoring Jack's silence with difficulty, she began setting up her warriors before she arrived.

There was a broken window at the top of the 1940s apartment building. She sent the hawks through it to wait at the top of the stairwell. The ocelot was almost there. She had used roofs as well as streets and had outpaced the others. The wolf was blocks back, trying to avoid being seen. The black and calico she kept with her, but she sent the ginger into the building to be two of her eyes. For the others she called rats from the surrounding buildings. Many waited to be renovated and housed her creatures. As her animals converged, she felt the warmth of her strength build.

By the time she climbed up the stairs of the subway station at Two hundredth, she was in place. She cycled through the consciousnesses of her animals, controlling them and holding them ready, and as she did, she tried to touch Cordelia. The girl was a blank without Jack to amplify her mind. With the part of herself that remained human and aware of why she was here, Bagabond urged Cordelia to use what she had been given to protect herself.

The black she had left to guard her car. He had been unhappy but she refused to risk him. The younger calico she took along but left up the block from the building. A combination of points of view told her that two men loitered at the main entrance of the partially renovated red-brick apartment house. The ocelot paced restlessly back and forth in the darkness of an alley beside the apartments. At the touch of a thought she sprang out and raced for the men, running silently for the hunt. She leaped for the closest guard and tore out his throat before he realized that he was being attacked. The other human was fast enough to pull his pistol, but his first shot was wild. He never got a chance for another. As she slunk into the five-story building, Bagabond made sure that no one was taking any notice of the noise or the bag lady. She jerked her head as the rhythmic wail of a car alarm began a few blocks away, but no one else reacted to it except the nervous ocelot.

Still trying vainly to get something from Cordelia, Bagabond sent the ocelot and the ginger ahead of her up the fire stairs. Moving quietly, she followed while tracking the presence of her creatures within and without the building. She spread a living net centered on Cordelia and a well-dressed Oriental man, confronting each other in a fourth-floor apartment. The rats scuttling through the walls and across the floors told her that the teenager was still alive.

As she climbed the fourth flight of stairs, she heard the voices echoing through the open door. The Oriental was interrogating Cordelia. She could not understand the words. Disrupting her concentration, Rosemary's face flashed across her mind. She mentally thrust it and the accompanying guilt away from her down into the submerged, fully human part of herself.

Rats broke from side rooms and ran down the hallway. Three guards stood outside in the bright light cast by the bare light bulbs in the ceiling. Heavy hitters in expensive tailored suits that normally hid the guns they had drawn. Bagabond wondered what these people feared from Cordelia.

The wolf was making his way up the stairs at the far end of the hall. The ocelot strained at her side. The sight of the rats had made the well-dressed killers nervous. She used her other eyes to look into the room where Cordelia still lay curled up on the floor as she was questioned. Damn her Catholic-martyr syndrome. Bagabond could not sense even stirrings of Cordelia's power. The girl was keeping her promise to herself or she was incapable of acting. A huge man who looked like a sumo wrestler and wore a Man Mountain Gentian T-shirt stood silently in the corner, but even through the rat's dim vision Bagabond could see the bloodlust in the way he moved constantly, clenching and unclenching his fists as he looked at Cordelia.

Abruptly Bagabond sent the ginger cat yowling down the hall. As she had hoped, the three men pulled their guns but held their shots when they saw it was just a cat.

"Goin' after the rats. Great!" One of the men voiced his hope as he reholstered his weapon. The other two were agreeing when the ocelot sprang away from Bagabond's side. One swipe of the ocelot's paw tore away most of a face and ripped the jugular before she used the shoulder of the dead man as a platform for her leap to the next. On the opposite side, one of the guards shot at the gray shape lunging across the scarred wooden floor, claws scrabbling for purchase. Only one shot creased the wolf's hindquarter before he was on his enemy, jaws closing on the man's throat. The last man had managed to wedge his forearm into the ocelot's mouth and was beating her with the butt of his gun when the wolf caught his free arm.

Bagabond knew the noise would alert the men inside. She could only hope that Cordelia would use the distraction to advantage in the short time before she could get there. The sumo was too close to Cordelia to stop.

When she slid behind the remains of the guards and into the apartment where they had been interrogating Cordelia,

Bagabond saw only a sharply tailored pants leg and an Italian shoe disappear into a connecting room. She didn't see the wrestler. Cordelia was wavering to her feet, saying something as Bagabond started forward to free her. The huge hand around her throat stopped her.

"Forget about me, you crazy bitch?" The sumo spoke with an English accent. Stepping completely out of a closet, he spun her toward him. Bagabond's breath was cut off and she felt her windpipe closing underneath his inhuman strength. She attacked him directly but her telepathy did not affect him. He was too human, she realized, in a part of her darkening mind that could still perceive irony. The ginger had already fastened her claws into his leg, but it had no effect. Bagabond called for the ocelot and the wolf, but her mental power was fading with her physical. She could not seem to override their desire to feast on their kills. As she considered all the deaths she had felt, she wondered how her own would be received by the wild ones. Would they remember her? She kicked at her tormentor, but she couldn't seem to get her legs untangled from her skirts and coat.

The wind of the hawks' passing brought her back to consciousness long enough to hear their hunting screams. She felt blood drip onto her face before she was flung away. She was blind, but through the eyes of the ginger lying across the room, she saw her attacker driven back toward the window. The shattering glass showered her as he crashed through to plunge forty feet to the ground. Bagabond thought she felt the building rock when he hit, but she decided that it had to be a hallucination from the oxygen deprivation.

The ocelot and the wolf crawled contritely over to her and leaned against her to give her strength. She could feel the rats running rampant throughout the building as the cats ran among them, scattering but not killing the vermin. As far as she could reach, her wild animals were going crazy. She did her best to bring them back to normal and sent those she could touch to their homes before returning to the bare apartment. Opening her eyes, she saw Cordelia, arms still tied behind her back, leaning over her.

"Girl, you got to take responsibility for yourself and what you are. I *ain't* goin' through this again. Not even for Jack. Either learn to use what you have or go live in a convent." Bagabond started to slide into the warm darkness again. She was not sure whether she had actually spoken to Cordelia or whether she had imagined it.

Rosemary was feeling increasingly afraid of the entire situation. Chris was up to something; she could feel it. She did not have to be a telepath like Bagabond to sense that she was in trouble. She had not seen any animals around her, not even a rat. It was not a good sign. Where the hell was Bagabond?

She deliberately slowed as she walked down the hallway. She tried to focus on her danger and use it. What was waiting for her in the filthy little room she was about to enter? Rosemary drew her own gun.

She tried the knob. The door was unlocked. She pushed it open onto the room and its occupant. The man who had been described to her as Croyd stood there, about to leave.

"Who the hell are you?" He was obviously surprised to see a woman. With the gun Rosemary gestured for him to sit back down on the iron-framed bed. She kept her back against the wall beside the door. "Christ, you're Maria Gambione!"

"I need to know what you actually found out." Rosemary leveled the gun on the man across the tiny room, holding it firmly just as she had always practiced. "You're not going anywhere."

Outside on the fire escape Chris waited for Rosemary to go down with the virus. Mentally he urged her to get closer to Croyd. He could not hear what they were saying. It did not matter as long as Croyd did to her what he had done to the capos. Chris knew Croyd had to have access to the virus somehow. Nothing else could have done *that*. Why didn't she close in?

He saw her gun go up. Croyd moved faster. Before Chris could get out of the way, Croyd had thrown the bedside lamp through the window and followed it out onto the fire escape. Chris scrambled backward, but in his haste to get away from Rosemary, Croyd was across the iron grating of the landing. Seeing Chris at last, Croyd tackled him and threw him down the next flight of steps. Chris gagged and tried to crawl away down the steps. A shot narrowly missed Croyd, and he clambered up the ladder two steps at a time.

Rosemary had frozen when Croyd went through the window. As the echoes of the crash rang through the flophouse, she heard her bodyguards coming for her. She followed Croyd out the broken window and saw him start up the fire escape. She fired at him more to keep him moving than to kill him. The only way out was down the escape. Chris was coughing and convulsing on the landing below her. As she heard her men break down the door behind her, she was running down the steps and jumping over her lover. She did not stop.

"Bastard!" she hissed at him as she left him behind. She was headed for the ground. She knew now that Chris's men would kill her on sight. It would take luck and fast moves, but there was just a chance she could lose the bodyguards and the men out front. It was her only chance.

Concerto for
Siren and Serotonin

VI

Croyd took a taxi crosstown, then hiked a circuitous route to his Morningside Heights apartment. There were no lights on within, and he entered quickly and quietly, painkillers, antihistamines, psychedelics, and a five-pound box of assorted chocolates all gift-wrapped together in a gaudy parcel beneath his arm. He flipped on the hall light and slipped into the bedroom.

"Veronica? You awake?" he whispered.

There was no reply, and he crossed to the bedside, lowered himself to a seated position, and reached out. His hand encountered only bedclothes.

"Veronica?" he said aloud.

No reply.

He turned on the bedside lamp. The bed was empty, her stuff gone. He looked about for a note. No. Nothing. Perhaps in the living room. Or the kitchen. Yes. Most likely she'd leave it in the refrigerator where he'd be certain to find it.

He rose, then halted. Was that a footstep? Back toward the living room?

"Veronica?"

No reply.

Foolish of him to have left the door open, he suddenly realized, though there had been no one in the hallway. . . .

He reached out and extinguished the lamp. He crossed to the door, dropped silently to the floor, moved his head outside at floor level, and drew it back quickly.

Empty. No one in the hall. No further sounds either.

He rose and stepped outside. He walked back toward the living room.

In the dim light from the hallway, as he rounded the

corner, he beheld a Bengal tiger, and its tail twitched once
before it sprang at him.

"Holy shit!" Croyd commented, dropping Veronica's present and leaping to the side.

Plaster shattered and fell as he caromed off the wall, an
orange and black shoulder grazed him in passing, and he
threw a punch that slid over the animal's back. He heard it
growl as he leaped into the living room. It turned quickly
and followed him, and he picked up a heavy chair and threw
it as the beast sprang again.

It roared as the chair struck it, and Croyd overturned a
heavy wooden table, raised it like a shield, and rushed with it
against the animal. The tiger shook itself, snarling, as it
batted the chair aside. It turned and caught the table's flat
surface upon a smooth expanse of shoulder muscle. Then it
swung a paw over the table's upper edge. Croyd ducked,
pushed forward.

The big cat fell back, dropped out of sight. Seconds crept
by like drugged cockroaches.

"Kitty?" he inquired.

Nothing.

He lowered the table a foot. With a roar the tiger sprang.
Croyd snapped the table upward, faster than he could remember ever having lifted a piece of furniture before. Its
edge caught the tiger a terrible blow beneath the jaw, and it
let out a human-sounding whimper as it was turned sideways
and fell to the floor. Croyd raised the table high and slammed
it down atop the beast, as if it were a giant flyswatter. He
raised it again. He halted. He stared.

No tiger.

"Kitty?" he repeated.

Nothing.

He lowered the table. Finally he set it aside. He moved
to the wall switch and threw it. Only then did he realize that
the front of his shirt was torn and bloody. Three furrows ran
down the left side of his chest from collarbone to hip.

On the floor, a bit of whiteness. . . .

Stooping, he touched the object, raised it, studied it. He
held one of those little folded paper figures—origami, he
remembered, the Japanese called them. This one was . . . a
paper tiger. He shivered at the same time as he chuckled.
This was almost supernatural. This was heavy shit. It oc-

curred to him then that he had just fought off another
ace—one with a power he did not understand—and he did
not like this a bit. Not with Veronica missing. Not with his
not even knowing which side had sent the stranger ace to
take him out.

He locked the door to the hallway. He opened Veronica's
present, took out the bottle of Percodans and tossed off a
couple before he hit the bathroom, stripped off his shirt, and
washed his chest. Then he fetched a beer from the refrigerator and washed down a French green with it, to provide the
Percs with some contrast. There was no note propped against
the milk carton or even in the egg drawer, and this made him
sad.

When the bleeding stopped, he washed again, taped a
dressing in place, and drew on a fresh shirt. He was not even
sure whether he had been followed or whether this had been
a stakeout. Either way, he wasn't going to stick around. He
hated abandoning Veronica if someone really had a make on
the place, but at the moment he had no choice. It was a very
familiar feeling: they were after him again.

Croyd rode subways and taxis and walked for over four
hours, crouched behind his mirrorshades, crissing and crossing the island in a pattern of evasion calculated to confuse
anybody. And for the first time in his life he saw his name up
in lights in Times Square.

CROYD CRENSON, said the flowing letters high on the
buildingside, CALL DR. T. EMERGENCY.

Croyd stood and stared, reading it over and over. When
he had convinced himself it was not a hallucination, he
shrugged. They ought to know he'd stop by and pay his
bill when he got a chance. It was damn humiliating, imply-
ing to the whole world that he was a deadbeat. They'd
probably even try to charge him for a bed, too, he guessed,
when broom closets should be a lot cheaper. Out to screw
him, the same as everyone else. They could damn well
wait.

Cursing, he ran for a subway entrance.

Heading south on the Broadway line, sucking on a pair of
purple hearts and a stray pyrahex he'd found at the bottom of
his pocket, Croyd was amazed and impressed that Senator

Hartmann actually did seem a man of the people, boarding
the train at the Canal Street Station that way. Then another
Senator Hartmann followed him. They glanced his way, con-
ferred for an instant, and one leaned out the door and
hollered something, and more Hartmanns came running.
There were tall Hartmanns, short Hartmanns, fat Hartmanns
and even a Hartmann with an extra appendage—seven
Hartmanns in all. And Croyd was not so unsophisticated as to
fail in realizing, this near Jokertown, that Hartmann's was the
Werewolves' face of the day.

The doors closed, the train began to move, the tallest
Hartmann turned, stared, and approached.

"You Croyd Crenson?" he asked.

"Nope," Croyd replied.

"I think you are."

Croyd shrugged. "Think whatever you want, but do it
someplace else if you want my vote."

"Get up."

"I am up. I'm a lot higher than you. And I'm up for
anything."

The tall Hartmann reached for him, and the
other Hartmanns began a swaying advance.

Croyd reached forward, caught the oncoming hand, and
drew it toward his face. There followed a crunching sound,
and the tall Hartmann screamed as Croyd jerked his head to
the side, then spat out the thumb he had just bitten off the
hand he held. Then he rose to his feet, still holding the
Werewolf's right wrist with his left hand. He jerked the man
forward and drove the fingers of his free hand deep into his
abdomen and began drawing them upward. Blood spurted
and ribs popped and protruded.

"Always following me," he said. "You're a real pain in the
ass, you know? Where's Veronica?"

The man commenced a coughing spasm. The other Werewolves halted as the blood began to flow. Croyd's hand
plunged again, downward this time. Red up to the elbow
now, he began drawing out a length of intestine. The others
began to gag, to back toward the rear of the car.

"This is a political statement," Croyd said as he raised the
gory Hartmann and tossed him after the others. "See you in
November, motherfuckers!"

* * *

Croyd exited quickly at the Wall Street Station, tore off his bloody shirt, and tossed it into a trash receptacle. He washed his hands in a public fountain before departing the area, and he offered a big black guy who'd said, "You *really* a Whitey!" fifty bucks for his shirt—a pale blue, long-sleeved polyester affair, which fit him fine. He trotted over to Nassau then, followed it north till it ran into Centre. He stopped in an OPEN ALL NIGHT Greek place and bought two giant styrofoam cups of coffee, one for each hand, to sip as he strolled.

He continued up to Canal and bore westward. Then he detoured several blocks to a café he knew, for steak and eggs and coffee and juice and more coffee. He sat beside the window and watched the street grow light and come alive. He took a black pill for medicinal purposes and a red one for good luck.

"Uh," he said to the waiter, "you're the sixth or seventh person I've seen wearing a surgical mask recently. . . ."

"Wild card virus," the man said. "It's around again."

"Just a few cases, here and there," Croyd said, "last I heard."

"Go listen again," the man responded. "It's close to a hundred—maybe over—already."

"Still," Croyd mused, "do you think a little strip of cloth like that will really do you any good?"

The waiter shrugged. "I figure it's better than nothing. . . . More coffee?"

"Yeah. Get me a dozen donuts to go, too, will you?"

"Sure."

He made his way to the Bowery via Broome Street, then on down toward Hester. As he drew nearer, he saw that the newsstand was not yet open, and Jube nowhere in sight. Pity. He'd a feeling Walrus might have some useful information or at least some good advice on dealing with the fact that both sides in the current gang war periodically took time out to shoot at him—say, every other day. Was it sunspots? Bad breath? It was rapidly ceasing to be cost effective for the Mob to keep chasing him to recover his fee for his investigation— and Siu Ma's people must have hit at him enough by now to have recovered a lot more face than he'd ever cost them.

Munching a donut, he passed on, heading for his Eldridge apartment. Later. No rush. He could talk to Jube by and by. Right now it would be restful to lean back in the big easy chair, his feet up on the ottoman, and close his eyes for a few minutes. . . .

"Shit!" he observed, tossing half a donut down the stairwell to a vacant basement flat as he turned the corner onto his block. Was it getting to be that time already?

Then he continued to turn with that rapid fluidity of movement that had come with the territory this time around, following the donut down into darkness where the asthmatic snuffling of some ancient dog would have been distracting but for the fact that he was viewing, even as he descended, a classical stakeout up the street near his pad.

"Son-of-a-bitch!" he added, just his head above ground level now, outline broken by a length of upright piping that supported the side railing.

One man sat in a parked car up past the building, in view of its front entrance. Another sat on a stoop, filing his nails, in command of an angled view of the rear of the building from across the side alley.

Croyd heard a panicked gasping as he swore, unlike any doggy sound with which he was familiar. Glancing downward and back into the shadows, he beheld the quivering, amorphous form of Snotman, generally conceded to be the most disgusting inhabitant of Jokertown, as he cringed in the corner and ate the remains of Croyd's donut.

Every square inch of the man's surface seemed covered with green mucus, which ran steadily from him and added to the stinking puddle in which he crouched. Whatever garments he had on were so saturated with it as to have become barely distinguishable—like his features.

"For Christ's sake! That's filthy and I was eating on it!" Croyd said. "Have a fresh one." He extended the bag toward Snotman, who did not move. "It's okay," he added, and finally he set the bag down on the bottom step and returned to watching the watchers.

Snotman finished the discarded fragment and remained still for some time. Finally, he asked, "For me?"

His voice was a liquid, snotty, snuffling thing.

"Yeah, finish 'em. I'm full," Croyd said. "I didn't know you could talk."

"Nobody to talk to," Snotman replied.

"Well—yeah. That's the breaks, I guess."

"People say I make them lose their appetites. Is that why you don't want the rest?"

"No," Croyd said. "I got a problem. I'm trying to figure what to do next. There're some guys up there have my place covered. I'm deciding whether to take them out or just go away. You don't bother me, even with that gunk all over you. I've looked as bad myself on occasion."

"You? How?"

"I'm Croyd Crenson, the one they call the Sleeper. I change appearance every time I sleep. Sometimes it's for the better, sometimes it isn't."

"Could I?"

"What? Oh, change again? I'm a special case, is what it is. I don't know any way I could share that with other people. Believe me, you wouldn't want a regular diet of it."

"Just once would be enough," Snotman answered, opening the bag and taking out a donut. "Why are you taking a pill? Are you sick?"

"No, it's just something to help me stay alert. I can't afford to sleep for a long time."

"Why not?"

"It's a long story. Very long."

"Nobody tells me stories anymore."

"What the hell. Why not?" Croyd said.

Blood Ties

IV

Baby, *your master is an idiot.*

No, master.

Yes, Baby.

Blaise lay curled among the tumbled pillows on the vast canopy bed that almost filled the bridge/stateroom aboard Tachyon's yacht. Two of the curving pearlescent walls presented a miniature schematic of New York City. Different-colored lines connected red markers. The third wall broke down the location of wild card cases by building and business. Chase Manhattan Bank Jokertown branch, three apartment buildings (one of which was in Harlem), Top Hat cleaners on the Bowery, restaurants, bars, drug stores, department stores.

It's a human vector.

Tachyon rose from the floor and dusted the seat of his pants, sensing irritation from his ship at this slur on her housekeeping. Sometimes ships had a skewed sense of priorities. An imputation of dust was far more significant than the announcement that a Typhoid Mary was threatening Manhattan.

Have I done well, master?

Extraordinarily well. I just wish I had not been so slow to see.

"Blaise, *kuket,* we're going now. Put your arm around my neck. Good lad."

He carried the child out of the ship. Pausing at the door of the warehouse, he fumbled with the lock and struggled with his sleeping burden. Tachyon was a small man, and his grandson already showed every indication that he would tower over his tiny forebear.

Into the sultry night. Two A.M. He could imagine what Victoria Queen was going to say to him when he woke her at this hour. But it had to be discussed, and with people he

395

could trust. Somewhere a human contagion slept or walked the streets of New York.

His arms tightened convulsively about the boy as the realization struck. *No one was safe.* While Blaise was playing in the park, walking to the clinic, eating in a restaurant, this monstrous sickness could pass by and endanger his child, his line, his future. He almost turned back to the ship. This evil could not pass *Baby.* He chided himself for hysteria. There were millions of people in greater Manhattan. What chance of actually encountering the carrier?

Depended upon the identity of the carrier.

And how to establish that? Ideal, it was probably a hopeless task.

"This is absolutely hopeless," said Victoria Queen.

"Thank you for that incredibly helpful observation." The chief of surgery and Tachyon exchanged sizzling glares.

Chrysalis flicked a nail against the rim of her glass, pulling out a single ringing tone. Finn took another bite of raw Quaker Oats.

"We interview the family and friends of every victim. We interview the surviving victims. We search for the common thread, some individual they all recall," said Tachyon.

"It would be an incredible long shot that any of them would remember," sighed Finn.

Tachyon turned the full blazing force of his lilac eyes on his assistant. "So are you suggesting that we wait and hope that this person notices that people are dying like flies all around him or her? And even that won't help." Tach shook his head as if disgusted by his own facetiousness. "The incubation period appears to be around twenty-four hours. This carrier, whoever it is, can have no notion of their power."

"Power," snorted Chrysalis.

"Yes, power. Clearly this person's wild card gift is to give wild card. The person probably contracted the virus during this latest outbreak. If it had happened earlier, we would have been facing this crisis months or even years ago."

"Doc." Finn tossed his heavy forelock out of his face. "This has to mean that the virus is mutating."

"Yes, I'm afraid you're correct. Dr. Corvisart will be ecstatic."

"Who?" asked Queen.

"A French researcher who was absolutely convinced that the virus was mutating. I tried to explain to him that there's only been one case of a constantly mutating virus, and that's because it is this man's power—"

"What? What is it?" asked Finn sharply at Tachyon's frozen expression.

The alien relaxed his frenzied grip on the edge of the desk. He and Chrysalis met each other's gaze. "You're thinking what I'm thinking."

"Ohhh, yes."

"Then why not enlighten those of us who aren't thinking," snapped Queen bitterly, who then flushed and quickly added, "In the peculiar way *you* think."

"There is one individual in this city who's an old hand at wild card. Who is reinfected with the virus every time he sleeps. How many times has he transformed over the past forty years? A dozen? Twenty? Thirty?"

"It would be the most unbelievable coincidence," warned Chrysalis.

"I agree, but it has to be investigated." Tachyon pushed to his feet.

Finn lurched to his feet. *"Sleep?"*

"Yes," said Tachyon rather impatiently.

The tiny centaur gave a long shake that began at his head, vibrated to his tail, and pulled a deep-throated groan from his lungs.

"He was here."

"WHAT!"

"Back in March. He came in to see you, but you weren't back yet. He was high on speed, and apparently he'd promised some girl he wouldn't go out with her cranked. He wanted help. I put him to sleep."

"How for the Ideal's sake? This could be critical."

"Brain entrainment and suggestion."

"When did he wake and leave?"

"Um, mid-May."

"May! And you didn't tell me!"

"I didn't think it was important."

"He's been awake a month," Chrysalis said to Tachyon.

"Do you still want us to do those interviews?" asked Queen.

"Yes, it might help us pinpoint his present physical form. I don't suppose you saw him when he left?"

"No, one morning he just wasn't there."

"Where did you stash him?" asked Chrysalis curiously.

"In the janitor's closet."

"Have we lost any janitors?" asked Tachyon with grave-yard humor.

"We were lucky, incredibly lucky," muttered Finn, crossing himself.

"People, this has got to be kept absolutely confidential. Can you imagine the panic if wind of this reaches the general populace?"

"Sooner or later the authorities are going to have to be informed," objected Queen.

"Not if Chrysalis and I succeed."

"I *hate* it when you're smug."

"Tachyon, she's got a point. We're going to feel like absolute shit if we can't find Croyd, or we find him and he's not the one. How many more people are going to die, Tachyon?" asked Chrysalis.

Tachyon splashed a liberal dollop of cognac into a glass, raised the blinds, and watched the sun trying valiantly to struggle through the layers of mist and smog.

"I think I'm justified in trying this alone first. What would I say to the mayor? Well, Your Honor, we think there's a wild card carrier. We think it's Croyd Crenson. No, sir, we don't know what he looks like because he changes every time he sleeps."

"I don't suppose we could try anything simple and silly like running ads on the radio and in the papers—'Croyd phone home'?" suggested Finn.

"Why not? I'm willing to try anything. The real question is how many amphetamines he's eaten in the past weeks." He turned away from the window to face Chrysalis. "You know what he's like toward the end of an episode."

"He's a psychotic," said Chrysalis bluntly.

"And usually paranoid, so if he starts hearing or reading ads, he's going to assume they're after him." The Takisian sighed. "And he'd be right."

Tachyon poured another drink and pulled a face as the brandy washed down.

"Great breakfast," said the owner of the Palace dryly.

"I'll break an egg in it if that will make you feel any better."

"You've been hitting the bottle pretty hard recently."

"You tell him," muttered Queen under her breath.

Tachyon glared at both of them. "Not to sound too terribly trite, but I have been under a great deal of pressure recently."

"You were an alcoholic, Tachyon. You shouldn't be drinking at all," said Chrysalis.

"Blood and Bone, what has gotten into you? One would think you'd joined a temperance league. Going to be down at Father Squid's beating on a tambourine? You're a saloonkeeper, Chrysalis."

He watched the increased wash of blood into those transparent cheeks. "I care, Tachyon, don't make me regret that. You're important to Jokertown." She plucked nervously at the arm of her chair. "Maybe even to the nation. Don't crap out on us and crawl back in a bottle. You've got the prestige to stand against crime bosses, and . . . other things. Nobody else in this fucking freak show has that."

Bitterness edged each word. He knew what it cost her to make that admission. She had a pride of self and place that rivaled his. Slowly he walked to her, forced himself to bend and place his cheek against hers. He couldn't help the involuntary closing of his eyes, but it wasn't as bad as he expected. Her skin, invisible though it was, was warm and soft. She could be any lovely woman. As long as his eyes were closed.

He stepped back and lifted her fingers to his lips. "Send out word to your network. This has to take precedence over anything else."

"Even the Fists and the Gambiones?"

"Yes. What profiteth us to gain Jokertown if we lose the whole bloody world?"

"I'll save you a tambourine."

"No, I want to be the whole damn trumpet section."

"Why am I not surprised?" said Queen to Finn.

Concerto for
Siren and Serotonin

VII

When Snotman grew ill, Croyd snapped the lock on the door behind him, letting him into the dusty ruin of a small two-room apartment whose owner was obviously using the place to store damaged furniture. He located a threadbare couch on which the glistening joker sprawled, quivering. He rinsed a jelly jar he found near a basin in the next room and took him a drink of water. Sweeping aside a mess of ancient drug paraphernalia, Croyd seated himself on a small cracked bench as the other sipped.

"You been sick?" Croyd asked him.

"No. I mean, I always feel like I've got a cold, but this is different. I feel sort of like I did a long time ago, when it all started."

Croyd covered the shivering joker with a pile of curtains he found in a corner, then seated himself again.

"Finish telling me what happened," Snotman said after a time.

"Oh, yeah."

Croyd popped a methamphet and a dex and continued his tale. When Snotman passed out, Croyd did not notice. He kept talking until he realized that Snotman's skin had gone dry. Then he grew still and watched, for the man's features seemed slowly to be rearranging themselves. Even speeded, Croyd was able to spot the onset of a wild card attack. But even speeded, this did not quite make sense. Snotman was already a joker, and Croyd had never heard of anyone—himself excluded—coming down with it a second time.

He shook his head, rose and paced, stepped outside. It was afternoon now, and he was hungry again. It took him a few moments to spot the new shift that had taken over

400

surveillance of his quarters. He decided against disposing of them. The most sensible thing to do, he guessed, would be to go and get a bite to eat, then come back and keep an eye on the now-transforming Snotman through his crisis, one way or the other. Then clear out, go deeper underground.

In the distance a siren wailed. Another Red Cross helicopter came and went, low, from the southeast, heading uptown. Memories of that first mad Wild Card Day swam in his head, and Croyd decided that perhaps he'd better acquire a new pad even before he ate. He knew just the sleaze-bin, not too far away, where he could get in off the streets and no questions asked, provided they had a vacancy—which was generally the case. He detoured to check it out.

Like a mating call, another siren answered the first, from the opposite direction. Croyd waved at the man who hung upside down by his feet from a lamppost, but the fellow took offense or grew frightened and flew away.

From somewhere he heard a loudspeaker mentioning his name, probably saying terrible things about him.

His fingers tightened on the fender of a parked car. The metal squealed as he pulled at it, tearing a wide strip loose. He turned then, bending it, folding it, blood dripping from a tear in his hand. He would find that speaker and destroy it, whether it was high on a buildingside or the top of a cop car. He would stop them from talking about him. He would . . .

That would give him away, though—he realized in a moment's clarity—to his enemies, who could be anybody. Anybody except the guy with the wild card virus, and Snotman couldn't be anybody's enemy just now. Croyd hurled the piece of metal across the street, then threw back his head and began to howl. Things were getting complicated again. And nasty. He needed something to calm his nerves.

He plunged his bloody hand into his pocket, withdrew a fistful of pills, and gulped them without looking to see what they were. He had to get presentable to go and get a room.

He ran his fingers through his hair, brushed off his clothes, began walking at a normal pace. It wasn't far.

Blood Ties

V

The man wrapped a webbed hand about Tachyon's wrist, indicated for a pad, and scrawled out, *How long you think I got?*

"A few days."

Tachyon noticed Tina Mixon's wince. He knew that she considered his frankness to border on brutality, but he didn't believe in lying to people. A man needed time to prepare himself for death. And these humans with their delicate sensibilities. They either wouldn't talk about death, or they shrouded it in euphemisms. On the other hand, they were not in the least backward about dealing out death.

The hiss of the respirator was loud in the room as the man laboriously wrote, *If you could find that woman.*

"She's vanished, Mr. Grogan. I'm sorry."

Use powers. Find her!

Tachyon bowed his head and recalled the scene (only three days ago? It seemed an eternity) that had met his disbelieving gaze. He had responded to word of a riot on the third floor. He had run into the ward, then frozen and stared down at the water washing over the tops of his shoes.

There must have been sixty people in a room designed for ten. Soaked and bedraggled jokers clung like survivors of a shipwreck to the beds. Orderlies disgruntledly slopped mops across the flooded floor. A sandy-haired man stood on one of the beds babbling hysterically while a pair of women jokers pawed at his knees and added their shrill cries to the general pandemonium

"A fucking vision. A fucking golden vision. And look at me!" screamed the sandy-haired man. "Look at me!"

"Why does it have to be a woman?" wailed a woman. "Maybe you got her power. Fuck me. FUCK ME!"

Tachy had ruthlessly mind-controlled her. And the babbling man, and anyone else who had seemed likely to make trouble. The remaining jokers had stared at him like targets at a county turkey shoot.

They were less intimidated now.

Like this pathetic blackmail from a dying man.

"I'm sorry," Tachyon said again to Grogan, and left the room.

And stumbled into a lurking pack of jokers.

"Good morning."

"What's good about it," growled a big joker with a mouthful of cilia in place of teeth. It made his diction mushy, and Tachyon had to strain to understand him.

"You're alive, Mr. Konopka, which is more than many unluckier ones can claim," the alien snapped. He pulled off his stethoscope and jerked it between his hands.

"You call this livin'?" said a woman. "I look like a monster, my husband's left me, I lost my job—"

"Everyone's got a story," said Tachyon shortly, heading down the hall. They followed him.

Konopka stepped in front of the Takisian and stopped him with a hard jab to the small alien's chest.

"What are you doing to find that woman?"

For a long moment Tachyon warred with conflicting emotions: to placate them with a soothing lie, or be damned to them, and tell them the truth.

The joker gave him another jab with a forefinger tipped with a long, sharp nail. "Huh? Huh? Answer up—"

Tach ran out of patience. "I'm doing precisely nothing to find that woman."

"You motherfucker, I'm gonna kill you." Konopka drew back a fist.

Another man cried, "You don't care about us!"

Tachyon whirled on him, seized him by the shoulders. "No! That's not true. Xuan, I care more than you can conceive. But I must also care for Jane. Look at you." He raked the crowd with a lilac-eyed glance. "You're like hunting *animals*."

"That girl can cure us. You gotta find her." The anger drained from Xuan, replaced with a humble pleading.

Konopka jerked the alien around to face him. "You owe it to us, Tachyon, because you made us what we are, and you can't do fuck to cure us!" There were shouts of agreement.

Tachyon glanced to the nurses' station, where Tina was dithering over the switchboard. He gave an infinitesimal shake of the head. All this situation needed was the arrival of security.

"All of you return to your rooms."

"No brush off, Tachyon!"

"Listen to me," he pleaded. "That girl is a person, a human being. Not a fucking machine designed to cure jokers. You would have killed her three days ago. Consider the terrible dilemma with which *she* is faced. Think of *her* too and not only of yourselves. How can I trust you when I can't even trust myself to do what is right and proper by Jane?"

Finn had popped out of an elevator and now stood with a foreleg upraised as if ready to paw the linoleum floor. With a low murmur the crowd began to disperse. All except Konopka. He gathered up a handful of the burgundy satin coat and lifted Tach's feet from the floor. Finn cantered daintily forward, whirled on his slender forelegs, and landed a kick square in the center of Konopka's ass. With a roar the joker dropped Tachyon and spun to face this new attack.

"Cut it out!" yelled Finn. "And get the hell back to your room." Konopka's fist lashed out. Finn danced back, but four legs are less dexterous than two. The blow landed.

"Nat ass-kisser!"

Tachyon dropped Konopka snoring to the floor.

"Why didn't you do that a long time ago?" asked Finn, rubbing at his reddening cheek.

"Possibly because I'm tired of victimizing them." Tachyon whirled, his long-tailed coat rustling around him. Finn had to trot to keep pace.

"It's not your fault."

"Which part of this mess? The creation of the virus? No, not entirely my fault. The fact that Croyd's become a carrier? Again, probably beyond my control. The fact that Jane has become the most hunted person in Jokertown? Maybe not. But she is my responsibility, and I've got to find her and protect her if I can." Tachyon slammed his fist into the elevator wall, breaking the skin across his knuckles.

Finn lifted his hand and blotted at the welling blood with a handkerchief. "Relax, we'll find her."

"Will we?" Tachyon licked reflectively at the blood. "More to the point, *should* we?"

* * *

"Ha! I blast you with my killer mind-attack. And I make it! You lose another life." Tachyon tossed the tiny cardboard marker into the discard pile. "And I can really do that too." Blaise's eyes glittered in the lamplight. "I bet if I worked hard I could kill with my mind."

Polyakov glanced up from his newspaper.

"It's not a talent to cultivate."

"Can you do it?"

"Drop it, Blaise."

"Can you?"

"I said drop it."

The small, round chin hardened, the lips narrowing into a mulish line. "Maybe I'll just have to practice on somebody since you won't—"

Tachyon came across the dining table and landed a slap that knocked the boy out of his chair.

"*Tachyon!*" bellowed the Russian.

"Blaise! Blaise! I'm sorry. So sorry. Are you all right?" Aghast, he gathered the child into his arms. "Oh, Ideal, forgive me."

The boy swung wildly, striking Tach above the eye. His esper ability poured off him in shuddering silver waves as he struggled to break his elder's shields. Tachyon quieted Blaise with a lick of his power.

"Listen to me. I'm horribly tired, and under a lot of stress. I know that's not an adequate excuse, but I offer it as an explanation. I don't want you to learn to kill. It does something to your soul because you are so closely linked with your victim. It's not like make-believe." He gestured back toward the abandoned Talisman game. "You have to burrow deep, tear away layer after layer of the person's mind before you can kill."

"Have you done it?" Blaise muttered around a swelling lip.

"Yes, and it haunts me to this day." Polyakov stepped to the alien's side and rested a hand on his shoulder. "I weighed Rabdan's life against the life of the Earth. He had to die, it was necessary but . . ." He hugged the child close. "You must learn to be kind, Blaise. Don't even joke about practicing on the humans. Our original sin was treating them as laboratory animals. Don't you—"

The trill of the phone interrupted him.

"Doctor. This is Jane."

"Jane, where—"

"No, no questions. Just listen. I have an address and a telephone number for Croyd. Only one. I heard the ads. I guess I can understand why you have to find him."

"Jane, I'm sorry I didn't help you before."

"It's okay. I was pretty strung out. You're not going to hurt him, are you? He's been a friend. I hate to think I'm betraying him, but..."

"More people will die if you don't. You're right to tell me."

"Okay. He's got an apartment on Eldridge. Three twenty-three Eldridge. Third floor. Five five five, four four nine one."

"Thank you, Jane, thank you so much. My dear child, we must—" But he was talking to the buzz of a disconnected line.

He replaced the receiver and stood face-to-face with a nasty moral dilemma. If... *when* they captured Croyd, and if he awoke in a new form minus the carrier power, well and good. But if this mutation carried over, then the decisions became harder. To keep the man in isolation for the rest of his life?

Or to kill him....

... A woman lying back among pillows and tangled sheets. A sheen of sweat across her dark breasts and belly. The moisture-matted hair of her mons—

The three-dimensional picture fragmented and vanished.

Sorry, squeaked Video in Tachyon's mind. *We got the wrong apartment.*

Wait, that might be Croyd.

He reached out and touched the woman's mind. It wasn't Croyd.

Floater and Video resumed their slow crawl across the back wall of the apartment building.

There were a few nervous laughs from the people in the van. Elmo shifted uncomfortably. His hazardous-environment suit was scarcely able to contain his bulk, and he looked rather like an ill-stuffed sausage. They had cobbled together suits for Troll and Ernie out of four other suits. So far the seals were holding, but Tachyon winced every time he considered the expense. Video and Floater each had suits, and Tachyon wore his Network-designed spacesuit.

It was impossible to protect Slither. They had tried a helmet and air supply, but the air tanks kept sliding around on her serpent's body, pulling loose the hoses. Tach had ordered her to stay out of the fight. She would be a final line of defense if Croyd got past them.

. . . Surprisingly neat room. A tall, thin man lounged on the sofa reading *Newsweek*. Ultrapale skin, odd eyes, brown hair with white roots showing. . . .

. . . Another man seated at the kitchen table playing solitaire. Wonderfully handsome, but an easily forgettable face for all that. . . .

Bill Lockwood.

Tachyon read a soul-deep sense of gratitude and a determination to protect . . . *Croyd!*

He switched his focus to the albino. Sweat broke out on his upper lip and stung his eyes as he struggled to touch the mind. Sliding his hand through the clear bubble of the helmet, he wiped perspiration and tried again. *Whirling darkness like a primordial black hole.* It was a mind block, but one of the oddest he'd ever felt. He spent another twenty minutes trying to find a way over, under, around, or through it. Finally he reluctantly concluded that it was more like an immunity than an actual shield.

He explained the situation to his troops, then added, "So we just go in and thump on him. How hard can it be? And remember, if you're not suited, *don't* go into that room."

They piled out. With a wave he motioned Slither and Ernie toward the rear alley. Then he and Troll and Elmo headed up the steps to the front door. There were buzzers, but since the lock was broken off the outer door, they didn't serve much purpose. Cautiously they stepped inside and started climbing for the third floor.

Fortunately the suit masked the smells, but Tach could imagine them. He had made too many house calls to just such buildings. The stink of rancid grease. The sickly-sweet scent of human and animal wastes clinging in the corners of the stairwells. Sweat, fear, poverty, and hopelessness—they too left a smell. The walls were graffiti-covered, slogans and howls of outrage in several languages.

I'm in position.

Video flashed him another picture of the room. Nothing had changed.

Window? Tachyon asked his recon team.

Open. In this heat what do you expect? sent back Floater.

Go in? asked Video.

Yes.

The alien motioned to Troll. The security chief took a grip on the knob, sucked in a breath, held it.

... The albino noticed Floater with Video riding piggy-back on his shoulders, crawling in the window. He rose with blinding speed, uttered an oath, and drew a gun....

"Now!" yelled Tachyon.

Troll forced the door. The lock broke with a scream of outraged metal and torn wood. Tach and Elmo tumbled into the room. The albino fired, and missed. Slither, disobeying or having completely forgotten her orders, came coiling up the fire escape like a hunting boa on a tree. She lashed out with her tufted tail and knocked the gun from the albino's hand.

"You fuckers!" Cards flew like frightened butterflies as the young man flung aside the table.

A right punch was coming in. Tachyon tried to deflect it with a quick outward block, but when his arm connected with Lockwood's, it stopped as if caught in a vise. Tach gasped. Troll, grunting with irritation, let loose with a wide, slow haymaker. His enormous fist slammed into Lockwood's jaw. No reaction. Tach and Troll stepped back, alarmed.

Croyd was trying to tie Slither into knots. Elmo waded in and was tossed contemptuously aside. He came back in, his arms driving like pistons. Ernie joined the fray. Floater was trying to scramble across the ceiling back to the window.

A sound like a side of beef hitting concrete. The pretty boy had landed a hit on Troll. The big joker doubled over. And Tachyon stared dismayed.

Thank you, Jesus, that he didn't hit me! came the hysterical little thought.

Troll drove two hard left/right punches into Lockwood's gut.

Nothing!

Lockwood wound up and delivered a punch to Tachyon's

head. The Network helmet withstood the blow, but the kinetic force threw the tiny alien across the room. He came up bruised and groaning against the far wall. Troll was raining punches on Lockwood. The young man grinned and hammered in a series of hits that drove Troll across the room. The big joker stood swaying, arms over his helmeted head. Lockwood kicked him hard in the groin, then brought both hands down on the back of Troll's neck.

When a tree falls in the forest this is just how it sounds, thought Tach inanely as nine feet of joker went down like a poleaxed ox.

"Shit," commented Floater from overhead.

Tachyon reached out with a powerful imperative. Silver lines of power flowed out from him but failed to wrap like a net about the man's mind. Instead the power sank like a stone in quicksand.

SLEEP!!!!!!!!!!

The power washed back toward him, struck his shields, and passed right through.

Boomerang power, was Tachyon's last conscious thought.

He was dancing the most intricate and wonderful triple minor set, but there were no other men in the dance. Just him, and a long line of women. Blythe and Saaba and Dani and Angelface and M'orat, and Jane and Talli, and Roulette and Peregrine and Victoria and—

Zabb grabbed him by the shoulder and tried to cut in.

Muttering and growling, Tach dug his cheek deeper into the pillow. The antiseptic smell and rough texture of the pillowcase infuriated him. *I won't endure a bed like this. How dare they? The infernal cheek!*

He forced up gummed lids, stared into Victoria Queen's frowning blue eyes.

Smiled up at her. "You dance divinely."

"Oh, wake up!" She jammed a needle into his arm.

"Ow!"

"Stimulant. Our hero. You finally meet someone with a superior mind-control power at positively the worst moment."

"He was *not* superior! That was my *own* power ricocheting back at me. Nothing else could have gotten past my—" He cut off, ashamed by his outraged justification, then continued in a chastised tone, "Did we get them?"

"No."

He dropped his face into his hands. "O ancestors, what a mess."

"Yes." She walked out.

Croyd escaped. And if Slither died? Another casualty of his failures.

The click of dainty hooves on tile. "What next, boss?"

"I commit suicide."

"Wrong answer."

"I go to the police."

"They'll freak," remarked the joker as he pulled tangles from his white mane.

"What choice do I have? I wanted to keep this secret, avoid panic, but Croyd now knows he's being hunted. He will go to ground. We must have manpower to find him. And this companion. Call Washington, have SCARE search their files for an ace with boomerang powers."

The Takisian rose stiffly from the bed. Winced as he explored a bruise on his elbow. Ran his hands through his tangled curls. "I handled this so badly."

"You couldn't know."

"How are the troops?" Finn bowed his head and inspected his hands. "What is it? What's happened? Troll? Slither?"

"Slither. She went into Black Queen reaction minutes after you went under."

"The incubation period . . ."

"Must be shortening."

"He's continuing to mutate the virus."

"So maybe it will mutate until it becomes nonviral?"

"I couldn't be so lucky. Everything I touch leads to death."

"Stop it! That's not true! We don't have time for you to feel guilty. If anyone's at fault—I am. I let him leave."

"You couldn't have known he'd become a carrier."

"My point exactly. What's done is done. Let's get on with the future."

"If there is one."

"We'll make it happen."

"How did you end up so optimistic and well adjusted?"

"I'm too dumb to be otherwise."

All the King's Horses

VI

The big corrugated metal garage door rattled overhead as it slid back in its tracks. The opener was old and noisy, but it still did its job. Dust and daylight filtered into the underground bunker. Tom turned off the flashlight and hung it on a hook in the wooden beam supporting the hard-packed dirt wall. His palms were sweaty. He wiped them on his jeans and stood regarding the metal hulks before him.

The hatch gaped open on his oldest shell, the armored Beetle. He'd spent the last week replacing vacuum tubes, oiling the camera tracks, and checking the wiring. It was as ready as it would ever be.

"Me and my big fucking mouth," Tom said to himself. His words echoed through the bunker.

He could have rented a truck, a big semi maybe. Joey would have helped. Back it up to the edge of the bunker, load the shells, get them over to Jokertown the easy way. But no, he had to go and tell Dutton he'd *fly* them over. No way the joker would ever believe him now if the damn things got delivered by UPS.

He looked at the open hatch, tried to imagine crawling into that blackness and sealing the door behind him, locking himself into that metal coffin, and he could feel the bile rise in the back of his throat. He couldn't.

Only he had no choice, did he? The junkyard wasn't his anymore. A crew would be arriving in less than three weeks to start clearing away all the shit that had accumulated here in the last forty years. If the shells were still lying around when they showed up with their bulldozers, the jig was seriously up.

Tom forced himself to walk forward. No big deal, he told himself. The shell was okay, he could get it across the bay, he'd done it a thousand times. So he had to do it one more time, that's all. One more time and he was free.

All the kings horses and all the king's men . . .

Tom bent at the knees, grasped the top edge of the hatch, and took a long, slow breath. The metal was cold between his fingers. He ducked his head and pulled himself inside, swinging the hatch closed behind him. The *clang* rang in his ears. It was pitch-dark inside the shell, and chilly. His mouth had gone dry, and he could feel his heart shuddering away in his chest.

He fumbled in the darkness for the seat, felt torn vinyl upholstery, squirmed toward it. He might as well be in a cave at the center of the earth, or dead and buried, it was so black. Faint lines of light leaked in around the outside of the hatch, but not enough to see by. Where the fuck was the power switch? The newer shells all had fingertip controls built into the armrests of the seat, but not this old bucket, oh, no. Tom groped in the darkness over his head and jammed his fingers painfully on something metal. Panic stirred inside him like a frightened animal. It was so fucking black, *where were the lights?*

Then, suddenly, he was falling.

The vertigo crashed over him like a wave. Tom grabbed the armrests hard, tried to tell himself it wasn't happening, but he could *feel* it. The darkness tumbled end over end. His stomach roiled, and he bent forward, cracking his forehead sharply against the curving wall of the shell. *"I'm not falling!"* he screamed loudly. The words rang in his ears as he fell, helpless, locked in his armored casket. His hands thrashed madly, fumbling against the wall, sliding over glass and vinyl, throwing switches everywhere as he gasped for breath.

All around him the TV screens woke to dim life.

The world steadied. Tom's breathing slowed. He wasn't falling, no, look out there, that was the bunker, he was sitting in the shell, safe on the ground at the bottom of a hole, that was all, he wasn't falling.

Fuzzy black-and-white images crowded the screens. The sets were a mismatch of sizes and brand names, there were obvious blind spots, one picture was locked into a slow vertical roll. Tom didn't care. He could see. He wasn't falling.

He found the tracking controls and set his external cameras to moving. The images on the screen shifted slowly as he scanned all around him. The other two shells, the empty husks, squatted a few feet away. He turned on the ventilation system, heard a fan begin to whir, felt fresh air wash over his face. Blood was dripping into his eyes. He'd cut himself in his panic. He wiped it away with the back of his hand, sagged back in the seat.

"Okay," he announced loudly. He'd gotten this far. The rest was candy. Up, up, and away. Out of the bunker, across New York Bay, one last flight, nothing simpler. He pushed up.

The shell rocked slowly from side to side, lifted maybe an inch off the ground, then settled back with a thump.

Tom grunted. *All the king's horses and all the king's men,* he thought. He summoned all his concentration, tried again to lift off. Nothing happened.

He sat there, grim-faced, staring unseeing at the washed-out black-and-white shapes on his television screens, and finally he admitted the truth. The truth he'd hidden from Joey DiAngelis, Xavier Desmond, and even from himself.

His shell wasn't the only thing that was broken.

For twenty-odd years he'd thought himself invulnerable once behind his armor. Tom Tudbury might have his doubts, his fears, his insecurities, but not the Turtle. His teke, nurtured by that sense of invincibility, had grown steadily greater, year after year after year, so long as he was inside his shell.

Until Wild Card Day.

They'd taken him out before he even knew what was happening.

He'd been high over the Hudson, answering a distress call, when some ace power had reached through his armor as if it didn't exist. Suddenly he'd felt sick, weak. He had to fight to keep from blacking out, and he could feel the massive shell stagger in midflight as his concentration wavered. A moment before his vision blurred, he'd glimpsed the boy in the hang glider slicing down from above. Then there'd been a tremendous loud *pop* that hurt his eardrums, and the shell had died.

Everything went. Cameras, computers, tape deck, ventilation system, all of it burned out or seized up in the same split second. An electromagnetic pulse, he'd read later in the papers, but all he'd known then was that he'd gone blind and helpless. For a moment he was too shocked to be afraid, punching wildly at his fingertip controls in the darkness, frantic to get the power back on.

He'd never even realized that they'd napalmed him.

But with the napalm the weakness came again. He lost it then; the shell began to tumble, plunging toward the river below. This time he *did* black out.

Tom pushed the memories away and ran his fingers through his hair. His breathing had gone ragged again, and he was covered with a fine sheen of sweat that made his shirt cling to his chest. *Face it,* he told himself, *you're terrified.*

It was no use. The Turtle was dead, and Tom Tudbury, he could juggle bars of soap and robot heads with the best of them, but no way was he going to lift a couple of tons of armor plate into the air. Give it up. Call Joey, dump the old shells into the bay, write it off. Forget the money, what's eighty thousand dollars? Not worth his life, that's for sure, Steve Bruder was going to make him rich anyway. The waters of New York Bay were wide and dark and cold, and it was a long way to Manhattan. He'd lucked out once, the god-damned shell had *exploded* as it fell to the bottom of the river, must have been the napalm or the water pressure or something, a freak accident, and the shock of the cold water had somehow revived him, and he'd struggled to the surface and let the current take him, and somehow, somehow, he'd made it to the shore in Jersey-City. He should have died.

His breakfast moved in the pit of his stomach, and for a moment Tom thought he would gag. Beaten, he unbuckled his seat belt. His hand was shaking. He turned off the fans, the tracking motors, the cameras. The darkness closed in around him.

The shell was supposed to make him invulnerable, but they'd turned it into a death trap. He couldn't take it up again. Not even for one last trip. He *couldn't.*

The blackness trembled around him. He felt as though he were going to fall again. He had to get out of here, *now,* he was suffocating. He could have died.

Only he hadn't.

The thought came out of nowhere, defiant. He could have died, but he hadn't died. He couldn't take the shell up again, but he had, that very night.

This very shell. When he'd finally made his way back to

the junkyard, he'd been half-drowned and exhausted and drunk with shock, but also strangely alive, exhilarated, high on the mere fact of his survival. He'd taken the shell out and crossed the bay and done loops over Jokertown, climbed right back on the horse that had thrown him, he'd showed them all, the Turtle was still alive, the Turtle had taken everything they could throw at him, they'd knocked him out and napalmed him and dropped him like a rock to the bottom of the fucking Hudson River, and *he was still alive*.

They'd cheered him in the streets.

Tom's hands reached out, flicked a switch, a second. The screens lit up again. The fans began to whir.

Don't do it, his fear whispered within him. *You can't. You'd be dead now if the shell hadn't blown—*

"It did blow," Tom said. The napalm, the water pressure, *something* . . .

The walls of his bedroom. Broken glass everywhere, his pillows ripped and torn, feathers floating in the air.

The water made a sullen gurgling sound somewhere in the close, hot blackness. The world twisted and turned, sinking. He was too weak and dizzy to move. He felt icy fingers on his legs, creeping up higher and higher, and then sudden shock as the water reached his crotch, jolting him awake. He tore away his seat harness with numb fingers, but too late, the cold caressed his chest, he lurched up and the floor tumbled and he lost his footing, and then the water was over his head and he couldn't breathe and everything was black, utterly black, as black as the grave, and he had to get out, he had to get *out* . . .

Cracks on the wall of his bedroom, more every time the nightmare came. And pictures in a magazine, fragments of armor plate torn and twisted, welds shattered, bolts torn loose, the whole shell shattered like an egg. The armor bent *outward*.

Fuck it all, he thought. *It was me. I did it.*

He looked into the nearest screen, gripped the armrests, and pushed down with his mind.

The shell rose smoothly up, through the bunker, through the garage door overhead, into the morning sky. Sunlight kissed the flaking green paint of its armor.

He came out of the eastern sky, out of Brooklyn, with the sun behind him. The trip was longer that way, when he circled over Staten Island and the Narrows, but it disguised the angle of his approach, and twenty years of turtling had taught him all the tricks. He came in over the great stone ramparts of the Brooklyn Bridge, low and fast, and on his screens he saw the morning strollers below look up in astonishment as his shadows washed across them. It was a sight the city had never seen before and would never see again: three Turtles sweeping across the East River, three iron specters from yesterday's headlines and the land of the dead, moving in tight formation, banking and turning as one, and sliding into a flamboyant double loop over the rooftops of Jokertown.

For Tom, in the center shell, the reactions down in the streets made it all worthwhile. At least he was going out in style; he'd like to see the magazines blame this one on Venus.

It'd been hell getting the other shells out of the bunker; gutted or not, their armor still lent them plenty of weight, and for a moment, hovering above the junkyard in Bayonne, he didn't think he'd be able to juggle all three. Then he had a better idea. Instead of trying to take them individually, he pictured them welded to the points of a giant invisible triangle, and he lifted the triangle into the air. After that it was candy.

Dutton had one camera crew on the Brooklyn Bridge, a second on the roof of the Famous Bowery Wild Card Dime Museum. With all the film they shot, there would be precious little question of authenticating the shells.

"All right," Tom announced through his loudspeakers after he had set the shells down on the wide, flat roof. "Show's over. Cut." Filming his approach and landing was one thing, but he wasn't going to have any footage of him climbing out of the hatch. Mask or no mask, that was a risk he didn't care to take.

Dutton, tall and dark with his cowl drawn up over his features, made a peremptory gesture with a gloved hand, and the camera crew—all jokers—loaded up their equipment and left the roof. When the last of them vanished down the stairs, Tom took a deep breath, slipped on his rubber frogface, killed the power, and crawled out into the morning sun.

After he'd emerged, he turned for one last look at what he was leaving behind. Out here, in daylight, they looked different than they had in the dimness of his bunker. Smaller, somehow. Shabbier. "Hard to walk away, isn't it?" Dutton asked him.

Tom turned. "Yes," he said. Beneath the cowl Dutton was wearing a leather lion mask with long golden hair. "You bought that mask at Holbrook's," Tom said.

"I own Holbrook's," Dutton replied. He studied the shells. "I wonder how we're going to get these inside."

Tom shrugged. "They got a fucking *whale* into the Museum of Natural History; a few turtles ought to be easy." He was not feeling nearly as nonchalant as he tried to sound. The Turtle had pissed off quite a few people over the years, everyone from street punks to Richard Milhous Nixon. If Dutton hadn't been discreet, any or all of them could be out there waiting for him, and even if they weren't, there was still the small matter of getting home with eighty thousand dollars in cash. "Let's do it," he said. "You got the money?"

"In my office," Dutton replied.

They went downstairs, Dutton leading, Tom following, looking around cautiously at every landing. It was cool and dim inside the building. "Closed again?" Tom asked.

"Business is off badly," Dutton admitted. "The city is afraid. This new wild card outbreak has driven the tourists away, and even the jokers are beginning to avoid crowds and public places."

When they reached the basement and entered the gloomy, stone-walled workshop, Tom saw that the museum was not entirely deserted. "We're preparing a number of new exhibits," Dutton explained as Tom paused to admire a slender, boyish young woman who was dressing a wax replica of Senator Hartmann. She had just finished knotting his tie with long, deft fingers. "This is for our Syrian diorama," Dutton said as the woman adjusted the senator's gray-checked sports coat. There was a ragged tear at one shoulder where a bullet had ripped through, and the surrounding fabric was carefully stained with fake blood.

"It looks very real," Tom said.

"Thank you," the young woman replied. She turned, smiling and extending her hand. Something was wrong with her eyes. They were all iris, a deep shiny red-black, half again the size of normal eyes. Yet she did not move like a blind person. "I'm Cathy, and I'd love to do you in wax," she said as Tom shook her hand. "Seated in one of your shells, maybe?" She tilted her head and pushed a strand of hair out of her strange dark eyes.

"Uh," said Tom, "I'd rather not."

"That's wise of you," Dutton said. "If Leo Barnett becomes president, some of your fellow aces may wish they'd kept a lower profile too. It doesn't pay to be too flamboyant these days."

"Barnett won't be elected," Tom said with some heat. He nodded at the wax figure. "Hartmann will stop him."

"Another vote for Senator Gregg," Cathy said, smiling. "If you ever change your mind about the statue, let me know."

"You'll be the first," Dutton told her. He took Tom by the arm. "Come," he urged. They passed other elements of the Syrian diorama in various states of assembly: Dr. Tachyon in full Arabian regalia, curled slippers on his feet; the giant Sayyid done in wax ten feet high; Carnifex in his blinding-white fighting togs. In another part of the room a technician labored over the mechanical ears on a huge elephant head that sat on a wooden table. Dutton passed him with a curt nod.

Then Tom saw something that stopped him dead. "Jesus fucking Christ," he said loudly. "That's . . ."

"Tom Miller," Dutton said. "But I believe he preferred to be called Gimli. Bound for our Hall of Infamy, I'm afraid."

The dwarf snarled up at them, one fist raised above his head as he harangued some crowd. His glass eyes, boiling with hate, seemed to follow them wherever they went. He wasn't wax.

"A brilliant piece of taxidermy," Dutton said. "We had to move quickly before decay set in. The skin was cracked in a dozen places, and everything inside had just dissolved—bones, muscles, internal organs, everything. This new wild card can be as merciless as the old."

"His *skin*," Tom said with revulsion.

"They have John Dillinger's penis in the Smithsonian," Dutton said calmly. "This way, please."

This time, when they reached Dutton's office, Tom accepted the offer of a drink.

Dutton had the money carefully banded and packed in a nondescript, rather shabby, green suitcase. "Tens, twenties, and fifties, a few hundreds," he said. "Would you like to count it?"

Tom just stared at all the crisp green bills, his drink forgotten in his hand. "No," he said softly after a long pause. "If it's not all there, I know where you live."

Dutton chuckled politely, went behind his desk, and produced a brown paper shopping bag with the museum logo on the side.

"What's that?" Tom asked.

"Why, the head. I was sure you'd want a bag."

Actually Tom had almost forgotten about Modular Man's head. "Oh, yeah," he said, taking the bag. "Sure." He looked inside. Modular Man stared back up at him. Quickly he closed the bag. "This will be fine," he said.

It was almost noon when he emerged from the museum, the green suitcase in his right hand and the shopping bag in his left. He stood blinking in the sunlight, then set off up the Bowery at a brisk pace, keeping a careful eye out to make certain he wasn't being followed. The streets were almost deserted, so he didn't think it would be too difficult to spot a tail.

By the third block Tom was pretty sure he was alone. What few people he'd seen were jokers wearing surgical masks or more elaborate face coverings, and they gave him, and each other, as wide a berth as possible. Still, he kept walking, just to be sure. The money was heavier than he had figured, and Modular Man surprisingly light, so he stopped twice to change hands.

When he reached the Funhouse, he set the suitcase and bag down, looked around carefully, saw no one. He peeled off his frog mask and jammed it in the pocket of his windbreaker.

The Funhouse was dark and padlocked. CLOSED UNTIL FURTHER NOTICE said the sign on the door. They'd shut their doors shortly after Xavier Desmond had been hospitalized, Tom knew. He'd read about it in the papers. It had saddened him immensely and made him feel even older than he felt already.

Bare-faced and nervous, shifting from foot to foot, Tom waited for a cab.

Traffic was very light, and the longer he waited, the more uneasy he grew. He gave fifty cents to a wino who stumbled up just to get rid of the man. Three punks in Demon Prince colors gave Tom and his suitcase a long, hard, speculative look. But his clothes were as shabby as the suitcase, and they must have decided that he wasn't worth the sweat.

Finally he got his cab.

He slid into the backseat of the big yellow Checker with a sigh of relief, the shopping bag on the seat beside him, the suitcase across his lap. "I'm going to Journal Square," he said. From there he could get another cab to take him back to Bayonne.

"Oh no, oh no," the cabbie said. He was dark-eyed, swarthy. Tom glanced at his hack's license. Pakistani. "No Jersey," the man said. "Oh no, do not go to Jersey."

Tom took a crumpled hundred from the pocket of his jeans. "Here," he said. "Keep the change."

The cabbie looked at the bill and broke into a broad smile. "Very good," he said. "Very good, New Jersey, oh yes, I am most pleasant." He put the cab in gear.

Tom was home free. He cranked down a window and settled back into his seat, enjoying the wind on his face and the pleasant heft of the suitcase on his lap.

A distant wail floated across the rooftops outside; high, thin, urgent.

"Oh, what is that?" the cabbie said, sounding puzzled.

"An air raid siren," Tom said. He leaned forward, alarmed. A second siren began to sound, nearer, loud and piercing. Cars were pulling over to the sidewalk. People in the streets stopped and looked up into bright, empty skies. Far off, Tom could hear other sirens joining the first two. The noise built and built. "Fuck," Tom said. He was remembering history. They'd sounded the air raid sirens the day that Jetboy had died, when the wild card had been played on an unsuspecting city. "Turn on the radio," he said.

"Oh, pardon, sir, does not work, oh no."

"Damn it," Tom swore. "Okay. Faster then. Get me to the Holland Tunnel."

The driver gunned it and ran a red light.

They were on Canal Street, four blocks from the Holland Tunnel, when the traffic came to a standstill.

The cab stopped behind a silver-gray Jaguar with its temporary license taped to the rear window. Nothing was moving. The cabbie hit his horn. Other horns sounded far up the street, mingling with the sound of the air raid sirens.

Behind them a rust-eaten Chevy van screeched to a halt and began to honk impatiently, over and over. The cabbie stuck his head out the window and screamed something in a language Tom did not know, but his meaning was clear. More traffic was piling up behind the van.

The cabdriver hit his horn again, then turned around long enough to tell Tom that it wasn't his fault. Tom had already figured out that much for himself. "Wait here," he said unnecessarily, since the traffic was locked bumper-to-bumper, none of it moving, and there wasn't room for the cabbie to pull out even if he'd wanted to.

Tom left the door open and stood on the center line, looking down Canal Street. Traffic was tied up as far as he could see, and the jam was growing rapidly behind them. Tom walked to the corner for a better look. The intersection was gridlocked, traffic lights cycling from red to green to yellow and back to red without anyone's moving an inch. Music blared from open car windows, a cacophony of stations and songs, all of it counterpointed by the horns and air raid sirens, but none of the radios were getting any news.

The driver of the Chevy van came up behind Tom. "Where the fuck are the cops?" he demanded. He was grossly fat with a jowly, pockmarked face. He looked as if he wanted to hit something, but he had a point. The police were nowhere to be seen. Somewhere up ahead a child began to cry, her voice as high and shrill as the sirens, wordless. It gave Tom a shiver of fear. This wasn't just a traffic jam, he thought. Something was wrong. Something was very, very wrong.

He went back to his cab. The driver was slamming his fist into the steering wheel, but he was the only one this side of Broadway who wasn't honking. "Horn broke," he explained.

"I'm getting out here," Tom said.

"No refund."

"Fuck you." Tom had been going to let the man keep the hundred anyway, but his tone pissed him off. He pulled the suitcase and shopping bag out of the backseat and gave the cabbie a finger as he headed up Canal on foot.

A well-dressed fiftyish woman sat behind the wheel of the silver Jaguar. "Do you know what's going on?" she asked.

Tom shrugged.

A lot of people were out of their cars now. A man in a Mercedes 450 SL stood with one foot in his car and one on the street, his cellular phone in his hand. "Nine-one-one's still busy," he told the people gathered around him.

"Fuckin' cops," someone complained.

Tom had reached the intersection when he saw the helicopter sweeping down Canal just above rooftop level. Dust whirled and old newspapers shivered in the gutters. The rotors were so *loud*, even at a distance. *I never made so much fucking noise*, Tom thought; something about the helicopter reminded him weirdly of the Turtle. He heard the crackle of a loudspeaker, the words lost in the street noise.

A pimpled teenager leaned out of a white Ford pickup with Jersey plates. "The Guard," he shouted. "That's a Guard chopper!" He waved at the helicopter.

The *whap-whap-whap* of the rotors mingled with the horns and sirens and shouting to drown out the loudspeakers. Horns began to fall silent. ". . . *your homes* . . ."

Someone began shouting obscenities.

The chopper dipped lower, came on. Even Tom saw the military markings now, the National Guard insignia. The loudspeakers boomed. ". . . *closed* . . . *repeat: Holland Tunnel is closed. Return to your homes peacefully.*"

Huge gusts of wind kicked up all around him as the helicopter passed directly overhead. Tom dropped to one knee and covered his face against the dust and dirt.

"*The tunnel is closed,*" he heard as the chopper receded. "*Do not attempt to leave Manhattan. Holland Tunnel is closed. Return to your homes peacefully.*"

When the copter reached the end of stalled traffic, two blocks farther back, it peeled off and rose high in the air, a small black shape in the sky, then circled back for another loop. The people in the streets looked at each other.

"They can't mean me, I'm from Iowa," a fat woman announced, as if it made a difference. Tom knew how she felt.

The cops had finally arrived. Two patrol cars edged down the sidewalk carefully, bypassing the worst of the congestion. A black policeman got out and started snapping orders. One or two people got back into their cars obediently. The rest surrounded the cop, all of them talking at once. Others, lots of them, had abandoned their vehicles. A stream of people headed up Canal Street, toward the entrance to the Holland Tunnel.

Tom went with them, moving along slower than most, struggling with the weight of his bags. He was sweating. A woman passed him at a dead run, looking ragged and near hysteria. The helicopter flew over again, loudspeakers blaring, warning the crowd to turn back.

"Martial law!" a truck driver shouted down from the cab of his semi. A wall of people formed around the truck, trapping Tom in their midst. He was shoved up against the tractor's rear wheel as the crowd pressed closer for news. "It just came over the CB," the trucker said. "The motherfuckers have declared martial law. Not just the Holland Tunnel. They shut down everything, all the bridges, the tunnels, even the Staten Island ferry. No one's getting off the island."

"Oh, god," someone said behind Tom, a man's voice, husky but raw with fear. "Oh, god, it's the wild card."

"We're all going to die," an old woman said. "I seen it in '46. They're just gonna keep us here."

"It's those jokers," suggested a man in a three-piece suit. "Barnett is right, they shouldn't be living with normal people, they spread disease."

"No," Tom said. "The wild card isn't contagious."

"Sez you. Oh, god, we probably all got it already."

"There's a carrier," the trucker shouted down. Tom could hear the crackle of his CB radio. "Some fucking joker. He's spreading it wherever he goes."

"That's not possible," Tom said.

"Goddamn joker-lover," someone shouted at him.

"I got to get home to my *babies*," a young woman wailed.

"Take it easy," Tom started to say, but it was too late, way too late. He heard crying, screaming, shouted obscenities. The crowd seemed to explode as people ran off in a dozen directions. Somebody slammed into him hard. Tom staggered back, then fell as he was buffeted from the side. He almost lost his grip on the suitcase, but he hung on grimly, even when a boot stomped painfully on his calf. He rolled under the truck. Feet rushed past him. He crawled between the wheels of the semi, dragging his bags behind him, and got to his feet on the sidewalk, half-dazed. *This is fucking crazy*, he thought.

Way down Canal, the helicopter began another pass. Tom watched it come, the crowd surging hysterically around him. *The chopper will calm them down*, he thought, *it has to*.

When the first tear gas canisters began to rain down into the street, trailing yellow smoke, he turned and dodged into the nearest alley and began to run.

The noise dwindled behind as Tom fled through alleys and side streets. He'd gone three blocks and was breathing hard when he noticed a cellar door ajar under a bookstore. He hesitated a moment, but when he heard the sound of running feet on the cross street, his mind was made up for him.

It was cool and quiet inside. Tom gratefully dropped the suitcase and sat cross-legged on the cement floor. He leaned back against the wall and listened. The air raid sirens had finally quieted, but he heard horns and an ambulance and the distant, angry rumble of shouts.

Off to his right he heard the scrape of a footstep.

Tom's head snapped around. "Who's there?"

There was only silence. The cellar was dark and gloomy. Tom got to his feet. He could swear he'd heard something. He took a step forward, froze, cocked his head. Then he was sure. Someone was back there, behind those boxes. He could hear the short, ragged sound of their breathing.

Tom wasn't going any closer. He backed toward the door and gave the boxes a hard telekinetic shove. The whole stack went over, cardboard ripping, and dozens of glossy paperback copies of *More Disgusting Joker Jokes* cascaded from a torn carton. There was a grunt of surprise and pain from behind the boxes.

Tom edged forward and pushed the top boxes in the feebly moving pile off to the side, using his hands this time.

"Don't hurt me!" a voice pleaded from under the books.

"No one's going to hurt you," Tom said. He shifted a torn box, spilling more paperbacks onto the floor. Half-buried underneath, a man curled in a fetal ball, arms locked protectively around his head. "Come on out of there."

"I wasn't doing nothing," the man on the floor said in a thin, whispery voice. "I just come in to hide."

"I was hiding, too," Tom said. "It's okay. Come on out."

The man stirred, unfolded, got warily to his feet. There was something dreadfully wrong with the way he moved. "I ain't so good to look at," he warned in that thin, rustling voice.

"I don't care," said Tom.

Walking in a painful crabbed sideways motion, the man edged forward into the light, and Tom got a good look at him. An instant of revulsion gave way to sudden, overwhelming pity. Even in the dim light in the back of the cellar, Tom could see how cruelly the joker's body had been twisted. One of his legs was much longer than the other, triple-jointed, and attached backward, so the knee bent in the wrong direction. The other leg, the "normal" one, ended in a clubfoot. A cluster of tiny vestigial hands grew from the swollen flesh of his right forearm. His skin was glossy black, bone-white, chocolate-brown, and copper-red in patches all over his body; there was no way to tell what race he'd belonged to originally. Only his face was normal. It was a beautiful face; blue-eyed, blond, strong. A movie star's face.

"I'm Mishmash," the joker whispered timidly.

But the movie star lips hadn't moved, and there was no life in those deep, clear blue eyes. Then Tom saw the second head, the hideous little monkey-face peeping cautiously out of the unbuttoned shirt. It sprouted crookedly from the joker's ample gut, as purple as an old bruise.

Tom felt nauseated. It must have showed on his face because Mishmash turned away. "Sorry," he muttered, "sorry."

"What happened?" Tom forced himself to ask. "Why are you hiding here?"

"I saw them," the joker told him, his back to Tom. "These guys. Nats. They had this joker; they were beating the hell out of him. They would of done me, too, only I snuck away. They said it was all our fault. I got to get home."

"Where do you live?" Tom asked.

Mishmash made a wet, muffled sound that might have been a laugh and half-turned. The little head twisted up to look at Tom. "Jokertown," he said.

"Yeah," Tom said, feeling very stupid. Of course he lived in Jokertown, where the fuck else could he live? "That's only a few blocks away. I'll take you there."

"You got a car?"

"No," Tom said. "We'll have to walk."

"I don't walk so good."

"We'll go slow," Tom said.

*   *   *

They went slow.

Dusk was falling when Tom finally emerged, cautiously, from the cellar refuge. The street had been quiet for hours, but Mishmash was too frightened to venture out until dark. "They'll hurt me," he kept saying.

Even when twilight began to gather, the joker was still reluctant to move. Tom went first to scout the block. There were lights in a few apartments, and he heard the sound of a television blaring from a third-story window, and more police sirens, far off in the distance. Otherwise the city seemed deathly quiet. He walked around the block slowly, moving from doorway to doorway like a GI in a war movie. There were no cars, no pedestrians, nothing. All the storefronts were dark, secured by accordion grills and steel shutters. Even the neighborhood bars were closed. Tom saw a few broken windows, and just around the corner the overturned, burned-out hulk of a police car sat square in the middle of the intersection. A huge Marlboro billboard had been defaced with red paint; KILL ALL JOKERS, it said. He decided not to take Mishmash down that street.

When he returned, the joker was waiting. He'd moved the suitcase and shopping bag to the doorway. "I told you not to touch those," Tom snapped in annoyance, and felt immediately guilty when he saw how Mishmash quailed under his voice.

He picked up the bags. "C'mon," he said, stepping back outside. Mishmash followed, his every step a hideous twisting dance. They went slowly. They went very slowly.

They stayed mostly to alleys and side streets south of Canal, resting frequently. The damned suitcase seemed to get heavier with each passing block.

They were catching their breath by a Dumpster just off Church Street when a tank rolled past the mouth of the alley, followed by a half dozen National Guardsmen on foot. One of them glanced to his left, saw Mishmash, and began to raise his rifle. Tom stood up, stepped in front of the joker. For an instant his eyes met the Guardsman's. He was only a kid, Tom saw, no more than nineteen or twenty. The boy looked at Tom for a long moment, then lowered his gun, nodded, and walked on.

Broadway was eerily deserted. A lone police paddy wagon

wove its way through an obstacle course of abandoned cars. Tom watched it pass while Mishmash cringed back behind some garbage cans. "Let's go," Tom said.

"They'll see us," Mishmash said. "They'll hurt me."

"No they won't," Tom promised. "Look at how dark it is."

They were halfway across Broadway, moving from car to car, when the streetlights came on, sudden and silent. The shadows were gone. Mishmash gave a single sharp bark of fear. "Move it," Tom told him urgently. They scrambled for the far side of the street.

"Hold it right there!"

The shout stopped them at the edge of the sidewalk. *Almost*, Tom thought, but almost only counts in horseshoes and grenades. He turned slowly.

The cop wore a white gauze surgical mask that muffled his voice, but his tone was still all business. His holster was unbuttoned, his gun already in hand.

"You don't have to—" Tom started nervously.

"Shut the fuck up," the cop said. "You're in violation of the curfew."

"Curfew?" Tom said.

"You heard me. Don't you listen to the radio?" He didn't wait for the answer. "Lemme see some ID."

Tom carefully lowered his bags to the ground. "I'm from Jersey," he said. "I was trying to get home, but they closed the tunnels." He fished out his wallet and handed it to the cop.

"Jersey," the cop said, studying the driver's license. He handed it back. "Why aren't you at Port Authority?"

"Port Authority?" Tom said, confused.

"The clearance center." The cop's tone was still gruff and impatient, but he'd evidently decided they weren't a threat. He holstered his gun. "Out-of-towners are supposed to report to Port Authority. You pass the medical, they'll give you a blue card and send you home. If I was you, I'd head up there."

Port Authority Bus Terminal was a zoo under the best of circumstances. Tom tried to imagine what it would be like now. Every tourist, commuter, and visitor in the city would be there, along with a lot of frightened Manhattanites pretending to be from out of town, all of them waiting their turn for a medical or fighting for a seat on one of the buses leaving the city, with the police and National Guard trying to keep order. You didn't need a lot of imagination to picture the kind of nightmare going on up at Forty-second Street. "I didn't know. I'll get right up there," Tom lied, "as soon as I get my friend home."

The cop gave Mishmash a hard look. "You're taking a big risk, buddy. The carrier's supposed to be some kind of albino, and nobody said anything about any extra heads, but all jokers look alike in the dark, right? Those Guard boys are real jumpy, too. They see a pair like you, they might decide to shoot first and check your IDs later."

"What the fuck is going on?" Tom said. It sounded worse than he could have imagined. "What is all this?"

"Do you good to turn on a radio once in a while," the cop said. "Might stop you getting your head shot off."

"Who are you looking for?"

"Some joker fuck, been spreading a new kind of wild card all over the city. He's freaky strong, and crazy. Dangerous. And he's got a friend with him, some new ace, looks normal but bullets bounce right off him. If I was you, I'd dump the geek and haul ass for Port Authority."

"I didn't do nothing," Mishmash whispered.

His voice was low, barely audible, but it was the first time he'd dared to speak, and the cop heard him well enough. "Shut the fuck up. I'm not in the mood for any joker lip. I want to hear you talk, I'll ask you a question."

Mishmash quailed. Tom was shocked by the loathing in the policeman's voice. "You got no call to talk to him that way."

It was a mistake, a big mistake. Above the surgical mask the policeman's eyes narrowed. "That so? What are you, one of those queers who likes to hump jokers?"

No, you asshole, Tom thought furiously, *I'm the Great and Powerful Turtle, and if I were in my shell right now, I'd pick you up and drop you in the garbage where you belong.* But what he said was, "Sorry, Officer. I didn't mean anything by it. It's been a rough day for everyone, right? Maybe we should just get going?" He tried to smile as he picked up the suitcase and shopping bag. "C'mon, Mishmash," he said.

"What's in those bags?" the cop said suddenly.

Modular Man's head and eighty thousand dollars in cash, Tom thought, but he didn't say it. He didn't think he'd broken any laws, but the truth would raise questions he wasn't prepared to answer. "Nothing," he told the cop. "Some clothes." But he'd hesitated too long.

"Why don't we have a look," the policeman replied.

"No," Tom blurted. "You can't. I mean, don't you need a search warrant or probable cause or something?"

"I got your fucking probable cause right here," the cop said, drawing his gun. "This is martial law, and we got authority to shoot looters on sight. Now lower the bags to the ground *slowly* and back off, asshole."

The moment seemed to last a long, long time. Then Tom did as he was told.

"Further back," the cop said. Tom retreated to the sidewalk. "You too, geek." Mishmash moved back next to Tom.

The policeman edged forward, bent over, and pulled one of the handles of the shopping bag to peer inside.

Modular Man's head flew up and smashed him in the face.

Blood squirted from the cop's nose with a sickening crunch to stain the white gauze of his mask. He gave a muffled screech and staggered back. The head bowled squarely into his gut, tumbling like a cannonball. The cop grunted as his feet went out from under him. He landed on his ass in the street.

The head swooped around him. The cop brought up his pistol with both hands and squeezed off a round. Glass shattered in a second-story window as the head came crashing into his temple. The cop swatted at it with the barrel of his pistol; then something jerked the gun right out his hand and sent it skittering off down a sewer.

"Son-of-a-bitch," the cop managed. He tried to struggle back to his feet, his eyes as glassy as Mod Man's. His nose was still bleeding; the surgical mask had turned a vivid red.

The head came at him again. This time he managed to grab it and hold it at bay, just inches from his face. The long cable dangling from the jagged neck took on a life of its own and snaked up into a bloody nostril. The cop screamed and grabbed for the cable. The head jumped forward; two foreheads cracked together hard. The cop went down. The head circled over him. The cop groaned and rolled over. He made no attempt to rise.

Tom started breathing again.

"Is he *dead*?" Mishmash asked in an eager whisper.

Tom's heart was still on adrenaline overdrive; it took a moment for the words to register. "Fuck," he said. What the hell had he *done*? It had all gone down so quickly.

Mod Man's head fell out of the air, hit the gutter, and rolled. Tom knelt over the fallen cop and felt for a pulse. "He's alive," Tom said. "Breathing is shallow, though. He might have a concussion, maybe even a cracked skull."

Mishmash crowded close. "Kill him."

Tom's head snapped back around and he stared at the joker in horror. "Are you crazy?"

The hideous little purple monkey-face was straining forward through his shirtfront. Moisture glistened on the hard, thin lips. "He was going to kill us. You heard him, you heard what he called us. He had no right. Kill him."

"No way," Tom said. He stood up, wiping his hands on his jeans compulsively. His high was gone now; he felt more than a little sick.

"He knows who you are," Mishmash whispered.

Tom had somehow managed to forget that. "Fuck fuck *fuck*," he swore. The cop had seen his driver's license.

"They'll come for you," Mishmash suggested. "They'll know you did it, and they'll come. Kill him. Go on, I won't tell."

Tom backed away, shaking his head. "No."

"Then I'll do it," Mishmash said. His lips peeled back over a mouthful of yellowed incisors, and the wrinkled face shot out and down, into the cop's throat. Mishmash's shirt sagged where his gut had been. The head worked at the soft flesh under the cop's chin, bobbing at the end of three feet of glistening transparent tube connecting it to the joker's torso. Tom heard wet, greedy sucking sounds. The cop's feet began to thrash feebly. Blood spurted, Mishmash swallowed and sucked, and a thick red wash began to travel up through the thick glassy flesh of his neck.

"*No!*" Tom screamed. "Stop it!"

The monkey-face continued to feed, but on top of the joker's body his second head, the movie-star head, turned to stare at Tom from clear blue eyes and smiled beatifically.

Tom reached out for Mishmash with his teke, or tried to, but there was nothing there. The fury that had filled him when the cop threatened them was gone; now there was only horror and fear, and his power had always deserted him when he was afraid. He stood helplessly, hands clenching and unclenching as Mishmash gnawed away with teeth as cruel and sharp as needles.

Then he leapt forward and grabbed the joker from behind, wrapping his arms around that twisted torso, pulling him back. For a moment they grappled. Tom was overweight and out of shape and had never been especially strong, but the joker's body was as weak as it was misshapen. They stumbled backward, Mishmash thrashing feebly in Tom's arms, until the head pulled free of the cop's torn throat with a soft *pop*. The joker hissed in fury. His long glistening neck coiled around, snakelike, over his left shoulder, as pale eyes glared down, insane with frustration. Blood was smeared all over the shrunken purplish face. Wet red teeth snapped wildly, but his neck wasn't long enough.

Tom spun him around and shoved him away. The joker's mismatched legs tangled under him, and he tripped and fell heavily into the gutter. "Get out of here!" Tom screamed. "Get out of here now or I'll give you the same thing I gave him."

Mishmash hissed, his head weaving back and forth. Then, as suddenly as it had come, the bloodlust was gone, and once more the joker cringed in fear. "Don't," he whispered, "please don't. I only wanted to help. Don't hurt me, mister." His neck shrunk slowly back into his shirt, a long, thick glass eel returning to its lair, until there was only the small scared face shivering between his buttons. By then Mishmash was back on his feet. He gave Tom one last pleading look, and then whirled and began to run, arms and legs working grotesquely.

Tom stopped the policeman's bleeding with a handkerchief. There was still a pulse, but it felt weak to him, and the man had obviously lost a lot of blood. He hoped it wasn't too late.

He looked around at the abandoned cars and headed toward a likely one. Joey had once shown him how to hot-wire an ignition; he sure as hell hoped he still remembered.

It was standing room only in the waiting room of the Jokertown Clinic. Tom pushed his suitcase up against a wall and sat on top of it. The shopping bag, with Modular Man's bloodied head stuck inside it, he shoved between his legs. The room was hot and noisy. He ignored the frightened people all around him, the screams of pain from the next room, and stared dully at the tiles on the floor, trying not to think. Perspiration covered his face under the clinging frog mask.

He'd been waiting a half hour when a fat, tusked newsboy in a porkpie hat and Hawaiian shirt entered the waiting room with an armful of papers. Tom bought a copy of tomorrow's *Jokertown Cry*, sat back on his suitcase, and began to read. He read every word in every story on every page, and then started all over again.

The headlines were full of martial law and the citywide manhunt for Croyd Crenson. Typhoid Croyd, the *Cry* called him; anyone coming in contact with the carrier risked drawing the wild card. No wonder everyone was so scared. Dr. Tachyon had told the authorities it was a mutant form, capable of reinfecting even stable aces and jokers.

The Turtle could bring him in, Tom thought. Anyone else, police or Guardsman or ace, risked infection and death if they tried to apprehend him, but the Turtle could take him in perfect safety, easy as candy. He didn't have to get real close to teke someone, and his shell gave him plenty of protection.

Only there was no shell, and the Turtle was dead.

Sixty-three people had required medical treatment after the rioting around the Holland Tunnel, and property damage was estimated at more than a million dollars, he read.

The Turtle could have dissipated that crowd without anyone's getting hurt. Just *talk* to them, dammit, take the time to quell their fears, and if things got out of hand, pry them apart with teke. You didn't need guns or tear gas.

Sporadic outbreaks of anti-joker violence had been reported throughout the city. Two jokers were dead, a dozen more had been hospitalized after beatings or stonings.

There was widespread looting in Harlem.

Arson had destroyed the storefront headquarters of Jokers for Jesus, and firemen responding to the alarm had been pelted with bricks and dogshit.

Leo Barnett was praying for the souls of the afflicted and calling for quarantine in the name of public health.

A twenty-year-old coed from Columbia had been gang-raped on a pool table in Squisher's Basement. More than a dozen jokers had watched from their barstools, and half of those had lined up to take their turns after the original rapists were done. Someone had told them they'd be cured of their deformities if they had sex with this woman.

The Turtle was dead, and Tom Tudbury sat on a battered old suitcase stuffed with eighty thousand dollars in cash as the world grew more and more insane.

All the king's horses and all the king's men, he thought.

He'd just finished his third pass through the newspaper when a shadow fell across him. Tom looked up and saw the hefty black nurse who had helped him carry the policeman in from the car. "Dr. Tachyon will see you now," she said.

Tom followed her back to a small cubicle off the emergency room, where Tachyon sat wearily behind a steel desk.

"Well?" Tom asked after the nurse had left.

"He'll live," Tach said. Lilac eyes lingered on the green, rubbery features of Tom's mask. "We are required by law to file a report on this sort of thing. The police will want to question you once the emergency has passed. We need a name."

"Thomas Tudbury," he said. He pulled off the mask and let it drop to the floor.

"Turtle," Tach blurted, surprised. He stood up.

The Turtle is dead, Tom thought, but he didn't say it.

Dr. Tachyon frowned. "Tom, what happened out there?"

"It's a long, ugly story. You want it, go into my fucking brain and take it. I don't want to talk about it."

Tach looked at him thoughtfully. Then the alien winced and sat down again.

"At least with the fucking Astronomer I could tell the good guys from the bad guys," Tom said.

"He has your name," Tach said.

"One of my names," Tom said. "Fuck it. I need your help."

Tach was still linked with his mind; the alien looked up sharply. "I will not do that."

Tom leaned forward across the desk, looming over the smaller man. "You will," he said. "You owe me, Tachyon. And there's no way I can kill myself without your help."

Mortality

by Walter Jon Williams

Run.

Consciousness stitched a lightning path across his mind. It seemed to come in bursts, like lines of text from a very fast laserprinter... but no, it was more complex than that. A master weaver was forming the largest and most intricate tapestry in the universe, all in a matter of seconds, and doing it all in his brain.

He opened his eyes. St. Elmo's fire shimmered before him like a polar aurora. A screaming noise assaulted his ears. Subsonics moved through his body like tidal waves.

The noise faded. Internals ran lightspeed checks. Radar painted an image in his brain, superimposed it on the visuals.

"All monitored systems are functioning," he found himself saying.

The St. Elmo's fluorescence faded, revealing sagging bare roofbeams, an half-open skylight with the glass painted black from the inside, diagrams tacked up helter-skelter, drooping electric cables. Electric fans made a busy stir in the air. Something in the room moved, imaged first by radar, then by visuals. He recognized the figure, the tall, white-haired man with the hawk nose and disdainful eyes. Maxim Travnicek. A frigid smile curled Travnicek's lips. He spoke with a middle-European accent.

"Welcome back, toaster. The land of the living awaits."

"I blew up." Modular Man examined this possibility with cold impartiality as he pulled on a jumpsuit. A fly buzzed in the distance.

"You blew up," said Travnicek. "Modular Man the invincible android blew himself to bits. In a big fight at Aces High with the Astronomer and the Egyptian Masons. Lucky I had a backup of your memory."

Memories poured over the android's macroatomic switches. Modular Man recognized Travnicek's new Jokertown loft, the one he'd moved into after being evicted from the bigger place on the Lower East Side. The place was stiflingly hot, and electric fans plugged into overworked extension cords did little to make the place seem like home. Equipment, the big flux generators and computers, were jammed together on home-built platforms and raw plywood shelving. The ultrasonics had burst the picture tubes in two of the monitors.

"The Astronomer?" he said. "He hadn't been seen in months. I have no recollection of his return."

Travnicek made a dismissive gesture. "The fight happened after I last backed up your memory."

"I blew up?" The android didn't want to think about this. "How could I blow up?"

"Right. A surprise to both of us. Half-intelligent microwave ovens aren't supposed to explode."

Travnicek sat on a thirdhand plastic chair, a cigarette in his hand. He was thinner than before, his reddened eyes sunk deep in hollows. He looked years older. His straight hair, usually combed back from his forehead, stuck out in tufts. He seemed to have been doing his own barbering.

Travnicek wore baggy, army-green surplus trousers and a cream-colored formal shirt with food stains and frills on the front. He wasn't wearing a tie.

The android had never seen Travnicek without a tie. Something must have happened to the man, he realized. And then a frightening thought came to him.

"How long have I been . . . ?"

"Dead?"

"Yes."

"You blew up last Wild Card Day. Now it's June fifteenth."

"Nine months." The android was horrified.

Travnicek seemed irritated. He threw away his cigarette and ground the stub into the bare plywood floor. "How long do you think it takes to *build* a blender of your capabilities? Jesus Christ, it took weeks just to decipher the notes I wrote last time." He gave an expansive wave of his hand. "*Look* at this place. I've been working day and night."

Fast food containers were everywhere, a bewildering variety that strongly represented Chinese places, pizza joints, and Kentucky Fried Chicken. Flies buzzed among the cartons. In and among the containers were bits of scrap, yellow legal paper, pieces of paper bags, torn cigarette cartons, and the insides of matchbooks. All with notes that Travnicek had made to himself during his fever of construction, half of them ground into the naked floor and covered with footprints. The electric fans Travnicek used to move the sluggish air in the place had done a good job of scattering them.

Travnicek stood up and turned away, lighting another cigarette. "The place needs a good cleaning," he said. "You know where the broom is."

"Yes, sir." Resigned to it.

"I've got about fifty bucks left after paying the rent on this fucking heap. Enough for a little celebration." He jingled change in his pockets. "Gotta make a little phone call." Travnicek leered. "You're not the only one with girlfriends."

Modular Man ran his internal checks again, looked down at his body in the half-zipped jumpsuit.

Nothing seemed out of place.

Still, he thought, something was wrong.

He went after the broom.

Half an hour later, carrying two plastic trash bags full of fast food cartons, the android opened the skylight, floated through it, crossed the roof, then dropped down the air shaft that led to the alley behind. His intention was to toss the trash in a Dumpster that he knew waited in the alley.

His feet touched broken concrete. Sounds echoed down the alley. Heavy breathing, a guttural moan. A strange, lyric, birdlike sound.

In Jokertown the sounds could mean anything. The victim of an assault bleeding against the brownstone wall; the sad and horrible joker Snotman struggling for breath; a derelict passed out and having a nightmare; a customer from Freakers who'd had too much liquor or too many grotesque sights and had stumbled away to upchuck his guts...

The android was cautious. He lowered the trash bags silently to the pavement and floated silently a few feet above the surface. Rotating his body to the horizontal, he peered out into the alleyway.

The heavy breathing was coming from Travnicek. He had a woman up against the wall, lunging into her with his trousers down around his ankles.

The woman wore an elaborate custom mask over her lower face: a joker. The upper half of her face was not disfigured, but it wasn't pretty, either. She was not young. She wore a tube top and a glittery silver jacket and a red miniskirt. Her plastic boots were white. The trilling sound came from behind the mask. Short-time in an alley was probably costing Travnicek about fifteen dollars.

Travnicek muttered something in Czech. The woman's face was impassive. She regarded the alley wall with dreamy eyes. The musical sound she was making was something she probably did all the time, a sound unconnected with what she was doing. The android decided he didn't want to watch this anymore.

He left the garbage in the airshaft. The trilling sound pursued him like a flight of birds.

Someone had stuck a red, white, and blue poster on the plastic hood over the pay phone: BARNETT FOR PRESIDENT. The android didn't know who Barnett was. His plastic fingertips jabbed the coin slot on the pay phone. There was a click, then a ringing signal. The android had long ago discovered an affinity with communications equipment.

"Hello."

"Alice? This is Modular Man."

A slight pause. "Not funny."

"This really is Modular Man. I'm back."

"Modular Man *blew up!*"

"My creator built me over again. I've got almost all the memories of the original." The android's eyes scanned the street, looking up and down. There were very few people on the street for a warm June afternoon. "You feature in a lot of those memories, Alice."

"Oh, god."

There was another long pause. The android noticed that the pedestrians on the street seemed to be giving one another a lot of space. One of them wore a gauze mask over his mouth and nose. Cars were few.

"Can I see you?" he asked.

"You were important for me, you know."

"I'm glad, Alice." The android sensed impending disappointment in his demotion to the past tense.

"I mean, every man I'd ever been involved with was so

demanding. Wanting this, wanting that. I never had any time to find out what *Alice* wanted. And then I meet this guy who's willing to give me all the space I need, who didn't want anything from me because he *can't* want anything, because he's a *machine*, you know, and because he can get me seated at the good tables at Aces High and because we can *fly* and dance with the moon..." There was a brief silence. "You were really important to me, Mod Man. But I can't see you. I'm married now."

A palpable sense of loss drifted like scuttering snow across the android's macroatomic switches. "I'm happy for you, Alice." A National Guard jeep cruised past, with four Guardsmen in combat gear. Modular Man, who had established good relations with the Guard during the Swarm attack, gave them a wave. The jeep slowed, its passengers looking at him without changing expression. Then they speeded up and moved on.

"I thought you were *dead*. You know?"

"I understand." He sensed an irresolution in her. "Can I call you later?"

"Only at work." Her voice was fast. "If you call me at home, Ralph might start asking questions. He knows about a lot of my past, but he might find an affair with a machine a little weird. I mean, *I* know it was okay, and *you* know, but I imagine it's a little strange explaining it to people."

"I understand."

"He's tolerant of alternate lifestyles, but I'm not sure how tolerant he'd be of *me* having one. Particularly one he'd never heard of or thought about."

"I'll call you, Alice."

"Good-bye."

She thought I didn't want anything for myself, the android thought as he hung up the phone. Somehow that made him sadder than anything.

His finger jabbed the coin slot again and dialed a California number. The phone rang twice before a recording announced the number had been disconnected. Cyndi had moved somewhere. Maybe, he thought, he'd call her agent later.

He dialed a New Haven number. "Hi, Kate," he said.

"Oh." He heard someone inhaling a cigarette. When the

voice came back, it was cheerful. "I always thought someone
would put you back together."

Relief poured into him. "Someone did. For good this
time, I hope."

A low chuckle. "It's hard to keep a good man down."

The android thought about that for a moment. "Maybe I
can see you," he said.

"I'm not coming to Manhattan. The bridges are closed
anyway."

"Bridges closed?"

"Bridges closed. Martial law. Panic in the streets. You
have been out of touch, haven't you?"

Modular Man looked up and down the street again. "I
guess so."

"There's a wild card outbreak, mostly in lower Manhattan.
Hundreds of people have drawn the Black Queen. It's a
mutant form. Supposedly it's spread by a carrier named
Croyd Crenson."

"The Sleeper? I've heard the name."

Kate sucked on the cigarette again. "They've closed the
bridges and tunnels to keep him from getting out. There's
martial law."

Which explained the Guard on the streets again. "Things
had seemed a little slow," Modular Man said. "But nobody
told me."

"Amazing."

"I guess if you're dead"—hollowly—"you don't get to
watch the news." He thought about this for a moment, then
tried to cheer himself up. "I could visit *you*. I can *fly*.
Roadblocks can't stop me."

"You might—" She cleared her throat. "You might be a
carrier, Mod Man." She tried to laugh. "Becoming a joker
would really wreck my burgeoning academic career."

"I can't be a carrier. I'm a machine."

"Oh." A surprised pause. "Sometimes I forget."

"Shall I come?"

"Um . . ." That cigarette sound again. "I'd better not. Not
till after comps."

"Comps?"

"Three days locked in a very small and cramped hell with
the dullest of the Roman poets, which come to think of it is

really saying something. I'm studying like mad. I really can't afford a social life till after I get my degree."

"Oh. I'll call you then, okay?"

"I'll be looking forward."

"Bye."

Modular Man hung up the phone. Other phone numbers rolled through his mind; but the first three had been sufficiently discouraging that he didn't really want to try again.

He looked up the near-vacant street. He could go to Aces High and maybe meet somebody, he thought.

Aces High. Where he'd died.

A coldness touched his mind at the thought. Quite suddenly he didn't want to go to Aces High at all.

Then he decided he needed to know.

Radar dish spinning, he rose silently into the air.

The android landed on the observation deck and stepped into the bar. Hiram Worchester, standing alone in the middle of the room, swung around suddenly, holding up a fist. . . . His eyes were dark holes in his doughy face. He looked at Modular Man for a long moment as if he didn't recognize him, then swallowed hard, lowered his hand, and almost visibly drew a smile onto his face.

"I thought you'd be rebuilt," he said.

The android smiled. "Takes a licking," he said. "Keeps on ticking."

"That's very good to hear." Hiram gave a grating chuckle that sounded as if it were coming from the tin horn of a gramophone. "Still, it's not every day a regular customer comes back from the dead. Your drinks and your next meal, Modular Man, are on Aces High."

Aside from Hiram the place was nearly deserted: only Wall Walker and two others were present.

"Thank you, Hiram." The android stepped to the bar and put his foot on the rail. The gesture felt familiar, warmly pleasant and homelike. He smiled at the bartender, whom he hadn't seen before, and said, "Zombie." Behind him, Hiram made a choking sound. He turned back to the fat man.

"A problem, Hiram?"

Hiram gave a nervous smile. "Not at all." He adjusted his bow tie, wiped imaginary sweat from his forehead. His pleasant tone was forced. It sounded as if it took great effort to talk. "I kept parts of you here for months," he said. "Your head came through more or less intact, though it wouldn't talk. I kept hoping your creator would appear and know how to reassemble them."

"He's secretive and wouldn't appear in public. But I'm sure he'd like the parts back."

Hiram looked at him with his deep, dead eyes. "Sorry. Someone stole them. A souvenir freak, I imagine."

"Oh. My creator will be disappointed."

"Your zombie, sir," said the bartender.

"Thank you." The android noticed that an autographed picture of Senator Hartmann had been moved from a corner of the bar to a prominent place above the bar.

"You must pardon me, Modular Man," Hiram said, "but I really ought to get back to the kitchens. Time and *rognons sautés au champagne* wait for no man."

"Sounds delectable," said the android. "Perhaps I'll have your *rognons* for dinner. Whatever they are." He watched as Hiram maneuvered his bulk toward the kitchen. There was something wrong with Hiram, he thought, something off-key in the way he reacted to things. The word *zombie*, the weird comment about the head. He seemed hollow, somehow. As if something was consuming his vast body from the inside. He was completely different from the way Modular Man remembered him.

So was Travnicek. So was everyone.

A chill eddied through his mind. Perhaps his earlier perceptions had been faulty in some way, his recorded memories subject to some unintended cybernetic bias. But it was just as likely that it was his current perceptions that were at fault. Maybe Travnicek's work was faulty.

Maybe he'd blow up again.

He left the bar and walked toward Wall Walker. Wall Walker was a fixture at Aces High, a thirtyish black man of no apparent occupation whose wild card enabled him to walk on the walls and ceiling. He wore a cloth domino mask that didn't go very far toward concealing his appearance, seemed to have plenty of money, and was, the android gathered, pleasant company. No one knew his real name. He looked up and smiled.

"Hi, Mod Man. You're looking good."

"May I join you?"

"I'm waiting for someone." His voice had what Modular Man thought to be a light West Indian accent. "But I don't mind company in the meantime."

Modular Man sat. Wall Walker regarded him from over the rim of a Sierra Porter. "I haven't seen you since you . . . exploded." He shook his head. "What a mess, mon."

Modular Man sipped his zombie. Taste receptors made a cataclysmic null sound in his mind. "I was wondering if you might be able to tell me about what happened that night."

The android's radar painted him the unmistakable image of Hiram stepping into the bar, glancing left and right in what seemed to be an anxious way, then stepping away.

"Oh. Yes. I daresay you would not remember, would you?" He frowned. "It was an accident, I think. You were trying to rescue Jane from the Astronomer, and you got in Croyd's way."

"Croyd? The same Croyd that's . . ."

"Spreading the virus? Yes. Same gentleman. He had the power to . . . make metal go limp, or some other such nonsense. He was trying to use it on the Astronomer and he couldn't control it and he hit you. You melted like the India-rubber man, and you started firing off tear gas and smoke, mon, and a few seconds later you exploded."

Modular Man was still for a few seconds while his circuits explored this possibility. "The Astronomer was made of metal?" he asked.

"No. Just an old fella, kinda frail."

"So Croyd's power wouldn't have worked anyway. Not on the Astronomer."

Wall Walker raised his hands. "People were shootin' off everything they had, mon. We had a full-grown *elephant* in here. The lights were out, the place was full of tear gas . . ."

"And Croyd fired off a wild card talent that could only work against *me*."

Wall Walker shrugged. The two other customers rose and left the bar. Modular Man thought for a moment.

"Who's Jane? The woman I was trying to rescue."

Wall Walker looked at him. "You don't remember her, either?"

"I don't think so."

"You were supposed to be guarding her. They call her Water Lily, mon."

"Oh." A qualified relief entered the android's mind. Here, at least, was something he could remember. "I met her briefly. During the Great Cloisters Raid. I thought her name was actually Lily, though." *Didn't I see you at the ape-escape?* he'd asked. Never saw her again. Maybe she'd have some answers.

"Seems to prefer that people call her Jane, mon. Was the name she used when she worked here."

I don't have a name, the android thought suddenly. *I've got this label, Modular Man, but it's a trademark, not a real name, not Bob or Simon or Michael. Sometimes people call me Mod Man, but that's just to make it easy on themselves. I don't really have a name.*

Sadness wafted through his mind.

"Do you know how to get ahold of this Jane person?" he asked. "I'd like to ask her some questions."

Wall Walker chuckled. "You and half the city, mon. She has disappeared and is probably running for her life. Word is she can heal Croyd's victims."

"Yes?"

"By fucking them."

"Oh."

Facts whirled hopelessly in the eddies of the android's mind. None of this made any sense at all. Croyd had blown him up and was now spreading death thoughout the city; the woman who could heal the harm Croyd was doing had fled from sight; Hiram and Travnicek were behaving oddly; and Alice had got married.

The android looked at Wall Walker carefully. "If this is all part of some strange joke," he said, "tell me now. Otherwise"— quite seriously—"I'll hurt you badly."

Wall Walker's eyes dilated. The android had the feeling he was not terribly intimidated. "I am not making it up, mon." His voice was emphatic, matter-of-fact. "This is not a fantasy, Mod Man. Croyd is spreading the Black Queen, Water Lily is on the run, there's martial law."

Suddenly there was shouting from the kitchen.

"I don't *know* where he went, damn it!" Hiram's voice. "He just walked out!"

"He was looking for you!" There was a sudden crash, as if a stack of pans had just toppled.

"I don't know! I don't know! He just walked out, goddammit!"

"He wouldn't walk out on *me*!"

"He walked out on both of us!"

"Jane wouldn't walk out!"

"They both left us!"

"I don't believe you!" More pans crashed.

"Out! Out! Get out of my place!" Hiram's voice was a scream. Suddenly he appeared, rushing out of the kitchen with another man in his arms. The man was Asian and wore a chef's uniform. He seemed light as a feather.

Hiram flung the man into the outside door. He didn't have enough weight to swing it open and began to drift to the floor. Hiram flushed. He rushed forward and pushed the man through the door.

There was a silence in the restaurant, filled only by the sound of Hiram's winded breaths. The restauranteur gave the bar a defiant glare, then stalked into his office. One of the customers rose hastily to pay for his drink and leave.

"Goddamn," the other customer said. He was a lanky, brown-haired man who looked uncomfortable in his well-tailored clothes. "I spent *twenty years* trying to get into this place, and look what happens when I finally get here."

Modular Man looked at Wall Walker. The black man gave him a rueful smile and said, "Standards fallin' all over."

The android took an odd comfort from the scene. Hiram *was* different. It wasn't just some programming glitch.

He turned his mind back to Wild Card Day. Circuits sifted possibilities. "Could Croyd have been working for the Astronomer?"

"Back on Wild Card Day?" Wall Walker seemed to find this thought interesting. "He *is* a mercenary of sorts—it's possible. But the Astronomer killed just about all of his own henchmen—a real bloodbath, mon—and Croyd is still with us."

"How do you know so much about Croyd?"

A smile. "I keep my ear to the ground, mon."

"What's he look like?" Modular Man intended to avoid him.

"I cannot give a description of what he looks like right now. Fella keeps changing appearance and abilities, understand, mon—his wild car. And last time he surfaced he had someone with him, a bodyguard or something, and no one knows which is which. Or who. One of them, Croyd or the other guy, he's an albino, mon. Probably got his hair dyed and shades over his eyes by now. The other is young, good-looking. But neither have been seen for a few days—no new cases of wild card—so whichever one is Croyd, he may be someone else now. He may not be carrying the plague anymore."

"In that case the emergency's over, right?"

"Guess so. There is still the gang war going on, though."

"I don't want to hear about it."

"And the elections. Even *I* don't believe who's running."

Seen on radar, Hiram appeared from his office, cast another anxious glance over the barroom, left again. Wall Walker's eyes tracked him over Modular Man's right shoulder. He looked concerned.

"Hiram's not doing well."

"I thought he seemed different."

"Business is way off, mon. Aces are not as fashionable as once we were. The Wild Card Day massacres were a real black eye for all wild talents. And then there was violence all *over* the bloody place on the WHO tour, a real cock-up, and Hiram took part . . . beg pardon, mon, that's something else you probably don't know about."

"Never mind," said the android.

"Okay. And now, the Croyd buggering up and dealing jokers and Black Queens all over town, a big reaction is going on. Soon it may not be . . . politically astute . . . to be seen in aces' company."

"I'm not an ace. I'm a machine."

"You fly, mon! You are abnormally strong, and you shoot energy bolts. Try and tell someone the difference."

"I suppose."

Someone walked into the bar. The radar image was strange enough that Modular Man turned his head to pick up on him visually.

The man's brown hair and beard hung almost to his ankles. He had a crucifix on a chain around his neck, outside the hair, and otherwise wore a dirty T-shirt, blue jean cutoffs, and was barefoot.

None of this was sufficiently abnormal to do more than suggest a wild card, but as the man ambled closer, Modular

Man saw the different-colored irises, orange-yellow-green, set one within the other like target symbols. His hands were deformed, the fingers thin and hairy. He held a six-ounce bottle of Coke in one hand.

"This is the man I need to see," Wall Walker said. "If you'll pardon me."

"See you later maybe." Modular Man stood up.

The hairy stranger walked up to the table and looked at Wall Walker and said, "I know you."

"You know me, Flattop."

Modular Man made his way to the bar and ordered another zombie. Hiram appeared and ejected Flattop for lacking proper footwear. When he left with Wall Walker, the android noticed that he had plugged the Coke bottle into the inside of his elbow joint, as if the bottle were a hypodermic needle, and left it there.

The bar was empty. Hiram seemed fretful and depressed, and the bartender echoed his boss's mood. The android made excuses and left.

He wouldn't drink zombies ever again. The associations were just too depressing.

"Yah. Gotta get us some money, right, food processor?" Maxim Travnicek was rooting through a pile of notes he'd written to himself during Modular Man's assemblage. "I want you to get to the patent office tomorrow. Get some forms. Shit, my foot itches." He rubbed the toe of his left shoe against his right calf.

"I could try to get on *Peregrine's Perch* tomorrow. Let everyone know I'm back. She only pays scale, but..."

"The bitch is pregnant, you know. Gonna pop any day now, from what I can see."

Something else I hadn't heard about, the android thought. *Wonderful*. Next he would discover that France had changed its name to Fredonia and moved to Asia.

"But you should see her tits! If you thought they were good before, you should see them now! Fantastic!"

"I'll fly over and visit her producer."

"Bosonic strings," Travnicek said. He had one of his notes in his hand but didn't seem to be looking at it. "Minus one to the Nth is minus one for the massless vector, so epsilon equals one." His eyes had glazed over. His body swayed back and forth. He seemed to have fallen into some kind of trance. "For superstrings," he went on, "minus one to the Nth is plus one for the massless vector, so epsilon equals minus one... All of the n times n antihermitian matrices taken together represent $U(n)$ in the complex case... Potential clash with unitarity..."

Cold terror washed over the android. He had never seen his creator do this before.

Travnicek went on in this mode for several minutes. Then he seemed to jerk awake. He turned to Modular Man.

"Did I say something?" he asked.

The android repeated it word for word. Travnicek listened with a frown. "That's open strings, okay," he said. "It's the ghost string operator that's the bitch. Did I say anything about Sigma sub plus one over two?"

"Sorry," said the android.

"Damn it." Travnicek shook his head. "I'm a physicist, not a mathematician. I've been working too hard. And my fucking foot keeps itching." He hopped to his camp bed, sat down, took off his shoe and sock. He began scratching between his toes.

"If I could get a handle on the fucking fermion-emission vertex I could solve that power-drain problem you have when you rotate out of the normal spectrum. Massless particles are easy, it's the..."

He stopped talking and stared at his foot.

Two of his toes had come off in his hand. Bluish ooze dripped deliberately from the wounds.

The android stared in disbelief.

Travnicek began to scream.

"The operators in question," said Travnicek, "are fermionic only in a two-dimensional world-sheet sense and not in the space-time D-dimensional sense." Lying on a gurney in the Rensselaer Clinic E-room, Travnicek had lapsed into a trance again. Modular Man wondered if this had anything to do with the "ghost operator" his creator had mentioned earlier.

"Truncating the spectrum to an even G parity sector... eliminates the tachyon from the spectrum..."

"It's wild card," Dr. Finn said to Modular Man. "There had scarcely been any doubt. "But it's strange. I don't understand the spectra." He glanced at a series of computer printouts. His hooves clicked nervously on the floor. "There seem to be *two* strains of wild card."

"Ghost-free light-cone gauge... Lorentz invariance is valid..."

"I've informed Tachyon," said Finn. He was a pony-size centaur, his human half wearing a white lab coat and stethoscope. He looked at Travnicek, then at the android. "Can you assume responsibility for this man, should we decide to give him the serum? Are you family?"

"I can't sign legal documents. I'm not a person, I'm a sixth-generation machine intelligence."

Finn absorbed this. "We'll wait for Tachyon," he decided.

The plastic curtains parted. The alien's violet eyes widened in surprise. "You're back," he said. Modular Man realized this was the first time he'd ever heard Tachyon use a contraction.

Tachyon was dressed in a white lab coat over which he wore a hussar jacket with enough gold lace to outfit the Ruritanian Royal Guard. Over it was strapped a Colt Python on a black gunbelt with silver-and-turquoise conchos. "You're carrying a six-gun," Modular Man said.

Tachyon recovered quickly from his surprise. He waved his hand carelessly. "There has been... harassment. We are coping, however, I am pleased to see you have been reassembled."

"Thank you. I've brought in a patient."

Tachyon took the printouts from the centaur and began glancing through them. "This is the first appearance of the wild card in three days," he remarked. "If we can discover where the patient was infected, we might be able to trace Croyd."

"Reparametrization invariance of the bosonic string!" Travnicek shouted. Sweat beaded on his forehead. "Preserve the covariant gauge!"

Tachyon's eyes narrowed as he glanced at the printouts. "There are two strains of wild card," Tachyon said. "One old infection, one new."

Modular Man looked at Travnicek in surprise. Probabilities poured through his mind. Travnicek had been a wild card all along. His ability to build Modular Man had been a function of his talent, not native genius.

Tachyon looked at Travnicek. "Can he be awakened from this state?"

"I don't know."

Tachyon leaned over the gurney, looked at Travnicek intently. Mental powers, Modular Man thought.

Travnicek gave a shout and batted the alien's arms away. He sat up and stared.

"It's that fucking Lorelei!" he said. "She's doing this to me, the bitch. Just because I wouldn't tip."

Tachyon looked at him. "Mister, ah..."

Travnicek brandished a finger. "Stop singing when we do it, I said, and maybe I'll tip! Who needs that kind of distraction?"

"Sir," Tachyon said. "We need a list of your contacts over the last few days."

Sweat poured down Travnicek's face. "I haven't seen anyone. I've been in the loft the last three days. Only ate a few slices of pizza from the fridge." His voice rose to a shriek. "It's that Lorelei, I tell you! She's doing it!"

"Are you sure this Lorelei is your only contact?"

"Jesus, yes!" Travnicek held out his hand. His two toes were still in his palm. "Look what the bitch is doing to me!"

"Do you know how to reach her? Where she might be hiding?"

"Shangri-la Outcalls. They're in the book. Just have them send her." Rage entered his eyes. "Five bucks for the taxi!"

Finn looked at Tachyon. "Could Croyd have become a female in the last three days?"

"Unlikely, but this remains the only lead we possess. If nothing else, this Lorelei might provide us with a lead to Croyd. Call the Squad. And the police."

"Sir." Finn's hooves rapped daintily on the tile floor as he left the curtained area. Tachyon's attention returned to Travnicek.

"Have you a wild card history?" he asked. "Any manifestations?"

"Of course not." Travnicek reached for his bare foot, then jerked his hand back. "I have no feeling in my toes. Goddamn it!"

"The reason I asked, sir—this is your second dose of wild card. You have a previous infection."

Travnicek's head snapped up. Sweat sprayed over Tachyon's coat. "What the hell do you mean, previous infection? I've had nothing of the sort."

"It would appear that you have. Your gene structure has been thoroughly infiltrated by the virus."

"I've never been sick in my life, you fucking quack."

"Sir," the android interrupted. "You have unusual abilities. Involving... reparametrization invariance of the bosonic string?"

Travnicek looked at him for a long moment. Then comprehension dawned, followed by horror.

"My God," he said.

"Sir," said Tachyon. "There is a serum. It has a twenty percent chance of success."

Travnicek continued to stare at the android. "Success," he said. "That means both infections go, right?"

"Yes. If it works at all. But there is a risk..."

Hooves tapped on the floor. Finn appeared through the curtains. "All set, Doc." He carried a case, which he opened. Bottles and hypodermics were revealed. "I've brought the serum. Also the release forms."

Travnicek appeared to notice the centaur for the first time. He shrank away. "Get away from me, you freak!"

Finn seemed embarrassed. Tachyon's face hardened, and he drew himself up. Angry hauteur burned in his face. "Dr. Finn is in charge here. He is a licensed physician—"

"I don't care if he's licensed to pull carriages in Central Park! A joker is *doing* this to me, and I'm not having a joker treat me!" Travnicek hesitated and looked at the toes in his hand. Decision entered his eyes. He flung the toes to the ground. "In fact, I'm not taking the fucking serum at all." He looked at the android. "Get me out of here. Now."

"Yes, sir." Dismay wafted through the android. He was not constructed so as to be able to refuse a direct command from his creator. He picked up Travnicek in his arms and rose into the air. Tachyon watched, arms folded in frozen, implacable hostility.

"Wait!" Finn's tone was desperate. "We need you to sign a release that you refused treatment!"

"Piss off!" barked Travnicek. Modular Man floated above the screens separating the E-room beds and began moving toward the entrance. A gray-faced joker child, waiting to have a splinter removed from his knee, stared upward with blank silver eyeballs. Finn followed, waving his forms and a pencil.

"Sir! I at least need your name!"

Modular Man butted through the swinging doors leading to the E-room and then past a surprised, green, seven-foot joker to the street door. Once outside he accelerated.

"After we get home," Travnicek said, "I want you to find Lorelei. Bring her to the loft and we'll make her turn off her wild card."

People on the night streets stared up as the android and his burden flew overhead. Half of them were wearing gauze masks. Modular Man's feeling of dismay intensified. "This is a viral infection, sir," he said. "I don't believe anyone is *doing* this to you."

"Jesus fucking Christ!" Travnicek slapped his forehead. "The two sons of bitches in the hallway! I forgot about them!" He grinned. "It's not the chippie after all. When I went downstairs to call Lorelei on the pay phone in the downstairs hall, I ran into these two guys coming up the stairs. I bumped into one of them in the hall. They went into the apartment right under us. One of them must be this Croyd guy."

"Was one an albino?"

"I didn't pay attention to them. They were wearing those surgical mask things anyway." He grew excited. "One of them was wearing dark glasses! And in a dark corridor! He must have been hiding his pink eyes!"

They had arrived at Travnicek's building. The android flew down the alley, circled into the airshaft, and rose to the building's flat roof. He opened the skylight and lowered Travnicek carefully through it. As he set Travnicek on his feet, he observed that two of the man's remaining toes were set at an odd angle.

Travnicek, oblivious to this fact, cackled as he paced back and forth. "I thought there was a joker in that apartment," he said. "I ran into one once on the stairs. All I cared about was that he didn't complain to the landlord about noise from the flux generators." One of his toes, cast adrift, rolled under a table. "He's right below," he said. "He's been *doing* this to me, and now the bastard is going to *pay*."

"He may not be able to control it," the android said. He was looking at the place where the toe had vanished, wondering if he should retrieve it. "He may not be able to reverse things."

Travnicek swung around. Sweat was pouring down his

face. His eyes were fevered. "He's going to stop what he's doing," he shouted, "or he's going to die!" His voice rose to a shriek. "I am *not* going to be a joker! I am a *genius*, and I intend to stay one! Find the bastard and bring him here!"

"Yes, sir." Resigned, the android stepped to the metal locker where his spare parts were kept. He twirled the combination knob, opened the door, and saw that the two grenade launchers were missing. Apparently he'd loaded one with sleep gas and the other with smoke grenades, and they'd been destroyed at Aces High. That left the dazzler, the 20mm cannon, and the microwave laser.

Croyd, he thought, had already destroyed him once.

He opened the zips on the shoulders of his jumpsuit and willed open the slots on his shoulders. He took the cannon and the laser and fixed them in place. The cannon was almost as tall as he was and heavy; he wove software patterns that compensated his balance accordingly. A drum of 20mm rounds was attached to the cannon. The bolt slammed back and forward and the first round was chambered.

He wondered if he was going to die again.

He turned on his flux fields. Ozone crackled around him. A faint St. Elmo's aura danced before his eyes.

Insubstantial, he melted through the floor.

The first thing the android saw was a television set. Its tube had imploded. An unstrung coat hanger was wired in place of one of the broken rabbit ears.

There was a camp bed in the middle of the floor. The mattress was wrapped in plastic. There were no sheets. Cheap furniture choked the rest of the room.

The android became substantial and hung suspended in the middle of the room. He heard voices in the back room. His weaponry swung toward the sound and locked into position.

"Something broke all the glass." The voice was fast, fervid, weirdly intense. "Something strange is going on."

"Maybe a sonic boom." Another voice, deeper. Certainly calmer.

"The *cups* on the *shelves?*" The voice was very insistent, talking so fast the words crowded on one another. "Something broke the *cups* on the *shelves*. Sonic booms don't do *that*. Not in New York. *Something else* must've done that." The man wouldn't let the subject alone.

Modular Man hovered to the doorway. Two men stood in the apartment's tiny kitchen, bent to peer into a small refrigerator. Milk and orange juice dripped from its sill.

The nearest man was young, dark-haired, movie-star handsome. He was dressed in blue jeans and a Levi's jacket. He had a piece of a broken juice container in his hand.

The other was a thin, pale, nervous man with pink eyes.

"Which one of you is Croyd Crenson?" asked the android.

The pink-eyed man turned and gave a shriek. "You blew up!" he shouted, and in a blur of speed he reached for a gun under his Levi's jacket.

Modular Man concluded this sure enough sounded like a guilty conscience. The ceiling was too low for him to maneuver over the first man, so he pushed out with an arm as he moved forward, intending to knock him into the refrigerator and get next to the albino.

The second man didn't move when the android shoved him. He didn't even shift his stance, partly stooped by the refrigerator. Modular Man stopped dead. He pushed harder. The man straightened and smiled and didn't move.

The presumed Croyd fired his automatic. The sound thundered in the small room. The first wild round missed, the second gouged plastic skin from the android's shoulder, the third and fourth shots hit Croyd's companion.

The man still didn't react, not even after being shot. The bullets didn't ricochet or flatten on impact, just dropped to the scarred linoleum.

Bullets don't work, the android thought. *Scratch the cannon.*

Modular Man backed up, dropped to the floor, fired a straight punch to the young man's chest. The man still didn't move, didn't even flinch. Croyd's bullets cracked as they cut the air. A couple of them hit his friend, none hit the android. The android punched again, full force. Same result.

The young man struck out, the return punch unnaturally fast. His fist caught Modular Man and knocked him back, out of the kitchen. The android drove through the old tin paneling of the far wall and partway through the slats on the other side. Paint flecks a dozen layers thick dropped like gray snow from the ancient walls. Red damage lights came alive in the android's mind.

Modular Man levered himself out of the wall—the long tube of the cannon got caught and required a wrench of the android's shoulders to free it. He saw the albino charging with superhuman speed, the refrigerator raised high. The android tried to get out of the way, but the wall hampered him and Croyd was moving very fast. The refrigerator drove Modular Man back through the wall again, widening the hole. Orange juice sloshed in the refrigerator's interior.

Modular Man cut in his flight generators and flew straight forward, seizing the refrigerator and using it as a battering ram. Croyd was caught off center and spun into the front room, arms flailing, before the camp bed caught the back of his knees and he crashed to the floor. The android kept going, driving the refrigerator full force into Croyd's companion.

The man still didn't move. St. Elmo's fire filled the hallway as the android's generators went to full power. The man still didn't move.

The hell with it. Go for Croyd.

The android let go of the refrigerator and altered his flight pattern to head for the albino, Very quickly, before he could move more than a few inches, the young man struck out with the other arm, a forearm slam against the top of the refrigerator.

Modular Man went through the wall again, across someone's apartment, into a fifteen-gallon fish tank, then into the exterior wall. Bits of the android's consciousness fragmented with shock. A green flood poured across the carpet. Tropical fish began to die.

A moment of time throbbed endlessly in his mind. He could not remember his purpose, could not recognize the scatter of bright scales that flapped helplessly before his gaze. Automatic systems slowly rerouted his memory.

The day and its long advent of despair returned. He pried himself from the wall. His energies needed replenishment. He couldn't go insubstantial for a while, and he shouldn't fly. The 20mm cannon hung bent over one shoulder. The laser seemed intact.

The apartment was decorated with care, featuring abstract prints, an Oriental carpet, more fish tanks. A mobile jangled near the ceiling. Its tenant seemed not to be home. Distantly he heard the sound of arriving police. The android stepped through the hole into Croyd's apartment, saw that the albino and his companion had left, and walked up the stairs to Travnicek's. On the way his consciousness disappeared twice, for half-second intervals. When he regained it, he moved faster.

He heard the heavy footsteps of police below.

Travnicek opened the door to his knock. Both his feet were bare, and all the toes had gone. Something blue and hairy was beginning to grow from each wound.

"Fucking coffee maker," said Travnicek.

The android knew it wasn't going to get any better.

"Croyd wasn't so much a problem as this other person." The android had his jumpsuit off, was repairing the gouge in his synthetic flesh. The cannon lay on a table. He would have to get a replacement from the army munitions depot where he'd found the first one.

Travnicek was laboring over broken components. He'd told the police that he'd heard shots but had been afraid to go downstairs to phone for help. They'd accepted his explanation without comment and never came into the apartment where the android had been hiding in a locker.

"Nothing's really badly damaged, toaster," Travnicek said. "Field monitor jarred loose. That's why you kept losing consciousness. I'll strap the bastard down this time. Otherwise, just a few dings here and there."

He straightened. His eyes glazed over. "Renormalization function switch damaged," he said. "Replace at once." He shook his head, frowned a moment, then turned to the android. "Open your chest again. I just remembered something."

Travnicek was scratching one of his hands near the finger joints. He looked down, realized what he was doing, and stopped. He seemed a little pale.

"After I get you fixed up," he said, "get on the goddamn streets. That Croyd guy is gonna be using his power to transform more people. That'll give you a fix on his location. I want you to be looking for him."

"Yes, sir." The android's chest opened. He noticed that his creator's neck was beginning to swell, and that his flesh now had a distinct blue cast.

He decided not to mention it.

* * *

The android patrolled all that night, searching the streets for familiar figures. His internal radio receiver was tuned to any alert, on both police and National Guard bands. From a early edition of the *Times* stolen from a pile near a closed newsstand, he found out that there had been a half dozen cases of wild card in the two hours following his battle with Croyd. Three of the cases had been in Jokertown, and the other three were people traveling together on a northbound number 4 Lexington Avenue express. Croyd and his companion had taken the subway at least as far as the Forty-second Street stop.

He also discovered from a copy of *Newsweek* he found in a trash basket that Croyd and his unknown protector had fought a group of jokers led by Tachyon to a standstill a few days before.

He wished he'd known that. Even though the article didn't give many details, maybe knowing the pair was dangerous would have made a difference.

As he hovered over the streets, eyes and radar casting for familiar images, he replayed the fight in the apartment. He'd tried to knock the unknown man away, and the man hadn't moved. Punches had struck him and then stopped. When the android had tried to bulldoze him with the refrigerator, motion had just stopped. Bullets hadn't bounced off the man, just lost their energy and fallen to the floor.

Lost their energy, the android thought. Lost their energy and died.

The unknown man, therefore, absorbed kinetic energy. Then he transformed it in an attack of his own. He had to get hit first, the android realized, because he seemed to need to absorb the android's attack before he could strike back.

Satisfaction moved through the android's mind. All he had to do to get around the other guy was not hit him. If he didn't have any energy to absorb, he couldn't do anything.

And if things went wrong, the android could use the microwave laser as a last resort. The unknown man absorbed kinetic energy, not radiation.

The android smiled. He had the next encounter aced.

All he had to do was find them.

At two thirty-one in the afternoon two people drew the Black Queen on Forty-seventh Street near Hammarskjöld

Plaza. The radio crackled with NYPD and National Guard commands to reinforce the guards on the United Nations building in case Croyd was intending to make some move on the UN.

Modular Man was overhead seconds after the alarm. Two victims were stretched on the street half a block apart, one lying still, his body turned into something monstrous, the other writhing in pain as his bones dissolved and he was crushed by the weight of his own body. Olive-green M.A.S.H. ambulances were responding, followed in the distance by a whooping city ambulance. There was nothing Modular Man could do for the victims. He flew a swift search pattern over the block, then began flying in widening circles. Another wild card victim to the west of the others on Third Avenue gave his search another focal point.

Then he saw one of his targets, Croyd's brown-haired companion. The man was dressed as the android had last seen him, in a Levi's jacket and jeans. He was walking east on Forty-eighth Street, having doubled back, and he was moving quickly, hands in his pockets and eyes fixed on the pedestrians ahead of him.

Modular Man flew behind the parapet of a building across the street, paralleling him, moving his head from cover every so often to keep tabs on his target. There was very little foot traffic and the android found him easy to follow. The young man did not look up. Ambulance sirens wailed in the distance.

The young man began moving north on Second Avenue. He walked for three blocks, then pushed through the revolving door of a large white-stone bank.

The android hovered over the building across the street while he decided what to do, then flew swiftly across Second Avenue and dropped to the pavement, careful not to make his movements visible from the bank's front door. People in white gauze masks gave him plenty of room on the sidewalk.

The android turned insubstantial and walked into the thick wall of the bank, then pushed his face through the far side. Croyd's guardian had walked across the bank lobby, past the teller cages, and was speaking to a pudgy, white-haired bank guard who sat on a stool near one of the back doors. He showed the guard a card and a key. The guard nodded, pressed a button, and a sliding door opened. The young man entered an elevator and the door shut behind him.

Modular Man stepped back from the building. Apparently Croyd's companion was heading for a safety deposit box. The android, to the audible gasps of a pair of pedestrians, dropped through the pavement.

Though his vision was dark, his internal navigation systems kept him aligned perfectly. He moved down, then forward. His upper head, containing eyes and radar, moved tentatively through a wall: the android perceived an enormous vault with a clerk behind a desk, her back to him. Stacks of fresh bills, each with a neat paper wrapper, stood on the desk.

Wrong vault. The android moved back, then to the side, then forward again, then pushed through a row of safety deposit boxes.

Right vault. Remaining insubstantial was draining his power reserves: he couldn't do this much longer.

Croyd's companion was marching with another guard to one large box. He and the guard inserted their keys, and the young man withdrew the box. The android memorized its location, then made note of the position of all the cameras and other security monitors.

His energy was running low. He moved back, rose up through the sidewalk, turned substantial, flew to the roof across the street, and lighted. It probably didn't matter what was in the deposit box, although if it proved relevant, he could always return.

Croyd's companion was in the bank for another ten minutes, allowing the android's energy to return fully. When the man emerged, he began retracing his steps south, turning west on Fiftieth Street to avoid the ambulances and military police setting up checkpoints on Forty-seventh, then hastened to Lexington Avenue, where he turned south again. The android followed, flitting from roof to roof. His quarry walked south to Forty-fourth, then headed west to enter one of the side entrances to Grand Central Station.

The android turned insubstantial and flew through the wall onto the second level of the station. He lighted on the polished marble balcony and watched his quarry move across the floor below.

The station was almost deserted. The entrances to the platforms were guarded by regular army Rangers in black berets. They were in full biological warfare rig, hoods and gas masks off but ready. Croyd's companion walked to a stairway leading down to the arcade level and descended.

The android followed, moving carefully, turning insubstantial when necessary in order to peer around corners. The young man moved lower, through a utility door with a smashed lock, then down into the train tunnels that stretched north from the station. Rusting iron supports held up what seemed to be half of Manhattan. Occasional bulbs provided dim light. The place smelled of damp and metal. The android, keeping his target in sight with radar, followed without difficulty.

He found a corpse, a man in several layers of shabby clothing whose body seemed to have calcified, leaving the derelict a huddled figure with his face permanently carved in a look of horror and pain. Croyd had been here all right. There was another body a hundred yards farther on, an elderly woman with her bags clutched around her. The android looked closer.

It wasn't the bag lady he had once known. The android was relieved.

"D'ja get it? D'ja get it?" The albino's eager voice rapped out of the darkness.

"Yeah."

"Lemme see."

"Bunch of keys. Envelope of cash."

"Gimme the deposit key."

The android crept nearer. An approaching train was rumbling closer, coming from the north.

"Here you go. You shouldn't have risked going out."

The albino's rapid-fire voice crackled with suspicion. "Didn't know if I could trust you. And your signature wasn't on the card."

"The guard barely looked at it. I think he was drunk."

"Gimme the gun."

"This thing's heavy. What is it?"

"Forty-four Automag. The most powerful handgun ever made." Croyd strapped a giant shoulder holster under his arm. "If the robot comes after us again," he said, "I wanna be able to dent him. This thing fires cut-down NATO rifle rounds."

"Jesus."

The albino said something then, but Modular Man couldn't hear it. The train was getting closer. Its headlight outlined iron stanchions. Croyd and his companion began moving toward Modular Man. The android silently flew upward to the dirty ceiling, hovering in the shadow of a girder.

Yellow light burned steadily on the iron pillars as the train ground steadily southward. The noise echoed in the cavernous room. Croyd and his bodyguard passed beneath the android.

Croyd looked up, warned somehow—maybe he'd seen the hovering android in his peripheral vision. The albino yelled something obscured by the sound of the train and clawed for his pistol with incredible speed. His companion began to turn.

Modular Man dropped from the ceiling, his arms going around the albino from behind. The train bathed the scene in garish cinema light. Croyd shouted, tried to throw himself from side to side. His strength was considerably more than that of a normal human, but not equal to that of the android. Modular Man rose into the air, his legs wrapping around Croyd's, and he began to fly south. Wind from the train pushed him on.

"Hey . . . !" The companion was running after, waving an arm. "Bring him back!" The huge gun, still jammed in Croyd's armpit, fired out and down through Croyd's coat. A ricochet struck bright sparks from an iron stanchion.

Croyd's guardian swerved. He leaped directly into the path of the train.

There was a burst of light, a crackling sound. The train stopped dead. The young man was hurled fifty feet farther down the track. When he hit the ground, a smaller burst of electricity jumped between him and the nearest rail.

The man jumped to his feet. In the bright light of the train's headlight the android could see his grin.

Modular Man made a brief calculation of the amount of kinetic energy possessed by a fully loaded train moving at fifteen or so miles per hour. Although Croyd's guardian hadn't absorbed all of it, and the excess had bled off in a burst of lightning—there were *some* limits on his power, fortunately—the total of what he *had* absorbed was appalling. The android's laser whined as it tracked toward the man standing on the tracks.

The man crouched, bracing his feet against the track, then jumped. His leap was aimed ahead of the android, to cut him off. The man tumbled in air—evidently he wasn't used to traveling this way—then hit a stanchion and fell to the ground. No electricity this time. He picked himself up and looked at the approaching android with clenched teeth. His clothing smoldered.

Swift calculations passed through macroatomic circuits, followed by lightspeed regret. Modular Man hadn't ever shot a real person before. He didn't want to now. But Croyd was killing people even in hiding, even in the tunnels deep under Grand Central. And if Croyd's guardian got his hands on the android, he could tear his alloy skeleton to bits.

The android fired. Then suddenly he was falling, his arms limp. Croyd tumbled to the ground. The android crashed to the ground at the young man's feet. The young man reached, seized him by the shoulders. The android tried to move, failed.

Modular Man realized that Croyd's protector didn't just absorb kinetic energy. He absorbed *any* kind of energy and could return it instantly.

Bad mistake, he thought.

Suddenly he was flying again. He crashed through the side of the commuter train, sprawled across several seats in a spill of glass and torn aluminum. Someone's briefcase tumbled to the aisle, papers flying. The android heard a scream. His sensors registered the smell of burning.

The few people on board—executives whose work forced them into the quarantined city—rushed to his aid. Lifting him from his ungainly sprawl across the seats, they laid him carefully in the aisle. "What's that on his head?" asked a white-haired man with a mustache.

Radar imaging was gone. Its control unit had been fried when Croyd's bodyguard returned the coherent microwave pulse. The monitor that controlled his ability to turn insubstantial was gone. His alloy underskin had a neat hole in it. The excess energy had blown a lot of circuit breakers. The android reset as many as possible and felt control return to his limbs. Some breakers wouldn't reset.

"Pardon me," he said, and stood up. People faded back. The train gave a jerk as it started moving again, and the android tumbled backward, arms windmilling, and sat down in the aisle. People rushed toward him again. He felt the helping hands on his right side but not on his left. Balance and coordination were still affected. He rerouted internal circuits, but still something was wrong.

"Excuse me." He unzipped and pulled off the upper half of his jumpsuit. Train passengers gasped. Plastic flesh was blackened around the wound. Modular Man opened his chest and reached inside with one hand. Someone turned away and began to be sick, but the other passengers seemed interested, one woman standing on a seat and craning her neck to peer into the android's interior through horn-rimmed spectacles.

The android removed one of his internal guidance units, saw melted connections, and sighed mentally. He returned the unit. The trip home was going to be pretty shaky. He certainly couldn't fly.

He looked up at the people on the train.

"Do any of you have five dollars for a taxi?" he asked.

The trip to Jokertown was humiliating and dangerous. Some of the passengers supported him out of the station, but even so he fell a few times. With some money given him by the man with the mustache, he took a taxi to the other side of the block from Travnicek's brownstone. He pushed the money through the slot in the taxi's bulletproof shield, then staggered out onto the sidewalk. He half-walked, half-crawled down the alley to Travnicek's building, then dragged himself up the fire escape to the roof. From there he crawled to the skylight and lowered himself down.

Travnicek lay on his camp bed, naked to the waist. His skin was light blue. Writhing cilia, covered with long hairs, grew from where his fingers and toes had been. A fly hummed over his head.

The swollen skin around his neck had split open, revealing a flower lei of organs. Some were recognizable—trumpet-shaped ears, yellowish eyes, some normal in size and some not—but others of the organs were not.

"The only left-moving ghosts," he muttered, "are the reparametrization ghosts." His voice was thick, indistinct. The android had the intuition that his lips might be growing together. And the words seemed half-unfamiliar, as if he no longer entirely comprehended their meaning.

"Sir," said Modular Man. "Sir. I've been injured again."

Travnicek sat up with a start. The eyes clustered around his neck swiveled to focus on the android. "Ah. Toaster. You look... very interesting... this way." The eyes in his skull were closed. Perhaps, the android thought, forever.

"I need repairs. Croyd's companion reflected my laser back at me."

"Why the fuck did you shoot him, blender? All forms of energy are the same. Same as *matter*, as far as that goes."

"I didn't know."

"Fucking moron. You'd think you'd pick up a little intelligence from me."

Travnicek jumped up from his cot, moving very fast, faster than a normal human. He caught hold of a roof beam with one hand, swung around it to stand on his head. He planted his feet on the ceiling, the hairy cilia splaying, and then removed his hand from the beam and hung inverted. Yellow eyes looked steadily at the android.

"Not bad, hey? Haven't felt this good in years." He moved carefully along the ceiling toward the android.

"Sir. Radar control is burned out. I've lost a stabilizer. My flux control is damaged."

"I hear you." His voice was serene, drifting. "In fact I don't just *hear* you, I perceive you in all sorts of ways. I'm not sure what some of them are just yet." Travnicek grabbed another roof beam, swung to the floor, dropped. The fly buzzed airily in the distance. Sadness swelled in the android's analog mind. A mounting hush of fear, like white noise, sizzled steadily in the background of his thoughts.

"Open your chest," Travnicek said. "Give me the monitor. There's a spare guidance unit in the cabinet."

"There's a hole in my chest."

The yellow eyes looked at him. The android waited for an outburst.

"Better patch it yourself," Travnicek said mildly. "When you have the time." He took the flux monitor and stepped to a workbench. "It's getting hard to think about all this," he said.

"Preserve your genius, sir." Modular Man tried not to let his desperation show. "Fight the infection. I'll get Croyd here."

A touch of vinegar entered Travnicek's voice. "Yah. You do that. Now let me worry about the fermionic coordinates, okay?"

"Yes, sir." Mildly reassured.

He staggered to the locker and began looking for a new gyroscope.

The BARNETT FOR PRESIDENT poster had been defaced. Someone had drawn a knife or fingernail file through the candidate's picture several times, then written JOKER DEATH over it in thick red letters. Next to it was a freehand drawing of an animal head—a black dog?—executed in thick felt tip.

"Hi. I need to talk."

Kate blew cigarette smoke. "Okay. For a little while."

"How are the Roman poets coming along?"

"If Latin weren't already a dead language, Statius would have killed it."

Modular Man was hunched over the public phone again. His gyroscope had been replaced and he could walk and fly.

Except for the heavy presence of the National Guard and Army, the streets were nearly deserted. Half the restaurants and cabarets in Jokertown were shut down.

"Kate," the android said, "I think I'm going to die."

There was a moment of startled silence. Then, "Tell me."

"My creator got infected by the wild card. He's turning into a joker and forgetting how to repair me. And he's sending me after the plague carrier, hoping the man can make it stop."

"Okay." Cautiously. "I'm following."

"He seems to think the man's deliberately doing this to him. But most people think the guy is just a carrier, and if that's true, and I bring him to my creator, the chances are nine to one that if my creator's reinfected, he'll draw the Black Queen and die."

"Yes."

"And the man I'm after—his name is Croyd—is the man who killed me the first time. And this time Croyd has a protector who is more powerful than he is. We're already fought twice, and they've beaten me both times. The last time I could easily have died. And my creator can't put me together again. He's losing his abilities. He may not be able to repair the damage from the *last* attack."

Kate drew on her cigarette, exhaled. "Mod Man," she said, "you need help."

"Yes. That's why I'm calling you."

"I mean other wild cards. You can't face these two alone."

"If I went to SCARE or someone, and we captured Croyd together, then I'd have to fight the SCARE aces to get him away. I'd be an outlaw."

"Maybe you could make some kind of deal with them."

"I'll think about it. I'll try." Despair wailed through him. "I'm going to *die*," he said.

"I'm sorry. Can't you—just leave?"

"I'm programmed to obey him. I can't refuse a direct order. And I'm programmed to battle the enemies of society. I don't have a choice in any of that. People like the Turtle, or Cyclone—it's their *decision* to do what they do. It was never mine. I'm not human that way."

"I see."

"Sooner or later I'm going to lose a fight. I don't heal like people, someone has to repair me. Any parts that get broken won't get fixed. If I don't die, I'll be a cripple, pieces falling off." Like Travnicek, he thought, and a cold shudder ran through his mind. "And even if I'm crippled," he went on, "I'll still have to fight. I *still* won't have any choice."

There was a long silence. "I don't know what to tell you." Her voice was choked.

"I was sort of immortal before," Modular Man said. "My creator was going to mass-produce me and sell me to the military. If any single unit was destroyed, the others would go on. They'd have identical programming; they'd still be *me*, at least mostly me. Now that's not going to happen."

"I'm sorry."

"What happens to machines when they die? I've been wondering that."

"I—"

"Your ancient philosophers never thought about that, right?"

"I suppose they didn't. But they had a lot to say about mortality in general. 'Must not all things be swallowed in death'—Plato, quoting Socrates."

"Thank you. That's really comforting."

"There's not a lot of comforting things to say about death. I'm sorry."

"I never really worried about it before. I'd never *died* before."

"Most of us don't get to come back even once. None of the others killed on Wild Card Day came back."

"This may be a temporary aberration. Normality may resume at any point."

The android realized he was shouting. The words echoed on the empty street. He swiftly wrote himself a piece of programming to keep his voice level.

Kate thought for a long moment. "Most of us have a lifetime to get used to the idea that we have to die. You've just had a few hours."

"I have a hard time getting my mind around it. There are all these feedback loops in my brain, and my thoughts keep going round and round. They're taking up more and more space."

"In other words, you're panicking."

"Am I?" He thought about this for a moment. "I suppose I am."

"The prospect of death, to misquote Samuel Johnson, is supposed to concentrate the mind wonderfully."

"I'll work at it." He suited action to words, swiftly putting an end to the runamuck computer logic that was smashing up against too many unknowns and infinities to do anything other than fill up his logic systems with macroatomic hash. A cooler and more systematic approach to the problem seemed indicated.

"Okay. That's done."

"That was fast."

"One point six six six seconds."

She laughed. "Not bad."

"I'm glad you recognized what was happening. I'm not really wired to deal with abstracts. I'd never got hung up that way before."

"You're still superhuman. No human could do that." She thought for a moment. "Do you know Millay? 'My candle burns at both ends; It will not last the night; But ah, my foes, and oh, my friends—It gives a lovely light.'"

The android considered this. "I suppose that, aesthetically, I might have produced an objectively lovely light when I blew up. The thought seems a bit barren of comfort, mainly I suppose because I wasn't there to see it."

"I think you missed my point." Patiently. "You are incredibly fast at both action and cognition. Your means of apprehending your surroundings are more complete and acute than those of a human. You have the capacity to experience your existence more thoroughly and intensely than anyone on the planet. Might this not compensate for any shortness of duration?"

The notion was encoded, spun into the maelstrom of the android's electronic mind, whirled like a leaf into a cold electronic torrent.

"I'll have to think about it," he said.

"You seemed to have crammed a lot of existence into the months you were on the planet. You had many of the experiences that people say lead to wisdom. War, comradeship, love, responsibility—even death."

The android gazed into the mutilated face of Barnett, the presidential candidate, and wondered who the man in the picture was. "I guess I kept busy," he said.

"There are a lot of people who would envy that existence."

"I'll try to bear that in mind."

"You burn very bright. Cherish that."

"I'll try."

"And you may not burn out. You fought the Swarm without taking serious injury, and there were hundreds of thousands of them. These are just a couple of guys."

"A couple of guys."

"You'll deal with it. I have confidence in you."

"Thank you." JOKER DEATH, the poster read. "I think you've given me something to consider."

"I hope I could help. Call me if you need to talk again."

"Thanks. You've really been of great assistance."

"Anytime."

Modular Man put the phone on the hook and rose silently into the sky. He rose into the darkness, drifted the several blocks to Travnicek's apartment, went in through the skylight. *Joker Death*, he thought.

Travnicek was lying on his bed, apparently asleep. The camp bed was surrounded by empty tins of food: apparently he'd been eating the stuff right from the cans. Some of the organs around Travnicek's neck had blossomed a bit, were making ultrasonic chirping sounds, the period of which decreased as the android dropped into the apartment. Sonar, the android thought. Travnicek opened the eyes around his neck.

"You," he said.

"Yes, sir."

"The module's rebuilt. I think. Some of my memories were kind of hazy."

Fear filled the android. A fly buzzed past and he chased it away with a flap of his arm. "I'll try it." He opened his jumpsuit and his chest, reached for the module that waited on the workbench.

"My brain seems to be evolving," Travnicek said. His voice was dreamy. "I think what's happening is that the virus is enlarging the brain sections concerned with sensory input. I'm perceiving things in every possible way now, very intensely. I've never experienced anything as intensely as I can just lying here, watching things." He gave a hollow laugh. "My god! I never knew that eating creamed corn from the can could be such a sensual experience!"

Modular Man inserted the module, ran test patterns. Relief flooded him. The monitor worked.

"Very good, sir," he said. "Hang on."

"You're so *interesting* this way," Travnicek said. The fly was wandering near the empty food cans.

There was sudden movement. One of the organs around Travnicek's neck uncoiled with lightning rapidity and caught the fly. The extrusion snapped back and stuffed the fly into Travnicek's mouth.

The android couldn't believe what he'd just seen.

"Wonderful," said Travnicek. Smacking his lips.

"Hang on, sir," Modular Man said again. His flux field crackled around him. He flew through the roof and into the blackness.

Arriving at the bank, the android turned insubstantial, burned every vault sensor with bursts from his microwave laser so that any guards couldn't see what happened next, then stepped into the vault, solidified himself, and ripped the deposit box from its resting place.

Suddenly he stopped. A yellow warning light glowed in his mind, flickered, turned red.

He tried to go insubstantial again. He rotated ninety degrees from the real for a fraction of a second, then he felt something go and he was solid again, standing in the bank vault. He could smell something burning.

The flux monitor was gone again. Travnicek's repairs hadn't been permanent. A chill eddy of fear rippled through

the android's mind at the thought that it might have happened
when he was in the steel-and-concrete wall of the vault.

He looked around, examined the door and the lock. If he
were found here in the morning, he thought, his reputation
as a do-gooder would definitely suffer.

It proved fortunate that vaults are made to prevent people
breaking in, not out. Forty-five minutes' patient work with
the microwave laser burned a hole in the laminated interior
of the door, gaining him access to the lock apparatus. He
reached through, touched the mechanism, felt an awareness
of its function. He glitched the electronics—easy as getting a
free telephone call—and the heavy bolts slid back.

He took the emergency stairs out, burning cameras as he
went. Once out he flew to the roof of a nearby building, tore
the box open, and examined the contents.

Long-term leases, he found, to several small apartments
in the New York area. Keys. Stacks of currency. Jewelry, gold
coins. Bottles containing hundreds of pills. A pair of pistols
and boxes of ammunition. Croyd's secret stash of money,
weapons, drugs, and the keys to his hideouts.

He thought for a long moment. Travnicek was deteriorat-
ing swiftly. The android was going to have to move fast, and
he was going to have to get some help.

"I don't want to have to do the scouting," Modular Man
said. "If they see me again, they'll run. And they'll spread the
plague while they do it."

"Very well." Tachyon's violet eyes glittered as his hands
played with the velvet lapels of his lavender jacket. His .357
and holster sat on the desk before him. On his office wall,
next to a set of honorary degrees, was a sign with red, white,
and blue lettering: THE MAN: HARTMANN. THE TIME: 1988. THE
PLAN: OUR CHILDREN'S FUTURE.

"My joker squad can be of use. Some of them should
prove capable of covert reconnaissance."

"Good. I should stay here with your most powerful people. Then we can move out together."

The contents of Croyd's deposit box were spread out on
Tachyon's desk and he looked at them. "There are only three
addresses actually in Manhattan," Tachyon said. "I suspect
he'd try for one of those first before trying the tunnels and
bridges. Blind Sophie can use her acute hearing to listen in

on what's going on behind a closed window, using the vibrations of the window glass as a diaphragm. Squish is a taxi driver, hence unobtrusive... he might be able to make inquiries that might seem suspicious from anyone else." Tachyon frowned. "Croyd's companion, however... that handsome young gentleman is going to prove difficult to deal with."

"I've fought him twice. But I think I know how his power works."

Tachyon stared. He leaned forward over the desk, pushing aside the pistol in its holster, his expression intent. "Tell me, sir."

"He absorbs energy, then returns it. He can only attack after he's already been hit. He absorbs all sorts of energy—kinetic, radiation..."

"Psionic," Tachyon murmured.

"But if you don't hit him first, he doesn't have any more strength than a normal person. So whatever we do, we can't attack him. Just ignore him, no matter how tempting a target he makes himself."

"Yes. Very good, Modular Man. You are to be commended."

The android looked at Tachyon and apprehension spun through his mind. "I need to get Croyd away as fast as possible. I can't catch the wild card from him, so I think I should deal with him solo—he's got enough strength to tear through your biochemical warfare suits. I'm powerful enough to subdue him if I don't have to worry about anyone else."

"The task is yours." Simply.

Triumph settled in the android. He was going to be able to seize Croyd and get him to Travnicek without interference.

Maybe things were looking up at last.

The phone rang on Tachyon's desk. The alien snatched it.

"Tachyon here." Modular Man saw Tachyon's violet eyes dilate with interest. "Very good. You are to be commended, Sophie. Stay there until we arrive." He returned the phone to its cradle. "Sophie believes they're in the Perry Street address. She can hear two people, and one of them is talking nonstop as if he was affected by stimulants."

The android jumped to his feet. His emergency pack had already been prepared, and he slung it on his back. Tachyon pressed a button on his telephone.

"Tell the squad to suit up," he said. "And after a decent interval, inform the police."

"I'll fly on ahead," the android said. He flung open the door and almost ran into a slim, erect black man who was standing just outside the door in the secretary's office. He wore a biochem suit and a feathered black-and-white death's-head mask. His smell was appalling, must and rotting flesh. A joker.

"Pardon me, sir," the man said. His voice was an educated, somewhat theatrical baritone. "Could you take me with you?"

Modular Man's software wove swift subroutines to eliminate the man's smell from his sensory input. "I don't believe I know you."

"Mr. Gravemold." A minute bow. "I am a member of the good doctor's joker squad."

"Can't you travel with them in the ambulance?"

The android sensed a smile behind the dramatic mask. "I'm afraid that in the close confines of an automobile, my scent becomes rather... overwhelming."

"I see your point."

"Gravemold." Tachyon's voice was strangled. "What are you doing in my secretary's office? Were you trying to eavesdrop?"

"That's *Mister* Gravemold, Doctor." The deep actor's voice was sharp.

"Beg pardon, I'm sure." Tachyon's voice was denasal.

"In answer to your question, I was waiting to speak to our artificial friend. I wished to spare the other squad members the burden of my... perfume."

"Right." Through clenched teeth. "Do as you please, Modular Man."

The android and Mr. Gravemold left the clinic at a fast trot, and then Modular Man wrapped his arms around the joker from behind and lifted him into the air. Air ruffled the feathers on Mr. Gravemold's mask.

"Sir," the android said. "Are there any abilities you have besides, ah..."

"My smell?" The deep voice was barren of amusement. "Indeed I have. As well as smelling as if I were dead, I have the powers of death. I can bring the cold of the grave to my enemies."

"That sounds . . . useful." Crazy, the android thought. The joker had been smelling his own perfume too long and it had driven him mad.

"I'm also fast and tough," Mr. Gravemold added.

"Good. So is Croyd." Quickly the android explained about the albino and his abilities, and also about the nature of his bodyguard. "Oh, yes," he added. "And Croyd is carrying a gun. A forty-four Automag."

"A preposterous weapon. He must be feeling insecure."

"Glad it doesn't bother you."

The Perry Street brownstone came in sight below. Modular Man dropped to the ground a few feet downwind of a slim, long-haired, middle-aged woman wearing shades and carrying a white cane. She was standing in the shadows by a doorstoop. The woman looked up. Her nose wrinkled.

"Gravemold," she said.

"*Mister* Gravemold, if you please."

"In that case," said Blind Sophie, "I'm *Miss* Yudkowski."

"I have never referred to you by any other name, madam."

A pair of ears, round like those of a cartoon mouse, seemed to inflate on either side of Sophie's head, rising like balloons past concealing strands of long, dark hair. She cocked her head toward Modular Man. "Hello, whoever you are. I didn't hear you till now."

"I didn't know I made any noise."

"You're a little late, gentlemen," Sophie said. "The two men left a couple minutes ago. Just after I got back from the telephone."

Annoyance flickered through the android's circuits. "Why didn't you tell us?"

"God forbid I should interfere with Mr. Gravemold correcting my speech."

"Where did they go?"

"They didn't say. I believe they took the back way out."

Without saying anything more Modular Man seized Mr. Gravemold again and rose into the sky. He swiftly quartered the district, radar searching out. Mr. Gravemold lay passively in his arms. Silent, the android thought, as the grave.

"We're on the way." Tachyon's voice crackled on Modular Man's receivers.

"There's a problem," Modular Man said, pulsing silent radio waves toward the clinic. He explained quickly.

"We shall continue heading in your direction, Modular Man," Tachyon said.

"There," said Mr. Gravemold, pointing. A pair of human-size radar images detached themselves from the shadow of a rusting iron pillar that helped support the deserted West Side Express Highway.

The android was surprised. The joker had incredibly good night vision. The android drifted silently toward the pair. He had to come within three hundred yards before he was certain the two were Croyd and his companion.

Uneasiness stirred him. The last time he'd almost died. *Burning bright*. Kate's voice echoed in his mind.

Each was burdened: the young man held a bulky parcel, and Croyd carried an outboard motor over one shoulder. Croyd was talking endlessly, but the android couldn't hear him. The two walked swiftly down a corroded concrete street and came to a stop at a chain link fence that cut off a Hudson River pier from the mainland. The albino put down his burden, inspected the padlock and chain that held the gate shut, and snapped the hasp with a quick twist of his fingers. The two moved through the gate and passed by a deserted guard box with shattered windows.

The pier was otherwise deserted. Except for a few ships caught here under quarantine, New York harbor was empty, a contrast to the blaze of activity on the Jersey shore.

"They're going to try to get off the island," said Mr. Gravemold.

"So it would seem."

"Put me down. We can deal with it."

"A moment. I've got to contact Tachyon." He sent Tachyon a radio message, heard no answer, and had to rise another five hundred feet before his pulse carried to the ambulance. Mr. Gravemold stirred restlessly.

"What are you doing, man? They're getting away. Put me down."

As soon as he heard an acknowledgment, Modular Man descended rapidly. Going to fight Croyd again, he thought. He remembered his first moments of existence, the confused fight around the Empire State Building, Cyndi's blond hair floating like a brilliant star above the ape's dark hand. Burning brightly, he thought.

He dropped Mr. Gravemold near the gate. The joker dusted himself off. "What was that all about?" he demanded.

"I'll explain later."

Both jumped at the sound of a moan from nearby. The android's alarm faded as he saw a pudgy, unconscious man lying near the fence, a bottle of bourbon near his tattooed hand. The drunk wore leather trousers and boots and an NYPD cap. His chest was bare and featured steel rings hanging from pierced nipples.

Modular Man fixed this sight in his memory. Cherish it, he thought.

"We can't wait," the joker said. "Those two will get away before the ambulance arrives."

Mr. Gravemold turned away and removed his mask. There was no facial deformity that Modular Man could see from behind. The joker put on his hood and gas mask and began to move with speed down the pier, following a pair of rusted railroad tracks. His feet stepped in surprising silence.

"Wait," said Modular Man. "They'll see you."

The joker paid no attention. He moved toward the edge of the pier, ducked under a railing, and disappeared. Alarm rattled in Modular Man's mind. He took to the air and did a half-roll under the pier.

Mr. Gravemold was still moving, walking inverted on the old, corroded planks, his pace brisk, the dark and silent Hudson rolling beneath his head. The android flew up next to him.

A possibility occurred to him. His mind ran scans, cross-checks.

The possibility was confirmed at greater than ninety percent. Build, talents, race, approximate age...everything matched. The accents were wildly different, and the voices substantially different as to tone and timbre, but scans of certain key words showed a surprising correspondence.

Why, Modular Man wondered, had Wall Walker made himself smell bad and disguised himself as a joker?

Or was that another manifestation of Wall Walker's wild card? Maybe he was Wall Walker part of the time, and then he started smelling bad and became Mr. Gravemold.

Maybe he was just crazy. Why else would someone disguise himself as a *joker*?

He decided not to mention his conclusions to the inverted ace beside him.

"You didn't mention you could walk upside down," he said.

"Did I not?" The voice was muffled by the mask. "Sometimes I'm a bit forgetful."

"Is there anything else you can do that I should know?"

Modular Man began to hear Croyd's voice. Mr. Gravemold looked at him. "Shhh. Be silent." The android sensed a grim smile behind the mask. "Silent as the grave."

They moved on. Mr. Gravemold moved easily through a tangle of wood and metal pier supports that loomed around them like the ribs of some giant, extinct animal. Croyd's voice grew louder. Modular Man remembered the shower of flaming stars that signaled the descent of the Swarm. Burning bright.

"Never had a fucking chance," Croyd said. "Jesus. Never learned a goddamn thing about the fucking world. Not algebra. Not anything." He laughed. "I taught *them* a thing or two. Stick with me, kid. We're gonna give 'em some *very interesting* lessons, you and me."

The android thought about Cyndi, Alice, the others. *Didn't I see you at the ape escape?* He thought about burning brightly and tried to make his movement precise, perfect. Tried to find the wonder in this situation, flying beneath a pier with the slick water waiting beneath him and a very likely insane, upside-down disguised ace walking purposefully beside him.

Halfway down the pier was a wooden ladder that reached down into the dark water. Croyd's voice seemed to come from just overhead.

"Okay, kid. Here we go. Just follow the ol' Sleeper. I know how to survive in this world."

Mr. Gravemold turned to the android and gestured. Despite the clumsiness of his suit, the meaning was clear: You fly over the opposite side of the pier, I'll wait here.

Great, the android thought. *I charge, and while they're killing me, Gravemold attacks from behind. Terrific.*

"Bring me the package, kid." Croyd's voice.

There seemed no time to engage in a debate with Mr. Gravemold. The android drifted backward across the pier, weaving his way through the metal supports, and then rose from the other side.

Croyd was standing by the ladder, facing his companion, and by coincidence, the android. Croyd's friend had a small knife out and had cut away the string and paper wrapping his package.

Croyd snapped to attention. "Shit! The robot!" His arm a blur of swift motion, he reached for his gun.

Not again, thought the android. He accelerated, heading straight for the albino.

Croyd made frantic tugging motions. The huge silver handgun seemed to have snagged in his armpit. His companion, without the unnatural speed possessed by the others, slowly turned and spun between Croyd and the charging android.

Choices rained on the android's circuits. He couldn't hit Croyd's bodyguard, not without charging him with energy, and he couldn't get to Croyd without going through the other. He dove for the surface of the pier, landed on his hands, tumbled. Splinters tore at his jumpsuit. He came to a halt at the young man's feet. The man stared at him.

There was a rip of fabric. With a triumphant cry Croyd jerked his gun free and leveled it. Black pills scattered like dirty snow, spilling from a torn inner pocket.

Mr. Gravemold rose behind Croyd, sudden and ominous as a specter. His gloved hand reached out and closed over the gun. He jerked it back, and the Automag went off with a sound like the end of the world.

The joker gave a yell as the gun's action slammed back under his hand. The gun clattered to the surface of the pier. The bullet, which had hit Croyd's bodyguard in the back, fell also.

Ooops, thought Modular Man.

The young man dived for him, right fist clenched. Modular Man rolled away. The man flopped on top of him, burning his power charge as he drove his fist into the planks. The android kicked up, throwing the man over onto his back. He had probably given him a small charge, but it wasn't enough to worry about.

Croyd in the meantime had slammed his elbow into Mr. Gravemold's sternum. The joker bounced back against the rail. Rusted nails moaned. Croyd scooped up the outboard engine, looked over his shoulder, and flung it full strength, not at his foes, but at his bodyguard. Trying to charge him up, the android thought.

He flew up into the engine's path. It thudded solidly into his shoulder, driving him back. Croyd's companion reached up and seized the android's feet. Fingers dug with desperate strength into his plastic flesh.

Mr. Gravemold flung himself off the rail, smashing Croyd from behind with a forearm. Croyd spun, his fingers talons. His pink eyes gleamed murderously. He clawed at the joker, trying to puncture his suit. Mr. Gravemold danced out of the way. Both were moving unnaturally fast.

Modular Man rose into the sky. The young man clung gamely to his legs. Kicking at him, the android thought, would only make him stronger.

Suddenly Croyd shuddered. He gasped, clutched at his middle. The balmy summer air suddenly turned a few degrees colder.

The cold of the grave, the android thought. It wasn't some fancy metaphor. The joker had actually meant what he said.

Lights flashed on the far end of the pier. A siren wailed. The ambulance from the Jokertown Clinic had arrived.

Croyd staggered back. He seized the package, flung it at Mr. Gravemold. The joker easily avoided it. It splashed into the water beyond.

"Death is cold, Mr Crenson," said Mr. Gravemold. His deep actor's voice rang past his gas mask, over the sound of the approaching ambulance. "Death is cold, and I am cold as death."

The joker raised a clenched fist, and the temperature dropped again. Mr. Gravemold, Modular Man realized, was stealing heat from the air. Croyd stumbled, went down on one knee. His white face had turned blue. His companion gave a cry of outrage and dropped to the surface of the pier with the Automag right in front him. He snatched up the gun and pointed it at the figure in the biochem suit.

Croyd fell flat on his face. His limbs twitched uncontrollably.

The android dove at maximum speed. The gun went off like a clap of thunder. A heavy slug caromed off Modular Man's metal substructure and tumbled away into the night. The bullet's energy began to spin the android. Unable to stop himself in time, he smashed through the guardrail and zoomed over the Hudson. He stabilized the spin and began to loop back toward the fight.

Ambulance lights flashed bright across the pier. Below, the package was inflating automatically at the touch of the water. A rubber raft.

Mr. Gravemold, still moving with unnatural speed, danced away from Croyd's bodyguard. The young man had difficulty tracking with the heavy gun. He fired twice and missed both times.

Mr. Gravemold raised his fist. "No!" Modular Man shouted.

The temperature dropped again. Croyd's bodyguard staggered and fell, the gun falling from his hand.

It worked, the android thought numbly. Then he realized that Mr. Gravemold's abilities didn't fire cold, but rather stole heat. With energy going out rather than in, the bodyguard's talent had nothing to work with.

Modular Man did a loop in air, came down on the albino, seized Croyd by collar and belt. Brakes shrieked as the ambulance came to a stop. Jokers in biochem suits spilled out. Laughter boomed from behind Mr. Gravemold's gas mask.

The android rose into the sky with his shivering burden and accelerated. Puzzled jokers, their face masks giving them tunnel vision, peered at the sky, trying to see where he and Croyd had gone.

Modular Man shook Croyd like a rag doll. *"Why did you blow me up?"* he shouted.

Croyd's teeth were chattering so hard it was difficult to understand him.

"Seemed like a good idea at the time."

Buildings sped beneath them. Fury raced through the android. He shook Croyd again. *"Why?"*

Croyd began to thrash. Modular Man suppressed the albino's uncoordinated movements with ease.

He had won, he realized. Carefully he tried to cherish the feeling.

Croyd was shivering uncontrollably as Modular Man lighted on a rooftop and took off the emergency pack he'd strapped to his back in the clinic. It contained a biochem suit, a blanket, a canvas tarpaulin, a sack, and some cord. The android wrapped the albino in a blanket before stuffing him into the biochem warfare suit.

"Who are you working for?" Croyd's teeth chattered louder than his voice. "The Mafia? The other guys?"

The android screamed at him. *"Why did you blow me up?"*

In the darkness Croyd's eyes were the color of blood. "Seemed like a good idea then," he said. "Better idea now."

A shivering fit struck him, and his teeth began to chatter like castanets. The albino's skin was a vivid turquoise, the same color as Travnicek's. He seemed barely conscious. The android closed the face mask and put a cloth flour sack over Croyd's head. He then wrapped Croyd in the canvas tarpaulin and tied him securely with the nylon cord. Even a person of unusual strength, the android thought, shouldn't be able to fight his way out of something that gave him no freedom of movement.

The android picked up his burden and flew on, spiraling down onto Travnicek's roof next to the skylight. Light shone upward through cracks in the black paint. He reached for the skylight.

"Over here, toaster."

Travnicek was standing naked atop the pointed roof of a water tower on the next building. His voice no longer came from his mouth, which seemed to be sealing up; one of the organs around his neck, one shaped like a speaking trumpet, had taken over that function. His middle-European accent had come through the transformation untouched.

"That's the Croyd person, yes?"

"That's correct." The android took his burden to the next roof and lowered it to a tarred surface still warm from the summer sunlight. Travnicek leaped the thirty feet from the top of the tower and landed effortlessly next to the bound figure. He bent, his organ-lei rustling as it focused on the albino. The sound of chattering teeth came from beneath the flour sack.

"I can *see* the viruses in there, right through that bag you've got over his head," Travnicek said. "I don't know how just yet, but I can see them. The wild cards are very alive, very eager to enter my body and... subvert my programming." A laugh floated from his speaking-trumpet. A mental chill flowed through the android at the noise, at how inhuman the laugh sounded without a throat to generate it.

Modular Man bent over the trembling figure of Croyd. "I will open the hood and mask. If you lean close, sir, and inhale, you should get another dose of the virus."

Travnicek laughed again. "You're a fool, toaster. A fool."

What rose in the android was not despair, but a bleak and hopeless confirmation of despair. "You ordered me to bring him. You *wanted* to be reinfected."

"That was before I realized what I was." The laugh came again. "I'm strong, I'm youthful, and I perceive the world in ways that no human ever dreamed were possible." He turned his back on the android and walked to the parapet. He stood on the edge of the roof and let the lights of Jokertown play on his azure skin. "This city is so *tasty*," he said. "I can *feel* the light, perceive motion and wind." His organ-lei rose toward the sky. "I can hear the stars singing. My senses range from the microscopic to the macrocosmic. Why should I want to lose this?"

"Your genius, sir. The genius that created *me*. If you don't regain it . . ."

"What good did it ever do me? What pleasure did it bring?" He laughed. "Years of bad food and no sleep, years of listening to voices babble in my head, years of no friendships, of fucking cheap tarts in alleyways because I didn't dare let them into my workplace . . . ." He gave a snarl and turned to the android.

"It's gonna change, blender. I'm gonna have a real *life* now. And the first thing, you get me some money."

"I—"

"*Real* money. A couple hundred thousand for a start. Just walk into a bank vault and grab it."

The android gazed at the garland of yellow eyes. "Yes, sir," he said.

"And get rid of that Croyd person. Where he won't bother anyone."

"Yes, sir."

Travnicek walked from the parapet to the iron base of the tower, then jumped six feet and clung to the side of the tower with hands and feet. He walked deliberately to its pointed crown and crouched, looking at the city.

"The world's my oyster," he said. "You're gonna open it for me."

The warm June night had gone cold. Croyd kicked and gave a yell. Modular Man picked him up and flew into the night, heading for the clinic.

A trumpet-flower laugh followed his silent ascent.

Travnicek, dressed in new custom-made clothing, stood with a woman on the observation deck of Aces High. Her hair was blond and curly, her dress light and low-cut and very nearly transparent. She wore white plastic boots. Travnicek leaned toward her, blue tongues lapping from his organ-lei, making wet tracks on her face. She shuddered and turned away.

"Fuck this, man. You're not paying me enough."

Travnicek reached into a pocket and pulled out a roll of bills. "How much *enough* do you want?" He held up a hundred-dollar bill.

The blond woman hesitated. Her face set into lines of determination. "A lot more."

Hiram wandered past like a ghost, his eyes tracking over the restaurant but seeing nothing.

"Jesus." A customer's voice drifted over the sound of the crowd. "Hiram never used to allow that kind of thing."

Modular Man winced and turned away. His seat near the window of the restaurant, within listening distance of the platform, gave him a far better view of Travnicek than he wanted.

There were some experiences he could not bring himself to cherish.

Kate looked over her shoulder at the twosome and lit a cigarette. "Quite an approach."

"It seems to work quite well."

She looked at him. "I detect a certain edge in your comment. Do you know the guy?"

"I have made his acquaintance."

"Okay. I won't ask."

Travnicek, laughing, handed the woman a roll of bills. His tongues, or whatever they were, continued to explore the woman. There were sounds of disgust from the bar.

Ignoring the fuss, the red-haired waitress stepped to the table. "Dessert?" she asked.

"Yes," said the android. "The crostata, the orange tart, and the chocolate sabayon pie."

"Yes, sir. And anything for the lady?"

Kate looked at Modular Man and stuck out her tongue. "Not for me. I'm counting calories."

"Very well. Coffee?"

"Yes. Thank you."

Kate tapped cigarette ash into an ashtray. She was a small woman, with straying brown hair and warm Jeanne Moreau eyes.

"I'm not sure even Epicurus would approve of all this gorging," she said.

"My days are numbered. I want to try everything." He smiled. "Besides, I don't gain calories."

"Just amps. I know." She reached out and squeezed his hand. "Are you all right? Now that you've fallen from Olympus and are living among the mortals?"

"I think I'm getting used to it. I'm still not certain I like it, though."

"And your creator?"

"His genius is gone."

"So you're on your own."

"No. I'm still compelled to obey him. Also to fight enemies of society in my spare time." *And break into safes,* he thought, though he didn't say it. *Wearing a disguise, so no one recognizes me.*

She looked troubled. "I wish there was something we could do."

"There appears not to be."

"Still." She took a drag on her cigarette. "You could learn physics. Metallurgy. That sort of thing. It could keep you going."

"Yes. I could enroll in night school."

"Why not full time?"

He shrugged. "Why not?"

Kate laughed. "They can bar a person from the classroom for not paying tuition. I don't know about a machine."

"Maybe I'll find out."

The android looked at his partner. "Thank you. You've helped me get things in perspective."

She smiled. "You're welcome. Anytime."

Someone's head appeared above the observation deck

balcony. Wall Walker's. The android started, remembering Mr. Gravemold. Why would someone disguise himself as a joker?

The young ace stepped over the balcony and entered the bar.

The waitress brought the dessert tray and a pot of coffee. Kate, looking balefully at the desserts, pushed back her chair. "Time for a bathroom check. And then"—she sighed—"I've got to get back to Statius and company."

The waitress moved the dessert tray to allow a customer to pass. The android recognized the nondescript brown-headed man who had been in the restaurant the day he'd spoken to Wall Walker. He nodded at the man but spoke to Kate.

"Thank you for joining me," he said. "I kept expecting an emergency of some sort to interrupt the dinner. An alien invasion, an ape escape, something."

Kate looked surprised. "Oh. You hadn't heard about the ape?"

The android's heart began to sink. "No. I hadn't."

"He's not an ape anymore. He—"

Modular Man raised a hand. "Spare me."

The lanky brown-haired customer looked at them. "In fact," he said, "*I'm* the ape."

The android looked at him. The man held out a hand. "Jeremiah Strauss," he said. "Pleased to meet you."

The android allowed his hand to be shaken. "Hi," he said.

"I don't do the ape anymore." Jeremiah Strauss seemed eager for company. "But I can still do Bogart. Watch this!"

The ex-ape began to concentrate. His features slowly began to rearrange themselves. "I'm not gonna play the sap for you, sweetheart," he lisped. His face looked like Bogart's must have looked in his coffin.

"Very good," Modular Man said, appalled.

"You wanna see Cagney?"

He looked at Kate, saw her glassy stare. "Maybe some other time."

Strauss seemed stricken. "Too eager, huh?" he said. "Sorry. I just haven't caught up yet. You think it was bad being dead for a year, man, trying being a giant ape for twenty. Jesus, last I heard, Ronald Reagan was an *actor*."

"Bathroom," Kate said. She looked at Strauss. "Nice to meet you."

She fled. Modular Man shook Strauss's hand and said good-bye

The waitress pushed the cart back to the table and handed him his desserts. "We had a message for you a couple days ago," she said. She gave him a wink. "A call from California. I thought maybe it would be a bad idea to give it to you when you were with another lady, though." She reached into a pocket and gave the android a pink message slip. A long-distance number was written at the top.

Welcome back. New phone number. Call soon. Love, Cyndi. P.S. Got your heart on?

Modular Man memorized the number, smiled, crumpled the paper.

Cherish, he thought.

"Thank you," he said. "If the lady should call again, tell her the answer is yes."

He reached for his desserts.

New experiences were everywhere.

Blood Ties

VI

If the situation hadn't been so deadly, it could have been funny. Modular Man vanishing over the rooftops with Croyd in his arms, and the joker squad and Tachyon gaping stupidly after him. Troll had cleared his throat, an explosion of sound like a road grader moving gravel. He offered the Takisian the limp figure of Bill Lockwood like a man presenting his prize catch.

"Well, at least we've got this one," he said timidly.

"Bloody lot of good it does us! Well, I suppose I must treat him," Tach had muttered pettishly, and they had all returned to the clinic.

A few hours later and the mystery man's body temperature was returned to near normal. He lay blinking groggily in the hospital bed confined by restraints. Tachyon drew up a chair and stared into the handsome, insipid face.

"You've given us a devil of a time, you know that. Why on earth did you protect Croyd so desperately? You're directly responsible for the deaths of hundreds of innocent people!"

To Tachyon's chagrin the young man's face screwed up, and he began to cry. "I was just lookin' out for Croyd," he blubbered while Tach mopped at the tears with his handkerchief. "He's the only person who's ever been good to me. He gave me his doughnuts. He made me an ace."

"Who the hell are you?"

"Aren't you gonna read my mind?"

"I'm too tired and cranky to read your mind." Tachyon sensed that in some inexplicable way he had let the man down.

"I'm . . . was Snotman—*but don't use that name*—I'm an ace now."

"Snot . . ." Tachyon's voice trailed away, and he helplessly shook his head.

Memories like a stuttering slide show racheted through his mind. The horrible mucus-covered figure fleeing from the baseball-bat-wielding bouncer at Freakers . . . the Demon Princes tormenting the miserable joker until blood had mingled with the green mucus . . . the disgusting adenoidal sounds emerging from dumpsters where Snotman slept.

"Oh, ships and ancestors, he made you an ace and you were so grateful . . ." Words again failed him.

"What's going to happen to me?" asked Bill Lockwood.

"I don't know."

There was a growing tumult in the hall: Troll bellowing like an outraged bull, and Tina's voice high and shrill. A name emerged from the cacophony . . . Tachyon's.

Modular Man was circling overhead with Croyd wrapped in a sheet like an outraged mummy. Tachyon and Troll tumbled into their suits, and the android thrust Croyd into the isolation chamber. Tachyon had prepared it weeks ago; prison security glass, a heavily reinforced steel door. They were ready.

Croyd punched his way through the glass in just under two minutes. And vanished beneath a pile of tackling bodies. Hours later the glass was replaced, and electrified mesh bolted to the wall.

Croyd punched through that in under a minute. Electricity seemed to act as a stimulant.

Troll looked up from where Croyd, bound hand and foot with steel shackles, lay beneath his nine-foot bulk. "Doc, I can't sit on him for the rest of my life."

They replaced the glass again. Tachyon discussed steel shutters with the security experts from Attica. They shrugged and pointed out that the walls would never bear the stress.

Then Finn had produced a wild and harebrained notion.

"Consider cows," he had remarked, pawing gently at the floor with a dainty forefoot. Victoria Queen had almost headed off for a sedative. "They're so stupid they won't walk over painted lines on the highway because they *think* it's a cattle guard."

"Yes, but Croyd is a man, not a cow," Tachyon explained patiently.

"But he's very suggestible."

"How would you know?"

"I put him to sleep with brain wave entrainment and suggestion, remember?"

They hooked him up and tried the same trick again. This time it didn't work. So they painted bars on the window. And on the door.

Croyd was very docile after that.

As long as no one came in the room.

Please go to sleep. Please, Croyd, go to sleep.

Tachyon had made this prayer every day for the past four days, but there was no response from the nervously pacing albino beyond the painted glass of the isolation chamber.

Tachyon had tried to give nature a little push. After the failure of brain wave entrainment he had pumped sleep gas into the room, drugged Croyd's food. And Croyd remained stubbornly and infectiously awake. And each hour he was awake the virus continued to mutate.

Croyd was a walking holocaust. And a decision had to be made. Tachyon stared down at his hands. Remembered the buck of the gun as he killed Claude Bonnell. Remembered the Burning Woman. Remembered Rabdan.

Ideal. I'm tired of dealing in death. Spare me, fathers, I don't want to do it again.

Peregrine smiled up at him from the hospital bed, then grimaced and bit down hard on her lip as another pain washed through her. Her blue eyes were overly bright, and her cheerful manner seemed more manic than natural. Tachyon sympathized. He had to struggle to keep his smile in place. In the next few hours she would give birth, and they both knew what that experience could do to the fetus now struggling to free itself from her swollen body.

He laid a gentle hand on the mound of her belly and felt the contraction shuddering through the muscles. "Cesarean might be easier on our boy."

"No. McCoy and I feel very strongly about this."

"Where is he?"

"Out getting coffee."

"You still insist on all this togetherness?"

"Yes."

"Husbands are a damned nuisance."

"I'd expect you to feel that way, Tachy darling." She managed to look almost sexy despite her condition. "And by

the way, we're not married." Another spasm, and she panted,
"How much longer?"

"You're just warming up."

"Terrific."

"Middle-aged mothers. It's harder on you."

"No encouragement, and now an insult."

"Sorry."

She reached out to him. "Tach, I was teasing."

"Try to rest. I'll see you in a few hours."

"It's a date."

Troll stuck his head around the office door. "You don't
need me, do you?"

"Why?"

"Trouble at the Chaos Club. The call just came in."

"No, go ahead."

"Strange, there hasn't been a peep out of these goons for
days. You'd think they'd have learned."

"Well, go and drive home the lesson again, Troll."

"You want to come?"

"Peregrine's in labor."

"Oh. See you later, Doc."

Tachyon checked with Tina and discovered they had
moved Peregrine to the delivery room. In the locker room he
stripped out of his peach and silver finery, shrugged into the
green surgical gown, and scrubbed.

The intercom buzzed. He flipped it on with an elbow.

"Boss," came Finn's voice. "It's raining jokers down here."

"I've got a baby to deliver."

"Oh, right." Finn hung up the phone. The emergency
room was filling up with young jokers sporting a variety of
cuts and bruises. More were streaming in. Finn trotted to the
nearest teen, then reared back when he noticed that the gash
across the boy's forehead was a clever makeup job.

A six-inch length of a switchblade glittered beneath Finn's
nose.

An ambulance roared into the bay and disgorged a party
of heavily armed men. Finn raised his hands. His mommy
didn't raise no dummy.

When the idea of seizing Tachyon's clinic had first been
proposed, Brennan had argued strenuously against the plan.

But the word filtered down from on high: Tachyon can lead us to a woman who can sleep with a joker and cure him. Find her. And Tachyon needs to be taught a lesson. Get him.

Brennan wasn't surprised by the order. A year ago Kien had been using the lovely Vietnamese girl Mai to cure jokers. All it took was money—a lot of it—and you were cured. Then Brennan had killed Scar and rescued Mai, and now a new girl had arisen to take her place. A girl who cured with sex. What joker male wouldn't pay a fortune to be cured by fucking a beautiful woman?

The real irony was that Brennan had been given command of the assault. After robbing Kien of his curing machine he was about to provide the crime boss with a new one. It was too bad about Tachyon and his clinic, but Brennan had his own agenda to pursue.

The only problem was that he'd been jumped over Danny Mao, and the Oriental didn't appreciate it. On the other hand it was an indication of how well regarded Brennan had become within Kien's byzantine network. The next step would probably be into the inner circle that surrounded Kien himself, and then Brennan's revenge would be within reach. So he couldn't refuse the assignment. He had worked too hard for too many years to pull down the facade that was Kien Phuc and reveal the rottenness that lay behind.

Brennan rammed a clip into his Browning High Power and touched the pockets of his vest, making sure his reloads were handy. It had been agreed that deaths would be kept to a minimum. Only one person was earmarked for death—Tachyon.

Eleven twenty-seven.

Brennan, riding with the driver, peered ahead at the clinic. They'd be pulling in soon. Too bad about Tachyon.

If you wish to find the unclouded truth, do not concern yourself with right and wrong.

He had his own agenda.

Right or wrong.

McCoy was holding up pretty well. At least he hadn't passed out and been carried out of the delivery room. He was even occasionally remembering to instruct Peri to pant, bear down, breathe. Her responses to these helpful reminders

were direct and uncomplimentary. Another brittle scream
tore from her throat, and she arched in the stirrups.

Tachyon, eyes flicking between monitors and her dilated
cervix, said softly, "You're doing fine, Peri. Just a little more
now."

He reached out and touched the unformed mind of the
child fighting its way down the birth canal. Fear, fury at
having its comfortable world so abruptly upset. (Definitely
Fortunato's child.) Tachyon stroked and soothed, watched the
heartbeat slow from its frenzied pounding.

*You're going to be all right, little man. Don't give me the
satisfaction of being right.*

How many times had he hunched between a mother's
knees, received a child, and had it turn to sludge in his
hands? Too many.

There was a crash that swung him around on the stool,
and the alien gaped in amazement at the three armed men
who had plunged through the doors of the delivery room.
Peregrine reared up on her elbows and eyed them with
loathing. "OH, CHRIST!"

"What the devil do you mean by this?"

Tach retreated slightly at the aggressive thrust of an Uzi
barrel in his direction. The two other intruders merely
gulped and stared with reddened faces at Peregrine's private
parts.

"You've broken the sterile integrity of this room. Get
out!"

"We're here for you."

"I'm a little busy right now. I'm delivering a baby. OUT!"
Tach made shooing motions with his gloved hands.

"Fuck this," yelled McCoy, doing just what Tachyon had
prayed he wouldn't.

Tach's mind control dropped the cameraman in his tracks,
and his seizure of the shootist sent the rounds spraying into
the ceiling. Glass from broken light fixtures tinkled all about
him.

"McCoy!" Peregrine struggled in Tina's grasp.

"Lay down! He's fine. He will live to be an idiot yet
another day."

"Release my man or I'll kill you. One of the two of us will
get you, or these women," shouted the nervous young Orien-

tal. Dr. Tachyon released the gunman. "Now you're coming with us."

"Gentlemen, I don't know why you're here, or who you are, but I will be at your disposal *after* I have delivered this child. I can't slip away down the drain. I have to exit through those doors, so kindly wait for me in the scrub room."

He pulled his stool back into position between Peri's legs and resumed his quiet external and internal monologue to mother and child.

"McCoy," panted the ace.

"Asleep."

Peri's screams and contractions were coming in waves. Tach didn't like her pressure, but . . . Suddenly baby slid free. Reaching into the vagina, he cradled the tiny head on his palm and helped slide John Fortune into his new world.

Tach tasted blood and realized he had bitten through his lower lip. He enfolded the child in waves of warmth and love and comfort. *Don't change! Don't transform! By the Ideal, don't transform!*

The baby lay in his hands, a perfectly formed man-child with a thick head of dark hair. The mucus was suctioned from the budlike mouth. Upending him, Tachyon massaged the tiny back, and a powerful yell erupted from the boy. Tach blinked away tears, wiped blood and mucus from the baby, and laid the child on his mother's flaccid stomach.

"He's all right. He's all right." Her fingers played gently across the bawling child.

"Yes, Peri, he's perfect. You were right."

The final details were handled; cord cut, child given a more thorough wash and wrapped in lamb's wool. Tachyon and Tina levered Peregrine onto a gurney, then heaved the snoring McCoy onto another. A face was thrust into the window of the delivery room. Tach hunched his shoulders and ignored it.

"Doctor, what's going on?" quavered Tina.

"I don't know, my dear, but I presume those armed gentlemen will tell me."

Brennan swept into the scrub room and stared at his men. They guiltily dropped the cigarette they had been sharing and studied the floor.

"Where's Tachyon?"

"In there."

"Why in there?"

"He was delivering a baby."

"God, it was gross."

"Embarrassing," amplified the third.

"He promised to—"

"Surrender to you. Yes, gentlemen, I did, and you behold me. Now, however, could you help me? I assume you have—" His eyes met Brennan's; he faltered, coughed, and resumed. "You have seized my orderlies, and I have a patient who needs to be taken to the nursery, and one who needs to go to her room."

You! My gods what are you doing here?

Seizing your clinic.

But why? WHY?

"So if you would be kind enough to assist with a gurney."

The outer conversation flowed on over the internal telepathic exchange.

The three men looked to Brennan. "Put them with the rest in the cafeteria."

"Cafeteria! Surely you're not moving the dangerously ill or the infants?"

"Don't be an idiot. They're no threat to us," said Brennan, disgusted.

"The man in isolation . . . you didn't release him?" asked Tachyon.

"No, he's our cover."

"Cover?"

"Why am I wasting time beating gums with you? Move it," shouted Brennan. "You can take the brat to the nursery, and we'll have a little talk."

Brennan, his Browning gripped tightly in his hand, and Tachyon, with John Fortune cradled in his arms, paced through the unnaturally silent halls.

The nursery staff had all been removed, so Tachyon prepared a bottle and fed the child. Brennan swung a chair around and straddled it, arms folded across the back.

"Now, what is this all about?" asked Tachyon with a mildness he didn't feel.

"Two things. You've upset a certain major player with your goon squad. You've also got an item that this player wants."

"Please stop talking like a third-rate goon in a B gangster movie. 'Item' indeed!" snorted the alien.

"Jane Lillian Dow."

"I don't know where she is."

"My boss thinks different."

"Your boss is wrong." Tachyon wiped away a trail of milk from the baby's chin. "I presume you have put about some story or another to explain the closure of the clinic?"

"Yes, we're telling people that the carrier's loose in the hospital."

"Clever." Tachyon shifted Johnny, studying the baby's slight epicanthic folds, and glanced significantly at Brennan's altered eyes. "I never asked why you wanted the surgery."

"I know. I appreciated that."

"I could have discovered, but I did not. I respected your privacy."

"Yeah, I know."

"And this is how you repay me?"

"I had to get into this . . . organization. I've risked everything for this."

Tachyon flung out a hand. "This? *This?* Invading my clinic, endangering my patients?"

"No, no, not this. Other . . . things. . . ." Brennan's voice trailed away.

"I wouldn't give you Jane even if I knew where she was."

"My orders are to start killing patients until you do."

Tachyon blanched and took a harder grip on the bottle. He flipped John over his shoulder and patted until the baby let out a loud belch, dribbling milk over the peach-colored material.

"Your orders are to kill *me* no matter what."

"STAY OUT OF MY HEAD!" Brennan swung away from Tachyon, clenched his fists between his thighs. "I won't do it."

"No, you will have someone else do it for you. What a very flexible mind you have, Captain. You would have made a good Takisian. Perhaps that is why I like you." He rose and laid Johnny in a crib.

"GODDAMN YOU!"

"Why?"

"You're all closing in on me, wrapping me in these bonds, holding me, smothering me."

"I wonder what your Jennifer would think of what you're doing?"

"DAMN IT! STAY OUT! JUST STAY THE FUCK OUT! I didn't want to care," he concluded quietly.

"It is the price you pay for being human, Brennan. Sometime you have to care."

"I do," he said, agonized.

"For death. Someday it might make an interesting change to choose the living."

"That's not fair," he cried after Tachyon's back. "What about Mai?"

"Mai is gone. This is here and now, and you are going to have to make a choice."

The hours crawled by. Tachyon's admiration for Bradly Latour Finn increased with each passing moment. The little joker comforted the old, jollied the young, and played games with the children. His insouciant grin never budged. Not when their increasingly nervous guards rained curses or blows onto his curly head. Not when Victoria Queen cried out hysterically:

"We're all going to *die*, and how can you be so fucking calm?"

"Too dumb to know different."

He trotted to Tachyon, gun muzzles following his progress through the crowded cafeteria. He paused briefly by a table where Deadhead was maintaining a constant babble. Nodded seriously for several seconds.

"I *couldn't* agree more."

"Sit down!" yelled one of their guards.

Finn backed delicately toward a chair. Wriggled his hindquarters. Sadly shook his head and trotted to Tach. The alien gasped in surprise as he noticed for the first time the joker's tail. It had been cut off just below the dock.

"Your tail!"

"It will adorn some Werewolf's jacket."

Idiotically, this upset Tachyon almost more than anything that had thus far happened. "Your tail," he mourned again.

"It'll grow. Besides, I was too proud of it anyway." He leaned in. "Doc, some of these people need medication."

"I know."

Tachyon slid off the table, and with his hand resting

lightly on Finn's withers, he walked to Brennan. It was an absurd picture. The tiny alien dressed in knee breeches, the lace cravat of his shirt untied and falling like a foaming waterfall, copper curls fluttering as he walked. The tiny palomino centaur prancing like a Lippizaner at his side.

"A number of these people are on medication. May I take some of my staff and obtain the drugs?"

"Drugs. Sounds good," laughed a Werewolf.

"Give us what we want," said Brennan.

"No."

"SHIT!" Danny Mao mashed out a cigarette on a cellophane-wrapped chef's salad. The hot tip burnt through the plastic and left a black smear on the cheese and the meat. "How long are we gonna sit here?"

"As long as it takes," replied Brennan shortly.

"Cowboy, let's kill a few of these ugly fuckers." Danny Mao eyed the huddled jokers with disgust. "We'd be doing most of them a favor."

Brennan rounded on Tachyon. "The girl."

"No."

Why are you doing this!

Why are you?

Twenty more minutes crawled agonizingly past. Tachyon, eyes half-closed, fingered a violin sonata on his knee, head beating time to the silent music.

"Cowboy, he's got a mind power. What's to say he's not calling the joker hit squad right now?"

Lee ranged himself with the only other Oriental in the group. "Danny's right."

"He won't call for help. He knows the risks of an assault from outside. How many of them"—Brennan's arm swept out to encompass the frightened patients and staff—"will be killed in the shooting?" He rounded on Tachyon, his gray eyes hard. "How many of them shall we kill as payment for treachery?"

"'Treachery.'" Tachyon savored the word. Lilac eyes met gray. The gray fell first.

"Okay, so you don't want to start offing sick old ladies," said Danny, eyeing one with disfavor. "Even if they are as ugly as an unwiped asshole. Why don't we use *him*?" A jerk of a thumb toward Deadhead, who was guiltily gobbling down a piece of pie, and keeping up the running monologue with himself. "That's what he's here for."

Brennan wiped sweat. "We don't know what Tachyon might do to him. It's an alien metabolism."

Danny stepped to an old man, gripped him by his stringy white hair, and thrust the barrel of his Colt Python into the toothless mouth. Victoria Queen whimpered. A rustle went through the hostages. Tachyon came half out of his chair, then subsided when he realized the Chinese man's focus was on Brennan.

"I don't think you've got what it takes, Cowboy," Danny said in a dangerously low tone. "I think it was a mistake putting you in charge. Now either you gather your stones and act, or *I* will."

"All right," shouted Brennan. "We'll use Deadhead."

Danny pulled his pistol from the joker's mouth and placed the tip of the barrel against Tachyon's throat. A gasp and a rustle ran through the prisoners.

"But not here. In his office. And Deadhead." The ace looked up and paused in his energetic chewing. "Bring a spoon."

Brennan left five men on guard in the cafeteria. He watched Tachyon studying the fifteen men who towered over him in the elevator. It was a look he knew—a man weighing the odds. And not liking the answer.

Isida, my roshi, what takes precedence? The quest of a man's soul, or the transitory friendships of this world?

There was no answer. Somehow Brennan had a feeling that even if the old man had been present, there still wouldn't have been an answer.

Tachyon's narrow face was composed. He was clearly resigned to death. Brennan doubted the alien would meet it quietly. He would try something before the end.

Deadhead belched and patted his stomach. "Wish I hadn't had that piece of pie. Hope I got room for this. Hey, how we gonna open his head?" Tachyon's eyes widened. Suddenly he doubled over and vomited onto Danny's shoes.

"Oh, shit!" yelled the Oriental.

"Mind reading's not such a great power, huh?" gritted Brennan. "You find out what's in store for you. Lee, go down to the operating room and bring a saw."

"Why don't we just take him down there?" whined the boy, holding his nose against the stink.

"Because I don't want to." Tension and fury crackled in the words.

They filed into Tachyon's office, Brennan carefully closing the door behind him. Danny pulled back the hammer on his gun and grinned back over his shoulder at Brennan.

"I'll handle this, Cowboy. You don't seem to have the stomach for it."

It wasn't a conscious decision. Brennan just reached out and snapped off the lights. New York's bright glow formed a square of silver around the tightly closed blinds, but the rest of the room was plunged into stygian darkness.

Tachyon hit the floor as two simultaneous muzzle flashes almost blinded him. A body fell across him.

"Shit! He's got a gun," he heard Brennan sing out.

He wished to god he had.

Thrusting with elbows and knees, Tachyon belly-crawled across the thick carpet. A foot took him hard in the ribs, and he bit back a gasp. The man took a header, discharging his Uzi in a long burst as he fell. Someone screamed.

Feeling for the knob, Tachyon seized it in a sweat-slick hand, threw open the door, and darted through. He slammed it quickly behind him, and bullets blasted through the thin wood, peppering his cheek with splinters. He ran.

Steadying himself with a hand, he swung around the corner just as the door burst open, and the pursuit began.

Again Brennan's voice. "Half of you come with me. We'll head him off."

Fifteen, becomes fourteen, becomes thirteen, becomes maybe twelve, if that first Uzi blast hit one of them. So call it six to one. Still terrible odds, and too many for mind control unless he could separate them, and he didn't like that idea at all.

So where to go?

"This is the Place of Death."

Tachyon jerked open the door to the stairs and leaped like a hunted deer, taking two steps at a time. They were one landing behind.

"But the buck lived . . . Because he came first, running for his life."

It was a desperate gamble. It had to be taken. Two floors

below huddled his people. If his pursuers remembered, returned to threaten them...

He fished out his keys, put on a final burst of speed. His breath was sobbing in his raw throat. He couldn't see Croyd through the wide observation window of the isolation room. The lock turned, and he waited, hand on the knob. The hunting pack burst out of the stairwell, baying with excitement.

"There he is!"

He entered the room with a forward roll. Flashed past Croyd, who was crouched waiting by the door. But not for a compact bundle, tucked in close and rolling. Tachyon bounced to his feet.

"Croyd, help me. They're after us!"

A hand reached out. Tach flowed through it, allowing the momentum to carry Croyd a good three feet past him. Avoidance was his only hope. If Croyd ever got a grip on him, the ace would break him like fragile glass. The red eyes were maddened, the pale face twisted, inhuman.

The hunters arrived. Tachyon threw himself into a long flat dive that carried him toward the bed. Croyd snarled, confused, questing. His eyes met those of the leading gun-man. The Uzi came up, but the man let out a wail like steam being vented from a locomotive and began to melt. Within seconds he had sunk to his knees in an ever-widening pool of frothing pink ooze.

Croyd's hand lashed out at another, connecting at the junction of shoulder and neck. Tachyon pressed desperately against the wall, heard bones crunch. The man collapsed with a broken neck. Screams filled the room.

Suddenly there was a flare of incandescence, and a hunter became a human torch. Within seconds all that was left was the stink of burnt tile and cooked flesh, and a blackened patch on the floor.

One of the three survivors got off a shot. The bullet buried itself in Croyd's bare foot. Throwing back his head, the albino howled in pain. He gripped the gun and ripped it from the man's hand. Croyd then proceeded to beat him with the barrel. Skin cracked and tore as the gunsight ripped into the tender flesh of his cheeks.

At Tachyon's feet another man writhed. The convulsions were so violent that he was literally bent like a bow, head to heels. Blood ran from his mouth where he had bitten through his tongue.

Black Queen. Without joker manifestation. Three out of seven. Blood and line, let me live. I want to live.

Fear was a living thing, gripping him by the throat, stopping the breath in his lungs. Tachyon struggled for air.

The boy, Lee, had been at the back of the pack. Terrified, he threw down his gun and fled. Croyd tossed aside his attacker, who collapsed like a bloody puppet, and raced in pursuit.

Tachyon, turning his head as if his neck were made of glass, eyed the carnage. Gazed down his own slim length. Gave a sob of joy. Pushing off the wall, he swept up an Uzi and ran into the hall. The window over the fire escape had been wrenched out of the wall. Leaning out he saw a shadowy figure vanishing between the Dumpsters in the alley. Hating himself, he fired, heard the whine of bullets ricocheting off brick and metal and no other sound. Croyd was gone.

His ankles had gone limp, and he almost fell. A strong arm slipped around his waist, and the Takisian gave a cry of terror. He lashed out with his mind power and froze as he recognized the mind.

"Brennan."

They had a few minutes before the police arrived. Tachyon sat behind his desk, poured two stiff brandies, and saluted the impassive human.

"I count you . . . friend. Thank you."

Brennan was canted back in his chair, booted feet propped on the desk. Danny's body sprawled on the carpet next to him.

"Took me a damn long time to make up my mind."

"You had much at stake. I am grateful."

"Shut up. You've thanked me enough. Well, I better get out of here." Brennan fished in his pocket, pulled out an ace of spades, and flipped the card onto the body. "Give them all something to think about."

"The police . . . and *who else*?"

"What do you mean?" Brennan tensed in the doorway.

"Who is behind this?" Silence stretched between them. "Daniel, I demand to know. You *owe* me that."

The human turned slowly back to face him. "It's dangerous."

"You're telling me something I don't already know? This man has preyed upon my people, my holding, and made war on *me*. It must stop."

"And how do you propose to accomplish that?"

"By making him believe that I am more dangerous to him than he is to me."

A smile quirked that strong mouth, vanished, began to grow by slow stages. Tachyon watched in fascination. It was the first time he'd ever seen Brennan smile.

"This is what I propose."

Order was restored. Finn treated patients for shock, Peregrine nursed her baby, statements were given, bodies or the remnants of bodies counted. The five men left on guard in the cafeteria had escaped, and also the horrifying Deadhead. A massive manhunt began for Croyd. Tachyon regretted and agonized over his decision. Perhaps he should have accepted death rather than release Croyd, but what a death . . . his brains consumed by that repellant creature. He decided he just wasn't that noble.

By five A.M. the alien was free to leave. He made preparations, collected the limousine, met Brennan. With the human driving they set out to Fifth Avenue and Seventy-third Street.

They parked in the alley behind the five-story gray-stone apartment building. Tachyon spread a lace tablecloth across the hood of the Lincoln and laid out breakfast: warm croissants, thermoses of hot tea and coffee. A selection of cheeses. Then, nibbling on a sliver of Camembert, he sent out the call. A siren's summons. Ten minutes later Kien Phuc stepped out the back door into the alley. Wyrm was with him. The joker reached for a gun, then hissed as Brennan slowly turned and notched a heavy broadhead hunting arrow in his bow and leveled it on Kien. Tachyon released the compulsion, and the Vietnamese waved his joker/ace down.

Tachyon spread his hands in welcome. "Won't you join me, Mr. Phuc? While our two lieutenants keep us and each other honest." Tachyon proffered a plate, shrugged when Kien remained motionless. "You have . . . irritated me, Mr. Phuc, but I was pleased when you tried your pathetic seizure of my clinic. It gave me the opportunity I had been seeking."

"For what?" Kien's voice grated out like rusty machinery starting after years of neglect.

"To warn you. I am a bad enemy to make," the alien said brightly, and spread jam on a croissant.

"What do you want?"

"First, to demonstrate how easily I can take your mind and compel you to do anything. Second, to make it clear to you that Jokertown is *my* territory, and third, to reach a truce."

"Truce?"

"I have my own interests to pursue, just as you have yours. Yours include prostitution and numbers running and the drug trade, but they will *not* include protection rackets and extortion and gun battles in my streets. I want my people safe."

Kien's eyes slid to Brennan. "Is this trained jackal yours?"

"Oh, no, he too has his own interests to pursue."

Brennan's gray eyes stared implacably into Kien's black ones. "I'm coming for you, Kien."

Tachyon smiled. "You have people who can kill me from the shadows. I have people who can do the same to you. Stalemate."

"You won't interfere with my business?"

"No." Tachyon sighed. "I suppose it shows a distressing lack of morality on my part, but I am not a crusader. Men will still crave women, and women will sell themselves to satisfy those cravings, and drugs will be sold and consumed. We are, alas, not angels. But I insist on peace in my streets." Tachyon lost his light, bantering tone. "There will be no more children dying in senseless gun battles in Jokertown. And my clinic and my patients will be safe."

"What about Jane Dow?"

"That chip is not up for discussion in this negotiation, Mr. Phuc."

Kien shrugged. "All right."

"Are we agreed?"

"I agree to your terms."

Tachyon grinned. "You should never plan a double cross in the presence of a telepath. Brennan, kill him." The Vietnamese blanched.

"Wait, no wait, wait!"

"All right, let us try it again. *Are we agreed?*"

"Not quite," Kien ground out. He stared at Brennan, who returned his gaze levelly. "I received a message from you some time ago." Brennan nodded. "This is my reply." Hate and fury laid a rough edge on the man's voice, and he pointed his half-hand at Brennan as if it were a weapon. "If you persist in annoying me, if, as you say, you bring me down, then I will have nothing left to live for. And then, I swear to you, this Wraith, this Jennifer Maloy, will die. Back off, Captain Brennan. Back off and leave me in peace or she *will* die. This is *my* promise to *you*."

Tachyon looked from Kien to Brennan. The archer's face was as hard and unyielding as a clenched fist.

"You weary me," snapped Tachyon. "Your threats weary me. Go!"

And he sent the Vietnamese and his jackal Wyrm trotting back into the building.

Tachyon was feeling pretty jaunty when he returned to the clinic. He paused to gleefully pat each stone lion, then trotted up the stairs. Croyd couldn't remain awake much longer. Surely his contagion power would fade in the next transformation. Kien was, for the moment, neutralized. Of course the Vietnamese would go back on his word, but perhaps by then Brennan would have achieved his goal, and Kien would no longer be a problem.

Tachyon headed into the basement and shut off the elaborate series of electronic locks that protected his private laboratory. It was here he manufactured the drug for Angelface and pursued his research for a perfected trump virus.

It was force of habit that drove him to draw blood and begin the XVTA-test. He was obviously fine. The Ideal and the percentages had been with him last night.

He slipped the slide into the electron microscope, focused, and read his fate in the tangled web of the wild card.

With a cry he swept a tray of slides and test tubes onto the floor. Beat his fists on the table, screaming out denial.

Calm, calm! Stress could trigger the virus.

Quietly he righted his stool, sat with folded hands, and considered. If it manifested, he would most likely die. Acceptable. He might become a joker. Unacceptable. The trump? A last resort.

Jane!

The irony of an impotent man being saved through sex struck him, and he laughed. When he realized they grew from hysteria, not humor, he stifled the wild whoops.

And the future?

Search for Jane. Remove as much stress as possible from his life. Go on living. The house Ilkazam did not breed cowards.

And most important: *Blaise*.

The boy was all he had now. His blood and seed were poisoned. There would be no other children.

Concerto for
Siren and Serotonin

VIII

Again they were after him. If you can't even trust your doctor, he wondered, who can you trust? The sirens' wails were almost a steady sheet of sound now.

He hurled chunks of concrete, broke streetlights, and dashed from alley to doorway. He crouched within parked cars. He watched the choppers go by, listening to the steady *phut-phut* of their blades. Every now and then he heard parts of appeals over some loudspeaker or other. They were talking to him, lying to him, asking him to turn himself in. He chuckled. That would be the day.

Was it all Tachy's fault again? An image flashed before his mind's eye, of Jetboy's small plane darting like a tiny fish among great, grazing whales there in the half-clouded sky of an afternoon. Back when it all began. What had ever happened to Joe Sarzanno?

He smelled smoke. Why did things always get burned in times of trouble? He rubbed his temples and yawned. Automatically he sought in his pocket after a pill, but there was nothing there. He tore open the door to a Coke machine before a darkened service station, broke into the coin box, then fed quarters back into the mechanism, collected a Coke for either hand, and walked away sipping.

After a time he found himself standing before the Jokertown Dime Museum, wanting to go inside and realizing that the place was closed.

He stood undecided for perhaps ten seconds. Then a siren sounded nearby. Probably just around the corner. He moved forward, snapped the lock, and entered. He left the price of admission on the little desk to his left and as an afterthought, tossed in something for the lock.

He sat on a bench for a while, watching shadows. Every now and then he rose, strolled, and returned. He saw again the golden butterfly, poised as if about to depart from the golden monkey wrench, both of them transmuted by the short-lived ace called Midas. He looked again at the jars of joker fetuses, and at a buckled section of a metal door bearing Devil John's hoofprint.

He walked among the Great Events in Wild Card History dioramas pressing the button over and over again at the Earth vs. Swarm display. Each time that he hit it, Modular Man fired his laser at a Swarm monster. Then he located one that made the statue of the Howler scream. . . .

It was not until his final Coke was down to its last swallow that he noticed the diminutive human skin, stuffed, displayed in a case. He pressed nearer, squinting, and read the card that identified it as having been found in an alley. He sucked in his breath as the recognition hit him.

"Poor Gimli," he said. "Who could have done this to you? And where are your insides? My stomach turns at it. Where are your wisecracks now? Go to Barnett, tell him to preach till all hell freezes. In the end it'll be his hide, too."

He turned away. He yawned again. His limbs were heavy. Rounding a corner, he beheld three metal shells, suspended by long cables in the middle of the air. He halted and regarded them, realizing immediately what they were.

On a whim he leaped and slapped the nearest of the three—an armor-plated VW body. It rang all about him and swayed slightly on its moorings, and he sprang a second time and slapped it again before another yawning jag seized him.

"Have shell, will travel," he muttered. "Always safe in there, weren't you, Turtle—so long as you didn't stick your neck out?"

He began to chuckle again, then stopped as he turned to the one he remembered most vividly—the sixties model—and he could not reach high enough to trace the peace symbol on its side, but " 'Make love, not war,' " he read, the motto painted into a flower-form mandala. "Shit, tell that to the guys trying to kill me.

"Always wondered what it looked like inside," he added,

and he leaped and hooked his fingers over the edge and drew himself upward.

The vehicle swayed but held his weight easily. In a minute he was sequestered within.

"Ah, sweet claustrophobia!" he sighed. "It *does* feel safe. I could . . ."

He closed his eyes. After a time he shimmered faintly.

"What Rough Beast..."

by Leanne C. Harper

Bagabond looked down at her friend Jack Robicheaux. The transformations were coming more slowly now and lasting longer. Right now he was human, and he would probably remain human for the next several days. She had spent some time wondering if she was partially to blame for his continuous transformations. Jack had known he could only communicate with her as an alligator. Even in his coma it was possible that he had realized that he had to change to tell her about Cordelia.

She looked up to catch C.C.'s gaze and shrugged. "I know I promised to stop feeling guilty. I'm going to miss him."

Both women looked up as Cordelia entered the hospital room.

"Good news, guys. Dr. Tacky says that Jack may be getting a little better. He's not sure, but he thinks that the time that Jack has been spending as a 'gator may be killing the virus." Cordelia crossed the hospital room to Jack's bed and leaned down to kiss him on the lips. "So there, *Oncle*. Don't you give up on me now."

C.C. Ryder and Bagabond exchanged surprised glances over Cordelia's head. Bagabond allowed a smile to sneak onto her face, camouflaged by the tangled hair.

The red-haired singer took Bagabond's hand. "Told ya so."

"What? Never mind. Y'all speak in shorthand anyway. Worse'n Cajuns. When are y'all leaving?" Cordelia stood by Jack's head, looking down as if she could see inside him.

"Plane leaves tomorrow. I dropped the itinerary off at your office this morning. So, if there's any change, you can get in touch immediately." C.C. looked up at her friend. "Suzanne will want to know right away."

"Do they have phones in Guatemala?"

"Yes, Cordelia." C.C. sighed.

"Bring me back an Indian?" Cordelia held her uncle's hand, but she grinned up disarmingly at Bagabond and C.C.

"We're going to help them, not arrange American wives."

"Who said anyt'ing about marriage?" Cordelia's quicksilver emotions turned serious. "Bagabond, I'll take care of him. I promise. I know you don't think much of me sometimes, but—"

"Just need to grow up. Don't make promises to yourself or anybody else that you can't keep. The world doesn't need any more saints." Cordelia blushed. Bagabond looked straight into the eyes of the younger woman. "'Sides, you don't think I'm going to leave Jack unguarded, do you?"

Bagabond swept open her coat and the black leaped out and shook himself before sitting down to begin preening his disturbed fur back into place. Cordelia knelt beside him and tried to scratch behind his ears. The cat backed away and leaped up onto Jack's bed and put his head beside Jack's on the pillow.

"Phones or no phones, tell the black if you need me. It's a long way, but I don't think that distance could stop us anymore. I feel bad going, though." Bagabond looked down at the floor.

"Dr. Tachyon will take care of Uncle Jack, with appropriate help from me and the black. He'd want you to go." Cordelia looked back at her uncle, lying pale and silent under the tubes and connections that kept him alive.

"I know. He'd say it would be good for me." Bagabond glanced at C.C., standing beside her. "I'm not used to all these people knowing what's good for me. But I always wanted to talk to a black jaguar, and no rock star should be without her bodyguard."

"Rock star." C.C. rolled her eyes toward heaven. "She keeps telling me that one jungle's like another. I don't know who's going to have the greatest culture shock: us or them. Poor guys are trying to build a new country. Just what they need, an aging 'rock star' and a bag lady."

Cordelia reached over and hugged C.C. "They could do a lot worse."

Bagabond watched her appraisingly, then held out her hand. Cordelia hesitated, then took it tightly between both of her own.

"You know how to take care of yourself. Don't cut off

something that's part of you." Bagabond raised her head to stare at Jack. "We both did, one way or another. He'd tell you the same. Don't become a cripple. It's not worth the effort."

"I think I figured that out, one night a while back." Cordelia released Bagabond's hand self-consciously. Bagabond walked up to Jack and gazed down on his peaceful face. She rested her hand on his cheek. With her hair hanging down around her face, no one else could see the words she made. She could only hope that Jack heard them, wherever he was. "I love you."

As they left the room, a man walked up to the door. It took Bagabond a moment to recognize him. "Michael."

He clutched a huge fruit basket that almost completely hid his face. What they could see was frightened. No one spoke.

"He's my friend, too." Michael lowered the basket a few inches. "Can I see him?"

Bagabond and Cordelia looked at each other, passing judgment on the man who had abandoned Jack months before. It was Cordelia who nodded their assent.

"We all love him."

Rocking back and forth, Rosemary Gambione wrung her hands as she sat on the bed waiting for the Shadow Fists' lawyer to make it official. It was all over. The Mafia had lost. The faces of the dead dons, the capos, even the soldiers, were with her now even in the daytime. The nightmare had become her reality.

She was sweating. Her little room sweltered in the August humidity of New York. On the bed her suitcase was packed and ready to go. Anywhere, as long as it was out of the city.

At the knock on her door she ran her hands down her jeans and grabbed her Walther. She had used it often in the last few months. It felt secure and heavy in her hands.

"Who?" She pulled the gun up to shove the damp hair out of her eyes.

"Swordfish. Or is there some other password you'd prefer?" The voice was elegant and a touch effete. Rosemary recognized it immediately from the phone calls that had set up this meeting. Holding the pistol in her right hand, she awkwardly opened the door with her left. Dressed in a custom-tailored white suit, the man she knew as Loophole sauntered into her room.

"Goodness." He looked at her gun for a moment before surveying the room. "Ah, well, these are troubled times in which we live, aren't they? Not even a desk, I see."

"Use the suitcase, Latham." Rosemary saw his head jerk slightly at the sound of his own name. She had seen him at every bar association dinner for years. She was surprised now that she had not recognized his voice.

"Quite. Much better than that 'Loophole' appellation with which I appear to be permanently associated. Please be seated, Ms. Gambione. Or is it Muldoon?"

"Gambione. Let's get this over with." Rosemary sat down across her suitcase from the lawyer, but she kept her Walther in her lap.

"By the way, my . . . associates are stationed throughout the building and on the street. To provide us with the privacy we need for our transaction."

Rosemary sighed and shook her head. "Loophole, I'm not going to take you hostage or kill you. What's the point? I just want to get this taken care of so I can leave. I don't want any more of my people dead. Let's see the contract."

Latham handed it over and studied her as she read it. Rosemary wondered if he was curious as to how low one of his own could sink. But then he had never seen her as a peer. If she hadn't wanted to keep those of her people who were left alive, killing Latham would be a particularly pleasurable form of suicide.

"It appears to be in order. The interests you represent take over my operations throughout the city, retaining my personnel—"

"Those who are left and still capable."

Rosemary's hand tightened on the gun. "Yeah, right. I'll sign it. Got a pen?"

"Of course." Latham extracted a Mont Blanc from his briefcase and carefully uncapped it for her. "Please . . ."

Rosemary laid the contract on her suitcase and in her last act as a Gambione, signed it. She saw her father's face in the background of the paper and her hand trembled. The signature was shaky, but it would keep her people safe.

Latham held up the contract and examined her signature. Rosemary couldn't tell if he was sneering at the wet imprints her hand had made or if it was simply his habitual expression. He was not sweating, she noticed. "I want the money and the ticket."

"It has all been arranged, my dear." Latham opened his briefcase again to stow away the contract and to remove two envelopes. The larger manila envelope was stuffed almost beyond its capacity. "Two hundred thousand and your passage to Cuba. I understand it is quite nice this time of year. I do hope you'll enjoy the voyage."

Latham stood and walked to the door. As he put his hand on the knob, he spoke again. "By the way, I had understood that you were looking for Mr. Mazzucchelli. My sources inform me that he can be found at the address in the envelope. Good luck."

Rosemary stared at the white envelope lying on her suitcase. She did not touch it. After a moment she looked up at Latham.

"Lagniappe." He shrugged. "The interests I represent are not without sympathy, my dear."

The door had been shut behind him for ten minutes before Rosemary picked up the white envelope. Turning it over, she saw the blood-red wax of the seal and smiled in pain.

One of the deals she had made was that the men who were entering the warehouse in front of her would be cared for in the best fashion possible. Most were not men anymore. They were the jokers that had survived the meeting with Croyd. She still wondered how Chris had arranged it.

When she had phoned their relatives to tell them about Chris, she had expected joy at this chance for revenge. She had received dull acceptance instead. Vengeance would be taken, but it would be taken because it was the proper thing to do, not because anyone, victim or guardian, could take any pleasure in it. She had been surprised, but now that she was here she understood. She was not pleased at what was about to happen. She felt nothing a all.

Earlier in the day she had found a side entrance and a route to the mezzanine of the abandoned Jokertown warehouse. If Chris had been there, she hadn't seen him. This time, as she took her vantage point, she heard the victims moving through the warehouse searching for him. The noises they made came close to nauseating her, but she forced herself to watch. It was her fault, after all.

The noises grew in volume. She spotted their prey and gasped. She had not expected this. What had been a thirty-year-old man was now a fur-covered, shambling thing. Its claws scrabbled on the concrete floor for purchase as it recognized that it was being pursued. As it turned its head to spot its enemies, the sharp teeth in the pointed muzzle glinted in the moonlight shining down through the shattered skylights. The only thing she recognized was the tangled rattail that still fell down his back.

His victims, her victims, shambled and oozed through the aisles of the warehouse toward the author of their pain. Did any of them still know what they had been or how they had become the warped creatures that closed in on the erstwhile Chris Mazzucchelli? An excited twittering erupted when Chris was spotted for the first time. He hissed at his pursuers, slashing the air with his outstretched claws. They were implacable. Even after he had drawn blood they came on, surrounding him carefully outside his reach.

Chris was backed into an area of the warehouse piled high with rusted machinery. He could not scale it, and his tormentors closed in for the kill. Rosemary tried to watch, but instead of remembering the man who had tried to kill her, she recalled the caring man she had taken as a lover. She stared down at the execution for only a moment before gagging and turning her back on the high-pitched screams that were followed by liquid gurgles.

Even the sounds were more than she could bear. Rosemary fled, but the noises pursued her long after she boarded the ship and curled up on the bed with her hands pressed against her ears.

Only the Dead
Know Jokertown

Epilogue

The new locks that Jennifer had had installed were so effica-
cious that Brennan couldn't let himself into her apartment.
That was good, he thought. She'd probably need them.

He sat on the fire escape landing outside her bedroom
window and watched the city traffic pass below him. He had
hated the city when he'd first arrived. Still did in fact, but
now he hated the thought of leaving even more.

And he had to leave. When he'd first come to the city,
nothing could've stopped him from bringing down Kien. He
would have sacrificed heaven and hell to get him. But now he
wasn't the same man. Now he had allowed himself to care,
and he had to pay the price for his weakness. Kien had won.
His vendetta was over. He watched the city move beneath his
feet, realizing for the first time how lonely the mountains
would be.

The warm spring afternoon had turned to dusk before a
small sound in the room behind him made him turn around.
Jennifer, home from the library, was looking out the window,
watching him. After a moment she crossed the room and
opened the window and Brennan ducked inside.

"Well," Jennifer said, "every few months you turn up just
like clockwork."

She was angry, and Brennan knew why. He hadn't seen
her since he'd foiled a Shadow Fists ambush at her apartment
in the wintertime. There'd been something of an unspoken
agreement between them that he'd come back to see her, but
he hadn't until now.

"I have to warn you." There was no easy way to say it.
"I'm leaving the city. Kien said he'll leave you alone, but I
don't trust him."

Jennifer frowned. "You're leaving because of me?"

Brennan shrugged. "Let's just say that I've chosen the living over the dead."

Her frown deepened. "He *did* use me to threaten you. He said he'd send his goons after me if you kept at him."

"Something like that," Brennan admitted. "He pointed out that he'd have nothing to live for if I brought him down. That there'd be nothing I could threaten him with to keep him from killing you."

Jennifer nodded slowly. "I see. Then my life means so much to you that you'd give up your vendetta, that you'd let Kien win?"

Brennan let out a deep breath and nodded.

Jennifer smiled. "It's good to know that. It'll make things easier."

"Things?" Brennan said suspiciously. "What things?"

"Things neither you nor Kien took into account. The fact that I won't allow myself to be held hostage by anyone. The fact that I can't be held hostage if no one knows where I am." She looked at Brennan for a long, long moment, and he felt a stab of pain at the love and beauty he saw on her face. "Good-bye, Daniel, and good hunting."

She ghosted. She stepped out of her clothes and through her bedroom wall and vanished. Brennan stared at the blank wall utterly confounded. She was gone, vanished like an exorcised specter.

"Wait—" he croaked, but it was too late. The room was empty, except for him and her belongings, abandoned and deserted now and forever. "Wait . . ."

He sat down heavily on the bed, overcome by shock and a sense of overwhelming loss that struck him with the force of a physical blow.

"You don't understand," he said aloud to the empty room, partly to himself, partly to a vanished Jennifer, struck with the force of his sudden insight. "Kien presented me with the choice, but I'm making it freely. I want you more than him. I want love more than hate . . . life more than death . . ."

His voice trailed off and he stared at the wall where Jennifer had vanished. His eyes nearly bugged out of their sockets when she stuck her head back through the wall.

"Good." She smiled. "I hoped you'd say something like that."

He shot off the bed. "Christ Almighty! Get back in here and get solid!"

"Why? Are you going to kiss me or slug me?"

"You'll have to take your chances," Brennan started to say, but her mouth covered his before he could get half the words out.

"You know," Jennifer said when they finally got their breath back, "it may be best to play Kien's game . . . at least for a little while."

Brennan nodded, his right arm tight around her waist, his left hand gently tracing the delicate curves of her jawline and chin.

"You're right." His voice, his eyes, were dreamy and strange-looking. Jennifer was startled, and then immensely pleased, to see happiness and perhaps even contentment in them. "I have a beautiful place in the Catskills I'd like you to see. And I haven't been back to New Mexico since . . . since . . . Christ has it really been that long?"

She smiled and kissed him again.

"And Kien?" she asked him when they broke apart.

Brennan shrugged. "He'll be here. I can wait." His smile came back, but there was a chill in it that both frightened and attracted her, drawing her like a moth to a dangerously burning flame. "It's what a hunter does best."

All the King's Horses

VII

"This is ridiculous." Bruder was in a fury. He had a pair of leather driving gloves in one hand, and he slapped them against his legs compulsively as he spoke. "Do you realize what you're doing? You're throwing away a fortune. *Millions* of dollars. Moreover, you're opening yourself up for a lawsuit. Tudbury and I were partners; this land ought to belong to me."

"That's not what the will says," Joey DiAngelis said. He was sitting on the rust-eaten hood of a 1957 Edsel Citation, a can of Schaefer in his hand, as Bruder paced back and forth in front of him.

"I'll contest the goddamned will," Bruder threatened. "Damn it, we took out loans together."

"The loans will be paid," Joey said. "Tuds was insured for a hundred grand. There's a lot left even after the funeral expenses. You'll be covered, Bruder. But you ain't getting the junkyard, that's mine."

Bruder pointed at him, gloves dangling from his hand. "If you think I won't take you to court, you better think again. I'm going to take everything you own, you asshole, including this shit-eating junkyard."

"Fuck you," Joey DiAngelis said. "So sue me, I don't give a shit. I can afford lawyers, too, Bruder. Tuds left me all the rest of his stuff, the house, the comic collection, his share of the business. I'll sell it all if I have to, but I'm keeping this junkyard."

Bruder scowled. "DiAngelis," he said, trying to sound a little more conciliatory, "listen to reason. Tudbury wanted to sell this place. What good is an abandoned junkyard? Think of all the people who need housing. This development will be an enormous boon to the whole city."

DiAngelis took a swig of beer. "You think I'm a moron or what? You're not building no shelter for the homeless. Tom showed me the plans. We're talking quarter-million-dollar townhouses, right?" He looked around at the acres of trash and rusted cars. "Well, fuck that shit. I grew up in this junkyard, Stevie boy. I like it just the way it is."

"Then you're an idiot," Bruder snapped.

"And you're on my property," Joey said. "You better get the fuck off, or I might get the urge to jam a tailpipe up that tight ass of yours." He crushed the beer can in his hand, tossed it aside, and slid off the hood of the Edsel. The two men stood toe to toe.

"You can't intimidate me, DiAngelis," Bruder said. "We're not kids in a schoolyard anymore. I'm bigger than you, and I work out three times a week. I've studied martial arts."

"Yeah," Joey said, "but I fight dirty." He grinned.

Bruder hesitated, then turned angrily on his heels and stalked back to his car. "You haven't heard the last of this!" he shouted, backing out.

Joey smiled as he watched him drive off.

After Bruder had gone, he went to his own car and pulled another Schaefer off the six-pack on the passenger seat. He drank the first swallow by the shore as the tide came in off the bay. It was a wet, windy, overcast day, and in an hour or so it was going to turn into a wet, windy, overcast night. Joey sat on a rock and watched the fading light paint rainbows in the oil slicks on the water, thinking of Tuds.

The wake and the funeral had both been closed casket, but Joey had gone into the back room after everyone else had left and told a junior mortician that he wanted to see the body. The wild card hadn't left much that looked like Tom. The corpse had skin like an armadillo, scaly and hard, and a faint greenish glow, like it was radioactive or some fucking thing. Its eyes were huge sacs of glistening pink gelatin, but it was wearing Tom's aviator frames, and he'd recognized the high school ring on the pinky of one webbed hand.

Not that there was any room for doubt. The body had been found in a Jokertown alley, wearing Tom's clothes and carrying all of Tom's ID, and Dr. Tachyon himself had done the autopsy and signed the death certificate, after comparing dental records.

Joey DiAngelis sighed, crushed another beer can in his

hand, and tossed it to the side. He remembered when he and Tom had built the first shell together. Back then they made beer cans out of steel, and you had to be strong to crush the motherfuckers. Now any old wimp could do it.

He grabbed the rest of his six-pack by an empty ring in the plastic holder and walked on back to the bunker.

The big door was open, and down inside the hole Joey saw the flare of an acetylene torch. He sat down with his legs over the edge and dangled the six-pack out in front of him. "Hey, Tuds," he shouted down, "you ready for a break?"

The blowtorch went out. Tom walked out from behind the framework of the huge new half-built shell. What a fucking monster, Joey thought again as he looked down at its skeleton; it was going to be almost twice as big as any previous shell, airtight, watertight, self-contained, computerized, armored to hell and gone, a hundred and fifty fucking thousand dollars' worth of shell, all the suitcase loot and most of the insurance settlement, too. Tuds was even making noises about cannibalizing that fucking head he'd brought back to see if he could figure out some way to fix the radar set and hook it into his hardware.

Tom pulled off his goggles. They left big pale circles around his eyes. "Asshole," he shouted up, "how many times I got to tell you, Tudbury is dead. There's no one home but us turtles."

"Fuck it then," Joey said. "Turtles don't drink beer."

"This one does. Give it here—that goddamn torch is *hot*." Joey dropped what was left of the six-pack.

Tom caught it, tore off a can, and opened it. Beer sprayed all over his face and hair. Joey laughed.

If you have any difficulty obtaining any of
the Titan range of books, you can order
direct from Titan Books Mail Order, 71
New Oxford Street, London, WC1A 1DG.
Tel: (01) 497 2150

Star Trek novels 1-31	£2.95 each
Next Generation novels 1-10	£2.95 each
Star Trek novels 32 onwards	£2.99 each
Next Generation novels 11 onwards	£2.99 each
Star Trek Giant novels 2-5	£3.95 each
Star Trek Giant novels 6 onwards	£3.99 each
The *Star Trek* Compendium	£8.95
Mr Scott's Guide to the Enterprise	£6.95
The *Star Trek* Interview Book	£5.95
Worlds of the Federation	£8.95
Captain's Log	£5.99
Thieves' World novels	£3.99 each
Wild Cards novels 1-4	£3.95 each
Wild Cards novels 5 onwards	£3.99 each
Thunderbirds novels	£2.95 each
Captain Scarlet novels	£2.95 each

For postage and packing:
on orders up to £5 add £1.20; orders up to £10 add £2;
orders up to £15 add £2.50; orders up to £20 add £2.70;
orders over £20 add £3.70.
Make cheques or postal orders payable to Titan Books.
NB. UK customers only.

While every effort is made to keep prices steady, Titan
Books reserves the right to change cover prices at short
notice from those listed here.